A Coffin for Dimitrios

Journey into Fear

The Light of Day

A Coffin for Dimitrios

Journey into Fear

The Light of Day

Eric Ambler

Quality Paperback Book Club
New York

A Coffin for Dimitrios

TO

ALAN AND FÉLICE HARVEY

CONTENTS

CONTENTS

"But the iniquity of oblivion blindely scattereth her poppy, and deals with the memory of men without distinction to merit of perpetuity . . . Without the favour of the everlasting register, the first man had been as unknown as the last, and Methuselah's long life had been his only Chronicle."

SIR THOMAS BROWNE: *Hydriotaphia*

CHAPTER I

ORIGINS OF

AN OBSESSION

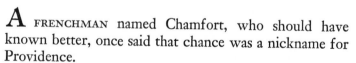

A FRENCHMAN named Chamfort, who should have known better, once said that chance was a nickname for Providence.

It is one of those convenient, question-begging aphorisms coined to discredit the unpleasant truth that chance plays an important, if not predominant, part in human affairs. Yet it was not entirely inexcusable. Inevitably, chance does occasionally operate with a sort of fumbling coherence readily mistakable for the workings of a self-conscious Providence.

3

The story of Dimitrios Makropoulos is an example of this.

The fact that a man like Latimer should so much as learn of the existence of a man like Dimitrios is alone grotesque. That he should actually see the dead body of Dimitrios, that he should spend weeks that he could ill afford probing into the man's shadowy history, and that he should ultimately find himself in the position of owing his life to a criminal's odd taste in interior decoration are breath-taking in their absurdity.

Yet, when these facts are seen side by side with the other facts in the case, it is difficult not to become lost in superstitious awe. Their very absurdity seems to prohibit the use of the words "chance" and "coincidence." For the sceptic there remains only one consolation: if there should be such a thing as a superhuman Law, it is administered with sub-human inefficiency. The choice of Latimer as its instrument could have been made only by an idiot.

During the first fifteen years of his adult life, Charles Latimer became a lecturer in political economy at a minor English university. By the time he was thirty-five he had, in addition, written three books. The first was a study of the influence of Proudhon on nineteenth century Italian political thought. The second was entitled: *The Gotha Programme of* 1875. The third was an assessment of the economic implications of Rosenberg's *Der Mythus des zwanzigsten Jahrhunderts*.

It was soon after he had finished correcting the bulky proofs of the last work, and in the hope of dispelling the black depression which was the aftermath of his temporary association with the philosophy of National Socialism and its prophet, Dr. Rosenberg, that he wrote his first detective story.

A Bloody Shovel was an immediate success. It was followed by *"I," said the Fly* and *Murder's Arms*. From the great army of university professors who write detective stories in their spare time, Latimer soon emerged as one of the shamefaced few who could make money at the sport. It was, perhaps, inevitable that, sooner or later, he would become a professional writer in name as well as in fact. Three things hastened the transition. The first was a disagreement with the university authorities over what he held to be a matter of principle. The second was an illness. The third was the fact that he happened to be unmarried. Not long after the publication of *No Doornail This* and following the illness, which had made inroads on his constitutional reserves, he wrote, with only mild reluctance, a letter of resignation and went abroad to complete his fifth detective story in the sun.

It was the week after he had finished that book's successor that he went to Turkey. He had spent a year in and near Athens and was longing for a change of scene. His health was much improved but the prospect of an English autumn was uninviting. At the suggestion of a Greek friend he took the steamer from the Piræus to Istanbul.

It was in Istanbul and from Colonel Haki that he first heard of Dimitrios.

A letter of introduction is an uneasy document. More often than not, the bearer of it is only casually acquainted with the giver who, in turn, may know the person to whom it is addressed even less well. The chances of its presentation having a satisfactory outcome for all three are slender.

Among the letters of introduction which Latimer carried with him to Istanbul was one to a Madame Chávez, who lived, he had been told, in a villa on the Bosphorus. Three days after he arrived, he wrote to her and received in reply an invitation to join a four day party at the villa. A trifle apprehensively, he accepted.

For Madame Chávez, the road from Buenos Ayres had been as liberally paved with gold as the road to it. A very handsome Turkish woman, she had successfully married and divorced a wealthy Argentine meat broker and, with a fraction of her gains from these transactions, had purchased a small palace which had once housed a minor Turkish royalty. It stood, remote and inconvenient of access, overlooking a bay of fantastic beauty and, apart from the fact that the supplies of fresh water were insufficient to serve even one of its nine bathrooms, was exquisitely appointed. But for the other guests and his hostess's Turkish habit of striking her servants violently in the face when they displeased her (which was often), Latimer, for whom such grandiose discomfort was a novelty, would have enjoyed himself.

The other guests were a very noisy pair of Marseillais, three Italians, two young Turkish naval officers and their "fiancées" of the moment and an assortment of Istanbul business men with their wives. The greater part of the time they spent in drinking Madame Chávez's seemingly inexhaustible supplies of Dutch gin and dancing to a gramophone attended by a servant who went on steadily playing records whether the guests happened to be dancing at the moment or not. On the pretext of ill-health, Latimer excused himself from much of the drinking and most of the dancing. He was generally ignored.

It was in the late afternoon of his last day there and he was sitting at the end of the vine-covered terrace out of earshot of the gramophone, when he saw a large chauffeur-driven touring car lurching up the long, dusty road to the villa. As it roared into the courtyard below, the occupant of the rear seat flung the door open and vaulted out before the car came to a standstill.

He was a tall man with lean, muscular cheeks whose pale tan contrasted well with a head of grey hair cropped Prussian fashion. A narrow frontal bone, a long beak of a nose and thin lips gave him a somewhat predatory air. He could not be less than fifty, Latimer thought, and studied the waist below the beautifully cut officer's uniform in the hope of detecting the corsets.

He watched the tall officer whip a silk handkerchief from his sleeve, flick some invisible dust from his immaculate patent-leather riding boots, tilt his cap raffishly and stride out of sight. Somewhere in the villa, a bell pealed.

Colonel Haki, for this was the officer's name, was an immediate success with the party. A quarter of an hour after his arrival, Madame Chávez, with an air of shy confusion clearly intended to inform her guests that she regarded herself as hopelessly compromised by the Colonel's unexpected appearance, led him on to the terrace and introduced him. All smiles and gallantry, he clicked heels, kissed hands, bowed, acknowledged the salutes of the naval officers and ogled the business men's wives. The performance so fascinated Latimer that, when his turn came to be introduced, the sound of his own name made him jump. The Colonel pump-handled his arm warmly.

"Damned pleased indeed to meet you, old boy," he said.

"*Monsieur le Colonel parle bien anglais*," explained Madame Chávez.

"*Quelques mots*," said Colonel Haki.

Latimer looked amiably into a pair of pale grey eyes. "How do you do?"

"Cheerio—all—the—best," replied the Colonel with grave courtesy, and passed on to kiss the hand of, and to run an appraising eye over, a stout girl in a bathing costume.

It was not until late in the evening that Latimer spoke to the Colonel again. The Colonel had injected a good deal of boisterous vitality into the party; cracking jokes, laughing loudly, making humorously brazen advances to the wives and rather more surreptitious ones to the unmarried women. From time to time his eye caught Latimer's and he grinned deprecatingly. "I've got to play the fool like this—it's expected of me," said the grin; "but don't think I like it." Then, long after dinner, when the guests had begun to take less interest in the dancing and more in the progress of a game of mixed strip poker, the Colonel took him by the arm and walked him on to the terrace.

"You must excuse me, Mr. Latimer," he said in French, "but I should very much like to talk with you. Those women—phew!" He slid a cigarette case under Latimer's nose. "A cigarette?"

"Thank you."

Colonel Haki glanced over his shoulder. "The other end of the terrace is more secluded," he said; and then, as they began to walk: "you know, I came up here to-day specially to see you. Madame told me you were here and really I could not resist the temptation of talking with the writer whose works I so much admire."

Latimer murmured a non-committal appreciation of the compliment. He was in a difficulty, for he had no means of knowing whether the Colonel was thinking in terms of political economy or detection. He had once startled and irritated a kindly old don who had professed interest in his "last book," by asking the old man whether he preferred his corpses shot or bludgeoned. It sounded affected to ask which set of books was under discussion.

Colonel Haki, however, did not wait to be questioned. "I get all the latest *romans policiers* sent to me from Paris," he went on. "I read nothing but *romans policiers*. I would like you to see my collection. Especially I like the English and American ones. All the best of them are translated into French. French writers themselves, I do not find sympathetic. French culture is not such as can produce a *roman policier* of the first order. I have just added your *Une Pelle Ensanglantée* to my library. Formidable! But I cannot quite understand the significance of the title."

Latimer spent some time trying to explain in French the meaning of "to call a spade a bloody shovel" and to translate the play on words which had given (to those readers with suitable minds) the essential clue to the murderer's identity in the very title.

Colonel Haki listened intently, nodding his head and saying: "Yes, I see, I see it clearly now," before Latimer had reached the point of the explanation.

"Monsieur," he said when Latimer had given up in despair, "I wonder whether you would do me the honour of lunching with me one day this week. I think," he added mysteriously, "that I may be able to help you."

Latimer did not see in what way he could be helped by Colonel Haki but said that he would be glad to lunch with him. They arranged to meet at the Pera Palace Hotel three days later.

It was not until the evening before it that Latimer thought very much more about the luncheon appointment. He was sitting in the lounge of his hotel with the manager of his bankers' Istanbul branch.

Collinson, he thought, was a pleasant fellow but a monotonous companion. His conversation consisted almost entirely of gossip about the doings of the English and American colonies in Istanbul. "Do you know the Fitzwilliams," he would say. "No? A pity, you'd like them. Well, the other day . . ." As a source of information about Kemal Ataturk's economic reforms he had proved a failure.

"By the way," said Latimer after listening to an account of the goings-on of the Turkish-born wife of an American car salesman, "do you know of a man named Colonel Haki?"

"Haki? What made you think of him?"

"I'm lunching with him to-morrow."

Collinson's eyebrows went up. "*Are* you, by Jove!" He scratched his chin. "Well, I know *of* him." He hesitated. "Haki's one of those people you hear a lot about in this place but never seem to get a line on. One of the people behind the scenes, if you get me. He's got more influence than a good many of the men who are supposed to be at the top at Ankara. He was one of the Gazi's own particular men in Anatolia in nineteen-nineteen, a deputy in the Provisional Government. I've heard stories about him then. Bloodthirsty devil by all accounts. There was something about torturing prisoners. But then both sides did that and I dare say it was the Sultan's boys that started it. I heard, too, that he can drink a couple of bottles of Scotch at a sitting and stay stone cold sober. Don't believe that though. How did you get on to him?"

Latimer explained. "What does he do for a living?" he added. "I don't understand these uniforms."

Collinson shrugged. "Well, I've *heard* on good authority that he's the head of the secret police, but that's probably just another story. That's the worst of this place. Can't believe a word they say in the Club. Why, only the other day . . ."

It was with rather more enthusiasm than before that Latimer went to his luncheon appointment the following day. He had judged Colonel Haki to be something of a ruffian and Collinson's vague information had tended to confirm that view.

The Colonel arrived, bursting with apologies, twenty minutes late, and hurried his guest straight into the restaurant. "We must have a whisky-soda immediately," he said and called loudly for a bottle of "Johnnie."

During most of the meal he talked about the detective stories he had read, his reactions to them, his opinions of the characters and his preference for murderers who shot their victims. At last, with an almost empty bottle of whisky at his elbow and a strawberry ice in front of him, he leaned forward across the table.

"I think, Mr. Latimer," he said again, "that I can help you."

For one wild moment Latimer wondered if he were going to be offered a job in the Turkish secret service; but he said: "That's very kind of you."

"It was my ambition," continued Colonel Haki, "to write a good *roman policier* of my own. I have often thought that I could do so if I had the time. That is the trouble—the time. I have found that out. But . . ." He paused impressively.

Latimer waited. He was always meeting people who felt that they could write detective stories if they had the time.

"But," repeated the Colonel, "I have the plot prepared; I would like to make you a present of it."

Latimer said that it was very good indeed of him.

The Colonel waved away his thanks. "Your books have given me so much pleasure, Mr. Latimer. I am glad to make you a present of an idea for a new one. I have not the time to use it myself, and, in any case," he added magnanimously, "you would make better use of it than I should."

Latimer mumbled incoherently.

"The scene of the story," pursued his host, his grey eyes fixed on Latimer's, "is an English country house belonging to the rich Lord Robinson. There is a party for the English week-end. In the middle of the party, Lord Robinson is discovered in the library sitting at his desk—shot through the temple. The wound is singed. A pool of blood has formed on the desk and it has soaked into a paper. The paper is a new Will which the Lord was about to sign. The old Will divided his money equally between six persons, his relations, who are at the party. The new Will, which he has been prevented from signing by the murderer's bullet, leaves all to one of those relations. Therefore" —he pointed his ice cream spoon accusingly—"one of the five other relations is the guilty one. That is logical, is it not?"

Latimer opened his mouth, then shut it again and nodded.

Colonel Haki grinned triumphantly. "That is the trick."

"The trick?"

"The Lord was murdered by none of the suspects, but by the butler, whose wife had been seduced by this Lord! What do you think of that, eh?"

"Very ingenious."

His host leaned back contentedly and smoothed out his tunic. "It is only a trick, but I am glad you like it. Of course, I have the whole plot worked out in detail. The *flic* is a High Commissioner of Scotland Yard. He seduces one of the suspects, a very pretty woman, and it is for her sake that he solves the mystery. It is quite artistic. But, as I say, I have the whole thing written out."

"I should be very interested," said Latimer with sincerity, "to read your notes."

"That is what I hoped you would say. Are you pressed for time?"

"Not a bit."

"Then let us go back to my office and I will show you what I have done. It is written in French."

Latimer hesitated only momentarily. He had nothing better to do, and it might be interesting to see Colonel Haki's office.

"I should like to go back with you," he said.

The Colonel's office was situated at the top of what might once have been a cheap hotel, but which, from the inside, was unmistakably a government building, in Galata. It was a large room at the end of a corridor. When they went in a uniformed clerk was bending over the desk. He straightened his back, clicked his heels and said something in Turkish. The Colonel answered him and nodded a dismissal.

The Colonel waved Latimer to a chair, gave him a cigarette and began rummaging in a drawer. At last he drew out a sheet or two of typewritten paper and held it out.

"There you are, Mr. Latimer. *The Clue of the Blood-stained Will*, I have called it, but I am not convinced that that is the best title. All the best titles have been used, I find. But I will think of some alternatives. Read it, and do not be afraid to say frankly what you think of it. If there are any details which you think should be altered, I will alter them."

Latimer took the sheets and read while the Colonel sat on the corner of his desk and swung a long, gleaming leg.

Latimer read through the sheets twice and then put them down. He was feeling ashamed of himself because he had wanted several times to laugh. He should not have come. Now that he *had* come, the best thing he could do was to leave as quickly as possible.

"I cannot suggest any improvements at the moment," he said slowly; "of course, it all wants thinking over; it is so easy to make mistakes with problems of this sort. There is so much to be thought of. Questions of British legal procedure, for instance . . ."

"Yes, yes, of course." Colonel Haki slid off the desk and sat down in his chair. "But you think you can use it, eh?"

"I am very grateful indeed for your generosity," said Latimer evasively.

"It is nothing. You shall send me a free copy of the book when it appears." He swung round in his chair and picked up the telephone. "I will have a copy made for you to take away."

Latimer sat back. Well, that was that! It could not take long to make a copy. He listened to the Colonel talking to someone over the telephone and saw him frown. The Colonel put the telephone down and turned to him.

"You will excuse me if I deal with a small matter?"

"Of course."

The Colonel drew a bulky manila file towards him and began to go through the papers inside it. Then he selected one and glanced down it. There was silence in the room.

Latimer, affecting preoccupation with his cigarette, glanced across the desk. Colonel Haki was slowly turning the pages inside the folder, and on his face was a look that Latimer had not seen there before. It was the look of the expert attending to the business he understood perfectly. There was a sort of watchful repose in his face that reminded Latimer of a very old and experienced cat contemplating a very young and inexperienced mouse. In that moment he revised his ideas about Colonel Haki. He had been feeling a little sorry for him as one feels sorry for anyone who has unconsciously made a fool of himself. He saw now that the Colonel stood in need of no such consideration. As his long, yellowish fingers turned the pages of the folder, Latimer remembered a sentence of Collinson's: "There was something about torturing prisoners." He knew suddenly that he was seeing the real

Colonel Haki for the first time. Then the Colonel looked up and his pale eyes rested thoughtfully on Latimer's tie.

For a moment Latimer had an uncomfortable suspicion that although the man across the desk appeared to be looking at his tie, he was actually looking into his mind. Then the Colonel's eyes moved upwards and he grinned slightly in a way that made Latimer feel as if he had been caught stealing something.

He said: "I wonder if you are interested in *real* murderers, Mr. Latimer."

CHAPTER II

THE DOSSIER
OF DIMITRIOS

L ATIMER felt himself redden. From the condescending professional he had been changed suddenly into the ridiculous amateur. It was a little disconcerting.

"Well, yes," he said slowly. "I suppose I am."

Colonel Haki pursed his lips. "You know, Mr. Latimer," he said, "I find the murderer in a *roman policier* much more sympathetic than a real murderer. In a *roman policier* there is a corpse, a number of suspects, a detective and a gallows. That is artistic. The real murderer is not artistic. I, who am a sort of policeman, tell you that

17

squarely." He tapped the folder on his desk. "Here is a real murderer. We have known of his existence for nearly twenty years. This is his dossier. We know of one murder he may have committed. There are doubtless others of which we, at any rate, know nothing. This man is typical. A dirty type, common, cowardly, scum. Murder, espionage, drugs—that is the history. There were also two affairs of assassination."

"Assassination! that argues a certain courage, surely?"

The Colonel laughed unpleasantly. "My dear friend, Dimitrios would have nothing to do with the actual shooting. No! His kind never risk their skins like that. They stay on the fringe of the plot. They are the professionals, the *entrepreneurs,* the links between the business men, the politicians who desire the end but are afraid of the means, and the fanatics, the idealists who are prepared to die for their convictions. The important thing to know about an assassination or an attempted assassination is not who fired the shot, but who paid for the bullet. It is the rats like Dimitrios who can best tell you that. They are always ready to talk to save themselves the inconvenience of a prison cell. Dimitrios would have been the same as any other. Courage!" He laughed again. "Dimitrios was a little cleverer than some of them. I'll grant you that. As far as I know, no government has ever caught him and there is no photograph in his dossier. But we knew him all right and so did Sofia and Belgrade and Paris and Athens. He was a great traveller, was Dimitrios."

"That sounds as though he's dead."

"Yes, he is dead." Colonel Haki turned the corners of his thin mouth down contemptuously. "A fisherman pulled his body out of the Bosphorus last night. It is believed that he had been knifed and thrown overboard from a ship. Like the scum he was, he was floating."

"At least," said Latimer, "he died by violence. That is something very like justice."

"Ah!" The Colonel leaned forward. "There is the writer speaking. Everything must be tidy, artistic, like a *roman policier*. Very well!" He pulled the dossier towards him and opened it. "Just listen, Mr. Latimer, to this. Then you shall tell me if it is artistic."

He began to read.

"Dimitrios Makropoulos." He stopped and looked up. "We have never been able to find out whether that was the surname of the family that adopted him or an alias. He was known usually as Dimitrios." He turned to the dossier again. "Dimitrios Makropoulos. Born eighteen eighty-nine in Larissa, Greece. Found abandoned. Parents unknown. Mother believed Roumanian. Registered as Greek subject and adopted by Greek family. Criminal record with Greek authorities. Details unobtainable." He looked up at Latimer. "That was before he came to our notice. We first heard of him at Izmir [1] in nineteen-twenty-two, a few days after our troops occupied the town. A *deunme* [2] named Sholem was found in his room with his throat cut. He was a money-lender and kept his money under the floorboards. These were ripped up and the money had been taken. There was much violence in Izmir at that time and little notice would have been taken by the military authorities. The thing might have been done by one of our soldiers. Then, another Jew, a relation of Sholem's, drew the attention of the military to a negro

[1] Smyrna.
[2] Jew turned Moslem.

named Dhris Mohammed, who had been spending money in the cafés and boasting that a Jew had lent him the money without interest. Inquiries were made and Dhris was arrested. His replies to the court-martial were unsatisfactory and he was condemned to death. Then he made a confession. He was a fig-packer and he said that one of his fellow workmen, whom he called Dimitrios, had told him of Sholem's wealth hidden under the floorboards of his room. They had planned the robbery together and had entered Sholem's room by night. It had been Dimitrios, he said, who had killed the Jew. He thought that Dimitrios, being registered as a Greek, had escaped and bought a passage on one of the refugee ships that waited at secret places along the coast."

He shrugged. "The authorities did not believe his story. We were at war with Greece, and it was the sort of story a guilty man might invent to save his neck. They found that there had been a fig-packer named Dimitrios, that his fellow workmen had disliked him and that he had disappeared." He grinned. "Quite a lot of Greeks named Dimitrios disappeared at that time. You could see their bodies in the streets and floating in the harbour. This negro's story was unprovable. He was hanged."

He paused. During this recital he had not once referred to the dossier.

"You have a very good memory for facts," commented Latimer.

The Colonel grinned again. "I was the President of the court-martial. It was through that that I was able to mark down Dimitrios later on. I was transferred a year later to the secret police. In nineteen twenty-four a plot to assassinate the Gazi was discovered. It was the year he abolished the Caliphate and the plot was outwardly the work of a group of religious fanatics. Actually the men behind it were agents of some people in the good graces of a neighbouring friendly government. They had good reasons for wishing the Gazi out of the way. The plot was discovered. The details are unimportant. But one of the agents who escaped was a man known as Dimitrios." He pushed the cigarettes towards Latimer. "Please smoke."

Latimer shook his head. "Was it the same Dimitrios?"

"It was. Now, tell me frankly, Mr. Latimer. Do you find anything artistic there? Could you make a good *roman policier* out of that? Is there anything there that could be of the slightest interest to a writer?"

"Police work interests me a great deal—naturally. But what happened to Dimitrios? How did the story end?"

Colonel Haki snapped his fingers. "Ah! I was waiting for you to ask that. I knew you would ask it. And my answer is this: it *didn't* end!"

"Then what happened?"

"I will tell you. The first problem was to identify Dimitrios of Izmir with Dimitrios of Edirné.[1] Accordingly we revived the affair of Sholem, issued a warrant for the arrest of a Greek fig-packer named Dimitrios on a charge of murder and, with that excuse, asked foreign police authorities for assistance. We did not learn much, but what we did learn was sufficient. Dimitrios had been concerned with the attempted assassination of Stambulisky in Bulgaria which had preceded the Macedonian officers' *putsch* in nineteen twenty-three. The Sofia police knew very little but that he was known there to be a Greek from Izmir. A woman with whom he had associated in Sofia

[1] Adrianople.

was questioned. She stated that she had had a letter from him a short time before. He had given no address, but as she had had very urgent reasons for wishing to get in touch with him she had looked at the postmark. It was from Edirné. The Sofia police obtained a rough description of him that agreed with that given by the negro in Izmir. The Greek police stated that he had had a criminal record prior to nineteen twenty-two and gave those particulars of his origin. The warrant is probably still in existence; but we did not find Dimitrios with it.

"It was not until two years later that we heard of him again. We received an inquiry from the Yugoslav Government concerning a Turkish subject named Dimitrios Talat. He was wanted, they said, for robbery; but an agent of ours in Belgrade reported that the robbery was the theft of some secret naval documents and that the charge the Yugoslavs hoped to bring against him was one of espionage on behalf of France. By the first name and the description issued by the Belgrade police we guessed that Talat was probably Dimitrios of Izmir. About the same time our Consul in Switzerland renewed the passport, issued apparently at Ankara, of a man named Talat. It is a common Turkish name; but when it came to entering the record of the renewal it was found from the number that no such passport had been issued. The passport had been forged." He spread out his hands. "You see, Mr. Latimer? There is your story. Incomplete. Inartistic. No detection, no suspects, no hidden motives, merely sordid."

"But interesting, nevertheless," objected Latimer. "What happened over the Talat business?"

"Still looking for the end of your story, Mr. Latimer?

All right, then. Nothing happened about Talat. It is just a name. We never heard it again. If he used the passport we don't know. It does not matter. We have Dimitrios. A corpse, it is true, but we have him. We shall probably never know who killed him. The ordinary police will doubtless make their inquiries and report to us that they have no hope of discovering the murderer. This dossier will go into the archives. It is just one of many similar cases."

"You said something about drugs."

Colonel Haki began to look bored. "Oh, yes. Dimitrios made a lot of money once I should think. Another unfinished story. About three years after the Belgrade affair we heard of him again. Nothing to do with us but the available information was added to the dossier as a routine matter." He referred to the dossier. "In nineteen twenty-nine, the League of Nations Advisory Committee on the illicit drug traffic received a report from the French government concerning the seizure of a large quantity of heroin at the Swiss frontier. It was concealed in a mattress in a sleeping car coming from Sofia. One of the car attendants was found to be responsible for the smuggling but all he could or would tell the police was that the drug was to have been collected in Paris by a man who worked at the rail terminus. He did not know the man's name and had never spoken to him; but he described him. The man in question was later arrested. Questioned, he admitted the charge but claimed that he knew nothing of the destination of the drug. He received one consignment a month which was collected by a third man. The police set a trap for this third man and caught him only to find that there was a fourth intermediary. They arrested six men in all in connection with that affair and only obtained one real clue. It was that the man at the head of this peddling organisation was a man known as Dimitrios. Through the medium of the Committee, the Bulgarian government then revealed that they had found a clandestine heroin laboratory at Radomir and had seized two hundred and thirty kilos of heroin ready for delivery. The consignee's name was Dimitrios. During the next year the French succeeded in discovering one or two other large heroin consignments bound for Dimitrios. But they did not get very much nearer to Dimitrios himself. There were difficulties. The stuff never seemed to come in the same way twice and by the end of that year, nineteen thirty, all they had to show in the way of arrests were a number of smugglers and some insignificant pedlars. Judging by the amounts of heroin they did find, Dimitrios must have been making huge sums for himself. Then, quite suddenly, about a year after that, Dimitrios went out of the drug business. The first news the police had of this was an anonymous letter which gave the names of all the principal members of the gang, their life histories and details of how evidence against every one of them might be obtained. The French police had a theory at the time. They said that Dimitrios himself had become a heroin addict. Whether that is true or not, the fact is that by December, the gang was rounded up. One of them, a woman, was already wanted for fraud. Some of them threatened to kill Dimitrios when they were released from prison but the most any of them could tell the police about him was that his surname was Makropoulos and that he had a flat in the seventeenth *arrondissement*. They never found the flat and they never found Dimitrios."

The clerk had come in and was standing by the desk.
"Ah," said the Colonel, "here is your copy."

Latimer took it and thanked him rather absently.

"And that was the last you heard of Dimitrios?" he
added.

"Oh, no. The last we heard of him was about a year
later. A Croat attempted to assassinate a Yugoslav politician in Zagreb. In the confession he made to the police,
he said that friends had obtained the pistol he used from a
man named Dimitrios in Rome. If it was Dimitrios of
Izmir he must have returned to his old profession. A dirty
type. There are a few more like him who should float in
the Bosphorus."

"You say you never had a photograph of him. How
did you identify him?"

"There was a French *carte d'identité* sewn inside the
lining of his coat. It was issued about a year ago at Lyons
to Dimitrios Makropoulos. It is a visitor's *carte* and he is
described as being without occupation. That might mean
anything. There was, of course, a photograph in it.
We've turned it over to the French. They say that it is
quite genuine." He pushed the dossier aside and stood up.
"There's an inquest to-morrow. I have to go and have a
look at the body in the police mortuary. That is a thing
you do not have to contend with in books, Mr. Latimer—
a list of regulations. A man is found floating in the Bosphorus. A police matter, clearly. But because this man
happens to be on my files, my organisation has to deal
with it also. I have my car waiting. Can I take you anywhere?"

"If my hotel isn't too much out of your way, I should
like to be taken there "

"Of course. You have the plot of your new book safely? Good. Then we are ready."

In the car, the Colonel elaborated on the virtues of *The Clue of the Bloodstained Will*. Latimer promised to keep in touch with him and let him know how the book progressed. The car pulled up outside his hotel. They had exchanged farewells and Latimer was about to get out when he hesitated and then dropped back into his seat.

"Look here, Colonel," he said, "I want to make what will seem to you a rather strange request."

The Colonel gestured expansively. "Anything."

"I have a fancy to see the body of this man Dimitrios. I wonder if it would be impossible for you to take me with you."

The Colonel frowned and then shrugged. "If you wish to come, by all means do so. But I do not see . . ."

"I have never," lied Latimer quickly, "seen either a dead man or a mortuary. I think that every detective story writer should see those things."

The Colonel's face cleared. "My dear fellow, of course he should. One cannot write about that which one has never seen." He signalled the chauffeur on. "Perhaps," he added as they drove off again, "we can incorporate a scene in a mortuary in your new book. I will think about it."

The mortuary was a small corrugated iron building in the precincts of a police station near the mosque of Nouri Osmanieh. A police official, collected *en route* by the Colonel, led them across the yard which separated it from the main building. The afternoon heat had set the air above the concrete quivering and Latimer began to wish that he had not come. It was not the weather for visiting corrugated iron mortuaries.

The official unlocked the door and opened it. A blast of hot, carbolic-laden air came out, as if from an oven, to meet them. Latimer took off his hat and followed the Colonel in.

There were no windows and light was supplied by a single high-powered electric lamp in an enamel reflector. On each side of a gangway which ran down the centre, there were four high, wooden trestle tables. All but three were bare. The three were draped with stiff, heavy tarpaulins which bulged slightly above the level of the other trestles. The heat was overpowering and Latimer felt the sweat begin to soak into his shirt and trickle down his legs.

"It's very hot," he said.

The Colonel shrugged and nodded towards the trestles. "They don't complain."

The official went to the nearest of the three trestles, leaned over it and dragged the tarpaulin back. The Colonel walked over and looked down. Latimer forced himself to follow.

The body lying on the trestle was that of a short, broad-shouldered man of about fifty. From where he stood near the foot of the table, Latimer could see very little of the face, only a section of putty-coloured flesh and a fringe of tousled grey hair. The body was wrapped in a mackintosh sheet. By the feet was a neat pile of crumpled clothing: some underwear, a shirt, socks, a flowered tie and a blue serge suit stained nearly grey by sea water. Beside this pile was a pair of narrow, pointed shoes, the soles of which had warped as they had dried.

Latimer took a step nearer so that he could see the face.

No one had troubled to close the eyes and the whites of them stared upwards at the light. The lower jaw had dropped slightly. It was not quite the face that Latimer had pictured; rather rounder and with thick lips instead of thin, a face that would work and quiver under the stress of emotion. The cheeks were loose and deeply lined. But it was too late now to form any judgment of the mind that had once been behind the face. The mind had gone.

The official had been speaking to the Colonel. Now he stopped.

"Killed by a knife wound in the stomach, according to the doctor," translated the Colonel. "Already dead when he got into the water."

"Where did the clothes come from?"

"Lyons, all except the suit and shoes which are Greek. Poor stuff."

He renewed his conversation with the official.

Latimer stared at the corpse. So this was Dimitrios. This was the man who had, perhaps, slit the throat of Sholem, the Jew turned Moslem. This was the man who had connived at assassinations, who had spied for France. This was the man who had trafficked in drugs, who had given a gun to a Croat terrorist and who, in the end, had himself died by violence. This putty-coloured bulk was the end of an Odyssey. Dimitrios had returned at last to the country whence he had set out so many years before.

So many years. Europe in labour had through its pain seen for an instant a new glory, and then had collapsed to welter again in the agonies of war and fear. Governments had risen and fallen; men and women had worked, had starved, had made speeches, had fought, had been tortured, had died. Hope had come and gone, a fugitive in the scented bosom of illusion. Men had learned to sniff the heady dreamstuff of the soul and wait impassively while the lathes turned the guns for their destruction. And through those years, Dimitrios had lived and breathed and come to terms with his strange gods. He had been a dangerous man. Now, in the loneliness of death, beside the squalid pile of clothes that was his estate, he was pitiable.

Latimer watched the two men as they discussed the filling-in of a printed form the official had produced. They turned to the clothes and began making an inventory of them.

Yet at some time Dimitrios had made money, much money. What had happened to it? Had he spent it or lost it? "Easy come, easy go," they said. But had Dimitrios been the sort of man to let money go easily, howsoever he had acquired it? They knew so little about him! A few odd facts about a few odd incidents in his life, that was all the dossier amounted to! No more. And for every one of the crimes recorded in the dossier there must have been others, perhaps even more serious. What had happened in those two- and three-year intervals which the dossier bridged so casually? And what had happened since he had been in Lyons a year ago? By what route had he travelled to keep his appointment with Nemesis?

They were not questions that Colonel Haki would bother even to ask, much less to answer. He was the professional, concerned only with the unfanciful business of disposing of a decomposing body. But there must be people who knew and knew of Dimitrios, his friends (if he had had any), and his enemies, people in Smyrna, people in Sofia, people in Belgrade, in Adrianople, in Paris, in Lyons, people all over Europe, who *could* answer them. If you could find those people and get the answers you would have the material for what would surely be the strangest of biographies.

Latimer's heart missed a beat. It would be an absurd thing to attempt, of course. Unthinkably foolish. If one did it one would begin with, say, Smyrna and try to follow one's man step by step from there, using the dossier as a rough guide. It would be an experiment in detection really. One would, no doubt, fail to discover anything new; but there would be valuable data to be gained even from failure. All the routine inquiries over which one skated so easily in one's novels one would have to make oneself. Not that any man in his senses would dream of going on such a wild goose chase—heavens no! But it was amusing to play with the idea and if one were a little tired of Istanbul . . .

He looked up and caught the Colonel's eye.

The Colonel grimaced a reference to the heat of the place. He had finished his business with the official. "Have you seen all you wanted to see?"

Latimer nodded.

Colonel Haki turned and looked at the body as if it were a piece of his own handiwork of which he was taking leave. For a moment or two he remained motionless. Then his right arm went out, and, grasping the dead man's hair, he lifted the head so that the sightless eyes stared into his.

"Ugly devil, isn't he?" he said. "Life is very strange. I've known about him for nearly twenty years and this is the first time I've met him face to face. Those eyes have seen some things I should like to see. It is a pity that the mouth can never speak about them."

He let the head go and it dropped back with a thud on to the table. Then, he drew out his silk handkerchief and wiped his fingers carefully. "The sooner he's in a coffin the better," he added as they walked away.

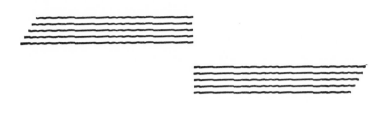

CHAPTER III

NINETEEN

TWENTY-TWO

I<small>N</small> the early hours of an August morning in nineteen twenty-two, the Turkish Nationalist Army under the command of Mustafa Kemal Pasha attacked the centre of the Greek army at Dumlu Punar on the plateau two hundred miles west of Smyrna. By the following morning, the Greek army had broken and was in headlong retreat towards Smyrna and the sea. In the days that followed, the retreat became a rout. Unable to destroy the Turkish army, the Greeks turned with frantic savagery to the business of destroying the Turkish population in the path

32

of their flight. From Alashehr to Smyrna they burnt and slaughtered. Not a village was left standing. Amid the smouldering ruins the pursuing Turks found the bodies of the villagers. Assisted by the few half-crazed Anatolian peasants who had survived, they took their revenge on the Greeks they were able to overtake. To the bodies of the Turkish women and children were added the mutilated carcasses of Greek stragglers. But the main Greek army had escaped by sea. Their lust for infidel blood still unsatisfied, the Turks swept on. On the ninth of September, they occupied Smyrna.

For a fortnight, refugees from the oncoming Turks had been pouring into the city to swell the already large Greek and Armenian populations. They had thought that the Greek army would turn and defend Smyrna. But the Greek army had fled. Now they were caught in a trap. The holocaust began.

The register of the Armenian Asia Minor Defence League had been seized by the occupying troops, and, on the night of the tenth, a party of regulars entered the Armenian quarters to find and kill those whose names appeared on the register. The Armenians resisted and the Turks ran amok. The massacre that followed acted like a signal. Encouraged by their officers, the Turkish troops descended next day upon the non-Turkish quarters of the city and began systematically to kill. Dragged from their houses and hiding places, men, women and children were butchered in the streets which soon became littered with mutilated bodies. The wooden walls of the churches, packed with refugees, were drenched with benzine and fired. The occupants who were not burnt alive were bayoneted as they tried to escape. In many parts looted houses had also been set on fire and now the flames began to spread.

At first, attempts were made to isolate the blaze. Then, the wind changed, blowing the fire away from the Turkish quarter, and further outbreaks were started by the troops. Soon, the whole city, with the exception of the Turkish quarter and a few houses near the Kassamba railway station, was burning fiercely The massacre continued with unabated ferocity. A cordon of troops was drawn round the city to keep the refugees within the burning area. The streams of panic-stricken fugitives were shot down pitilessly or driven back into the inferno. The narrow, gutted streets became so choked with corpses that, even had the would-be rescue parties been able to endure the sickening stench that arose, they could not have passed along them. Smyrna was changed from a city into a charnel-house. Many refugees had tried to reach ships in the inner harbour. Shot, drowned, mangled by propellers, their bodies floated hideously in the blood-tinged water. But the quayside was still crowded with those trying frantically to escape from the blazing waterfront buildings toppling above them a few yards behind. It was said that the screams of these people were heard a mile out at sea. *Giaur Izmir*—infidel Smyrna—had atoned for its sins.

By the time that dawn broke on the fifteenth of September, over one hundred and twenty thousand persons had perished; but somewhere amidst that horror had been Dimitrios, alive.

As, sixteen years later, his train drew into Smyrna, Latimer came to the conclusion that he was being a fool. It was not a conclusion that he had reached hastily or without weighing carefully all the available evidence. It was a conclusion that he disliked exceedingly. Yet there were two hard facts that were inescapable. In the first place, he might have asked Colonel Haki for assistance in gaining access to the records of the court-martial and confession of Dhris Mohammed but had not been able to think of a reasonable excuse for doing so. In the second place, he knew so little Turkish that, even assuming that he could gain access to the records without Colonel Haki's help, he would be unable to read them. To have set out at all on this fantastic and slightly undignified wild goose chase was bad enough. To have set out without, so to speak, a gun and ammunition with which to make the killing was crass idiocy. Had he not been installed within an hour of his arrival in an excellent hotel, had his room not possessed a very comfortable bed and a view across the gulf to the sun-drenched, khaki hills that lay beyond it and, above all, had he not been offered a dry Martini by the French proprietor who greeted him, he would have abandoned his experiment in detection and returned forthwith to Istanbul. As it was . . . Dimitrios or no Dimitrios, he might as well see something of Smyrna now that he was in the place. He partly unpacked his suit-cases.

On his second morning in Smyrna, he went to the proprietor of his hotel and asked to be put in touch with a good interpreter.

Fedor Muishkin was a self-important little Russian of about sixty with a thick, pendulous underlip which flapped and quivered as he talked. He had an office on the waterfront and earned his living by translating business documents and interpreting for the masters and pursers of foreign cargo vessels using the port. He had been a Men-shevik and had fled from Odessa in nineteen-nineteen; but although, as the hotel proprietor pointed out sardonically, he now declared himself in sympathy with the Soviets, he had preferred not to return to Russia. A humbug, mind you; but at the same time a good interpreter. If you wanted an interpreter, Muishkin was the man.

Muishkin himself also said that he was the man. He had a high-pitched, husky voice and scratched himself a great deal. His English was accurate but larded with slang phrases that never seemed quite to fit their contexts. He said: "If there is anything I can do for you just give me the wire. I'm dirt cheap."

"I want," Latimer explained, "to trace the record of a Greek who left here in September, nineteen twenty-two."

The other's eyebrows went up. "Nineteen twenty-two, eh? A Greek who left here?" He chuckled breathlessly. "A good many of them left here then." He spat on one forefinger and drew it across his throat. "Like that! It was damnawful the way those Turks treated those Greeks. Bloody!"

"This man got away on a refugee ship. His name was Dimitrios. He was believed to have conspired with a ne-gro named Dhris Mohammed to murder a moneylender named Sholem. The negro was tried by a military court and hanged. Dimitrios got away. I want to inspect, if I can, the records of the evidence taken at the trial, the confession of the negro and the inquiries concerning Dimitrios."

Muishkin stared. "Dimitrios?"

"Yes."

"Nineteen twenty-two?"

"Yes." Latimer's heart jumped. "Why? Did you happen to know him?"

The Russian appeared to be about to say something and then to change his mind. He shook his head. "No. I was thinking that it was a very common name. Have you permission to examine the police archives?"

"No. I was hoping that you might be able to advise me as to the best way of getting permission. I realise, of course, that your business is only concerned with making translations, but if you could help me in this matter I should be very grateful."

Muishkin pinched his lower lip thoughtfully. "Perhaps if you were to approach the British Vice-Consul and request him to secure permission . . . ?" He broke off. "But excuse me," he said; "why do you want these records? I ask, not because I cannot mind my own damn business, but that question may be asked by the police. Now," he went on slowly, "if it were a *legal* matter and quite above board and Bristol fashion, I have a friend with influence who might arrange the matter quite cheap."

Latimer felt himself redden. "As it happens," he said as casually as he could, "it *is* a legal matter. I could, of course, go to the Consul, but if you care to arrange this business for me then I shall be saved the trouble."

"A pleasure. I shall speak to my friend to-day. The police, you understand, are damnawful and if I go to them myself it will cost plenty. I like to protect my clients."

"That's very good of you."

"Don't mention it." A faraway look came into his eyes. "I like you British, you know. You understand how to do business. You do not haggle like those damn Greeks. When a man says cash with order you pay cash with order. A deposit? O.K. The British play fair. There is a mutual confidence between all parties. A chap can do his best work under such circumstances. He feels . . ."

"How much?" interrupted Latimer.

"Five hundred piastres?" He said it hesitantly. His eyes were mournful. Here was an artist who had no confidence in himself, a child in business matters, happy only in his work.

Latimer thought for a moment. Five hundred piastres was less than a pound. Cheap enough. Then he detected a gleam in the mournful eyes.

"Two hundred and fifty," he said firmly.

Muishkin threw up his hands in despair. He had to live. There was his friend, too. He had great influence.

Soon after, having paid over one hundred and fifty piastres on account of a finally agreed price of three hundred (including fifty piastres for the influential friend), Latimer left. He walked back along the quayside not unpleased with his morning's work. He would have preferred, it was true, to have examined the records himself and to have seen the translation done. He would have felt more like an investigator and less like an inquisitive tourist; but there it was. There was always the chance, of course, that Muishkin might have in mind the pocketing of an easy one hundred and fifty piastres; but somehow he did not think so. He was susceptible to impressions and the Russian had impressed him as being fundamentally, if not superficially, honest. And there could be no question of his being deceived by manufactured documents. Colonel Haki had told him enough about the Dhris Mohammed court-martial to enable him to detect that sort of fraud. The only thing that could go wrong was that the friend would prove unworthy of his fifty piastres.

The following day, Muishkin arrived, sweating profusely, very shortly before the time of the evening meal, and Latimer was drinking an aperitif. Muishkin came towards him waving his arms and rolling his eyes despairingly and, throwing himself into an armchair, emitted a loud gasp of exhaustion.

"What a day! Such heat!" he said.

"Have you got the translation?"

Muishkin nodded wearily, put his hand in his inside pocket and drew out a bundle of papers.

"Will you have a drink?" said Latimer.

The Russian's eyes flickered open and he looked round like a man regaining consciousness. He said: "If you like. I will have an absinthe, please. *Avec de la glace.*"

The waiter took the order and Latimer sat back to inspect his purchase.

The translation was handwritten and covered twelve large sheets of paper. Latimer glanced through the first two or three pages. There was no doubt that it was all genuine. He began to read it carefully.

NATIONAL GOVERNMENT OF TURKEY
TRIBUNAL OF INDEPENDENCE

By order of the officer commanding the garrison of Izmir, acting under the Decree Law promulgated at Ankara on the eighteenth day of the sixth month of nineteen twenty-two in the new calendar.

Summary of evidence taken before the Deputy Presi-

dent of the Tribunal, Major-of-Brigade Zia Haki, on the sixth day of the tenth month of nineteen twenty-two in the new calendar.

"The Jew, Zakari, complains that the murder of his cousin, Sholem, was the work of Dhris Mohammed, a negro fig-packer of Buja.

"Last week, a patrol belonging to the sixtieth regiment discovered the body of Sholem, a Deunme moneylender, in his room in an unnamed street near the Old Mosque. His throat had been cut. Although this man was neither the son of True Believers nor of good reputation, our vigilant police instituted inquiries and discovered that his money had been taken.

"Several days later, the complainant, Zakari, informed the Commandant of Police that he had been in a café and seen the man Dhris showing handfuls of Greek money. He knew Dhris for a poor man and was surprised. Later, when Dhris had become drunk, he heard him boast that the Jew Sholem had lent him money without interest. At that time he knew nothing of the death of Sholem but when his relations told him of it he remembered what he had seen and heard.

"Evidence was heard from Abdul Hakk, the owner of the Bar Cristal, who said that Dhris had shown this Greek money, a matter of several hundreds of drachmas, and had boasted that he had had it from the Jew Sholem without interest. He had thought this strange for Sholem was a hard man.

"A dock-worker named Ismail also deposed that he had heard this from the prisoner.

"Asked to explain how he came into possession of the money, the murderer at first denied that he had had the money or that he had ever seen Sholem and said that as a True Believer, he was hated by the Jew Zakari. He said that Abdul Hakk and Ismail had also lied.

"Questioned sternly by the Deputy-President of the Tribunal, he then admitted that he had had the money and that it had been given to him by Sholem for a service he had done. But he could not explain what this service had been and his manner became strange and agitated. He denied killing Sholem and in a blasphemous way called upon the True God to witness his innocence.

"The Deputy-President then ordered that the prisoner be hanged, the other members of the Tribunal agreeing that this was right and just."

Latimer had come to the end of a page. He looked at Muishkin. The Russian had swallowed the absinthe and was examining the glass. He caught Latimer's eye. "Absinthe," he said, "is very good indeed. So cooling."

"Will you have another?"

"If you like." He smiled and indicated the papers in Latimer's hand. "That's all right, eh?"

"Oh yes, it looks all right. But they are a little vague about their dates, aren't they? There is no doctor's report either, and no attempt to fix the time of the murder. As for the evidence, it seems fantastically feeble to me. Nothing was proved."

Muishkin looked surprised. "But why bother to prove? This negro was obviously guilty. Best to hang him."

"I see. Well, if you don't mind, I'll go on glancing through it."

Muishkin shrugged, stretched himself luxuriously and signalled to the waiter. Latimer turned a page and went on reading.

STATEMENT MADE BY THE MURDERER, DHRIS MO-
HAMMED, IN THE PRESENCE OF THE GUARD-
COMMANDANT OF THE BARRACKS IN IZMIR AND
OTHER TRUE WITNESSES.

"It is said in the book that he shall not prosper who makes lies and I say these things in order to prove my innocence and to save myself from the gallows. I have lied but now I will tell the truth. I am a True Believer. There is no god but God.

"I did not kill Sholem. I tell you I did not kill him. Why should I lie now? Yes, I will explain. It was not I but Dimitrios who killed Sholem.

"I will tell you about Dimitrios and you will believe me. Dimitrios is a Greek. To Greeks he is a Greek but to True Believers he says that he is also a Believer and that it is only with the authorities that he is a Greek because of some papers signed by his foster-parents.

"Dimitrios worked with others of us in the packing sheds and he was hated by many for his violence and for his bitter tongue. But I am a man who loves other men as brothers and I would speak with Dimitrios sometimes as he worked and tell him of the religion of God. And he would listen.

"Then, when the Greeks were fleeing before the victorious army of the True God, Dimitrios came to my house and asked me to hide him from the terror of the Greeks. He said that he was a True Believer. So I hid him. Then, our glorious army came to our aid. But Dimitrios did not go because he was, by reason of this paper signed by his foster-parents, a Greek and in fear of his life. So he stayed in my house and when he went out dressed like a Turk. Then, one day, he said certain things to me. There was the Jew Sholem, he said, who had much money, Greek pieces and some gold, hidden below the floor of his room. It was the time, he said, to take our revenge upon those who had insulted the True God and His Prophet. It was wrong, he said, that a pig of a Jew should have the money rightfully belonging to True Believers. He proposed that we should go secretly to Sholem, bind him and take his money.

"At first I was afraid, but he put heart into me, reminding me of the book which says that whosoever fights for the religion of God, whether he be slain or victorious, will surely find a great reward. This is now my reward: to be hanged like a dog.

"Yes, I will go on. That night after the curfew we went to the place where Sholem lived and crept up the stairs to his room. The door was bolted. Then Dimitrios knocked and called out that it was a patrol to search the house and Sholem opened the door. He had been in bed and he was grumbling at being woken from his sleep. When he saw us he called upon God and tried to close the door. But Dimitrios seized him and held him while I went in as we had arranged and searched for the loose board which concealed the money. Dimitrios dragged the old man across the bed and kept him down with his knee.

"I soon found the loose board and turned round full of joy to tell Dimitrios. He had his back turned towards me and was pressing down on Sholem with the blanket to stifle his cries. He had said that he himself would bind Sholem with rope which we had brought. I saw him now draw out his knife. I thought that he was meaning to cut the rope for some purpose and I said nothing. Then, before I could speak, he drove the knife into the old Jew's neck and pulled it across his throat.

"I saw the blood bubble and spurt out as if from a fountain and Sholem rolled over. Dimitrios stood away and watched him for a moment then he looked at me. I asked him what he had done and he answered that it was necessary to kill Sholem for fear that he should point us out to the police. Sholem was still moving on the bed and the blood was still bubbling, but Dimitrios said that he was certainly dead. After that, we took the money.

"Then, Dimitrios said that it was better that we should not go together but that each should take his share and go separately. That was agreed. I was afraid then, for Dimitrios had a knife and I had none and I thought he meant to kill me. I wondered why he had told me of the money. He had said that he needed a companion to search for the money while he held Sholem. But I could see that he had meant from the first to kill Sholem. Why then had he brought me? He could have found the money for himself after he had killed the Jew. But we divided the money equally and he smiled and did not try to kill me. We left the place separately. He had told me the day before that there were Greek ships lying off the coast near Smyrna and that he had overheard a man saying that the captains of these ships were taking refugees who could pay. I think that he escaped on one of those ships.

"I see now that I was a fool of fools and that he was

right to smile at me. He knew that when my purse becomes full my head becomes empty. He knew, God's curses fall upon him, that when I sin by becoming drunk I cannot stop my tongue from wagging. I did not kill Sholem. It was Dimitrios the Greek who killed him. Dimitrios . . ." (*here followed a stream of unprintable obscenities*). "There is no doubt in what I say. As God is God and as Mohammed is His Prophet, I swear that I have said the truth. For the love of God, have mercy."

A note was appended to this, saying that the confession had been signed with a thumb print and witnessed. The record went on:

"The murderer was asked for a description of this Dimitrios and said:

" 'He has the look of a Greek but I do not think he is one because he hates his own countrymen. He is shorter than I am and his hair is long and straight. His face is very still and he speaks very little. His eyes are brown and tired-looking. Many men are afraid of him but I do not understand this as he is not strong and I could break him with my two hands.'

"N.B. The height of this man is 185 centimetres.

"Inquiries have been made concerning the man Dimitrios at the packing sheds. He is known and disliked. Nothing has been heard of him for several weeks and he is presumed to have died in the fire. This seems likely.

"The murderer was executed on the ninth day of the tenth month of nineteen twenty-two in the new calendar."

Latimer returned to the confession and examined it thoughtfully. It rang true; there was no doubt about that. There was a circumstantial feeling about it. The negro, Dhris, had obviously been a very stupid man. Could he have invented those details about the scene in Sholem's room? A guilty man inventing a tale would surely have embroidered it differently. And there was his fear that Dimitrios might have been going to kill him. If he himself had been responsible for the killing he would not have thought of that. Colonel Haki had said that it was the sort of story that a man might invent to save his neck. Fear did stimulate even the most sluggish imaginations; but did it stimulate them in quite that sort of way? The authorities obviously had not cared very much whether the story was or was not true. Their inquiries had been pitiably half-hearted; yet even so they had tended to confirm the negro's story. Dimitrios had been presumed to have died in the fire. There was no evidence offered to support the presumption. It had, no doubt, been easier to hang Dhris Mohammed than to conduct, amidst all the terrible confusion of those October days, a search for a hypothetical Greek named Dimitrios. Dimitrios had, of course, counted on that fact. But for the accident of the Colonel's transfer to the secret police, he would never have been connected with the affair.

Latimer had once seen a zoophysicist friend of his build up the complete skeleton of a prehistoric animal from a fragment of fossilised bone. It had taken the zoophysicist nearly two years and Latimer, the economist, had marvelled at the man's inexhaustible enthusiasm for the task. Now, for the first time, he understood that enthusiasm. He had unearthed a single twisted fragment of the mind of Dimitrios and now he wanted to complete the structure. The fragment was small enough but it was substantial. The wretched Dhris had never had a chance. Dimitrios had used the negro's dull wits, had played upon his religious fanaticism, his simplicity, his cupidity with a skill that was terrifying. "We divided the money equally and he smiled and did not try to kill me." Dimitrios had smiled. And the negro had been too preoccupied with his fear of the man whom he could have broken with his two hands to wonder about that smile until it was too late. The brown, tired-looking eyes had watched Dhris Mohammed and understood him perfectly.

Latimer folded up the papers, put them in his pocket and turned to Muishkin.

"One hundred and fifty piastres, I owe you."

"Right," said Muishkin into his glass. He had ordered and was now finishing his third absinthe. He set down his glass and took the money from Latimer. "I like you," he said seriously; "you have no *snobisme*. Now you will have a drink with me, eh?"

Latimer glanced at his watch. "Why not have some dinner with me first?"

"Good!" Muishkin clambered laboriously to his feet. "Good," he repeated and Latimer saw that his eyes were unnaturally bright.

At the Russian's suggestion they went out to a restaurant, a place of subdued lights and red plush and gilt and stained mirrors, where French food was served. It was crowded and the atmosphere was thick with cigarette smoke. They sat down in upholstered chairs which exuded wafts of stale scent.

"*Ton*," said Muishkin looking round. He seized the menu and after some deliberation chose the most expensive dish on it. With their food they drank a syrupy, resinous Smyrna wine. Muishkin began to talk about his life. Odessa, nineteen eighteen. Stambul, nineteen nineteen. Smyrna, nineteen twenty-one. Bolsheviks. Wrangel's army. Kiev. A woman they called The Butcher. They used the abattoir as a prison because the prison had become an abattoir. Terrible, damnawful atrocities. Allied army of occupation. The English sporting. American relief. Bed bugs. Typhus. Vickers guns. The Greeks—God, those Greeks! Fortunes waiting to be picked up. Kemalists. His voice droned on while outside, through the cigarette smoke, beyond the red plush and the gilt and the white table-cloths, the amethyst twilight had deepened into night.

Another bottle of syrupy wine arrived. Latimer began to feel sleepy.

"And after so much madness, where are we now?" demanded Muishkin. His English had been steadily deteriorating. Now, his lower lip wet and quivering with emotion, he fixed Latimer with the unwavering stare of the drunk about to become philosophical. "Where now?" he repeated and thumped the table.

"In Smyrna," said Latimer and realised suddenly that he had drunk too much of the wine.

Muishkin shook his head irritably. "We grade rapidly to damnawful hell," he declared. "Are you a Marxist?"

"No."

Muishkin leaned forward confidentially. "Neither me." He plucked at Latimer's sleeve. His lip trembled violently. "I'm a swindler."

"Are you?"

"Yes." Tears began to form in his eyes. "I damn well swindled you."

"Did you?"

"Yes." He fumbled in his pocket. "You are no snob.

You must take back fifty piastres."

"What for?"

"Take them back." The tears began to course down his cheeks and mingle with the sweat collecting on the point of his chin. "I swindled you, Mister. There was no damn friend to pay, no permission, nothing."

"Do you mean that you made up those records yourself?"

Muishkin sat up sharply. *"Je ne suis pas un faussaire,"* he asserted. He wagged a finger in Latimer's face. "This type came to me three months ago. By paying large bribes—" the finger stabbed emphatically "—large bribes, he had obtained the permissions to examine the archives for the dossier on the murder of Sholem. The dossier was in the old Arabic script and he brought photographs of the pages to me to translate. He took the photographs back, but I kept the translation on file. You see? I swindled you. You paid fifty piastres too much. Faugh!" He snapped his fingers. "I could have swindled five hundred piastres, and you would have paid. I am too soft."

"What did he want with this information?"

Muishkin looked sulky. "I can mind my own damn nose in the business."

"What did he look like?"

"He looked like a Frenchman."

"What sort of a Frenchman?"

But Muishkin's head had sagged forward on to his chest and he did not answer. Then, after a moment or two, he raised his head and stared blankly at Latimer. His face was livid and Latimer guessed that he would very shortly be sick. His lips moved.

"Je ne suis pas un faussaire," he muttered; "three hun-

dred piastres, dirt cheap!" He stood up suddenly, murmured, *"Excusez-moi,"* and walked rapidly in the direction of the toilet.

Latimer waited for a time then paid the bill and went to investigate. There was another entrance to the toilet and Muishkin had gone. Latimer walked back to his hotel.

From the balcony outside the window of his room, he could see over the bay to the hills beyond. A moon had risen and its reflection gleamed through the tangle of crane jibs along the quay where the steamers berthed. The seachlights of a Turkish cruiser anchored in the roadstead outside the inner port swung round like long white fingers, brushed the summits of the hills and were extinguished. Out in the harbour and on the slopes above the town pinpoints of light twinkled. A slight warm breeze off the sea had begun to stir the leaves of a rubber tree in the garden below him. In another room of the hotel a woman laughed. Somewhere in the distance a gramophone was playing a tango. The turntable was revolving too quickly and the sound was shrill and congested.

Latimer lit a final cigarette and wondered for the hundredth time what the man who looked like a Frenchman had wanted with the dossier of the Sholem murder. At last he pitched his cigarette away and shrugged. One thing was certain: he could not possibly have been interested in Dimitrios.

CHAPTER IV

MR. PETERS

Two days later, Latimer left Smyrna. He did not see Muishkin again.

The situation in which a person, imagining fondly that he is in charge of his own destiny, is, in fact, the sport of circumstances beyond his control, is always fascinating. It is the essential element in most good theatre from the *Œdipus* of Sophocles to *East Lynne*. When, however, that person is oneself and one is examining the situation in retrospect, the fascination becomes a trifle morbid. Thus, when Latimer used afterwards to look back upon those two days in Smyrna, it was not so much his ignorance of the part he was playing but the bliss which accompanied the ignorance that so appalled him. He had gone into the business believing his eyes to be wide open, whereas, actually, they had been tightly shut. That, no doubt, could not have been helped. The galling part was that he had failed for so long to perceive the fact. Of course, he did himself less than justice; but his self-esteem had been punctured; he had been transferred without his knowledge from the role of sophisticated, impersonal weigher of facts to that of active participator in a melodrama.

Of the imminence of that humiliation, however, he had no inkling when, on the morning after his dinner with Muishkin, he sat down with a pencil and a notebook to arrange the material for his experiment in detection.

Some time early in October nineteen twenty-two, Dimitrios had left Smyrna. He had had money and had probably purchased a passage on a Greek steamer. The next time Colonel Haki had heard of him he had been in Adrianople two years later. In that interim, however, the Bulgarian police had had trouble with him in Sofia in connection with the attempted assassination of Stambulisky. Latimer was a little hazy as to the precise date of that attempt but he began to jot down a rough chronological table.

TIME	PLACE	REMARKS	SOURCE OF INFORMATION
1922 (October)	-Smyrna	Sholem	Police Archives
1923 (early part)	-Sofia	Stambulisky	Colonel Haki
1924 - -	-Adrianople	Kemal attempt	Colonel Haki
1926 - -	-Belgrade	Espionage for France	Colonel Haki
1926 - -	-Switzerland	Talat passport	Colonel Haki
1929-31 (?) -	-Paris	Drugs	Colonel Haki
1932 - -	-Zagreb	Croat assassin	Colonel Haki
1937 - -	-Lyons	*Carte d'identité*	Colonel Haki
1938 - -	-Istanbul	Murdered	Colonel Haki

The immediate problem, then, was quite clear-cut. In the six months following the murder of Sholem, Dimitrios had escaped from Smyrna, made his way to Sofia and become involved in a plot to assassinate the Bulgarian Prime Minister. Latimer found it a trifle difficult to form any estimate of the time required to become involved in a plot to kill a Prime Minister; but it was fairly certain that Dimitrios must have arrived in Sofia soon after his departure from Smyrna. If he had indeed escaped by Greek steamer he must have gone first to the Piræus and Athens. From Athens he could have reached Sofia overland, via Salonika, or by sea, via the Dardanelles and the Golden Horn to Bourgaz or Varna, Bulgaria's Black Sea port. Istanbul at that time was in Allied hands. He would have had nothing to fear from the Allies. The question was: what had induced him to go to Sofia?

However, the logical course now was to go to Athens and tackle the job of picking up the trail there. It would not be easy. Even if attempts had been made to record the presence of every refugee among the tens of thousands who had arrived, it was more than probable that what records still existed, if any, were incomplete. There was no point, however, in anticipating failure. He had several valuable friends in Athens and if there was a record in existence it was fairly certain that he would be able to get access to it. He shut up his notebook.

When the weekly boat to the Piræus left Smyrna the following day, Latimer was among the passengers.

During the months following the Turkish occupation of Smyrna, more than eight hundred thousand Greeks returned to their country. They came, boatload after boatload of them, packed on the decks and in the holds. Many of them were naked and starving. Some still carried in their arms the dead children they had had no time to bury. With them came the germs of typhus and smallpox.

War-weary and ruined, gripped by a food shortage and starved of medical supplies, their motherland received them. In the hastily improvised refugee camps they died like flies. Outside Athens, on the Piræus, in Salonika, masses of humanity lay rotting in the cold of a Greek winter. Then, the Fourth Assembly of the League of Nations, in session in Geneva, voted one hundred thousand gold francs to the Nansen relief organisation for immediate use in Greece. The work of salvage began. Huge refugee settlements were organised. Food was brought and clothing and medical supplies. The epidemics were stopped. The survivors began to sort themselves into new communities. For the first time in history, large scale disaster had been halted by goodwill and reason. It seemed as if the human animal were at last discovering a conscience, as if it were at last becoming aware of its humanity.

All this and more, Latimer heard from a friend, one Siantos, in Athens. When, however, he came to the point of his inquiries, Siantos pursed his lips.

"A complete register of those who arrived from Smyrna? That is a tall order. If you had seen them come . . . So many and in such a state . . ." And then followed the inevitable question. "Why are you interested?"

It had occurred to Latimer that this question was going to crop up again and again. He had accordingly prepared his explanation. To have told the truth, to have explained that he was trying, for purely academic reasons, to trace the history of a dead criminal named Dimitrios would have been a long and uneasy business. He was, in any case, not anxious to have a second opinion on his prospects of success. His own was depressing enough. What had seemed a fascinating idea in a Turkish mortuary might well, in the bright, warm light of a Greek autumn, appear merely absurd. Much simpler to avoid the issue altogether.

He answered: "It is in connection with a new book I am writing. A matter of detail that must be checked. I want to see if it is possible to trace an individual refugee after so long."

Siantos said that he understood and Latimer grinned ashamedly to himself. The fact that one was a writer could be relied upon to explain away the most curious extravagances.

He had gone to Siantos because he knew that the man had a Government post of some importance in Athens; but now his first disappointment was in store for him. A week went by and, at the end of it, Siantos was able to tell him only that a register was in existence, that it was in the custody of the municipal authorities and that it was not open to inspection by unauthorised persons. Permission would have to be obtained. It took another week, a week of waiting, of sitting in *kafenios*, of being introduced to thirsty gentlemen with connections in the municipal offices. At last, however, the permission was forthcoming and the following day Latimer presented himself at the bureau in which the records were housed.

The inquiry office was a bare tiled room with a counter at one end. Behind the counter sat the official in charge. He shrugged over the information Latimer had to give him. A fig-packer named Dimitrios? October nineteen twenty-two? It was impossible. The register had been compiled alphabetically by surname.

Latimer's heart sank. All his trouble, then, was to go for nothing. He had thanked the man and was turning away when he had an idea. There was just a remote chance . . .

He turned back to the official. "The surname," he said, "may have been Makropoulos."

He was dimly aware, as he said it, that behind him a man had entered the inquiry office through the door leading to the street. The sun was streaming obliquely into the room and for an instant a long, distorted shadow twisted across the tiles as the new-comer passed the window.

"Dimitrios Makropoulos?" repeated the official. "That is better. If there was a person of that name on the register we will find him. It is a question of patience and organisation. Please come this way."

He raised the flap of the counter for Latimer to go through. As he did so he glanced over Latimer's shoulder.

"Gone!" he exclaimed. "I have no assistance in my work of organisation here. The whole burden falls upon my shoulders. Yet people have no patience. I am engaged for a moment. They cannot wait." He shrugged. "That is their affair. I do my duty. If you will follow me, please."

Latimer followed him down a flight of stone stairs into an extensive basement occupied by row upon row of steel cabinets.

"Organisation," commented the official; "that is the secret of modern statecraft. Organisation will make a

greater Greece. A new empire. But patience is necessary." He led the way to a series of small cabinets in one
corner of the basement, pulled open one of the drawers
and began with his finger-nail to flick over a series of
cards. At last he stopped at a card and examined it carefully before closing the drawer. "Makropoulos. If there
is a record of this man we shall find it in drawer number
sixteen. That is organisation."

In drawer number sixteen, however, they drew blank.
The official threw up his hands in despair and searched
again without success. Then inspiration came to Latimer.

"Try under the name of Talat," he said desperately.

"But that is a Turkish name."

"I know it. But try it."

The official shrugged. There was another reference to
the main index. "Drawer twenty-seven," announced the
official a little impatiently; "are you sure that this man
came to Athens? Many went to Salonika. Why not this
fig-packer?"

This was precisely the question that Latimer had been
asking himself. He said nothing and watched the official's
finger-nail flicking over another series of cards. Suddenly
it stopped.

"Have you found it?" said Latimer quickly.

The official pulled out a card. "Here is one," he said.
"The man was a fig-packer, but the name is Dimitrios
Tala*dis*."

"Let me see." Latimer took the card. Dimitrios Taladis! There it was in black and white. He had found out
something that Colonel Haki did not know. Dimitrios had
used the name Talat before nineteen twenty-six. There
could be no doubt that it *was* Dimitrios. He had merely

tacked a Greek suffix on to the name. He stared at the card. And there were here some other things that Colonel Haki did not know.

He looked up at the beaming official. "Can I copy this?"

"Of course. Patience and organisation, you see. My organisation is for use. But I must not let the record out of my sight. That is the regulation."

Under the now somewhat mystified eyes of the apostle of organisation and patience Latimer began to copy the wording on the card into his note-book, translating it as he did so into English. He wrote:

NUMBER T.53462

NATIONAL RELIEF ORGANISATION
Refugee Section: ATHINAI

Sex: Male. *Name:* Dimitrios Taladis. *Born:* Salonika, 1889. *Occupation:* Fig-packer. *Parents:* believed dead. *Identity Papers or Passport:* Identity card lost. Said to have been issued at Smyrna. *Nationality:* Greek. *Arrived:* October 1, 1922. *Coming from:* Smyrna. *On examination:* Able-bodied. No disease. Without money. Assigned to camp at Tabouria. Temporary identity paper issued. *Note:* Left Tabouria on own initiative, November 29th, 1922. Warrant for arrest, on charge of robbery and attempted murder, issued in Athinai, November 30th, 1922. Believed to have escaped by sea.

Yes, that was Dimitrios all right. The date of his birth agreed with that supplied by the Greek police (and based on information gained prior to nineteen twenty-two) to Colonel Haki. The place of birth, however, was differ-

ent. According to the Turkish dossier it had been Larissa.
Why had Dimitrios bothered to change it? If he were
giving a false name, he must have seen that the chances of
its falsity being discovered by reference to the registration records were as great for Salonika as for Larissa.

Salonika eighteen eighty-nine! Why Salonika? Then
Latimer remembered. Of course! It was quite simple. In
eighteen eighty-nine Salonika had been in Turkish territory, a part of the Ottoman Empire. The registration
records of that period would, in all probability, not be
available to the Greek authorities. Dimitrios had certainly
been no fool. But why had he picked on the name Taladis? Why had he not chosen a typical Greek name? The
Turkish "Talat" must have had some special association
for him. As for his identity card issued in Smyrna, that
would naturally be "lost" since, presumably, it had been
issued to him in the name of Makropoulos by which he
was already known to the Greek police.

The date of his arrival fitted in with the vague allusions
to time made in the court-martial. Unlike the majority
of his fellow refugees, he had been able-bodied and free
from disease when he had arrived. Naturally. Thanks to
Sholem's Greek money, he had been able to buy a passage
to the Piræus and travel in comparative comfort instead of
being loaded on to a refugee ship with thousands of others.
Dimitrios had known how to look after himself. The fig-
packer had packed enough figs. Dimitrios the Man had
been emerging from his chrysalis. No doubt he had had
a substantial amount of Sholem's money left when he had
arrived. Yet to the relief authorities he had been "without money." That had been sensible of him. He might
otherwise have been forced to buy food and clothing for

stupid fools who had failed to provide, as he had provided, for the future. His expenses had been heavy enough as it was; so heavy that another Sholem had been needed. No doubt he had regretted Dhris Mohammed's half share.

"Believed to have escaped by sea." With the proceeds of the second robbery added to the balance from the first, he had no doubt been able to pay for his passage to Bourgaz. It would obviously have been too risky for him to have gone overland. He had only temporary identity papers and might have been stopped at the frontier, whereas in Bourgaz, the same papers issued by an international relief commission with considerable prestige would have enabled him to get through.

The official's much-advertised patience was showing signs of wearing thin. Latimer handed over the card, expressed his thanks in a suitable manner and returned thoughtfully to his hotel.

He was feeling pleased with himself. He had discovered some new information about Dimitrios and he had discovered it through his own efforts. It had been, it was true, an obvious piece of routine inquiry; but, in the best Scotland Yard tradition, it had called for patience and persistence. Besides, if he had not thought of trying the Talat name . . . He wished that he could have sent a report of his investigations to Colonel Haki, but that was out of the question. The Colonel would probably fail to understand the spirit in which the experiment in detection was being made. In any case, Dimitrios himself would by this time be mouldering below ground, his dossier sealed and forgotten in the archives of the Turkish secret police. The main thing was now to tackle the Sofia affair.

He tried to remember what he knew about post-war

Bulgarian politics and speedily came to the conclusion that it was very little. In nineteen twenty-three Stambulisky had, he knew, been head of a government of liberal tendencies; but of just how liberal those tendencies had been he had no idea. There had been an attempted assassination and later a military *coup d'état* carried out at the instigation, if not under the leadership of the I.M.R.O., the International Macedonian Revolutionary Organisation. Stambulisky had fled from Sofia, tried to organise a counter-revolution and been killed. That was the gist of the affair, he thought. But of the rights and wrongs of it (if any such distinction were possible), of the nature of the political forces involved, he was quite ignorant. That state of affairs would have to be remedied; and the place in which to remedy it would be Sofia.

That evening he asked Siantos to dinner. Latimer knew him for a vain, generous soul who liked discussing his friends' problems and was flattered when, by making judicious use of his official position, he could help them. After giving thanks for the assistance in the matter of the municipal register, Latimer broached the subject of Sofia.

"I am going to trespass on your kindness still further, my dear Siantos."

"So much the better."

"Do you know anyone in Sofia? I want a letter of introduction to an intelligent newspaper man there who could give me some inside information about Bulgarian politics in nineteen twenty-three."

Siantos smoothed his gleaming white hair and grinned admiringly. "You writers have bizarre tastes. Something might be done. Do you want a Greek or a Bulgar?"

"Greek for preference. I don't speak Bulgarian."

Siantos was thoughtful for a moment. "There is a man in Sofia named Marukakis," he said at last. "He is the Sofia correspondent of a French news agency. I do not know him myself, but I might be able to get a letter to him from a friend of mine." They were sitting in a restaurant, and now Siantos glanced round furtively and lowered his voice. "There is only one trouble about him from your point of view. I happen to know that he has . . ." The voice sunk still lower in tone. Latimer was prepared for nothing less horrible than leprosy. ". . . Communist tendencies," concluded Siantos in a whisper.

Latimer raised his eyebrows. "I don't regard that as a drawback. All the Communists I have ever met have been highly intelligent."

Siantos looked shocked. "How can that be? It is dangerous to say such things, my friend. Marxist thought is forbidden in Greece."

"When can I have that letter?"

Siantos sighed. "Bizarre!" he remarked. "I will get it for you to-morrow. You writers . . . !"

Within a week the letter of introduction had been obtained, and Latimer, having secured Greek exit and Bulgarian ingress visas, boarded a night train for Sofia.

The train was not crowded and he had hoped to have a sleeping car compartment to himself; but five minutes before the train was due to start, luggage was carried in and deposited above the empty berth. The owner of the luggage followed very soon after it.

"I must apologise for intruding on your privacy," he said to Latimer in English.

He was a fat, unhealthy-looking man of about fifty-five. He had turned to tip the porter before he spoke, and the first thing about him that impressed Latimer was that the seat of his trousers sagged absurdly, making his walk reminiscent of that of the hind legs of an elephant. Then Latimer saw his face and forgot about the trousers. There was the sort of sallow shapelessness about it that derives from simultaneous over-eating and under-sleeping. From above two heavy satchels of flesh peered a pair of pale-blue, bloodshot eyes that seemed to be permanently weeping. The nose was rubbery and indeterminate. It was the mouth that gave the face expression. The lips were pallid and undefined, seeming thicker than they really were. Pressed together over unnaturally white and regular false teeth, they were set permanently in a saccharine smile. In conjunction with the weeping eyes above it, it created an impression of sweet patience in adversity, quite startling in its intensity. Here, it said, was a man who had suffered, who had been buffeted by fiendishly vindictive Fates as no other man had been buffeted, yet who had retained his humble faith in the essential goodness of Man: here, it said, was a martyr who smiled through the flames,—smiled yet who could not but weep for the misery of others as he did so. He reminded Latimer of a high church priest he had known in England who had been unfrocked for embezzling the altar fund.

"The berth was unoccupied," Latimer pointed out; "there is no question of your intruding." He noted with an inward sigh that the man breathed very heavily and noisily through congested nostrils. He would probably snore.

The new-comer sat down on his berth and shook his head slowly. "How good of you to put it that way! How little kindliness there is in the world these days! How little thought for others!" The bloodshot eyes met Latimer's. "May I ask how far you are going?"

"Sofia."

"Sofia. So? A beautiful city, beautiful. I am continuing to Bucaresti. I do hope that we shall have a pleasant journey together."

Latimer said that he hoped so too. The fat man's English was very accurate, but he spoke it with an atrocious accent which Latimer could not place. It was thick and slightly guttural, as though he were speaking with his mouth full of cake. Occasionally, too, the accurate English would give out in the middle of a difficult sentence, which would be completed in very fluent French or German. Latimer gained the impression that the man had learned his English from books.

The fat man turned and began to unpack a small attaché-case containing a pair of woollen pyjamas, some bed socks and a dog-eared paper-backed book. Latimer managed to see the title of the book. It was called *Pearls of Everyday Wisdom* and was in French. The fat man arranged these things carefully on the shelf and then produced a packet of thin Greek cheroots.

"Will you allow me to smoke, please?" he said, extending the packet.

"Please do. But I won't smoke just now myself, thank you."

The train had begun to gather speed and the attendant came in to make up their beds. When he had gone, Latimer partially undressed and lay down on his bed.

The fat man picked up the book and then put it down again.

"You know," he said, "the moment the attendant told me that there was an Englishman on the train, I knew that I should have a pleasant journey." The smile came into play, sweet and compassionate, a spiritual pat on the head.

"It's very good of you to say so."

"Oh, no, that is how I feel."

"You speak very good English."

"English is the most beautiful language, I think. Shakespeare, H. G. Wells—you have some great English writers. But I cannot yet express all my ideas in English. I am, as you will have noticed, more at ease with French."

"But your own language . . . ?"

The fat man spread out large, soft hands on one of which twinkled a rather grubby diamond ring. "I am a citizen of the world," he said. "To me, all countries, all languages are beautiful. If only men could live as brothers, without hatred, seeing only the beautiful things. But no! There are always Communists etcetera."

Latimer said: "I think I'll go to sleep now."

"Sleep!" apostrophized his companion raptly; "the great mercy vouchsafed to us poor humans. My name," he added inconsequentially, "is Mister Peters."

"It has been very pleasant to have met you, Mr. Peters," returned Latimer firmly. "We get into Sofia so early that I shan't trouble to undress."

He switched off the main light in the compartment leaving only the dark blue emergency light glowing and the small reading lights over the berths. Then he stripped a blanket off his bed and wrapped it round him.

Mr. Peters had watched these preparations in wistful silence. Now, he began to undress, balancing himself dexterously against the lurching of the train as he put on his pyjamas. At last he clambered into his bed and lay still for a moment, the breath whistling through his nostrils. Then he turned over on his side, groped for his book and began to read. Latimer switched off his own reading lamp. A few moments later he was asleep.

The train reached the frontier in the early hours of the morning and he was awakened by the attendant for his papers. Mr. Peters was still reading. His papers had already been examined by the Greek and Bulgarian officials in the corridor outside and Latimer did not have an opportunity of ascertaining the nationality of the citizen of the world. A Bulgarian customs official put his head in the compartment, frowned at their suit-cases and then withdrew. Soon the train moved on over the frontier. Dozing fitfully, Latimer saw the thin strip of sky between the blinds turn blue-black and then grey. The train was due in Sofia at seven. When, at last, he rose to dress and collect his belongings, he saw that Mr. Peters had switched off his reading lamp and had his eyes closed. As the train began to rattle over the network of points outside Sofia, he gently slid the compartment door open.

Mr. Peters stirred and opened his eyes.

"I'm sorry," said Latimer, "I tried not to waken you."

In the semi-darkness of the compartment, the fat man's smile looked like a clown's grimace. "Please don't trouble yourself about me," he said. "I was not asleep. I meant to tell you that the best hotel for you to stay at would be the Slavianska Besseda."

"That's very kind of you; but I wired a reservation from Athens to the Grand Palace. It was recommended to me. Do you know it?"

"Yes. I think it is quite good." The train began to slow down. "Good-bye, Mr. Latimer."

"Good-bye."

In his eagerness to get to a bath and some breakfast it did not occur to Latimer to wonder how Mr. Peters had discovered his name.

CHAPTER V

NINETEEN

TWENTY-THREE

Latimer had thought carefully about the problem which awaited him in Sofia.

In Smyrna and Athens it had been simply a matter of gaining access to written records. Any competent private inquiry agents could have found out as much. Now, however, things were different. Dimitrios had, to be sure, a police record in Sofia; but, according to Colonel Haki, the Bulgarian police had known very little about him. That they had, indeed, thought him of very little importance was shown by the fact that it was not until they

68

had received the Colonel's inquiry that they had troubled to get a description of him from the woman with whom he was known to have associated. Obviously it was what the police had *not* got in their records, rather than what they had got, which would be interesting. As the Colonel had pointed out, the important thing to know about an assassination was not who had fired the shot but who had paid for the bullet. What information the ordinary police had would no doubt be helpful; but their business would have been with shot-firing rather than bullet-buying. The first thing he had to find out was who had or might have stood to gain by the death of Stambulisky. Until he had that basic information it was idle to speculate as to the part Dimitrios had played. That the information, even if he did obtain it, might turn out to be quite useless as a basis for anything but a Communist pamphlet, was a contingency that he was not for the moment prepared to consider. He was beginning to like his experiment and was unwilling to abandon it easily. If it were to die, he would see that it died hard.

On the afternoon of his arrival he sought out Marukakis at the office of the French news agency and presented his letter of introduction.

The Greek was a dark, lean man of middle age with intelligent, rather bulbous eyes and a way of bringing his lips together at the end of a sentence as though amazed at his own lack of discretion. He greeted Latimer with the watchful courtesy of a negotiator in an armed truce. He spoke in French.

"What information is it that you need, Monsieur?"

"As much as you can give me about the Stambulisky affair of nineteen twenty-three."

Marukakis raised his eyebrows. "So long ago? I shall have to refresh my memory. No, it is no trouble, I will gladly help you. Give me an hour."

"If you could have dinner with me at my hotel this evening, I should be delighted."

"Where are you staying?"

"The Grand Palace."

"We can get a better dinner than that at a fraction of the cost. If you like, I will call for you at eight o'clock and take you to the place. Agreed?"

"Certainly."

"Good. At eight o'clock then. *Au 'voir.*"

He arrived punctually at eight o'clock and led the way in silence across the Boulevard Maria-Louise and up the Rue Alabinska to a small side-street. Half way along it there was a grocer's shop. Marukakis stopped. He looked suddenly self-conscious. "It does not look very much," he said doubtfully; "but the food is sometimes very good. Would you rather go to a better place?"

"Oh no, I'll leave it to you."

Marukakis looked relieved. "I thought that I had better ask you," he said and pushed open the door of the shop.

Two of the tables were occupied by a group of men and women noisily eating soup. They sat down at a third. A moustachioed man in shirt sleeves and a green baize apron lounged over and addressed them in voluble Bulgarian.

"I think you had better order," said Latimer.

Marukakis said something to the waiter who twirled his moustache and lounged away shouting at a dark opening in the wall that looked like the entrance to the cellar. A voice could be heard faintly acknowledging the order.

The man returned with a bottle and three glasses.

"I have ordered vodka," said Marukakis. "I hope you like it."

"Very much."

"Good."

The waiter filled the three glasses, took one for himself, nodded to Latimer and, throwing back his head, poured the vodka down his throat. Then he walked away.

"*A votre santé*," said Marukakis politely. "Now," he went on as they set their glasses down, "that we have drunk together and that we are comrades, I will make a bargain with you. I will give you the information and then you shall tell me why you want it. Does that go?"

"It goes."

"Very well then."

Soup was put before them. It was thick and highly spiced and mixed with sour cream. As they ate it Marukakis began to talk.

In a dying civilisation, political prestige is the reward not of the shrewdest diagnostician but of the man with the best bedside manner. It is the decoration conferred on mediocrity by ignorance. Yet there remains one sort of political prestige that may still be worn with a certain pathetic dignity; it is that given to the liberal-minded leader of a party of conflicting doctrinaire extremists. His dignity is that of all doomed men: for, whether the two extremes proceed to mutual destruction or whether one of them prevails, doomed he is, either to suffer the hatred of the people or to die a martyr.

Thus it was with Monsieur Stambulisky, leader of the Bulgarian Peasant Agrarian Party, Prime Minister and

Minister for Foreign Affairs. The Agrarian Party, faced by organised reaction, was immobilised, rendered powerless by its own internal conflicts. It died without firing a shot in its own defence.

The end began soon after Stambulisky returned to Sofia early in January nineteen twenty-three, from the Lausanne Conference.

On January the twenty-third, the Yugoslav (then Serbian) Government lodged an official protest in Sofia against a series of armed raids carried out by Bulgarian *comitadji* over the Yugoslav frontier. A few days later, on February the fifth, during a performance celebrating the foundation of the National Theatre in Sofia at which the King and Princesses were present, a bomb was thrown into a box in which sat several government ministers. The bomb exploded. Several persons were injured.

Both the authors and objects of these outrages were readily apparent.

From the start, Stambulisky's policy towards the Yugoslav Government had been one of appeasement and conciliation. Relations between the two countries had been improving rapidly. But an objection to this improvement came from the Macedonian Autonomists, represented by the notorious Macedonian Revolutionary Committee, which operated in both Yugoslavia and in Bulgaria. Fearing that friendly relations between the two countries might lead to joint action against them, the Macedonians set to work systematically to poison those relations and to destroy their enemy Stambulisky. The attacks of the *comitadji* and the theatre incident inaugurated a period of organised terrorism.

On March the eighth, Stambulisky played his trump

card by announcing that the Narodno Sobranie would be dissolved on the thirteenth and that new elections would be held in April.

This was disaster for the reactionary parties. Bulgaria was prospering under the Agrarian Government. The peasants were solidly behind Stambulisky. An election would have established him even more securely. The funds of the Macedonian Revolutionary Committee increased suddenly.

Almost immediately an attempt was made to assassinate Stambulisky and his Minister of Railways, Atanassoff, at Haskovo on the Thracian frontier. It was frustrated only at the last moment. Several police officials responsible for suppressing the activities of the *comitadji*, including the Prefect of Petrich, were threatened with death. In the face of these menaces, the elections were postponed.

Then, on June the fourth, the Sofia police discovered a plot to assassinate not only Stambulisky but also Muravieff, the War Minister, and Stoyanoff, the Minister of the Interior. A young army officer, believed to have been given the job of killing Stoyanoff, was shot dead by the police in a gun fight. Other young officers, also under the orders of the terrorist Committee, were known to have arrived in Sofia, and a search for them was made. The police were beginning to lose control of the situation.

Now was the time for the Agrarian Party to have acted, to have armed their peasant supporters. But they did not do so. Instead, they played politics among themselves. For them, the enemy was the Macedonian Revolutionary Committee, a terrorist gang, a small organisation quite incapable of ousting a government entrenched behind hundreds of thousands of peasant votes. They failed to per-

ceive that the activities of the Committee had been merely
the smoke-screen behind which the reactionary parties
had been steadily making their preparations for an offensive. They very soon paid for this lack of perception.

At midnight on June the eighth all was calm. By four
o'clock on the morning of the ninth, all the members of
the Stambulisky Government, with the exception of Stambulisky himself, were in prison and martial law had been
declared. The leaders of this *coup d'état* were the reac-
tionaries Zankoff and Rouseff, neither of whom had ever
been connected with the Macedonian Committee.

Too late, Stambulisky tried to rally his peasants to their
own defence. Several weeks later he was surrounded with
a few followers in a country house some hundreds of miles
from Sofia and captured. Shortly afterwards and in circumstances which are still obscure, he was shot.

It was in this way that, as Marukakis talked, Latimer
sorted out the facts in his own mind. The Greek was a
fast talker but liable, if he saw the chance, to turn from
fact to revolutionary theory. Latimer was drinking his
third glass of tea when the recital ended.

For a moment or two he was silent. At last he said:
"Do you know who put up the money for the Committee?"

Marukakis grinned. "Rumours began to circulate some
time after. There were many explanations offered; but,
in my opinion, the most reasonable and, incidentally, the
only one I was able to find any evidence for, was that the
money had been advanced by the bank which held the
Committee's funds. It is called the Eurasian Credit
Trust."

"You mean that this bank advanced the money on behalf of a third party?"

"No, I don't. The bank advanced the money on its own behalf. I happened to find out that it had been badly caught owing to the rise in the value of the *Lev* under the Stambulisky administration. In the early part of nineteen twenty-three, before the trouble started in earnest, the *Lev* doubled its value in two months. It was about eight hundred to the pound sterling and it rose to about four hundred. I could look up the actual figures if you are interested. Anyone who had been selling the *Lev* for delivery in three months or more, counting on a fall, would face huge losses. The Eurasian Credit Trust was not, nor is for that matter, the sort of bank to accept a loss like that."

"What sort of a bank is it?"

"It is registered in Monaco which means not only that it pays no taxes in the countries in which it operates but also that its balance sheet is not published and that it is impossible to find out anything about it. There are lots more like that in Europe. Its head office is in Paris but it operates in the Balkans. Amongst other things it finances the clandestine manufacture of heroin in Bulgaria for illicit export."

"Do you think that it financed the Zankoff *coup d'ètat*?"

"Possibly. At any rate it financed the conditions that made the *coup d'état* possible. It was an open secret that the attempt on Stambulisky and Atanassoff at Haskovo was the work of foreign gunmen imported and paid by someone specially for the purpose. A lot of people said, too, that although there was a lot of talking and threatening, the trouble would have died down if it had not been for foreign *agents provocateurs*."

This was better than Latimer had hoped.

"Is there any way in which I can get details of the Haskovo affair?"

Marukakis shrugged. "It is over fifteen years old. The police might tell you something but I doubt it. If I knew what you wanted to know . . ."

Latimer made up his mind. "Very well, I said I would tell you why I wanted this information and I will." He went on hurriedly. "When I was in Stambul some weeks ago I had lunch with a man who happened to be the chief of the Turkish Secret Police. He was interested in detective stories and wanted me to use a plot he had thought of. We were discussing the respective merits of real and fictional murderers when, to illustrate his point, he read me the dossier of a man named Dimitrios Makropoulos or Dimitrios Talat. The man had been a scoundrel and a cutthroat of the worst sort. He had murdered a man in Smyrna and arranged to have another man hanged for it. He had been involved in three attempted assassinations including that of Stambulisky. He had been a French spy and he had organised a gang of drug pedlars in Paris. The day before I heard of him he had been found floating dead in the Bosphorus. He had been knifed in the stomach. For some reason or other I was curious to see him and persuaded this man to take me with him to the mortuary. Dimitrios was there on a table with his clothes piled up beside him.

"It may have been that I had had a good lunch and was feeling stupid but I suddenly had a curious desire to know more about Dimitrios. As you know, I write detective stories. I told myself that if, for once, I tried doing some detecting myself instead of merely writing about other people doing it, I might get some interesting results. My idea was to try to fill in some of the gaps in the dossier. But that was only an excuse. I did not care to admit to myself then that my interest was nothing to do with detection. It is difficult to explain but I see now that my curiosity about Dimitrios was that of the biographer rather than of the detective. There was an emotional element in it, too. I wanted to explain Dimitrios, to account for him, to understand his mind. Merely to label him with disapproval was not enough. I saw him not as a corpse in a mortuary but as a man, not as an isolate, a phenomenon, but as a unit in a disintegrating social system."

He paused. "Well, there you are, Marukakis! That is why I am in Sofia, why I am wasting your time with questions about things that happened fifteen years ago. I am gathering material for a biography that will never be written, when I ought to be producing a detective story. It sounds unlikely enough to me. To you it must sound fantastic. But it is my explanation."

He sat back feeling very foolish. It would have been better to have told a carefully thought out lie.

Marukakis had been staring at his tea. Now he looked up.

"What is your own private explanation of your interest in this Dimitrios?"

"I've just told you."

"No. I think not. You deceive yourself. You hope *au fond* that by rationalizing Dimitrios, by explaining him, you will also explain that disintegrating social system you spoke about."

"That is very ingenious; but, if you will forgive my saying so, a little over-simplified. I don't think that I can accept it."

Marukakis shrugged. "It is my opinion."

"It is very good of you to believe me."

"Why should I not believe you? It is too absurd for disbelief. What do you know of Dimitrios in Bulgaria?"

"Very little. He was, I am told, an intermediary in an attempt to assassinate Stambulisky. That is to say there is no evidence to show that he was going to do any shooting himself. He left Athens, wanted by the police for robbery and attempted murder, towards the end of November nineteen twenty-two. I found that out myself. I also believe that he came to Bulgaria by sea. He was known to the Sofia police. I know that because in nineteen twenty-four the Turkish secret police made inquiries about him in connection with another matter. The police here questioned a woman with whom he was known to have associated."

"If she were still here and alive it would be interesting to talk to her."

"It would. I've traced Dimitrios in Smyrna and in Athens where he called himself Taladis, but so far I have not talked to anyone who ever saw him alive. Unfortunately, I do not even know the woman's name."

"The police records would contain it. If you like I will make inquiries."

"I cannot ask you to take the trouble. If I like to waste my time reading police records there is nothing to prevent my doing so, but there is no reason why I should waste your time too."

"There is plenty to prevent your wasting your time reading police records. In the first place, you cannot read

Bulgarian and in the second place, the police would make difficulties. I am, God help me, an accredited journalist working for a French news agency. I have certain privileges. Besides—" he grinned—"absurd as it is, your detecting intrigues me. The baroque in human affairs is always interesting don't you think?" He looked round. The restaurant had emptied. The waiter was sitting asleep with his feet on one of the tables. Marukakis sighed. "We shall have to wake the poor devil to pay him."

On his third day in Sofia, Latimer received a letter from Marukakis.

My dear Mr. Latimer, (he wrote in French)
  Here, as I promised, is a précis of all the information about Dimitrios Makropoulos which I have been able to obtain from the police. It is not, as you will see, complete. That is interesting, don't you think! Whether the woman can be found or not, I cannot say until I have made friends with a few more policemen. Perhaps we could meet tomorrow.
  Assuring you of my most distinguished sentiments.

                                        N. Marukakis.

Attached to this letter was the précis:

POLICE ARCHIVES, SOFIA 1922–4

Dimitrios Makropoulos. *Citizenship:* Greek. *Place of birth:* Salonika. *Date:* 1889. *Trade:* Described as fig-packer. *Entry:* Varna, December 22nd 1922, off Italian steamer *Isola Bella. Passport or Identity Card:* Relief Commission Identity Card No. T53462.

At police inspection of papers in Café Spetzi, rue Perotska, Sofia, June 6th 1923, was in company of woman named Irana Preveza, Greek-born Bulgar. D. M. known associate of foreign criminals. Proscribed for deportation, June 7th 1923. Released at request and on assurances of A. Vazoff, June 7th 1923.

In September 1924 request received from Turkish Government for information relating to a fig-packer named 'Dimitrios' wanted on a charge of murder. Above information supplied a month later. Irana Preveza when questioned reported receiving letter from Makropoulos at Adrianople. She gave following description:

Height: 182 centimetres. *Eyes:* brown. *Complexion:* dark, clean-shaven. *Hair:* dark and straight. *Distinguishing marks:* none.

At the foot of this *précis,* Marukakis had added a handwritten note.

N.B. This is an ordinary police dossier only. Reference is made to a second dossier on the secret file but it is forbidden to inspect this.

Latimer sighed. The second dossier contained, no doubt, the details of the part played by Dimitrios in the events of nineteen twenty-three. The Bulgarian authorities had evidently known more about Dimitrios than they had been prepared to confide to the Turkish police. To know that the information was in existence, yet to be unable to get at it was really most irritating.

However, there was much food for thought in what information was available. The most obvious tit-bit was

that on board the Italian steamer *Isola Bella* in December
1922, between the Piræus and Varna in the Black Sea, the
Relief Commission Identity Card number T.53462 had
suffered an alteration. "Dimitrios Taladis" had become
"Dimitrios Makropoulos." Either Dimitrios had discovered a talent for forgery or he had met and employed
someone with such a talent.

Irana Preveza! A real clue that and one that would
have to be followed up very carefully. If she were still
alive there must surely be some way of finding her. For
the moment, however, that task would have to be left to
Marukakis. Incidentally, the fact that she was of Greek
extraction was suggestive, Dimitrios would probably not
have spoken Bulgar.

"Known associate of foreign criminals," was distinctly
vague. What sort of criminals? Of what foreign nationality? And to what extent had he associated with them?
And why had attempts been made to deport him just two
days before the Zankoff *coup d'état?* Had Dimitrios been
one of the suspected assassins for whom the Sofia police
had been searching during that critical week? Colonel
Haki had pooh-poohed the idea of his being an assassin at
all. "His kind never risk their skins like that." But Colonel Haki had not known everything about Dimitrios.
And who on earth was the obliging A. Vazoff who had so
promptly and effectively intervened on behalf of Dimitrios? The answers to those questions were, no doubt,
in that secret second dossier. Most irritating!

He had sent a note to Marukakis, and on the following
morning received a telephone call from him. They arranged to meet again for dinner that evening.

"Have you got any farther with the police?"

"Yes. I will tell you everything when we meet this evening. Good-bye."

By the time the evening came, Latimer was feeling very much as he had once used to feel while waiting for examination results: a little excited, a little apprehensive and very much irritated at the decorous delay in publishing information which had been in existence for several days. He smiled rather sourly at Marukakis.

"It is really very good of you to take so much trouble."

Marukakis flourished a hand. "Nonsense, my dear friend. I told you I was interested. Shall we go to the grocer's shop again? We can talk there quietly."

From then until the arrival of the tea he talked incessantly about the position of the Scandinavian countries in the event of a major European War. Latimer began to feel as baleful as one of his own murderers.

"And now," said the Greek at last, "as to this question of your Dimitrios, we are going on a little trip to-night."

"What do you mean?"

"I said that I would make friends with some policeman and I have done so. As a result I have found out where Irana Preveza is now. It was not very difficult. She turns out to be very well known—to the police."

Latimer felt his heart begin to beat a little faster. "Where is she?" he demanded.

"About five minutes' walk away from here. She is the proprietress of a *Nachtlokal* called *La Vierge St. Marie.*"

"*Nachtlokal?*"

He grinned. "Well, you could call it a night club."

"I see."

"She has not always had her own place. For many years

she worked either on her own or for other houses. But she grew too old. She had money saved, and so she started her own place. About fifty years of age, but looks younger. The police have quite an affection for her. She does not get up until ten in the evening, so we must wait a little before we try our luck at talking to her. Did you read her description of Dimitrios? No distinguishing marks! That made me laugh."

"Did it occur to you to wonder how she knew that his height was exactly one hundred and eighty-two centimetres?"

Marukakis frowned. "Why should it?"

"Very few people know even their own heights exactly."

"What is your idea?"

"I think that that description came from the second dossier you mentioned, and not from the woman."

"And so?"

"Just a moment. Do you know who A. Vazoff is?"

"I meant to tell you. I asked the same question. He was a lawyer."

"Was?"

"He died three years ago. He left much money. It was claimed by a nephew living in Bucaresti. He had no relations living here." Marukakis paused and then, with an elaborate air of simplicity, added: "He used to be on the board of directors of the Eurasian Credit Trust. I was keeping that as a little surprise for you later, but you may have it now. I found out from the files. Eurasian Credit Trust was not registered in Monaco until nineteen twenty-six. The list of directors prior to that date is still in existence and open to inspection if you know where to find it."

"But," spluttered Latimer, "this is most important. Don't you see what . . ."

Marukakis interrupted him by calling for the bill. Then he glanced at Latimer slyly. "You know," he said, "you English are sublime. You are the only nation in the world that believes that it has a monopoly of ordinary common sense."

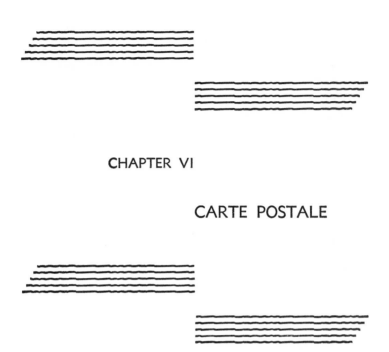

CHAPTER VI

CARTE POSTALE

La Vierge St. Marie was situated, with somewhat dingy logic, in a street of houses behind the church of *Sveta Nedelja*. The street was narrow, sloping and poorly lit. At first it seemed unnaturally silent. But behind the silence there were whispers of music and laughter—whispers that would start out suddenly as a door opened and then be smothered as it closed again. Two men came out of a doorway ahead of them, lit cigarettes and walked quickly away. The footsteps of another pedestrian approached and then stopped as their owner went into one of the houses.

"Not many people about now," commented Marukakis; "too early."

Most of the doors were panelled with translucent glass
and had dim lights showing through them. On some of
the panels the number of the house was painted; painted
rather more elaborately than was necessary for ordinary
purposes. Other doors bore names. There was *Wonder-
bar, O.K., Jymmies Bar, Stambul, Torquemada, Vitocha,
Le Viol de Lucrece* and, higher up the hill, *La Vierge St.
Marie.*

For a moment they stood outside it. The door looked
less shabby than some of the others. Latimer felt to see if
his wallet was safe in his pocket as Marukakis pushed open
the door and led the way in.

They found themselves in a low-ceilinged room about
thirty feet square. At regular intervals round the pale blue
walls were placed oval mirrors supported by *papier-maché*
cherubim. The spaces between the mirrors were deco-
rated haphazard with highly stylised pictures, painted on
the walls, of monocled men with straw-coloured hair and
nude torsos, and women in tailor-made costumes and
check stockings. In one corner of the room was a minute
bar; in the opposite corner the platform on which sat the
band—four listless negroes in white "Argentine" blouses.
Near them was a blue plush curtained doorway. The rest
of the wall space was taken up by small cubicles which
rose to the shoulder height of those sitting at the tables
set inside them. A few more tables encroached on the
dance-floor in the centre.

When they came in there were about a dozen persons
seated in the cubicles. The band was still playing and two
girls who looked as though they might presently form

part of the cabaret were dancing solemnly together.

"Too early," repeated Marukakis disappointedly. "But it will be gayer soon."

A waiter swept them to one of the cubicles and hurried away, to reappear a moment or two later with a bottle of champagne.

"Have you got plenty of money with you?" murmured Marukakis; "we shall have to pay at least two hundred leva for this poison."

Latimer nodded. Two hundred leva was about ten shillings.

The band stopped. The two girls finished their dance, and one of them caught Latimer's eye. They walked over to the cubicle and stood smiling down. Marukakis said something. Still smiling, the two shrugged their shoulders and went away. Marukakis looked doubtfully at Latimer.

"I said that we had business to discuss, but that we would entertain them later. Of course, if you don't want to be bothered with them . . ."

"I don't," said Latimer firmly and then shuddered as he drank some of the champagne.

Marukakis sighed. "It seems a pity. We shall have to pay for the champagne. Someone may as well drink it."

"Where is La Preveza?"

"She will be down at any moment now, I should think. Of course," he added thoughtfully, "we could go up to her." He raised his eyes significantly towards the ceiling. "It is really quite refined, this place. Everything seems to be most discreet."

"If she will be down here soon there seems to be no point in our going up." He felt an austere prig and wished that the champagne had been drinkable.

"Just so," said Marukakis gloomily.

But an hour and a half passed by before the proprietress of *La Vierge St. Marie* put in an appearance. During that time things certainly did become gayer. More people arrived, mostly men, although among them were one or two peculiar-looking women. An obvious pimp, who looked very sober, brought in a couple of Germans who looked very drunk and might have been commercial travellers on the spree. A pair of rather sinister young men sat down and ordered Vichy water. There was a certain amount of coming and going through the plush-curtained door. The cubicles were all occupied and extra tables were set up on the dance-floor which soon became a congested mass of swaying, sweating couples. Presently, however, the floor was cleared and a number of the girls who had disappeared some minutes before to replace their clothes with a bunch or two of artificial primroses and a great deal of sun-tan powder, did a short dance. They were followed by a youth dressed as a woman who sang songs in German; then they reappeared without their primroses to do another dance. This concluded the cabaret and the audience swarmed back on to the dance-floor. The atmosphere thickened, became hotter and hotter.

Through smarting eyes Latimer was idly watching one of the sinister young men offering the other a pinch of what might have been snuff, but which was not, and wondering whether he should make another attempt to slake his thirst with the champagne, when suddenly Marukakis touched his arm.

"That will be her," he said.

Latimer looked across the room. For a moment a

couple on the extreme corner of the dance-floor obstructed the view; then the couple moved an inch or two, and he saw her standing motionless by the curtained door by which she had entered.

She possessed that odd blowzy quality that is independent of good clothes and well-dressed hair and skilful maquillage. Her figure was full but good and she held herself well; her dress was probably expensive, her thick, dark hair looked as though it had spent the past two hours in the hands of a hairdresser. Yet she remained, unmistakably and irrevocably, a slattern. There was something temporary, an air of suspended animation, about her. It seemed as if at any moment the hair should begin to straggle, the dress slip down negligently over one soft, creamy shoulder, the hand with the diamond cluster ring which now hung loosely at her side reach up to pluck at pink silk shoulder straps and pat abstractedly at the hair. You saw it in her dark eyes. The mouth was firm and good-humoured in the loose, raddled flesh about it; but the eyes were humid with sleep and the carelessness of sleep. Now they were open and watchful, moving about while the mouth smiled a greeting here and there. Latimer watched her turn suddenly and go towards the bar.

Marukakis beckoned to the waiter and said something to him. The man hesitated and then nodded. Latimer saw him weave his way towards where Madame Preveza was talking to a fat man with his arm round one of the cabaret girls. The waiter whispered something. Madame Preveza stopped talking and looked at him. He pointed towards Latimer and Marukakis, and for a moment her eyes rested dispassionately on them. Then she turned away, said a word to the waiter and resumed her conversation.

"She'll come in a minute," said Marukakis.

Soon she left the fat man and went on making her tour of the room, nodding, smiling indulgently. At last she reached their table. Involuntarily, Latimer got to his feet. The eyes studied his face.

"You wished to speak with me, messieurs?" Her voice was husky, a little harsh, and she spoke in strongly accented French.

"We should be honoured if you would sit at our table for a moment," said Marukakis.

"Of course." She sat down beside him. Immediately the waiter came up. She waved him away and looked at Latimer. "I have not seen you before, monsieur. Your friend I have seen, but not in my place." She looked sideways at Marukakis. "Are you going to write about me in the Paris newspapers, monsieur? If so, you must see the rest of my entertainment—you and your friend."

Marukakis smiled. "No, madame. We are trespassing on your hospitality to ask for some information."

"Information?" A blank look had come into the dark eyes. "I know nothing of any interest to anybody."

"Your discretion is famous, madame. This, however, concerns a man, now dead and buried, whom you knew over fifteen years ago."

She laughed shortly and Latimer saw that her teeth were bad. She laughed again, uproariously, so that her body shook. It was an ugly sound that tore away her slumberous dignity, leaving her old. She coughed a little as the laughter died away. "You pay the most delicate compliments, monsieur," she gasped. "Fifteen years! You expect me to remember a man that long? Holy Mother of Christ, I think you shall buy me a drink after all."

Latimer beckoned to the waiter. "What will you drink, Madame?"

"Champagne. Not this filth. The waiter will know. Fifteen years!" She was still amused.

"We hardly dared to hope that you would remember," said Marukakis a trifle coldly. "But if a name means anything to you . . . it was Dimitrios—Dimitrios Makropoulos."

She had been lighting a cigarette. Now she stopped still with the burning match in her fingers. Her eyes were on the end of the cigarette. For several seconds the only movement that Latimer saw in her face was the corners of her mouth turning slowly downward. It seemed to him that the noise about them had receded suddenly, that there was cotton wool in his ears. Then she slowly turned the match between her fingers and dropped it on to the plate in front of her. The eyes did not move. Then, very softly, she said: "I don't like you here. Get out—both of you!"

"But . . ."

"Get out!" Still she did not raise her voice or move her head.

Marukakis looked across at Latimer, shrugged and stood up. Latimer followed suit. She glared up at them sullenly. "Sit down," she snapped; "do you think I want a scene here?"

They sat down. "If you will explain, madame," said Marukakis acidly, "how we can get out without standing up we should be grateful."

The fingers of her right hand moved quickly and grasped the stem of a glass. For a moment Latimer thought that she was going to break it in the Greek's face. Then her fingers relaxed and she said something in Greek too rapid for Latimer to understand.

Marukakis shook his head. "No, he is nothing to do with the police," Latimer heard him reply. "He is a writer of books and he seeks information."

"Why?"

"He is curious. He saw the dead body of Dimitrios Makropoulos in Stambul a month or two ago, and he is curious about him."

She turned to Latimer and gripped his sleeve urgently. "He is dead? You are sure he is dead? You actually saw his body?"

He nodded. Her manner made him feel oddly like the doctor who descends the stairs to announce that all is over. "He had been stabbed and thrown into the sea," he added and cursed himself for putting it so clumsily. In her eyes was an emotion he could not quite identify. Perhaps, in her way, she had loved him. A slice of life! Tears should follow.

But there were no tears. She said.

"Had he any money on him?"

Slowly, uncomprehendingly, Latimer shook his head.

"*Merde!*" she said viciously; "the son of a diseased camel owed me a thousand French francs. Now I shall never see it back. *Salop!* Get out, both of you, before I have you thrown out!"

It was nearly half-past three before Latimer and Marukakis left *La Vierge St. Marie.*

The preceding two hours they had spent in Madame Preveza's private office, a beflowered room filled with furniture: a walnut grand piano draped in a white silk shawl with a fringe and pen painted birds in the corners of it, small tables loaded with bric-a-brac, many chairs, a browning palm tree in a bamboo stand, a chaise-longue and a large roll-top desk in Spanish oak. They had reached it, under her guidance, via the curtained door, a flight of stairs and a dimly lit corridor with numbered doors on either side of it and a smell that had reminded Latimer of an expensive nursing home during visiting hours.

The invitation had been the very last thing that he had expected. It had come close on the heels of her final exhortation to them to "get out." She had become plaintive; apologised. A thousand francs was a thousand francs. Now she would never see it. Her eyes had filled with tears. To Latimer she had seemed fantastic. The money had been owing since nineteen twenty-three. She could not seriously have expected its return after fifteen years. Perhaps somewhere in her mind she had kept intact the romantic illusion that one day Dimitrios would walk in and scatter thousand franc notes like leaves about her. The fairy tale gesture! Latimer's news had shattered that illusion and when her first anger had gone she had felt herself in need of sympathy. Forgotten had been their request for information about Dimitrios. The bearers of the bad news must know how bad their news had been. She had been saying farewell to a legend. An audience had been necessary, an audience who would understand what a foolish, generous woman she was. Their drinks she had said, rubbing salt in the wound, were on the house.

They had seated themselves side by side on the chaise-longue while she had rummaged in the roll-top desk. From one of the innumerable pigeon-holes she had produced a small dog-eared notebook. The pages of it had rustled through her fingers. Then:

"February the fifteenth, nineteen twenty-three," she had said suddenly. The notebook had shut with a snap and her eyes had moved upwards calling upon Heaven to testify to the accuracy of the date. "That was when the money became due to me. A thousand francs and he promised faithfully that he would pay me. It was due to me and he had received it. Sooner than make a big scene —for I detest big scenes—I said that he could borrow it. And he said that he would repay me, that in a matter of weeks he would be getting plenty of money. And he did get that money but he did not pay me my thousand francs. After all I had done for him, too!

"I picked that man up out of the gutter, Messieurs. That was in December. Dear Christ, it was cold. In the eastern provinces people were dying quicker than you could have machine-gunned them—and I have seen people machine-gunned. At that time I had no place like this, you understand. Of course, I was a girl then. Often I used to be asked to pose for photographs. There was one that was my favourite. I had on just a simple drape of white chiffon, caught in at the waist with a girdle, and a crown of small white flowers. In my right hand which rested—so—upon a pretty, white column, I held a single red rose. It was used for postcards, *pour les amoureux,* and the photographer coloured the rose and printed a very pretty poem at the bottom of the card." The dark, moist lids had drooped over her eyes and she had recited softly:

"*Je veux que mon coeur vous serve d'oreiller,*
"*Et à votre bonheur je saurai veiller.*

"Very pretty, don't you think?" The ghost of a smile

had tightened her lips. "I burnt all my photographs several years ago. Sometimes I am sorry for that but I think that I was right. It is not good to be reminded always of the past. That is why, Messieurs, I was angry to-night when you spoke of Dimitrios; for he is of the past. One must think of the present and of the future.

"But Dimitrios was not a man that one forgets easily. I have known many men but I have been afraid of only two men in my life. One of them was the man I married and the other was Dimitrios. One deceives oneself, you know. One thinks that one wants to be understood when one wants only to be half-understood. If a person really understands you, you fear him. My husband understood me because he loved me and I feared him because of that. But when he grew tired of loving me I could laugh at him and no longer fear him. But Dimitrios was different. Dimitrios understood me better than I understood myself; but he did not love me. I do not think he could love anyone. I thought that one day I should be able to laugh at him too, but that day never came. You could not laugh at Dimitrios. I found that out. When he had gone I hated him and told myself that it was because of the thousand francs he owed to me. I wrote it down in my book as proof. But I was lying to myself. He owed me more than a thousand francs. He had always cheated me over the money. It was because I feared him and could not understand him as he understood me that I hated him.

"I was living in a hotel then. A filthy place, full of scum. The *patron* was a dirty bully, but friendly with the police; and while one paid for one's room one was safe, even if one's papers were not in order.

"One afternoon I was resting when I heard the *patron*

shouting at someone in the next room. The walls were thin and I could hear everything. At first I paid no attention, for he was always shouting at someone, but after a while I began to listen because they were speaking in Greek and I understand Greek. The *patron* was threatening to call in the police if the room were not paid for. I could not hear what was said in reply for the other man spoke softly; but at last the *patron* went out and there was quiet. I was half-asleep when suddenly I heard the handle of my door being tried. The door was bolted. I watched the handle turn slowly as it was released again. Then there was a knock.

"I asked who was there but there was no answer. I thought that perhaps it was one of my friends and that he had not heard me so I went to the door and unbolted it. Outside was Dimitrios.

"He asked in Greek if he could come in. I asked him what he wanted and he said that he wanted to talk to me. I asked him how he knew that I spoke Greek but he did not answer. I knew now that he must be the man in the next room. I had passed him once or twice on the stairs and he had always seemed very polite and nervous as he stood aside for me. But now he was not nervous. I said that I was resting and that he could come to see me later if he wished. But he smiled and pushed the door open and came in and leaned against the wall.

"I told him to get out, that I would call the *patron;* but he only smiled and stayed where he was. He asked me then whether I had heard what the *patron* had said and I replied that I had not heard. I had a pistol in the drawer of my table and I went to it; but he seemed to guess what I was thinking for he moved across the room as if by accident and leaned against the table as if he owned the place. Then he asked me to lend him some money.

"I was never a fool. I had a thousand leva pinned high up in the curtain but only a few coins in my bag. I said that I had no money. He seemed not to take any notice of that and began to tell me that he had not eaten anything since the day before, that he had no money and that he felt ill. But all the time he talked his eyes were moving, looking at the things in the room. I can see him now. His face was smooth and oval and pale and he had very brown, anxious eyes that made you think of a doctor's eyes when he is doing something to you that hurts. He frightened me. I told him again that I had no money but that I had some bread if he wanted it. He said: 'Give me the bread.'

"I got the bread from the drawer and gave it to him. He ate it slowly, still leaning against the table. When he had finished he asked for a cigarette. I gave him one. Then he said that I needed a protector. I knew then what he was after. I said that I could manage my own affairs. He said that I was a fool and that he could prove it. If I would do as he said he would get five thousand leva that day and give me half of it. I asked what he wanted me to do. He told me to write a note that he would dictate. It was addressed to a man whose name I had never heard and simply asked for five thousand leva. I thought he must be mad and to get rid of him I wrote the note and signed it 'Irana.' He said that he would meet me at a café that evening.

"I did not trouble to keep the appointment. The next morning he came again to my room. This time I would not let him in. He was very angry and said that he had two thousand five hundred leva for me. Of course, I did not believe him but he pushed a thousand leva note under the door and said that I should have the rest when I let him in. So I let him in. He gave me immediately another fifteen hundred leva. I asked him where he had got it and he said that he had delivered the note himself to the man who had given him the money immediately.

"I have always been discreet. I am not interested in the real names of my friends. Dimitrios had followed one of them to his home, had found out his real name and that he was an important man and then with my note in his hand had threatened to tell his wife and daughters of our friendship unless he paid.

"I was very angry. I said that for the sake of two thousand five hundred leva, I had lost one of my good friends. Dimitrios said that he could get me richer friends. He said, too, that he had given the money to me to show that he was serious and that he could have written the note himself and gone to my friend without telling me.

"I saw that this was true. I saw also that he might go to other friends unless I agreed with him. So Dimitrios became my protector and he *did* bring me richer friends. And he bought himself very smart clothes and sometimes went to the best cafés.

"But soon, someone I knew told me that he had become involved in politics and that he often went to certain cafés that the police watched. I told him that he was a fool, but he took no notice. He said that soon he would make a lot of money. Often he left Sofia for several days at a time. He did not tell me when he went and I did not ask. But I knew that he had made important friends, for, once, when the police were making difficulties about his papers, he laughed and told me not to worry about the police. They would not dare to touch him, he said.

"But one morning he came to me in great agitation. He looked as if he had been travelling all night and had not shaved for several days. I had never seen him so nervous. He took me by the wrists and said that if anyone asked me I must say that he had been with me for the last three days. I had not seen him for over a week but I had to agree and he went to sleep in my room.

"Nobody asked me about him; but later that day I read in the newspaper that an attempt had been made on Stambulisky at Haskovo and I guessed where Dimitrios had been. I was frightened. An old friend of mine, whom I had known before Dimitrios, wanted to give me an apartment of my own. When Dimitrios had had his sleep and gone, I went to my friend and said that I would take this apartment.

"I was afraid when I had done it, but that night I met Dimitrios and told him. I had expected him to be angry but he was quite calm and said that it would be best for me. Yet I could not tell what he was thinking because he always looked the same, like a doctor when he is doing something to you that hurts. I took courage and reminded him that we had some business to settle. He agreed and said that he would meet me three days later to give me all the money that was due to me."

"Three days later I waited for him in the café and he did not come. Several weeks after that I saw him and he said that he had been away but that if I would meet him on the following day, he would pay me the money he owed. The meeting place was a café in the Rue Perotska, a low place that I did not like.

"This time he came as he had promised. He said that he was in difficulties about money, that he had a great sum coming to him and that he would pay me within a few weeks.

"I wondered why he had kept the appointment merely to tell me that; but later I understood why. He had come to ask me a favour. He had to have certain letters received by someone he could trust. They were not his letters but those of a friend of his, a Turk named Talat. If this friend could give the address of my apartment, Dimitrios himself would collect the letters when he paid me my money.

"I agreed. I could do nothing else. It meant that if Dimitrios had to collect these letters from me he would have to pay me the money. But I knew in my heart and he knew too that he could have collected the letters and not paid me a sou and I could have done nothing.

"We were sitting there drinking coffee—for Dimitrios was very mean in cafés—when the police came in to inspect papers. It was quite usual at that time but it was not good to be found in that café because of its reputation. Dimitrios had his papers in order but because he was a foreigner they took his name and mine because I was with him. When they had gone he was very angry; but I think he was angry not because of their taking his name but because they had taken my name as being with him. He was much put out and told me not to trouble about the letters as he would arrange for them with someone else. We left the café and that was the last time I saw him."

She had had a Mandarine-Curaçao in front of her and now she had drunk it down thirstily. Latimer had cleared his throat.

"And the last you heard of him?"

Suspicion had flickered for an instant in her eyes. Latimer had said: "Dimitrios is dead, Madame. Fifteen years have gone by. Times have changed in Sofia."

Her queer, taut smile had hovered on her lips.

" 'Dimitrios is dead, Madame.' That sounds very curious to me. It is difficult to think of Dimitrios as dead. How did he look?"

"His hair was grey. He was wearing clothes bought in Greece and in France. Poor stuff." Unconsciously he had echoed Colonel Haki's phrase.

"Then he did not become rich?"

"He did once become rich, in Paris, but he lost his money."

She had laughed. "That must have hurt him." And then suspicion again: "You know a lot about Dimitrios, Monsieur. If he is dead . . . I don't understand."

"My friend is a writer," Marukakis had put in; "he is naturally interested in human nature."

"What do you write?"

"Detective stories."

She had shrugged. "You do not need to know human nature for that. It is for love stories and romances that one must know human nature. *Romans policiers* are ugly. *Folle Farine* I think is a lovely story. Do you like it?"

"Very much."

"I have read it seventeen times. It is the best of Ouida's books and I have read them all. One day I shall write my memoirs. I have seen a lot of human nature you know." The smile had become a trifle arch and she had sighed and fingered a diamond brooch.

"But you wish to know more of Dimitrios. Very well. I heard of Dimitrios again a year later. One day I received a letter from him, from Adrianople. He gave a Poste Restante address. The letter asked me if I had received any letters for this Talat. If I had I was to write saying so but to keep the letters. He said that I was to tell nobody that I had heard from him. He promised again to pay me the money he owed me. I had no letters addressed to Talat and wrote to tell him so. I also said that I needed the money because, now that he had gone away, I had lost all my friends. That was a lie but I thought that by flattering him I would perhaps get the money. I should have known Dimitrios better. He did not even reply.

"A few weeks after that a man came to see me. A type of *fonctionnaire* he was, very severe and businesslike. His clothes looked expensive. He said that the police would probably be coming to question me about Dimitrios.

"I was frightened at that but he said that I had nothing to fear. Only I must be careful what I said to them. He told me what to say: how I must describe Dimitrios so that the police would be satisfied. I showed him the letter from Adrianople and it seemed to amuse him. He said that I could tell the police about the letter coming from Adrianople but that I must say nothing about this name Talat. He said that the letter was a dangerous thing to keep and burnt it. That made me angry but he gave me a thousand leva note and asked me if I liked Dimitrios, if I was a friend. I said that I hated him. Then he said that friendship was a great thing and that he would give me five thousand leva to say what he had told me to the police."

She had shrugged. "That is being serious, Messieurs. Five thousand leva! When the police came I said what this man had asked me to say and the following day an envelope with five thousand leva in it arrived by post. There was nothing else in the envelope, no letter. That was all right. But listen! About two years later I saw this man in the street. I went up to him; but the *salop* pretended that he had not seen me before and called the police to me. Friendship is a great thing."

She had picked up the book and put it back in its pigeon hole.

"If you will excuse me, Messieurs, it is time I returned to my guests. I think I have talked too much. You see, I know nothing about Dimitrios that is of any interest."

"We have been most interested, Madame."

She had smiled. "If you are not in a hurry, Messieurs, I can show you more interesting things than Dimitrios. I have two most amusing girls who . . ."

"We are a little pressed for time, Madame. Another night we should be delighted. Perhaps you would allow us to pay for your drinks."

She had smiled. "As you wish, Messieurs, but it has been most agreeable talking to you. No, no, please! I have a superstition about money being shown in my own private room. Please arrange it with the waiter at your table. You will excuse me if I don't come down with you? I have a little business to attend to. *Au 'voir, Monsieur. Au 'voir, Monsieur. A bientôt.*"

The dark, humid eyes had rested on them affectionately. Latimer had found himself feeling absurdly distressed at the leave-taking.

It had been a *gérant* who had responded to their request for a bill. He had had a brisk, cheerful manner.

"Eleven hundred leva, Messieurs."

"What!"

"The price you arranged with Madame, Messieurs."

"You know," Marukakis remarked as they waited for their change, "I think one does wrong to disapprove altogether of Dimitrios. He had his points."

"Dimitrios was employed by Vazoff acting on behalf of the Eurasian Credit Trust to do work in connection with getting rid of Stambulisky. It would be interesting to know how they recruited him, but that is a thing we shall never know. However, they must have found him satisfactory because they employed him to do similar work in Adrianople. He probably used the name Talat there."

"The Turkish police did not know that. They heard of him simply as 'Dimitrios,'" put in Latimer. "What I cannot understand is why Vazoff—it obviously was Vazoff who visited La Preveza in nineteen twenty-four—allowed her to tell the police that she had had that letter from Adrianople."

"For only one reason, surely. Because Dimitrios was no longer in Adrianople." Marukakis stifled a yawn. "It's been a curious evening."

They were standing outside Latimer's hotel. The night air was cold. "I think I'll go in now," he said.

"You'll be leaving Sofia?"

"For Belgrade. Yes."

"Then you are still interested in Dimitrios?"

"Oh, yes." Latimer hesitated. "I can't tell you how grateful I am to you for your help. It has been a miserable waste of time for you."

Marukakis laughed and then grinned apologetically.

He said: "I was laughing at myself for envying you your Dimitrios. If you find out any more about him in Belgrade I should like you to write to me. Would you do that?"

"Of course."

But Latimer was not to reach Belgrade.

He thanked Marukakis again and they shook hands; then he went into the hotel. His room was on the second floor. Key in hand, he climbed the stairs. Along the heavily carpeted corridors his footsteps made no sound. He put the key in the lock, turned it and opened the door.

He had been expecting darkness and the lights in the room were switched on. That startled him a little. The thought flashed through his mind that perhaps he had mistaken the room; but an instant later he saw something which disposed of that notion. That something was chaos.

Strewn about the floor in utter confusion were the contents of his suitcases. Draped carelessly over a chair were the bedclothes. On the mattress, stripped of their bindings, were the few English books he had brought with him from Athens. The room looked as if a cageful of chimpanzees had been turned loose in it.

Dazed, Latimer took two steps forward into the room. Then a slight sound to the right of him made him turn his head. The next moment his heart jolted sickeningly.

The door leading to the bathroom was open. Standing just inside it, a disembowelled tube of toothpaste in one hand, a massive Lüger pistol held loosely in the other and on his lips a sweet, sad smile, was Mr. Peters.

CHAPTER VII

HALF A MILLION

FRANCS

Mr. Peters took a firmer grasp of his pistol.

"Would you be so good," he said gently, "as to shut the door behind you? I think that if you stretched out your right arm you could do it without moving your feet." The pistol was now levelled in an unmistakable fashion.

Latimer obeyed. Now, at last, he felt very frightened indeed. He was afraid that he was going to be hurt; he could already feel the doctor probing for the bullet. He would insist on an anæsthetic. He was afraid that Mr. Peters was not used to the pistol, that he might fire acci-

106

dentally. He was afraid of moving his hand too quickly lest the sudden movement should be misinterpreted. The door closed. He began to shake from head to foot and could not decide whether it was anger, fear or shock that made him do so. Suddenly he made up his mind to say something.

"What the hell does this mean?" he demanded harshly and then swore. It was not what he had intended to say and he was a man who very rarely swore. He was sure now that it was anger that was making him tremble. He glowered into Mr. Peters' wet eyes.

The fat man lowered his pistol and sat down on the edge of the mattress.

"This is most awkward," he said unhappily. "I did not expect you back so soon. Your *maison close* must have proved disappointing. The inevitable Armenian girls, of course. Appealing enough for a while and then merely dull. I often think that perhaps this great world of ours would be a better, finer place if . . ." He broke off. "But we can talk about that another time." Carefully he put the remains of the toothpaste tube on the bedside table. "I had hoped to get things tidied a little before I left," he added.

Latimer decided to play for time. "Including the books, Mr. Peters?"

"Ah, yes, the books!" He shook his head despondently. "An act of vandalism. A book is a lovely thing, a garden stocked with beautiful flowers, a magic carpet on which to fly away to unknown climes. I am sorry. But it was necessary."

"What was necessary? What are you talking about?"

Mr. Peters smiled a sad, long-suffering smile. "A little

frankness, Mr. Latimer, *please*. There could be only one reason why your room should be searched and you know it as well as I do. I can see your difficulty, of course. You are wondering exactly where I stand. If it is any consolation to you, however, I may say that my difficulty is in wondering exactly where *you* stand."

This was fantastic. In his exasperation, Latimer forgot his fears. He took a deep breath.

"Now look here, Mr. Peters, or whatever your name is, I am very tired and I want to go to bed. If I remember correctly, I travelled with you in a train from Athens several days ago. You were, I believe, going to Bucharest. I, on the other hand, got off here in Sofia. I have been out with a friend. I return to my hotel to find my room in a disgusting mess, my books destroyed and you flourishing a pistol in my face. I conclude that you are either a sneak thief or a drunk. But for your pistol, of which I am, I confess, afraid, I should already have rung for assistance. But it seems to me on reflection that thieves do not ordinarily meet their victims in first class sleeping cars, nor do they tear books to pieces. Again, you do not appear to be drunk. I begin, naturally, to wonder if, after all, you may not be mad. If you are, of course, I can do nothing but humour you and hope for the best. But if you are comparatively sane I must ask you once more for an explanation. I repeat, Mr. Peters; what the hell does this mean?"

Mr. Peters' tear-filled eyes were half-closed. "Perfect," he said raptly; "perfect! No, no, Mr. Latimer, keep away from the bell push, please. That is better. You know, for a moment I was almost convinced of your sincerity. Almost. But, of course, not quite. It really is not kind of you to try to deceive me. Not kind, not considerate and such a waste of time."

Latimer took a step forward. "Now listen to me . . ."

The Lüger jerked upwards. The smile left Mr. Peters' mouth and his flaccid lips parted slightly. He looked adenoidal and very dangerous. Latimer stepped back quickly. The smile slowly returned.

"Come now, Mr. Latimer. A little frankness, please. I have the best of intentions towards you. I did not seek this interview. But since you have returned so unexpectedly, since I could no longer meet you on a basis of, may I say, disinterested friendship, let us be frank with one another." He leaned forward a little. "Why are you so interested in Dimitrios?"

"Dimitrios!"

"Yes, dear Mr. Latimer, Dimitrios. You have come from the Levant. Dimitrios came from there. In Athens you were very energetically seeking his record in the relief commission archives. Here in Sofia you have employed an agent to trace his police record. Why? Wait before you answer. I have no animosity towards you. I bear you no ill-will. Let that be clear. But, as it happens, I too am interested in Dimitrios and because of that I am interested in you. Now, Mr. Latimer, tell me frankly where you stand. What—forgive the expression, please— is your game?"

Latimer was silent for a moment. He was trying to think quickly and not succeeding. He was confused. He had come to regard Dimitrios as his own property, a problem as academic as that of the authorship of an anonymous sixteenth century lyric. And now, here was the odious

Mr. Peters, with his shabby god and his smiles and his Lüger pistol, claiming acquaintance with the problem as though he, Latimer, were the interloper. There was, of course, no reason why he should be surprised. Dimitrios must have been known to many persons. Yet he had felt instinctively that they must all have died with Dimitrios. Absurd, no doubt, but . . .

"Well, Mr. Latimer." The fat man's smile had lost none of its sweetness, but there was an edge to his husky voice that made Latimer think of a small boy pulling the legs off flies.

"I think," he said slowly, "that if I am going to answer questions, I ought to be allowed to ask some. In other words, Mr. Peters, if you will tell me what *your* game is, I will tell you about mine. I have nothing at all to hide, but I have a curiosity to satisfy. Do you mind telling me what you hoped to find here—in the bindings of my books or in the tube of toothpaste?"

"I was looking for an answer to my question, Mr. Latimer. But all I found was this." He held up a sheet of paper. It was the chronological table which Latimer had jotted down in Smyrna. As far as he remembered, he had left it folded in a book he had been reading. "You see, Mr. Latimer, I felt that if you hid papers between the leaves of books, you might also hide more interesting papers in the bindings."

"It wasn't intended to be hidden."

But Mr. Peters took no notice. He held up the paper delicately between a finger and thumb—a schoolmaster about to consider a schoolboy essay. He shook his head.

"And is this all you know about Dimitrios, Mr. Latimer?"

"No."

"Ah!" He gazed pathetically at Latimer's tie. "Now who, I wonder, is this Colonel Haki, who seems so well informed and so indiscreet? The name is Turkish. And poor Dimitrios was taken from us at Istanbul, was he not? And you have come from Istanbul, haven't you?"

Involuntarily, Latimer nodded and then could have kicked himself, for Mr. Peters' smile broadened.

"Thank you, Mr. Latimer. I can see that you are prepared to be helpful. Now let us see. You were in Istanbul, and so was Dimitrios, and so was Colonel Haki. There is a note here about a passport in the name of Talat. Another Turkish name. And there is Adrianople and the phrase 'Kemal attempt.' 'Attempt'—ah, yes! Now, I wonder if you translated that word literally from the French '*attentat.*' You won't tell me? Well, well. I think that perhaps we may take that for granted. You know it almost looks as if you have been reading a Turkish police dossier. Now, doesn't it, eh?"

Latimer had begun to feel rather foolish. He said: "I don't think you're going to get very far that way. You're forgetting that for every question you ask you're going to have to answer one. For example, I should very much like to know whether you ever actually met Dimitrios."

Mr. Peters contemplated him for a moment without speaking. Then: "I don't think that you are very sure of yourself, Mr. Latimer," he said slowly. "I have an idea that I could tell you much more than you could tell me." He dropped the Lüger into his overcoat pocket and got to his feet. "I think I must be going," he added.

This was not at all what Latimer expected or wanted, but he said "Good night" calmly enough.

The fat man walked towards the door. But there he stopped. "Istanbul," Latimer heard him murmur thoughtfully. "Istanbul. Smyrna nineteen twenty-two, Athens the same year, Sofia nineteen twenty-three. Adrianople—no, because he comes from Turkey." He turned round quickly. "Now, I wonder . . ." He paused, and then seemed to make up his mind. "I wonder if it would be very stupid of me to imagine that you might be thinking of going to Belgrade in the near future. Would it, Mr. Latimer?"

Latimer was taken by surprise, and, even as he began to say very decidedly that it would be more than stupid of Mr. Peters to imagine any such thing, he knew by the other's triumphant smile that his surprise had been detected and interpreted.

"You will like Belgrade," Mr. Peters continued happily; "such a beautiful city. The views from the Terazija and the Kalemegdan! Magnificent!"

Latimer pulled the bedclothes off the chair and sat down facing him.

"Mr. Peters," he said, "in Smyrna I had occasion to examine certain fifteen-year-old police records. I afterwards found out that those same records had been examined three months previously by someone else. I wonder if you would like to tell me if that someone else was you."

But the fat man's watery eyes were staring into vacancy. A slight frown gathered on his forehead. He said, as though he were listening to Latimer's voice for mistakes in intonation: "Would you mind repeating that question?"

Latimer repeated the question.

There was another pause. Then Mr. Peters shook his head decidedly. "No, Mr. Latimer, it was not I."

"But you were yourself making inquiries about Dimitrios in Athens, weren't you, Mr. Peters? You were the person who came into the bureau while I was asking about Dimitrios, weren't you? You made a rather hurried exit, I seem to remember. Unfortunately I did not see it, but the official there commented on it. And it was design, not accident, that brought you to Sofia on the train by which I was travelling, wasn't it? You also took care to find out from me—very neatly, I admit—at which hotel I was staying, before I got off the train. That's right, isn't it?"

Mr. Peters was smiling sunnily again. He nodded. "Yes, Mr. Latimer, all quite right. I know everything that you have done since you left the record bureau in Athens. I have already told you that I am interested in anyone who is interested in Dimitrios. Of course, you found out all about this man who had been before you in Smyrna?"

The last sentence was put in a little too casually. Latimer said: "No, Mr. Peters, I did not."

"But surely you were interested?"

"Not very."

The fat man sighed. "I do not think that you are being frank with me. How much better if . . ."

"Listen!" Latimer interrupted rudely. "I'm going to be frank. You are doing your level best to pump me. I'm not going to be pumped. Let that be clear. I made you an offer. You answer my questions and I'll answer yours. The only questions you've answered so far have been questions to which I had already guessed the answers. I still want to know why you are interested in this dead man Dimitrios. You said that you could tell me more than I could tell you. That may be so. But *I* have an idea, Mr. Peters, that it is more important for you to have my answers than it is for me to have your answers. Breaking into hotel rooms and making this sort of mess isn't the sort of thing any man does in a spirit of idle inquiry. To be honest, I cannot for the life of me conceive of any reason for your interest in Dimitrios. It did not occur to me that perhaps Dimitrios had kept some of that money he earned in Paris. . . . You know about that, I expect?" And in response to a faint nod from Mr. Peters: "Yes, I thought you might. But, as I say, it did occur to me that Dimitrios might have hidden his treasure and that you were interested in finding out where. Unfortunately my own information disposes of that possibility. His belongings were on the mortuary table beside him, and there wasn't a penny piece there. Just a bundle of cheap clothes. And as for . . ."

But Mr. Peters had stepped forward and was staring down at him with a peculiar expression on his face. Latimer allowed the sentence he had begun to trail off lamely into silence. "What is the matter?" he added.

"Did I understand you to say," said the fat man slowly, "that you actually saw the body of Dimitrios in the mortuary?"

"Yes; what of it? Have I carelessly let slip another useful piece of information?"

But Mr. Peters did not answer. He had produced one of his thin cheroots and was lighting it carefully. Suddenly he blew out a jet of smoke and started to waddle slowly up and down the room, his eyes screwed up as if he were in great pain. He began to talk.

"Mr. Latimer, we must reach an understanding. We

must stop this quarrelling." He halted in his tracks and looked down at Latimer again. "It is absolutely essential, Mr. Latimer," he said, "that I know what you are after. No, no, please! Don't interrupt me. I admit that I probably need your answers more than you need mine. But I cannot give you mine at present. Yes, yes, I heard what you said. But I am talking seriously. Listen, please.

"You are interested in the history of Dimitrios. You are thinking of going to Belgrade to find out more about him. You cannot deny that. Now, both of us know that Dimitrios was in Belgrade in nineteen twenty-six. Also, I can tell you that he was never there after nineteen twenty-six. Why are you interested? You will not tell me. Very well. I will tell you something more. If you go to Belgrade you will not discover a single trace of Dimitrios. Furthermore, you may find yourself in trouble with the authorities if you pursue the matter. There is only one man who could and would, under certain circumstances, tell you what you want to know. He is a Pole, and he lives near Geneva.

"Now then! I will give you his name and I will give you a letter to him. I will do that for you. But first I must know why you want this information. I thought at first that you might perhaps be connected with the Turkish police—there are so many Englishmen in the Near Eastern police departments these days—but that possibility I no longer consider. Your passport describes you as a writer, but that is a very elastic term. Who are you, Mr. Latimer, and what is your game?"

He paused expectantly. Latimer stared back at him with what he hoped was an inscrutable expression. Mr. Peters, unabashed, went on:

"Naturally, when I ask what your game is, I use the phrase in a specific sense. Your game is, of course, to get money. But that is not the answer I need. Are you a rich man, Mr. Latimer? No? Then what I have to say may be simplified. I am proposing an alliance, Mr. Latimer, a pooling of resources. I am aware of certain facts which I cannot tell you about at the moment. You, on the other hand, possess an important piece of information. You may not know that it is important, but nevertheless it *is*. Now, my facts alone are not worth a great deal. Your piece of information is quite valueless without my facts. The two together, however, are worth at the very least"— he stroked his chin—"at the very least five thousand English pounds, a million French francs." He smiled triumphantly. "What do you say to that?"

"You will forgive me," replied Latimer coldly, "if I say that I cannot understand what you're talking about, won't you? Not that it makes any difference whether you do or don't. I am *tired*, Mr. Peters, *very* tired. I want badly to go to bed." He got to his feet and, pulling the bedclothes on to the bed, began to remake it. "There is, I suppose, no reason why you should not know why I am interested in Dimitrios," he went on as he dragged a sheet into position. "The reason is certainly nothing to do with money. I write detective stories for a living. In Stambul I heard from a Colonel Haki, who is something to do with the police there, about a criminal named Dimitrios, who had been found dead in the Bosphorus. Partly for amusement—the sort of amusement that one derives from cross-word puzzles—partly from a desire to try my hand at practical detection, I set out to trace the man's history. That is all. I don't expect you to understand it. You are probably wondering at the moment why I couldn't think of a more convincing story. I am sorry. If you don't like the truth, you can lump it."

Mr. Peters had listened in silence. Now he waddled to the window, pitched out his cheroot and faced Latimer across the bed.

"Detective stories! Now, that is most interesting to me, Mr. Latimer. I am so fond of them. I wonder if you would tell me the names of some of your books."

Latimer gave him several titles.

"And your publisher?"

"English, American, French, Swedish, Norwegian, Dutch or Hungarian?"

"Hungarian, please."

Latimer told him.

Mr. Peters nodded slowly. "A good firm, I believe." He seemed to reach a decision. "Have you a pen and paper, Mr. Latimer?"

Latimer nodded wearily towards the writing-table. The other went to it and sat down. As he finished making the bed and began to collect his belongings from the floor, Latimer heard the hotel pen scratching over a piece of the hotel paper. Mr. Peters was keeping his word.

At last he finished and the chair creaked as he got up. Latimer, who was replacing some shoe trees, straightened his back. Mr. Peters had recovered his smile. Good will oozed from him like sweat.

"Here, Mr. Latimer," he announced, "are three pieces of paper. On the first one is written the name of the man of whom I spoke to you. His name is Grodek—Wladyslaw Grodek. He lives just outside Geneva. The second is a letter to him. If you present that letter he will know that you are a friend of mine and that he can be frank with you. He is retired now, so I think I may safely tell you that he was at one time the most successful professional agent in Europe. More secret naval and military information has passed through his hands than through those of any other one man. It was always accurate, what is more. He dealt with quite a number of governments. His headquarters were in Brussels. To an author I should think he would be very interesting. You will like him, I think. He is a great lover of animals. A beautiful character *au fond*. Incidentally, it was he who employed Dimitrios in nineteen twenty-six."

"I see. Thank you very much. What about the third piece of paper?"

Mr. Peters hesitated. His smile became a little smug. "I think you said that you were not rich."

"No, I am not rich."

"Half a million francs, two thousand five hundred English pounds, would be useful to you?"

"Undoubtedly."

"Well, then, Mr. Latimer, when you have tired of Geneva I want you to—how do you say?—to kill two birds with one stone." He pulled Latimer's chronological table from his pocket. "On this list of yours you have other dates besides nineteen twenty-six still to be accounted for if you are to know what there is to know about Dimitrios. The place to account for them is Paris. That is the first thing. The second is that if you will come to Paris, if you will put yourself in touch with me there, if you will consider, then, the pooling of resources, the alliance that I have already proposed to you, I can definitely guarantee that in a very few days you will have at least two thousand five hundred English pounds to pay into your account—half a million French francs!"

"I do wish," retorted Latimer irritably, "that you would be a little more explicit. Half a million francs for doing what? Who is going to pay this money? You are far too mysterious, Mr. Peters—far too mysterious to be true."

Mr. Peters' smile tightened. Here was a Christian, reviled but unembittered, waiting steadfastly for the lions to be admitted into the arena.

"Mr. Latimer," he said gently, "I know that you do not trust me. That is the reason why I have given you Grodek's address and that letter to him. I want to give you concrete evidence of my goodwill towards you, to prove that my word is to be trusted. And I want to show that I trust you, that I believe what you have told me. At the moment I cannot say more. But if you will believe in and trust me, if you will come to Paris, then here, on this piece of paper, is an àddress. When you arrive send a *pneumatique* to me. Do not call, for it is the address of a friend. If you will simply send a *pneumatique* giving me your address, I will be able to explain everything. It is perfectly simple."

It was time, Latimer decided, to get rid of Mr. Peters.

"Well," he said, "this is all very confusing. You seem to me to have jumped to a lot of conclusions. I had not definitely arranged to go to Belgrade. It is not certain that I shall have time to go to Geneva. As for going on to Paris, that is a thing which I could not possibly consider at the moment. I have a great deal of work to do, of course, and . . ."

Mr. Peters buttoned up his overcoat. "Of course." And then, with a curious urgency in his tone: "But if you *should* find time to come to Paris, do please send me that *pneumatique*. I have put you to so much trouble, I should like to make restitution in a practical way. Half a million francs is worth considering, eh? And I would guarantee it. But we must trust one another. That is most important." He held out his hand. "Good night, Mr. Latimer. I won't say 'good-bye.' "

Latimer took the hand. It was dry and very soft.

"Good night."

At the door he half turned. "Half a million francs, Mr. Latimer, will buy a lot of good things. I do hope that we shall meet in Paris. Good night."

"I hope so, too. Good night."

The door closed and Mr. Peters was gone; but to Latimer's overwrought imagination it seemed as if his smile, like the Cheshire cat's, remained behind him, floating in the air. He leaned against the door and surveyed for an instant the upturned suit-cases. Outside it was beginning to get light. He looked at his watch. Five o'clock. The business of clearing up the room could wait. He undressed and got into bed.

CHAPTER VIII

GRODEK

Iᴛ was eleven o'clock when Latimer, having been awake for about a quarter of an hour, finally opened his eyes. There, on the bedside table, were Mr. Peters' three pieces of paper. They were an unpleasant reminder that he had some thinking to do and some decisions to make. But for their presence and the fact that in the morning light his room looked like a rag-picker's workshop, he might have dismissed his recollections of the visitation as being no more than part of the bad dreams which had troubled his sleep. He would have liked so to dismiss them. But Mr. Peters, with his mystery, his absurd references to half millions of francs, his threats and his hintings, was not so

121

easily disposed of. He . . .

Latimer sat up in bed and reached for the three pieces of paper.

The first, as Peters had said, contained the Geneva address:

Wladyslaw Grodek,
Villa Acacias
Chambésy.
(At 7 km. from Geneva.)

The writing was scratchy, florid and difficult to read. The figure seven was made with a stroke across the middle in the French way.

He turned hopefully to the letter. It consisted of only six lines and was written in a language and with an alphabet which he did not recognise, but which he concluded was probably Polish. It began, as far as he could see, without any preliminary "Dear Grodek," and ended with an indecipherable initial. In the middle of the second line he made out his own name spelt with what looked like a "Y" instead of an "I." He sighed. He could, of course, take the thing to a bureau and have it translated, but Mr. Peters would no doubt have thought of that, and it was unlikely that the result would supply any sort of answer to the questions that he, Latimer, badly wanted answered: the questions of who and what was Mr. Peters.

He turned to the second address:

Mr. Peters,
aux soins de Caillé,
3, Impasse des Huit Anges,
Paris 7.

And that brought his thoughts back to their starting point. Why, in the name of all that was reasonable, should Mr. Peters want him to go to Paris? What was this information that was worth so much money? Who was going to pay for it?

He tried to remember at exactly what point in their encounter Mr. Peters had changed his tactics so abruptly. He had an idea that it had been when he had said something about having seen Dimitrios in the mortuary. But there could surely be nothing in that. Could it have been his reference to the "treasure" of Dimitrios that had . . .

He snapped his fingers. Of course! What a fool not to think of it before! He had been ignoring an important fact. Dimitrios had not died a natural death. *Dimitrios had been murdered.*

Colonel Haki's doubts of the possibility of tracing the murderer and his own preoccupation with the past had caused him to lose sight of the fact or, at any rate, to see in it no more than a logical ending to an ugly story. He had failed to take into account the two consequent facts; that the murderer was still at large (and probably alive) and that there must have been a motive for the murder.

A murderer and a motive. The motive would be monetary gain. What money? Naturally, the money that had been made out of the drug-peddling business in Paris, the money that had so unaccountably disappeared. Mr. Peters' references to half millions of francs did not seem quite as fantastic when you looked at the problem from that point of view. As for the murderer—why not Peters?

But at that Latimer frowned. Dimitrios had been stabbed. He began to reconstruct the picture in his mind, to see Peters stabbing someone. Yet the picture seemed wrong. It was difficult to see Peters wielding a stabbing knife. The difficulty made him begin to think again. There really was no reason at all even to suspect Peters of the murder. And even if there had been a reason, the fact of Peters' murdering Dimitrios for his money still did not explain the connection (if a connection existed) between that money and the half millions of francs (if they existed). And, anyway, what was this mysterious piece of information he was supposed to possess? It was all very like being faced by an algebraic problem containing many unknown quantities and having only one biquadratic equation with which to solve it. If he *were* to solve it . . .

Now why should Peters be so anxious for him to go to Paris? Surely it would have been just as simple to have pooled their resources (whatever that might mean) in Sofia. Confound Mr. Peters! Latimer got out of bed and turned on his bath. Sitting in the hot, slightly rusty water he reduced his predicament to its essentials.

He had a choice of two courses of action.

He could go back to Athens, work on his new book and put Dimitrios and Marukakis and Mr. Peters and this Grodek out of his mind. Or, he could go to Geneva, see Grodek (if there were such a person) and postpone making any decision about Mr. Peters' proposals.

The first course was obviously the sensible one. After all, the justification of his researches into the past life of Dimitrios had been that he was making an impersonal experiment in detection. The experiment must not be allowed to become an obsession. He had found out some interesting things about the man. Honour should be satisfied. And it was high time he got on with the book. He had his living to earn and no amount of information about

Dimitrios and Mr. Peters or anyone else would compensate for a lean bank balance six months hence. As for the half a million francs, that could not be taken seriously. Yes, he would return to Athens at once.

He got out of the bath and began to dry himself.

On the other hand there was the matter of Mr. Peters to be cleared up. He could not reasonably be expected to leave these things as they were and hurry off to write a detective story. It was too much to ask of any man. Besides, here was *real* murder: not neat, tidy book-murder with corpse and clues and suspects and hangman, but murder over which a chief of police shrugged his shoulders, wiped his hands and consigned the stinking victim to a coffin. Yes, that was it. It was real. Dimitrios was or had been real. Here were no strutting paper figures, but tangible evocative men and women, as real as Proudhon, Montesquieu and Rosa Luxemburg.

Aloud Latimer murmured: "Comfortable, very comfortable! You want to go to Geneva. You don't want to work. You're feeling lazy and your curiosity has been aroused."

He shaved, dressed, collected his belongings, packed and went downstairs to inquire about the trains to Athens. The reception clerk brought him a time-table and found the Athens page.

Latimer stared at it in silence for a moment. Then:

"Supposing," he said slowly, "that I wanted to go to Geneva from here."

On his second evening in Geneva, Latimer received a letter bearing the Chambésy postmark. It was from

Wladyslaw Grodek and was in answer to a letter Latimer had sent enclosing Mr. Peters' note.

Herr Grodek wrote briefly and in French:

> *Villa Acacias,*
> *Chambésy.*
> *Friday.*

My dear Mr. Latimer,

I should be pleased if you could come to the Villa Acacias for luncheon to-morrow. Unless I hear that you cannot come, my chauffeur will call at your hotel at eleven-thirty.

Please accept the expression of my most distinguished sentiments.

> *Grodek.*

The chauffeur arrived punctually, saluted, ushered Latimer ceremoniously into a huge chocolate-coloured *coupé de ville*, and drove off through the rain as if he were escaping from the scene of a crime.

Idly, Latimer surveyed the interior of the car. Everything about it from the inlaid wood panelling and ivory fittings to the too-comfortable upholstery suggested money, a great deal of money. Money, he reflected, that, if Peters were to be believed, had been made out of espionage. Unreasonably he found it odd that there should be no evidence in the car of the sinister origin of its purchase price. He wondered what Herr Grodek would look like. He might possibly have a pointed white beard. Peters had said that he was a Polish national, a great lover of animals and a beautiful character *au fond*. Did that mean that superficially he was an ugly character? As for his alleged love of animals, that meant nothing. Great animal lovers were sometimes pathetic in their hatred of humanity. Would a professional spy, uninspired by any patriotic motives, hate the world he worked in? A stupid question.

For a time they travelled along the road which ran by the northerly shore of the lake; but at Pregny they turned to the left and began to climb a long hill. About a kilometre farther on, the car swung off into a narrow lane through a pine forest. They stopped before a pair of iron gates which the chauffeur got out to open. Then they drove on up a steep drive with a right-angle turn in the middle to stop at last before a large, ugly *chalet*.

The chauffeur opened the door and he got out and walked towards the door of the house. As he did so it was opened by a stout, cheerful-looking woman who looked as though she might be the housekeeper. He went in.

He found himself in a small lobby no more than six feet wide. On one wall was a row of clothes pegs draped carelessly with hats and coats, a woman's and a man's, a climbing rope and an odd ski-stick. Against the opposite wall were stacked three pairs of well-greased skis.

The housekeeper took his coat and hat and he walked through the lobby into a large room.

It was built rather like an inn with stairs leading to a gallery which ran along two sides of the room, and a vast cowled fireplace. A wood fire roared in the grate and the pinewood floor was covered with thick rugs. It was very warm and clean.

With a smiling assurance that Herr Grodek would be down immediately, the housekeeper withdrew. There were arm chairs in front of the fire and Latimer walked towards them. As he did so there was a quick rustle and a Siamese cat leaped on to the back of the nearest chair and stared at him with hostile blue eyes. It was joined by another. Latimer moved towards them and they drew back arching their backs. Giving them a wide berth, Latimer made his way to the fire. The cats watched him narrowly. The logs shifted restlessly in the grate. There was a moment's silence; then Herr Grodek came down the stairs.

The first thing that drew Latimer's attention to the fact was that the cats lifted their heads suddenly, stared over his shoulder and then jumped lightly to the floor. He looked round. The man had reached the foot of the stairs. Now he turned and walked towards Latimer with his hand outstretched and words of apology on his lips.

He was a tall, broad-shouldered man of about sixty with thinning grey hair still tinged with the original straw colour which had matched the fair, clean-shaven cheeks and blue-grey eyes. His face was pear-shaped, tapering from a broad forehead, past a small tight mouth to a chin which receded almost into the neck. You might have put him down as an Englishman or Dane of more than average intelligence; a retired consulting engineer, perhaps. In his slippers and his thick baggy tweeds and with his vigorous, decisive movements he looked like a man enjoying the well-earned fruits of a blameless and worthy career.

He said: "Excuse me, please, Monsieur. I did not hear the car arrive."

His French, though curiously accented, was very ready and Latimer found the fact incongruous. The small mouth would have been more at home with English.

"It is very kind of you to receive me so hospitably,

Monsieur Grodek. I don't know what Peters said in his letter, because . . ."

"Because," interrupted the tall man heartily, "you very wisely have never troubled to learn Polish. I can sympathise with you. It is a horrible tongue. You have introduced yourself to Anton and Simone here." He indicated the cats. "I am convinced that they resent the fact that I do not speak Siamese. Do you like cats? Anton and Simone have critical intelligence, I am sure of it. They are not like ordinary cats, are you, *mes enfants?*" He seized one of them and held it up for Latimer's inspection. *"Ah, Simone cherie, comme tu es mignonne! Comme tu es bête!"* He released it so that it stood on the palms of his hands. *"Allez vite! Va promener avec ton vrai amant, ton cher Anton!"* The cat jumped to the floor and stalked indignantly away. Grodek dusted his hands lightly together. "Beautiful, aren't they! And so human. They become ill-tempered when the weather is bad. I wish so much that we could have had a fine day for your visit, Monsieur. When the sun is shining the view from here is very pretty."

Latimer said that he had guessed from what he had seen that it would be. He was puzzled. Both his host and his reception were totally unlike those he had expected. Grodek might look like a retired consulting engineer, but he had a quality which seemed to render the simile absurd. It was a quality that derived somehow from the contrast between his appearance and his quick, neat gestures, the urgency of his small lips. You could picture him without effort in the role of lover; which was a thing, Latimer reflected, that you could say of few men of sixty and few of under sixty. He wondered about the woman whose belongings he had seen in the entrance lobby. He added lamely: "It must be agreeable here in the summer."

Grodek nodded. He had opened a cupboard by the fireplace. "Agreeable enough. What will you drink? English whisky?"

"Thank you."

"Good. I, too, prefer it as an aperitif."

He began to splash whisky into two tumblers. "In the summer I work outside. That is very good for me but not good for my work, I think. Do you find that you can work out of doors?"

"No, I don't. The flies. . . ."

"Exactly! the flies. I am writing a book, you know."

"Indeed. Your memoirs?"

Grodek looked up from the bottle of soda water he was opening and Latimer saw a glint of amusement in his eyes as he shook his head. "No, Monsieur. A Life of St. Francis. I confidently expect to be dead before it is finished."

"It must be a very exhaustive study."

"Oh yes." He handed Latimer a drink. "You see, the advantage of St. Francis from my point of view is that he has been written about so extensively that I need not go to sources for my material. There is no original research for me to do. The work therefore serves its purpose in permitting me to live here in almost absolute idleness with an easy conscience." He raised his glass. "*A votre santé.*"

"*A la vôtre.*" Latimer was beginning to wonder if his host were, after all, no more than an affected ass. He drank a little of his whisky. "I wonder," he said, "if Peters mentioned the purpose of my visit to you in the letter I brought with me from Sofia."

"No, Monsieur, he did not. But I received a letter from him yesterday which did mention it." He was putting down his glass and he gave Latimer a sidelong look as he added: "It interested me very much." And then: "Have you known Peters long?"

There was an unmistakable hesitation at the name. Latimer guessed that the other's lips had been framing a word of a different shape.

"I have met him once or twice. Once in a train, once in my hotel. And you, Monsieur? You must know him very well."

Grodek raised his eyebrows. "And what makes you so sure of that, Monsieur?"

Latimer smiled easily because he felt uneasy. He had, he felt, committed some sort of indiscretion. "If he had not known you very well he would surely not have given me an introduction to you or asked you to give me information of so confidential a character." He felt pleased with that speech.

"Monsieur," said Herr Grodek; "I wonder what your attitude would be if I were to ask an impertinent question; if I were, for instance, to ask you to tell me seriously if a literary interest in human frailty were your only reason for approaching me."

Latimer felt himself redden. "I can assure you . . ." he began.

"I am quite certain that you can," Grodek interrupted smoothly. "But—forgive me—what are your assurances worth?"

"I can only give you my word, Monsieur, to treat any information you may give me as confidential," retorted Latimer stiffly.

The other sighed. "I don't think I have made myself quite clear," he said carefully. "The information itself is nothing. What happened in Belgrade in nineteen twenty-six is of little importance now. It is my own position of which I am thinking. To be frank, our friend Peters has been a little indiscreet in sending you to me. He admits it but craves my indulgence and asks me as a favour—he recalls that I am under a slight obligation to him—to give you the information you need about Dimitrios Talat. He explains that you are a writer and that your interest is merely that of a writer. Very well! There is one thing, however, which I find inexplicable." He paused, picked up his glass and drained it. "As a student of human behaviour, Monsieur," he went on, "you must have noticed that most persons have behind their actions one stimulus which tends to dominate all others. With some of us it is vanity, with others the gratification of the senses, with still others the desire for money, and so on. Er—Peters happens to be one of those with the money stimulus very highly developed. Without being unkind to him, I think I may tell you that he has the miser's love of money for its own sake. Do not misunderstand me, please. I do not say that he will act only under that money stimulus. What I mean is that I cannot from my knowledge of Peters imagine him going to the trouble of sending you here to me and writing to me in the way he has written, in the interests of the English detective story. You see my point? I am a little suspicious, Monsieur. I still have enemies in this world. Supposing, therefore, that you tell me just what your relations with our friend Peters are. Would you like to do that?"

"I should be delighted to do so. Unfortunately I cannot do so. And for a very simple reason. I don't know what those relations are myself."

Grodek's eyes hardened. "I was not joking, Monsieur."

"Nor was I. I have been investigating the history of this man Dimitrios. While doing so I have met Peters. For some reason that I do not know of, he, too, is interested in Dimitrios. He overheard me making inquiries in the relief commission archives in Athens. He then followed me to Sofia and approached me there—behind a pistol, I may add—for an explanation of my interest in this man, who, by the way, was murdered some weeks ago before I ever heard of him. He followed this up with an offer. He said that if I would meet him in Paris and collaborate with him in some scheme he had in mind we should each profit to the extent of half a million francs. He said that I possessed a piece of information which, though valueless by itself, would, when used in conjunction with information in his possession, be of great value. I did not believe him and refused to have anything to do with his scheme. Accordingly, as an inducement to me and as evidence of his goodwill, he gave me the note to you. I had told him, you see, that my interest was that of a writer and admitted that I was about to go to Belgrade to collect more information there if I could. He told me that you were the only person who could supply it."

Grodek's eyebrows went up. "I don't want to seem too inquisitive, Monsieur, but I should like to know how you knew that Dimitrios Talat was in Belgrade in nineteen twenty-six."

"I was told by a Turkish official with whom I became friendly in Istanbul. He described the man's history to me; his history, that is, as far as it was known in Istanbul."

"I see. And what, may I ask, is this so valuable piece of information in your possession?"

"I don't know."

Grodek frowned. "Come now, Monsieur. You ask me for my confidences. The least you can do is to give me yours."

"I am telling you the truth. I don't know. I talked fairly freely to Peters. Then, at one point in the conversation, he became excited."

"At what point?"

"I was explaining, I think, how I knew that Dimitrios had no money when he died. It was after that that he started talking about this million francs."

"And how *did* you know?"

"Because when I saw the body everything taken from it was on the mortuary table. Everything, that is, except his *carte d'identité* which had been removed from the lining of his coat and forwarded to the French authorities. There was no money. Not a penny."

For several seconds Grodek stared at him. Then he walked over to the cupboard where the drinks were kept. "Another drink, Monsieur?"

He poured the drinks out in silence, handed Latimer his and raised his glass solemnly. "A toast, Monsieur. To the English detective story!"

Amused, Latimer raised his glass to his lips. His host had done the same. Suddenly, however, he choked and, dragging a handkerchief from his pocket, set his glass down again. To his surprise, Latimer saw that the man was laughing.

"Forgive me, Monsieur," he gasped; "a thought crossed my mind that made me laugh. It was"--he hesitated a fraction of a second—"it was the thought of our friend Peters confronting you with a pistol. He is quite terrified of firearms."

"He seemed to keep his fears to himself quite successfully." Latimer spoke a trifle irritably. He had a suspicion that there was another joke somewhere, the point of which he had missed.

"A clever man, Peters." Grodek chuckled and patted Latimer on the shoulder. He seemed suddenly in excellent spirits. "My dear chap, please don't say that I have offended you. Look, we will have luncheon now. I hope you will like it. Are you hungry? Greta is really a splendid cook and there is nothing Swiss about my wines. Afterwards, I will tell you about Dimitrios and the trouble he caused me, and Belgrade and nineteen twenty-six. Does that please you?"

"It's very good of you to put yourself out like this."

He thought that Grodek was about to laugh again, but the Pole seemed to change his mind. He became instead very solemn. "It is a pleasure, Monsieur. Peters is a very good friend of mine. Besides, I like you personally, and we have so few visitors here." He hesitated. "May I be permitted as a friend to give you a word of advice, Monsieur?"

"Please do."

"Then, if I were in your place, Monsieur, I should be inclined to take our friend Peters at his word and go to Paris."

Latimer was perplexed. "I don't know . . ." he began slowly.

But the housekeeper, Greta, had come into the room.

"Luncheon!" exclaimed Grodek with satisfaction.

Later, when he had an opportunity of asking Grodek to explain his "word of advice," Latimer forgot to do so. By that time he had other things to think about.

CHAPTER IX

BELGRADE, 1926

MEN have learned to distrust their imaginations. It is, therefore, strange to them when they chance to discover that a world conceived in the imagination, outside experience, does exist in fact. The afternoon which Latimer spent at the Villa Acacias, listening to Wladyslaw Grodek, he recalls as, in that sense, one of the strangest of his life. In a letter (written in French) to the Greek, Marukakis, which he began that evening, while the whole thing was still fresh in his mind, and finished on the following day, the Sunday, he placed it on record.

137

Geneva.
Saturday.

My dear Marukakis,

I remember that I promised to write to you to let you know if I discovered anything more about Dimitrios. I wonder if you will be as surprised as I am that I have actually done so. Discovered something, I mean; for I intended to write to you in any case to thank you again for the help you gave me in Sofia.

When I left you there, I was bound, you may remember, for Belgrade. Why, then, am I writing from Geneva?

I was afraid that you would ask that question.

My dear fellow, I wish that I knew the answer. I know part of it. The man, the professional spy, who employed Dimitrios in Belgrade in nineteen twenty-six, lives just outside Geneva. I saw him to-day and talked with him about Dimitrios. I can even explain how I got into touch with him. I was introduced. But just why I was introduced and just what the man who introduced us hopes to get out of it I cannot imagine. I shall, I hope, discover those things eventually. Meanwhile, let me say that if you find this mystery irritating, I find it no less so. Let me tell you about Dimitrios.

Did you ever believe in the existence of the "master" spy? Until to-day I most certainly did not. Now I do. The reason for this is that I have spent the greater part of to-day talking to one. I cannot tell you his name, so I shall call him, in the best spy-story tradition, "G."

G. was a "master" spy (he has retired now) in the same sense that the printer my publisher uses is a "master" printer. He was an employer of spy labour. His work was mainly (though not entirely) administrative in character.

Now I know that a lot of nonsense is talked and written about spies and espionage, but let me try to put the question to you as G. put it to me.

He began by quoting Napoleon as saying that in war the basic element of all successful strategy was surprise.

G. is, I should say, a confirmed Napoleon-quoter. No doubt Napoleon did say that or something like it. I am quite sure he wasn't the first military leader to do so. Alexander, Cæsar, Genghis Khan and Frederick of Prussia all had the same idea. In nineteen eighteen Foch thought of it, too. But to return to G.

G. says that "the experiences of the 1914–18 conflict" showed that in a future war (that sounds so beautifully distant, doesn't it?) the mobility and striking power of modern armies and navies and the existence of air forces would render the element of surprise more important than ever; so important, in fact, that it was possible that the people who got in with a surprise attack first might win the war. It was more than ever necessary to guard against surprise, to guard against it, moreover, *before* the war had started.

Now, there are roughly twenty-seven independent states in Europe. Each has an army and an air force and most have some sort of navy as well. For its own security, each of those armies, air forces and navies must know what each corresponding force in each of the other twenty-six countries is doing—what its strength is, what its efficiency is, what secret preparations it is making. That means spies —armies of them.

In nineteen twenty-six G. was employed by Italy; and in the spring of that year he set up house in Belgrade.

Relations between Yugoslavia and Italy were strained at the time. The Italian seizure of Fiume was still as fresh in Yugoslav minds as the bombardment of Corfu; there were rumours, too (not unfounded as it was learned later in the year) that Mussolini contemplated occupying Albania.

Italy, on her side, was suspicious of Yugoslavia. Fiume was held under Yugoslav guns. A Yugoslav Albania alongside the Straits of Otranto was an unthinkable proposition. An independent Albania was tolerable only as long as it was under a predominantly Italian influence. It might be desirable to make certain of things. But the Yugoslavs might put up a fight. Reports from Italian agents in Belgrade indicated that in the event of war Yugoslavia intended to protect her seaboard by bottling herself up in the Adriatic with minefields laid just north of the Straits of Otranto.

I don't know much about these things, but apparently one does not have to lay a couple of hundred miles' worth of mines to make a two-hundred-mile wide corridor of sea impassable. One just lays one or two small fields without letting one's enemy know just where. It is necessary, then, for them to find out the positions of those minefields.

That, then, was G.'s job in Belgrade. Italian agents found out about the minefields. G., the expert spy, was commissioned to do the real work of discovering where they were to be laid, without—a most important point this —without letting the Yugoslavs find out that he had done so. If they did find out, of course, they would promptly change the positions.

In that last part of his task G. failed. The reason for his failure was Dimitrios.

It has always seemed to me that a spy's job must be an extraordinarily difficult one. What I mean is this. If I were sent to Belgrade by the British Government with orders to get hold of the details of a secret mine-laying project for the Straits of Otranto, I should not even know where to start. Supposing I knew, as G. knew, that the details were recorded by means of markings on a navigational chart of the Straits. Very well. How many copies of the chart are kept? I would not know. Where are they kept? I would not know. I might reasonably suppose that at least one copy would be kept somewhere in the Ministry of Marine; but the Ministry of Marine is a large place. Moreover, the chart will almost certainly be under lock and key. And even if, as seems unlikely, I were able to find in which room it is kept and how to get to it, how should I set about obtaining a copy of it without letting the Yugoslavs know that I had done so?

When I tell you that within a month of his arrival in Belgrade, G. had not only found out where a copy of the chart was kept, but had also made up his mind how he was going to copy that copy *without the Yugoslavs knowing,* you will see that he is entitled to describe himself as competent.

How did he do it? What ingenious manœuvre, what subtle trick made it possible? I shall try to break the news gently.

Posing as a German, the representative of an optical instrument-maker in Dresden, he struck up an acquaintance with a clerk in the Submarine Defence Department (which dealt with submarine nets, booms, mine-laying and mine-sweeping) of the Ministry of Marine!

Pitiful, wasn't it! The amazing thing is that he himself regards it as a very astute move. His sense of humour is quite paralysed. When I asked him if he ever read spy stories, he said that he did not, as they always seemed to him very naïve. But there is worse to come.

He struck up this acquaintance by going to the Ministry and asking the door-keeper to direct him to the Department of Supply, a perfectly normal request for an outsider to make. Having got past the door-keeper, he stopped someone in a corridor, said that he had been directed to the Submarine Defence Department and had got lost and asked to be re-directed. Having got to the S.D. Department, he marched in and asked if it was the Department of Supply. They said that it was not, and out he went. He was in there not more than a minute, but in that time he had cast a quick eye over the personnel of the department, or, at all events, those of them he could see. He marked down three. That evening he waited outside the Ministry until the first of them came out. This man he followed home. Having found out his name and as much as he could about him, he repeated the process on succeeding evenings with the other two. Then he made his choice. It fell on a man named Bulić.

Now, G.'s actual methods may have lacked subtlety; but there was considerable subtlety in the way he employed them. He himself is quite oblivious of any distinction here. He is not the first successful man to misunderstand the reasons for his own success.

G.'s first piece of subtlety lay in his choice of Bulić as a tool.

Bulić was a disagreeable, conceited man of between

forty and fifty, older than most of his fellow clerks and disliked by them. His wife was ten years younger than he, dissatisfied and pretty. He suffered from catarrh. He was in the habit of going to a café for a drink when he left the Ministry for the day, and it was in this café that G. made his acquaintance by the simple process of asking him for a match, offering him a cigar and, finally, buying him a drink.

You may imagine that a clerk in a government department dealing with highly confidential matters would naturally tend to be suspicious of café acquaintances who tried to pump him about his work. G. was ready to deal with those suspicions long before they had entered Bulić's head.

The acquaintance ripened. G. would be in the café every evening when Bulić entered. They would carry on a desultory conversation. G., as a stranger to Belgrade, would ask Bulić's advice about this and that. He would pay for Bulić's drinks. He let Bulić condescend to him. Sometimes they would play a game of chess. Bulić would win. At other times they would play four-pack *bezique* with other frequenters of the café. Then, one evening, G. told Bulić a story.

He had been told by a mutual acquaintance, he said, that he, Bulić held an important post in the Ministry of Marine.

For Bulić the "mutual acquaintance" could have been one of several men with whom they played cards and exchanged opinions and who were vaguely aware that he worked in the Ministry. He frowned and opened his mouth. He was probably about to enter a mock-modest qualification of the adjective "important." But G. swept on. As chief salesman for a highly respectable firm of optical instrument makers, he was deputed to obtain an order due to be placed by the Ministry of Marine for binoculars. He had submitted his quotation and had hopes of securing the order but, as Bulić would know, there was nothing like a friend at court in these affairs. If, therefore, the good and influential Bulić would bring pressure to bear to see that the Dresden company secured the order, Bulić would be in pocket to the tune of twenty thousand dinar.[1]

Consider that proposition from Bulić's point of view. Here was he, an insignificant clerk, being flattered by the representative of a great German company and promised twenty thousand dinar, as much as he ordinarily earned in six months, for doing precisely nothing. If the quotation were already submitted, there was nothing to be done there. It would stand its chance with the other quotations. If the Dresden company secured the order he would be twenty thousand dinar in pocket without having compromised himself in any way. If they lost it *he* would lose nothing except the respect of this stupid and misinformed German.

G. admits that Bulić did make a half-hearted effort to be honest. He mumbled something about his not being sure that his influence could help. This, G. chose to treat as an attempt to increase the bribe. Bulić protested that no such thought had been in his mind. He was lost. Within five minutes he had agreed.

In the days that followed, Bulić and G. became close friends. G. ran no risk. Bulić could not know that no quotation had been submitted by the Dresden company

[1] The Yugoslav *dinar* is worth a little less than the French franc.

as all quotations received by the Department of Supply were confidential until the order was placed. If he were inquisitive enough to make inquiries, he would find, as G. had found by previous reference to the *Official Gazette*, that quotations for binoculars had actually been asked for by the Department of Supply.

G. now got to work.

Bulić, remember, had to play the part assigned to him by G., the part of influential official. G., furthermore, began to make himself very amiable by entertaining Bulić and the pretty but stupid Madame Bulić at expensive restaurants and night clubs. The pair responded like thirsty plants to rain. Could Bulić be cautious when, having had the best part of a bottle of sweet champagne, he found himself involved in an argument about Italy's overwhelming naval strength and her threat to Yugoslavia's seaboard? It was unlikely. He was a little drunk. His wife was present. For the first time in his dreary life, his judgment was being treated with the deference due to it. Besides, he had his part to play. It would not do to seem to be ignorant of what was going on behind the scenes. He began to brag. He himself had seen the very plans that in operation would immobilise Italy's fleet in the Adriatic. Naturally, he had to be discreet, but . . .

By the end of that evening G. knew that Bulić had access to a copy of the chart. He had also made up his mind that Bulić was going to get that copy for him.

He made his plans carefully. Then he looked round for a suitable man to carry them out. He needed a go-between. He found Dimitrios.

Just how G. came to hear of Dimitrios is not clear. I fancy that he was anxious not to compromise any of

his old associates. One can conceive that his reticence
might be understandable. Anyway, Dimitrios was recommended to him. I asked in what business the recom-
mender was engaged. I hoped, I admit to be able to find
some link with the Eurasian Credit Trust episode. But
G. became vague. It was so very long ago. But he remembered the verbal testimonial which accompanied the
recommendation.

Dimitrios Talat was a Greek-speaking Turk with an
"effective" passport and a reputation for being "useful"
and at the same time discreet. He was also said to have had
experience in "financial work of a confidential nature."

If one did not happen to know just what he was useful
for and the nature of the financial work he had done,
one might have supposed that the man under discussion
was some sort of accountant. But there is, it seems, a jar-
gon in these affairs. G. understood it and decided that Dimitrios was the man for the job in hand. He wrote to Dimitrios—he gave me the address as though it were a sort
of American Express poste restante—care of the Eurasian
Credit Trust in Bucharest!

Dimitrios arrived in Belgrade five days later and presented himself at G.'s house just off the Knez Miletina.

G. remembers the occasion very well. Dimitrios, he
says, was a man of medium height who might have been
almost any age between thirty-five and fifty—he was actually thirty-seven. He was smartly dressed and . . . But
I had better quote G.'s own words:

"He was chic in an expensive way, and his hair was
becoming grey at the sides of his head. He had a sleek,
satisfied, confident air and something about the eyes that
I recognised immediately. The man was a pimp. I can

always recognise it. Do not ask me how. I have a woman's instinct for these things."

So there you have it. Dimitrios had prospered. Had there been any more Madame Prevezas? We shall never know. At all events, G. detected the pimp in Dimitrios and was not displeased. A pimp, he reasoned, could be relied upon not to fool about with women to the detriment of the business in hand. Also Dimitrios was of pleasing address. I think that I had better quote G. again:

"He could wear his clothes gracefully. Also he looked intelligent. I was pleased by this because I did not care to employ riff-raff from the gutters. Sometimes it was necessary but I never liked it. They did not always understand my curious temperament."

G., you see, was fussy.

Dimitrios had not wasted his time. He could now speak both German and French with reasonable accuracy. He said:

"I came as soon as I received your letter. I was busy in Bucharest but I was glad to get your letter as I had heard of you."

G. explained carefully and with circumspection (it did not do to give too much away to a prospective employee) what he wanted done. Dimitrios listened unemotionally. When G. had finished, he asked how much he was to be paid.

"Thirty thousand dinar," said G.

"Fifty thousand," said Dimitrios, "and I would prefer to have it in Swiss francs."

They compromised on forty thousand to be paid in Swiss francs. Dimitrios smiled and shrugged his agreement.

Meanwhile, Bulić was finding life more pleasant than it had ever been before. He was being entertained at rich places. His wife, warmed by unfamiliar luxury, no longer looked at him with contempt and distaste in her eyes. With the money they saved on the meals provided by the stupid German she could drink her favourite cognac; and when she drank she became friendly and agreeable. In a week's time, moreover, he might become the possessor of twenty thousand dinar. There was a chance. He felt very well, he said one night, and added that cheap food was bad for his catarrh. That was the nearest he came to forgetting to play his part.

The order for the binoculars was given to a Czech firm. The *Official Gazette*, in which the fact was announced, was published at noon. At one minute past noon, G. had a copy and was on his way to an engraver on whose bench lay a half-finished copper die. By six o'clock he was waiting opposite the entrance to the Ministry. Soon after six, Bulić appeared. He had seen the *Official Gazette*. A copy was under his arm. His dejection was visible from where G. stood. G. began to follow him.

Ordinarily, Bulić would have crossed the road before many minutes had passed, to get to his café. To-night he hesitated and then walked straight on. He was not anxious to meet the man from Dresden.

G. turned down a side street and hailed a taxi. Within two minutes his taxi had made a detour and was approaching Bulić. Suddenly, he signalled to the driver to stop, bounded out on to the pavement and embraced Bulić delightedly. Before the bewildered clerk could protest, he was bundled into the taxi and G. was pouring congratulations and thanks into his ear and pressing a cheque for twenty thousand dinar into his hand.

"But I thought you'd lost the order," mumbles Bulić at last.

G. laughs as if at a huge joke. "Lost it!" And then he "understands." "Of course! I forgot to tell you. The quotation was submitted through a Czech subsidiary of ours. Look, does this explain it?" He thrusts one of the newly printed cards into Bulić's hand. "I don't use this card often. Most people know that these Czechs are owned by our company in Dresden." He brushes the matter aside. "But we must have a drink immediately. Driver!"

That night they celebrated. His first bewilderment over, Bulić took full advantage of the situation. He became drunk. He began to brag of the potency of his influence in the Ministry until even G., who had every reason for satisfaction, was hard put to it to remain civil.

But towards the end of the evening, he drew Bulić aside. Estimates, he said, had been invited for rangefinders. Could he, Bulić, assist? Of course he could. And now Bulić became cunning. Now that the value of his cooperation had been established, he had a right to expect something on account.

G. had not anticipated this, but, secretly amused, he agreed at once. Bulić received another cheque; this time it was for ten thousand dinar. The understanding was that he should be paid a further ten thousand when the order was placed with G.'s "employers."

Bulić was now wealthier than ever before. He had thirty thousand dinar. Two evenings later, in the supper room of a fashionable hotel, G. introduced him to a Freiherr von Kiessling. The Freiherr von Kiessling's other name was, needless to say, Dimitrios.

"You would have thought," says G., "that he had been living in such places all his life. For all I know, he may have been doing so. His manner was perfect. When I introduced Bulić as an important official in the Ministry of Marine, he condescended magnificently. With Madame Bulić he was superb. He might have been greeting a princess. But I saw the way his fingers moved across the palm of her hand as he bent to kiss the back of it."

Dimitrios had displayed himself in the supper room before G. had affected to claim acquaintance with him in order to give G. time to prepare the ground. The "Freiherr," G. told the Bulićs after he had drawn their attention to Dimitrios, was a very important man. Something of a mystery, perhaps; but a very important factor in international big business. He was enormously rich and was believed to control as many as twenty-seven companies. He might be a useful man to know.

The Bulićs were enchanted to be presented to him. When the "Freiherr" agreed to drink a glass of champagne at their table, they felt themselves honoured indeed. In their halting German they strove to make themselves agreeable. This, Bulić must have felt, was what he had been waiting for all his life: at last he was in touch with the people who counted, the real people, the people who made men and broke them, the people who might make him. Perhaps he saw himself a director of one of the "Freiherr's" companies, with a fine house and others dependent on him, loyal servants who would respect him as a man as well as a master. When, the next morning, he went to his stool in the Ministry, there must have been joy in his heart, joy made all the sweeter by the faint misgivings, the slight prickings of conscience which could so easily be stilled. After all, G. had received his money's worth. He, Bulić, had nothing to lose. Besides, you never knew what might come of it all. Men had taken stranger paths to fortune.

The "Freiherr" had been good enough to say that he would have supper with Herr G. and his two charming friends two evenings later.

I questioned G. about this. Would it not have been better to have struck while the iron was hot? Two days gave the Bulićs time to think. "Precisely," was G.'s reply; "time to think of the good things to come, to prepare themselves for the feast, to dream." He became preternaturally solemn at the thought and then, grinning, suddenly quoted Goethe at me. *Ach! warum, ihr Götter, ist unendlich, alles, alles, endlich unser Glück nur?* G., you see, lays claim to a sense of humour.

That supper was the critical moment for him. Dimitrios got to work on Madame. It was such a pleasure to meet such pleasant people as Madame—and, of course, her husband. She—and her husband, naturally—must certainly come and stay with him in Bavaria next month. He preferred it to his Paris house and Cannes was sometimes chilly in the spring. Madame would enjoy Bavaria; and so, no doubt, would her husband. That was, if he could tear himself away from the Ministry.

Crude, simple stuff, no doubt; but the Bulićs were crude, simple people. Madame lapped it up with her sweet champagne while Bulić became sulky. Then the great moment arrived.

The flower girl stopped by the table with her tray of orchids. Dimitrios turned round and, selecting the largest and most expensive bloom, handed it with a little flourish to Madame Bulić with a request that she accept it as a token of his esteem. Madame would accept it. Dimitrios drew out his wallet to pay. The next moment a thick wad of thousand dinar notes fell from his breast pocket on to the table.

With a word of apology Dimitrios put the money back in his pocket. G., taking his cue, remarked that it was rather a lot of money to carry in one's pocket and asked if the "Freiherr" always carried as much. No, he did not. He had won the money at Alessandro's earlier in the evening and had forgotten to leave it upstairs in his room. Did Madame know Alessandro's? She did not. Both the Bulićs were silent as the "Freiherr" talked on: they had never seen so much money before. In the "Freiherr's" opinion Alessandro's was the most reliable gambling place in Belgradè. It was your own luck not the croupier's skill that mattered at Alessandro's. Personally he was having a run of luck that evening—this with velvety eyes on Madame—and had won a little more than usual. He hesitated at that point. And then: "As you have never been in the place, I should be delighted if you would accompany me as my guests later."

Of course, they went; and, of course, they were expected and preparations had been made. Dimitrios had arranged everything. No roulette—it is difficult to cheat a man at roulette—but there was *trente et quarante*. The minimum stake was two hundred and fifty dinar.

They had drinks and watched the play for a time. Then G. decided that he would play a little. They watched him win twice. Then the "Freiherr" asked Madame if she would like to play. She looked at her husband. He said, apologetically, that he had very little money with him. But Dimitrios was ready for that. No trouble at all, Herr Bulić! He personally was well known to Alessandro. Any friend of his could be accommodated. If he should happen to lose a few dinar, Alessandro would take a cheque or a note.

The farce went on. Alessandro was summoned and introduced. The situation was explained to him. He raised protesting hands. Any friend of the "Freiherr" need not even ask such a thing. Besides, he had not yet played. Time to talk of such things if he had a little bad luck.

G. thinks that if Dimitrios had allowed the two to talk to one another for even a moment, they would not have played. Two hundred and fifty dinar was the minimum stake, and not even the possession of thirty thousand could overcome their consciousness of the value in terms of food and rent of two hundred and fifty. But Dimitrios did not give them a chance to exchange misgivings. Instead, as they were waiting at the table behind G.'s chair, he murmured to Bulić that if he, Bulić, had time, he, the "Freiherr," would like to talk business with him over luncheon one day that week.

It was beautifully timed. It could, I feel, have meant only one thing to Bulić: "My dear Bulić, there really is no need for you to concern yourself over a paltry few hundred dinar. I am interested in you, and that means that your fortune is made. Please do not disappoint me by showing yourself less important than you seem now."

Madame Bulić began to play.

Her first two hundred and fifty she lost on *couleur*. The second won on *inverse*. Then, Dimitrios, advising greater caution, suggested that she play *à cheval*. There was a *refait* and then a second *refait*. Ultimately she lost again.

At the end of an hour the five thousand dinar's worth of chips she had been given had gone. Dimitrios, sympathising with her for her "bad luck," pushed across some five hundred dinar chips from a pile in front of him and begged that she would play with them "for luck."

The tortured Bulić may have had the idea that these were a gift, for he made only the faintest sound of protest. That they had not been a gift he was presently to discover. Madame Bulić, thoroughly miserable now and becoming a little untidy, played on. She won a little; she lost more. At half-past two Bulić signed a promissory note to Alessandro for twelve thousand dinar. G. bought them a drink.

It is easy to picture the scene between the Bulićs when at last they were alone—the recriminations, the tears, the interminable arguments—only too easy. Yet, bad as things were, the gloom was not unrelieved; for Bulić was to lunch the following day with the "Freiherr." And they were to talk business.

They did talk business. Dimitrios had been told to be encouraging. No doubt he was. Hints of big deals afoot, of opportunities for making fabulous sums for those who were in the know, talk of castles in Bavaria—it would all be there. Bulić had only to listen and let his heart beat faster. What did twelve thousand dinar matter? You had to think in millions.

All the same, it was Dimitrios who raised the subject of his guest's debt to Alessandro. He supposed that Bulić would be going along that very night to settle it. He personally would be playing again. One could not, after all,

win so much without giving Alessandro a chance to lose
some more. Supposing that they went along together—
just the two of them. Women were bad gamblers.

When they met that night Bulić had nearly thirty-five
thousand dinar in his pocket. He must have added his
savings to G.'s thirty thousand. When Dimitrios reported
to G.—in the early hours of the following morning—he
said that Bulić had, in spite of Alessandro's protests, insisted on redeeming his promissory note before he started
to play. "I pay my debts," he told Dimitrios proudly.
The balance of the money he spent, with a flourish, on
five hundred dinar chips. To-night he was going to make
a killing. He refused a drink. He meant to keep a cool
head.

G. grinned at this and perhaps he was wise to do so.
Pity is sometimes too uncomfortable; and I do find Bulić
pitiable. You may say that he was a weak fool. So he
was. But Providence is never quite as calculating as were
G. and Dimitrios. It may bludgeon away at a man, but it
never feels between his ribs with a knife. Bulić had no
chance. They understood him and used their understanding with devilish skill. With the cards as neatly stacked
against me as they were against him, I should perhaps be
no less weak, no less foolish. It is a comfort to me to believe that the occasion is unlikely to arise.

Inevitably he lost. He began to play with just over
forty chips. It took him two hours of winning and losing
to get rid of them. Then, quite calmly, he took another
twenty on credit. He said that his luck must change. The
poor wretch did not even suspect that he might be being
cheated. Why should he suspect? The "Freiherr" was
losing even more than he was. He doubled his stakes and

survived for forty minutes. He borrowed again and lost again. He had lost thirty-eight thousand dinar more than he had in the world when, white and sweating, he decided to stop.

After that it was plain sailing for Dimitrios. The following night Bulić returned. They let him win thirty thousand back. The third night he lost another fourteen thousand. On the fourth night, when he was about twenty-five thousand in debt, Alessandro asked for his money. Bulić promised to redeem his notes within a week. The first person to whom he went for help was G.

G. was sympathetic. Twenty-five thousand was a lot of money, wasn't it? Of course, any money he used in connection with orders received was his employers', and he was not empowered to do what he liked with it. But he himself could spare two hundred and fifty for a few days if it were any help. He would have liked to do more, but . . . Bulić took the two hundred and fifty.

With it G. gave him a word of advice. The "Freiherr" was the man to get him out of his difficulty. He never lent money—with him it was a question of principle, he believed—but he had a reputation for helping his friends by putting them in the way of earning quite substantial sums. Why not have a talk with him?

The "talk" between Bulić and Dimitrios took place after a dinner for which Bulić paid and in the "Freiherr's" hotel sitting-room. G. was out of sight in the adjoining bedroom.

When Bulić at last got to the point, he asked about Alessandro. Would he insist on his money? What would happen if he were not paid?

Dimitrios affected surprise. There was no question, he

hoped, of Alessandro's not being paid. After all, it was on his personal recommendation that Alessandro had given credit in the first place. He would not like there to be any unpleasantness. What sort of unpleasantness? Well, Alessandro held the promissory notes and could take the matter to the police. He hoped sincerely that that would not happen.

Bulić was hoping so, too. Now, he had everything to lose, including his post at the Ministry. It might even come out that he had taken money from G. That might even mean prison. Would they believe that he had done nothing in return for those thirty thousand dinar? It was madness to expect them to do so. His only chance was to get the money from the "Freiherr"—somehow.

To his pleas for a loan Dimitrios shook his head. No. That would simply make matters worse, for then he would owe the money to a friend instead of to an enemy; besides, it was a matter of principle with him. At the same time, he wanted to help. There was just one way; but would Herr Bulić feel disposed to take it? That was the question. He scarcely liked to mention the matter; but, since Herr Bulić pressed him, he knew of certain persons who were interested in obtaining some information from the Ministry of Marine that could not be obtained through the usual channels. They could probably be persuaded to pay as much as fifty thousand dinar for this information if they could rely upon its being accurate.

G. said that he attributed quite a lot of the success of his plan (he deems it successful in the same way that a surgeon deems an operation successful when the patient leaves the operating theatre alive) to his careful use of figures. Every sum from the original twenty thousand dinar to the amounts of the successive debts to Alessandro (who was an Italian agent) and the final amount offered by Dimitrios was carefully calculated with an eye to its psychological value. That final fifty thousand, for example. Its appeal to Bulić was two-fold. It would pay off his debt and still leave him with nearly as much as he had had before he met the "Freiherr." To the incentive of fear they added that of greed.

But Bulić did not give in immediately. When he heard exactly what the information was, he became frightened and angry. The anger was dealt with very efficiently by Dimitrios. If Bulić had begun to entertain doubts about the *bona fides* of the "Freiherr" those doubts were now made certainties; for when he shouted "dirty spy," the "Freiherr's" easy charm deserted him. Bulić was kicked in the abdomen and then, as he bent forward retching, in the face. Gasping for breath and with pain and bleeding at the mouth, he was flung into a chair while Dimitrios explained coldly that the only risk he ran was in not doing as he was told.

His instructions were simple. Bulić was to get a copy of the chart and bring it to the hotel when he left the Ministry the following evening. An hour later the chart would be returned to him to replace in the morning. That was all. He would be paid when he brought the chart. He was warned of the consequences to himself if he should decide to go to the authorities with his story, reminded of the fifty thousand that awaited him and dismissed.

He duly returned the following night with the chart folded in four under his coat. Dimitrios took the chart in to G. and returned to keep watch on Bulić while it was

photographed and the negative developed. Apparently
Bulić had nothing to say. When G. had finished he took
the money and the chart from Dimitrios and went without a word.

G. says that in the bedroom at that moment, when he
heard the door close behind Bulić and as he held the negative up to the light, he was feeling very pleased with himself. Expenses had been low; there had been no wasted
effort; there had been no tiresome delays; everybody, even
Bulić, had done well out of the business. It only remained
to hope that Bulić would restore the chart safely. There
was really no reason why he should not do so. A very
satisfactory affair from every point of view.

And then Dimitrios came into the room.

It was at that moment that G. realised that he had made
one mistake.

"My wages," said Dimitrios, and held out his hand.

G. met his employee's eyes and nodded. He needed a
gun and he had not got one. "We'll go to my house now,"
he said and started towards the door.

Dimitrios shook his head deliberately. "My wages are
in your pocket."

"Not your wages. Only mine."

Dimitrios produced a revolver. A smile played about
his lips. "What I want is in your pocket, *mein Herr*. Put
your hands behind your head."

G. obeyed. Dimitrios walked towards him. G., looking steadily into those brown anxious eyes, saw that he
was in danger. Two feet in front of him Dimitrios
stopped. "Please be careful, *mein Herr*."

The smile disappeared. Dimitrios stepped forward suddenly and, jamming his revolver into G.'s stomach,

snatched the negative from G.'s pocket with his free hand. Then, as suddenly, he stood back. "You may go," he said.

G. went. Dimitrios, in turn, had made *his* mistake.

All that night men, hastily recruited from the criminal cafés, scoured Belgrade for Dimitrios. But Dimitrios had disappeared. G. never saw him again.

What happened to the negative? Let me give you G.'s own words:

"When the morning came and my men had failed to find him, I knew what I must do. I felt very bitter. After all my careful work it was most disappointing. But there was nothing else for it. I had known for a week that Dimitrios had got into touch with a French agent. The negative would be in that agent's hands by now. I really had no choice. A friend of mine in the German Embassy was able to oblige me. The Germans were anxious to please Belgrade at the time. What more natural than that they should pass on an item of information interesting to the Yugoslav government?"

"Do you mean," I said, "that you deliberately arranged for the Yugoslav authorities to be informed of the removal of the chart and of the fact that it had been photographed?"

"Unfortunately, it was the only thing I could do. You see, I had to render the chart worthless. It was really very foolish of Dimitrios to let me go; but he was inexperienced. He probably thought that I should blackmail Bulić into bringing the chart out again. But I realised that I should not be paid much for bringing in information already in the possession of the French. Besides, my reputation would have suffered. I was very bitter about the whole affair. The only amusing aspect of it was that the French had paid over to Dimitrios half the agreed price for the chart before they discovered that the information on it had been rendered obsolete by my little *démarche*."

"What about Bulić?"

G. pulled a face. "Yes, I was sorry about that. I always have felt a certain responsibility towards those who work for me. He was arrested almost at once. There was no doubt as to which of the Ministry copies had been used. They were kept rolled in metal cylinders. Bulić had folded this one to bring it out of the Ministry. It was the only one with creases in it. His finger-prints did the rest. Very wisely he told the authorities all he knew about Dimitrios. As a result they sent him to prison for life instead of shooting him. I quite expected him to implicate me, but he did not. I was a little surprised. After all it was I who introduced him to Dimitrios. I wondered at the time whether it was because he was unwilling to face an additional charge of accepting bribes or because he felt grateful to me for lending him that two hundred and fifty dinar. Probably he did not connect me with the business of the chart at all. In any case, I was pleased. I still had work to do in Belgrade, and being wanted by the police, even under another name, might have complicated my life. I have never been able to bring myself to wear disguises."

I asked him one more question. Here is his answer:

"Oh, yes, I obtained the new charts as soon as they had been made. In quite a different way, of course. With so much of my money invested in the enterprise I could not return empty handed. It is always the same: for one reason or another there are always these delays, these wastages of effort and money. You may say that I was careless in my handling of Dimitrios. That would be unjust. It was a small error of judgment on my part, that is all. I counted on his being like all the other fools in the world, on his being too greedy; I thought he would wait until he had had from me the forty thousand dinar due to him before he tried to take the photograph as well. He took me by surprise. That error of judgment cost me a lot of money."

"It cost Bulić his liberty." I am afraid I said it a trifle vindictively, for he frowned.

"My dear Monsieur Latimer," he retorted stiffly, "Bulić was a traitor and he was rewarded according to his deserts. One cannot sentimentalise over him. In war there are always casualties. Bulić was very lucky. I should certainly have used him again, and he might ultimately have been shot. As it was, he went to prison. For all I know he is still in prison. I do not wish to seem callous, but I must say that he is better off there. His liberty? Rubbish! He had none to lose. As for his wife, I have no doubt that she has done better for herself. She always gave me the impression of wanting to do so. I do not blame her. He was an objectionable man. I seem to remember that he tended to dribble as he ate. What is more, he was a nuisance. You would have thought, would you not, that on leaving Dimitrios that evening he would have gone there and then to Alessandro to pay his debt? He did not do so. When he was arrested late the following day he still had the fifty thousand dinar in his pocket. More waste. It is at times like those, my friend, that one needs one's sense of humour."

Well, my dear Marukakis, that is all. It is, I think, more

than enough. For me, wandering among the ghosts of old lies, there is comfort in the thought that you might write to me and tell me that all this was worth finding out. You might. For myself, I begin to wonder. It is such a poor story, isn't it? There is no hero, no heroine; there are only knaves and fools. Or do I mean only fools?

But it really is too early in the afternoon to pose such questions. Besides, I have packing to do. In a few days I shall send you a post card with my name and new address on it in the hope that you will have time to write. In any case, we shall, I hope, meet again very soon. *Croyez en mes meilleurs souvenirs.*

Charles Latimer.

CHAPTER X

THE EIGHT ANGELS

It was on a slate-grey November day that Latimer arrived in Paris.

As his taxi crossed the bridge to the Ile de la Cité, he saw for a moment a panorama of low, black clouds moving quickly in the chill, dusty wind. The long façade of the houses on the Quai de Corse were still and secretive. It was as if each window concealed a watcher. There seemed to be few people about. Paris, in that late autumn afternoon, had the macabre formality of a steel engraving.

It depressed him, and as he climbed the stairs of his hotel in the Quai Voltaire he wished fervently that he had gone back to Athens.

His room was cold. It was too early for an aperitif. He had been able to eat enough of his meal on the train to render an early dinner unnecessary. He decided to inspect the outside of number three, Impasse des Huit Anges. With some difficulty he found the Impasse tucked away in a side street off the Rue de Rennes.

It was a wide, cobbled passage shaped like an L and flanked at the entrance by a pair of tall iron gates. They were fastened back, against the walls that supported them, with heavy staples, and had evidently not been shut for years. A row of spiked railings separated one side of the Impasse from the blank side-wall of the adjoining block of houses. Another blank cement wall, unguarded by railings but protected by the words "DEFENSE D'AFFICHER, LOI DU 10 AVIL 1929" in weatherbeaten black paint, faced it.

There were only three houses in the Impasse. They were grouped out of sight of the road, in the foot of the L, and looked out through the narrow gap between the building on which bill-posting was forbidden and the back of a hotel over which drainpipes writhed like snakes, on to yet another sightless expanse of cement. Life in the Impasse des Huit Anges would, Latimer thought, be rather like a rehearsal for Eternity. That others before him had found it so was suggested by the fact that, of the three houses, two were shuttered and obviously quite empty, while the third, number three, was occupied on the fourth and top floors only.

Feeling as if he were trespassing, Latimer walked slowly across the irregular cobbles to the entrance of number three.

The door was open and he could see along a tiled corridor to a small, dank yard at the back. The concierge's room, to the right of the door, was empty and showed no signs of having been used recently. Beside it, on the wall, was nailed a dusty board with four brass name slots screwed to it. Three of the slots were empty. In the fourth was a grimy piece of paper with the name "CAILLÉ" clumsily printed on it in violet ink.

There was nothing to be learned from this but the fact, which Latimer had not doubted, that Mr. Peters' accommodation address existed. He turned and walked back to the street. In the Rue de Rennes he found a post office where he bought a *pneumatique* letter-card, wrote in it his name and that of his hotel, addressed it to Mr. Peters and dropped it down the chute. He also sent a post card to Marukakis. What happened now depended to a great extent on Mr. Peters. But there was something he could and should do: that was to find out what, if anything, the Paris newspapers had had to say about the breaking up in December nineteen thirty-one of a drug-peddling gang.

At nine o'clock the following morning, being without word from Peters, he decided to spend the morning with newspaper files.

The paper he finally selected for detailed reading had made a number of references to the case. The first was dated November 29, 1931. It was headed: "DRUG TRAF-FICKERS ARRESTED," and went on:

"A man and a woman engaged in the distribution of drugs to addicts were arrested yesterday in the Alésia quarter. They are said to be members of a notorious foreign gang. The police expect to make further arrests within a few days."

That was all. It read curiously, Latimer thought. Those three bald sentences looked as if they had been lifted out of a longer report. The absence of names, too, was odd. Police censorship, perhaps.

The next reference appeared on December the fourth under the heading: "DRUG GANG, THREE MORE ARRESTS."

"Three members of a criminal drug distributing organisation were arrested late last night in a café near the Porte d'Orleans. *Agents* entering the café to make the arrests were compelled to fire on one of the men who was armed and who made a desperate attempt to escape. He was slightly wounded. The other two, one of whom was a foreigner, did not resist.

"This brings the number of drug gang arrests to five, for it is believed that the three men arrested last night belonged to the same gang as the man and woman arrested a week ago in the Alésia quarter.

"The police state that still more arrests are likely to be made, as the Bureau Général des Stupéfiants has in its possession evidence implicating the actual organisers of the gang.

"Monsieur Auguste Lafon, director of the Bureau, said: 'We have known of this gang for some time and have conducted painstaking investigations into their activities. We could have made arrests but we held our hands. It was the leaders, the big criminals whom we wanted. Without leaders, with their sources of supply cut off, the army of drug pedlars that infests Paris will be powerless to carry on their nefarious trade. We intend to smash this gang and others like it.' "

Then, on December the eleventh, the newspaper reported:

DRUG GANG SMASHED

NEW ARRESTS

———

"Now we have them all," says Lafon

THE COUNCIL OF SEVEN

———

"Six men and one woman are now under arrest as a result of the attack launched by Monsieur Lafon, director of the Bureau Général des Stupéfiants, on a notorious gang of foreign drug traffickers operating in Paris and Marseilles.

"The attack began with the arrest two weeks ago of a woman and her male accomplice in the Alésia quarter. It reached its climax yesterday with the arrest in Marseilles of two men believed to be the remaining members of the gang's 'Council of Seven,' which was responsible for the organisation of this criminal enterprise.

"At the request of the police we have hitherto remained silent as to the names of those arrested as it was desired not to put the others on their guard. Now that restriction has been lifted.

"The woman, Lydia Prokofievna, is a Russian who is believed to have come to France from Turkey with a Nansen passport in 1924. She is known in criminal circles as 'The Grand Duchess.' The man arrested with her was a Dutchman named Manus Visser who, through his association with Prokofievna, was sometimes referred to as 'Monsieur le Duc.'

"The names of the other five under arrest are; Luis

Galindo, a naturalised Frenchman of Mexican origin, who now lies in hospital with a bullet wound in the thigh, Jean-Baptiste Lenôtre, a Frenchman from Bordeaux, and Jacob Werner, a Belgian, who were arrested with Galindo, Pierre Lamare or 'Jo-jo,' a Niçois, and Frederik Petersen, a Dane, who were arrested in Marseilles.

"In a statement to the press last night, Monsieur Lafon said: 'Now we have them all. The gang is smashed. We have cut off the head and with it the brains. The body will now die a speedy death. It is finished.'

"Lamare and Petersen are to be questioned by the examining magistrate to-day. It is expected that there will be a mass-trial of the prisoners."

In England, Latimer reflected, Monsieur Lafon would have found himself in serious trouble. It hardly seemed worthwhile trying the accused after he and the press between them had already pronounced the verdict. But then, the accused was always guilty in a French trial. To give him a trial at all was, practically speaking, merely to ask him whether he had anything to say before he was sentenced.

With the arrest of the "Council of Seven," interest in the case seemed to wane. The fact that "The Grand Duchess" had been transferred to Nice to stand trial there for a fraud committed three years previously may have been responsible for this. The trial of the men was dealt with briefly. All were sentenced: Galindo, Lenôtre and Werner to fines of five thousand francs and three months' imprisonment, Lamare, Petersen and Visser to fines of two thousand francs and one month's imprisonment.

Latimer was amazed by the lightness of the sentences. Lafon was outraged but not amazed. But for the existence of a set of obsolete and wholly ridiculous laws, he thundered, the whole six would have been imprisoned for life.

The newspaper did not mention the fact that the police had failed to find Dimitrios. That was not surprising. The police were not going to tell the press that the arrests were made possible only by a dossier obligingly supplied by some anonymous well-wisher whom they suspected of being the leader of the gang. All the same, it was irritating to Latimer to find that he knew more than the newspaper he had relied upon to clarify the affair for him.

He was about to shut the file in disgust when his attention was caught by an illustration. It was a smudgy reproduction of a photograph of three of the prisoners being led from the court by detectives to whom they were handcuffed. All three had turned their faces away from the camera but the fact of their being handcuffed had prevented them from concealing themselves effectively.

Latimer left the newspaper office in better spirits than those in which he had entered it.

At his hotel a message awaited him. Unless he sent a *pneumatique* making other arrangements, Mr. Peters would call upon him at six o'clock that evening.

Mr. Peters arrived soon after half-past five. He greeted Latimer effusively.

"My *dear* Mr. Latimer! I cannot tell you how pleased I am to see you. Our last meeting took place under such inauspicious circumstances that I hardly dare hope . . . But let us talk of pleasanter things. Welcome to Paris! Have you had a good journey? You are looking well. Tell me, what did you think of Grodek? He wrote telling me how charming and sympathetic you were. A good fellow, isn't he? Those cats of his! He worships them."

"He was very helpful. Do, please, sit down."

"I knew he would be."

For Latimer, Mr. Peters' sweet smile was like the greeting of an old and detested acquaintance. "He was also mysterious. He urged me to come to Paris to see you."

"Did he?" Mr. Peters did not seem pleased. His smile faded a little. "And what else did he say, Mr. Latimer?"

"He said that you were a clever man. He seemed to find something I said about you amusing."

Mr. Peters sat down carefully on the bed. His smile had quite gone. "And what was it you said?"

"He insisted upon knowing what business I had with you. I told him all I could. As I knew nothing," went on Latimer spitefully, "I felt that I could safely confide in him. If you do not like that, I am sorry. You must remember that I am still in complete ignorance concerning this precious scheme of yours."

"Grodek did not tell you?"

"No. Could he have done so?"

The smile once more tightened his soft lips. It was as if some obscene plant had turned its face to the sun. "Yes, Mr. Latimer, he could have done so. What you have told me explains the flippant tone of his letter to me. I am glad you satisfied his curiosity. The rich are so often covetous of others' goods in this world of ours. Grodek is a dear friend of mine but it is just as well that he knows that we stand in no need of assistance. He might otherwise be tempted by the prospect of gain."

Latimer regarded him thoughtfully for a moment. Then:

"Have you got your pistol with you, Mr. Peters?"

The fat man looked horrified. "Dear me no, Mr. Latimer. Why should I bring such a thing on a friendly visit to you?"

"Good," said Latimer curtly. He backed towards the door and turned the key in the lock. The key he put in his pocket. "Now then," he went on grimly, "I don't want to seem a bad host but there are limits to my patience. I have come a long way to see you and I still don't know why. I want to know why."

"And so you shall."

"I've heard that before," answered Latimer rudely. "Now before you start beating about the bush again there are one or two things *you* should know. I am not a violent man, Mr. Peters. To be honest with you, I dread violence. But there are times when the most peace-loving among us must use it. This may be one of them. I am younger than you and, I should say, in better condition. If you persist in being mysterious I shall attack you. That is the first thing.

"The second is that I know who you are. Your name is not Peters but Petersen, Frederik Petersen. You were a member of the drug-peddling gang organised by Dimitrios and you were arrested in December nineteen thirty-one, fined two thousand francs and sentenced to one month's imprisonment."

Mr. Peters' smile was tortured. "Did Grodek tell you this?" He asked the question gently and sorrowfully. The word "Grodek" might have been another way of saying "Judas."

"No. I saw a picture of you this morning in a newspaper file."

"A newspaper. Ah, yes! I could not believe that my friend Grodek . . ."

"You don't deny it?"

"Oh, no. It is the truth."

"Well then, Mr. Petersen . . ."

"Peters, Mr. Latimer. I decided to change the name."

"All right then—Peters. We come to my third point. When I was in Istanbul I heard some interesting things about the end of that gang. It was said that Dimitrios betrayed the lot of you by sending to the police, anonymously, a dossier convicting the seven of you. Is that true?"

"Dimitrios behaved very badly to us all," said Mr. Peters huskily.

"It was also said that Dimitrios had become an addict himself. Is that true?"

"Unhappily, it is. Otherwise I do not think he would have betrayed us. We were making so much money for him."

"I was also told that there was talk of vengeance, that you all threatened to kill Dimitrios as soon as you were free."

"*I* did not threaten," Mr. Peters corrected him. "Some of the others did so. Galindo, for example, was always a hot-head."

"I see. You did not threaten; you preferred to act."

"I don't understand you, Mr. Latimer." And he looked as if he really did not understand.

"No? Let me put it to you this way. Dimitrios was murdered near Istanbul roughly two months ago. Very shortly after the time when the murder could have taken

place, you were in Athens. That is not very far from
Istanbul, is it? Dimitrios, it is said, died a poor man. Now
is that likely? As you have just pointed out, his gang
made a lot of money for him in nineteen thirty-one. From
what I have heard of him, he was not the man to lose
money he had made. Do you know what is in my mind,
Mr. Peters? I am wondering whether it would not be
reasonable to suppose that you killed Dimitrios for his
money. What have you to say to that?"

Mr. Peters did not answer for a moment but contemplated Latimer unhappily in the manner of a good shep-
herd about to admonish an erring lamb.

Then he said: "Mr. Latimer, I think that you are very
indiscreet."

"Do you?"

"And also very fortunate. Just suppose that I had, as
you suggest, killed Dimitrios. Think what I should be
forced to do. I should be forced to kill you also, now
shouldn't I?" He put his hand in his breast pocket. It
emerged holding the Lüger pistol. "You see, I lied to you
just now. I admit it. I was so curious to know what you
were going to do if you thought that I was unarmed. Besides, it seemed so impolite to come here carrying a pistol.
The fact that I did not bring the pistol with me because
of you would be a difficult one to prove. So I lied. Do
you understand my feelings a little? I am so anxious to
have your confidence."

"All of which is as skilful a reply to an accusation of
murder as one could wish for."

Mr. Peters put away his pistol wearily. "Mr. Latimer,
this is not a detective story. There is no *need* to be so
stupid. Even if you cannot be discreet, at least use your

imagination. Is it likely that Dimitrios would make a Will in my favour? No. Then how do you suppose that I could kill him for his money? People in these days do not keep their wealth in treasure chests. Come now, Mr. Latimer, let us please be sensible. Let us eat dinner together and then talk business. I suggest that after dinner we drink coffee in my apartment—it is a little more comfortable than this room—though if you would prefer to go to a café I shall understand. You probably disapprove of me. I really cannot blame you. But at least let us cultivate the illusion of friendship."

For a moment Latimer felt himself warming to Mr. Peters. True, the last part of his appeal had been accompanied by an almost visible accretion of self-pity; but he had not smiled. Besides, the man had already made him feel a fool: it would be too much if he made him feel a prig as well. At the same time . . .

"I am as hungry as you," he said; "and I can see no reason why I should prefer a café to your apartment. At the same time, Mr. Peters, anxious though I am to be friendly, I feel that I should warn you now that unless I have, this evening, a satisfactory explanation of your asking me to meet you here in Paris, I shall—half a million francs or no half a million francs—leave by the first available train. Is that clear?"

Mr. Peters' smile returned. "It could not be clearer, Mr. Latimer. And may I say how much I appreciate your frankness?"

"Where shall we dine? There is a Danish place near here, isn't there?"

Mr. Peters struggled into his overcoat. "No, Mr. Latimer, as you are doubtless well aware, there is not." He sighed unhappily. "It is unkind of you to make fun of me. And in any case I prefer French cooking."

Mr. Peters' capacity for making him feel a fool was, Latimer reflected as they descended the stairs, remarkable.

At Mr. Peters' suggestion and expense they ate in a cheap restaurant in the Rue Jacob. Afterwards they went to the Impasse des Huit Anges.

"What about Caillé?" said Latimer as they climbed the dusty stairs.

"He is away. At the moment I am in sole possession."

"I see."

Mr. Peters, who was breathing heavily by the time they had reached the second landing, paused for a moment. "You have concluded, I suppose, that I am Caillé."

"Yes."

Mr. Peters began to climb again. The stairs creaked under his weight. Latimer, following two or three stairs behind, was reminded of a circus elephant picking its way unwillingly up a pyramid of coloured blocks to perform a balancing trick. They reached the fourth floor. Mr. Peters stopped and, standing panting before a battered door, hauled out a bunch of keys. A moment later he pushed open the door, pressed a switch and waved Latimer in.

The room ran from front to back of the house and was divided into two by a curtain to the left of the door. The half beyond the curtain was of a different shape from that which contained the door as it included the space between the end of the landing, the rear wall and the next house. The space formed an alcove. At each end of the room was a tall French window.

But if it was, architecturally speaking, the sort of room

that one would expect to find in a French house of that type and age, it was in every other respect fantastic.

The first thing that Latimer saw was the dividing curtain. It was of imitation cloth of gold. The walls and ceiling were distempered an angry blue and bespattered with gold five-pointed stars. Scattered all over the floor, so that not a square inch of it showed, were cheap Moroccan rugs. They overlapped a good deal so that in places there were humps of three and even four thicknesses of rug. There were three huge divans piled high with cushions, some tooled leather ottoman seats and a Moroccan table with a brass tray upon it. In one corner stood an enormous brass gong. The light came from fretted oak lanterns. In the centre of it all stood a small chromium-plated electric radiator. There was a choking smell of upholstery dust.

"Home!" said Mr. Peters. "Take your things off, Mr. Latimer; would you like to see the rest of the place?"

"Very much."

"Outwardly, just another uncomfortable French house," commented Mr. Peters as he toiled up the stairs again; "actually an oasis in a desert of discomfort. This is my bedroom."

Latimer had another glimpse of French Morocco. This time it was adorned by a pair of crumpled flannel pyjamas.

"And the toilet."

Latimer looked at the toilet and learned that his host had a spare set of false teeth.

"Now," said Mr. Peters, "I will show you something curious."

He led the way out on to the landing. Facing them was

a large clothes cupboard. He opened the door and struck
a match. Along the back of the cupboard was a row of
metal clothes pegs. Grasping the centre one, he turned it
like a latch and pulled. The back of the cupboard swung
towards them and Latimer felt the night air on his face and
heard the noises of the city.

"There is a narrow iron platform running along the
outside wall to the next house," explained Mr. Peters.
"There is another cupboard there like this one. You can
see nothing because there are only blank walls facing us.
Equally, no one could see us should we choose to leave
that way. It was Dimitrios who had this done."

"Dimitrios!"

"Dimitrios owned all three of these houses. They were
kept empty for reasons of privacy. Sometimes, they were
used as stores. These two floors were used for meetings.
Morally, no doubt, the houses still belong to Dimitrios.
Fortunately for me, he took the precaution of buying
them in my name. I also conducted the negotiations. The
police never found out about them. I was able, therefore,
to move in when I came out of prison. In case Dimitrios
should ever wonder what had happened to his property,
I took the precaution of buying them from myself in the
name of Caillé. Do you like Algerian coffee?"

"Yes."

"It takes a little longer to prepare than French but I
prefer it. Shall we go downstairs again?"

They went downstairs. Having seen Latimer uncomfortably ensconced amid a sea of cushions, Mr. Peters disappeared into the alcove.

Latimer got rid of some of the cushions and looked

about him. It was odd to feel that the house had once belonged to Dimitrios. Yet the evidence around him of the
tenancy of the preposterous Mr. Peters was a good deal
odder. There was a small (fretted) shelf above his head.
On it were paper-bound books. There was *Pearls of
Everyday Wisdom*. That was the one he had been reading in the train from Athens. There was, besides, Plato's
Symposium, in French and uncut, an anthology called
Poèmes Erotiques, which had no author's name on it and
had been cut, Æsop's Fables in English, Mrs. Humphry
Ward's *Robert Elsmere* in French, a German Gazetteer,
and several books by Dr. Frank Crane in a language which
Latimer took to be Danish.

Mr. Peters came back carrying a Moroccan tray on
which were a curious looking coffee percolator, a spirit
lamp, two cups and a Moroccan cigarette box. The spirit
lamp he lighted and put under the percolator. The cigarettes he placed beside Latimer on the divan. Then he
reached up above Latimer's head, brought down one of
the Danish books and flicked over one or two of the pages.
A small photograph fluttered to the floor. He picked it
up and handed it to Latimer.

"Do you recognise him, Mr. Latimer?"

It was a faded head and shoulders photograph of a
middle aged man with . . .

Latimer looked up. "It's Dimitrios!" he exclaimed.
"Where did you get it?"

Mr. Peters took the photograph from Latimer's fingers.
"You recognise it? Good." He sat down on one of the
ottoman seats and adjusted the spirit lamp. Then he
looked up. If it had been possible for Mr. Peters' wet,

lustreless eyes to gleam, Latimer would have said that they were gleaming with pleasure.

"Help yourself to cigarettes, Mr. Latimer," he said. "I am going to tell you a story."

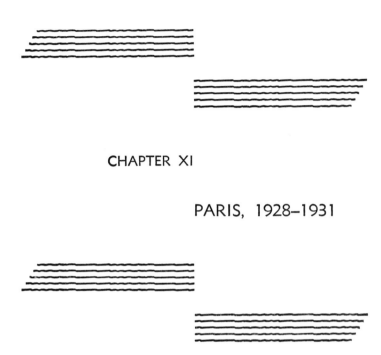

CHAPTER XI

PARIS, 1928–1931

Yes, Mr. Latimer, most of us go through life without knowing what we want of it. But Dimitrios, you know, was not like that. Dimitrios knew exactly what he wanted. He wanted money and he wanted power. Just those two things; as much of them as he could get. The curious thing is that I helped him to get them.

"It was in nineteen twenty-eight that I first set eyes on Dimitrios. It was here in Paris. I was, at the time, the part-owner, with a man named Giraud, of a *boîte* in the rue Blanche. We called it *Le Kasbah Parisien* and it was a very gay and cosy place with divans and amber lights and rugs. I had met Giraud in Marrakesh and we decided that

181

everything should be just like a place we knew there. Everything was Moroccan; everything, that is, except the band for dancing which was South American.

"We opened it in nineteen twenty-six which was a good year in Paris. The Americans and English, but especially the Americans, had money to spend on champagne and the French used to come, too. Most Frenchmen are sentimental about Morocco unless they have done their military service there. And the *Kasbah was* Morocco. We had Arab and Senegalese waiters and the champagne actually came from Meknes. It was a little sweet for the Americans but very nice all the same and quite cheap.

"For two years we made money and then, as is the way with such places, the clientèle began to change in character. We had more French and fewer Americans, more *maquereaux* and fewer gentlemen, more *poules* and fewer *chic* ladies. We still made a profit but it was not as great and we had to do more for it. I began to think that it was time to move on.

"It was Giraud who brought Dimitrios to *Le Kasbah*.

"I had met Giraud when I was in Marrakesh. He was a half-caste, his mother being an Arab and his father a French soldier. He was born in Algiers and had a French passport.

"I do not know exactly how he met Dimitrios. I think that it was at some *boîte* higher up the rue Blanche; for we did not open until eleven o'clock and Giraud liked to dance at other places beforehand. But, one evening, he brought Dimitrios into *Le Kasbah* and then took me aside. He remarked that profits had been getting smaller and said that we could make some money for ourselves if we

did business with this friend of his, Dimitrios Makropoulos.

"The first time I saw Dimitrios I was not impressed by
him. He was, I thought, just such a type of *maquereau* as
I had seen before. His clothes fitted tightly and he had
greying hair and polished fingernails and he looked at
women in a way that those who came to *Le Kasbah* would
not like. But I went over to his table with Giraud and we
shook hands. Then he pointed to the chair beside him and
told me to sit down. One would have thought that I was a
waiter instead of the *patron*."

He turned his watery eyes to Latimer. "You may
think, Mr. Latimer, that, for one who was not impressed,
I remember the occasion very clearly. That is true. I do
remember it clearly. You understand, I did not then
know Dimitrios as I came to know him later. He made
his impression without seeming to do so. At the time he
irritated me. Without sitting down, I asked him what he
wanted.

"For a moment he looked at me. He had very soft,
brown eyes, you know. Then he said: 'I want champagne, my friend. Have you any objection? I can pay
for it, you know. Are you going to be polite to me or
shall I take my business proposals to more intelligent
people?'

"I am an even-tempered man. I do not like trouble. I
often think how much pleasanter a place this world of ours
would be if people were polite and softly spoken with one
another. But there are times when it is difficult. I told
Dimitrios that nothing would induce me to be polite to
him and that he could go when he pleased.

"But for Giraud he would have gone and I should not be sitting here talking to you. Giraud sat down at the table with him, apologising for me. Dimitrios was watching me while Giraud was speaking, and I could see that he was wondering about me.

"I was now quite sure that I did not want to do business of any kind with this Dimitrios; but because of Giraud I agreed to listen, and we sat down together while Dimitrios told us what his proposal was. He talked very convincingly, and at last I agreed to do what he wanted. We had been in association with Dimitrios for several months, when one day . . ."

"Just a moment," interrupted Latimer; "what was this association? Was this the beginning of the drug peddling?"

Mr. Peters hesitated and frowned. "No, Mr. Latimer, it was not. Dimitrios was connected at the time with what I believe you call the white slave traffic. It is such an interesting phrase to me. 'Traffic'—a word full of horrible significance. 'White slave'—consider the implications of the adjective. Does anyone talk nowadays about the *coloured* slave traffic? I think not. Yet the majority of the women involved are coloured. I fail to see why the consequences of the traffic should be any more disagreeable to a white girl from a Bucharest slum than to a negro girl from Dakar or a Chinese girl from Harbin. The League of Nations Committee is unprejudiced enough to appreciate that aspect of the question. They are intelligent enough, too, to mistrust the word 'slave.' They refer to the 'traffic in women.'

"I have never liked the business. It is impossible to treat human beings as one would treat ordinary inanimate merchandise. There is always trouble. There is always the possibility, too, that in an isolated case the adjective 'white' might have a religious instead of a merely racial application. From my experience, I should say that the possibility is remote; but there it is. I may be illogical and sentimental, but I should not care to be associated with anything like that. Besides, the overhead expenses of a trafficker in what is considered a fair way of business are enormous. There are always false birth, marriage and death certificates to be obtained and travelling expenses and bribes to pay quite apart from the cost of maintaining several identities. You have no idea of the cost of forged documents, Mr. Latimer. There used to be three recognised sources of supply: one in Zürich, one in Amsterdam and one in Brussels. All neutrals! Odd, isn't it? You used to be able to get a false-real Danish passport—that is, a real Danish passport treated chemically to remove the original entries and photograph and then filled in with new ones—for, let me see, about two thousand francs at the present rate of exchange. A real-false—manufactured from start to finish by the agent—would have cost you a little less, say fifteen hundred. Nowadays you would have to pay twice as much. Most of the business is done here in Paris now. It is the refugees, of course. The point is that a trafficker needs plenty of capital. If he is known there are always plenty of people willing to provide it, but they expect fantastic dividends. It is better to have one's own capital.

"Dimitrios had his own capital; but he also had access to capital which was not his own. He represented certain very rich men. He was never at a loss for money. When he came to Giraud and me he was in a different sort of difficulty. Owing to League of Nations activities the laws in quite a number of countries had been altered and tightened up in such a way that it was sometimes very difficult indeed to get women from one place to another. All very praiseworthy, but a great nuisance to men like Dimitrios. It was not that it made it impossible for them to do their business. It didn't. But it made things more complicated and expensive for them.

"Before Dimitrios came to us he had had a very simple technique. He knew people in Alexandria who would advise him about their requirements. Then he would go to, say, Poland, recruit the women, take them to France on their own passports and then ship them from Marseilles. That was all. It was enough to say that the girls were going to fulfil a theatrical engagement. When the regulations were tightened up, however, it was no longer as simple. The night he came to *Le Kasbah* he told us that he had just encountered his first trouble. He had recruited twelve women from a *Madame* in Vilna, but the Poles would not let him bring them out without guarantees as to their destination and the respectability of their future employment. Respectability! But that was the law.

"Naturally, Dimitrios had told the Polish authorities that he would provide the guarantees. It would have been fatal for him not to have done so, for then he would have been suspect. Somehow he had to obtain the guarantees. That was where Giraud and I came in. We were to say that we were employing the girls as cabaret dancers and deal with any inquiries that might be made by the Polish Consular authorities. As long as they stayed in Paris for a week or so, we were perfectly safe. If inquiries were made after that we knew nothing. They had completed their engagement and gone. Where they had gone to was no business of ours.

"That was the way Dimitrios put it to us. He said that for our part of the affair he would pay us five thousand francs. It was money easily earned, but I was doubtful; and it was Giraud who finally persuaded me to agree. But I told Dimitrios that my agreement only applied to this particular case and that I could not consider myself committed to helping him again. Giraud grumbled, but agreed to accept the condition.

"A month later Dimitrios came to see us again, paid us the balance of the five thousand francs and said that he had another job for us. I objected; but, as Giraud immediately pointed out, we had had no trouble on the first occasion and my objection was not very firm. The money was useful. It paid the South Americans for a week.

"I believe now that Dimitrios lied to us about that first five thousand francs. I do not think that we earned it. I think he gave it to us simply to gain our confidence. It was like him to do a thing like that. Another man might try to trick you into serving his ends; but Dimitrios bought you. Yet he bought you cheaply. He set one's common sense fighting against one's instinctive suspicions of him.

"I have said that we earned that first five thousand francs without trouble. The second caused us a lot of trouble. The Polish authorities made some *chi-chi* and we had the police visiting us and asking questions. Worse, we had to have these women in *Le Kasbah* to prove that we were employing them. They could not dance a step and were a great inconvenience to us, as we had to be amiable to them in case one should go to the police and tell the truth. They drank champagne all the time, and if

Dimitrios had not agreed to pay for it we should have lost money.

"He was, of course, very apologetic and said that there had been a mistake. He paid us ten thousand francs for our trouble and promised that if we would continue to help him there would be no more Polish girls and no more *chi-chi*. After some argument we agreed, and for several months we were paid our ten thousand francs. We had during that time only occasional visits from the police, and there was no unpleasantness. But at last we had trouble again. This time it was because of the Italian authorities. Both Giraud and I were questioned by the examining magistrate for the district and kept for a day at the Commissariat. The day after that I quarrelled with Giraud.

"I say that I quarrelled. It would be more correct to say that our quarrel became open. He was crude and stupid and he sometimes tried to cheat me. He was suspicious, too; suspicious in a loud, stupid way like an animal; and he encouraged the wrong sort of clientèle. His friends were detestable; *maquereaux*, all of them. He used to call people '*mon gar*.' He would have been better as the *patron* of a *bistro*. For all I know he may be one now; but I think it more likely that he is in a prison. He often became violent when he was angry and sometimes injured people badly.

"That day after our unpleasantness with the police I said that we should have no more to do with this business of the women. That made him angry. He said that we should be fools to give up ten thousand francs a month because of a few police and that I was too nervous for his taste. I understood his point of view. He had had much to do with the police both in Marrakesh and Algiers, and he had a contempt for them. As long as he could keep out of prison and make money he was satisfied. I have never thought that way. I do not like the police to be interested in me, even though they cannot arrest me. Giraud was right. I was nervous. But although I understood his point of view I could not agree with it, and I said so. I also said that, if he wished, he could buy my share in *Le Kasbah Parisien* for the amount of money I had originally invested.

"It was a sacrifice on my part, you know, but I was tired of Giraud and wanted to be rid of him. I did get rid of him. He agreed immediately. That night we saw Dimitrios and explained the situation to him. Giraud was delighted with his bargain and enjoyed himself very much cracking clumsy jokes at my expense. Dimitrios smiled at these jokes; but when Giraud left us alone for a moment, he asked me to leave soon after he did and meet him at a café as he had something to say to me.

"I very nearly did not go. On the whole, I think that it was as well that I did go. I profited by my association with Dimitrios. There are, I think, very few associates of Dimitrios who could say as much; but I was lucky. Besides, I think that he had a respect for my intelligence. Generally he could bluff me, but not always.

"He was waiting in the café for me, and I sat down beside him and asked him what he wanted. I was never polite to him.

"He said: 'I think you are wise to leave Giraud. The business with the women has become too dangerous. It was always difficult. Now I have finished with it.'

"I asked him if he proposed to tell Giraud that and he smiled.

" 'Not yet,' he said; 'not until you have your money from him.'

"I said suspiciously that he was very kind, but he shook his head impatiently. 'Giraud is a fool,' he said. 'If you had not been there with him, I should have made other arrangements about the women. Now, I am offering you a chance to work with me. I should be a fool if I made you angry with me to begin with by costing you your investment in *Le Kasbah*.'

"Then he asked me if I knew anything about the heroin business. I did know a little about it. He then told me that he had sufficient capital to buy twenty kilogrammes a month and finance its distribution in Paris and asked me if I were interested in working for him.

"Now, twenty kilogrammes of heroin is a serious thing, Mr. Latimer. It is worth a lot of money. I asked him how he proposed to distribute so much. He said that, for the moment, that would be his affair. What he wanted me to do was to negotiate the purchases abroad and find ways of bringing it into the country. If I agreed to his proposal I was to begin by going to Bulgaria as his representative, dealing with suppliers there of whom he already knew and arranging for the transport of the stuff to Paris. He offered me ten per cent. of the value of every kilo I supplied him with.

"I said that I would think it over, but my mind was already made up. With the price of heroin as it was then, I knew that I would make nearly twenty thousand francs a month. I knew also that he was going to make a great deal more than that for himself. Even if, with my commission and expenses, he had to pay in effect fifteen thousand francs a kilo for the stuff, it would be good business for him. Selling heroin by the gramme in Paris, one can get nearly one hundred thousand francs a kilo for it. With the commissions to the actual pedlars and others, he would make not less than thirty thousand francs on each kilo. That meant over half a million francs a month for him. Capital is a wonderful thing if one knows just what to do with it and does not mind a little risk.

"In the September of nineteen twenty-eight I went to Bulgaria for Dimitrios with instructions from him to get the first twenty kilos to him by November. He had already begun to make arrangements with agents and pedlars. The sooner I could get the stuff the better.

"Dimitrios had given me the name of a man in Sofia who would put me in touch with the suppliers. This man did so. He also arranged for the credits with which I was to make the purchases. He . . ."

Latimer had an idea. He said suddenly: "What was this man's name?"

Mr. Peters frowned at the interruption. "I do not think that you ought to ask me that, Mr. Latimer."

"Was it Vazoff?"

Mr. Peters' eyes watered at him. "Yes, it was."

"And were the credits arranged through the Eurasian Credit Trust?"

"You evidently know a great deal more than I had thought." Mr. Peters was obviously not pleased by the fact. "May I ask . . . ?"

"I was guessing. But you need not have worried about compromising Vazoff. He died three years ago."

"I am aware of it. Did you guess that Vazoff was dead? And how much more guessing have you done, Mr. Latimer?"

"That is all. Please continue."

"Frankness . . ." began Mr. Peters and then stopped and drank his coffee. "We will return to the subject," he said at last. "Yes, Mr. Latimer, I admit that you are right. Through Vazoff, I purchased the supplies Dimitrios needed and paid for them with drafts on Eurasian Credit Trust of Sofia. There was no difficulty about that. My real task was to transport the stuff to France. I decided to send it by rail to Salonika and ship it from there to Marseilles."

"As heroin?"

"Obviously not. But I must confess it was difficult to know how to disguise it. The only goods which come into France from Bulgaria regularly, and which would not, therefore, be subject to special examination by the French Customs, were things like grain and tobacco and attar of roses. Dimitrios was pressing for delivery and I was at my wits' end." He paused dramatically.

"Well, how *did* you smuggle it?"

"In a coffin, Mr. Latimer. The French, I reflected, are a race with a great respect for the solemnity of death. Have you ever attended a French funeral? *Pompe funèbre*, you know. It is most impressive. No Customs official, I felt certain, would care to play the ghoul. I purchased the coffin in Sofia. It was a beautiful thing with very fine carving on it. I also purchased a suit of mourning clothes and accompanied the coffin myself. I am a man who responds very readily to emotion and really I was most moved by the marks of simple respect for my grief shown by the stevedores who handled the coffin at the dock. Not even my own personal luggage was examined at the Customs.

"I had warned Dimitrios, and a hearse was waiting for me and the coffin. I was pleased by my success, but Dimitrios, when I saw him, shrugged. I could not, he said very reasonably, arrive in France with a coffin every month. I think he thought the whole affair a little unbusinesslike. He was right, of course. He had, however, a suggestion. There was an Italian shipping line which ran one cargo steamer a month from Varna to Genoa. The stuff could be shipped to Genoa in small cases and manifested as special tobacco consigned to France. That would prevent the Italian Customs examining it. There was a man in Nice who could arrange for the transport of the stuff from Genoa by bribing the warehouse people to release it from bond and then smuggling it through by road. I wished to know how that would affect my financial interest in the supplies. He said that I should lose nothing as there was other work for me to do.

"It was curious how we all accepted his leadership almost without question. Yes, he had the money; but there was more than that to it. He dominated us because he knew precisely what he wanted and precisely how to get it with the least possible trouble and at the lowest possible cost. He knew how to find the people to work for him, too; and, when he had found them, he knew how to handle them.

"There were seven of us who took our instructions directly from Dimitrios and not one was the sort of person to take instructions easily. For instance, Visser, the Dutchman, had sold German machine guns to the Chinese, spied for the Japanese and served a term of imprisonment for killing a coolie in Batavia. He was not an easy man to handle. It was he who made the arrangements with the clubs and bars through which we reached the addicts.

"You see, the system of distribution was very carefully organised. Both Lenôtre and Galindo had for several years been peddling drugs which they bought from a man in the employ of a big French wholesale drug manufacturer. That sort of thing used to be quite easy before the nineteen thirty-one regulations. Both those men knew well those who needed the stuff and where to find them. Before Dimitrios came on the scene they had been dealing mostly in morphine and cocaine and always they had been handicapped by limited supplies. When Dimitrios offered them unlimited supplies of heroin they were quite ready to abandon the wholesale chemist and sell their clients heroin.

"But that was only one part of the business. Drug addicts, you know, are always very eager to get other people to take drugs too. Consequently, your circle of consumers is ever widening. It is most important, as you may imagine, to see that when you are approached by new customers they are not representatives of the *Brigade des Stupéfiants* or other similar undesirables. That was where Visser's work came in. The would-be buyer would come to, say, Lenôtre in the first place on the recommendation of a regular customer known to Lenôtre. But, on being asked for drugs, Lenôtre would pretend to be astonished. Drugs? He knew nothing of such things. Personally, he never used them. But, if one did use them, he had heard that the place to go to was the So-and-So Bar. At the So-and-So Bar, which would be on Visser's list, the prospective customer would receive much the same sort of answer. Drugs? No. Nothing of that kind at the So-and-So Bar but if it should be possible to call in again the following night, there might possibly be someone who could help. The following night, the Grand Duchess would be there.

"She was a curious woman. She had been brought into the business by Visser and was, I think, the only one of us Dimitrios had not found for himself. She was very clever. Her capacity for weighing up complete strangers was extraordinary. She could, I think, tell the most cleverly disguised detective just by looking at him across a room. It was her business to examine the person who wanted to buy and decide whether he or she should be supplied or not and how much was to be charged. She was very valuable to us.

"The other man was the Belgian, Werner. It was he who dealt with the small pedlars. He had been a chemist at one time and he used, I believe, to dilute the heroin with pigments under the pretext of testing its purity. Dimitrios never mentioned that part of the business.

"Some dilution very soon became necessary. Within six months of our beginning, I had had to increase the monthly heroin supply to fifty kilos. And I had other work to do. Lenôtre and Galindo had reported in the early stages that, if they were to get all the business they knew of, they would have to have morphine and cocaine to sell as well as heroin. Morphine addicts did not always like heroin and cocaine addicts would sometimes refuse it if they could get cocaine elsewhere. I had then to arrange for supplies of morphine and cocaine. The morphine problem was a simple one as it could be supplied at the same time and by the same people as the heroin; but the cocaine was a different matter. For that, it was necessary to go to Germany. I had plenty to do.

"We had our troubles, of course. They usually came to my part of the business. By the time we had been operating for a year, I had made several alternative arrangements for bringing in our supplies. In addition to the Genoa route for heroin and morphine which Lamare handled, I had come to terms with a sleeping car attendant on the Orient Express. He used to take the stuff aboard at Sofia and deliver it when the train was shunted into the siding in Paris. It was not a very safe route and I had to take elaborate precautions to protect myself in case of trouble, but it was rapid. Cocaine used to come in in cases of machinery from Germany. We had also begun to receive consignments of heroin from an Istanbul factory. These were brought by a cargo boat which left them floating outside the port of Marseilles in anchored containers for Lamare to collect at night.

"There was one week of disaster. In the last week of the June of nineteen twenty-nine, fifteen kilos of heroin were seized on the Orient Express and the police arrested six of my men including the sleeping car attendant. That would have been bad enough; but during the same week Lamare had to abandon a consignment of forty kilos of heroin and morphine near Sospel. He himself escaped but we were in a serious difficulty, for the loss of those fifty-five kilos meant that we were left with only eight kilos to meet commitments for over fifty. None was due on the Istanbul boat for several days. We were in despair. Lenôtre and Galindo and Werner had a terrible time. Two of Galindo's clientele committed suicide and in one of the bars there was a *fracas* in which Werner had his head cut.

"I did the best I could. I went to Sofia myself and brought back ten kilos in a trunk; but that was not enough. Dimitrios did not, I must say, blame me. It would have been unfair to have done so. But he was angry. He decided that, in future, reserve stocks must be held. It was soon after that week that he bought these houses. Until then we had always met him in a room over a café near the Porte d'Orleans. Now he said that these houses should be our headquarters. We never knew where he lived and could never get in touch with him until he chose to telephone one or other of us. We were to discover later that this ignorance of his address put us at a disastrous disadvantage. But other things happened before we made that discovery.

"The task of creating stocks was left to me. It was by no means easy. If we were both to create stocks and to maintain existing supplies we had to increase the size of the consignments. That meant that there was a greater risk of seizure. It also meant that we had to find more new methods of bringing the stuff in. Things were complicated, too, by the Bulgarian Government's closing down the factory at Radomir from which we drew the bulk of our supplies. It soon opened again in a different part of the country; but inevitably there were delays. We were forced to rely more and more upon Istanbul.

"It was a trying time. In two months we lost by seizure no less than ninety kilos of heroin, twenty of morphine and five of cocaine. But, in spite of ups and downs, the stock increased steadily. By the end of nineteen thirty, we had, beneath the floorboards of those houses next door, two hundred and fifty kilos of heroin, two hundred odd kilos of morphine, ninety kilos of cocaine and a small quantity of prepared Turkish opium."

Mr. Peters poured out the remainder of the coffee and extinguished the spirit lamp. Then he took a cigarette, wetted the end of it with his tongue and lit it.

"Have you ever known a drug addict, Mr. Latimer?" he asked suddenly.

"I don't think so."

"Ah, you don't *think* so. You do not know for certain. Yes, it is possible for a drug taker to conceal his little weakness for quite a time. But he—and especially *she*—cannot conceal it indefinitely, you know. The process is always roughly the same. It begins as an experiment. Half a gramme, perhaps, is taken through the nostrils. It may make you feel sick the first time; but you will try again and the next time it will be as it should be. A delicious sensation, warm, brilliant. Time stands still; but the mind moves at a tremendous pace and, it seems to you, with incredible efficiency. You were stupid; you become highly intelligent. You were unhappy; you become carefree. What you do not like you forget; and what you do like you experience with an intensity of pleasure undreamed of. Three hours of Paradise. And afterwards it is not too bad; not nearly as bad as it was when you had too much champagne. You want to be quiet; you feel a little ill at ease; that is all. Soon you are yourself again. Nothing has happened to you except that you have enjoyed yourself amazingly. If you do not wish to take the drug again, you tell yourself you need not do so. As an intelligent person you are superior to the stuff. Then, therefore, there is no logical reason why you should not enjoy yourself again, is there? Of course there isn't! And so you do. But this time it is a little disappointing. Your half a gramme was not quite enough. Disappointment must be dealt with. You must wander in Paradise just once more before you decide not to take the stuff again. A trifle more; nearly a gramme perhaps. Paradise again and still you don't feel any the worse for it. And since you don't feel any the worse for it, why not continue? Everybody knows that the stuff does ultimately have a bad effect on you; but the moment you detect any bad effects *you* will stop. Only fools become addicts. One and a half grammes. It really is something to look forward to in life. Only three months ago everything was so dreary; but now . . . Two grammes. Naturally, as you are taking a little more it is only reasonable to expect to feel a little ill and depressed afterwards. It's four months now. You must stop soon. Two and a half grammes. Your nose and throat get so dry these days. Other people seem to get on your nerves, too. Perhaps it is because you are sleeping so badly. They make too much noise. They talk so loudly. And what are they saying? Yes, *what?* Things about *you*, vicious lies. You can see it in their faces. Three grammes. And there are other things to be considered; other dangers. You have to be careful. Food tastes horrible. You cannot remember things that you have to do; important things. Even if you should happen to remember them, there are so many other things to worry you apart from this beastliness of having to live. For instance, your nose keeps running: that is, it is not really running but you think it must be, so you have to keep touching it to make sure. Another thing: there is always a fly annoying you. This terrible fly never *will* leave you alone and in peace. It is on your face, on your hand, on your neck. You must pull yourself together. Three and a half grammes. You see the idea, Mr. Latimer?"

"You don't seem to approve of drug-taking."

"Approve!" Mr. Peters stared, aghast. "It is terrible, *terrible*! Lives are ruined. They lose the power to work yet they must find money to pay for their special stuff. Under such circumstances people become desperate and may even do something criminal to get it. I see what is in your mind, Mr. Latimer. You feel that it is strange that I should have been connected with, that I should have made money out of, a thing of which I disapprove so sternly. But consider. If *I* had not made the money, someone else would have done so. Not one of those unfortunate creatures would have been any better off and I should have lost money."

"What about this ever-increasing clientèle of yours? You cannot pretend that all of those your organisation supplied were habitual drug-takers before you went to work."

"Of course they were not. But that side of the business was nothing to do with *me*. That was Lenôtre and Galindo. And I may tell you that Lenôtre and Galindo and Werner, too, were themselves addicts. They used cocaine. It is harder on the constitution but, whereas one can become a dangerous heroin addict in a few months, one can spend several years killing oneself with cocaine."

"What did Dimitrios take?"

"Heroin. It was a great surprise to us the first time we noticed it. We would meet him in this room as a rule at about six o'clock in the evening. It was on one of those evenings in the spring of nineteen thirty-one when we had our surprise.

"Dimitrios arrived late. That in itself was unusual; but we took little notice of it. As a rule, at these meetings, he would sit very quietly with his eyes half-closed, looking a little troubled as though he had a headache, so that even when one became used to him one constantly wished to ask if all was well with him. Watching him sometimes I used to be amazed at myself for allowing myself to be led by him. Then I would see his face change as he turned to meet some objection from Visser —it was always Visser who objected—and I would understand. Visser was a violent man and quick and cunning as well; but he seemed a child beside Dimitrios. Once when Dimitrios had been making a fool of him, Visser pulled out a pistol. He was white with rage. I could see his finger squeezing the trigger. If I had been Dimitrios, I should have prayed. But Dimitrios only smiled in the insolent way he had and, turning his back on Visser, began to talk to me about some business matter. Dimitrios was always quiet like that, even when he was angry.

"That was why we were so surprised that evening. He came in late and he stood inside the door looking at us for nearly a minute. Then he walked over to his place and sat down. Visser had been saying something about the *patron* of a café who had been making trouble and now he went on. There was nothing remarkable about what he was saying. I think he was telling Galindo that he must stop using the café as it was unsafe.

"Suddenly, Dimitrios leaned across the table, shouted *'Imbecile!'* and spat in Visser's face.

"Visser was as surprised as the rest of us. He opened his mouth to speak but Dimitrios did not give him time to say anything. Before we could grasp what was happening, he was accusing Visser of the most fantastic things. The words poured out and he spat again like a guttersnipe.

"Visser went white and got to his feet with his hand in the pocket where he kept his pistol; but Lenôtre, who was beside him, got up, too, and whispered something to him which made Visser take his hand from his pocket. Lenôtre was used to people who had been taking drugs and he and Galindo and Werner had recognised the signs as soon as Dimitrios had entered the room. But Dimitrios had seen Lenôtre whisper and turned to him. From Lenôtre he came to the rest of us. We were fools, he told us, if we thought that he did not know that we were plotting against him. He called us a lot of very unpleasant names in French and Greek. Then he began to boast that he was cleverer than the rest of us together, that but for him we should be starving, that he alone was responsible for our success (which was true though we did not like to be told it) and that he could do with us as he wished. He went on for half an hour, abusing us and boasting alternately. None of us said a word. Then, as suddenly as he had started, he stopped, stood up and walked out of the room.

"I suppose that we should have been prepared for treachery after that. Heroin addicts have a reputation for it. Yet we were not prepared. I think it may have been that we were so conscious of the amount of money he was making. I only know that, when he had gone, Lenôtre and Galindo laughed and asked Werner if the boss were paying for the stuff he used. Even Visser grinned. A joke was made of it, you see.

"Next time we saw Dimitrios he was quite normal and

no reference was made to his outburst. But as the months went by, although we had no more outbursts, he became bad-tempered and little difficulties would make him angry. His appearance was changing, too. He looked thin and ill and his eyes were dull. He did not always come to the meetings.

"Then, we had our second warning.

"Early in September, he announced suddenly that he proposed to reduce the consignments for the next three months and use our stock. This startled us and there were many objections. I was one of the objectors. I had had a great deal of trouble building up the stock and did not want to see it distributed without reason. The others reminded him of the trouble they had had when supplies ran out before. But Dimitrios would not listen. He had been warned, he said, that there was to be a new drive by the police. Not only, he said, would so large a stock compromise us seriously if it were discovered; but its seizure would be a serious financial loss. He, too, was sorry to see it go but it was best to play for safety.

"I do not think that the notion that he might be liquidating his assets before he got out occurred to any of us; and you may say that for people of experience we were very trusting. You would be right to say that. With the exception of Visser we seemed always to be on the defensive in our dealings with Dimitrios. Even Lydia, who understood so much about people, was defeated by him. As for Visser, he was too paralysed by his own conceit to believe that anyone, even a drug-addict, could betray him. Besides, why should we suspect him? We were making money, but he was making more, much more. What logical reason was there for suspecting him? Who could possibly have foreseen that he would behave like a madman?"

He shrugged. "You know the rest. He turned informer. We were all arrested. I was in Marseilles with Lamare when we were caught. The police were quite clever. They watched us for a week before they took us. They hoped, I think, to catch us with some of the stuff. Luckily, we noticed them the day before we were due to take delivery of a big consignment from Istanbul. Lenôtre and Galindo and Werner were not so lucky. They had some of the stuff in their pockets. The police tried, of course, to make me tell them about Dimitrios and showed me the dossier he had sent them. They might as well have asked me for the moon. Visser, I found out later, knew more than the rest of us, but he did not tell the police what it was. He had other ideas. He told the police that Dimitrios had had an apartment in the seventeenth arrondissement. That was a lie. Visser wanted to get a lighter sentence than the rest of us. He did not. He died not long ago, poor fellow." Mr. Peters heaved a sigh and produced one of his cheroots.

Latimer touched his second cup of coffee. It was quite cold. He took a cigarette and accepted a light from his host's match.

"Well?" he said when he saw that the cheroot was alight. "What then? I am still waiting to hear how I am to earn a half a million francs."

Mr. Peters smiled as if he were presiding at a Sunday School treat and Latimer had asked for a second currant bun. "That, Mr. Latimer, is part of another story."

"What story?"

"The story of what happened to Dimitrios after he disappeared from view."

"Well, what *did* happen to him?" Latimer demanded testily.

Without replying, Mr. Peters picked up the photograph that lay on the table and handed it to him again.

Latimer looked at it and frowned. "Yes, I've seen this. It's Dimitrios all right. What about it?"

Mr. Peters smiled very sweetly and gently. "That, Mr. Latimer, is a photograph of Manus Visser."

"What on earth do you mean?"

"I told you that Visser had other ideas about using the knowledge he had been clever enough to acquire about Dimitrios. What you saw on the mortuary table in Istanbul, Mr. Latimer, was Visser after he had tried to put those ideas into practice."

"But it was Dimitrios. I saw . . ."

"You saw the body of Visser, Mr. Latimer, after Dimitrios had killed him. Dimitrios himself, I am glad to say, is alive and in good health."

CHAPTER XII

MONSIEUR C. K.

Latimer stared. His jaw had dropped and he knew that he looked ridiculous and that there was nothing to be done about the fact. Dimitrios was alive. It did not even occur to him to question the statement seriously. He knew instinctively that it was true. It was as if a doctor had warned him that he was suffering from a dangerous disease of the symptoms of which he had been only vaguely aware. He was surprised beyond words, resentful, curious and a little frightened; while his mind began to work feverishly to meet and deal with a new and strange set of conditions. He shut his mouth, then opened it again to say, feebly: "I can't believe it."

206

Mr. Peters was clearly gratified by the effect of his announcement.

"I scarcely hoped," he said, "that you would have had no suspicions of the truth. Grodek, of course, understood. He had been puzzled by certain questions I asked him some time ago. When you came he was even more curious. That was why he wanted to know so much. But as soon as you told him that you had seen the body in Istanbul, he understood. He saw at once that the one thing that rendered you unique from my point of view was the fact of your having seen the face of the man buried as Dimitrios. It was obvious. Not to you, perhaps. I suppose that when one sees a perfect stranger on a mortuary slab and a policeman tells one that his name is Dimitrios Makropoulos, one assumes, if one has your respect for the police, that one has the truth of the matter. I *knew* that it was not Dimitrios you saw. But—I could not prove it. You, on the other hand, can. *You* can identify Manus Visser." He paused significantly and then, as Latimer made no comment, added: "How did they identify him as Dimitrios?"

"There was a French *carte d'identité*, issued in Lyons a year ago to Dimitrios Makropoulos, sewn inside the lining of his coat." Latimer spoke mechanically. He was thinking of Grodek's toast to the English detective story and of Grodek's inability to stop himself laughing at his own joke. Heavens! what a fool the man must have thought him!

"A French *carte d'identité*!" echoed Mr. Peters. "That I find amusing. Very amusing."

"It had been pronounced genuine by the French authorities and it had a photograph in it."

Mr. Peters smiled tolerantly. "I could get you a dozen genuine French *cartes d'identité*, Mr. Latimer, each in the name of Dimitrios Makropoulos and each with a different photograph. Look!" He drew a green *permis de séjour* from his pocket, opened it and, with his fingers over the space taken up by the identifying particulars, displayed the photograph in it. "Does that look very much like me, Mr. Latimer?"

Latimer shook his head.

"And yet," declared Mr. Peters, "it *is* a genuine photograph of me taken three years ago. I made no effort to deceive. It is simply that I am not *photogénique*, that is all. Very few men are. The camera is a consistent liar. Dimitrios could have used photographs of anyone with the same type of face as Visser. That photograph I showed you a few moments ago is of someone like Visser."

"If Dimitrios is still alive, where is he?"

"Here in Paris." Mr. Peters leaned forward and patted Latimer's knee. "You have been very reasonable, Mr. Latimer," he said kindly. "I shall tell you everything."

"It's very good of you," said Latimer bitterly.

"No, no! You have a *right* to know," said Mr. Peters warmly. He pursed his lips with the air of one who knows justice when he sees it. "I shall tell you everything," he said again and lit another cheroot.

"As you may imagine," he went on, "we were all very angry with Dimitrios. Some of us threatened revenge. But, Mr. Latimer, I have never been one to beat my head against a wall. Dimitrios had disappeared and there was no way of finding him. The indignities of prison life a memory, I purged my heart of malice and went abroad to regain my sense of proportion. I became a wanderer,

Mr. Latimer. A little business here, a little business there, travel and meditation—that was my life. Two years ago I met Visser in Rome.

"I had not, of course, seen him for five years. Poor fellow! he had had a bad time. A few months after his release from prison he was pressed for money and forged a cheque. They sent him back to prison for three years and then, when he came out, deported him. He was almost penniless and he could not work in France where he knew useful people. I could not blame him for feeling bitter.

"He asked me to lend him money. We had met in a café and he told me that he had to go to Zürich to buy a new passport but that he had no money. His Dutch passport was useless because it was in his real name. I would have liked to have helped him; for, although I had never liked him very much, I felt sorry for him; but I decided to refuse.

"At my refusal he became angry and accused me of not trusting him to pay a debt of honour, which was a foolish way for him to talk. Then he pleaded with me. He could prove, he said, that he would be able to repay the money and began to tell me some interesting things.

"I have said that Visser had known a little more about Dimitrios than the rest of us. That was true. He had taken a lot of trouble finding it out. It was just after that evening when he had pulled out a pistol to threaten Dimitrios and Dimitrios had turned his back upon him. Nobody had treated him like that before and he wished to know more about the man who had humiliated him: that, at least, is what I believe. He himself said that he had suspected that Dimitrios would betray us; but that, I knew, was nonsense. Whatever his reason, however, he decided to follow Dimitrios when he left the Impasse.

"The first night that he tried he was unsuccessful. There was a large closed car waiting at the entrance to the Impasse and Dimitrios was driven off in it before Visser could find a taxi in which to follow. The second night he had a hired car ready. He did not come to the meeting but waited for Dimitrios in the Rue de Rennes. When the closed car appeared, Visser drove off after it. Dimitrios stopped outside a big apartment house in the Avenue de Wagram and went inside while the big car drove away. Visser noted the address and about a week later, at a time when he knew that Dimitrios would be here in this room, he called at the apartment house and asked for Monsieur Makropoulos. Naturally, the concièrge knew of no one of that name but Visser gave him money and described Dimitrios and found that he had an apartment there in the name of Rougemont.

"Now Visser, for all his conceit, was no fool. He knew that Dimitrios would have foreseen that he might be followed and guessed that the Rougemont apartment was not his only place. Accordingly he set himself to watch Monsieur Rougemont's comings and goings. It was not long before he discovered that there was another way out of the apartment house at the rear and that Dimitrios used to leave that way.

"One night when Dimitrios left by the back entrance Visser followed him. He did not have far to go. He found that Dimitrios lived in a big house just off the Avenue Hoche. It belonged, he found, to a titled and very *chic* woman. I shall call her Madame la Comtesse. Later Visser saw Dimitrios leave with her for the opera. Dimitrios was *en grande tenue* and they had a large Hispano to take them there.

"At that point Visser lost interest. He knew where Dimitrios lived. No doubt he felt that he had in some way obtained his revenge by discovering that much. He must, too, have been tired of waiting about in the streets. His curiosity was satisfied. What he had discovered was, after all, very much what he might have expected to discover. Dimitrios was a man with a large income. He was spending it in the same way as other men with large incomes.

"They told me that, when Visser was arrested in Paris, he said very little about Dimitrios. Yet he must have had ugly thoughts, for he was by nature a violent man and very conceited. It would have been useless, in any case, for him to have tried to have Dimitrios arrested, for he could only have sent them to the apartment in the Avenue de Wagram and the house of Madame la Comtesse off the Avenue Hoche and he knew that Dimitrios would have gone away. He had, as I said, other ideas about his knowledge.

"I think that, to begin with, he had intended to kill Dimitrios when he found him; but as he began to get short of money his hatred of Dimitrios became more reasonable. He probably remembered the Hispano and the luxury of the house of Madame la Comtesse. She would perhaps be worried to hear that her friend made his money by selling heroin and Dimitrios might be ready to pay good money to save her that worry. But it was easier to think about Dimitrios and his money than it was to find them. For several months after he was released from prison early in nineteen thirty-two, Visser looked for

Dimitrios. The apartment in the Avenue de Wagram was no longer occupied. The house of Madame la Comtesse was shut up and the concièrge said that she was in Biarritz. Visser went to Biarritz and found that she was staying with friends. Dimitrios was not with her. Visser returned to Paris. Then he had what I think was quite a good idea. He himself was pleased with it. Unfortunately for him, it came a little too late. He remembered one day that Dimitrios had been a drug addict, and it occurred to him that Dimitrios might have done what many other wealthy addicts do when their addiction reaches an advanced stage. He might have entered a clinic to be cured.

"There are five private clinics near Paris which specialise in such cures. On the pretext of making inquiries as to terms on behalf of an imaginary brother, Visser went to each one in turn, saying that he had been recommended by friends of Monsieur Rougemont. At the fourth his idea was proved to be good. The doctor in charge asked after the health of Monsieur Rougemont.

"I think that Visser derived a certain vulgar satisfaction from the thought of Dimitrios being cured of a heroin addiction. The cure is terrible, you know. The doctors go on giving the patient drugs, but gradually reduce the quantity. For him the torture is almost unbearable. He yawns and sweats and shivers for days, but he does not sleep and he cannot eat. He longs for death and babbles of suicide; but he has not the strength left to commit it. He shrieks and screams for his drug and it is withheld. He . . . But I must not bore you with horrors, Mr. Latimer. The cure lasts three months and costs five thousand francs a week. When it is over the patient may forget the torture and start taking drugs again. Or he may be wiser and forget Paradise. Dimitrios, it seems, was wise.

"He had left the clinic four months before Visser visited it; and so Visser had to think of another good idea. He *did* think of it, but it involved going to Biarritz again and he had no money. He forged a cheque, cashed it and set off again. He reasoned that as Dimitrios and Madame la Comtesse had been friends, she would probably know his present whereabouts. But he could not simply go to her and ask for his address. Even if he could have invented a pretext for doing so, he did not know under what name Dimitrios was known to her. There were difficulties, you see. But he found a way to overcome them. For several days he watched the villa where she was staying. Then, when he had found out enough about it, he broke into her room one afternoon, when the house was empty except for two drowsy servants, and looked through her baggage. He was looking for letters.

"Dimitrios had never liked written records in our business, and he never corresponded with any of us. But Visser had remembered that on one occasion Dimitrios had scribbled an address for Werner on a piece of paper. I remembered the occasion myself. The writing had been curious: quite uneducated, with clumsy, badly formed letters and many flourishes. It was this writing that Visser was looking for. He found it. There were nine letters in the writing. All were from an expensive hotel in Rome. I beg your pardon, Mr. Latimer. You said something?"

"I can tell you what he was doing in Rome. He was organising the assassination of a Yugoslav politician."

Mr. Peters did not seem impressed. "Very likely," he said indifferently; "he would not be where he is to-day without that special organising ability of his. Where was I? Ah, yes! the letters.

"All were from Rome and all were signed with initials which I shall tell you were 'C. K.' The letters themselves were not what Visser had expected. They were very formal and stilted and brief. Most of them said no more than that the writer was in good health, that business was interesting and that he hoped to see his dear friend soon. No *tu-toi*, you know. But in one he said that he had met a relation by marriage of the Italian royal family and in another that he had been presented to a Rumanian diplomat with a title. He was very pleased with these encounters, it seems. It was all very *snob*, and Visser felt that Dimitrios would certainly wish to buy his friendship. He noted the name of the hotel and, leaving everything as he found it, went back to Paris *en route* for Rome. He arrived in Paris the following morning. The police were waiting for him. He was not, I should think, a very clever forger.

"But you may imagine the poor fellow's feelings. During the three interminable years that followed he thought of nothing but Dimitrios; of how near he had been to him and how far he was now. He seemed, for some strange reason, to regard Dimitrios as the one responsible for his being in prison again. The idea served to feed his hatred of him and strengthen his resolve to make him pay. He was, I think, a little mad. As soon as he was free he got a little money in Holland and went to Rome. He was over three years behind Dimitrios, but he was determined to catch up with him. He went to the hotel and, posing as a Dutch private detective, asked to be permitted to see the records of those who had stayed there three years before.

The *affiches* had, of course, gone to the police, but they had the bills for the period in question and he had the initials. He was able to discover the name which Dimitrios had used. Dimitrios had also left a forwarding address. It was a Poste Restante in Paris.

"Visser was now in a new difficulty. He knew the name; but that was useless unless he could get into France to trace the owner of it. It was no use his writing his demands for money. Dimitrios would not go on calling for letters for three years. And yet he could not enter France without being turned at the frontier or risking another term of imprisonment. He had somehow to get a new name and a new passport, and he had no money with which to do so.

"I lent him three thousand francs; and I will confess to you, Mr. Latimer, that I felt myself to be truly stupid. Yet I was sorry for him. He was not the Visser I had known in Paris. Prison had broken him. Once his passions had been in his eyes, but now they were in his mouth and cheeks. One felt he was getting old. I gave him the money out of pity and to get rid of him. I did not believe his story. I never expected to hear from him again. You may, therefore, imagine my astonishment when, a year ago, I received here a letter from him enclosing a *mandat* for the three thousand francs.

"The letter was very short. It said: 'I have found him as I said I would. Here, with my profound thanks, is the money you lent me. It is worth three thousand francs to surprise you.' That was all. He did not sign it. He gave no address. The *mandat* had been bought in Nice and posted there.

"That letter made me think, Mr. Latimer. Visser had

recovered his conceit. He could afford to indulge it to the extent of three thousand francs. That meant that he had a great deal more money. Conceited persons dream of such gestures, but they very rarely make them. Dimitrios must have paid; and since he was not a fool he must have had a very good reason for paying.

"I was idle at the time, Mr. Latimer; idle and a little restless. It might be interesting, I thought, to find Dimitrios for myself and share in Visser's good fortune. It was not greed that prompted me, Mr. Latimer; I should not like you to think that. I was *interested*. Besides, I felt that Dimitrios owed me something for the discomforts and indignities I had experienced because of him. For two days I played with the idea. Then, on the third day I made up my mind. I set out for Rome.

"As you may imagine, Mr. Latimer, I had a difficult time and many disappointments. I had the initials, which Visser, in his eagerness to convince me, had revealed, but the only thing I knew about the hotel was that it was expensive. There are, unfortunately, a great many expensive hotels in Rome. I began to investigate them one after the other; but when, at the fifth hotel, they refused, for some reason, to let me see the bills for nineteen thirty-two, I abandoned the attempt. Instead, I went to an Italian friend of mine in one of the Ministries. He was able to use his influence on my behalf and, after a lot of *chi-chi* and expense, I was permitted to inspect the Ministry of Interior archives for nineteen thirty-two. I found out the name Dimitrios was using, and I also found out what Visser had not found out—that Dimitrios had taken the course, which I myself took in nineteen thirty-two, of purchasing the citizenship of a certain South American republic which is sympathetic in such matters if one's pocket-book is fat enough. Dimitrios and I had become fellow citizens.

"I must confess, Mr. Latimer, that I went back to Paris with hope in my heart. I was to be bitterly disappointed. Our consul was not helpful. He said that he had never heard of Señor C. K. And yet another disappointment awaited me. The house of Madame la Comtesse off the Avenue Hoche had been empty for two years.

"You would think, would you not, that it would be easy to find out where a *chic* and wealthy woman was? It was most difficult. The *Bottin* gave nothing. Apparently she had no house in Paris. I was, I will confess, about to abandon the search when I found a way out of my difficulty. I reflected that a fashionable woman like Madame la Comtesse would be certain to have gone somewhere for the winter sports season that was just over. Accordingly, I commissioned Hachettes to purchase for me a copy of every French, Swiss, German and Italian winter sports and social magazine which had been published during the previous three months.

"It was a desperate idea, but it yielded results. You have no idea how many such magazines there are, Mr. Latimer. It took me a little over a week to go through them all carefully, and I can assure you that by the middle of that week I was very nearly a social-democrat. By the end of it, however, I had recovered my sense of humour. If repetition makes nonsense of words it makes even more fantastic nonsense of smiling faces, even if their owners are rich. Besides, I had found what I wanted. In one of the German magazines for February there was a small paragraph which said that Madame la Comtesse was at St.

Anton for the winter sports. In a French magazine there
was a *couturier's* picture of her in skating clothes. I went
to St. Anton. There are not many hotels there, and I soon
found that Monsieur C. K. had been in St. Anton at the
same time. He had given an address in Cannes.

"At Cannes I found that Monsieur C. K. had a villa on
the Estoril, but that he himself was abroad on business at
the moment. I was not discontented. Dimitrios would
return to his villa sooner or later. Meanwhile I set myself
to discover something about Monsieur C. K.

"I have always said, Mr. Latimer, that the art of being
successful in this life of ours is the art of knowing the
people who will be useful to one. I have in my time met
and done business with many important people—people,
you know, who are informed of what goes on and why—
and I have always taken care to be helpful to them. It
has paid me.

"So, where Visser might have had to prowl about in the
darkness in search of his information, I was able to get
mine from a friend. It proved easier than I had expected
to do so, for I found that, in certain circles, Dimitrios,
with the name of Monsieur C. K., had become quite important. In fact, when I learned just how important he
had become, I was pleasantly surprised. I began to realise
that Visser must be living on the money he got from
Dimitrios. Yet what did Visser know? Only that Dimitrios had dealt illegally in drugs; a fact that it would be
difficult for him to prove. He knew nothing about the
dealings in women. I did. There must, I reasoned, be
other things, too, which Dimitrios would prefer not to
be generally known. If, before I approached Dimitrios,
I could find out some of those things, my financial posi-

tion would be very strong indeed. I decided to see some more of my friends.

"Two of them were able to help me. Grodek was one. A Rumanian friend of mine was another. You know of Grodek's acquaintance with Dimitrios when he called himself Talat. The Rumanian friend told me that in nineteen twenty-five Dimitrios had had questionable financial dealings with Codreanu, the lamented leader of the Rumanian Iron Guard, and that he was known to, but not wanted by, the Bulgarian police.

"Now there was nothing criminal about any of those affairs. Indeed, Grodek's information depressed me some - what. It was unlikely that the Yugoslav Government would apply for extradition after so many years; while, as for the French, they might hold that, as Dimitrios had rendered some sort of service to the Republic in nineteen twenty-six, he was entitled to a little tolerance in the matter of dealings in drugs and women. I decided to see what I could find out in Greece. A week after I arrived in Athens and while I was still trying unsuccessfully to trace in the official records a reference to my particular Dimitrios, I read in an Athens paper of the discovery, by the Istanbul police, of the body of a Greek from Smyrna with the name of Dimitrios Makropoulos."

He raised his eyes to Latimer's. "Do you begin to see, Mr. Latimer, why I found your interest in Dimitrios a little difficult to explain?" And then, as Latimer nodded: "I, too, of course, inspected the Relief Commission dossier; but I followed you to Sofia instead of going to Smyrna. I wonder if you would care to tell me now what you found out from the police records there?"

"Dimitrios was suspected of murdering a money-lender

named Sholem in Smyrna in nineteen twenty-two. He escaped to Greece. Two years later, he was involved in an attempt to assassinate Kemal. He escaped again, but the Turks used the murder as a pretext for issuing a warrant for his arrest."

"A murder in Smyrna! That makes it even clearer." Mr. Peters smiled. "A wonderful man, Dimitrios, don't you think? So economical."

"What do you mean?"

"Let me finish my story and you will see. As soon as I read that newspaper paragraph, I sent a telegram to a friend in Paris asking him to let me know the whereabouts of Monsieur C.K. He replied two days later, saying that Monsieur C.K. had just returned to Cannes after an Ægean cruise with a party of friends in a Greek diesel yacht which he had chartered two months previously.

"Do you see now what had happened, Mr. Latimer? You tell me that the *carte d'identité* was a year old when they found it on the body. That means that it was obtained a few weeks before Visser sent me that three thousand francs. You see, from the moment Visser found Dimitrios, he was doomed. Dimitrios must have made up his mind at once to kill him. You can see why. Visser was dangerous. He was such a conceited fellow. He might have blurted out indiscretions at any time when he had been drinking and wanted to boast. He would have to be killed.

"Yet, see how clever Dimitrios was! He could have killed Visser at once, no doubt. But he did not do so. His economical mind had evolved a better plan. If it were necessary to kill Visser, could he not dispose of the body in some advantageous way? Why not use it to safeguard himself against the consequences of that old indiscretion in Smyrna? It was unlikely that there would be consequences, but here was his chance to make certain of the fact. The body of the villain, Dimitrios Makropoulos, would be delivered to the Turkish police. Dimitrios, the murderer, would be dead and Monsieur C.K. would be left alive to cultivate his garden. But he would require a certain amount of co-operation from Visser himself. The man would have to be lulled into feeling secure. So, Dimitrios smiled and paid up and set about getting the identity card which was to go with Visser's dead body. Nine months later, in June, he invited his good friend Visser to join him on a yatching trip."

"Yes, but how could he have committed the murder on the yachting trip? What about the crew? What about the other passengers?"

Mr. Peters looked knowing. "Let me tell you, Mr. Latimer, what I should have done if I had been Dimitrios. I should have begun by chartering a Greek yacht. There would be a reason for its being a Greek yacht: its home port would be the Piræus.

"I should have arranged for my friends, including Visser, to join the yacht at Naples. Then I should have taken them on their cruise and returned a month later to Naples, where I should have announced that the cruise would end. They would disembark; but I should stay on board saying that I was returning with the yacht to the Piræus. Then I should take Visser aside privately and tell him that I had some very secret business to transact in Istanbul, that I proposed to go there on the yacht and that I should be glad of his company. I should ask him not to tell the disembarking passengers who might be angry because I had not asked them and to return to the yacht when they had gone. To poor, conceited Visser, the invitation would be irresistible.

"To the captain I should say that Visser and I would leave the yacht at Istanbul and return overland, after we had transacted our business, to Paris. He would sail the yacht back to the Piræus. At Istanbul Visser and I would go ashore together. I should have left word with the crew that we would send for our baggage when we had decided where we should be staying for the night. Then, I should have taken him to a *boîte* I know of in a street off the Grande Rue de Pera; and later that night I should find myself poorer by ten thousand French francs, while Visser would be at the bottom of the Bosphorus at a place where the current would carry him, when he was rotten enough to float, out to Seraglio Point. Then I should take a room in a hotel in the name and with the passport of Visser, and send a porter to the yacht with a note authorising him to collect both Visser's luggage and mine. As Visser, I would leave the hotel in the morning for the station. His baggage, which I should have searched overnight to see that there was nothing in it to identify it as Visser's, I would deposit in the *consigne*. Then I would take the train to Paris. If inquiries about Visser are ever made in Istanbul, he left by train for Paris. But who is going to inquire? My friends believe he left the yacht at Naples. The captain and crew of the yacht are not interested. Visser has a false passport, he is a criminal: such a type has an obvious reason for disappearing of his own free will. Finish!"

Mr. Peters spread out his hands. "That is how it would occur to me to deal with such a situation. Perhaps Dimitrios managed it a little differently; but that is what might well have happened. There is one thing, however, that I am quite sure he did. You remember telling me that some months before you arrived in Smyrna, someone examined the same police records that you examined there? That must have been Dimitrios. He was always very cautious. No doubt he was anxious to find out how much they knew about his appearance, before he left Visser for them to find."

"But that man I told you about looked like a Frenchman."

Mr. Peters smiled reproachfully. "Then you were *not* quite frank with me in Sofia, Mr. Latimer. You *did* inquire about this mysterious man." He shrugged. "Dimitrios does look like a Frenchman now. His clothes are French."

"You've seen him recently?"

"Yesterday. Though he did not see me."

"You know exactly where he is in Paris, then?"

"Exactly. As soon as I discovered his new business I knew where to find him here."

"And, now that you have found him, what next?"

Mr. Peters frowned. "Come now, Mr. Latimer. I am sure that you are not quite as obtuse as all that. You know and can prove that the man buried in Istanbul is not Dimitrios. If necessary you could identify Visser's photographs on the police files. I, on the other hand, know what Dimitrios is calling himself now and where to find him. Our joint silence would be worth a lot of money to Dimitrios. With Visser's fate in mind, we shall know, too, how to deal with the matter. We shall demand a million francs. Dimitrios will pay us, believing that we shall come back for more. We shall not be as foolish as to endanger our lives in that way. We shall rest content with half a million each—nearly three thousand pounds sterling, Mr. Latimer—and quietly disappear."

"I see. Blackmail on a cash basis. No credit. But why bring me into the business? The Turkish police could identify Visser without my help."

"How? They identified him as Dimitrios and buried him. They have seen perhaps a dozen or more dead bodies since then. Weeks have gone by. Are they going to remember Visser's face well enough to justify their beginning expensive extradition proceedings against a rich foreigner because of their fourteen years old suspicions about a sixteen years old murder? My dear Mr. Latimer! Dimitrios would laugh at me. He would do with me as he did with Visser: give me a few thousand francs here and there to keep me from making myself a nuisance with the French police and to keep me quiet until, for safety's sake, I could be killed. But you have seen Visser's body and identified it. You have seen the police records in Smyrna. He knows nothing about you. He will have to pay or run an unknown risk. He is too cautious for that. Listen. In the first place, it is essential that Dimitrios does not discover our identities. He will know me, of course, but he will not know my present name. In your case, we shall invent a name. Mr. Smith, perhaps, as you are English. I shall approach Dimitrios in the name of Petersen and we shall arrange to meet him outside Paris at a place of our own choosing to receive our million francs. That is the last that he will see of either of us."

Latimer laughed but not very heartily. "And do you really suppose that I shall agree to this plan of yours?"

"If, Mr. Latimer, your trained mind can evolve a more ingenious plan, I shall be only too happy to . . ."

"My trained mind, Mr. Peters, is concerned with wondering how best to convey this information which you have given me to the police."

Mr. Peters' smile became thin. "The police? What information, Mr. Latimer?" he inquired softly.

"Why, the information that . . ." Latimer began impatiently and then stopped, frowning.

"Quite so," nodded Mr. Peters approvingly. "You have no real information to convey. If you go to the Turkish police they will no doubt send to the French police for Visser's photographs and record your identification. What then? Dimitrios will be found to be alive. That is all. I have not, you may remember, told you the name that Dimitrios uses now or even his initials. It would be impossible for you to trace him from Rome as Visser and I traced him. Nor do you know the name of Madame la Comtesse. As for the French police, I do not think that they would be interested either in the fate of a deported Dutch criminal or excited by the knowledge that somewhere in France there is a Greek using a false name who killed a man in Smyrna in nineteen twenty-two. You see, Mr. Latimer, you cannot act without me. If, of course, Dimitrios should prove difficult, then it might be desirable to take the police into our confidence. But I do not think that Dimitrios will be difficult. He is very intelligent. In any case, Mr. Latimer, why throw away three thousand pounds?"

Latimer considered him for a moment. Then he said: "Has it occurred to you that I might not want that particular three thousand pounds? I think, my friend, that prolonged association with criminals has made it difficult for you to follow some trains of thought."

"This moral rectitude . . ." began Mr. Peters wearily. Then he seemed to change his mind. He cleared his throat. "If you wished," he said with the calculated *bonhommie* of one who reasons with a drunken friend, "we could inform the police *after* we had secured the money. Even if Dimitrios were able to prove that he had paid money to us, he could not, however unpleasant he wished to be, tell the police our names or how to find us. In fact, I think that that would be a very wise move on our part, Mr. Latimer. We should then be quite sure that Dimitrios was no longer dangerous. We could supply the police anonymously with a dossier as Dimitrios did in nineteen thirty-one. The retribution would be just." Then his face fell. "Ah, no. It is impossible. I am afraid that the suspicions of your Turkish friends might fall upon you, Mr. Latimer. We could not risk that, could we!"

But Latimer was scarcely listening. He knew that what he had made up his mind to say was foolish and he was trying to justify its folly. Peters was right. There was nothing he could do to bring Dimitrios to justice. He was left with a choice. Either he could go back to Athens and leave Peters to make the best deal he could with Dimitrios or he could stay in Paris to see the last act of the grotesque comedy in which he now found himself playing a part. The first alternative being unthinkable, he was committed to the second. He really had no choice. To gain time he had taken and lighted a cigarette. Now he looked up from it.

"All right," he said slowly; "I'll do what you want.

But there are conditions."

"Conditions?" Mr. Peters' lips tightened. "I think that a half share is more than generous, Mr. Latimer. Why my trouble and expenses alone . . . !"

"Just a moment. I was saying, Mr. Peters, that there are conditions. The first should be very easy for you to fulfil. It is simply that you yourself retain all the money that you are able to squeeze from Dimitrios. The second . . ." he went on and then paused. He had the momentary pleasure of seeing Mr. Peters disconcerted. Then, he saw the watery eyes narrow quite appreciably. Mr. Peters' words as they issued from his mouth were charged with suspicion.

"I don't think I quite understand, Mr. Latimer. If this is a clumsy trick . . ."

"Oh no. There is no trick, clumsy or otherwise, Mr. Peters. 'Moral rectitude' was your phrase, wasn't it? It will do. I am prepared, you see, to assist in blackmailing a person when that person is Dimitrios; but I am not prepared to share in the profits. So much the better for you, of course."

Mr. Peters nodded thoughtfully. "Yes, I see that you might think like that. So much the better for me, as you say. But what is the other condition?"

"Equally inoffensive. You have referred mysteriously to Dimitrios's having become a person of importance. I make my helping you get your million francs conditional on your telling me exactly *what* he has become."

Mr. Peters thought for a moment, then shrugged. "Very well. I see no reason why I should not tell you. It so happens that the knowledge cannot possibly be of any help to you in discovering his present identity. The Eurasian Credit Trust is registered in Monaco and the details of its registration are not therefore open to inspection. Dimitrios is a member of the Board of Directors."

CHAPTER XIII

RENDEZVOUS

I<small>T</small> was two o'clock in the morning when Latimer left the Impasse des Huits Anges and began to walk slowly in the direction of the Quai Voltaire.

At the corner of the Boulevard St. Germain there was a café open. He went inside and was served with a glass of beer by the bored mute behind the zinc. He drank some of his beer and gazed vacantly about him like a person who has strayed into a museum for shelter from the rain. He wished that he had gone to bed after all. He paid for his beer and took a taxi back to his hotel. He was tired, of course: that was the trouble.

In his room, Latimer sat down by the window and

gazed out across the black river to the lights which it reflected and the faint glow in the sky beyond the Louvre. His mind was haunted by the past, by the confession of Dhris, the negro, and by the memories of Irana Preveza, by the tragedy of Bulić and by a tale of white crystals travelling west to Paris, bringing money to the fig-packer of Izmir. Three human beings had died horribly and countless others had lived horribly that Dimitrios might take his ease. If there *were* such a thing as Evil, then this man. . . .

But it was useless to try to explain him in terms of Good and Evil. They were no more than baroque abstractions. Good Business and Bad Business were the elements of the new theology. Dimitrios was not evil. He was logical and consistent; as logical and consistent in the European jungle as the poison gas called Lewisite and the shattered bodies of children killed in the bombardment of an open town. The logic of Michael Angelo's *David*, Beethoven's quartets and Einstein's physics had been replaced by that of the *Stock Exchange Year Book* and Hitler's *Mein Kampf*.

Yet, Latimer reflected, although you could not stop people buying and selling Lewisite, although you could do no more than "deplore" a number of slaughtered children, there were in existence means of preventing one particular aspect of the principle of expediency from doing too much damage. Most international criminals were beyond the reach of man-made laws; but Dimitrios happened to be within reach of one law. He had committed at least two murders and had therefore broken the law as surely as if he had been starving and had stolen a loaf of bread.

It was easy enough, however, to say that he was within reach of the Law: it was not as easy to see how the Law was to be informed of the fact. As Mr. Peters had so carefully pointed out, he, Latimer, had no information to give the police. But was that an altogether true picture of the situation? He *had* some information. He knew that Dimitrios was alive and that he was a director of the Eurasian Credit Trust, that he knew a French Countess who had had a house off the Avenue Hoche and that he or she had had an Hispana Suiza car, that both of them had been in St. Anton that year for the winter sports and that he had chartered a Greek yacht in June, that he had a villa on the Estoril and that he was now the citizen of a South American republic. Surely, then, it must be possible to find the person with those particular attributes. Even if the names of the directors of the Eurasian Credit Trust were unobtainable, it ought to be possible to get the names of the men who had chartered Greek yachts in June, of the wealthy South Americans with villas on the Estoril and of the South American visitors to St. Anton in February. If you could get those lists, all you would have to do would be to see which names (if there should be more than one) were common to the three.

But how did you get the lists? Besides, even if you could persuade the Turkish police to exhume Visser and then apply officially for all that information, what sort of proof would you have that the man you had concluded to be Dimitrios, was in fact, Dimitrios? And supposing that you could convince Colonel Haki of the truth, would he have enough evidence to justify the French extraditing a director of the powerful Eurasian Credit Trust? If it had taken twelve years to secure the acquittal of Dreyfus, it could take at least as many years to secure the conviction of Dimitrios.

He undressed wearily and got into bed.

It looked as if he were committed to Mr. Peters' black-mailing scheme. Lying in a comfortable bed with his eyes closed, he found the fact that in a few days' time he would be, technically speaking, one of the worst sorts of criminals no more than odd. Yet, at the back of his mind there was a certain discomfort. When the reason for it dawned on him, he was mildly shocked. The simple truth was that he was feeling afraid of Dimitrios. Dimitrios was a dangerous man; more dangerous by far than he had been in Smyrna and Athens and Sofia because he now had more to lose. Visser had blackmailed him and died. Now, he, Latimer, was going to blackmail him. Dimitrios had never hesitated to kill a man if he had deemed it necessary to do so; and, if he had deemed it necessary in the case of a man who threatened to expose him as a drug pedlar, would he hesitate in the case of two men who threatened to expose him as a murderer?

It was most important to see that, hesitation or no hesitation, he was not given the opportunity. Mr. Peters had proposed the taking of elaborate precautions.

The first contact with Dimitrios was to be established by letter. Latimer had seen a draft of the letter and had found it gratifyingly similar in tone to a letter he himself had written for a blackmailer in one of his books. It began, with sinister cordiality, by trusting that, after all these years, Monsieur C.K. had not forgotten the writer and the pleasant and profitable times they had spent together, went on to say how pleasing it was to hear that he was so successful and hoped sincerely that he would be able to

meet the writer who would be at the So-and-so Hotel at
nine o'clock on the Thursday evening of that week. The
writer concluded with an expression of his *"plus sincere
amitié"* and a significant little postscript to the effect that
he had chanced to meet someone who had known their
mutual friend Visser quite well, that this person was most
anxious to meet Monsieur K. and that it would be so unfortunate if Monsieur K. could not arrange to keep the appointment on Thursday evening.

Dimitrios would receive that letter on the Thursday
morning. At half past eight on the Thursday evening,
"Mr. Petersen" and "Mr. Smith" would arrive at the hotel chosen for the interview and "Mr. Petersen" would
take a room. There they would await the arrival of Dimitrios. When the situation had been explained, Dimitrios
would be informed that he would receive instructions as
to the payment of the million francs on the following
morning and told to go. "Mr. Petersen" and "Mr. Smith"
would then leave.

Precautions would now have to be taken to see that
they were not followed and identified. Mr. Peters had
not specified what sort of precautions but had given assurances that there would be no difficulties.

That same evening, a second letter would be posted to
Dimitrios telling him to send a messenger with the million francs, in *mille* notes to a specified point on the road
outside the cemetery of Neuilly at eleven o'clock on the
Friday night. There would be a hired car waiting for
him there with two men in it. The two men would have
been recruited for the purpose by Mr. Peters. Their business would be to pick up the messenger and drive along
the Quai National in the direction of Suresnes until they

were quite sure that they were not being followed and then to make for a point on the Avenue de la Reine near the Porte de St. Cloud where "Mr. Petersen" and "Mr. Smith" would be waiting to receive the money. The two men would then drive the messenger back to Neuilly. The letter would specify that the messenger must be a woman.

Latimer had been puzzled by this last provision. Mr. Peters had justified it by pointing out that if Dimitrios came himself there was just a chance that he might prove too clever for the men in the car and that "Mr. Petersen" and "Mr. Smith" would end up lying in the Avenue de la Reine with bullets in their backs. Descriptions were unreliable and the two men would have no certain means of knowing in the dark if a man presenting himself as the messenger were Dimitrios or not. They could make no such mistake about a woman.

Yes, Latimer reflected, it was absurd to imagine that there could be any danger from Dimitrios. The only thing he had to look forward to was the meeting with this curious man whose path he had stumbled across. It would be strange, after he had heard so much about him, to meet him face to face; strange to see the hand which had packed figs and driven the knife into Sholem's throat, the eyes which Irana Preveza and Wladyslaw Grodek and Mr. Peters had remembered so well. It would be as if a waxwork in a chamber of horrors had come to life.

For a time he stared at the narrow gap between the curtains. It was getting light. Very soon he fell asleep.

He was disturbed towards eleven by a telephone call from Mr. Peters, who said that the letter to Dimitrios had been posted and asked if they could have dinner together "to discuss our plans for to-morrow." Latimer was under the impression that their plans had already been discussed, but he agreed. The afternoon he spent alone at the Vincennes Zoo. The subsequent dinner was tedious. Little was said about their plans, and Latimer concluded that the invitation had been another of Mr. Peters' precautions. He was making sure that his collaborator, who now had no financial interest in the business, had not changed his mind about collaborating.

On the pretext of having a headache, Latimer escaped soon after ten o'clock and went to bed. When he awoke the following morning he actually had a headache and concluded that the carafe burgundy which his host had recommended so warmly at dinner had been even cheaper than it had tasted. As his mind crept slowly back to consciousness he had, too, a feeling that something unpleasant had happened. Then he remembered. Of course! Dimitrios had by now received the first letter.

He sat up in bed to think about it and, after a moment or two, came to the profound conclusion that if it were easy enough to hate and despise blackmailing when one wrote and read about it, the act of blackmailing itself called for rather more moral hardihood, more firmness of purpose, than he, at any rate, possessed. It made no difference to remind oneself that Dimitrios was a criminal. Blackmail was blackmail, just as murder was murder. Macbeth would probably have hesitated at the last minute to kill a criminal Duncan just as much as he hesitated to kill the Duncan whose virtues pleaded like angels. Fortunately, or unfortunately, he, Latimer, had a Lady Macbeth in the person of Mr. Peters. He decided to go out to breakfast.

The day seemed interminable. Mr. Peters had said that he had arrangements to make in connection with the car and the men to drive in it, and that he would meet Latimer at a quarter to eight, after dinner. Latimer spent the morning walking aimlessly in the Bois and, in the afternoon, went to a cinema.

It was toward six o'clock and after he had left the cinema that he began to notice a slight breathless feeling in the region of the solar plexus. It was as if someone had dealt him a light blow there. He concluded that it was Mr. Peters' corrosive burgundy fighting a rearguard action and stopped in one of the cafés on the Champs Elysées for an *infusion*. But the feeling persisted, and he found himself becoming more and more conscious of it. Then, as his gaze rested for a moment on a party of four men and women talking excitedly and laughing over some joke, he realised what was the matter with him. He did not want to meet Mr. Peters. He did not want to go on this blackmailing expedition. He did not want to face a man in whose mind the uppermost thought would be to kill him as quickly and quietly as possible. The trouble was not in his stomach. He had cold feet.

The realisation annoyed him. Why should he be afraid? There was nothing to be afraid of. This man Dimitrios was a clever and dangerous criminal, but he was far from being superhuman. If a man like Peters could . . . but then Peters was used to this sort of thing. He, Latimer, was not. He ought to have gone to the police as soon as he had discovered that Dimitrios was alive and risked being thought a troublesome crank. He should have realised before that, with Mr. Peters' revelations, the whole affair had taken on a completely different complexion. that it

was no longer one in which an amateur criminologist (and
a fiction writer at that) should meddle. You could not
deal with real murderers in this irresponsible fashion.
His bargain with Mr. Peters, for example: what would
an English judge say to that? He could almost hear the
words:

*"As for the actions of this man Latimer, he has given
an explanation of them which you may find difficult to
believe. He is, we have been told, an intelligent man, a
scholar who has held responsible posts in universities in
this country and written works of scholarship. He is,
moreover, a successful author of a type of fiction which,
even if it is properly regarded by the average man as no
more than the pabulum of adolescent minds, has, at least,
the virtue of accepting the proposition that it is the business of right-thinking men and women to assist the police,
should the opportunity present itself, in preventing crime
and in capturing criminals. If you accept Latimer's explanation, you must conclude that he deliberately conspired with Peters to defeat the ends of justice and to act
as an accessory before the fact of the crime of blackmail
for the sole purpose of pursuing researches which he states
had no object other than the satisfaction of his curiosity.
You may ask yourselves if that would not have been the
conduct of a mentally unbalanced child rather than that
of an intelligent man. You must also weigh carefully the
suggestion of the prosecution that Latimer did in fact
share in the proceeds of this blackmailing scheme and that
his explanation is no more than an effort to minimise his
part in the affair."*

No doubt a French judge could make it sound even
worse.

It was still too early for dinner. He left the café and walked in the direction of the Opera. In any case, he reflected, it was too late now to do anything. He was committed to helping Mr. Peters. But was it too late? If he went to the police now, this minute, something could surely be done.

He stopped. This minute! There had been an *agent* sauntering along the street through which he had just come. He retraced his steps. Yes, there was the man, leaning against the wall, swinging his baton and talking to someone inside a doorway. Latimer hesitated again, then crossed the road and asked to be directed to the police *Poste*. It was three streets away, he was told. He set off again.

The entrance to the *Poste* was narrow and almost entirely concealed by a group of three *agents* deep in a conversation which they did not interrupt as they made way for him. Inside was an enamelled plate indicating that inquiries should be made on the first floor and pointing to a flight of stairs with a thin iron banister rail on one side and a wall with a long, greasy stain on it on the other. The place smelt strongly of camphor and faintly of excrement. From a room adjacent to the entrance hall came a murmur of voices and the clacking of a typewriter.

His resolution ebbing with every step, he went up the stairs to a room divided into two by a high wooden counter, the outer edges of which had been worn smooth and shiny by the palms of innumerable hands. Behind the counter a man in uniform was peering with the aid of a hand-mirror into the inside of his mouth.

Latimer paused. He had yet to make up his mind how he was going to begin. If he said: "I was going to blackmail a murderer to-night, but I have decided to hand him over to you instead," there was more than a chance that they would think him mad or drunk. In spite of the urgent need for immediate action, he would have to make some show of beginning at the beginning. "I was in Istanbul some weeks ago and was told of a murder committed there in nineteen twenty-two. Quite by chance, I have found that the man who did it is here in Paris and is being blackmailed." Something like that. The uniformed man caught a glimpse of him in the mirror and turned sharply round.

"What do you want?"

"I should like to see Monsieur le Commissaire."

"What for?"

"I have some information to give him."

The man frowned impatiently. "What information? Please be precise."

"It concerns a case of blackmail."

"You are being blackmailed?"

"No. Someone else is. It is a very complicated and serious affair."

"Your *carte d'identité*, please."

"I have no *carte d'identité*. I am a temporary visitor. I entered France four days ago."

"Your passport, then."

"It is at my hotel."

The man stiffened. The frown of irritation left his face. Here was something that he understood and with which long experience had enabled him to deal. He spoke with easy assurance.

"That is very serious, Monsieur. You realise that? Are you English?"

"Yes."

He drew a deep breath. "You must understand, Monsieur, that your papers must always be in your pocket. It is the law. If you saw a street accident and were required as a witness, the *agent* would ask to see your papers before you were permitted to leave the scene of the accident. If you had not got them, he could, if he wished, arrest you. If you were in a *boîte de nuit* and the police entered to inspect papers, you would certainly be arrested if you carried none. It is the law, you understand? I shall have to take the necessary particulars. Give me your name and that of your hotel, please."

Latimer did so. The man noted them down, picked up a telephone and asked for "*Septième*." There was a pause, then he read out Latimer's name and address and asked for confirmation that they were genuine. There was another pause, of a minute or two this time, before he began to nod his head and say: "*Bien, bien*." Then he listened for a moment, said: "*Oui, c'est ça*," and put the telephone back on its hook. He returned to Latimer.

"It is in order," he said; "but you must present yourself with your passport at the Commissariat of the Seventh Arrondissement within twenty-four hours. As for this complaint of yours, you can make that at the same time. Please remember," he went on tapping his pencil on the counter for emphasis, "that your passport must always be carried. It is obligatory to do so. You are English, and so nothing more need be made of the affair; but you must report to the Commissariat in your arrondissement, and in future always remember to carry your passport. *Au 'voir*, Monsieur." He nodded benevolently with an air of knowing his duty to be well done.

Latimer went out in a very bad temper. Officious ass! But the man was right, of course. It had been absurd of him to go into the place without his passport. Complaint, indeed! In a sense he had had a narrow escape. He might have had to tell his story to the man. He might well have been under arrest by now. As it was, he had not told his story and was still a potential blackmailer.

Yet the visit to the police *Poste* had eased his conscience considerably. He did not feel quite as irresponsible as he had felt before. He had made an effort to bring the police into the affair. It had been an abortive effort; but short of collecting his passport from the other side of Paris and starting all over again (and that, he decided comfortably, was out of the question) there was nothing more he could do. He was due to meet Mr. Peters at a quarter to eight in a café in the Boulevard Hausmann. But by the time he had finished a very light dinner the curious feeling had returned to his solar plexus and the two brandies which he had with his coffee were intended to do more than pass the time. It was a pity, he reflected as he went to keep his appointment, that he could not accept even a small share of the million francs. The cost of satisfying his curiosity was proving, in terms of frayed nerves and an uneasy conscience, practically prohibitive.

Mr. Peters arrived ten minutes late with a large, cheap-looking suit-case and the too matter-of-fact air of a surgeon about to perform a difficult operation. He said, "Ah, Mr. Latimer!" and sitting down at the table, ordered a raspberry liqueur.

"Is everything all right?" Latimer felt that the question was a little theatrical, but he really wanted to know the answer to it.

"So far, yes. Naturally, I have had no word from him because I gave no address. We shall see."

"What have you got in the suit-case?"

"Old newspapers. It is better to arrive at a hotel with a suit-case. I do not wish to have to fill up an *affiche* unless I am compelled to do so. I decided finally upon a hotel near to the Ledru-Rollin Metro. Very convenient."

"Why can't we go by taxi?"

"We shall go by taxi. But," added Mr. Peters significantly, "we shall return by the Metro. You will see." His liqueur arrived. He poured it down his throat, shuddered, licked his lips and said that it was time to go.

The hotel chosen by Mr. Peters for the meeting with Dimitrios was in a street just off the Avenue Ledru. It was small and dirty. A man in his shirt-sleeves came out of a room marked "Bureau," chewing a mouthful of food.

"I telephoned for a room," said Mr. Peters.

"Monsieur Petersen?"

"Yes."

The man looked them both up and down. "It is a large room. Fifteen francs for one. Twenty francs for two. Service, twelve and a half per cent."

"This gentleman is not staying with me."

The man took a key from a rack just inside the Bureau and, taking Mr. Peters' suit-case, led the way upstairs to a room on the second floor. Mr. Peters looked inside it and nodded.

"Yes, this will do. A friend of mine will call for me here soon. Ask him to come up, please."

The man withdrew. Mr. Peters sat on the bed and looked round approvingly. "Quite nice," he said, "and very cheap."

"Yes, it is."

It was a long, narrow room with an old hair carpet, an iron bedstead, a wardrobe, two bent wood chairs, a small table, a screen and an enamelled iron *bidet*. The carpet was red; but by the washbasin was a threadbare patch, black and shiny with use. The wall-paper depicted a trellis supporting a creeping plant, a number of purple discs and some shapeless pink objects of a vaguely clinical character. The curtains were thick and blue and hung on brass rings.

Mr. Peters looked at his watch. "Twenty-five minutes before he is due. We had better make ourselves comfortable. Would you like the bed?"

"No, thank you. I suppose you will do the talking."

"I think it will be best." Mr. Peters drew his Lüger pistol from his breast pocket, examined it to see that it was loaded and then dropped it into the right-hand pocket of his overcoat.

Latimer watched these preparations in silence. He was now feeling quite sick. He said suddenly: "I don't like this."

"Nor do I," said Mr. Peters soothingly; "but we must take precautions. It is unlikely, I think, that they will be needed. You need have no fears."

Latimer remembered an American gangster picture that he had once seen.

"What is to prevent him from walking in here and shooting us both?"

Mr. Peters smiled tolerantly. "Now, now! You must not let your imagination run away with you, Mr. Latimer. Dimitrios would not do that. It would be too noisy and dangerous for him. Remember, the man downstairs will have seen him. Besides, that would not be his way."

"What is his way?"

"Dimitrios is a very cautious man. He thinks very carefully before he acts."

"He has had all day to think carefully."

"Yes, but he does not yet know how much we know, and if anyone else knows what we know. He would have to discover those things. Leave everything to me, Mr. Latimer. I understand Dimitrios."

Latimer was about to point out that Visser had probably had the same idea, and then decided not to do so. He had another, more personal, misgiving to air.

"You said that when Dimitrios paid us the million francs that would be the last he heard of us. Has it occurred to you that he may not be content to let things rest in that way? When he finds that we don't come back for more money he may decide to come after us."

"After Mr. Smith and Mr. Petersen? We should be difficult to find under those names, my dear Mr. Latimer."

"But he knows your face already. He will see mine. He could recognise our faces, whatever we chose to call ourselves."

"But first he would have to find out where we were."

"My photograph has appeared once or twice in newspapers. It may do so again. Or supposing my publisher decided to spread my photograph over the wrapper of a book. Dimitrios might easily happen to see it. There have been stranger coincidences."

Mr. Peters pursed his lips. "I think you exaggerate, but"—he shrugged—"since you feel nervous perhaps you had better keep your face hidden. Do you wear spectacles?"

"For reading."

"Then put them on. Wear your hat, too, and turn up the collar of your coat. You might sit in the corner of the room where it is not so light. In front of the screen. It will blur the outlines of your face. There."

Latimer obeyed. When he was in position, with his collar buttoned across his chin and his hat tilted forward over his eyes, Mr. Peters surveyed him from the door and nodded.

"It will do. I still think it unnecessary; but it will do. After making all these preparations we shall feel very foolish if he does not come."

Latimer, who was feeling very foolish anyway, grunted. "Is there any likelihood of his not coming?"

"Who knows?" Mr. Peters sat on the bed again. "A dozen things might happen to prevent him. He might not, for some reason, have received my letter. He may have left Paris yesterday. But, if he has received the letter, I think that he will come." He looked at his watch again. "Eight forty-five. If he *is* coming, he will soon be here."

They fell silent. Mr. Peters began to trim his nails with a pair of pocket scissors.

Except for the clicking of the scissors and the sound of Mr. Peters' heavy breathing, the silence in the room was complete. To Latimer it seemed almost tangible; a dark grey fluid that oozed from the corners of the room. He began to hear the watch ticking on his wrist. He waited for what seemed an eternity before looking at it. When he did look it was ten minutes to nine. Another eternity. He tried to think of something to say to Mr. Peters to pass the time. He tried counting the complete parallelograms in the pattern of the wall-paper between the wardrobe and the window. Now he thought he could hear Mr. Peters' watch ticking. The muffled sound of someone moving a chair and walking about in the room overhead seemed to intensify the silence. Four minutes to nine.

Then, so suddenly that the sound seemed as loud as a pistol shot, one of the stairs outside the door creaked.

Mr. Peters stopped trimming his nails and, dropping the scissors on the bed, put his right hand in his overcoat pocket.

There was a pause. His heart beating painfully, Latimer gazed rigidly at the door. There was a soft knock.

Mr. Peters stood up and, with his hand still in his pocket, went to the door and opened it.

Latimer saw him stare for a moment into the semi-darkness of the landing and then stand back.

Dimitrios walked into the room.

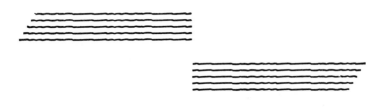

CHAPTER XIV

THE MASK
OF DIMITRIOS

A MAN's features, the bone structure and the tissue which covers it, are the product of a biological process; but his face he creates for himself. It is a statement of his habitual emotional attitude; the attitude which his desires need for their fulfilment and which his fears demand for their protection from prying eyes. He wears it like a devil mask; a device to evoke in others the emotions complementary to his own. If he is afraid, then he must be feared; if he desires, then he must be desired. It is a screen to hide his mind's nakedness. Only a few

247

men, painters, have been able to see the mind through the face. Other men in their judgments reach out for the evidence of word and deed that will explain the mask before their eyes. Yet, though they understand instinctively that the mask cannot be the man behind it, they are generally shocked by a demonstration of the fact. The duplicity of others must always be shocking when one is unconscious of one's own.

So, when at last Latimer saw Dimitrios and tried to read in the face of the man staring across the room at him the evil which he felt should be there, it was of that sense of shock which he was conscious. Hat in hand, in his dark, neat French clothes, with his slim, erect figure and sleek grey hair, Dimitrios was a picture of distinguished respectability.

His distinction was that of a relatively unimportant guest at a large diplomatic reception. He gave the impression of being slightly taller than the one hundred and eighty-two centimetres with which the Bulgarian police had credited him. His skin had the creamy pallor which succeeds in middle age a youthful sallowness. With his high cheekbones, thin nose and beak-like upper lip he might well have been the member of an Eastern European legation. It was only the expression of his eyes that fitted in with any of Latimer's preconceived ideas about his appearance.

They were very brown and seemed at first to be a little screwed up, as if he were short-sighted or worried. But there was no corresponding frown or contraction of the eyebrows; and Latimer saw that the expression of anxiety or short-sightedness was an optical illusion due to the height of the cheekbones and the way the eyes were set in the head. Actually, the face was utterly expressionless, as impassive as that of a lizard.

For a moment the brown eyes rested on Latimer; then, as Mr. Peters closed the door behind him Dimitrios turned his head and said in strongly accented French: "Present me to your friend. I do not think that I have seen him before."

Latimer very nearly jumped. The face of Dimitrios might not be revealing, but the voice certainly was. It was very coarse and sharp, with an acrid quality that made nonsense of any grace implicit in the words it produced. He spoke very softly, and it occurred to Latimer that the man was aware of the ugliness of his voice and tried to conceal it. He failed. Its promise was as deadly as the rattle of a rattlesnake.

"This is Monsieur Smith," said Mr. Peters. "There is a chair behind you. You may sit down."

Dimitrios ignored the suggestion. "Monsieur Smith! An Englishman. It appears that you knew Monsieur Visser."

"I have *seen* Visser."

"That is what we wanted to talk to you about, Dimitrios," said Mr. Peters.

"Yes?" Dimitrios sat down on the spare chair. "Then talk and be quick. I have an appointment to keep. I cannot waste time in this way."

Mr. Peters shook his head sorrowfully. "You have not changed at all, Dimitrios. Always impetuous, always a little unkind. After all these years no word of greeting, no word of regret for all the unhappiness you caused me.

You know, it was most unkind of you to hand us all over to the police like that. We were your friends. Why did you do it?"

"You still talk too much," said Dimitrios. "What is it you want?"

Mr. Peters sat down carefully on the edge of the bed. "Since you insist on making this a purely business meeting—we want money."

The brown eyes flickered towards him. "Naturally. What do you want to give me for it?"

"Our silence, Dimitrios. It is very valuable."

"Indeed? How valuable?"

"It is worth at the very least a million francs."

Dimitrios sat back in the chair and crossed his legs. "And who is going to pay you that for it?"

"You are, Dimitrios. And you are going to be glad to get it so cheaply."

Then Dimitrios smiled.

It was a slow tightening of the small, thin lips; nothing more. Yet there was something inexpressibly savage about it; something that made Latimer feel glad that it was Mr. Peters who had to face it. At that moment, he felt, Dimitrios was far more appropriate to a gathering of man-eating tigers than to a diplomatic reception, however large. The smile faded. "I think," he said, "that you shall tell me now precisely what you mean."

To Latimer, who would, he knew, have responded promptly to the menace in the man's voice, Mr. Peters' bland hesitation was maddeningly reckless. He appeared to be enjoying himself.

"It is so difficult to know where to begin."

There was no reply. Mr. Peters waited for a moment

and then shrugged. "There are," he went on, "so many things that the police would be glad to know. For instance, I might tell them who it was who sent them that dossier in nineteen thirty-one. And it would be such a surprise for them to know that a respectable director of the Eurasian Credit Trust was really the Dimitrios Makropoulos who used to send women to Alexandria."

Latimer thought that he saw Dimitrios relax a little in his chair. "And you expect me to pay you a million francs for that? My good Petersen, you are childish."

Mr. Peters smiled. "Very likely, Dimitrios. You were always inclined to despise my simple approach to the problems of this life of ours. But our silence on those matters would be worth a great deal to you, would it not?"

Dimitrios considered him for a moment. Then: "Why don't you come to the point, Petersen? Or perhaps you are only preparing the way for your Englishman." He turned his head. "What have you to say, Monsieur Smith? Or is neither of you very sure of himself?"

"Petersen is speaking for me," mumbled Latimer. He wished fervently that Mr. Peters would get the business over.

"May I continue?" inquired Mr. Peters.

"Go on."

"The Yugoslav police, too, might be interested in you. If we were to tell them where Monsieur Talat . . ."

"*Par example!*" Dimitrios laughed malignantly. "So Grodek has been talking. Not a sou for that, my friend. Is there any more?"

"Athens, nineteen twenty-two. Does that mean anything to you, Dimitrios? The name was Taladis, if you remember. The charge was robbery and attempted murder. Is that so amusing?"

Into Mr. Peters' face had come the look of unsmiling, adenoidal viciousness that Latimer had seen for a moment or two in Sofia. Dimitrios stared at him unblinkingly. In an instant the atmosphere had become deadly with a naked hatred that to Latimer was quite horrible. He felt as he had once felt when, as a child, he had seen a street fight between two middle-aged men. He saw Mr. Peters draw the Lüger from his pocket and weigh it in his hands.

"You have nothing to say to that, Dimitrios? Then I shall go on. A little earlier that year you murdered a man in Smyrna, a moneylender. What was his name, Monsieur Smith?"

"Sholem."

"Sholem, of course. Monsieur Smith was clever enough to discover that, Dimitrios. A good piece of work, don't you think? Monsieur Smith, you know, is very friendly with the Turkish police; almost, one might say, in their confidence. Do you still think that a million francs is a lot to pay, Dimitrios?"

Dimitrios did not look at either of them. "The murderer of Sholem was hanged," he said slowly.

Mr. Peters raised his eyebrows. "Can that be true, Monsieur Smith?"

"A negro named Dhris Mohammed was hanged for the murder, but he made a confession implicating Monsieur Makropoulos. An order was issued for his arrest in nineteen twenty-four. The charge was murder; for the Turkish police were anxious to catch him for another reason. He had been concerned in an attempt to assassinate Kemal in Adrianople."

"You see, Dimitrios, we are very well informed. Shall we continue?" He paused. Dimitrios still stared straight in front of him. Not a muscle of his face moved. Mr. Peters looked across at Latimer. "Dimitrios is impressed, I think. I feel sure he would like us to continue." He went on.

"Monsieur Smith has told you that he saw Visser. It was in a mortuary in Istanbul that he saw him. As I told you, he is very friendly with the Turkish police, and they showed him the body. They told him that it was the body of a criminal named Dimitrios Makropoulos. It was foolish of them to be so easily deceived, was it not? But even Monsieur Smith was deceived for a while. Fortunately I was able to tell him that Dimitrios was still alive." He paused. "You do not wish to comment? Very well. Perhaps you would like to hear how I discovered where you were and who you were." Another silence. "No? Perhaps you would like to know how I knew that you were in Istanbul at the time poor, silly Visser was killed; or how easily Monsieur Smith was able to identify a photograph of Visser with the dead man he saw in the mortuary." Another silence. "No? Perhaps you would like to be told how easy it would be for us to arouse the interest of the Turkish police in the curious case of a dead murderer who is alive, or of the Greek police in the case of the refugee from Smyrna who left Tabouria so suddenly. I wonder if you are thinking that it would be difficult for us to prove that you *are* Dimitrios Makropoulos, or Taladis, or Talat, or Rougemont, after such a long time has elapsed. Are you thinking that, Dimitrios? You do not wish to answer? Then let me tell you that it would be quite easy for us to prove. I could identify you as Makropoulos, and so could Werner or Lenôtre or Galindo or the Grand Duchess. One of them is sure to be alive and within reach of the police. Any of them would be glad to help to hang you. Monsieur Smith can swear that the man buried in Istanbul is Visser. Then there is the crew of the yacht you chartered in June. They knew that Visser went with you to Istanbul. There is the concièrge in the Avenue de Wagram. He knew you as Rougemont. Your present passport would not be a very good protection to a man with so many false names, would it? And even if you submitted to a little *chantage* from the French and Greek police, Monsieur Smith's Turkish friends would not be as accommodating. Do you think that a million francs is too much to pay for saving you from the hangman, Dimitrios?"

He stopped. For several long seconds Dimitrios continued to stare at the wall. Then at last he stirred and looked at his small gloved hands. His words, when they came, were like stones dropped one by one into a stagnant pool. "I am wondering," he said, "why you ask so little. Is this million all that you are asking?"

Mr. Peters sniggered. "You mean, are we going to the police when we have the million? Oh, no, Dimitrios. We shall be fair with you. This million is only a preliminary gesture of good will. There will be other opportunities for you. But you will not find us greedy."

"I am sure of that. You would not want me to become desperate, I think. Are you the only ones who have this curious delusion that I killed Visser?"

"There is no one else. I shall want the million in *mille* notes to-morrow."

"So soon?"

"You will receive instructions as to how you are to give them to us, by post, in the morning. If the instructions are not followed exactly you will not be given a second chance. The police will be approached immediately. Do you understand?"

"Perfectly."

As Dimitrios stood up an idea seemed to occur to him. He turned to Latimer. "You have been very silent, Monsieur. I wonder if you have been understanding that your life is in your friend Petersen's hands. If, for example, he decided to tell me your real name and where you might be found, I should very likely have you killed."

Mr. Peters showed his white false teeth. "Why should I deprive myself of Monsieur Smith's help? Monsieur Smith is invaluable. He can prove that Visser is dead. Without him you could breathe again."

Dimitrios took no notice of the interruption. "Well, Monsieur Smith?"

Latimer looked up into the brown anxious-seeming eyes and thought of Madame Preveza's phrase. They were certainly the eyes of a man ready to do something that hurt, but they could have belonged to no doctor. There was murder in them.

"I can assure you," he said, "that Petersen has no inducement to kill me. You see . . ."

"You see," put in Mr. Peters quickly, "we are not fools, Dimitrios. You can go now."

"Of course." Dimitrios went towards the door, but at the threshold he paused.

"What is it?" said Mr. Peters.

"I should like to ask Monsieur Smith two questions."

"Well?"

"How was this man whom you took to be Visser dressed when he was found?"

"In a cheap blue serge suit. A French *carte d'identité*, issued at Lyons a year previously, was sewn into the lining. The suit was of Greek manufacture, but the shirt and underwear were French."

"And how was he killed?"

"He had been stabbed in the side and then thrown into the water."

Mr. Peters smiled. "Are you satisfied, Dimitrios?"

Dimitrios stared at him. "Visser," he said slowly, "was too greedy. You will not be too greedy, will you, Petersen?"

Mr. Peters gave him stare for stare. "I shall be very careful," he said. "You have no more questions to ask? Good. You will receive your instructions in the morning."

Dimitrios went without another word. Mr. Peters shut the door, waited a moment or two, then, very gently opened it again. Motioning to Latimer to remain where he was, he disappeared on to the landing. Latimer heard the stairs creak. A minute later he returned.

"He has gone," he announced. "In a few minutes we, too, shall go." He sat down again on the bed, lit one of his cheroots and blew the smoke out as luxuriously as if he had just been released from bondage. His sweet smile came out again like a rose after a storm. "Well," he said, "that was Dimitrios about whom you have heard such a great deal. What did you think of him?"

"I didn't know what to think. Perhaps, if I had not known so much about him, I should have disliked him less. I don't know. It is difficult to be reasonable about a man who is obviously wondering how quickly he can murder you." He hesitated. "I did not realise that you hated him so much."

Mr. Peters did not smile. "I assure you, Mr. Latimer, that it was a surprise to me to realise it. I did not like him. I did not trust him. After the way he betrayed us all, that was understandable. It was not until I saw him in this room just now that I realised that I hated him enough to kill him. If I were a superstitious man, I should wonder if perhaps the spirit of poor Visser had entered into me." He stopped, then added "*Salop!*" under his breath. He was silent for a moment. Then he looked up. "Mr. Latimer, I must make an admission. I must tell you that even if you had agreed to the offer I made you, you would not have received your half million. I should not have paid you." He shut his mouth tightly as if he were prepared to receive a blow.

"So I imagine," said Latimer dryly. "I very nearly accepted the offer just to see how you would cheat me. I take it that you would have made the real time for the delivery of the money an hour or so earlier than you would have told me, and that, by the time I arrived on the scene, you and the money would have gone. Was that it?"

Mr. Peters winced. "It was very wise of you not to trust me, but very unkind. But I suppose that I cannot blame you. But it was not to abase myself that I admitted to having tried to deceive you. It was to defend myself. I would like to ask you a question."

"Well?"

"Was it—forgive me—was it the thought that I might betray you to Dimitrios that made you refuse my offer to share the money with you?"

"It never occurred to me."

"I am glad," said Mr. Peters solemnly. "I should not like you to think that of me. You may dislike me, but I should not care to be thought cold-blooded. I may tell you that the thought did not occur to me either. There you see Dimitrios! We have discussed this matter, you and I. We have mistrusted one another and looked for betrayal. Yet it is Dimitrios who puts this thought in our heads. I have met many wicked and violent men, Mr. Latimer, but I tell you that Dimitrios is unique. Why do you think he suggested to you that I might betray you?"

"I imagine that he was acting on the principle that the best way to fight two allies is to get them to fight each other."

Mr. Peters smiled. "No, Mr. Latimer. That would have been too obvious a trick for Dimitrios. He was suggesting to you in a very delicate way that *I* was the unnecessary partner and that you could remove me very easily by telling him where I could be found."

"Do you mean that he was offering to kill you for me?"

"Exactly. He would have only you to deal with then. He does not know, of course," added Mr. Peters thoughtfully, "that you do not know his present name." He stood up and put on his hat. "No, Mr. Latimer, I do not like Dimitrios. Do not misunderstand me, please. I have no moral rectitude. But Dimitrios is a savage beast. Even now, though I know that I have taken every precaution, I am afraid. I shall take his million and go. If I could allow you to hand him over to the police when I have done with him, I would do so. He would not hesitate if the situation were reversed. But it is impossible."

"Why?"

Mr. Peters looked at him curiously. "Dimitrios seems to have had a strange effect on you. No, to tell the police afterwards would be too dangerous. If we were asked to explain the million francs—and we could not expect Dimitrios to remain silent about them—we should be embarrassed. A pity. Shall we go now? I shall leave the money for the room on the table. They can take the suitcase for a *pourboire*."

They went downstairs in silence. As they deposited the key, the man in his shirt-sleeves appeared with an *affiche* for Mr. Peters to complete. Mr. Peters waved him away. He would, he said, fill it in when he returned.

In the street he halted and faced Latimer.

"Have you ever been followed?"

"Not to my knowledge."

"Then you will be followed now. I do not suppose that Dimitrios had any real hope of our leading him to our homes, but he was always thorough." He glanced over Latimer's shoulder. "Ah, yes. He was there when we arrived. Do not look round, Mr. Latimer. A man wearing a grey mackintosh and a dark soft hat. You will see him in a minute."

The hollow feeling which had disappeared with the departure of Dimitrios jolted back into its position in Latimer's stomach. "What are we to do?"

"Return by Metro, as I said before."

"What good will that do?"

"You will see in a minute."

The Ledru-Rollin Metro station was about a hundred yards away. As they walked toward it the muscles in Latimer's calves tightened and he had a ridiculous desire to run. He felt himself walking stiffly and self-consciously.

"Do not look round," said Mr. Peters again.

They walked down the steps to the Metro. "Keep close to me now," said Mr. Peters.

He bought two second-class tickets and they walked on down the tunnel in the direction of the trains.

It was a long tunnel. As they pushed their way through the spring barriers, Latimer felt that he could reasonably glance behind him. He did so, and caught a glimpse of a shabby young man in a grey raincoat about thirty feet behind them. Now the tunnel split into two. One way was labelled: "*Direction* Pte. de Charenton," the other: "*Direction* Balard." Mr. Peters stopped.

"It would be wise now," he said, "if we appeared to be about to take leave of one another." He glanced out of the corners of his eyes. "Yes, he has stopped. He is wondering what is going to happen. Talk, please, Mr. Latimer, but not too loudly. I want to listen."

"Listen to what?"

"The trains. I spent half an hour here listening to them this morning."

"What on earth for? I don't see . . ."

Mr. Peters gripped his arm and he stopped. In the distance he could hear the rumble of an approaching train.

"*Direction* Balard," muttered Mr. Peters suddenly. "Come along. Keep close to me and do not walk too quickly."

They went on down the right-hand tunnel. The rumble of the train grew louder. They rounded a bend in the tunnel. Ahead was the green automatic gate.

"*Vite!*" cried Mr. Peters.

The train was by now almost in the station. The automatic door began to swing slowly across the entrance to the platform. As Latimer reached it and passed through with about three inches to spare, he heard, above the hiss and screech of pneumatic brakes, the sound of running feet. He looked round. Although Mr. Peters' stomach had suffered some compression, he had squeezed himself through on to the platform. But the man in the grey raincoat had, in spite of his last-minute sprint, left it too late. He now stood, red in the face with anger, shaking his fists at them from the other side of the automatic gate.

They got into the train a trifle breathlessly.

"Excellent!" puffed Mr. Peters happily. "Now do you see what I meant, Mr. Latimer?"

"Very ingenious."

The noise of the train made further conversation impossible.

Mr. Peters touched his arm. They were at Chatelet. They got out and took the Porte d'Orléans *correspond-ance* to St. Placide. As they walked down the Rue de Rennes, Mr. Peters hummed softly. They passed a café.

Mr. Peters stopped humming. "Would you like some coffee, Mr. Latimer?"

"No, thanks. What about your letter to Dimitrios?"

Mr. Peters tapped his pocket. "It is already written. Eleven o'clock is the time. The junction of the Avenue de la Reine and the Boulevard Jean Jaurès is the place. Would you like to be there, or are you leaving Paris tomorrow?" And then, without giving Latimer a chance to reply: "I shall be sorry to say good-bye to you, Mr. Latimer. I find you so sympathetic. Our association has, on the whole, been most agreeable. It has also been profitable to me." He sighed. "I feel a little guilty, Mr. Latimer. You have been so patient and helpful and yet you go un-rewarded. You would not," he inquired a trifle anxiously, "accept a thousand francs of the money? It would help to pay your expenses."

"No, thank you."

"No, of course not. Then, at least, Mr. Latimer, let me give you a glass of wine. That is it! A celebration! Come, Mr. Latimer. There is no taste in nothing. Let us collect the money together to-morrow night. You will have the satisfaction of seeing a little blood squeezed from this swine Dimitrios. Then we will celebrate with a glass of wine. What do you say to that?"

They had stopped at the corner of the street which contained the Impasse. Latimer looked into Mr. Peters' watery eyes. "I should say," he said deliberately, "that you are wondering if there is a chance that Dimitrios might decide to call your bluff and thinking that it might be a good idea to have me in Paris until you have the money actually in your pocket."

Mr. Peters' eyes slowly closed. "Mr. Latimer," he said bitterly, "I did not think . . . I would not have thought that you could have put such a construction on . . ."

"All right, I'll stay." Irritably, Latimer interrupted him. He had wasted so many days: another one would make no difference. "I'll come with you to-morrow, but only on these conditions. The wine must be champagne; it must come from France, not Meknes, and it must be a vintage *cuvée* of either nineteen nineteen, twenty or twenty-one. A bottle," he added vindictively, "will cost you at least one hundred francs."

Mr. Peters opened his eyes. He smiled bravely. "You shall have it, Mr. Latimer," he said.

CHAPTER XV

THE STRANGE TOWN

M̲ʀ. Pᴇᴛᴇʀs and Latimer took up their positions at the corner of the Avenue de la Reine and the Boulevard Jean Jaurès at half-past ten, the hour at which the hired car was due to pick up the messenger from Dimitrios opposite the Neuilly cemetery.

It was a cold night, and as it began to rain soon after they arrived, they stood for shelter just inside the *porte cochère* of a building a few yards along the Avenue in the direction of the Pont St. Cloud.

"How long will they be getting here?" Latimer asked.

"I said that I would expect them by eleven. That gives them half an hour to drive from Neuilly. They could do it in less, but I told them to make quite certain that they were not followed. If they are in doubt they will return to Neuilly. They will take no chances. The car is a Renault *coupé-de-ville*. We must have patience."

They waited in silence. Now and again Mr. Peters would stir as a car that might have been the hired Renault approached from the direction of the river. The rain trickling down the slope formed by the subsidence of the cobbles formed puddles about their feet.

Suddenly Mr. Peters grunted: *"Attention!"*

"Are they coming?"

"Yes."

Latimer looked over Mr. Peters' shoulder. A large Renault was approaching from the left. As he looked it began to slow down as if the driver were uncertain of the way. It passed them, the rain glistening in the beams of the headlights, and stopped a few yards farther on. The outline of the driver's head and shoulders were just visible in the darkness, but blinds were pulled down over the rear windows. Mr. Peters put his hand in his overcoat pocket.

"Wait here, please," he said to Latimer, and walked towards the car.

"Ca va?" Latimer heard him say to the driver. There was an answering *"Oui."* Mr. Peters opened the rear door and leaned forward.

Almost immediately he withdrew a pace and closed the door. In his left hand was a package. *"Attendez,"* he said, and walked back to where Latimer was standing.

"All right?" said Latimer.

"I think so. Will you strike a match, please?"

Latimer did so. The package was the size of a large

book, about two inches thick and was wrapped in blue paper and tied with string. Mr. Peters tore away the paper at one of the corners and exposed a solid wad of *mille* notes. He sighed. "Beautiful!"

"Aren't you going to count them?"

"That pleasure," said Mr. Peters seriously, "I shall reserve for the comfort of my home." He crammed the package into his overcoat pocket, stepped on to the pavement and raised his hand. The Renault started with a jerk, swung round in a wide circle and splashed away on its return journey. Mr. Peters watched it go with a smile.

"A very pretty woman," he said. "I wonder who she can be. But I prefer the million francs. Now, Mr. Latimer, a taxi and then your favourite champagne. We have earned it, I think."

They found a taxi near the Porte de St. Cloud. Mr. Peters enlarged on his success.

"With a type like Dimitrios it is necessary only to be firm and circumspect. We put the matter to him squarely; we let him see that he has no choice but to agree to our demands, and it is done. A million francs. Very nice! One almost wishes that one had demanded two million. But it would have been unwise to be too greedy. As it is, he believes that we shall make fresh demands and that he has time to deal with us as he dealt with Visser. He will find that he has deceived himself. This is very satisfactory to me, Mr. Latimer: as satisfying to my pride as it is to my pocket. I feel, too, that I have, in some measure, avenged poor Visser's death. I have suffered. Now I have my reward." He patted his pocket. "It would be amusing to see Dimitrios when at last he realises how he has been tricked. A pity that we shall not be there."

"Shall you leave Paris immediately?"

"I think so. I have a fancy to see something of South America. Not my own adopted fatherland, of course. It is one of the terms of my citizenship that I never enter the country. A hard condition, for I would like for sentimental reasons to see the country of my adoption. But it cannot be altered. I am a citizen of the world and must remain so. Perhaps I shall buy an estate somewhere, a place where I shall be able to pass my days in peace when I am old. You are a young man, Mr. Latimer. When one is my age, the years seem shorter and one feels that one is soon to reach a destination. It is as if one were approaching a strange town late at night when one is sorry to be leaving the warm train for an unknown hotel and wishing that the journey would never end."

He glanced out of the window. "We are nearly home. I have your champagne. It was, as you warned me, very expensive. But I have no priggish objections to a little luxury. It is sometimes agreeable and, even when it is disagreeable, it serves to make us appreciate simplicity. Ah!" The taxi had stopped at the end of the Impasse. "I have no change, Mr. Latimer. That seems odd with a million francs in one's pocket, does it not? Will you pay, please?"

They walked down the Impasse.

"I think," said Mr. Peters, "that I shall sell these houses before I go to South America. One does not want property on one's hands that is not yielding a profit."

"Won't they be rather difficult to sell? The view from the windows is a little depressing, isn't it?"

"It is not necessary to be always looking out of the windows. They could be made into very nice houses."

They began the long climb up the stairs. On the second

landing Mr. Peters paused for breath, took off his overcoat and got out his keys. They continued the climb to
his door.

He opened it, switched on the light, and then, going
straight to the largest divan, took the package from his
overcoat pocket and undid the string. With loving care
he extracted the notes from the wrappings and held them
up. For once his smile was real.

"There, Mr. Latimer! A million francs! Have you ever
seen so much money at once before? Nearly six thousand
English pounds!" He stood up. "But we must have our
little celebration. Take off your coat and I will get the
champagne. I hope that you will like it. I have no ice,
but I put it in a bowl of water. It will be quite cool."

He walked towards the curtained-off part of the room.

Latimer had turned away to take off his coat. Suddenly
he became aware that Mr. Peters was still on the same side
of the curtain and that he was standing motionless. He
glanced round.

For a moment he thought that he was going to faint.
The blood seemed to drain away suddenly from his head,
leaving it hollow and light. A steel band seemed to tighten
round his chest. He felt that he wanted to cry out, but all
he could do was to stare.

Mr. Peters was standing with his back to him, and his
hands were raised above his head. Facing him in the gap
between the gold curtains was Dimitrios, with a revolver
in his hand.

Dimitrios stepped forward and sideways so that Latimer was no longer partly covered by Mr. Peters. Latimer
dropped his coat and put up his hands. Dimitrios raised
his eyebrows.

"It is not flattering," he said, "for you to look so surprised to see me, Petersen. Or should I call you Caillé?"

Mr. Peters said nothing. Latimer could not see his face, but he saw his throat move as if he were swallowing.

The brown eyes flickered to Latimer. "I am glad that the Englishman is here, too, Petersen. I am saved the trouble of persuading you to give me his name and address. Monsieur Smith, who knows so many things and who was so anxious to keep his face hidden, is now shown to be as easy to deal with as you are, Petersen. You were always too ingenious, Petersen. I told you so once before. It was on the occasion when you brought a coffin from Salonika. You remember? Ingenuity is never a substitute for intelligence, you know. Did you really think that I should not see through you?" His lips twisted. "Poor Dimitrios! He is very simple. He will think that I, clever Petersen, will come back for more, like any other blackmailer. He will not guess that I may be bluffing him. But, just to make sure that he does not guess, I will do what no other blackmailer ever did. I will tell him that I *shall* come back for more. Poor Dimitrios is such a fool that he will believe me. Poor Dimitrios has no intelligence. Even if he finds out from the records that, within a month of my coming out of prison, I had succeeded in selling three unsaleable houses to someone named Caillé, he will not dream of suspecting that I, clever Petersen, am also Caillé. Did you not know, Petersen, that before I bought these houses in your name they had been empty for ten years? You are such a fool."

He paused. The anxious brown eyes narrowed. The mouth tightened. Latimer knew that Dimitrios was going to kill Mr. Peters and that there was nothing that he could do about it. The wild beating of his heart seemed to be suffocating him.

"Drop the money, Petersen."

The wad of notes hit the carpet and spread out like a fan.

Dimitrios raised the revolver.

Suddenly, Mr. Peters seemed to realise what was about to happen. He cried out: "No! You must . . ."

Then Dimitrios fired. He fired twice and with the ear-splitting noise of the explosions Latimer heard one of the bullets thud into Mr. Peters' body.

Mr. Peters emitted a long-drawn-out retching sound and sank forward on to his hands and knees with blood pouring from his neck.

Dimitrios stared at Latimer. "Now you," he said.

At that moment Latimer jumped.

Why he chose that particular moment to jump he never knew. He never even knew what prompted him to jump at all. He supposed that it was an instinctive attempt to save himself. Why, however, his instinct for self-preservation should have led him to jump in the direction of the revolver which Dimitrios was about to fire is inexplicable. But he did jump, and the jump did save his life; for, as his right foot left the floor, a fraction of a second before Dimitrios pressed the trigger, he stumbled over one of Mr. Peters' thick tufts of rug and the shot went over his head into the wall.

Half dazed and with his forehead scorched by the blast from the muzzle of the revolver, he hurled himself at Dimitrios. They went down together with their hands at each other's throats, but immediately Dimitrios brought his knee up into Latimer's stomach and rolled clear of him.

He had dropped his revolver, and now he went to pick it up. Gasping for breath, Latimer scrambled towards the nearest movable object, which happened to be the heavy brass tray on top of one of the Moroccan tables, and flung it at Dimitrios. The edge of it hit the side of his head as he was reaching for the revolver and he reeled; but the blow stopped him for barely a second. Latimer threw the wooden part of the table at him and dashed forward. Dimitrios staggered back as the table caught his shoulder. The next moment Latimer had the revolver and was standing back, still trying to get his breath, but with his finger on the trigger.

His face sheet-white, Dimitrios came towards him. Latimer raised the revolver.

"If you move again, I shall fire."

Dimitrios stood still. His brown eyes stared into Latimer's. His grey hair was tousled; his scarf had come out of his coat; he looked dangerous. Latimer was beginning to recover his breath, but his knees felt horribly weak, his ears were singing and the air he breathed reeked sickeningly of cordite fumes. It was for him to make the next move, and he felt frightened and helpless.

"If you move," he repeated, "I shall fire."

He saw the brown eyes flicker towards the notes on the floor and then back to him. "What are you going to do?" said Dimitrios suddenly. "If the police come we shall both have something to explain. If you shoot me you will get only that million. If you will release me I will give you another million as well. That would be good for you."

Latimer took no notice. He edged sideways towards the wall, until he could glance quickly at Mr. Peters.

Mr. Peters had crawled towards the divan on which his overcoat lay, and was now leaning against it with his eyes half closed. He was breathing stertorously through the mouth. One bullet had torn a great gaping wound in the side of his neck from which the blood was welling. The second had hit him full in the chest and scorched the clothing. The wound was a round purple mess about two inches in diameter. It was bleeding very little. Mr. Peters' lips moved.

Keeping his eyes fixed on Dimitrios, Latimer moved round until he was alongside Mr. Peters.

"How do you feel?" he said.

It was a stupid question, and he knew it the moment the words had left his mouth. He tried desperately to collect his wits. A man had been shot and he had the man who shot him. He . . .

"My pistol," muttered Mr. Peters; "get my pistol. Overcoat." He said something else that was inaudible.

Cautiously, Latimer worked his way round to the overcoat and fumbled for the pistol. Dimitrios watched with a thin ghastly smile on his lips. Latimer found the pistol and handed it to Mr. Peters. He grasped it with both hands and snicked back the safety catch.

"Now," he muttered, "go and get police."

"Someone will have heard the shots," said Latimer soothingly. "The police will be here soon."

"Won't find us," whispered Mr. Peters. "Get police."

Latimer hesitated. What Mr. Peters said was true. The Impasse was hemmed in by blank walls. The shots might have been heard, but unless someone had happened to be passing the entrance to the Impasse during the few seconds in which they were fired, nobody would know where the sounds had come from.

"All right," he said. "Where is the telephone?"

"No telephone."

"But . . ." He hesitated again. It might take ten minutes to find a policeman. Could he leave a badly wounded Mr. Peters to watch a man like Dimitrios? But there was nothing else for it. Mr. Peters needed a doctor. The sooner Dimitrios was under lock and key the better. He knew that Dimitrios understood his predicament and the knowledge did not please him. He glanced at Mr. Peters. He had the Lüger resting on one knee and pointed at Dimitrios. The blood was still pouring from his neck. If a doctor did not attend to him soon he would bleed to death.

"All right," he said. "I'll be as quick as I can."

He went towards the door.

"One moment, Monsieur." There was an urgency in the harsh voice that made Latimer pause.

"Well?"

"If you go he will shoot me. Don't you see that? Why not accept my offer?"

Latimer opened the door. "If you try any tricks you will certainly be shot." He looked again at the wounded man, huddled over the Lüger. "I shall be back with the police. Don't shoot unless you have to."

Then, as he made to go, Dimitrios laughed. Involuntarily, Latimer turned. "I should save that laugh for the executioner," he snapped. "You will need it."

"I was thinking," said Dimitrios, "that in the end one is always defeated by stupidity. If it is not one's own it is the stupidity of others." His face changed. "Five million, monsieur," he shouted angrily. "Is it not enough or do you want this carrion to kill me?"

Latimer stared at him for a moment. The man was almost convincing. Then he remembered that others had been convinced by Dimitrios. He waited no longer. He heard Dimitrios shout something after him as he shut the door.

He was half-way down the stairs when he heard the shots. There were four of them. Three cracked out in quick succession. Then, there was a pause before the last one. His heart in his mouth, he turned and ran back up to the room. It was only later that he found anything curious in the fact that, as he raced up the stairs, the fear uppermost in his mind was for Mr. Peters.

Dimitrios was not a pleasant sight. Only one of the bullets from Mr. Peters' Lüger had missed. Two had lodged in the body. The fourth, evidently fired at him after he had fallen to the floor, had hit him between the eyes and almost blown the top of his head off. His body was still twitching.

The Lüger slipped from Mr. Peters' fingers and he was leaning, with his head on the edge of the divan, opening and shutting his mouth like a stranded fish. As Latimer stood there he choked suddenly and blood trickled from his mouth.

Scarcely knowing what he was doing, Latimer blundered through the curtain. Dimitrios was dead; Mr. Peters was dying; and all he, Latimer, could think about was the effort required not to faint or vomit. He strove to pull himself together. He must do something. Mr. Peters must have water. Wounded men always needed water. There was a wash-basin and beside it were some glasses. He filled one and carried it back into the room.

Mr. Peters had not moved. His mouth and eyes were open. Latimer knelt down beside him and poured a little water into the mouth. It ran out again. He put down the glass and felt for the pulse. There was none.

Latimer got quickly to his feet and looked at his hands. There was blood on them. He went back to the wash-basin, rinsed them and dried them on a small, dirty towel which hung from a hook.

He should, he knew, call the police immediately. Two men had killed each other. That was a matter for the police. Yet . . . what was he going to say to them? How was he going to explain his own presence there in that shambles? Could he say that he had been passing the end of the Impasse and had heard the shots? But someone might have noticed him with Mr. Peters. There was the taxi-driver who had brought them. And when they found that Dimitrios had that day obtained a million francs from his bank . . . there would be endless questionings. Supposing they suspected him.

His brain seemed to clear suddenly. He must get out at once and he must leave no traces of his presence there. He thought quickly. The revolver in his pocket belonged to Dimitrios. It had his finger-prints on it. He took it out of his pocket, put on his gloves and wiped it all over carefully with his handkerchief. Then, setting his teeth, he went back into the room, knelt down beside Dimitrios and, taking his right hand, pressed the fingers round the butt and trigger. Removing the fingers and holding the revolver by the barrel, he then put it near the body on the floor.

He considered the *mille* notes strewn over the rug like so much waste-paper. To whom did they belong—Dimitrios or Mr. Peters? There was Sholem's money there and the money stolen in Athens in nineteen twenty-two. There was the fee for helping to assassinate Stambulisky and the money of which Madame Preveza had been cheated. There was the price of the charts Bulić had stolen and part of the profits from the white slave and drug traffics. To whom did it belong? Well, the police would decide. Best to leave it as it was. It would give them something to think about.

There was, however, the glass of water. It must be emptied, dried and replaced with the other glasses. He looked round. Was there anything else? No. Nothing at all? Yes, one thing. His finger-prints were on the tray and the table. He wiped them. Nothing more? Yes. Finger-prints on the door-knobs. He wiped them. Anything else? No. He carried the glass to the wash-basin. The glass dried and replaced, he turned to go. It was then that he noticed the champagne which Mr. Peters had bought for their celebration standing in a bowl of water. It was a Verzy 1921—a half-bottle.

No one saw him leave the Impasse. He went to a café in the Rue de Rennes and ordered a cognac.

Now he began to tremble from head to foot. He had been a fool. He ought to have gone to the police. It was still not too late to go to them. Supposing the bodies remained undiscovered. They might lie there for weeks in that ghastly room with the blue walls and gold stars and rugs, while the blood congealed and hardened and collected dust and the flesh began to rot. It was horrible to think of. If only there were some way of telling the police. An anonymous letter would be too dangerous. The police would know immediately that a third person had been concerned in the affair and would not be satisfied with the simple explanation that the two men had killed each other. Then he had an idea. The main thing was to get the police to the house. Why they went was unimportant.

There was an evening paper in the rack. He took it to his table and read it through feverishly. There were two news items in it which suited his purpose. One was a report of the theft of some valuable furs from a warehouse in the Avenue de la Republique; the other was an account of the smashing of the shop window of a jeweller in the Avenue de Clichy and the escape of two men with a tray of rings.

He decided that the first would suit his purpose best, and, summoning the waiter, ordered another cognac together with writing materials. He drank the brandy at a gulp and put his gloves on. Then, taking a sheet of the letter paper, he examined it carefully. It was ordinary, cheap café notepaper. Having satisfied himself that there was no distinguishing mark of any kind on it, he wrote across the middle of it in capital letters: "FAITES DES ENQUETES SUR CAILLE—3, IMPASSE DES HUITS ANGES." Then he tore the report of the fur robbery out of the paper, folded it inside the note and put the two in an envelope, which he addressed to the Commissaire of Police of the Seventh Arrondissement. Leaving the café, he bought a stamp at a tobacco kiosk and posted the letter.

It was not until four o'clock that morning, when he had lain awake in bed for two hours, that the nerves of his stomach succumbed at last to the strain which had been put upon them and he was sick.

Two days later a paragraph appeared in three of the Paris morning papers saying that the body of a South American named Frederik Peters, together with that of a man, at present unidentified, but believed to be a South American also, had been found in an apartment off the Rue de Rennes. Both men, the paragraph continued, had been shot and it was thought that they had killed one another in a revolver fight following a quarrel over money, a considerable sum of which was found in the apartment. It was the only reference to the affair, the attention of the public being divided at the time between a new international crisis and a hatchet murder in the suburbs.

Latimer did not see the paragraph until several days later.

Soon after nine o'clock on the morning of the day on which the police received his note, he left his hotel for the Gare de l'Est and the Orient express. A letter had arrived for him by the first post. It had a Bulgarian stamp and a Sofia postmark and was obviously from Marukakis. He put it in his pocket unread. It was not until later in the day, when the express was racing through the hills west of Belfort, that he remembered it. He opened it and began to read:

My Dear Friend,

Your letter delighted me. I was so pleased to get it. I was also a little surprised, for—forgive me, please—I did not seriously expect you to succeed in the difficult task which you had set yourself. The years bury so much of our wisdom that they are bound to bury most of our folly with it. Some time I hope to hear from you how a folly buried in Belgrade comes to be unearthed in Geneva.

I was interested in the reference to the Eurasian Credit Trust. Here is something that will interest you.

There has been recently, as you may know, a great deal of tension between this country and Yugoslavia. The Serbs, you know, have reason to feel tense. If Germany and vassal Hungary attacked her from the north, Italy attacked her through Albania from the south and by sea from the west, and Bulgaria attacked her from the east, she would be quickly finished. Her only chance would lie in the Russians outflanking the Germans and Hungarians with an attack launched through Rumania along the Bukovina railway. But has Bulgaria anything to fear from Yugoslavia? Is she a danger to Bulgaria? The idea is absurd. Yet, for the past three months or four, there has been here a stream of propaganda to the effect that Yugoslavia is planning to attack Bulgaria. "The menace across the frontier" is a typical phrase.

If such things were not so dangerous one would laugh. But one recognizes the technique. Such propaganda always begins with words but soon it proceeds to deeds. When there are no facts to support lies, facts must be made.

Two weeks ago there took place the inevitable frontier incident. Some Bulgarian peasants were fired upon by Yugoslavs (alleged to be soldiers), and one of the peasants was killed. There is much popular indignation, an outcry against the devilish Serbs. The newspaper offices are very busy. A week later the Government announces fresh purchases of anti-aircraft guns to strengthen the defences of the western Provinces. The purchases are made from a Belgian firm with the help of a loan negotiated by the Eurasian Credit Trust.

Yesterday a curious news item comes into this office.

As a result of careful investigations by the Yugoslav Government, it is shown that the four men who fired on the peasants were not Yugoslav soldiers, nor even Yugoslav subjects. They were of various nationalities and two had previously been imprisoned in Poland for terrorist activities. They had been paid to create the incident by a man about whom none of them knows anything more than that he came from Paris.

But there is more. Within an hour of that news item reaching Paris, I had instructions from the head office there to suppress the item and send out a *démenti* to all subscribers taking our French news. That is amusing, is it not? One would not have thought that such a rich organisation as the Eruasian Credit Trust would be so sensitive.

As for your Dimitrios: what can one say?

A writer of plays once said that there are some situations that one cannot use on the stage; situations in which the audience can feel neither approval or disapproval, sympathy or antipathy; situations out of which there is no possible way that is not humiliating or distressing and from which there is no truth, however bitter, to be extracted. He was, you may say, one of those unhappy men who are confounded by the difference between the stupid vulgarities of real life and the ideal existence of the imagination. That may be. Yet, I have been wondering if, for once, I do not find myself in sympathy with him. Can one explain Dimitrios or must one turn away disgusted and defeated? I am tempted to find reason and justice in the fact that he died as violently and indecently as he lived. But that is too ingenuous a way out. It does not explain Dimitrios; it only apologises for him. Special sorts of conditions must exist for the creation of the special sort of criminal that he typified. I have tried to define those conditions—but unsuccessfully. All I do know is that while might is right, while chaos and anarchy masquerade as order and enlightenment, those conditions will obtain.

What is the remedy? But I can see you yawning and remember that if I bore you you will not write to me again and tell me whether you are enjoying your stay in Paris, whether you have found any more Bulićs or Prevezas and whether we shall see you soon in Sofia. My latest information is that war will not break out until the spring; so there will be time for some ski-ing. Late January is quite good here. The roads are terrible, but the runs, when one gets to them, are quite good. I shall look forward eagerly to learning from you when you will come.

With my most sincere regards

N. Marukakis.

Latimer folded the letter and put it in his pocket. A good fellow, Marukakis! He must write to him when he had the time. But just at the moment there were more important matters to be considered.

He needed, and badly, a motive, a neat method of committing a murder and an entertaining crew of suspects. Yes, the suspects must certainly be entertaining. His last book had been a trifle heavy. He must inject a little more humour into this one. As for the motive, money was always, of course, the soundest basis. A pity that Wills and life insurance were so outmoded. Supposing a man murdered an old lady so that his wife should have a private income. It might be worth thinking about. The scene? Well, there was always plenty of fun to be got out of an English country village, wasn't there? The time? Summer; with cricket matches on the village green, garden parties at the vicarage, the clink of tea-cups and the sweet smell of grass on a July evening. That was the sort of thing people liked to hear about. It was the sort of thing that he himself would like to hear about.

He looked out of the window. The sun had gone and the hills were receding slowly into the night sky. They would be slowing down for Belfort soon. Two more days to go! He ought to get some sort of a plot worked out in that time.

The train ran into a tunnel.

Journey into Fear

FOR LOUISE

Verily I have seene divers become mad and senseless for feare: yea and in him, who is most settled and best resolved, it is certaine that whilest his fit continueth, it begetteth many strange dazelings, and terrible amazements in him.

MONTAIGNE

JOURNEY INTO FEAR

CHAPTER ONE

THE STEAMER, *Sestri Levante*, stood high above the dock side, and the watery sleet, carried on the wind blustering down from the Black Sea, had drenched even the small shelter deck. In the after well the Turkish stevedores, with sacking tied round their shoulders, were still loading cargo.

Graham saw the steward carry his suit-case through a door marked PASSEGGIERI, and turned aside to see if the two men who had shaken hands with him at the foot of the gangway were still there. They had not come aboard lest the uniform of one of them should draw attention to him. Now they were walking away across the crane lines towards the warehouses and the dock gates beyond. As they reached the shelter of the first shed they looked back. He raised his left arm and saw an answering wave. They walked on out of sight.

For a moment he stood there shivering and staring out of the mist that shrouded the domes and spires of Stambul. Behind the rumble and clatter of the winches, the

3

Turkish foreman was shouting plaintively in bad Italian to one of the ship's officers. Graham remembered that he had been told to go to his cabin and stay there until the ship sailed. He followed the steward through the door.

The man was waiting for him at the head of a short flight of stairs. There was no sign of any of the nine other passengers.

"*Cinque, signore?*"

"Yes."

"*Da queste parte.*"

Graham followed him below.

Number five was a small cabin with a single bunk, a combined wardrobe and washing cabinet, and only just enough floor space left over to take him and his suit-case. The port-hole fittings were caked with verdigris, and there was a strong smell of paint. The steward man-handled the suit-case under the bunk, and squeezed out into the alley-way.

"*Favorisca di darmi il suo biglietto ed il suo passaporto, signore. Li portero al Commissario.*"

Graham gave him the ticket and passport, and, pointing to the port-hole, made the motions of unscrewing and opening it.

The steward said, "*Subito, signore,*" and went away.

Graham sat down wearily on the bunk. It was the first time for nearly twenty-four hours that he had been left alone to think. He took his right hand carefully out of his overcoat pocket, and looked at the bandages swathed round it. It throbbed and ached abominably. If that was what a bullet graze felt like, he thanked his stars that the bullet had not really hit him.

He looked round the cabin, accepting his presence in it as he had accepted so many other absurdities since he had returned to his hotel in Pera the night before. The acceptance was unquestioning. He felt only as if he had lost something valuable. In fact, he had lost nothing of any value but a sliver of skin and cartilage from the back of his right hand. All that had happened to him was that he had discovered the fear of death.

By the husbands of his wife's friends, Graham was considered lucky. He had a highly paid job with a big armaments manufacturing concern, a pleasant house in the country an hour's drive from his office, and a wife whom everyone liked. Not that he didn't deserve it all. He was, though you would never think it to look at him, a brilliant engineer; quite an important one if some of the things you heard were true; something to do with guns. He went abroad a good deal on business. He was a quiet, likeable sort of chap, and generous with his whisky. You couldn't, of course, imagine yourself getting to know him very well (it was hard to say which was worse—his golf or his bridge), but he was always friendly. Nothing effusive; just friendly; a bit like an expensive dentist trying to take your mind off things. He looked rather like an expensive dentist, too, when you came to think of it: thin and slightly stooping, with well-cut clothes, a good smile, and hair going a bit grey. But if it was difficult to imagine a woman like Stephanie marrying him for anything except his salary, you had to admit that they got on extraordinarily well together. It only went to show . . .

Graham himself also thought that he was lucky. From his father, a diabetic school-master, he had inherited, at the age of seventeen, an easy-going disposition, five hundred pounds in cash from a life insurance policy, and a good mathematical brain. The first legacy had enabled him to endure without resentment the ministrations of a reluctant and cantankerous guardian; the second had made it possible for him to use the scholarship he had won to a university; the third resulted in his securing in his middle twenties a science doctorate. The subject of his thesis had been a problem in ballistics, and an abridged version of it had appeared in a technical journal. By the time he was thirty he was in charge of one of his employers' experimental departments, and a little surprised that he should be paid so much money for doing something that he liked doing. That same year he had married Stephanie.

It never occurred to him to doubt that his attitude towards his wife was that of any other man towards a wife to whom he has been married for ten years. He had married her because he had been tired of living in furnished rooms, and had assumed (correctly) that she had married him to get away from her father—a disagreeable and impecunious doctor. He was pleased by her good looks, her good humour, and her capacity for keeping servants and making friends, and if he sometimes found the friends tiresome, was inclined to blame himself rather than them. She, on her part, accepted the fact that he was more interested in his work than in anyone or anything else as a matter of course and without resentment. She liked her life exactly as it was. They lived in an atmosphere of good-natured affection and mutual tolerance, and thought their marriage as successful as one could reasonably expect a marriage to be.

The outbreak of war in September nineteen thirty-nine had little effect on the Graham household. Having spent the previous two years with the certain knowledge that such an outbreak was as inevitable as the going down of the sun, Graham was neither astonished nor dismayed when it occurred. He had calculated to a nicety its probable effects on his private life, and by October he was able to conclude that his calculations had been correct. For him, the war meant more work; but that was all. It touched neither his economic nor his personal security. He could not, under any circumstances, become liable for combatant military service. The chances of a German bomber unloading its cargo anywhere near either his house or his office were remote enough to be disregarded. When he learned, just three weeks after the signing of the Anglo-Turkish treaty of alliance, that he was to go to Turkey on company business, he was troubled only by the dismal prospect of spending Christmas away from home.

He had been thirty-two when he had made his first business trip abroad. It had been a success. His employers had discovered that, in addition to his technical ability, he had the faculty, unusual in a man with his particular qualifications, of making himself amiable to—and liked by—foreign government officials. In the years that followed, occasional trips abroad had become part of his working life. He enjoyed them. He liked the actual business of getting to a strange city almost as much as he liked discovering its strangeness. He liked meeting men of other nationalities, learning smatterings of their languages, and being appalled at his lack of understanding of both. He had acquired a wholesome dislike of the word "typical."

Towards the middle of November, he reached Istanbul, by train from Paris, and left it almost immediately for Izmir and, later, Gallipoli. By the end of December he had finished his work in those two places, and on the first of January took a train back to Istanbul, the starting point of his journey home.

He had had a trying six weeks. His job had been a difficult one made more difficult by his having to discuss highly technical subjects through interpreters. The horror of the Anatolian earthquake disaster had upset him nearly as much as it had upset his hosts. Finally, the train service from Gallipoli to Istanbul had been disorganized by floods. By the time he arrived back in Istanbul he was feeling tired and depressed.

He was met at the station by Kopeikin, the company's representative in Turkey.

Kopeikin had arrived in Istanbul with sixty-five thousand other Russian refugees in nineteen twenty-four, and had been, by turns, card-sharper, part owner of a brothel, and army clothing contractor before he had secured—the Managing Director alone knew how—the lucrative agency he now held. Graham liked him. He was a plump, exuberant man with large projecting ears, irrepressible high spirits, and a vast fund of low cunning.

He wrung Graham's hand enthusiastically. "Have you had a bad trip? I am so sorry. It is good to see you back again. How did you get on with Fethi?"

"Very well, I think. I imagined something much worse from your description of him."

"My dear fellow, you underrate your charm of manner. He is known to be difficult. But he is important. Now everything will go smoothly. But we will talk business over a drink. I have engaged a room for you—a room with a bath, at the Adler-Palace, as before. For to-night I have arranged a farewell dinner. The expense is mine."

"It's very good of you."

"A great pleasure, my dear fellow. Afterwards we will amuse ourselves a little. There is a box that is very popular at the moment—Le Jockey Cabaret. You will like it, I think. It is very nicely arranged, and the people who go there are quite nice. No riff-raff. Is this your luggage?"

Graham's heart sank. He had expected to have dinner with Kopeikin, but he had been promising himself that about ten o'clock he would have a hot bath and go to bed with a Tauchnitz detective story. The last thing he wanted to do was to "amuse" himself at Le Jockey Cabaret, or any other night place. He said, as they followed the porter out to Kopeikin's car: "I think that perhaps I ought to get to bed early to-night, Kopeikin. I've got four nights in a train in front of me."

"My dear fellow, it will do you good to be late. Besides, your train does not go until eleven to-morrow morning, and I have reserved a sleeper for you. You can sleep all the way to Paris if you feel tired."

Over dinner at the Pera Palace Hotel, Kopeikin gave war news. For him, the Soviets were still "the July assassins" of Nicholas the Second, and Graham heard much of Finnish victories and Russian defeats. The Germans had sunk more British ships and lost more submarines. The Dutch, the Danes, the Swedes and the Norwegians were looking to their defences. The world awaited a bloody Spring. They went on to talk about the earthquake. It was half-past ten when Kopeikin announced that it was time for them to leave for Le Jockey Cabaret.

It was in the Beyoglu quarter; just off the Grande Rue de Pera, and in a street of buildings obviously designed by a French architect of the middle nineteen twenties. Kopeikin took his arm affectionately as they went in.

"It is a very nice place, this," he said. "Serge, the proprietor, is a friend of mine, so they will not cheat us. I will introduce you to him."

For the man he was, Graham's knowledge of the night life of cities was surprisingly extensive. For some reason, the nature of which he could never discover, his foreign hosts always seemed to consider that the only form of entertainment acceptable to an English engineer was that to be found in the rather less reputable *Nachtlokalen*. He had been in such places in Buenos Aires and in Madrid, in Valparaiso and in Bucharest, in Rome and in Mexico; and he could not remember one that was very much different from any of the others. He could remember the business acquaintances with whom he had sat far into the early morning hours drinking outrageously expensive drinks; but the places themselves had merged in his mind's eye into one prototypical picture of a smoke-filled basement room with a platform for the band at one end, a small space for dancing surrounded by tables, and a bar with stools, where the drinks were alleged to be cheaper, to one side.

He did not expect Le Jockey Cabaret to be any different. It was not.

The mural decorations seemed to have caught the spirit of the street outside. They consisted of a series of immense vorticisms involving sky-scrapers at camera angles, coloured saxophone players, green all-seeing eyes, telephones, Easter Island masks, and ash-blond hermaphrodites with long cigarette holders. The place was crowded and very noisy. Serge was a sharp-featured Russian with bristly grey hair and the air of one whose feelings were constantly on the point of getting the better of his judgment. To Graham, looking at his eyes, it seemed unlikely that they ever did: but he greeted them graciously enough, and showed them to a table beside the dance floor. Kopeikin ordered a bottle of brandy.

The band brought an American dance tune, which they had been playing with painful zeal, to an abrupt end and began, with more success, to play a rumba.

"It is very gay here," said Kopeikin. "Would you like to dance? There are plenty of girls. Say which you fancy and I will speak to Serge."

"Oh, don't bother. I really don't think I ought to stay long."

"You must stop thinking about your journey. Drink some more brandy and you will feel better." He got to his feet. "I shall dance now and find a nice girl for you."

Graham felt guilty. He should, he knew, be displaying more enthusiasm. Kopeikin was, after all, being extraordinarily kind. It could be no pleasure for him to try to entertain a train-weary Englishman who would have preferred to be in bed. He drank some more brandy determinedly. More people were arriving. He saw Serge greet them warmly and then, when their backs were turned, issue a furtive instruction to the waiter who was to serve them: a drab little reminder that Le Jockey Cabaret was in business neither for his own pleasure nor for theirs. He turned his head to watch Kopeikin dancing.

The girl was thin and dark and had large teeth. Her red satin evening dress drooped on her as if it had been made for a bigger woman. She smiled a great deal. Kopeikin held her slightly away from him and talked all the time they were dancing. To Graham, he seemed, despite the grossness of his body, to be the only man on the floor who was completely self-possessed. He was the ex-brothel-proprietor dealing with something he understood perfectly. When the music stopped he brought the girl over to their table.

"This is Maria," he said. "She is an Arab. You would not think it to look at her, would you?"

"No, you wouldn't."

"She speaks a little French."

"*Enchanté, Mademoiselle.*"

"*Monsieur.*" Her voice was unexpectedly harsh, but her smile was pleasant. She was obviously good natured.

"Poor child!" Kopeikin's tone was that of a governess who hoped that her charge would not disgrace her before visitors. "She has only just recovered from a sore throat. But she is a very nice girl and has good manners. *Assieds-toi,* Maria."

She sat down beside Graham. "*Je prends du champagne,*" she said.

"*Oui, oui, mon enfant. Plus tard,*" said Kopeikin

vaguely. "She gets extra commission if we order champagne," he remarked to Graham, and poured out some brandy for her.

She took it without comment, raised it to her lips, and said, "*Skål!*"

"She thinks you are a Swede," said Kopeikin.

"Why?"

"She likes Swedes, so I said you were a Swede." He chuckled. "You cannot say that the Turkish agent does nothing for the company."

She had been listening to them with an uncomprehending smile. Now, the music began again and, turning to Graham, she asked him if he would like to dance.

She danced well; well enough for him to feel that he, too, was dancing well. He felt less depressed and asked her to dance again. The second time she pressed her thin body hard against him. He saw a grubby shoulder strap begin to work its way out from under the red satin and smelt the heat of her body behind the scent she used. He found that he was getting tired of her.

She began to talk. Did he know Istanbul well? Had he been there before? Did he know Paris? And London? He was lucky. She had never been to those places. She hoped to go to them. And to Stockholm, too. Had he many friends in Istanbul? She asked because there was a gentleman who had come in just after him and his friend who seemed to know him. This gentleman kept looking at him.

Graham had been wondering how soon he could get away. He realised suddenly that she was waiting for him to say something. His mind had caught her last remark.

"Who keeps looking at me?"

"We cannot see him now. The gentleman is sitting at the bar."

"No doubt he's looking at you." There seemed nothing else to say.

But she was evidently serious. "It is in you that he is interested, Monsieur. It is the one with the handkerchief in his hand."

They had reached a point on the floor from which he could see the bar. The man was sitting on a stool with a glass of vermouth in front of him.

He was a short, thin man with a stupid face: very bony with large nostrils, prominent cheekbones, and full lips pressed together as if he had sore gums or were trying to keep his temper. He was intensely pale and his small, deep-set eyes and thinning, curly hair seemed in consequence darker than they were. The hair was plastered in streaks across his skull. He wore a crumpled brown suit with lumpy padded shoulders, a soft shirt with an almost invisible collar, and a new grey tie. As Graham watched him he wiped his upper lip with the handkerchief as if the heat of the place were making him sweat.

"He doesn't seem to be looking at me now," Graham said. "Anyway, I don't know him, I'm afraid."

"I did not think so, Monsieur." She pressed his arm to her side with her elbow. "But I wished to be sure. I do not know him either, but I know the type. You are a stranger here, Monsieur, and you perhaps have money in your pocket. Istanbul is not like Stockholm. When such types look at you more than once, it is advisable to be careful. You are strong, but a knife in the back is the same for a strong man as for a small one."

Her solemnity was ludicrous. He laughed; but he looked again at the man by the bar. He was sipping at his vermouth; an inoffensive creature. The girl was probably trying, rather clumsily, to demonstrate that her own intentions were good.

He said: "I don't think that I need worry."

She relaxed the pressure on his arm. "Perhaps not, Monsieur." She seemed suddenly to lose interest in the subject. The band stopped and they returned to the table.

"She dances very nicely, doesn't she?" said Kopeikin.

"Very."

She smiled at them, sat down and finished her drink as if she were thirsty. Then she sat back. "We are three," she said and counted round with one finger to make sure they understood; "would you like me to bring a friend of mine to have a drink with us? She is very sympathetic. She is my greatest friend."

"Later, perhaps," said Kopeikin. He poured her out another drink.

At that moment, the band played a resounding "chord-on" and most of the lights went out. A spotlight quivered on the floor in front of the platform.

"The attractions," said Maria. "It is very good."

Serge stepped into the spotlight and pattered off a long announcement in Turkish which ended in a flourish of the hand towards a door beside the platform. Two dark young men in pale blue dinner jackets promptly dashed out on to the floor and proceeded to do an energetic tap dance. They were soon breathless and their hair became dishevelled, but the applause, when they had finished, was lukewarm. Then they put on false beards and, pretending to be old men, did some tumbling. The audience was only slightly more enthusiastic. They retired, rather angrily Graham thought, dripping with perspiration. They were followed by a handsome coloured woman with long thin legs who proved to be a contortionist. Her contortions were ingeniously obscene and evoked gusts of laughter. In response to shouts, she followed her contortions with a snake dance. This was not so successful, as the snake, produced from a gilt wicker crate as cautiously as if it had been a fully grown anaconda, proved to be a small and rather senile python with a tendency to fall asleep in its mistress's hands. It was finally bundled back into its crate while she did some more contortions. When she had gone, the proprietor stepped once more into the spotlight and made an announcement that was greeted with clapping.

The girl put her lips to Graham's ear. "It is Josette and her partner, José. They are dancers from Paris. This is their last night here. They have had a great success."

The spotlight became pink and swept to the entrance door. There was a roll of drums. Then, as the band struck up the Blue Danube waltz, the dancers glided on to the floor.

For the weary Graham, their dance was as much a part of the cellar convention as the bar and the platform for the band: it was something to justify the prices of the drinks: a demonstration of the fact that, by applying the laws of classical mechanics, one small, unhealthy looking man with a broad sash round his waist could handle an eight stone woman as if she were a child. Josette and her partner were remarkable only in that, although they carried out the standard "specialty" routine rather less efficiently than usual, they managed to do so with considerably more effect.

She was a slim woman with beautiful arms and shoulders and a mass of gleaming fair hair. Her heavily lidded eyes, almost closed as she danced, and the rather full lips, fixed in a theatrical half-smile, contradicted in a curious way the swift neatness of her movements. Graham saw that she was not a dancer but a woman who had been trained to dance and who did so with a sort of indolent sensuality, conscious of her young-looking body, her long legs, and the muscles below the smooth surfaces of her thighs and stomach. If her performance did not succeed as a dance, as an *attraction* at Le Jockey Cabaret it succeeded perfectly and in spite of her partner.

He was a dark, preoccupied man with tight, disagreeable lips, a smooth sallow face, and an irritating way of sticking his tongue hard in his cheek as he prepared to exert himself. He moved badly and was clumsy, his fingers shifting uncertainly as he grasped her for the lifts as if he were uncertain of the point of balance. He was constantly steadying himself.

But the audience was not looking at him, and when they had finished called loudly for an encore. It was given. The band played another "chord-on." Mademoiselle Josette took a bow and was presented with a bouquet of flowers by Serge. She returned several times and bowed and kissed her hand.

"She is quite charming, isn't she?" Kopeikin said in English as the lights went up. "I promised you that this place was amusing."

"She's quite good. But it's a pity about the moth-eaten Valentino."

"José? He does well for himself. Would you like to have her to the table for a drink?"

"Very much. But won't it be rather expensive?"

"Gracious no! She does not get commission."

"Will she come?"

"Of course. The *patron* introduced me. I know her well. You might take to her, I think. This Arab is a little stupid. No doubt Josette is stupid, too; but she is very attractive in her way. If I had not learned too much when I was too young, I should like her myself."

Maria stared after him as he went across the floor, and remained silent for a moment. Then she said: "He is very good, that friend of yours."

Graham was not quite sure whether it was a statement, a question, or a feeble attempt to make conversation. He nodded. "Very good."

She smiled. "He knows the proprietor well. If you desire it, he will ask Serge to let me go when you wish instead of when the place closes."

He smiled as regretfully as he could. "I'm afraid, Maria, that I have to pack my luggage and catch a train in the morning."

She smiled again. "It does not matter. But I specially like the Swedes. May I have some more brandy, Monsieur?"

"Of course." He refilled her glass.

She drank half of it. "Do you like Mademoiselle Josette?"

"She dances very well."

"She is very sympathetic. That is because she has a success. When people have a success they are sympathetic. José, nobody likes. He is a Spaniard from Morocco, and very jealous. They are all the same. I do not know how she stands him."

"I thought you said they were Parisians."

"They have danced in Paris. She is from Hungary. She speaks languages—German, Spanish, English—but not Swedish, I think. She has had many rich lovers." She paused. "Are you a business man, Monsieur?"

"No, an engineer." He realised, with some amusement, that Maria was less stupid than she seemed, and that she knew exactly why Kopeikin had left them. He was being warned, indirectly but unmistakably, that Mademoiselle Josette was very expensive, that communication with her would be difficult, and that he would have a jealous Spaniard to deal with.

She drained her glass again, and stared vaguely in the direction of the bar. "My friend is looking very lonely," she said. She turned her head and looked directly at him. "Will you give me a hundred piastres, Monsieur?"

"What for?"

"A tip, Monsieur." She smiled, but in not quite so friendly a fashion as before.

He gave her a hundred piastre note. She folded it up, put it in her bag, and stood up. "Will you excuse me, please? I wish to speak to my friend. I will come back if you wish." She smiled.

He saw her red satin dress disappear in the crowd gathered round the bar. Kopeikin returned almost immediately.

"Where is the Arab?"

"She's gone to speak to her best friend. I gave her a hundred piastres."

"A hundred! Fifty would have been plenty. But perhaps it is as well. Josette asks us to have a drink with her in her dressing-room. She is leaving Istanbul to-morrow, and does not wish to come out here. She will have to speak to so many people, and she has packing to do."

"Shan't we be rather a nuisance?"

"My dear fellow, she is anxious to meet you. She saw you while she was dancing. When I told her that you were an Englishman, she was delighted. We can leave these drinks here."

Mademoiselle Josette's dressing-room was a space about eight feet square, partitioned off from the other half of what appeared to be the proprietor's office by a brown curtain. The three solid walls were covered with faded pink wall-paper with stripes of blue: there were greasy patches here and there where people had leaned against them. The room contained two bent-wood chairs and two rickety dressing tables littered with cream jars and dirty make-up towels. There was a mixed smell of stale cigarette smoke, face powder, and damp upholstery.

As they went in in response to a grunt of *"Entrez"* from the partner, José, he got up from his dressing table. Still wiping the grease paint from his face, he walked out without a glance at them. For some reason, Kopeikin winked at Graham. Josette was leaning forward in her chair dabbing intently at one of her eyebrows with a swab of damp cotton-wool. She had discarded her costume, and put on a rose velvet house-coat. Her hair hung down loosely about her head as if she had shaken it out and brushed it. It was really, Graham thought, very beautiful hair. She began to speak in slow, careful English, punctuating the words with dabs.

"Please excuse me. It is this filthy paint. It . . . *Merde!*"

She threw the swab down impatiently, stood up suddenly, and turned to face them.

In the hard light of the unshaded bulb above her head she looked smaller than she had looked on the dance floor; and a trifle haggard. Graham, thinking of his Stephanie's rather buxom good looks, reflected that the woman before him would probably be quite plain in ten years' time. He was in the habit of comparing other women with his wife. As a method of disguising from himself the fact that other women still interested him, it was usually effective. But Josette was unusual. What she might look like in ten years' time was altogether beside the point. At that moment she was a very attractive, self-possessed woman with a soft, smiling mouth, slightly protuberant blue eyes, and a sleepy vitality that seemed to fill the room.

"This, my dear Josette," said Kopeikin, "is Mr. Graham."

"I enjoyed your dancing very much, Mademoiselle," he said.

"So Kopeikin told me." She shrugged. "It could be better, I think, but it is very good of you to say that you like it. It is nonsense to say that Englishmen are not polite." She flourished her hand round the room. "I do not like to ask you to sit down in this filth, but please try to make yourself comfortable. There is José's chair for Kopeikin, and if you could push José's things away, the corner of his table will be for you. It is too bad that we cannot sit together in comfort outside, but there are so many of these men who make some *chichi* if one does not stop and drink some of their champagne. The champagne here is filthy. I do not wish to leave Istanbul with a headache. How long do you stay here, Mr. Graham?"

"I, too, leave to-morrow." She amused him. Her posturing was absurd. Within the space of a minute she had been a great actress receiving wealthy suitors, a friendly woman of the world, and a disillusioned genius of the dance. Every movement, every piece of affectation was calculated: it was as if she were still dancing.

Now she became a serious student of affairs. "It is terrible, this travelling. And you go back to your war. I am sorry. These filthy Nazis. It is such a pity that there must be wars. And if it is not wars, it is earthquakes. Always death. It is so bad for business. I am not interested in death. Kopeikin is, I think. Perhaps it is because he is a Russian."

"I think nothing of death," said Kopeikin. "I am concerned only that the waiter shall bring the drinks I ordered. Will you have a cigarette?"

"Please, yes. The waiters here are filthy. There must be much better places than this in London, Mr. Graham."

"The waiters there are very bad, too. Waiters are, I think, mostly very bad. But I should have thought you had been to London. Your English . . ."

Her smile tolerated his indiscretion, the depths of which he could not know. As well to have asked the Pompadour who paid her bills. "I learned it from an American and in Italy. I have a great sympathy for Americans. They are so clever in business, and yet so generous and sincere. I think it is most important to be sincere. Was it amusing dancing with that little Maria, Mr. Graham?"

"She dances very well. She seems to admire you very much. She says that you have a great success. You do, of course."

"A great success! Here?" The disillusioned genius raised her eyebrows. "I hope you gave her a good tip, Mr. Graham."

"He gave her twice as much as was necessary," said Kopeikin. "Ah, here are the drinks!"

They talked for a time about people whom Graham did not know, and about the war. He saw that behind her posturing she was quick and shrewd, and wondered if the American in Italy had ever regretted his "sincerity." After a while Kopeikin raised his glass.

"I drink," he said pompously, "to your two journeys." He lowered his glass suddenly without drinking. "No, it is absurd," he said, irritably. "My heart is not in the toast. I cannot help thinking that it is a pity that there should be two journeys. You are both going to Paris. You are both friends of mine, and so you have"—he patted his stomach—"much in common."

Graham smiled, trying not to look startled. She was certainly very attractive, and it was pleasant to sit facing her as he was; but the idea that the acquaintance might be extended had simply not occurred to him. He was confused by it. He saw that she was watching him with amusement in her eyes, and had an uncomfortable feeling that she knew exactly what was passing through his mind.

He put the best face on the situation that he could. "I was hoping to suggest the same thing. I think you should have left me to suggest it, Kopeikin. Mademoiselle will wonder if I am as sincere as an American." He smiled at her. "I am leaving by the eleven o'clock train."

"And in the first class, Mr. Graham?"

"Yes."

She put out her cigarette. "Then there are two obvious reasons why we cannot travel together. I am not leaving by that train and, in any case, I travel in the second class. It is perhaps just as well. José would wish to play cards with you all the way, and you would lose your money."

There was no doubt that she expected them to finish their drinks and go. Graham felt oddly disappointed. He would have liked to stay. He knew, besides, that he had behaved awkwardly.

"Perhaps," he said, "we could meet in Paris."

"Perhaps." She stood up and smiled kindly at him. "I shall stay at the Hotel des Belges near Trinité, if it is still open. I shall hope to meet you again. Kopeikin tells me that as an engineer you are very well known."

"Kopeikin exaggerates—just as he exaggerated when he said that we should not hinder you and your partner in your packing. I hope you have a pleasant journey."

"It has been so good to meet you. It was so kind of you, Kopeikin, to bring Mr. Graham to see me."

"It was his idea," said Kopeikin. "Good-bye, my dear Josette, and *bon voyage*. We should like to stay, but it is late, and I insisted on Mr. Graham's getting some sleep. He would stay talking until he missed the train if I permitted it."

She laughed. "You are very nice, Kopeikin. When I come next to Istanbul, I shall tell you first. *Au 'voir*, Mr. Graham, and *bon voyage*." She held out her hand.

"The Hotel des Belges near Trinité," he said: "I shall remember." He spoke very little less than the truth. During the ten minutes that his taxi would take to get from the Gare de l'Est to the Gare St. Lazare, he probably would remember.

She pressed his fingers gently. "I'm sure you will," she said. "*Au 'voir*, Kopeikin. You know the way?"

"I think," said Kopeikin, as they waited for their bill, "I think that I am a little disappointed in you, my dear fellow. You made an excellent impression. She was yours for the asking. You had only to ask her the time of her train."

"I am quite sure that I made no impression at all. Frankly, she embarrassed me. I don't understand women of that sort."

"That sort of woman, as you put it, likes a man who is embarrassed by her. Your diffidence was charming."

"Heavens! Anyway, I said that I would see her in Paris."

"My dear fellow, she knows perfectly well that you have not the smallest intention of seeing her in Paris. It is a pity. She is, I know, quite particular. You were lucky, and you chose to ignore the fact."

"Good gracious, man, you seem to forget that I'm a married man!"

Kopeikin threw up his hands. "The English point of view! One cannot reason; one can only stand amazed." He sighed profoundly. "Here comes the bill."

On their way out they passed Maria sitting at the bar with her best friend, a mournful-looking Turkish girl. They received a smile. Graham noticed that the man in the crumpled brown suit had gone.

It was cold in the street. A wind was beginning to moan through the telephone wires bracketed on the wall. At three o'clock in the morning the city of Sulyman the Magnificent was like a railway station after the last train had gone.

"We shall be having snow," said Kopeikin. "Your hotel is quite near. We will walk if you like. It is to be hoped," he went on as they began to walk, "that you will miss the snow on your journey. Last year there was a Simplon Orient express delayed for three days near Salonika."

"I shall take a bottle of brandy with me."

Kopeikin grunted. "Still, I do not envy you the journey. I think perhaps I am getting old. Besides, travelling at this time . . ."

"Oh, I'm a good traveller. I don't get bored easily."

"I was not thinking of boredom. So many unpleasant things can happen in war time."

"I suppose so."

Kopeikin buttoned up his overcoat collar. "To give you only one example . . .

"During the last war an Austrian friend of mine was returning to Berlin from Zürich, where he had been doing some business. He sat in the train with a man who said that he was a Swiss from Lugano. They talked a lot on the journey. This Swiss told my friend about his wife and his children, his business, and his home. He seemed a very nice man. But soon after they had crossed the frontier, the train stopped at a small station and soldiers came on with police. They arrested the Swiss. My friend had also to leave the train as he was with the Swiss. He was not alarmed. His papers were in order. He was a good Austrian. But the man from Lugano was terrified. He turned very pale and cried like a child. They told my friend afterwards that the man was not a Swiss but an Italian spy and that he would be shot. My friend was upset. You see, one can always tell when a man is speaking about something he loves, and there was no doubt that all that this man had said about his wife and children was true: all except one thing—they were in Italy instead of Switzerland. War," he added solemnly, "is unpleasant."

"Quite so." They had stopped outside the Adler-Palace Hotel. "Will you come in for a drink?"

Kopeikin shook his head. "It is kind of you to suggest it, but you must get some sleep. I feel guilty now at having kept you out so late, but I have enjoyed our evening together."

"So have I. I'm very grateful to you."

"A great pleasure. No farewells now. I shall take you to the station in the morning. Can you be ready by ten?"

"Easily."

"Then good night, my dear fellow."

"Good night, Kopeikin."

Graham went inside, stopped at the hall porter's desk for his key and to tell the night porter to call him at eight. Then, as the power for the lift was switched off at night, he climbed wearily up the stairs to his room on the second floor.

It was at the end of the corridor. He put the key in the lock, turned it, pushed the door open and, with his right hand, felt along the wall for the light switch.

The next moment there was a splinter of flame in the darkness and an ear-splitting detonation. A piece of plaster from the wall beside him stung his cheek. Before he could move or even think, the flame and the noise came again and it seemed as if a bar of white-hot metal had been suddenly pressed against the back of his hand. He cried out with pain and stumbled forward out of the light from the corridor into the darkness of the room. Another shot scattered plaster behind him.

There was silence. He was half leaning, half crouching against the wall by the bed, his ears singing from the din of the explosions. He was dimly aware that the window was open and that someone was moving by it. His hand seemed to be numb, but he could feel blood beginning to trickle between his fingers.

He remained motionless, his heart hammering at his head. The air reeked of cordite fumes. Then, as his eyes became used to the darkness, he saw that whoever had been at the window had left by it.

There would, he knew, be another light switch beside the bed. With his left hand he fumbled along the wall towards it. Then his hand touched the telephone. Hardly knowing what he was doing, he picked it up.

He heard a click as the night porter plugged in at the switchboard.

"Room thirty-six," he said and was surprised to find that he was shouting. "Something has happened. I need help."

He put the telephone down, blundered towards the bathroom and switched on the light there. The blood was pouring from a great gash across the back of his hand. Through the waves of nausea flowing from his stomach to his head, he could hear doors being flung open and excited voices in the corridor. Someone started hammering at the door.

CHAPTER TWO

THE STEVEDORES had finished loading and were battening down. One winch was still working but it was hoisting the steel bearers into place. The bulkhead against which Graham was leaning vibrated as they thudded into their sockets. Another passenger had come aboard and the steward had shown him to a cabin farther along the alleyway. The newcomer had a low, grumbling voice and had addressed the steward in hesitant Italian.

Graham stood up and with his unbandaged hand fumbled in his pocket for a cigarette. He was beginning to find the cabin oppressive. He looked at his watch. The ship would not be sailing for another hour. He wished he had asked Kopeikin to come aboard with him. He tried to think of his wife in England, to picture her sitting with her friends having tea; but it was as if someone behind him were holding a stereoscope to his mind's eyes; someone who was steadily sliding picture after picture between him and the rest of his life to cut him off from it;

pictures of Kopeikin and Le Jockey Cabaret, of Maria and the man in the crumpled suit, of Josette and her partner, of stabbing flames in a sea of darkness and of pale, frightened faces in the hotel corridor. He had not known then what he knew now, what he learnt in the cold, beastly dawn that had followed. The whole thing had seemed different then: unpleasant, decidedly unpleasant, but reasonable, accountable. Now he felt as if a doctor had told him that he was suffering from some horrible and deadly disease; as if he had become part of a different world, a world of which he knew nothing but that it was detestable.

The hand holding the match to his cigarette was trembling. "What I need," he thought, "is sleep."

As the waves of nausea subsided and he stood there in the bathroom, shivering, sounds began once more to penetrate the blanket of cotton wool that seemed to have enveloped his brain. There was a sort of irregular thudding coming from a long distance. He realised that someone was still knocking at the bedroom door.

He wrapped a face towel round his hand, went back into the bedroom and switched on the light. As he did so, the knocking ceased and there was a clinking of metal. Someone had got a pass key. The door burst open.

It was the night porter who came in first, blinking round uncertainly. Behind him in the corridor were the people from the neighbouring rooms, drawing back now for fear of seeing what they hoped to see. A small, dark man in a red dressing gown over blue striped pyjamas pushed past the night porter. Graham recognised the man who had shown him to his room.

"There were shots," he began in French. Then he saw Graham's hand and went white. "I . . . You are wounded. You are . . ."

Graham sat down on the bed. "Not seriously. If you will send for a doctor to bandage my hand properly, I will tell you what has happened. But first: the man who fired the shots left through the window. You might try and catch him. What is below the window?"

"But . . ." began the man shrilly. He stopped, visibly pulling himself together. Then he turned to the night porter and said something in Turkish. The porter went out, shutting the door behind him. There was a burst of excited chatter from outside.

"The next thing," said Graham, "is to send for the manager."

"Pardon, Monsieur, he has been sent for. I am the Assistant Manager." He wrung his hands. "What has happened? Your hand, Monsieur. . . . But the doctor will be here immediately."

"Good. You'd better know what happened. I have been out this evening with a friend. I returned a few minutes ago. As I opened the door here, someone standing there just inside the window fired three shots at me. The second one hit my hand. The other two hit the wall. I heard him moving but I did not see his face. I imagine that he was a thief and that my unexpected return disturbed him."

"It is an outrage!" said the Assistant Manager hotly. His face changed. "A thief! Has anything been stolen, Monsieur?"

"I haven't looked. My suitcase is over there. It was locked."

The Assistant Manager hurried across the room and went down on his knees beside the suitcase. "It is still locked," he reported with a sigh of relief.

Graham fumbled in his pocket. "Here are the keys. You'd better open it."

The man obeyed. Graham glanced at the contents of the case. "It has not been touched."

"A blessing!" He hesitated. He was obviously thinking fast. "You say that your hand is not seriously hurt, Monsieur?"

"I don't think it is."

"It is a great relief. When the shots were heard, Monsieur, we feared an unbelievable horror. You may imagine. . . . But this is bad enough." He went to the window and looked out. "The pig! He must have escaped through the gardens immediately. Useless to search for him." He shrugged despairingly. "He is gone now, and there is nothing to be done. I need not tell you, Monsieur, how profoundly we regret that this thing should happen to you in the Adler-Palace. Never before has such a thing happened here." He hesitated again and then went on quickly: "Naturally, Monsieur, we shall do everything in our power to alleviate the distress which has been caused to you. I have told the porter to bring some whisky for you when he has telephoned for the doctor. English whisky! We have a special supply. Happily, nothing has been stolen. We could not, of course, have foreseen that an accident of such a kind should happen; but we shall ourselves see that the best medical attention is given. And there will, of course, be no question of any charge for your stay here. But . . .''

"But you don't want to call in the police and involve the hotel. Is that it?"

The Assistant Manager smiled nervously. "No good can be done, Monsieur. The police would merely ask questions and make inconveniences for all." Inspiration came to him. "For *all*, Monsieur," he repeated emphatically. "You are a business man. You wish to leave Istanbul this morning. But if the police are brought in, it might be difficult. There would be, inevitably, delays. And for what purpose?"

"They might catch the man who shot me."

"But how, Monsieur? You did not see his face. You cannot identify him. There is nothing stolen by which he could be traced."

Graham hesitated. "But what about this doctor you are getting? Supposing he reports to the police the fact that there is someone here with a bullet wound."

"The doctor's services, Monsieur, will be paid for liberally by the management."

There was a knock at the door and the porter came in with whisky, soda-water, and glasses which he set down on the table. He said something to the Assistant Manager who nodded and then motioned him out.

"The doctor is on his way, Monsieur."

"Very well. No, I don't want any whisky. But drink some yourself. You look as though you need it. I should like to make a telephone call. Will you tell the porter to telephone the Crystal Apartments in the rue d'Italie? The number is forty-four, nine hundred and seven, I think. I want to speak to Monsieur Kopeikin."

"Certainly, Monsieur. Anything you wish." He went to the door and called after the porter. There was another incomprehensible exchange. The Assistant Manager came back and helped himself generously to the whisky.

"I think," he said, returning to the charge, "that you are wise not to invoke the police, Monsieur. Nothing has been stolen. Your injury is not serious. There will be no trouble. It is thus and thus with the police here, you understand."

"I haven't yet decided what to do," snapped Graham. His head was aching violently and his hand was beginning to throb. He was getting tired of the Assistant Manager.

The telephone bell rang. He moved along the bed and picked up the telephone.

"Is that you, Kopeikin?"

He heard a mystified grunt. "Graham? What is it? I have only just this moment come in. Where are you?"

"Sitting on my bed. Listen! Something stupid has happened. There was a burglar in my room when I got up here. He took pot shots at me with a gun before escaping via the window. One of them hit me in the hand."

"Merciful God! Are you badly hurt?"

"No. It just took a slice of the back of my right hand. I don't feel too good, though. It gave me a nasty shock."

"My dear fellow! Please tell me exactly what has happened."

Graham told him. "My suitcase was locked," he went

on, "and nothing is missing. I must have got back just a minute or so too soon. But there are complications. The noise seems to have roused half the hotel, including the Assistant Manager who is now standing about drinking whisky. They've sent for a doctor to bandage me up, but that's all. They made no attempt to get out after the man. Not, I suppose, that it would have done any good if they had, but at least they might have seen him. I didn't. They say he must have got away by the gardens. The point is that they won't call in the police unless I turn nasty and insist. Naturally, they don't want police tramping about the place, giving the hotel a bad name. They put it to me that the police would prevent my travelling on the eleven o'clock train if I lodged a complaint. I expect they would. But I don't know the laws of this place; and I don't want to put myself in a false position by failing to lodge a complaint. They propose, I gather, to square the doctor. But that's their look-out. What do *I* do?"

There was a short silence. Then: "I think," said Kopeikin, slowly, "that you should do nothing at the moment. Leave the matter to me. I will speak to a friend of mine about it. He is connected with the police, and has great influence. As soon as I have spoken to him, I will come to your hotel."

"But there's no need for you to do that, Kopeikin. I . . ."

"Excuse me, my dear fellow, there is every need. Let the doctor attend to your wound and then stay in your room until I arrive."

"I wasn't going out," said Graham, acidly; but Kopeikin had rung off.

As he hung up the telephone, the doctor arrived. He was thin and quiet, with a sallow face, and wore an overcoat with a black lamb's wool collar over his pyjamas. Behind him came the Manager, a heavy, disagreeable-looking man who obviously suspected that the whole thing was a hoax concocted expressly to annoy him.

He gave Graham a hostile stare, but before he could open his mouth his assistant was pouring out an account of what had occurred. There was a lot of gesturing and rolling of eyes. The Manager exclaimed as he listened, and looked at Graham with less hostility and more apprehension. At last the assistant paused, and then broke meaningly into French.

"Monsieur leaves Istanbul by the eleven o'clock train, and so does not wish to have the trouble and inconvenience of taking this matter to the police. I think you will agree, Monsieur le Directeur, that his attitude is wise."

"Very wise," agreed the Manager pontifically, "and most discreet." He squared his shoulders. "Monsieur, we infinitely regret that you should have been put to such pain, discomfort and indignity. But not even the most luxurious hotel can fortify itself against thieves who climb through windows. Nevertheless," he went on, "the Hotel Adler-Palace recognises its responsibilities towards its guests. We shall do everything humanly possible to arrange the affair."

"If it would be humanly possible to instruct the doctor then to attend to my hand, I should be grateful."

"Ah yes. The doctor. A thousand pardons."

The doctor, who had been standing gloomily in the background, now came forward and began snapping out instructions in Turkish. The windows were promptly shut, the heating turned up, and the Assistant Manager dispatched on an errand. He returned, almost immediately, with an enamel bowl which was then filled with hot water from the bathroom. The doctor removed the towel from Graham's hand, sponged the blood away, and inspected the wound. Then he looked up and said something to the Manager.

"He says, Monsieur," reported the Manager, complacently, "that it is not serious—no more than a little scratch."

"I already knew that. If you wish to go back to bed, please do so. But I should like some hot coffee. I am cold."

"Immediately, Monsieur." He snapped his fingers to the Assistant Manager, who scuttled out. "And if there is anything else, Monsieur?"

"No, thank you. Nothing. Good night."

"At your service, Monsieur. It is all most regrettable. Good night."

He went. The doctor cleaned the wound carefully, and began to dress it. Graham wished that he had not telephoned Kopeikin. The fuss was over. It was now nearly four o'clock. But for the fact that Kopeikin had promised to call in to see him, he might have had a few hours' sleep. He was yawning repeatedly. The doctor finished the dressing, patted it reassuringly, and looked up. His lips worked.

"*Maintenant*," he said laboriously, "*il faut dormir.*"

Graham nodded. The doctor got to his feet and re-packed his bag with the air of a man who has done every-thing possible for a difficult patient. Then he looked at his watch and sighed. "*Très tard*," he said. "*Giteceğ-im. Adiyo, efendi.*"

Graham mustered his Turkish. "*Adiyo, hekim efendi. Cok tesekkür ederim.*"

"*Birsey değil. Adiyo.*" He bowed and went.

A moment later, the Assistant Manager bustled in with the coffee, set it down with a businesslike flourish clearly intended to indicate that he, too, was about to return to his bed, and collected the bottle of whisky.

"You may leave that," said Graham; "a friend is on his way to see me. You might tell the porter . . ."

But as he spoke, the telephone rang, and the night porter announced that Kopeikin had arrived. The As-sistant Manager retired.

Kopeikin came into the room looking preternaturally grave.

"My dear fellow!" was his greeting. He looked round. "Where is the doctor?"

"He's just left. Just a graze. Nothing serious. I feel a bit jumpy but, apart from that, I'm all right. It's really very good of you to turn out like this. The grateful management has presented me with a bottle of whisky. Sit down and help yourself. I'm having coffee."

Kopeikin sank into the arm-chair. "Tell me exactly how it happened."

Graham told him. Kopeikin heaved himself out of the arm-chair and walked over to the window. Suddenly he stooped and picked something up. He held it up: a small brass cartridge case.

"A nine millimetre calibre self-loading pistol," he remarked. "An unpleasant thing!" He dropped it on the floor again, opened the window and looked out.

Graham sighed. "I really don't think it's any good playing detectives, Kopeikin. The man was in the room; I disturbed him, and he shot at me. Come in, shut that window, and drink some whisky."

"Gladly, my dear fellow, gladly. You must excuse my curiosity."

Graham realised that he was being a little ungracious. "It's extremely kind of you, Kopeikin, to take so much trouble. I seem to have made a lot of fuss about nothing."

"It is good that you have." He frowned. "Unfortunately a lot more fuss must be made."

"You think we ought to call in the police? I don't see that it can do any good. Besides, my train goes at eleven. I don't want to miss it."

Kopeikin drank some whisky and put his glass down with a bang. "I am afraid, my dear fellow, that you cannot under any circumstances leave on the eleven o'clock train."

"What on earth do you mean? Of course I can. I'm perfectly all right."

Kopeikin looked at him curiously. "Fortunately you are. But that does not alter facts."

"Facts?"

"Did you notice that both your windows and the shutters outside have been forced open?"

"I didn't. I didn't look. But what of it?"

"If you will look out of the window you will see that there is a terrace below which gives on the garden. Above the terrace there is a steel framework which reaches almost to the second floor balconies. In the summer it is covered with straw matting so that people can eat and drink on the terrace, out of the sun. This man obviously climbed up by the framework. It would be easy. I could almost do it myself. He could reach the balconies of all the rooms on this floor of the hotel that way. But can you tell me why he chooses to break into one of the few rooms with both shutters and windows locked?"

"Of course I can't. I've always heard that criminals were fools."

"You say nothing was stolen. Your suitcase was not even opened. A coincidence that you should return just in time to prevent him."

"A lucky coincidence. For goodness' sake, Kopeikin, let's talk about something else. The man's escaped. That's the end of it."

Kopeikin shook his head. "I'm afraid not, my dear fellow. Does he not seem to you to have been a very curious thief? He behaves like no other hotel thief ever behaved. He breaks in, and through a locked window as well. If you had been in bed, he would certainly have awakened you. He must, therefore, have known beforehand that you were not there. He must also have discovered your room number. Have you anything so obviously valuable that a thief finds it worth his while to make such preparations? No. A curious thief! He carries, too, a pistol weighing at least a kilogramme with which he fires three shots at you."

"Well?"

Kopeikin bounced angrily out of his chair. "My dear fellow, does it not occur to you that this man was shooting to kill you, and that he came here for no other purpose?"

Graham laughed. "Then all I can say is that he was a pretty bad shot. Now you listen to me carefully, Kopeikin. Have you ever heard the legend about Americans and Englishmen? It persists in every country in the world where English isn't spoken. The story is that all Americans and Englishmen are millionaires, and that they always leave vast amounts of loose cash about the place. And now, if you don't mind, I'm going to try to snatch a few hours' sleep. It was very good of you to come round, Kopeikin, and I'm very grateful, but now . . ."

"Have you ever," demanded Kopeikin, "tried firing a heavy pistol in a dark room at a man who's just come through the door? There's no direct light from the corridor outside. Merely a glow of light. Have you ever tried? No. You might be able to see the man, but it's quite another thing to hit him. Under these circumstances even a good shot might miss first time as this man missed. That miss would unnerve him. He does not perhaps know that Englishmen do not usually carry firearms. You may fire back. He fires again, quickly, and clips your hand. You probably cry out with the pain. He probably thinks that he has wounded you seriously. He fires another shot for luck, and goes."

"Nonsense, Kopeikin! You must be out of your senses. What conceivable reason could anyone have for wanting to kill me? I'm the most harmless man alive."

Kopeikin glared at him stonily. "Are you?"

"Now what does *that* mean?"

But Kopeikin ignored the question. He finished his whisky. "I told you that I was going to telephone a friend of mine. I did so." He buttoned up his coat deliberately. "I am sorry to tell you, my dear fellow, that you must come with me to see him immediately. I have been trying to break the news to you gently, but now I must be frank. A man tried to murder you to-night. Something must be done about it at once."

Graham got to his feet. "Are you mad?"

"No, my dear fellow, I am not. You ask me why anyone should want to murder you. There is an excellent reason. Unfortunately, I cannot be more explicit. I have my official instructions."

Graham sat down. "Kopeikin, *I* shall go crazy in a minute. Will you kindly tell me what you are babbling about? Friend? Murder? Official instructions? What is all this nonsense?"

Kopeikin was looking acutely embarrassed. "I am sorry, my dear fellow. I can understand your feelings. Let me tell you this much. This friend of mine is not, strictly speaking, a friend at all. In fact, I dislike him. But his name is Colonel Haki, and he is the head of the Turkish secret police. His office is in Galata, and he is expecting us to meet him there now to discuss this affair. I may also tell you that I anticipated that you might not wish to go, and told him so. He said, forgive me, that if you did not go you would be fetched. My dear fellow, it is no use your being angry. The circumstances are exceptional. If I had not known that it was necessary both in your interests and in mine to telephone him, I would not have done so. Now then, my dear fellow, I have a taxi outside. We ought to be going."

Graham got slowly to his feet again. "Very well. I must say, Kopeikin, that you have surprised me. Friendly concern, I could understand and appreciate. But this . . . Hysteria is the last thing I should have expected from you. To get the head of the secret police out of bed at this hour seems to me a fantastic thing to do. I can only hope that he doesn't object to being made a fool of."

Kopeikin flushed. "I am neither hysterical nor fantastic, my friend. I have something unpleasant to do, and I am doing it. If you will forgive my saying so, I think . . ."

"I can forgive almost anything except stupidity," snapped Graham. "However, this is your affair. Do you mind helping me on with my overcoat?"

They drove to Galata in grim silence. Kopeikin was sulking. Graham sat hunched up in his corner staring out miserably at the cold, dark streets, and wishing that he had not telephoned Kopeikin. It was, he kept telling himself, absurd enough to be shot at by a hotel sneak thief: to be bundled out in the early hours of the morning to tell the head of the secret police about it was worse than absurd; it was ludicrous. He felt, too, concerned on Kopeikin's account. The man might be behaving like an idiot; but it was not very pleasant to think of him making an ass of himself before a man who might well be able to do him harm in his business. Besides, he, Graham, had been rude.

He turned his head. "What's this Colonel Haki like?"

Kopeikin grunted. "Very *chic* and polished—a ladies' man. There is also a legend that he can drink two bottles of whisky without getting drunk. It may be true. He was one of Ataturk's men, a deputy in the provisional government of nineteen-nineteen. There is also another legend—that he killed prisoners by tying them together in pairs and throwing them into the river to save both food and ammunition. I do not believe everything I hear, nor am I a prig, but, as I told you, I do not like him. He is, however, very clever. But you will be able to judge for yourself. You can speak French to him."

"I still don't see . . ."

"You will."

They pulled up soon afterwards behind a big American car which almost blocked the narrow street into which they had turned. They got out. Graham found himself standing in front of a pair of double doors which might have been the entrance to a cheap hotel. Kopeikin pressed a bell push.

One of the doors was opened almost immediately by a sleepy-looking caretaker who had obviously only just been roused from his bed.

"*Haki efendi evde midir*," said Kopeikin.

"*Efendi var-dir. Yokari.*" The man pointed to the stairs.

They went up.

Colonel Haki's office was a large room at the end of a corridor on the top floor of the building. The Colonel himself walked down the corridor to meet them.

He was a tall man with lean, muscular cheeks, a small mouth and grey hair cropped Prussian fashion. A narrow frontal bone, a long beak of a nose and a slight stoop gave him a somewhat vultural air. He wore a very well-cut officer's tunic with full riding breeches and very tight, shiny cavalry boots; he walked with the slight swagger of a man who is used to riding. But for the intense pallor of his face and the fact that it was unshaven, there was nothing about him to show that he had recently been asleep. His eyes were grey and very wide-awake. They surveyed Graham with interest.

"Ah! *Nasil-siniz. Fransizca konus-abilir misin.* Yes? Delighted, Mr. Graham. Your wound, of course." Graham found his unbandaged hand being gripped with considerable force by long rubbery fingers. "I hope that it is not too painful. Something must be done about this rascal who tries to kill you."

"I'm afraid," said Graham, "that we have disturbed your rest unnecessarily, Colonel. The man stole nothing."

Colonel Haki looked quickly at Kopeikin.

"I have told him nothing," said Kopeikin placidly. "At your suggestion, Colonel, you may remember. I regret to say that he thinks that I am either mad or hysterical."

Colonel Haki chuckled. "It is the lot of you Russians to be misunderstood. Let us go into my office where we can talk."

They followed him: Graham with the growing conviction that he was involved in a nightmare and that he would presently wake up to find himself at his dentist's. The corridor was, indeed, as bare and featureless as the corridors of a dream. It smelt strongly, however, of stale cigarette smoke.

The Colonel's office was large and chilly. They sat

down facing him across his desk. He pushed a box of cigarettes towards them, lounged back in his chair and crossed his legs.

"You must realise, Mr. Graham," he said suddenly, "that an attempt was made to kill you to-night."

"Why?" demanded Graham irritably. "I'm sorry, but I don't see it. I returned to my room to find that a man had got in through the window. Obviously he was some sort of thief. I disturbed him. He fired at me and then escaped. That is all."

"You have not, I understand, reported the matter to the police."

"I did not consider that reporting it could do any good. I did not see the man's face. Besides, I am leaving for England this morning on the eleven o'clock train. I did not wish to delay myself. If I have broken the law in any way I am sorry."

"*Zarar yok!* It does not matter." The Colonel lit a cigarette and blew smoke at the ceiling. "I have a duty to do, Mr. Graham," he said. "That duty is to protect you. I am afraid that you cannot leave on the eleven o'clock train."

"But protect me from *what*?"

"I will ask you questions, Mr. Graham. It will be simpler. You are in the employ of Messrs. Cator and Bliss, Ltd., the English armament manufacturers?"

"Yes. Kopeikin here is the company's Turkish agent."

"Quite so. You are, I believe, Mr. Graham, a naval ordnance expert."

Graham hesitated. He had the engineer's dislike of the word "expert." His managing director sometimes applied it to him when writing to foreign naval authorities; but he could, on those occasions, console himself with the reflection that his managing director would describe him as a full-blooded Zulu to impress a customer. At other times he found the word unreasonably irritating.

"Well, Mr. Graham?"

"I'm an engineer. Naval ordnance happens to be my subject."

"As you please. The point is that Messrs. Cator and Bliss, Ltd., have contracted to do some work for my Government. Good. Now, Mr. Graham, I do not know exactly what that work is"—he waved his cigarette airily—"that is the affair of the Ministry of Marine. But I have been told some things. I know that certain of our naval vessels are to be rearmed with new guns and torpedo tubes and that you were sent to discuss the matter with our dockyard experts. I also know that our authorities stipulated that the new equipment should be delivered by the spring. Your company agreed to that stipulation. Are you aware of it?"

"I have been aware of nothing else for the past two months."

"*Iyi dir!* Now I may tell you, Mr. Graham, that the reason for that stipulation as to time was not mere caprice on the part of our Ministry of Marine. The international situation demands that we have that new equipment in our dockyards by the time in question."

"I know that, too."

"Excellent. Then you will understand what I am about to say. The naval authorities of Germany and Italy and Russia are perfectly well aware of the fact that these vessels are being rearmed and I have no doubt that the moment the work is done, or even before, their agents will discover the details known at the moment only to a few men, yourself among them. That is unimportant. No navy can keep that sort of secret: no navy expects to do so. We might even consider it advisable, for various reasons, to publish the details ourselves. But"—he raised a long, well-manicured finger—"at the moment you are in a curious position, Mr. Graham."

"That, at least, I can believe."

The Colonel's small grey eyes rested on him coldly. "I am not here to make jokes, Mr. Graham."

"I beg your pardon."

"Not at all. Please take another cigarette. I was saying that at the moment your position is curious. Tell me! Have you ever regarded yourself as indispensable in your business, Mr. Graham?"

Graham laughed. "Certainly not. I could tell you the names of dozens of other men with my particular qualifications."

"Then," said Colonel Haki, "allow me to inform you, Mr. Graham, that for once in your life you *are* indispensable. Let us suppose for the moment that your thief's shooting had been a little more accurate and that at this moment you were, instead of sitting talking with me, lying in hospital on an operating table with a bullet in your lungs. What would be the effect on this business you are engaged in now?"

"Naturally, the company would send another man out immediately."

Colonel Haki affected a look of theatrical astonishment. "So? That would be splendid. So typically British! Sporting! One man falls—immediately another, undaunted, takes his place. But wait!" The Colonel held up a forbidding arm. "Is it necessary? Surely, Mr. Kopeikin here could arrange to have your papers taken to England. No doubt your colleagues there could find out from your notes, your sketches, your drawings, exactly what they wanted to know even though your company did not build the ships in question, eh?"

Graham flushed. "I gather from your tone that you know perfectly well that the matter could not be dealt with so simply. I was forbidden, in any case, to put certain things on paper."

Colonel Haki tilted his chair. "Yes, Mr. Graham,"—he smiled cheerfully—"I do know that. Another expert would have to be sent out to do some of your work over again." His chair came forward with a crash. "And meanwhile," he said through his teeth, "the spring would be here and those ships would still be lying in the dockyards of Izmir and Gallipoli, waiting for their new guns and torpedo tubes. Listen to me, Mr. Graham! Turkey and Great Britain are allies. It is in the interests of your country's enemies that, when the snow melts and the rain ceases, Turkish naval strength should be exactly what it is now. *Exactly what it is now!* They will do anything to see that it is so. *Anything*, Mr. Graham! Do you understand?"

Graham felt something tightening in his chest. He had to force himself to smile. "A little melodramatic, aren't you? We have no proof that what you say is true. And, after all, this is real life, not . . ." He hesitated.

"Not what, Mr. Graham?" The Colonel was watching him like a cat about to streak after a mouse.

". . . the cinema, I was going to say, only it sounded a little impolite."

Colonel Haki stood up quickly. "Melodrama! Proof! Real life! The cinema! Impolite!" His lips curled round the words as if they were obscene. "Do you think I care what you say, Mr. Graham? It's your carcass I am inter-ested in. Alive, it's worth something to the Turkish Republic. I'm going to see that it stays alive as long as I've any control over it. There is a war on in Europe. Do you understand *that*?"

Graham said nothing.

The Colonel stared at him for a moment and then went on quietly. "A little more than a week ago, while you were still in Gallipoli, we discovered—that is, my agents discovered—a plot to murder you there. The whole thing was very clumsy and amateurish. You were to be kidnapped and knifed. Fortunately, we are not fools. *We* do not dismiss as melodramatic anything that does not please us. We were able to persuade the arrested men to tell us that they had been paid by a German agent in Sofia —a man named Moeller about whom we have known for some time. He used to call himself an American until the American Legation objected. His name was Fielding then. I imagine that he claims any name and nationality that happens to suit him. However, I called Mr. Kopeikin in to see me and told him about it but suggested that nothing should be said about it to you. The less these things are talked about the better and, besides, there was nothing to be gained by upsetting you while you were so hard at work. I think I made a mistake. I had reason to believe that this Moeller's further efforts would be directed elsewhere. When Mr. Kopeikin, very wisely, telephoned me immediately he knew of this fresh attempt, I realised that I had underestimated the determination of this gentleman in Sofia. He tried again. I have no doubt that he will try a third time if we give him a chance." He leaned back in his chair. "Do you understand now, Mr. Graham? Has your excellent brain grasped what I have been trying to say? It is perfectly simple! Someone is trying to kill you."

CHAPTER THREE

ON THE RARE OCCASIONS—when matters concerned with insurance policies had been under consideration—on which Graham had thought about his own death, it had been to reaffirm the conviction that he would die of natural causes and in bed. Accidents did happen, of course; but he was a careful driver, an imaginative pedestrian and a strong swimmer; he neither rode horses nor climbed mountains; he was not subject to attacks of dizziness; he did not hunt big game and he had never had even the smallest desire to jump in front of an approaching train. He had felt, on the whole, that the conviction was not unreasonable. The idea that anyone else in the world might so much as hope for his death had never occurred to him. If it had done so he would probably have hastened to consult a nerve specialist. Confronted by the proposition that someone was, in fact, not merely hoping for his death but deliberately trying to murder him, he was as profoundly shocked as if he had been presented with incontrovertible proofs that a^2 no longer equalled $b^2 + c^2$ or that his wife had a lover.

He was a man who had always been inclined to think well of his fellow creatures; and the first involuntary thought that came into his head was that he must have done something particularly reprehensible for anyone to want to murder him. The mere fact that he was doing his job could not be sufficient reason. He was not dangerous. Besides, he had a wife dependent on him. It was impossible that anyone should wish to kill him. There must be some horrible mistake.

He heard himself saying: "Yes. I understand."

He didn't understand, of course. It was absurd. He saw Colonel Haki looking at him with a frosty little smile on his small mouth.

"A shock, Mr. Graham? You do not like it, eh? It is not pleasant. War is war. But it is one thing to be a soldier in the trenches: the enemy is not trying to kill you in particular because you are Mr. Graham: the man next to you will do as well: it is all impersonal. When you are a marked man it is not so easy to keep your courage. I understand, believe me. But you have advantages over the soldier. You have only to defend yourself. You do not have to go into the open and attack. And you have no trench or fort to hold. You may run away without being a coward. You must reach London safely. But it is a long way from Istanbul to London. You must, like the soldier, take precautions against surprise. You must know your enemy. You follow me?"

"Yes. I follow you."

His brain was icily calm now, but it seemed to have

lost control of his body. He knew that he must try to look as if he were taking it all very philosophically, but his mouth kept filling with saliva, so that he was swallowing repeatedly, and his hands and legs were trembling. He told himself that he was behaving like a schoolboy. A man had fired three shots at him. What difference did it make whether the man had been a thief or an intending murderer? He had fired three shots, and that was that. But all the same, it did somehow make a difference . . .

"Then," Colonel Haki was saying, "let us begin with what has just happened." He was obviously enjoying himself. "According to Mr. Kopeikin, you did not see the man who shot at you."

"No, I didn't. The room was in darkness."

Kopeikin chipped in. "He left cartridge cases behind him. Nine millimetre calibre ejected from a self-loading pistol."

"That does not help a great deal. You noticed nothing about him, Mr. Graham?"

"Nothing, I'm afraid. It was all over so quickly. He had gone before I realised it."

"But he had probably been in the room for some time waiting for you. You didn't notice any perfume in the room?"

"All I could smell was cordite."

"What time did you arrive in Istanbul?"

"At about six p.m."

"And you did not return to your hotel until three o'clock this morning. Please tell me where you were during that time."

"Certainly. I spent the time with Kopeikin. He met me at the station, and we drove in a taxi to the Adler-Palace, where I left my suitcase and had a wash. We then had some drinks and dined. Where did we have the drinks, Kopeikin?"

"At the Rumca Bar."

"Yes, that was it. We went on to the Pera Palace to dine. Just before eleven we left there, and went on to Le Jockey Cabaret."

"Le Jockey Cabaret! You surprise me! What did you do there?"

"We danced with an Arab girl named Maria, and saw the cabaret."

"We? Was there, then, only one girl between you?"

"I was rather tired, and did not want to dance much. Later we had a drink with one of the cabaret dancers, Josette, in her dressing-room." To Graham it all sounded rather like the evidence of detectives in a divorce case.

"A nice girl, this Josette?"

"Very attractive."

The Colonel laughed: the doctor keeping the patient's spirits up. "Blonde or brunette?"

"Blonde."

"Ah! I must visit Le Jockey. I have missed something. And what happened then?"

"Kopeikin and I left the place. We walked back to the Adler-Palace together where Kopeikin left me to go on to his apartment."

The Colonel looked humorously astonished. "You left this dancing blonde?"—he snapped his fingers—"just like that? There were no—little games?"

"No. No little games."

"Ah, but you have told me that you were tired." He swung round suddenly in his chair to face Kopeikin. "These women—this Arab and this Josette—what do you know of them?"

Kopeikin stroked his chin. "I know Serge, the proprietor of Le Jockey Cabaret. He introduced me to Josette some time ago. She is a Hungarian, I believe. I know nothing against her. The Arab girl is from a house in Alexandria."

"Very well. We will see about them later." He turned again to Graham. "Now, Mr. Graham, we shall see what we can find out from you about the enemy. You were tired, you say?"

"Yes."

"But you kept your eyes open, eh?"

"I suppose so."

"Let us hope so. You realise that you must have been followed from the moment you left Gallipoli?"

"I hadn't realised that."

"It must be so. They knew your hotel and your room in it. They were waiting for you to return. They must have known of every movement you made since you arrived."

He got up suddenly and, going to a filing cabinet in the corner, extracted from it a yellow maníila folder. He brought it back and dropped it on the desk in front of Graham. "Inside that folder, Mr. Graham, you will find photographs of fifteen men. Some of the photographs are clear; most are very blurred and indistinct. You will have to do the best you can. I want you to cast your mind back to the time you boarded the train at Gallipoli yesterday, and remember every face you saw, even casually, between that time and three o'clock this morning. Then I want you to look at those photographs and see if you recognise any of the faces there. Afterwards Mr. Kopeikin can look at them, but I wish you to see them first."

Graham opened the folder. There was a series of thin white cards in it. Each was about the size of the folder, and had a photograph gummed to the top half of it. The prints were all the same size, but they had obviously been copied from original photographs of varying sizes. One was an enlargement of part of a photograph of a group of men standing in front of some trees. Underneath each print was a paragraph or two of typewritten matter in Turkish: presumably the description of the man in question.

Most of the photographs were, as the Colonel had said, blurred. One or two of the faces were, indeed, no more than blobs of grey with dark patches marking the eyes and mouths. Those that were clear looked like prison photographs. The men in them stared sullenly at their tormentors. There was one of a negro wearing a tarboosh with his mouth wide open as if he were shouting at someone to the right of the camera. Graham turned the cards over, slowly and hopelessly. If he had ever seen any of these men in his life, he could not recognise them now.

The next moment his heart jolted violently. He was looking at a photograph taken in very strong sunshine of a man in a hard straw hat standing in front of what might have been a shop, and looking over his shoulder at the camera. His right arm and his body below the waist were out of the picture, and what was in was rather out of focus; in addition the photograph looked as if it had been taken at least ten years previously; but there was no mistaking the doughy, characterless features, the long-suffering mouth, the small deep-set eyes. It was the man in the crumpled suit.

"Well, Mr. Graham!"

"This man. He was at Le Jockey Cabaret. It was the Arab girl who drew my attention to him while we were dancing. She said that he came in just after Kopeikin and me, and that he kept looking at me. She warned me against him. She seemed to think that he might stick a knife in my back and take my wallet."

"Did she know him?"

"No. She said that she recognised the type."

Colonel Haki took the card and leaned back. "That was very intelligent of her. Did you see this man, Mr. Kopeikin?"

Kopeikin looked, and then shook his head.

"Very well." Colonel Haki dropped the card on the desk in front of him. "You need not trouble to look at any more of the photographs, gentlemen. I know now what I wanted to know. This is the only one of the fifteen that interests us. The rest I put with it merely to make sure that you identified this one of your own accord."

"Who is he?"

"He is a Roumanian by birth. His name is supposed to be Petre Banat; but as Banat is the name of a Roumanian province, I think it very probable that he never had a family name. We know, indeed, very little about him. But what we do know is enough. He is a professional gunman. Ten years ago he was convicted, in Jassy, of helping to kick a man to death, and was sent to prison for two years. Soon after he came out of prison he joined Codreanu's Iron Guard. In nineteen thirty-three he was charged with the assassination of a police official at Bucova. It appears that he walked into the official's house one Sunday afternoon, shot the man dead, wounded his wife, and then calmly walked out again. He is a careful man, but he knew that he was safe. The trial was a farce. The court-room was filled with Iron Guards with pistols, who threatened to shoot the judge and everyone connected with the trial if Banat were convicted. He was acquitted. There were many such trials in Roumania at that time. Banat was afterwards responsible for at least four other murders in Roumania. When the Iron Guard was proscribed, however, he escaped from the country, and has not returned there. He spent some time in France until the French police deported him. Then he went to Belgrade. But he got into trouble there, too, and has since moved about Eastern Europe.

"There are men who are natural killers. Banat is one of them. He is very fond of gambling, and is always short of money. At one time it was said that his price for killing a man was as little as five thousand French francs and expenses.

"But all that is of no interest to you, Mr. Graham. The point is that Banat is here in Istanbul. I may tell you that we receive regular reports on the activities of this man Moeller in Sofia. About a week ago it was reported that he had been in touch with Banat, and that Banat had afterwards left Sofia. I will admit to you, Mr. Graham, that I did not attach any importance to the fact. To be frank, it was another aspect of this agent's activities which was interesting me at the time. It was not until Mr. Kopeikin telephoned me that I remembered Banat and wondered if, by any chance, he had come to Istanbul. We know now that he is here. We know also that Moeller saw him just after those other arrangements for killing you had been upset. There can be no doubt, I think, that it was Banat who was waiting for you in your room at the Adler-Palace."

Graham strove to seem unimpressed. "He looked harmless enough."

"That," said Colonel Haki, sagely, "is because you are not experienced, Mr. Graham. The real killer is not a mere brute. He may be quite sensitive. Have you studied abnormal psychology?"

"I'm afraid not."

"It is very interesting. Apart from detective stories, Krafft-Ebing and Stekel are my favourite reading. I have my own theory about men such as Banat. I believe that they are perverts with an *idée fixe* about the father whom they identify not with a virile god"—he held up a cautionary finger—"but with their own impotence. When they kill, they are thus killing their own weakness. There is no doubt of it, I think."

"Very interesting, I feel sure. But can't you arrest this man?"

Colonel Haki cocked one gleaming boot over the arm of his chair, and pursed his lips. "That raises an awkward problem, Mr. Graham. In the first place, we have to find him. He will certainly be travelling with a false passport and under a false name. I can and, of course, will circulate his description to the frontier posts so that we shall know if he leaves the country, but as for arresting him . . . You see, Mr. Graham, the so-called democratic forms of government have serious drawbacks for a man in my position. It is impossible to arrest and detain people without absurd legal formalities." He threw up his hands —a patriot bemoaning his country's decadence. "On what charge can we arrest him? We have no evidence against him. We could, no doubt, invent a charge and then apologise, but what good will it do? No! I regret it, but we can do nothing about Banat. I do not think it matters a great deal. What we must think of now is the future. We must consider how to get you home safely."

"I have, as I have already told you, a sleeping berth on the eleven o'clock train. I fail to see why I shouldn't use it. It seems to me that the sooner I leave here the better."

Colonel Haki frowned. "Let me tell you, Mr. Graham, that if you were to take that or any other train, you would be dead before you reached Belgrade. Don't imagine for one moment that the presence of other travellers would deter them. You must not underrate the enemy, Mr. Graham. It is a fatal mistake. In a train you would be caught like a rat in a trap. Picture it for yourself! There are innumerable stops between the Turkish and French frontiers. Your assassin might get on the train at any of them. Imagine yourself sitting there for hour after hour after hour trying to stay awake lest you should

be knifed while you slept; not daring to leave the compartment for fear of being shot down in the corridor;
living in terror of everyone—from the man sitting opposite to you in the restaurant car to the Customs officials.
Picture it, Mr. Graham, and then reflect that a trans-
continental train is the safest place in the world in which
to kill a man. Consider the position! These people do not
wish you to reach England. So they decide, very wisely
and logically, to kill you. They have tried twice and
failed. They will wait now to see what you will do. They
will not try again in this country. They will know that
you will now be too well protected. They will wait until
you come out in the open. No! I am afraid that you cannot travel by train."

"Then I don't see. . . ."

"If," continued the Colonel, "the air line services had
not been suspended we could send you by aeroplane to
Brindisi. But they *are* suspended—the earthquake, you
understand. Everything is disorganized. The planes are
being used for relief work. But we can do without them.
It will be best if you go by sea."

"But surely . . ."

"There is an Italian shipping line which runs a weekly
service of small cargo boats between here and Genoa.
Sometimes, when there is a cargo, they go up as far as
Constanza, but usually they run only as far as here, calling at the Piræus on the way. They carry a few passengers, fifteen at the most, and we can make sure that
every one of them is harmless before the boat is given its
clearance papers. When you get to Genoa, you will have
only the short train journey between Genoa and the

French frontier to put you out of reach of German agents."

"But as you yourself pointed out, time is an important factor. To-day is the second. I am due back on the eighth. If I have to wait for boats I shall be days late. Besides, the journey itself will take at least a week."

"There will be no delay, Mr. Graham," sighed the Colonel. "I am not stupid. I telephoned the port police before you arrived. There is a boat leaving in two days' time for Marseilles. It would have been better if you could have travelled on that even though it does not ordinarily take passengers. But the Italian boat leaves to-day at four-thirty in the afternoon. You will be able to stretch your legs in Athens to-morrow afternoon. You will dock in Genoa early Saturday morning. You can, if you wish and if your visas are in order, be in London by Monday morning. As I have told you, a marked man has advantages over his enemies: he can run away—disappear. In the middle of the Mediterranean, you will be as safe as you are in this office."

Graham hesitated. He glanced at Kopeikin; but the Russian was staring at his finger nails.

"Well, I don't know, Colonel. This is all very good of you, but I can't help thinking that, in view of the circumstances which you have explained to me, I ought to get in touch with the British Consul here, or with the British Embassy, before deciding anything."

Colonel Haki lit a cigarette. "And what do you expect the Consul or the Ambassador to do? Send you home in a cruiser?" He laughed unpleasantly. "My dear Mr. Graham, I am not asking you to decide anything. I am telling you what you must do. You are, I must again remind you, of great value to my country in your present state of health. You must allow me to protect my country's interests in my own way. I think that you are probably tired now and a little upset. I do not wish to harass you, but I must explain that, if you do not agree to follow my instructions, I shall have no alternative but to arrest you, have an order issued for your deportation and put you on board the *Sestri Levante* under guard. I hope that I make myself clear."

Graham felt himself reddening. "Quite clear. Would you like to handcuff me now? It will save a lot of trouble. You need . . ."

"I think," put in Kopeikin hastily, "that I should do as the Colonel suggests, my dear fellow. It is the best thing."

"I prefer to be my own judge of that, Kopeikin." He looked from one to the other of them angrily. He felt confused and wretched. Things had been moving too quickly for him. Colonel Haki he disliked intensely. Kopeikin seemed to be no longer capable of thinking for himself. He felt that they were making decisions with the glib irresponsibility of schoolboys planning a game of Red Indians. And yet the devil of it was that those conclusions were inescapably logical. His life was threatened. All they were asking him to do was to go home by another and safer route. It was a reasonable request but. . . . Then he shrugged his shoulders. "All right. I seem to have no choice."

"Exactly, Mr. Graham." The Colonel smoothed out his tunic with the air of one who has reasoned wisely with a child. "Now we can make our arrangements. As soon as the shipping company's offices are open Mr. Kopeikin can arrange for your passage and obtain a refund for your railway ticket. I will see that the names and particulars of the other passengers are submitted to me for approval before the ship sails. You need have no fears, Mr. Graham, of your fellow travellers. But I am afraid that you will not find them very *chic* or the boat very comfortable. This line is actually the cheapest route to and from Istanbul if you live in the west. But you will not, I am sure, mind a little discomfort if you have peace of mind to compensate for it."

"As long as I get back to England by the eighth, I don't care how I travel."

"That is the right spirit. And now I suggest that you remain in this building until it is time for you to leave. We will make you as comfortable as possible. Mr. Kopeikin can collect your suitcase from the hotel. I will see that a doctor looks at your hand later on to see that it is still all right." He looked at his watch. "The concièrge can make us some coffee now. Later, he can get some food for you from the restaurant round the corner." He stood up. "I will go and see about it now. We cannot save you from bullets to let you die of starvation, eh?"

"It's very kind of you," said Graham; and then, as the Colonel disappeared down the corridor: "I owe you an apolegy Kopeikin. I behaved badly."

Kopeikin looked distressed. "My dear fellow! You cannot be blamed. I am glad everything has been settled so quickly."

"Quickly, yes." He hesitated. "Is this man Haki to be trusted?"

"You do not like him either, eh?" Kopeikin chuckled. "I would not trust him with a woman; but with you— yes."

"You approve of my going on this boat?"

"I do. By the way, my dear fellow," he went on mildly, "have you a gun in your luggage?"

"Good heavens, no!"

"Then you had better take this." He pulled a small revolver out of his overcoat pocket. "I put it in my pocket when I came out after you telephoned. It is fully loaded."

"But I shan't need it."

"No, but it will make you feel better to have it."

"I doubt that. Still. . . ." He took the revolver and stared at it distastefully. "I've never fired one of these things, you know."

"It is easy. You release the safety catch, point it, pull the trigger and hope for the best."

"All the same . . ."

"Put it in your pocket. You can give it to the French Customs officials at Modano."

Colonel Haki returned. "The coffee is being prepared. Now, Mr. Graham, we will decide how you are to amuse yourself until it is time for you to go." He caught sight of the revolver in Graham's hand. "Ah-ha! You are arming yourself!" He grinned. "A little melodrama is sometimes unavoidable, eh, Mr. Graham?"

The decks were silent now and Graham could hear the sounds within the ship: people talking, doors slamming, quick businesslike footsteps in the alleyways. There

was not long to wait now. Outside it was getting dark.
He looked back upon a day which had seemed interminable, surprised that he could remember so little of it.

Most of it he had spent in Colonel Haki's office, his
brain hovering uncertainly on the brink of sleep. He had
smoked innumerable cigarettes and read some fortnight
old French newspapers. There had been an article in one
of them, he remembered, about the French mandate in
the Cameroons. A doctor had been, reported favourably
on the state of his wound, dressed it and gone. Kopeikin
had brought him his suitcase and he had made a bloody
attempt to shave with his left hand. In the absence of
Colonel Haki they had shared a cool and soggy meal from
the restaurant. The Colonel had returned at two to inform him that there were nine other passengers travelling on the boat, four of them women, that none of them
had booked for the journey less than three days previously, and that they were all harmless.

The gangway was down now and the last of the nine,
a couple who sounded middle-aged and spoke French, had
come aboard and were in the cabin next to his. Their
voices penetrated the thin wooden bulkhead with dis-
maying ease. He could hear almost every sound they
made. They had argued incessantly, in whispers at first
as if they had been in church; but the novelty of their
surroundings soon wore off and they spoke in ordinary
tones.

"The sheets are damp."

"No, it is simply that they are cold. In any case it does
not matter."

"You think not? You think not?" She made a noise

in her throat. "You may sleep as you wish, but do not complain to me about your kidneys."

"Cold sheets do not harm the kidneys, *chérie*."

"We have paid for our tickets. We are entitled to comfort."

"If you never sleep in a worse place you will be lucky. This is not the *Normandie*."

"That is evident." The washing cabinet clicked open. "Ah! Look at this. Look! Do you expect me to wash in it?"

"It is only necessary to run the water. A little dust."

"Dust! It is *dirty*. Filthy! It is for the steward to clean it. I will not touch it. Go and fetch him while I unpack the luggage. My dresses will be crushed. Where is the W.C.?"

"At the end of the corridor."

"Then find the steward. There is no room for two while I unpack. We should have gone by train."

"Naturally. But it is I who must pay. It is I who must give the steward a tip."

"It is you who make too much noise. Quickly. Do you want to disturb everyone?"

The man went out and the woman sighed loudly. Graham wondered whether they would talk all night. And one or both of them might snore. He would have to cough loudly once or twice so that they would realise how thin the partition was. But it was strangely comforting to hear people talking about damp sheets and dirty wash basins and W.C.'s as if—the phrase was in his mind before he realised it—as if they were matters of life and death.

Life and death! He got to his feet and found himself staring at the framed instructions for lifeboat drill.

"CINTURE DI SALVATAGGIO, CEINTURES DE SAUVETAGE, RET-TUNGSGÜRTEL. LIFEBELTS. . . . *In case of danger, the signal will be given by six short blasts on the whistle followed by one long blast and the ringing of alarm bells. Passengers should then put on their lifebelts and assemble at boat station number 4.*"

He had seen the same sort of thing dozens of times before but now he read it carefully. The paper it was printed on was yellow with age. The lifebelt on top of the washing cabinet looked as if it had not been moved for years. It was all ludicrously reassuring. "*In case of danger. . . .*" In case! But you couldn't get away from danger! It was all about you, all the time. You could live in ignorance of it for years: you might go to the end of your days believing that some things couldn't possibly happen to *you*, that death could only come to you with the sweet reason of disease or an "act of God": but it was there just the same, waiting to make nonsense of all your comfortable ideas about your relations with time and chance, ready to remind you—in case you had forgotten —that civilisation was a word and that you still lived in the jungle.

The ship swayed gently. There was a faint clanging from the engine room telegraph. The floor began to vibrate. Through the smeared glass of the porthole he saw a light begin to move. The vibration ceased for a moment or two; then the engines went astern and the water glass rattled in its bracket on the wall. Another pause and then the engines went ahead again, slowly and steadily. They were free of the land. With a sigh of relief he opened the cabin door and went up on deck.

It was cold but the ship had turned and was taking the wind on her port side. She seemed stationary on the oily water of the harbour but the dock lights were sliding past them and receding. He drew the cold air into his lungs. It was good to be out of the cabin. His thoughts no longer seemed to worry him. Istanbul, Le Jockey Cabaret, the man in the crumpled suit, the Adler-Palace and its manager, Colonel Haki—they were all behind him. He could forget about them.

He began to pace slowly along the deck. He would, he told himself, be able to laugh at the whole business soon. It was already half-forgotten; there was already an air of the fantastic about it. He might almost have dreamed it. He was back in the ordinary world: he was on his way home.

He passed one of his fellow passengers, the first he had seen, an elderly man leaning on the rail staring at the lights of Istanbul coming into view as they cleared the mole. Now, as he reached the end of the deck and turned about, he saw that a woman in a fur coat had just come out of the saloon door and was walking towards him.

The light on the deck was dim and she was within a few yards of him before he recognised her.

It was Josette.

CHAPTER FOUR

For a moment they stared blankly at one another. Then she laughed. "Merciful God! It is the Englishman. Excuse me, but this is extraordinary."

"Yes, isn't it."

"And what happened to your first-class compartment on the Orient Express?"

He smiled. "Kopeikin thought that a little sea air would do me good."

"And you needed doing good?" The straw-coloured hair was covered with a woollen scarf tied under the chin, but she held her head back to look at him as if she were wearing a hat that shaded her eyes.

"Evidently." On the whole, he decided, she looked a good deal less attractive than she had looked in her dressing-room. The fur coat was shapeless, and the scarf did not suit her. "Since we are talking about trains," he added, "what happened to your second-class compartment?"

She frowned with a smile at the corners of her mouth. "This way is so much less expensive. Did I say that I was travelling by train?"

Graham flushed. "No, of course not." He realised that he was being rather rude. "In any case, I am delighted to see you again so soon. I have been wondering what I should do if I found that the Hotel des Belges was closed."

She looked at him archly. "Ah! You were really going to telephone me, then?"

"Of course. It was understood, wasn't it?"

She discarded the arch look and replaced it with a pout. "I do not think that you are sincere after all. Tell me truthfully why you are on this boat."

She began to walk along the deck. He could do nothing but fall in step beside her.

"You don't believe me?"

She lifted her shoulders elaborately. "You need not tell me if you do not wish to. I am not inquisitive."

He thought he saw her difficulty. From her point of view there could be only two explanations of his presence on the boat: either his claim to be travelling first class on the Orient Express had been a pretentious lie intended to impress her—in which case he would have very little money—or he had somehow discovered that she was travelling on the boat, and had abandoned the luxury of the Orient Express in order to pursue her—in which case he would probably have plenty of money. He had a sudden absurd desire to startle her with the truth.

"Very well," he said. "I am travelling this way to avoid someone who is trying to shoot me."

She stopped dead. "I think it is too cold out here," she

said calmly. "I shall go in."

He was so surprised that he laughed.

She turned on him quickly. "You should not make such stupid jokes."

There was no doubt about it; she was genuinely angry. He held up his bandaged hand. "A bullet grazed it."

She frowned. "You are very bad. If you have hurt your hand I am sorry, but you should not make jokes about it. It is very dangerous."

"Dangerous!"

"You will have bad luck, and so shall I. It is very bad luck to joke in that way."

"Oh, I see." He grinned. "I am not superstitious."

"That is because you do not know. I would sooner see a raven flying than joke about killing. If you wish me to like you, you must not say such things."

"I apologise," said Graham, mildly. "Actually I cut my hand with a razor."

"Ah, they are dangerous things! In Algiers José saw a man with his throat cut from ear to ear with a razor."

"Suicide?"

"No, no! It was his *petite amie* who did it. There was a lot of blood. José will tell you about it if you ask him. It was very sad."

"Yes, I can imagine. José is travelling with you, then?"

"Naturally." And then, with a sidelong look: "He is my husband."

Her husband! That explained why she "put up with" José. It also explained why Colonel Haki had omitted to tell him that the "dancing blonde" was travelling on the boat. Graham remembered the promptitude with which

José had retired from the dressing-room. That, no doubt, had been a matter of business. *Attractions* at a place like Le Jockey Cabaret were not quite so attractive if they were known to have husbands in the vicinity. He said: "Kopeikin didn't tell me that you were married."

"Kopeikin is very nice, but he does not know everything. But I will tell you confidentially that with José and me it is an arrangement. We are partners, nothing more. He is jealous about me only when I neglect business for pleasure."

She said it indifferently, as if she were discussing a clause in her contract.

"Are you going to dance in Paris now?"

"I do not know. I hope so; but so much is closed on account of the war."

"What will you do if you can't get an engagement?"

"What do you think? I shall starve. I have done it before." She smiled bravely. "It is good for the figure." She pressed her hands on her hips and looked at him, inviting his considered opinion. "Do you not think it would be good for my figure to starve a little? One grows fat in Istanbul." She posed. "You see?"

Graham nearly laughed. The picture being presented for his approval had all the simple allure of a full-page drawing in *La Vie Parisienne*. Here was the "business man's" dream come true: the beautiful blonde dancer. married but unloved, in need of protection: something expensive going cheap.

"A dancer's must be a very hard life," he said dryly.

"Ah, yes! Many people think that it is so gay. If they knew!"

"Yes, of course. It is getting a little cold, isn't it? Shall we go inside and have a drink?"

"That would be nice." She added with a tremendous air of candour: "I am so glad we are travelling together. I was afraid that I was going to be bored. Now, I shall enjoy myself."

He felt that his answering smile was probably rather sickly. He was beginning to have an uncomfortable suspicion that he was making a fool of himself. "We go this way, I think," he said.

The *salone* was a narrow room about thirty feet long, with entrances from the shelter deck and from the landing at the head of the stairs to the cabins. There were grey upholstered *banquettes* round the walls and, at one end, three round dining tables bolted down. Evidently there was no separate dining-room. Some chairs, a card table, a shaky writing desk, a radio, a piano and a threadbare carpet completed the furnishings. Opening off the room at the far end was a cubby hole with half doors. The lower door had a strip of wood screwed to the top of it to make a counter. This was the bar. Inside it, the steward was opening cartons of cigarettes. Except for him, the place was deserted. They sat down.

"What would you like to drink, Mrs. . . .," began Graham tentatively.

She laughed. "José's name is Gallindo, but I detest it. You must call me Josette. I would like some English whisky and a cigarette, please."

"Two whiskies," said Graham.

The steward put his head out and frowned at them. "Viski? *E molto caro*," he said warningly; "*très cher.*

Cinque lire. Five lire each. Vair dear."

"Yes, it is, but we will have them just the same."

The steward retired into the bar, and made a lot of noise with the bottles.

"He is very angry," said Josette. "He is not used to people who order whisky." She had obviously derived a good deal of satisfaction from the ordering of the whisky, and the discomfiture of the steward. In the light of the saloon her fur coat looked cheap and old; but she had unbuttoned it and arranged it round her shoulders as if it had been a thousand guinea mink. He began, against his better judgment, to feel sorry for her.

"How long have you been dancing?"

"Since I was ten. That is twenty years ago. You see," she remarked, complacently, "I do not lie to you about my age. I was born in Serbia, but I say that I am Hungarian because it sounds better. My mother and father were very poor."

"But honest, no doubt."

She looked faintly puzzled. "Oh no, my father was not at all honest. He was a dancer, and he stole some money from someone in the troupe. They put him in prison. Then the war came, and my mother took me to Paris. A very rich man took care of us for a time, and we had a very nice apartment." She gave a nostalgic sigh: an impoverished *grande dame* lamenting past glories. "But he lost his money, and so my mother had to dance again. My mother died when we were in Madrid, and I was sent back to Paris, to a convent. It was terrible there. I do not know what happened to my father. I think perhaps he was killed in the war."

"And what about José?"

"I met him in Berlin when I was dancing there. He did not like his partner. She was," she added simply, "a terrible bitch."

"Was this long ago?"

"Oh, yes. Three years. We have been to a great many places." She examined him with affectionate concern. "But you are tired. You look tired. You have cut your face, too."

"I tried to shave with one hand."

"Have you got a very nice house in England?"

"My wife likes it."

"*Oh là-là!* And do you like your wife?"

"Very much."

"I do not think," she said reflectively, "that I would like to go to England. So much rain and fog. I like Paris. There is nothing better to live in than an apartment in Paris. It is not expensive."

"No?"

"For twelve hundred francs a month one can have a very nice apartment. In Rome it is not so cheap. I had an apartment in Rome that was very nice, but it cost fifteen hundred lire. My fiancé was very rich. He sold automobiles."

"That was before you married José?"

"Of course. We were going to be married but there was some trouble about his divorce from his wife in America. He always said that he would fix it, but in the end it was impossible. I was very sorry. I had that apartment for a year."

"And that was how you learned English?"

"Yes, but I had learned a little in that terrible convent." She frowned. "But I tell you everything about myself. About you I know nothing except that you have a nice house and a wife, and that you are an engineer. You ask questions, but you tell me nothing. I still do not know why you are here. It is very bad of you."

But he did not have to reply to this. Another passenger had entered the saloon, and was advancing towards them, clearly with the intention of making their acquaintance.

He was short, broad-shouldered and unkempt, with a heavy jowl and a fringe of scurfy grey hair round a bald pate. He had a smile, fixed like that of a ventriloquist's doll: a standing apology for the iniquity of his existence.

The boat had begun to roll slightly; but from the way he clutched for support at the backs of chairs as he crossed the room, it might have been riding out a full gale.

"There is lot of movement, eh?" he said in English, and subsided into a chair. "Ah! That is better, eh?" He looked at Josette with obvious interest, but turned to Graham before he spoke again. "I hear English spoken so I am interested at once," he said. "You are English, sir?"

"Yes. And you?"

"Turkish. I also go to London. Trade is very good. I go to sell tobacco. My name is Mr. Kuvetli, sir."

"My name is Graham. This is Señora Gallindo."

"So good," said Mr. Kuvetli. Without getting up from his chair, he bowed from the waist. "I don't speak English very well," he added, unnecessarily.

"It is a very difficult language," said Josette, coldly. She was obviously displeased by the intrusion.

"My wife," continued Mr. Kuvetli, "does not speak English any. So I do not bring her with me. She has not been to England."

"But you have?"

"Yes, sir. Three times, and to sell tobacco. I do not sell much before, but now I sell lot. It is war. United States ships do not come to England any more. English ships bring guns and aeroplanes from U.S. and have no room for tobacco, so England now buys lot of tobacco from Turkey. It is good business for my boss. Firm of Pazar and Co."

"It must be."

"He would come to England himself, but cannot speak English any. Or he cannot write. He is very ignorant. I reply to all favours from England and elsewhere abroad. But he knows lot about tobacco. We produce best." He plunged his hand into his pocket and produced a leather cigarette case. "Please try cigarette made from tobacco by Pazar and Co." He extended the case to Josette.

She shook her head. *"Tesekkür ederim."*

The Turkish phrase irritated Graham. It seemed to belittle the man's polite efforts to speak a language foreign to him.

"Ah!" said Mr. Kuvetli, "you speak my language. That is very good. You have been long in Turkey?"

"Dört ay." She turned to Graham. "I would like one of *your* cigarettes, please."

It was a deliberate insult but Mr. Kuvetli only smiled a little more. Graham took one of the cigarettes.

"Thank you very much. It's very good of you. Will you have a drink, Mr. Kuvetli?"

"Ah, no, thank you. I must go to arrange my cabin before it is dinner."

"Then later, perhaps."

"Yes, please." With a broadened smile and a bow to each of them he got to his feet and made his way to the door.

Graham lit his cigarette. "Was it absolutely necessary to be so rude? Why drive the man away?"

She frowned. "Turks! I do not like them. They are"—she ransacked the automobile salesman's vocabulary for an epithet—"they are goddamned dagoes. See how thick his skin is! He does not get angry. He only smiles."

"Yes, he behaved very well."

"I do not understand it," she burst out angrily. "In the last war you fought with France against the Turks. In the convent they told me much about it. They are heathen animals, these Turks. There were the Armenian atrocities and the Syrian atrocities and the Smyrna atrocities. Turks killed babies with their bayonets. But now it is all different. You like the Turks. They are your allies and you buy tobacco from them. It is the English hypocrisy. I am a Serb. I have a longer memory."

"Does your memory go back to nineteen twelve? I was thinking of the Serbian atrocities in Turkish villages. Most armies commit what are called atrocities at some time or other. They usually call them reprisals."

"Including the British army, perhaps?"

"You would have to ask an Indian or an Afrikander about that. But every country has its madmen. Some countries have more than others. And when you give such men a license to kill they are not always particular about the way they kill. But I am afraid that the rest of their fellow countrymen remain human beings. Personally, I like the Turks."

She was clearly angry with him. He suspected that her rudeness to Mr. Kuvetli had been calculated to earn his approval and that she was annoyed because he had not responded in the way she had expected. "It is stuffy in here," she said, "and there is a smell of cooking. I should like to walk outside again. You may come with me if you wish."

Graham seized the opportunity. He said, as they walked towards the door: "I think that I should unpack my suitcase. I shall hope to see you at dinner."

Her expression changed quickly. She became an international beauty humouring, with a tolerant smile, the extravagances of a love-sick boy. "As you wish José will be with me later. I shall introduce you to him. He will want to play cards."

"Yes, I remember you told me that he would. I shall have to try to remember a game that I can play well."

She shrugged. "He will win in any case. But I have warned you."

"I shall remember that when I lose."

He returned to his cabin and stayed there until the steward came round beating a gong to announce dinner. When he went upstairs he was feeling better. He had changed his clothes. He had managed to complete the shave which he had begun in the morning. He had an appetite. He was prepared to take an interest in his fellow passengers.

Most of them were already in their places when he entered the saloon.

The ship's officers evidently ate in their own quarters. Only two of the dining tables were laid. At one of them sat Mr. Kuvetli, a man and woman who looked as if they might be the French couple from the cabin next to his, Josette, and with her a very sleek José. Graham smiled courteously at the assembly and received in return a loud "good evening" from Mr. Kuvetli, a lift of the eyebrows from Josette, a cool nod from José, and a blank stare from the French couple. There was about them an air of tension which seemed to him to be more than the ordinary restraint of passengers on a boat sitting down together for the first time. The steward showed him to the other table.

One of the places was already filled by the elderly man whom he had passed on his walk round the deck. He was a thick, round-shouldered man with a pale heavy face, white hair and a long upper lip. As Graham sat down next to him he looked up. Graham met a pair of prominent pale blue eyes.

"Mr. Graham?"

"Yes. Good evening."

"My name is Haller. Doctor Fritz Haller. I should explain that I am a German, a good German, and that I am on my way back to my country." He spoke very good, deliberate English in a deep voice.

Graham realised that the occupants of the other table were staring at them in breathless silence. He understood now their air of tension.

He said calmly: "I am an Englishman. But I gather you knew that."

"Yes, I knew it." Haller turned to the food in front of

him. "The Allies seem to be here in force and unhappily the steward is an imbecile. The two French people at the next table were placed here. They objected to eating with the enemy, insulted me and moved. If you wish to do the same I suggest that you do so now. Everyone is expecting the scene."

"So I see." Graham cursed the steward silently.

"On the other hand," Haller continued, breaking his bread, "you may find the situation humorous. I do myself. Perhaps I am not as patriotic as I should be. No doubt I should insult you before you insult me; but, quite apart from the unfair differences in our ages, I can think of no effective way of insulting you. One must understand a person thoroughly before one can insult him effectively. The French lady, for example, called me a filthy Bosche. I am unmoved. I bathed this morning and I have no unpleasant habits."

"I see your point. But . . ."

"But there is a matter of etiquette involved. Quite so. Fortunately, I must leave that to you. Move or not, as you choose. Your presence here would not embarrass me. If it were understood that we were to exclude international politics from our conversation we might even pass the next half-hour in a civilised manner. However, as the newcomer on the scene, it is for you to decide."

Graham picked up the menu. "I believe it is the custom for belligerents on neutral ground to ignore each other if possible and in any case to avoid embarrassing the neutrals in question. Thanks to the steward, we cannot ignore each other. There seems to be no reason why we should make a difficult situation unpleasant. No doubt we can rearrange the seating before the next meal."

Haller nodded approval. "Very sensible. I must admit that I am glad of your company to-night. My wife suffers from the sea and will stay in her cabin this evening. I think that Italian cooking is very monotonous without conversation."

"I am inclined to agree with you." Graham smiled intentionally and heard a rustle from the next table. He also heard an exclamation of disgust from the Frenchwoman. He was annoyed to find that the sound made him feel guilty.

"You seem," said Haller, "to have earned some disapproval. It is partly my fault. I am sorry. Perhaps it is that I am old, but I find it extremely difficult to identify men with their ideas. I can dislike, even hate an idea, but the man who has it seems to be still a man."

"Have you been long in Turkey?"

"A few weeks. I came there from Persia."

"Oil?"

"No, Mr. Graham, archeology. I was investigating the early pre-Islamic cultures. The little I have been able to discover seems to suggest that some of the tribes who moved westward to the plains of Iran about four thousand years ago assimilated the Sumerian culture and preserved it almost intact until long after the fall of Babylon. The form of perpetuation of the Adonis myth alone was instructive. The weeping for Tammuz was always a focal point of the pre-historic religions—the cult of the dying and risen god. Tammuz, Osiris and Adonis are the same Sumerian deity personified by three different races. But the Sumerians called this god Dumuzida. So did some of the pre-Islamic tribes of Iran! And they had a most interesting variation of the Sumerian epic of Gilgamish and Enkidu which I had not heard about before. But forgive me, I am boring you already."

"Not at all," said Graham politely. "Were you in Persia for long?"

"Two years only. I would have stayed another year but for the war."

"Did it make so much difference?"

Haller pursed his lips. "There was a financial question. But even without that I think that I might not have stayed. We can learn only in the expectation of life. Europe is too preoccupied with its destruction to concern itself with such things: a condemned man is interested only in himself, the passage of hours and such intimations of immortality as he can conjure from the recesses of his mind."

"I should have thought that a preoccupation with the past. . . ."

"Ah yes, I know. The scholar in his study can ignore the noise in the market place. Perhaps—if he is a theologian or a biologist or an antiquarian. I am none of those things. I helped in the search for a logic of history. We should have made of the past a mirror with which to see round the corner that separates us from the future. Unfortunately, it no longer matters what we could have seen. We are returning the way we came. Human understanding is re-entering the monastery."

"Forgive me but I thought you said that you were a *good* German."

He chuckled. "I am old. I can afford the luxury of despair."

"Still, in your place, I think that I should have stayed in Persia and luxuriated at a distance."

"The climate, unfortunately, is not suitable for any sort of luxuriating. It is either very hot or very cold. My wife found it particularly trying. Are you a soldier, Mr. Graham?"

"No, an engineer."

"That is much the same thing. I have a son in the army. He has always been a soldier. I have never understood why he should be my son. As a lad of fourteen he disapproved of me because I had no duelling scars. He disapproved of the English, too, I am afraid. We lived for some time in Oxford while I was doing some work there. A beautiful city! Do you live in London?"

"No, in the North."

"I have visited Manchester and Leeds. I preferred Oxford. I live in Berlin myself. I don't think it is any uglier than London." He glanced at Graham's hand. "You seem to have had an accident."

"Yes. Fortunately it's just as easy to eat ravioli with the left hand."

"There is that to be said for it, I suppose. Will you have some of this wine?"

"I don't think so, thank you."

"Yes, you're wise. The best Italian wines never leave Italy." He dropped his voice. "Ah! Here are the other two passengers."

They looked like mother and son. The woman was about fifty and unmistakably Italian. Her face was very hollow and pale and she carried herself as if she had been seriously ill. Her son, a handsome lad of eighteen or so, was very attentive to her and glared defensively at Graham, who had risen to draw back her chair for her. They both wore black.

Haller greeted them in Italian to which the boy replied briefly. The woman inclined her head to them but did not speak. It was obvious that they wished to be left to themselves. They conferred in whispers over the menu. Graham could hear José talking at the next table.

"War!" he was saying in thick, glutinous French; "it makes it very difficult for all to earn money. Let Germany have all the territory she desires. Let her choke herself with territory. Then let us go to Berlin and enjoy ourselves. It is ridiculous to fight. It is not businesslike."

"Ha!" said the Frenchman. "You, a Spaniard, say that! Ha! That is very good. Magnificent!"

"In the civil war," said José, "I took no sides. I had my work to do, my living to earn. It was madness. I did not go to Spain."

"War is terrible," said Mr. Kuvetli.

"But if the Reds had won . . ." began the Frenchman.

"Ah yes!" exclaimed his wife. "If the Reds had won. . . . They were anti-Christ. They burnt churches and broke sacred images and relics. They violated nuns and murdered priests."

"It was all very bad for business," repeated José obstinately. "I know a man in Bilbao who had a big business. It was all finished by the war. War is very stupid."

"The voice of the fool," murmured Haller, "with the tongue of the wise. I think that I will go and see how my wife is. Will you excuse me, please?"

Graham finished his meal virtually alone. Haller did

not return. The mother and son opposite to him ate with their heads bent over their plates. They seemed to be in communion over some private sorrow. He felt as if he were intruding. As soon as he had finished he left the saloon, put on his overcoat and went out on deck to get some air before going to bed.

The lights on the land were distant now, and the ship was rustling through the sea before the wind. He found the companionway up to the boat deck and stood for a time in the lee of a ventilator idly watching a man with a lamp on the well deck below tapping the wedges which secured the hatch tarpaulins. Soon the man finished his task, and Graham was left to wonder how he was going to pass the time on the boat. He made up his mind to get some books in Athens the following day. According to Kopeikin, they would dock at the Piræus at about two o'clock in the afternoon, and sail again at five. He would have plenty of time to take the tram into Athens, buy some English cigarettes and books, send a telegram to Stephanie and get back to the dock.

He lit a cigarette, telling himself that he would smoke it and then go to bed; but, even as he threw the match away, he saw that Josette and José had come on to the deck, and that the girl had seen him. It was too late to retreat. They were coming over to him.

"So you are here," she said accusingly. "This is José."

José, who was wearing a very tight black overcoat and a grey soft hat with a curly brim, nodded reluctantly, and said: "*Enchanté, Monsieur,*" with the air of a busy man whose time is being wasted.

"José does not speak English," she explained.

"There is no reason why he should. It is a pleasure to meet you, Señor Gallindo," he went on in Spanish. "I very much enjoyed the dancing of you and your wife."

José laughed rudely. "It is nothing. The place was impossible."

"José was angry all the time because Coco—the negress with the snake, you remember?—had more money from Serge than we did, although we were the principal attraction."

José said something unprintable, in Spanish.

"She was," said Josette, "Serge's lover. You smile, but it is true. Is it not true, José?"

José made a loud noise with his lips.

"José is very vulgar," commented Josette. "But it is true about Serge and Coco. It is a very *drôle* story. There was a great joke about Fifi, the snake. Coco was very fond of Fifi, and always used to take it to bed with her. But Serge did not know that until he became her lover. Coco says that when he found Fifi in the bed, he fainted. She made him increase her wages to double before she would consent to Fifi's sleeping alone in its basket. Serge is no fool: even José says that Serge is no fool; but Coco treats him like dirt. It is because she has a very great temper that she is able to do it."

"He needs to hit her with his fist," said José.

"Ah! *Salop!*" She turned to Graham. "And you! Do you agree with José?"

"I have no experience of snake dancers."

"Ah! You do not answer. You are brutes, you men!"

She was obviously amusing herself at his expense. He said to José: "Have you made this trip before?"

José stared suspiciously. "No. Why? Have you?"

"Oh no."

José lit a cigarette. "I am already very tired of this ship," he announced. "It is dull and dirty, and it vibrates excessively. Also the cabins are too near the lavabos. Do you play poker?"

"I *have* played. But I don't play very well."

"I told you!" cried Josette.

"She thinks," said José sourly, "that because I win I cheat. I do not care a damn what she thinks. People are not compelled by law to play cards with me. Why should they squeal like stuck pigs when they lose?"

"It is," Graham admitted, tactfully, "illogical."

"We will play now if you like," said José, as if someone had accused him of refusing a challenge.

"If you don't mind, I'd sooner leave it until to-morrow. I'm rather tired to-night. In fact, I think that if you will excuse me I shall get to bed now."

"So soon!" Josette pouted, and broke into English. "There is only one interesting person on the boat, and he goes to bed. It is too bad. Ah yes, you are being very bad. Why did you sit next to that German at dinner?"

"He did not object to my sitting beside him. Why should *I* object? He is a very pleasant and intelligent old fellow."

"He is a German. For you no German should be pleasant or intelligent. It is as the French people were saying. The English are not serious about these things."

José turned suddenly on his heel. "It is very boring to listen to English," he said, "and I am cold. I shall go and drink some brandy."

Graham was beginning to apologise when the girl cut him short. "He is very unpleasant to-day. It is because he is disappointed. He thought there were going to be some pretty little girls for him to roll his eyes at. He always has a great success with pretty little girls—and old women."

She had spoken loudly, and in French. José, who had reached the top of the companionway, turned and belched deliberately before descending.

"He is gone," said Josette. "I am glad. He has very bad manners." She drew in her breath, and looked up at the clouds. "It is a lovely night. I do not see why you wish to go to bed. It is early."

"I'm very tired."

"You cannot be too tired to walk across the deck with me."

"Of course not."

There was a corner of the deck below the bridge where it was very dark. She stopped there, turned abruptly and leaned with her back to the rail so that he was facing her.

"I think you are angry with me?"

"Good gracious, no! Why should I be?"

"Because I was rude to your little Turk."

"He's not *my* little Turk."

"But you are angry?"

"Of course not."

She sighed. "You are very mysterious. You have still not told me why you are travelling on this boat. I am very interested to know. It cannot be because it is cheap. Your clothes are expensive!"

He could not see her face, only a vague outline of her;

but he could smell the scent she was using, and the mustiness of the fur coat. He said: "I can't think why you should be interested."

"But you know perfectly well that I am."

She had come an inch or two nearer to him. He knew that, if he wanted to do so, he could kiss her and that she would return the kiss. He knew also that it would be no idle peck, but a declaration that their relationship was to be the subject of discussion. He was surprised to find that he did not reject the idea instantaneously, that the immediate prospect of feeling her full smooth lips against his was more than attractive. He was cold and tired: she was near, and he could sense the warmth of her body. It could do no one any harm if . . . He said: "Are you travelling to Paris via Modane?"

"Yes. But why ask? It is the way to Paris."

"When we get to Modane I will tell you exactly why I travelled this way, if you are still interested."

She turned and they walked on. "Perhaps it is not so important," she said. "You must not think I am inquisitive." They reached the companionway. Her attitude towards him had changed perceptibly. She looked at him with friendly concern. "Yes, my dear sir, you are tired. I should not have asked you to stay up here. I shall finish my walk alone. Good night."

"Good night, Señora."

She smiled. "Señora! You must not be so unkind. Good night."

He went below amused and irritated by his thoughts. Outside the door of the saloon he came face to face with Mr. Kuvetli.

Mr. Kuvetli broadened his smile. "First officer says we shall have good weather, sir."

"Splendid." He remembered with a sinking heart that he had invited the man to have a drink. "Will you join me in a drink?"

"Oh no, thank you. Not now." Mr. Kuvetli placed one hand on his chest. "Matter of fact, I have pain because of wine at table. Very strong acid stuff!"

"So I should imagine. Until to-morrow, then."

"Yes, Mr. Graham. You will be glad to arrive back at your home, eh?" He seemed to want to talk.

"Oh yes, very glad."

"You go to Athens when we stop to-morrow?"

"I was thinking of doing so."

"Do you know Athens well, I suppose?"

"I've been there before."

Mr. Kuvetli hesitated. His smile became oily. "You are in a position to do me service, Mr. Graham."

"Oh yes?"

"I do not know Athens. I have never been. Would you allow me to go with you?"

"Yes, of course. I should be glad of company. But I was only going to buy some English books and cigarettes."

"I am most grateful."

"Not at all. We get in just after lunch, don't we?"

"Yes, yes. That is quite right. But I will find out exact time. You leave that to me."

"Then that's settled. I think I shall go to bed now. Good night, Mr. Kuvetli."

"Good night, sir. And I thank you for your favour."

"Not at all. Good night."

JOURNEY INTO FEAR   95

He went to his cabin, rang for the steward and said
that he wanted his breakfast coffee in his cabin at nine-
thirty. Then he undressed and got into his bunk.

For a few minutes he lay on his back enjoying the
gradual relaxing of his muscles. Now, at last, he could
forget Haki, Kopeikin, Banat, and the rest of it. He was
back in his own life, and could sleep. The phrase "asleep
almost as soon as his head touched the pillow" passed
through his mind. That was how it would be with him.
God knew he was tired enough. He turned on his side.
But sleep did not come so easily. His brain would not
stop working. It was as if the needle were trapped in one
groove on the record. He'd made a fool of himself with
that wretched woman Josette. He'd made a fool . . .
He jerked his thoughts forward. Ah yes! He was committed to three unalloyed hours of Mr. Kuvetli's company. But that was to-morrow. And now, sleep. But
his hand was throbbing again, and there seemed to be a
lot of noise going on. That boor José was right. The
vibration *was* excessive. The cabins *were* too near the
lavatories. There were footsteps overhead, too: people
walking round the shelter deck. Round and round. Why,
for Heaven's sake, must people always be walking?

He had been lying awake for half an hour when the
French couple entered their cabin.

They were quiet for a minute or two, and he could
only hear the sounds they made as they moved about the
cabin, and an occasional grunted comment. Then the
woman began.

"Well, that is the first evening over! Three more! It is
too much to think of."

"It will pass." A yawn. "What is the matter with the Italian woman and her son?"

"You did not hear? Her husband was killed in the earthquake at Erzurum. The first officer told me. He is very nice, but I had hoped that there would be at least one French person to talk to."

"There are people who speak French. The little Turk speaks it very well. And there are the others."

"They are not French. That girl and that man—the Spaniard. They say that they are dancers, but I ask you."

"She is pretty."

"Certainly. I do not dispute it. But you need not think little thoughts. She is interested in the Englishman. I do not like him. He does not look like an Englishman."

"You think the English are all *milords* with sporting clothes and monocles. Ha! I saw the Tommies in nineteen fifteen. They are all small and ugly with very loud voices. They talk very quickly. This type is more like the officers who are thin and slow, and look as if things do not smell very nice."

"This type is not an English officer. He likes the Germans."

"You exaggerate. An old man like that! I would have sat with him myself."

"Ah! So you say. I will not believe it."

"No? When you are a soldier you do not call the Bosche 'the filthy Bosche.' That is for the women, the civilians."

"You are mad. They are filthy. They are beasts like those in Spain who violated nuns and murdered priests."

"But, my little one, you forget that there were many

of Hitler's Bosches who fought *against* the Reds in Spain. You forget. You are not logical."

"They are not the same as those who attack France. They were Catholic Germans."

"You are ridiculous! Was I not hit in the guts by a bullet fired by a Bavarian Catholic in 'seventeen? You make me tired. You are ridiculous. Be silent."

"No, it is you who . . ."

They went on. Graham heard little more. Before he could make up his mind to cough loudly, he was asleep.

He awoke only once in the night. The vibration had ceased. He looked at his watch, saw that the time was half-past two, and guessed that they had stopped at Chanaq to drop the pilot. A few minutes later, as the engines started again, he went to sleep again.

It was not until the steward brought his coffee seven hours later that he learned that the pilot cutter from Chanaq had brought a telegram for him.

It was addressed: "GRAHAM, VAPUR SESTRI LEVANTE, CANAKKALE." He read:

"H. REQUESTS ME INFORM YOU B. LEFT FOR SOFIA HOUR AGO. ALL WELL. BEST WISHES. KOPEIKIN."

It had been handed in at Beyoglu at seven o'clock the previous evening.

CHAPTER FIVE

IT WAS an Ægean day: intensely coloured in the sun and with small pink clouds drifting in a bleached indigo sky. A stiff breeze was blowing and the amethyst of the sea was broken with white. The *Sestri Levante* was burying her stem in it and lifting clouds of spray which the breeze whipped across the well-deck like hail. The steward had told him that they were within sight of the island of Makronisi and as he went out on deck he saw it: a thin golden line shimmering in the sun and stretched out ahead of them like a sand bar at the entrance to a lagoon.

There were two other persons on that side of the deck. There was Haller and with him, on his arm, a small desiccated woman with thin grey hair, who was evidently his wife. They were steadying themselves at the rail and he was holding his head up to the wind as if to draw strength from it. He had his hat off and the white hair quivered with the air streaming through it.

Evidently they had not seen him. He made his way up to the boat deck. The breeze there was stronger. Mr. Kuvetli and the French couple stood by the rail clutching at their hats and watching the gulls following the ship. Mr. Kuvetli saw him immediately and waved. He went over to them.

"Good morning. *Madame. Monsieur.*"

They greeted him guardedly but Mr. Kuvetli was enthusiastic.

"It *is* good morning, eh? You sleep well? I look forward to our excursion this afternoon. Permit me to present Monsieur and Madame Mathis. Monsieur Graham."

There was handshaking. Mathis was a sharp-featured man of fifty or so with lean jaws and a permanent frown. But his smile, when it came, was good and his eyes were alive. The frown was the badge of his ascendancy over his wife. She had bony hips and wore an expression which said that she was determined to keep her temper however sorely it were tried. She was like her voice.

"Monsieur Mathis," said Mr. Kuvetli, whose French was a good deal more certain than his English, "is from Eskeshehir, where he has been working with the French railway company."

"It is a bad climate for the lungs," said Mathis. "Do you know Eskeshehir, Monsieur Graham?"

"I was there for a few minutes only."

"That would have been quite enough for me," said Madame Mathis. "We have been there three years. It was never any better than the day we arrived."

"The Turks are a great people," said her husband. "They are hard and they endure. But we shall be glad to return to France. Do you come from London, Monsieur?"

"No, the North of England. I have been in Turkey for a few weeks on business."

"To us, war will be strange after so many years. They say that the towns in France are darker than the last time."

"The towns are damnably dark both in France and in England. If you do not have to go out at night it is better to stay in."

"It is war," said Mathis sententiously.

"It is the filthy Bosche," said his wife.

"War," put in Mr. Kuvetli, stroking an unshaven chin, "is a terrible thing. There is no doubt of it. But the Allies must win."

"The Bosche is strong," said Mathis. "It is easy to say that the Allies must win, but they yet have the fighting to do. And do we yet know whom we are going to fight or where? There is a front in the East as well as in the West. We do not yet know the truth. When that is known the war will be over."

"It is not for us to ask questions," said his wife.

His lips twisted and in his brown eyes was the bitterness of years. "You are right. It is not for us to ask questions. And why? Because the only people who can give us the answers are the bankers and the politicians at the top, the boys with the shares in the big factories which make war materials. They will not give us answers. Why? Because they know that if the soldiers of France and England knew those answers they would not fight."

His wife reddened. "You are mad! Naturally the men of France would fight to defend us from the filthy

Bosche." She glanced at Graham. "It is bad to say that France would not fight. We are not cowards."

"No, but neither are we fools." He turned quickly to Graham. "Have you heard of Briey, Monsieur? From the mines of the Briey district comes ninety per cent. of France's iron ore. In nineteen fourteen those mines were captured by the Germans, who worked them for the iron they needed. They worked them hard. They have admitted since that without the iron they mined at Briey they would have been finished in nineteen seventeen. Yes, they worked Briey hard. I, who was at Verdun, can tell you that. Night after night we watched the glare in the sky from the blast furnaces of Briey a few kilometres away; the blast furnaces that were feeding the German guns. Our artillery and our bombing aeroplanes could have blown those furnaces to pieces in a week. But our artillery remained silent; an airman who dropped one bomb on the Briey area was court-martialled. Why?" His voice rose. "I will tell you why, Monsieur. Because there were orders that Briey was not to be touched. Whose orders? Nobody knew. The orders came from someone at the top. The Ministry of War said that it was the generals. The generals said that it was the Ministry of War. We did not find out the facts until after the war. The orders had been issued by Monsieur de Wendel of the Comité des Forges who owned the Briey mines and blast furnaces. We were fighting for our lives, but our lives were less important than that the property of Monsieur de Wendel should be preserved to make fat profits. No, it is not good for those who fight to know too much. Speeches, yes! The truth, no!"

His wife sniggered. "It is always the same. Let someone mention the war and he begins to talk about Briey—
something that happened twenty-four years ago."

"And why not?" he demanded. "Things have not
changed so much. Because we do not know about such
things until after they have happened it does not mean
that things like it are not happening now. When I think
of war I think also of Briey and the glare of the blast furnaces in the sky to remind myself that I am an ordinary
man who must not believe all that he is told. I see the
newspapers from France with the blanks in them to show
where the censor has been at work. They tell me certain
things, these newspapers. France, they say, is fighting
with England against Hitler and the Nazis for democracy
and liberty."

"And you don't believe that?" Graham asked.

"I believe that *the peoples* of France and England are so
fighting, but is that the same thing? I think of Briey and
wonder. Those same newspapers once told me that the
Germans were not taking ore from the Briey mines and
that all was well. I am an invalid of the last war. I do
not have to fight in this one. But I can think."

His wife laughed again. "Ha! It will be different when
he gets to France again. He talks like a fool but you
should take no notice, Messieurs. He is a good Frenchman. He won the Croix de Guerre."

He winked. "A little piece of silver outside the chest
to serenade the little piece of steel inside, eh? It is the
women, I think, who should fight these wars. They are
more ferocious as patriots than the men."

"And what do you think, Mr. Kuvetli?" said Graham.

"Me? Ah, please!" Mr. Kuvetli looked apologetic. "I am neutral, you understand. I know nothing. I have no opinion." He spread out his hands. "I sell tobacco. Export business. That is enough."

The Frenchman's eyebrows went up. "Tobacco? So? I arranged a great deal of transport for the tobacco companies. What company is that?"

"Pazar of Istanbul."

"Pazar? " Mathis looked slightly puzzled. "I don't think . . ."

But Mr. Kuvetli interrupted him. "Ah! See! There is Greece!"

They looked. There, sure enough, was Greece. It looked like a low bank of cloud on the horizon beyond the end of the golden line of Makronisi, a line that was contracting slowly as the ship ploughed on its way through the Zea channel.

"Beautiful day!" enthused Mr. Kuvetli. "Magnificent!" He drew a deep breath and exhaled loudly. "I anticipate very much to see Athens. We get to Piræus at two o'clock."

"Are you and Madame going ashore?" said Graham to Mathis.

"No, I think not. It is too short a time." He turned his coat collar up and shivered. "I agree that it is a beautiful day, but it is cold."

"If you did not stand talking so much," said his wife, "you would keep warm. And you have no scarf."

"Very well, very well!" he said irritably. "We will go below. Excuse us, please."

"I think that I, too, will go," said Mr. Kuvetli. "Are

you coming down, Mr. Graham?"

"I'll stay a little." He would have enough of Mr. Kuvetli later.

"Then at two o'clock."

"Yes."

When they had gone he looked at his watch, saw that it was eleven-thirty, and made up his mind to walk round the boat deck ten times before he went down for a drink. He was, he decided as he began to walk, a good deal better for his night's rest. For one thing, his hand had ceased throbbing and he could bend the fingers a little, without pain. More important, however, was the fact that the feeling of moving in a nightmare which he had had the previous day had now gone. He felt whole again and cheerful. Yesterday was years away. There was, of course, his bandaged hand to remind him of it but the wound no longer seemed significant. Yesterday it had been a part of something horrible. To-day it was a cut on the back of his hand, a cut which would take a few days to heal. Meanwhile he was on his way home, back to his work. As for Mademoiselle Josette, he had had, fortunately, enough sense left not to behave really stupidly. That he should actually have wanted, even momentarily, to kiss her was fantastic enough. However, there were extenuating circumstances. He had been tired and confused; and, while she was a woman whose needs and methods of fulfilling them were only too apparent, she was undeniably attractive in a blowzy way.

He had completed his fourth circuit when the subject of these reflections appeared on the deck. She had on a camel hair coat instead of the fur, a green cotton scarf round her head in place of the woollen one, and wore sports shoes with cork "platform" soles. She waited for him to come over to her.

He smiled and nodded. "Good morning."

She raised her eyebrows. "Good morning! Is that all you have to say?"

He was startled. "What should I say?"

"You have disappointed me. I thought that all Englishmen got out of bed early to eat a great English breakfast. I get out of bed at ten but you are nowhere to be found. The steward says that you are still in your cabin."

"Unfortunately they don't serve English breakfasts on this boat. I made do with coffee and drank it in bed."

She frowned. "Now, you do not ask why I wished to see you. Is it so natural that I should wish to see you as soon as I left my bed?"

The mock severity was appalling. Graham said: "I'm afraid I didn't take you seriously. Why *should* you want to find me?"

"Ah, that is better. It is not good but it is better. Are you going into Athens this afternoon?"

"Yes."

"I wished to ask you if you would let me come with you."

"I see. I should be . . ."

"But now it is too late."

"I'm so sorry," said Graham happily. "I should have been delighted to take you."

She shrugged. "It is too late. Mr. Kuvetli, the little

Turk, has asked me and, *faut de mieux*, I accepted. I do not like him but he knows Athens very well. It will be interesting."

"Yes, I should think it would be."

"He is a very interesting man."

"Evidently."

"Of course, I might be able to persuade him . . ."

"Unfortunately, there is a difficulty. Last night Mr. Kuvetli asked me if I minded his going with me as he had never been in Athens before."

It gave him a great deal of pleasure to say it; but she was disconcerted only momentarily. She burst out laughing.

"You are not at all polite. Not at all. You let me say what you know to be untrue. You do not stop me. You are unkind." She laughed again. "But it is a good joke."

"I'm really very sorry."

"You are too kind. I wished only to be friendly to you. I do not care whether I go to Athens or not."

"I'm sure Mr. Kuvetli would be delighted if you came with us. So should I, of course. You probably know a great deal more about Athens than I do."

Her eyes narrowed suddenly. "What, please, do you mean by that?"

He had not meant anything at all beyond the plain statement. He said, with a smile that he intended to be reassuring: "I mean that you have probably danced there."

She stared at him sullenly for a moment. He felt the smile, still clinging fatuously to his lips, fading. She said slowly: "I do not think I like you as much as I thought. I do not think that you understand me at all."

"It's possible. I've known you for such a short time."

"Because a woman is an artiste," she said angrily, "you think that she must be of the *milieu*."

"Not at all. The idea hadn't occurred to me. Would you like to walk round the deck?"

She did not move. "I am beginning to think that I do not like you at all."

"I'm sorry. I was looking forward to your company on the journey."

"But you have Mr. Kuvetli," she said viciously.

"Yes, that's true. Unfortunately, he's not as attractive as you are."

She laughed sarcastically. "Oh, you have seen that I am attractive? That is very good. I am so pleased. I am honoured."

"I seem to have offended you," he said. "I apologise."

She waved one hand airily. "Do not trouble. I think that it is perhaps because you are stupid. You wish to walk. Very well, we will walk."

"Splendid."

They had taken three steps when she stopped again and faced him. "Why do you have to take this little Turk to Athens?" she demanded. "Tell him that you cannot go. If you were polite you would do that."

"And take you? Is that the idea?"

"If you asked me, I would go with you. I am bored with this ship and I like to speak English."

"I'm afraid that Mr. Kuvetli might not think it so polite."

"If you liked me it would not matter to you about Mr. Kuvetli." She shrugged. "But I understand. It does not matter. I think that you are very unkind, but it does not matter. I am bored."

"I'm sorry."

"Yes, you are sorry. That is all right. But I am still bored. Let us walk." And then, as they began to walk: "José thinks that you are indiscreet."

"Does he? Why?"

"That old German you talked to. How do you know that he is not a spy?"

He laughed outright. "A spy! What an extraordinary idea!"

She glanced at him coldly. "And why is it extraordinary?"

"If you had talked to him you would know quite well that he couldn't possibly be anything of the sort."

"Perhaps not. José is always very suspicious of people. He always believes that they are lying about themselves."

"Frankly, I should be inclined to accept José's disapproval of a person as a recommendation."

"Oh, he does not disapprove. He is just interested. He likes to find things out about people. He thinks that we are all animals. He is never shocked by anything people do."

"He sounds very stupid."

"You do not understand José. He does not think of good things and evil things as they do in the convent, but only of things. He says that a thing that is good for one person may be evil for another, so that it is stupid to talk of good and evil."

"But people sometimes do good things simply because those things *are* good."

"Only because they feel nice when they do them—that is what José says."

"What about the people who stop themselves from doing evil because it *is* evil?"

"José says that if a person *really* needs to do something he will not trouble about what others may think of him. If he is really hungry, he will steal. If he is in real danger, he will kill. If he is really afraid, he will be cruel. He says that it was people who were safe and well fed who invented good and evil so that they would not have to worry about the people who were hungry and unsafe. What a man does depends on what he needs. It is simple. You are not a murderer. You say that murder is evil. José would say that you are as much a murderer as Landru or Weidmann and that it is just that fortune has not made it necessary for you to murder anyone. Someone once told him that there was a German proverb which said that a man is an ape in velvet. He always likes to repeat it."

"And do you agree with José? I don't mean about my being a potential murderer. I mean about why people are what they are."

"I do not agree or disagree. I do not care. For me, some people are nice, some people are sometimes nice and others are not at all nice." She looked at him out of the corners of her eyes. "You are sometimes nice."

"What do you think about yourself?"

She smiled. "Me? Oh, I am sometimes nice, too. When people are nice to me, I am a little angel." She added: "José thinks that he is as clever as God."

"Yes, I can see that he would."

"You do not like him. I am not surprised. It is only

the old women who like José."

"Do *you* like him?"

"He is my partner. With us it is business."

"Yes, you told me that before. But do you *like* him?"

"He makes me laugh sometimes. He says amusing things about people. You remember Serge? José said that Serge would steal straw from his mother's kennel. It made me laugh very much."

"It must have done. Would you like a drink now?"

She looked at a small silver watch on her wrist and said that she would.

They went down. One of the ship's officers was leaning by the bar with a beer in his hand, talking to the steward. As Graham ordered the drinks, the officer turned his attention to Josette. He obviously counted on being successful with women: his dark eyes did not leave hers while he was talking to her. Graham, listening to the Italian with bored incomprehension, was ignored. He was content to be ignored. He got on with his drink. It was not until the gong sounded for lunch and Haller came in that he remembered that he had done nothing about changing his place at table.

The German nodded in a friendly way as Graham sat down beside him. "I did not expect to have your company to-day."

"I completely forgot to speak to the steward. If you . . ."

"No, please. I take it as a compliment."

"How is your wife?"

"Better, though she is not yet prepared to face a meal. But she took a walk this morning. I showed her the sea.

This is the way Xerxes' great ships sailed to their defeat at Salamis. For those Persians that grey mass on the horizon was the country of Themistocles and the Attic Greeks of Marathon. You will think that it is my German sentimentality but I must say that the fact that for me that grey mass is the country of Venizelos and Metaxas is as regrettable as it could be. I was at the German Institute in Athens for several years when I was young."

"Shall you go ashore this afternoon?"

"I do not think so. Athens can only remind me of what I know already—that I am old. Do you know the city?"

"A little. I know Salamis better."

"That is now their big naval base, isn't it?"

Graham said yes rather too carelessly. Haller glanced sideways and smiled slightly. "I beg your pardon. I see that I am on the point of being indiscreet."

"I shall go ashore to get some books and cigarettes. Can I get anything for you?"

"It is very kind of you, but there is nothing. Are you going alone?"

"Mr. Kuvetli, the Turkish gentleman at the next table, has asked me to show him round. He has never been to Athens."

Haller raised his eyebrows. "Kuvetli? So that is his name. I talked with him this morning. He speaks German quite well and knows Berlin a little."

"He speaks English, too, and very good French. He seems to have travelled a lot."

Haller grunted. "I should have thought that a Turk who had travelled a lot would have been to Athens."

"He sells tobacco. Greece grows its own tobacco."

"Yes, of course. I had not thought of that. I am apt to forget that most people who travel do so not to see but to sell. I talked with him for twenty minutes. He has a way of talking without saying anything. His conversation consists of agreements or indisputable statements."

"I suppose it's something to do with his being a salesman. 'The world is my customer and the customer is always right.'"

"He interests me. In my opinion he is too simple to be true. The smile is a little too stupid, the conversation a little too evasive. He tells you some things about himself within the first minutes of your meeting him and then tells you no more. That is curious. A man who begins by telling you about himself usually goes on doing so. Besides, who ever heard of a simple Turkish business man? No, he makes me think of a man who has set out to create a definite impression of himself in people's minds. He is a man who wishes to be underrated."

"But why? He's not selling us tobacco."

"Perhaps, as you suggest, he regards the world as his customer. But you will have an opportunity of probing a little this afternoon." He smiled. "You see, I assume, quite unwarrantably, that you are interested. I must ask your pardon. I am a bad traveller who has had to do a great deal of travelling. To pass the time I have learned to play a game. I compare my own first impressions of my fellow travellers with what I can find out about them."

"If you are right you score a point? If you are wrong you lose one?"

"Precisely. Actually I enjoy losing more than winning. It is an old man's game, you see."

"And what is your impression of Señor Gallindo?"

Haller frowned. "I am afraid that I am only too right about that gentleman. He is not really very interesting."

"He has a theory that all men are potential murderers and is fond of quoting a German proverb to the effect that a man is an ape in velvet."

"It does not surprise me," was the acid reply. "Every man must justify himself somehow."

"Aren't you a little severe?"

"Perhaps. I regret to say that I find Señor Gallindo a very ill-mannered person."

Graham's reply was interrupted by the entrance of the man himself, looking as if he had just got out of bed. He was followed by the Italian mother and son. The conversation became desultory and over-polite.

The *Sestri Levante* was tied up alongside the new wharf on the north side of the harbour of the Piræus soon after two o'clock. As, with Mr. Kuvetli, Graham stood on the deck waiting for the passenger gangway to be hoisted into position, he saw that Josette and José had left the saloon and were standing behind him. José nodded to them suspiciously as if he were afraid that they were thinking of borrowing money from him. The girl smiled. It was the tolerant smile that sees a friend disregarding good advice.

Mr. Kuvetli spoke up eagerly. "Are you going ashore, Monsieur-dame?"

"Why should we?" demanded José. "It is a waste of time to go."

But Mr. Kuvetli was not sensitive. "Ah! Then you know Athens, you and your wife?"

"Too well. It is a dirty town."

"I have not seen it. I was thinking that if you and Madame were going, we might all go together." He beamed round expectantly.

José set his teeth and rolled his eyes as if he were being tortured. "I have already said that we are *not* going."

"But it is very kind of you to suggest it," Josette put in graciously.

The Mathis came out of the saloon. "Ah!" he greeted them. "The adventurers! Do not forget that we leave at five. We shall not wait for you."

The gangway thudded into position and Mr. Kuvetli clambered down it nervously. Graham followed. He was beginning to wish that he had decided to stay on board. At the foot of the gangway he turned and looked up— the inevitable movement of a passenger leaving a ship. Mathis waved his hand.

"He is very amiable, Monsieur Mathis," said Mr. Kuvetli.

"Very."

Beyond the Customs shed there was a fly-blown old Fiat landaulet with a notice on it in French, Italian, English and Greek, saying that an hour's tour of the sights and antiquities of Athens for four persons cost five hundred drachmes.

Graham stopped. He thought of the electric trains and trams he would have to clamber on to, of the hill up to the Acropolis, of the walking he would have to do, of the exhausting boredom of sightseeing on foot. Any way of avoiding the worst of it was, he decided, worth thirty shillingsworth of drachmes.

"I think," he said, "that we will take this car."

Mr. Kuvetli looked worried. "There is no other way? It is very expensive."

"That's all right. I'll pay."

"But it is you who do favour to me. I must pay."

"Oh, I should have taken a car in any case. Five hundred drachmes is not really expensive."

Mr. Kuvetli's eyes opened very wide. "Five hundred? But that is for four persons. We are two."

Graham laughed. "I doubt if the driver will look at it that way. I don't suppose it costs him any less to take two instead of four."

Mr. Kuvetli looked apologetic. "I have little Greek. You will permit me to ask him?"

"Of course. Go ahead."

The driver, a predatory looking man wearing a suit several sizes too small for him and highly polished tan shoes without socks, had leapt out at their approach and was holding the door open. Now he began to shout. "*Allez! Allez! Allez!*" he exhorted them; "*très bon marché. Cinque-cento, solamente.*"

Mr. Kuvetli strode forward, a stout, grubby little Daniel going out to do battle with a lean Goliath in stained blue serge. He began to speak.

He spoke Greek fluently; there was no doubt of it. Graham saw the surprised look on the driver's face replaced by one of fury as a torrent of words poured from Mr. Kuvetli's lips. He was disparaging the car. He began to point. He pointed to every defect in the thing from a patch of rust on the luggage grid to a small tear in the upholstery, from a crack in the windshield to a worn patch on the running board. He paused for breath and the angry driver seized the opportunity of replying. He shouted and thumped the door panels with his fist to emphasise his remarks and made long streamlining gestures. Mr. Kuvetli smiled sceptically and returned to the attack. The driver spat on the ground and counterattacked. Mr. Kuvetli replied with a short, sharp burst of fire. The driver flung up his hands, disgusted but defeated.

Mr. Kuvetli turned to Graham. "Price," he reported simply, "is now three hundred drachmes. It is too much, I think, but it will take time to reduce more. But if you think . . ."

"It seems a very fair price," said Graham hurriedly.

Mr. Kuvetli shrugged. "Perhaps. It could be reduced more, but . . ." He turned and nodded to the driver, who suddenly grinned broadly. They got into the cab.

"Did you say," said Graham, as they drove off, "that you had never been in Greece before?"

Mr. Kuvetli's smile was bland. "I know little Greek," he said. "I was born in Izmir."

The tour began. The Greek drove fast and with dash, twitching the wheel playfully in the direction of slow moving pedestrians, so that they had to run for their lives, and flinging a running commentary over his right shoulder as he went. They stopped for a moment on the road by the Theseion and again on the Acropolis where they got out and walked round. Here, Mr. Kuvetli's curiosity seemed inexhaustible. He insisted on a century by century history of the Parthenon and prowled round the museum as if he would have liked to spend the rest of the day there; but at last they got back into the car and were whisked round to the theatre of Dionysos, the arch of Hadrian, the Olympieion, and the Royal Palace. It was, by now, four o'clock and Mr. Kuvetli had been asking questions and saying "very nice" and "*formidable*" for well over the allotted hour. At Graham's suggestion they stopped in the Syntagma, changed some money and paid off the driver, adding that if he liked to wait in the square he could earn another fifty drachmes by driving them back to the wharf later. The driver agreed. Graham bought his cigarettes and books and sent his telegram. There was a band playing on the terrace of one of the cafés when they got back to the square and at Mr. Kuvetli's suggestion they sat down at a table to drink coffee before returning to the port.

Mr. Kuvetli surveyed the square regretfully. "It is very nice," he said with a sigh. "One would like to stay longer. So many magnificent ruins we have seen!"

Graham remembered what Haller had said at lunch about Mr. Kuvetli's evasions. "Which is your favourite city, Mr. Kuvetli?"

"Ah, that is difficult to say. All cities have their magnificences. I like all cities." He breathed the air. "It is most kind of you to bring me here to-day, Mr. Graham."

Graham stuck to the point. "A great pleasure. But surely you have some preference."

Mr. Kuvetli looked anxious. "It is so difficult. I like London very much."

"Personally I like Paris better."

"Ah, yes. Paris is also magnificent."

Feeling rather baffled, Graham sipped his coffee. Then he had another idea. "What do you think of Señor Gallindo, Mr. Kuvetli?"

"Señor Gallindo? It is so difficult. I do not know him. His manner is strange."

"His manner," said Graham, "is damnably offensive. Don't you agree?"

"I do not like Señor Gallindo very much," conceded Mr. Kuvetli. "But he is Spanish."

"What can that have to do with it? The Spanish are an exceedingly polite race."

"Ah, I have not been to Spain." He looked at his watch. "It is quarter-past four now. Perhaps we should go, eh? It has been very nice this afternoon."

Graham nodded wearily. If Haller wanted Mr. Kuvetli "probed" he could do the probing himself. His, Graham's, personal opinion was that Mr. Kuvetli was an ordinary bore whose conversation, such as it was, sounded a little unreal because he used languages with which he was unfamiliar.

Mr. Kuvetli insisted on paying for the coffee; Mr. Kuvetli insisted on paying the fare back to the wharf. By a quarter to five they were on board again. An hour later Graham stood on deck watching the pilot's boat chugging back towards the greying land. The Frenchman, Mathis, who was leaning on the rail a few feet away, turned his head.

"Well, that's *that!* Two more days and we shall be in Genoa. Did you enjoy your excursion ashore this afternoon, Monsieur?"

"Oh, yes, thank you. It was . . ."

But he never finished telling Monsieur Mathis what it was. A man had come out of the saloon door some yards away and was standing blinking at the setting sun which streamed across the sea towards them.

"Ah, yes," said Mathis. "We have acquired another passenger. He arrived while you were ashore this afternoon. I expect that he is a Greek."

Graham did not, could not, answer. He knew that the man standing there with the golden light of the sun on his face was not a Greek. He knew, too, that beneath the dark grey raincoat the man wore there was a crumpled brown suit with lumpy padded shoulders; that below the high-crowned soft hat and above the pale, doughy features with the self-conscious mouth was thinning curly hair. He knew that this man's name was Banat.

CHAPTER SIX

GRAHAM STOOD THERE motionless. His body was tingling as if some violent mechanical shock had been transmitted to it through his heels. He heard Mathis' voice a long way away, asking him what the matter was.

He said: "I don't feel well. Will you excuse me, please?"

He saw apprehension flicker over the Frenchman's face and thought: "He thinks I'm going to be sick." But he did not wait for Mathis to say anything. He turned and, without looking again at the man by the saloon door, walked to the door at the other end of the deck and went below to his cabin.

He locked the door when he got inside. He was shaking from head to foot. He sat down on the bunk and tried to pull himself together. He told himself: "There's no need to get worried. There's a way out of this. You've got to think."

120

Somehow Banat had discovered that he was on the *Sestri Levante*. It could not have been very difficult. An inquiry made at the Wagon-Lit and shipping company offices would have been enough. The man had then taken a ticket for Sofia, left the train when it crossed the Greek frontier, and taken another train via Salonika to Athens.

He pulled Kopeikin's telegram out of his pocket and stared at it. "All well!" The fools! The bloody fools! He'd distrusted this ship business from the start. He ought to have relied on his instinct and insisted on seeing the British Consul. If it had not been for that conceited imbecile Haki . . . But now he was caught like a rat in a trap. Banat wouldn't miss twice. My God, no! The man was a professional murderer. He would have his reputation to consider—to say nothing of his fee.

A curious but vaguely familiar feeling began to steal over him: a feeling that was dimly associated with the smell of antiseptics and the singing of a kettle. With a sudden rush of horror, he remembered. It had happened years ago. They had been trying out an experimental fourteen-inch gun on the proving ground. The second time they fired it, it had burst. There had been something wrong with the breech mechanism. It had killed two men outright and badly injured a third. This third man had looked like a great clot of blood lying there on the concrete. But the clot of blood had screamed: screamed steadily until the ambulance had come and a doctor had used a hypodermic. It had been a thin, high, inhuman sound; just like the singing of a kettle. The doctor had said that the man was unconscious even though he was screaming. Before they had examined the remains of the gun, the concrete had been swabbed down with a solution of lysol. He hadn't eaten any lunch. In the afternoon it had begun to rain. He . . .

He realised suddenly that he was swearing. The words were dropping from his lips in a steady stream: a meaningless succession of obscenities. He stood up quickly. He was losing his head. Something had got to be done; and done quickly. If he could get off the ship . . .

He wrenched the cabin door open and went out into the alleyway. The Purser was the man to see first. The Purser's office was on the same deck. He went straight to it.

The door of the office was ajar and the Purser, a tall, middle-aged Italian with the stump of a cigar in his mouth, was sitting in his shirt-sleeves before a typewriter and a stack of copies of Bills of Lading. He was copying details of the Bills on to the ruled sheet in the typewriter. He looked up with a frown as Graham knocked. He was busy.

"*Signore?*"

"Do you speak English?"

"No, *Signore.*"

"French?"

"Yes. What is it you wish?"

"I want to see the Captain at once."

"For what reason, Monsieur?"

"It is absolutely necessary that I am put ashore immediately."

The Purser put his cigar down and turned in his swivel chair.

"My French is not very good," he said calmly. "Do

you mind repeating . . . ?"

"I want to be put ashore."

"Monsieur Graham, is it?"

"Yes."

"I regret, Monsieur Graham. It is too late. The pilot boat has gone. You should have . . ."

"I know. But it is absolutely necessary that I go ashore now. No, I am not mad. I realise that under ordinary circumstances it would be out of the question. But the circumstances are exceptional. I am ready to pay for the loss of time and the inconvenience caused."

The Purser looked bewildered. "But why? Are you ill?"

"No, I . . ." He stopped and could have bitten his tongue off. There was no doctor aboard and the threat of some infectious disease might have been sufficient. But it was too late now. "If you will arrange for me to see the Captain at once, I will explain why. I can assure you that my reasons are good ones."

"I am afraid," said the Purser stiffly, "that it is out of the question. You do not understand . . ."

"All I am asking," interrupted Graham desperately, "is that you put back a short way and ask for a pilot boat. I am willing and able to pay."

The Purser smiled in an exasperated way. "This is a ship, Monsieur, not a taxi. We carry cargo and run to a schedule. You are not ill and . . ."

"I have already said that my reasons are excellent. If you will allow me to see the Captain . . ."

"It is quite useless to argue, Monsieur. I do not doubt your willingness or ability to pay the cost of a boat from the harbour. Unfortunately that is not the important thing. You say that you are not ill but that you have reasons. As you can only have thought of those reasons within the last ten minutes, you must not be angry if I say that they cannot be of very grave importance. Let me assure you, Monsieur, that nothing but proved and evident reasons of life and death will suffice to stop any ship for the convenience of one passenger. Naturally, if you can give me any such reasons I will place them before the Captain immediately. If not, then I am afraid your reasons must wait until we get to Genoa."

"I assure you . . ."

The Purser smiled sorrowfully. "I do not question the good faith of your assurances, Monsieur, but I regret to say that we need more than assurances."

"Very well," snapped Graham, "since you insist on details I will tell you. I have just found that there is a man on this ship who is here for the express purpose of murdering me."

The Purser's face went blank. "Indeed, Monsieur?"

"Yes, I . . ." Something in the man's eyes stopped him. "I suppose you've decided that I'm either mad or drunk," he concluded.

"Not at all, Monsieur." But what he was thinking was as plain as a pikestaff. He was thinking that Graham was just another of the poor lunatics with whom his work sometimes brought him in contact. They were a nuisance, because they wasted time. But he was tolerant. It was useless to be angry with a lunatic. Besides, dealing with them always seemed to emphasize his own sanity and intelligence: the sanity and intelligence which, had the owners been less short sighted, would long ago have taken him to a seat on the board of directors. And they made good stories to tell his friends when he got home. "Imagine, Beppo! There was this Englishman, looking sane but really mad. He thought that someone was trying to murder him! Imagine! It is the whisky, you know. I said to him . . ." But meanwhile he would have to be humoured, to be dealt with tactfully. "Not at all, Monsieur," he repeated.

Graham began to lose control of his temper. "You asked me for my reasons. I am giving them to you."

"And I am listening carefully, Monsieur."

"There is someone on this ship who is here to murder me."

"And his name, Monsieur?"

"Banat. B-A-N-A-T. He is a Roumanian. He . . ."

"One moment, Monsieur." The Purser got a sheet of paper out of a drawer and ran a pencil down the names on it with ostentatious care. Then he looked up. "There is no one of that name or nationality on the ship, Monsieur."

"I was about to tell you, when you interrupted me, that the man is travelling on a false passport."

"Then, please . . ."

"He is the passenger who came aboard this afternoon."

The Purser looked at the paper again. "Cabin number nine. That is Monsieur Mavrodopoulos. He is a Greek business man."

"That may be what his passport says. His real name is Banat and he is a Roumanian."

The Purser remained polite with obvious difficulty.

"Have you any proof of that, Monsieur?"

"If you radio Colonel Haki of the Turkish police at Istanbul, he will confirm what I say."

"This is an Italian ship, Monsieur. We are not in Turkish territorial waters. We can refer such a matter only to the Italian police. In any case, we carry wireless only for navigational purposes. This is not the *Rex* or the *Conte di Savoia*, you understand. This matter must be left until we reach Genoa. The police there will deal with your accusation concerning the passport."

"I don't care a damn about his passport," said Graham violently. "I'm telling you that the man intends to kill me."

"And why?"

"Because he has been paid to do so; that is why. Now do you understand?"

The Purser got to his feet. He had been tolerant. Now the time had come to be firm. "No, Monsieur, I do *not* understand."

"Then if you cannot understand, let me speak to the Captain."

"That will not be necessary, Monsieur. I understand enough." He looked Graham in the eyes. "In my opinion there are two *charitable* explanations of this matter. Either you have mistaken this Monsieur Mavrodopoulos for someone else, or you have had a bad dream. If it is the former, I advise you not to repeat your mistake to anyone else. I am discreet, but if Monsieur Mavrodopoulos should hear of it he might regard it as a reflection upon his honour. If it is the second, I suggest that you lie down in your cabin for a while. And remember that nobody is going to murder you on this ship. There are too many people about."

"But don't you see . . . ?" shouted Graham.

"I see," said the Purser grimly, "that there is another less charitable explanation of this matter. You may have invented this story simply because for some private reason you wish to be put ashore. If that is true, I am sorry. It is a ridiculous story. In any case, the ship stops at Genoa and not before. And now, if you will excuse me, I have work to do."

"I demand to see the Captain."

"If you will close the door as you leave," said the Purser happily.

Almost sick with anger and fear, Graham went back to his cabin.

He lit a cigarette and tried to think reasonably. He should have gone straight to the Captain. He could still go straight to the Captain. For a moment he considered doing so. If he . . . But it would be useless and unnecessarily humiliating. The Captain, even if he could get to him and make him understand, would probably receive his story with even less sympathy. And he would still have no proof that what he said was true. Even if he could persuade the Captain that there was some truth in what he was saying, that he was not, in fact, suffering from some form of delusional insanity, the answer would be the same: "Nobody is going to murder you on this ship. There are too many people about."

Too many people about! They did not know Banat. The man who had walked into a police official's house in broad daylight, shot the official and his wife and then calmly walked out again, was not going to be unnerved so easily. Passengers had disappeared from ships in mid-ocean before. Sometimes their bodies had been washed ashore, and sometimes they hadn't. Sometimes the disappearances had been explained, and sometimes they hadn't. What would there be to connect this disappearance of an English engineer (who had behaved very queerly) from a ship at sea with Mr. Mavrodopoulos, a Greek business man? Nothing. And even if the body of the English engineer were washed ashore before the fish had rendered it unidentifiable and it were found that he had been killed before he had entered the water, who was going to prove that Mr. Mavrodopoulos—if by that time there were anything left of Mr. Mavrodopoulos but the ashes of his passport—had been responsible for the killing? Nobody.

He thought of the telegram he had sent in Athens that afternoon. "Home Monday," he had said. Home Monday! He looked at his unbandaged hand and moved the fingers of it. By Monday they could be dead and beginning to decompose with the rest of the entity which called itself Graham. Stephanie would be upset, but she'd get over it quickly. She was resilient and sensible. But there wouldn't be much money for her. She'd have to sell the house. He should have taken out more insurance. If only he'd known. But of course it was just because you *didn't* know, that there *were* such things as insurance companies. Still, he could do nothing now but hope that it would be over quickly, that it wouldn't be painful.

He shivered and began to swear again. Then he pulled himself up sharply. He'd *got* to think of some way out. And not only for his own sake and Stephanie's. There

was the job he had to do. "It is in the interests of your
country's enemies that when the snow melts and the rain
ceases, Turkish naval strength shall be exactly what it is
now. They will do anything to see that it is so." Anything! Behind Banat was the German agent in Sofia and
behind him was Germany and the Nazis. Yes, he'd *got*
to think of some way out. If other Englishmen could die
for their country, surely he could manage to stay alive for
it. Then another of Colonel Haki's statements came back
to him. "You have advantages over the soldier. You have
only to defend yourself. You do not have to go into the
open. You may run away without being a coward."

Well he couldn't run away now; but the rest of it was
true enough. He didn't have to go out into the open. He
could stay here in the cabin; have his meals here; keep
the door locked. He could defend himself, too, if need be.
Yes, by God! He had Kopeikin's revolver.

He had put it among the clothes in his suitcase. Now,
thanking his stars that he had not refused to take it, he
got it out and weighed it in his hand.

For Graham a gun was a series of mathematical expres-
sions resolved in such a way as to enable one man, by
touching a button, to project an armour-piercing shell so
that it hit a target several miles away plumb in the middle.
It was a piece of machinery no more and no less significant than a vacuum cleaner or a bacon slicer. It had no
nationality and no loyalties. It was neither awe-inspiring
nor symbolic of anything except the owner's ability to
pay for it. His interest in the men who had to fire the
products of his skill as in the men who had to suffer their
fire (and, thanks to his employers' tireless international-

ism, the same sets of men often had to do both) had always been detached. To him who knew what even one four-inch shell could accomplish in the way of destruction, it seemed that they should be—could only be—nerveless cyphers. That they were not was an evergreen source of astonishment to him. His attitude towards them was as uncomprehending as that of the stoker of a crematorium towards the solemnity of the grave.

But this revolver was different. It wasn't impersonal. There was a relationship between it and the human body. It had, perhaps, an effective range of twenty-five yards or less. That meant that you could see the face of the man at whom you fired it both before and after you fired it. You could see and hear his agony. You couldn't think of honour and glory with a revolver in your hand, but only of killing and being killed. There was no machine to serve. Life and death were there in your hand in the shape of an elementary arrangement of springs and levers and a few grammes of lead and cordite.

He had never handled a revolver in his life before. He examined it carefully. Stamped above the trigger guard was "Made in U.S.A." and the name of an American typewriter manufacturer. There were two small sliding bosses on the other side. One was the safety catch. The other, when moved, released the breech which dropped sideways and showed that there were cartridges in all six chambers. It was beautifully made. He took the cartridges out and pulled the trigger once or twice experimentally. It was not easy with his bandaged hand, but it could be done. He put the cartridges back.

He felt better now. Banat might be a professional

killer, but he was as susceptible to bullets as any other man. And *he* had to make the first move. One had to look at things from his point of view. He'd failed in Istanbul and he'd had to catch up with the victim again. He'd managed to get aboard the boat on which the victim was travelling. But did that really help him very much? What he had done in Roumania as a member of the Iron Guard was beside the point now. A man could afford to be bold when he was protected by an army of thugs and an intimidated judge. It was true that passengers were sometimes lost off ships at sea; but those ships were big liners, not two thousand ton cargo boats. It really would be very difficult to kill a man on a boat of that size without anyone discovering that you had done so. You might be able to do it; that is if you could get your victim alone on deck at night. You could knife him and push him over the side. But you would have to get him there first, and there was more than a chance that you would be seen from the bridge. Or heard: a knifed man might make a lot of noise before he reached the water. And if you cut his throat there would be a lot of blood left behind to be accounted for. Besides, that was always assuming that you could use a knife so skilfully. Banat was a gunman, not a cut-throat. That confounded Purser was right. There were too many people about for anyone to murder him on the ship. As long as he was careful he would be all right. The real danger would begin when he got off the ship at Genoa.

Obviously the thing for him to do there would be to go straight to the British Consul, explain all the circumstances, and secure police protection as far as the frontier.

Yes, that was it. He had one priceless advantage over the enemy. *Banat did not know that he was identified.* He would be assuming that the victim was unsuspecting, that he could bide his time, that he could do his work between Genoa and the French frontier. By the time he discovered his mistake it would be too late for him to do anything about rectifying it. The only thing now was to see that he did not discover the mistake too soon.

Supposing, for instance, that Banat had noticed his hasty retreat from the deck. His blood ran cold at the idea. But no, the man had not been looking. The supposition showed, though, how careful he had to be. It was out of the question for him to skulk in his cabin for the rest of the trip. That would arouse immediate suspicion. He would have to look as unsuspecting as he could and yet take care not to expose himself to any sort of attack. He must make sure that if he were not in his cabin with the door locked, he was with or near one of the other passengers. He must even be amiable to "Monsieur Mavrodopoulos."

He unbuttoned his jacket and put the revolver in his hip pocket. It bulged absurdly and uncomfortably. He took the wallet out of his breast pocket and put the revolver there. That was uncomfortable, too, and the shape of it could be seen from the outside. Banat must not see that he was armed. The revolver could stay in the cabin.

He put it back in his suitcase and stood up, bracing himself. He'd go straight up to the saloon and have a drink now. If Banat were there, so much the better. A drink would help to ease the strain of the first encounter. He knew that it would be a strain. He had to face a man who had tried once to kill him and who was going to try again, and behave as if he had never seen or heard of him before. His stomach was already responding to the prospect. But he had to keep calm. His life, he told himself, might depend on his behaving normally. And the longer he hung about thinking it over, the less normal he would be. Better get it over with now.

He lit a cigarette, opened the cabin door and went straight upstairs to the saloon.

Banat was not there. He could have laughed aloud with relief. Josette and José were there with drinks in front of them, listening to Mathis.

"And so," he was saying vehemently, "it goes on. The big newspapers of the Right are owned by those whose interest it is to see that France spends her wealth on arms and that the ordinary people do not understand too much of what goes on behind the scenes. I am glad to be going back to France because it is my country. But do not ask me to love those who have my country in the palms of their hands. Ah, no!"

His wife was listening with tight-lipped disapproval. José was openly yawning. Josette was nodding sympathetically but her face lit up with relief when she saw Graham. "And where has our Englishman been?" she said immediately. "Mr. Kuvetli has told everyone what a magnificent time you both had."

"I've been in my cabin recovering from the afternoon's excitements."

Mathis did not look very pleased at the interruption but said agreeably enough: "I was afraid that you were ill, Monsieur. Are you better now?"

"Oh yes, thanks."

"You have been ill?" demanded Josette.

"I felt tired."

"It is the ventilation," said Madame Mathis promptly. "I myself have felt a nausea and a headache since I got on the ship. We should complain. But"—she made a derogatory gesture in the direction of her husband—"as long as he is comfortable all is well."

Mathis grinned. "Bah! It is seasickness."

"You are ridiculous. If I am sick it is of you."

José made a loud plopping noise with his tongue and leaned back in his chair, his closed eyes and tightened lips calling upon Heaven to deliver him from domesticity.

Graham ordered a whisky.

"Whisky?" José sat up whistling astonishment. "The Englishman drinks whisky!" he announced and then, pursing his lips and screwing up his face to express congenital aristocratic idiocy, added: "Some viskee, pliz, ol' bhoy!" He looked round, grinning, for applause.

"That is his idea of an Englishman," Josette explained. "He is very stupid."

"Oh I don't think so," said Graham; "he has never been to England. A great many English people who have never been to Spain are under the impression that all Spaniards smell of garlic."

Mathis giggled.

José half rose in his chair. "Do you intend to be insulting?" he demanded.

"Not at all. I was merely pointing out that these misconceptions exist. You, for instance, do not smell of garlic at all."

José subsided into his chair again. "I am glad to hear you say so," he said ominously. "If I thought . . ."

"Ah! Be silent!" Josette broke in. "You make yourself look a fool."

To Graham's relief the subject was disposed of by the entrance of Mr. Kuvetli. He was beaming happily.

"I come," he said to Graham, "to ask you to have drink with me."

"That's very good of you but I've just ordered a drink. Supposing you have one with me."

"Most kind. I will take vermouth, please." He sat down. "You have seen we have new passenger?"

"Yes, Monsieur Mathis pointed him out to me." He turned to the steward bringing him his whisky and ordered Mr. Kuvetli's vermouth.

"He is Greek gentleman. Name of Mavrodopoulos. He is business man."

"What business is he in?" Graham found, to his relief, that he could talk of Monsieur Mavrodopoulos quite calmly.

"That I do not know."

"That I do not care," said Josette. "I have just seen him. Ugh!"

"What's the matter with him?"

"She likes only men who look clean and simple," said José vindictively. "This Greek looks dirty. He would probably smell dirty too, but he uses a cheap perfume." He kissed his fingers to the air. "*Nuit de Petits Gars! Numero soixante-neuf! Cinq francs la bouteille.*"

Madame Mathis' face froze.

"You are disgusting, José," said Josette. "Besides, your

own perfume cost only fifty francs a bottle. It is filthy. And you must not say such things. You will offend Madame here who is not used to your jokes."

But Madame Mathis had already taken offence. "It is disgraceful," she said angrily, "that such things should be said when there are women present. With men alone it would not be polite."

"Ah yes!" said Mathis. "My wife and I are not hypocrites but there are some things that should not be said." He looked as if he were pleased to be able, for once, to side with his wife. Her surprise was almost pathetic. They proceeded to make the most of the occasion.

She said: "Monsieur Gallindo should apologize."

"I must insist," said Mathis, "that you apologize to my wife."

José stared at them in angry astonishment. "Apologize? What for?"

"He will apologize," said Josette. She turned to him and broke into Spanish. "Apologize, you dirty fool. Do you want trouble? Don't you see he's showing off to the woman? He would break you in pieces."

José shrugged. "Very well." He looked insolently at the Mathises. "I apologize. What for, I do not know, but I apologize."

"My wife accepts the apology," said Mathis stiffly. "It is not gracious but it is accepted."

"An officer says," remarked Mr. Kuvetli tactfully, "that we shall not be able to see Messina because it will be dark."

But this elephantine change of subject was unnecessary

for at that moment Banat came through the door from the promenade deck.

He stood there for an instant looking at them, his rain-coat hanging open, his hat in his hand, like a man who has strayed into a picture gallery out of the rain. His white face was drawn from lack of sleep, there were circles under the small deep-set eyes, the full lips were twisted slightly as if he had a headache.

Graham's heart drummed sickeningly at the base of his skull. This was the executioner. The hand with the hat in it was the hand which had fired the shots which had grazed his own hand, now outstretched to pick up a glass of whisky. This was the man who had killed men for as little as five thousand francs and his expenses.

He felt the blood leaving his face. He had only glanced quickly at the man but the whole picture of him was in his mind; the whole picture from the dusty tan shoes to the new tie with the filthy soft collar and the tired, frowsty, stupid face. He drank some of his whisky and saw that Mr. Kuvetli was bestowing his smile on the new-comer. The others were staring blankly.

Banat walked slowly over to the bar.

"*Bon soir, Monsieur*," said Mr. Kuvetli.

"*Bon soir*." It was grunted almost inaudibly as if he were anxious not to commit himself to accepting something he did not want. He reached the bar and murmured something to the steward.

He had passed close to Madame Mathis and Graham saw her frown. Then he himself caught the smell of scent. It was attar of roses and very strong. He remembered

Colonel Haki's question as to whether he had noticed any perfume in his room at the Adler-Palace after the attacks. Here was the explanation. The man reeked of scent. The smell of it would stay with the things he touched.

"Are you going far, Monsieur?" said Mr. Kuvetli.

The man eyed him. "No. Genoa."

"It is a beautiful city."

Banat turned without answering to the drink the steward had poured out for him. He had not once looked at Graham.

"You are not looking well," said Josette severely. "I do not think you are sincere when you say that you are only tired."

"You are tired?" said Mr. Kuvetli in French. "Ah, it is my fault. Always with ancient monuments it is necessary to walk." He seemed to have given Banat up as a bad job.

"Oh, I enjoyed the walk."

"It is the ventilation," Madame Mathis repeated stubbornly.

"There *is*," conceded her husband, "a certain stuffiness." He addressed himself very pointedly to exclude José from his audience. "But what can one expect for so little money?"

"So little!" exclaimed José. "That is very good. It is quite expensive enough for me. I am not a millionaire."

Mathis flushed angrily. "There are more expensive ways of travelling from Istanbul to Genoa."

"There is always a more expensive way of doing anything," retorted José.

Josette said quickly: "My husband always exaggerates."

"Travelling is very expensive to-day," pronounced Mr. Kuvetli.

"But . . ."

The argument rambled on, pointless and stupid; a mask for the antagonism between José and the Mathis. Graham listened with half his mind. He knew that sooner or later Banat must look at him and he wanted to see that look. Not that it would tell him anything that he did not already know, but he wanted to see it just the same. He could look at Mathis and yet see Banat out of the corner of his eye. Banat raised the glass of brandy to his lips and drank some of it; then, as he put the glass down, he looked directly at Graham.

Graham leaned back in his chair.

". . . but," Mathis was saying, "compare the service one receives. On the train there is a *couchette* in a compartment with others. One sleeps—perhaps. There is waiting at Belgrade for the coaches from Bucharest and at Trieste for the coaches from Budapest. There are passport examinations in the middle of the night and terrible food in the day. There is the noise and there is the dust and soot. I cannot conceive . . ."

Graham drained his glass. Banat was inspecting him: secretly, as the hangman inspects the man whom he is to execute the following morning; mentally weighing him, looking at his neck, calculating the drop.

"Travelling is very expensive to-day," said Mr. Kuvetli again.

At that moment the dinner gong sounded. Banat put

his glass down and went out of the room. The Mathis followed. Graham saw that Josette was looking at him curiously. He got to his feet. There was a smell of food coming from the kitchen. The Italian woman and her son came in and sat down at the table. The thought of food made him feel ill.

"You are sure you feel well?" said Josette as they went to the dinner tables. "You do not look it."

"Quite sure." He cast about desperately for something else to say and uttered the first words that came into his head: "Madame Mathis is right. The ventilation is not good. Perhaps we could walk on deck after dinner is over."

She raised her eyebrows. "Ah, now I know that you cannot be well! You are polite. But very well, I will go with you."

He smiled fatuously, went on to his table, and exchanged reserved greetings with the two Italians. It was not until he sat down that he noticed that an extra place had been laid beside them.

His first impulse was to get up and walk out. The fact that Banat was on the ship was bad enough: to have to eat at the same table would be intolerable. But everything depended upon his behaving normally. He would *have* to stay. He must try and think of Banat as Monsieur Mavrodopoulos, a Greek business man, whom he had never seen or heard of before. He must . . .

Haller came in and sat down beside him. "Good evening, Mr. Graham. And did you enjoy Athens this afternoon?"

"Yes, thanks. Mr. Kuvetli was suitably impressed."

"Ah, yes, of course. You were doing duty as a guide. You must be feeling tired."

"To tell you the truth, my courage failed me. I hired a car. The chauffeur did the guiding. As Mr. Kuvetli speaks fluent Greek, the whole thing went off quite satisfactorily."

"He speaks Greek and yet he has never been to Athens?"

"It appears that he was born in Smyrna. Apart from that, I regret to say, I discovered nothing. My own private opinion is that he is a bore."

"That is disappointing. I had hopes . . . However, it cannot be helped. To tell you the truth, I wished afterwards that I had come with you. You went up to the Parthenon, of course."

"Yes."

Haller smiled apologetically. "When you reach my age you sometimes think of the approach of death. I thought this afternoon how much I would have liked to have seen the Parthenon just once more. I doubt if I shall have another opportunity of doing so. I used to spend hours standing in the shade by the Propylæa looking at it and trying to understand the men who built it. I was young then and did not know how difficult it is for Western man to understand the dream-heavy classical soul. They are so far apart. The god of superlative shape has been replaced by the god of superlative force and between the two conceptions there is all space. The destiny idea symbolised by the Doric columns is incomprehensible to the children of Faust. For us . . ." He broke off. "Excuse me. I see that we have another passenger.

I suppose that he is to sit here."

Graham forced himself to look up.

Banat had come in and was standing looking at the tables. The steward, carrying plates of soup, appeared behind him and motioned him towards the place next to the Italian woman. Banat approached, looked round the table, and sat down. He nodded to them, smiling slightly.

"Mavrodopoulos," he said. "*Je parle français un petit peu.*"

His voice was toneless and husky and he spoke with a slight lisp. The smell of attar of roses came across the table.

Graham nodded distantly. Now that the moment had come he felt quite calm.

Haller's look of strangled disgust was almost funny. He said pompously: "Haller. Beside you are Signora and Signor Beronelli. This is Monsieur Graham."

Banat nodded to them again and said: "I have travelled a long way to-day. From Salonika."

Graham made an effort. "I should have thought," he said, "that it would have been easier to go to Genoa by train from Salonika." He felt oddly breathless as he said it and his voice sounded strange in his own ears.

There was a bowl of raisins in the centre of the table and Banat put some in his mouth before replying. "I don't like trains," he said shortly. He looked at Haller. "You are a German, Monsieur?"

Haller frowned. "I am."

"It is a good country, Germany." He turned his attention to Signora Beronelli. "Italy is good, too." He took some more raisins.

The woman smiled and inclined her head. The boy looked angry.

"And what," said Graham, "do you think about England?"

The small tired eyes stared into his coldly. "I have never seen England." The eyes wandered away round the table. "When I was last in Rome," he said, "I saw a magnificent parade of the Italian army with guns and armoured cars and aeroplanes." He swallowed his raisins. "The aeroplanes were a great sight and made one think of God."

"And why should they do that, Monsieur?" demanded Haller. Evidently he did not like Monsieur Mavrodopoulos.

"They made one think of God. That is all I know. You feel it in the stomach. A thunderstorm makes one think of God, too. But these aeroplanes were better than a storm. They shook the air like paper."

Watching the full self-conscious lips enunciating these absurdities, Graham wondered if an English jury, trying the man for murder, would find him insane. Probably not: he killed for money; and the Law did not think that a man who killed for money was insane. And yet he *was* insane. His was the insanity of the sub-conscious mind running naked, of the "throw back," of the mind which could discover the majesty of God in thunder and lightning, the roar of bombing planes, or the firing of a five hundred pound shell; the awe-inspired insanity of the primæval swamp. Killing, for this man, *could* be a business. Once, no doubt, he had been surprised that people should be prepared to pay so handsomely for the doing of something they could do so easily for themselves. But, of course, he would have ended by concluding, with other successful business men, that he was cleverer than his fellows. His mental approach to the business of killing would be that of the lavatory attendant to the business of attending to his lavatories or of the stockbroker towards the business of taking his commission: purely practical.

"Are you going to Rome now?" said Haller politely. It was the heavy politeness of an old man with a young fool.

"I go to Genoa," said Banat.

"I understand," said Graham, "that the thing to see at Genoa is the cemetery."

Banat spat out a raisin seed. "That is so? Why?" Obviously, that sort of remark was not going to disconcert him.

"It is supposed to be very large, very well arranged, and planted with very fine cypresses."

"Perhaps I shall go."

The waiter brought soup. Haller turned rather ostentatiously to Graham and began once more to talk about the Parthenon. It seemed that he liked arranging his thoughts aloud. The resultant monologue demanded practically nothing of the listener but an occasional nod. From the Parthenon he wandered to pre-Hellenic remains, the Aryan hero tales, and the Vedic religion. Graham ate mechanically, listened, and watched Banat. The man put his food in his mouth as if he enjoyed it. Then, as he chewed, he would look round the room like a dog over a plate of scraps. There was something pathetic about him. He was—Graham realised it with a shock—pathetic in the way that a monkey, in its likeness to man, could be pathetic. He was not insane. He was an animal and dangerous.

The meal came to an end. Haller, as usual, went to his wife. Thankful for the opportunity, Graham left at the same time, got his overcoat, and went out on deck.

The wind had dropped and the roll of the ship was long and slow. She was making good speed and the water sliding along her plates was hissing and bubbling as if they were red hot. It was a cold, clear night.

The smell of attar of roses was at the back of his throat and in his nostrils. He drew the fresh unscented air into his lungs with conscious pleasure. He was, he told himself, over the first hurdle. He had sat face to face with Banat and talked to him without giving himself away. The man could not possibly suspect that he was known and understood. The rest of it would be easy. He had only to keep his head.

There was a step behind him and he swung round quickly, his nerves jumping.

It was Josette. She came towards him smiling. "Ah! So this is your politeness. You ask me to walk with you, but you do not wait for me. I have to find you. You are very bad."

"I'm sorry. It was so stuffy in the saloon that . . ."

"It is not at all stuffy in the saloon, as you know perfectly well." She linked her arm in his. "Now we will walk and you shall tell me what is *really* the matter."

He looked at her quickly. "What is *really* the matter! What do you mean?"

She became the *grande dame*. "So you are not going to tell me. You will not tell me how you came to be on this ship. You will not tell me what has happened to-day to make you so nervous."

"Nervous! But . . ."

"Yes, Monsieur Graham, nervous!" She abandoned the *grande dame* with a shrug. "I am sorry but I have seen people who are afraid before. They do not look at all like people who are tired or people who feel faint in a stuffy room. They have a special look about them. Their faces look very small and grey round the mouth and they cannot keep their hands still." They had reached the stairs to the boat deck. She turned and looked at him. "Shall we go up?"

He nodded. He would have nodded if she had suggested that they jump overboard. He could think of only one thing. If *she* knew a frightened man when she saw one, then so did Banat. And if Banat had noticed. . . . But he couldn't have noticed. He couldn't. He . . .

They were on the boat deck now and she took his arm again.

"It is a very nice night," she said. "I am glad that we can walk like this. I was afraid this morning that I had annoyed you. I did not really wish to go to Athens. That officer who thinks he is so nice asked me to go with him but I did not. But I would have gone if you had asked me. I do not say that to flatter you. I tell you the truth."

"It's very kind of you," he muttered.

She mimicked him. " 'It's very kind of you.' Ah, you are so solemn. It is as if you did not like me."

He managed to smile. "Oh, I like you, all right."

"But you do not trust me? I understand. You see me dancing in Le Jockey Cabaret and you say, because you are so experienced: 'Ah! I must be careful of this lady.' Eh? But I am a friend. You are so silly."

"Yes, I am silly."

"But you *do* like me?"

"Yes, I like you." A stupid, fantastic suggestion was taking root in his mind.

"Then you must trust me, also."

"Yes, I must." It was absurd, of course. He couldn't trust her. Her motives were as transparent as the day. He couldn't trust anybody. He was alone; damnably alone. If he had someone to talk to about it, it wouldn't be so bad. Now supposing Banat had seen that he was nervous and concluded that he was on his guard. Had he or hadn't he seen? She could tell him that.

"What are you thinking about?"

"To-morrow." She said that she was a friend. If there was one thing he needed now, it was, God knew, a friend. Any friend. Someone to talk to, to discuss it with. Nobody knew about it but him. If anything happened to him there would be nobody to accuse Banat. He would go scot free to collect his wages. She was right. It was stupid to distrust her simply because she danced in night places. After all, Kopeikin had liked her and he was no fool about women.

They had reached the corner below the bridge structure. She stopped as he had known she would.

"If we stay here," she said, "I shall get cold. It will be better if we go on walking round and round and round the deck."

"I thought you wanted to ask me questions."

"I have told you I am not inquisitive."

"So you did. Do you remember that yesterday evening I told you that I came on this ship to avoid someone who was trying to shoot me and that this"—he held up his right hand—"was a bullet wound?"

"Yes. I remember. It was a bad joke."

"A very bad joke. Unfortunately, it happened to be true."

It was out now. He could not see her face but he heard her draw in her breath sharply and felt her fingers dig into his arm.

"You are lying to me."

"I'm afraid not."

"But you are an engineer," she said accusingly. "You said so. What have you done that someone should wish to kill you?"

"I have done nothing." He hesitated. "I just happen to be on important business. Some business competitors don't want me to return to England."

"Now you are lying."

"Yes, I am lying, but not very much. I *am* on important business and there *are* some people who do not want me to get back to England. They employed men to kill me while I was in Gallipoli but the Turkish police arrested these men before they could try. Then they employed a professional killer to do the job. When I got back to my hotel after I left Le Jockey Cabaret the other night, he was waiting for me. He shot at me and missed everything except my hand."

She was breathing quickly. "It is atrocious! A bestiality! Does Kopeikin know of it?"

"Yes. It was partly his idea that I should travel on this boat."

"But who are these people?"

"I only know of one. His name is Moeller and he lives in Sofia. The Turkish police told me that he is a German agent."

"The *salop*! But he cannot touch you now."

"Unfortunately he can. While I was ashore with Kuvetli this afternoon, another passenger came aboard."

"The little man who smells? Mavrodopoulos? But. . . ."

"His real name is Banat and he is the professional killer who shot at me in Istanbul."

"But how do you know?" she demanded breathlessly.

"He was at Le Jockey Cabaret watching me. He had followed me there to see that I was out of the way before he broke into my room at the hotel. It was dark in the room when he shot at me, but the police showed me his photograph later and I identified him."

She was silent for a moment. Then she said slowly: "It is not very nice. That little man is a dirty type."

"No, it is not very nice."

"You must go to the Captain."

"Thanks. I've tried to see the Captain once. I got as far as the Purser. He thinks I'm either crazy, drunk, or lying."

"What are you going to do?"

"Nothing for the moment. He doesn't know that I know who he is. I think that he will wait until we get to Genoa before he tries again. When we get there I shall go to the British Consul and ask him to advise the police."

"But I think he *does* know that you suspect him. When we were in the *salone* before dinner and the Frenchman was talking about trains, this man was watching you. Mr. Kuvetli was watching you also. You looked so curious, you see."

His stomach turned over. "You mean, I suppose, that I looked frightened to death. I was frightened. I admit it. Why shouldn't I? I am not used to people trying to kill me." His voice had risen. He felt himself shaking with a sort of hysterical anger.

She gripped his arm again. "Ssh! You must not speak so loudly." And then: "Does it matter so much that he knows?"

"If he knows, it means that he will have to act before we get to Genoa."

"On this little ship? He would not dare." She paused. "José has a revolver in his box. I will try to get it for you."

"I've got a revolver."

"Where?"

"It's in my suitcase. It shows in my pocket. I did not want him to see that I knew I was in danger."

"If you carry the revolver you will be in no danger. Let him see it. If a dog sees that you are nervous, he will bite you. With types like that you must show that you are dangerous and then they are afraid." She took his other arm. "Ah, you do not need to worry. You will get to Genoa and you will go to the British Consul. You can ignore this dirty beast with the perfume. By the time you get to Paris you will have forgotten him."

"If I get to Paris."

"You are impossible. Why should you not get to Paris?"

"You think I'm a fool."

"I think perhaps you are tired. Your wound . . ."

"It was only a graze."

"Ah, but it is not the size of the wound. It is the shock."

He wanted suddenly to laugh. It was true what she was saying. He hadn't really got over that hellish night with Kopeikin and Haki. His nerves were on edge. He was worrying unnecessarily. He said: "When we get to Paris, Josette, I shall give you the best dinner it is possible to buy."

She came close to him. "I don't want you to give me anything, *chéri.* I want you to like me. You *do* like me?"

"Of course I like you. I told you so."

"Yes, you told me so."

His left hand touched the belt on her coat. Her body moved suddenly pressing against his. The next moment his arms were round her and he was kissing her.

When his arms grew tired, she leaned back, half against him, half against the rail.

"Do you feel better, *chéri?*"

"Yes, I feel better."

"Then I will have a cigarette."

He gave her the cigarette and she looked at him across the light of the match. "Are you thinking of this lady in England who is your wife?"

"No."

"But you *will* think of her?"

"If you keep talking about her I shall have to think about her."

"I see. For you I am part of the journey from Istanbul to London. Like Mr. Kuvetli."

"Not quite like Mr. Kuvetli. I shan't kiss Mr. Kuvetli if I can help it."

"What do you think about me?"

"I think that you're very attractive. I like your hair and your eyes and the scent you use."

"That is very nice. Shall I tell you something, *chéri?*"

"What?"

She began to speak very softly. "This boat is very small; the cabins are very small; the walls are very thin; and there are people everywhere."

"Yes?"

"Paris is very large and there are nice hotels there with big rooms and thick walls. One need not see anyone one does not wish to see. And do you know, *chéri,* that if one is making a journey from Istanbul to London and one arrives in Paris, it is sometimes necessary to wait a week before continuing the journey?"

"That's a long time."

"It is because of the war, you see. There are always difficulties. People have to wait days and days for permission to leave France. There is a special stamp that must be put in your passport, and they will not let you on the train to England until you have that stamp. You have to go to the Préfecture for it and there is a great deal of *chi-chi.* You have to stay in Paris until the old women in the Préfecture can find time to deal with your application."

"Very annoying."

She sighed. "We could pass that week or ten days very

nicely. I do not mean at the Hotel des Belges. That is a dirty place. But there is the Ritz Hotel and the Lancaster Hotel and the Georges Cinque. . . ." She paused and he knew that he was expected to say something.

He said it. "And the Crillon and the Meurice."

She squeezed his arm. "You are very nice. But you understand me? An apartment is cheaper, but for so little time that is impossible. One cannot enjoy oneself in a cheap hotel. All the same I do not like extravagance. There are nice hotels for less than it costs at the Ritz or the Georges Cinque and one has more money to spend on eating and dancing at nice places. Even in war time there are nice places." The burning end of her cigarette made an impatient gesture. "But I must not talk about money. You will make the old women at the Préfecture give you your permit too soon and then I shall be disappointed."

He said: "You know, Josette, I shall begin in a minute to think that you are really serious."

"And you think that I am not?" She was indignant.

"I'm quite sure of it."

She burst out laughing. "You can be rude very politely. I shall tell José that. It will amuse him."

"I don't think I want to amuse José. Shall we go down?"

"Ah, you are angry! You think that I have been making a fool of you."

"Not a bit."

"Then kiss me."

Some moments later she said softly: "I like you very much. I would not mind very much a room for fifty francs a day. But the Hotel des Belges is terrible. I do not want to go back there. You are not angry with me?"

"No, I am not angry with you." Her body was soft and warm and infinitely yielding. She had made him feel as if Banat and the rest of the journey really did not matter. He felt both grateful to and sorry for her. He made up his mind that, when he got to Paris, he would buy her a handbag and slip a thousand franc note in it before he gave it to her. He said: "It's all right. You needn't go back to the Hotel des Belges."

When at last they went down to the saloon it was after ten. José and Mr. Kuvetli were there playing cards.

José was playing with thin-lipped concentration and took no notice of them; but Mr. Kuvetli looked up. His smile was sickly.

"Madame," he said ruefully, "your husband plays cards very well."

"He has had a lot of practice."

"Ah, yes, I am sure." He played a card. José slapped another one on top of it triumphantly. Mr. Kuvetli's face fell.

"It is my game," said José and gathered up some money from the table. "You have lost eighty-four lire. If we had been playing for lire instead of centesimi I should have won eight thousand four hundred lire. That would be interesting. Shall we play another game?"

"I think that I will go to bed now," said Mr. Kuvetli hurriedly. "Good night, Messieurs-dame." He went.

José sucked his teeth as if the game had left an unpleasant taste in his mouth. "Everyone goes to bed early on this filthy boat," he said. "It is very boring." He looked up at Graham. "Do you want to play?"

"I'm sorry to say that I must go to bed, too."

José shrugged. "Very well. Good-bye." He glanced at Josette and began to deal two hands. "I will play a game with you."

She looked at Graham and smiled hopelessly. "If I do not he will be disagreeable. Good night, Monsieur."

Graham smiled and said good night. He was not unrelieved.

He got to his cabin feeling a good deal more cheerful than he had felt when he had left it earlier in the evening.

How sensible she was! And how stupid he'd been! With men like Banat it was dangerous to be subtle. If a dog saw that you were nervous, he bit you. From now on he would carry the revolver. What was more, he would use it if Banat tried any funny business. You had to meet force with force.

He bent down to pull his suitcase from under the bunk. He was going to get the revolver out then and there.

Suddenly he stopped. For an instant his nostrils had caught the sweet cloying smell of attar of roses.

The smell had been faint, almost imperceptible, and he could not detect it again. For a moment he remained motionless, telling himself that he must have imagined it. Then panic seized him.

With shaking fingers he tore at the latches on the suitcase and flung back the lid.

The revolver was gone.

CHAPTER SEVEN

He undressed slowly, got into his bunk and lay there staring at the cracks in the asbestos round a steam pipe which crossed the ceiling. He could taste Josette's lipstick in his mouth. The taste was all that was left to remind him of the self-assurance with which he had returned to the cabin; the self-assurance which had been swept away by fear welling up into his mind like blood from a severed artery; fear that clotted, paralysing thought. Only his senses seemed alive.

On the other side of the partition, Mathis finished brushing his teeth and there was a lot of grunting and creaking as he clambered into the upper berth. At last he lay back with a sigh.

"Another day!"

"So much the better. Is the porthole open?"

"Unmistakably. There is a very disagreeable current of air on my back."

"We do not want to be ill like the Englishman."

"That was nothing to do with the air. It was seasickness. He would not admit it because it would not be correct for an Englishman to be seasick. The English like to think that they are all great sailors. He is *drôle* but I like him."

"That is because he listens to your nonsense. He is polite—too polite. He and that German greet each other now as if they were friends. *That* is not correct. If this Gallindo . . ."

"Oh, we have talked enough about him."

"Signora Beronelli said that he knocked against her on the stairs and went on without apologising."

"He is a filthy type."

There was a silence. Then:

"Robert!"

"I am nearly asleep."

"You remember that I said that the husband of Signora Beronelli was killed in the earthquake?"

"What about it?"

"I talked to her this evening. It is a terrible story. It was not the earthquake that killed him. He was shot."

"Why?"

"She does not wish everyone to know. You must say nothing of it."

"Well?"

"It was during the first earthquake. After the great shocks were over they went back to their house from the fields in which they had taken refuge. The house was in ruins. There was part of one wall standing and he made a shelter against it with some boards. They found some food that had been in the house but the tanks had been broken and there was no water. He left her with the boy, their son, and went to look for water. Some friends who had a house near theirs were away in Istanbul. That house, too, had fallen, but he went among the ruins to find the water tanks. He found them and one of them had not been broken. He had nothing to take the water back in so he searched for a jug or a tin. He found a jug. It was of silver and had been partly crushed by the falling stones. After the earthquake, soldiers had been sent to patrol the streets to prevent looting, of which there was a great deal because valuable things were lying everywhere in the ruins. As he was standing there trying to straighten the jug, a soldier arrested him. Signora Beronelli knew nothing of this and when he did not come back she and her son went to look for him. But there was such chaos that she could do nothing. The next day she heard that he had been shot. Is that not a terrible tragedy?"

"Yes, it is a tragedy. Such things happen."

"If the good God had killed him in the earthquake she could bear it more easily. But for him to be shot . . . ! She is very brave. She does not blame the soldiers. With so much chaos they cannot be blamed. It was the Will of the good God."

"He is a comedian. I have noticed it before."

"Do not blaspheme."

"It is *you* who blaspheme. You talk of the good God as if He were a waiter with a fly-swatter. He hits at the flies and kills some. But one escapes. Ah, *le salaud*! The waiter hits again and the fly is paste with the others. The good God is not like that. He does not make earthquakes and tragedies. He is of the mind."

"You are insupportable. Have you no pity for the poor woman?"

"Yes, I pity her. But will it help her if we hold another burial service? Will it help her if I stay awake arguing instead of going to sleep as I wish? She told you this because she likes to talk of it. Poor soul! It eases her mind to become the heroine of a tragedy. The fact becomes less real. But if there is no audience, there is no tragedy. If she tells me, I, too, will be a good audience. Tears will come into my eyes. But you are not the heroine. Go to sleep."

"You are a beast without imagination."

"Beasts must sleep. Good night, *chérie!*"

"Camel!"

There was no answer. After a moment or two he sighed heavily and turned over in his bunk. Soon he began gently to snore.

For a time Graham lay awake listening to the rush of the sea outside and the steady throb of the engines. A waiter with a fly-swatter! In Berlin there was a man whom he had never seen and whose name he did not know, who had condemned him to death; in Sofia there was a man named Moeller who had been instructed to carry out the sentence; and here, a few yards away in cabin number nine, was the executioner with a nine milli-metre calibre self-loading pistol, ready, now that he had disarmed the condemned man, to do his work and collect his money. The whole thing was as impersonal, as dis-passionate, as justice itself. To attempt to defeat it seemed as futile as to argue with the hangman on the scaffold.

He tried to think of Stephanie and found that he could

not. The things of which she was a part, his house, his friends, had ceased to exist. He was a man alone, transported into a strange land with death for its frontiers: alone but for the one person to whom he could speak of its terrors. She was sanity. She was reality. He needed her. Stephanie he did not need. She was a face and a voice dimly remembered with the other faces and voices of a world he had once known.

His mind wandered away into an uneasy doze. Then he dreamed that he was falling down a precipice and awoke with a start. He switched on the light and picked up one of the books he had bought that afternoon. It was a detective story. He read a few pages and then put it down. He was not going to be able to read himself to sleep with news of "neat, slightly bleeding" holes in the right temples of corpses lying "grotesquely twisted in the final agony of death."

He got out of his bunk, wrapped himself in a blanket, and sat down to smoke a cigarette. He would, he decided, spend the rest of the night like that: sitting and smoking cigarettes. Lying prone increased his sense of helplessness. If only he had a revolver.

It seemed to him as he sat there that the having or not having of a revolver was really as important to a man as the having or not having of sight. That he should have survived for so many years without one could only be due to chance. Without a revolver a man was as defenceless as a tethered goat in a jungle. What an incredible fool he had been to leave the thing in his suitcase! If only . . .

And then he remembered something Josette had said: "José has a revolver in his box. I will try to get it for you."

He drew a deep breath. He was saved. José had a revolver. Josette would get it for him. All would be well. She would probably be on deck by ten. He would wait until he was sure of finding her there, tell her what had happened, and ask her to get the revolver there and then. With luck he would have it in his pocket within half an hour or so of his leaving his cabin. He would be able to sit down to luncheon with the thing bulging in his pocket. Banat would get a surprise. Thank goodness for José's suspicious nature!

He yawned and put out his cigarette. It would be stupid to sit there all night: stupid, uncomfortable, and dull. He felt sleepy, too. He put the blanket back on the bunk and lay down once more. Within five minutes he was asleep.

When he again awoke, a crescent of sunlight slanting through the porthole was rising and falling on the white paint of the bulkhead. He lay there watching it until he had to get up to unlock the door for the steward bringing his coffee. It was nine o'clock. He drank the coffee slowly, smoked a cigarette, and had a hot sea water bath. By the time he was dressed it was close on ten o'clock. He put on his coat and left the cabin.

The alleyway on to which the cabins opened was only just wide enough for two persons to pass. It formed three sides of a square, the fourth side of which was taken up by the stairs to the saloon and shelter deck and two small spaces in which stood a pair of dusty palms in earthen-ware tubs. He was within a yard or two of the end of the alleyway when he came face to face with Banat.

The man had turned into the alleyway from the space at the foot of the stairs, and by taking a pace backwards he could have given Graham room to pass; but he made no attempt to do so. When he saw Graham, he stopped. Then, very slowly, he put his hands in his pockets and leaned against the steel bulkhead. Graham could either turn round and go back the way he had come or stay where he was. His heart pounding at his ribs, he stayed where he was.

Banat nodded. "Good morning, Monsieur. It is very fine weather to-day, eh?"

"Very fine."

"For you, an Englishman, it must be very agreeable to see the sun." He had shaved and his pasty jowl gleamed with unrinsed soap. The smell of attar of roses came from him in waves.

"Most agreeable. Excuse me." He went to push by to the stairs.

Banat moved, as if by accident, blocking the way. "It is so narrow! One person must give way to the other, eh?"

"Just so. Do you want to go by?"

Banat shook his head. "No. There is no hurry. I was so anxious to ask you, Monsieur, about your hand. I noticed it last night. What is the matter with it?"

Graham met the small, dangerous eyes staring inso-lently into his. Banat knew that he was unarmed and was trying to unnerve him as well. And he was succeeding.

Graham had a sudden desire to smash his knuckles into the pale, stupid face. He controlled himself with an effort.

"It is a small wound," he said calmly. And then his pent up feelings got the better of him. "A bullet wound, to be exact," he added. "Some dirty little thief took a shot at me in Istanbul. He was either a bad shot or frightened. He missed."

The small eyes did not flicker but an ugly little smile twisted the mouth. Banat said slowly: "A dirty little thief, eh? You must look after yourself carefully. You must be ready to shoot back next time."

"I shall shoot back. There is not the slightest doubt of that."

The smile widened. "You carry a pistol, then?"

"Naturally. And now, if you will excuse me . . ." He walked forward intending to shoulder the other man out of the way if he did not move. But Banat moved. He was grinning now. "Be very careful, Monsieur," he said, and laughed.

Graham had reached the foot of the stairs. He paused and looked back. "I don't think it will be necessary," he said deliberately. "These scum don't risk their skins with an armed man." He used the word *excrément*.

The grin faded from Banat's face. Without replying he turned and went on to his cabin.

By the time Graham reached the deck, reaction had set in. His legs seemed to have gone to jelly and he was sweating. The unexpectedness of the encounter had helped and, all things considered, he had not come out of it too badly. He'd put up a bluff. Banat might conceivably be wondering if, after all, he had a second revolver. But bluff wasn't going to go very far now. The gloves were off. His bluff might be called. Now, whatever happened, he *must* get José's revolver.

He walked quickly round the shelter deck. Haller was there with his wife on his arm, walking slowly. He said good morning; but Graham did not want to talk to anyone but the girl. She was not on the shelter deck. He went on up to the boat deck.

She was there, but talking to the young officer. The Mathis and Mr. Kuvetli were a few yards away. Out of the corner of his eye he saw them look at him expectantly but he pretended not to have seen them and walked over to Josette.

She greeted him with a smile and a meaning look intended to convey that she was bored with her companion. The young Italian scowled a good morning and made to take up the conversation where Graham had interrupted it.

But Graham was in no mood for courtesies. "You must excuse me, Monsieur," he said in French; "I have a message for Madame from her husband."

The officer nodded and stood aside politely.

Graham raised his eyebrows. "It is a *private* message, Monsieur."

The officer flushed angrily and looked at Josette. She nodded to him in a kindly way and said something to him in Italian. He flashed his teeth at her, scowled once more at Graham and stalked on.

She giggled. "You were really very unkind to that poor boy. He was getting on so nicely. Could you think of nothing better than a message from José?"

"I said the first thing that came into my head. I had to speak to you."

She nodded approvingly. "That is very nice." She looked at him slyly. "I was afraid that you would spend the night being angry with yourself because of last night. But you must not look so solemn. Madame Mathis is very interested in us."

"I'm feeling solemn. Something has happened."

The smile faded from her lips. "Something serious?"

"Something serious. I . . ."

She glanced over his shoulder. "It will be better if we walk up and down and look as if we are talking about the sea and the sun. Otherwise they will be gossiping. I do not care what people say, you understand. But it would be embarrassing."

"Very well." And then, as they began to walk: "When I got back to my cabin last night I found that my revolver had been stolen from my suitcase."

She stopped. "This is true?"

"Quite true."

She began to walk again. "It may have been the steward."

"No. Banat had been in my cabin. I could smell that scent of his."

She was silent for a moment. Then: "Have you told anyone?"

"It's no use my making a complaint. The revolver will be at the bottom of the sea by now. I have no proof that Banat took it. Besides, they wouldn't listen to me after the scene I made with the Purser yesterday."

"What are you going to do?"

"Ask you to do something for me."

She looked at him quickly. "What?"

"You said last night that José had a revolver and that you might be able to get it for me."

"You are serious?"

"Never more so in all my life."

She bit her lip. "But what am I to say to José if he finds that it is gone?"

"Will he find out?"

"He may do."

He began to get angry. "It was, I think, your idea that you should get it for me."

"It is so necessary that you should have a revolver? There is nothing that he can do."

"It was also your idea that I should carry a revolver."

She looked sullen. "I was frightened by what you said about this man. But that was because it was dark. Now that it is daytime it is different." She smiled suddenly. "Ah, my friend, do not be so serious. Think of the nice time we will have in Paris together. This man is not going to make any trouble."

"I'm afraid he is." He told her about his encounter by the stairs, and added: "Besides, why did he steal my revolver if he doesn't intend to make trouble?"

She hesitated. Then she said slowly: "Very well, I will try."

"Now?"

"Yes, if you wish. It is in his box in the cabin. He is in the *salone* reading. Do you want to wait here for me?"

"No, I'll wait on the deck below. I don't want to have

to talk to these people here just now."

They went down and stood for a moment by the rail at the foot of the companionway.

"I'll stay here." He pressed her hand. "My dear Josette, I can't tell you how grateful I am to you for this."

She smiled as if at a small boy to whom she had promised sweets. "You shall tell me that in Paris."

He watched her go and then turned to lean against the rail. She could not be more than five minutes. He stared for a time at the long, curling bow wave streaming out and away to meet the transverse wave from the stern and be broken by it into froth. He looked at his watch. Three minutes. Someone clattered down the companionway.

"Good morning, Mr. Graham. You feel all right today, eh?" It was Mr. Kuvetli.

Graham turned his head. "Yes, thanks."

"Monsieur and Madame Mathis are hopeful to play some bridge this afternoon. Do you play?"

"Yes, I play." He was not, he knew, being very gracious but he was terrified lest Mr. Kuvetli should attach himself to him.

"Then perhaps we make party of four, eh?"

"By all means."

"I do not play well. Is very difficult game."

"Yes." Out of the corner of his eye he saw Josette step through the door from the landing on to the deck.

Mr. Kuvetli's eyes flickered in her direction. He leered. "This afternoon then, Mr. Graham."

"I shall look forward to it."

Mr. Kuvetli went. Josette came up to him.

"What was he saying?"

"He was asking me to play bridge." Something in her face set his heart going like a trip hammer. "You've got it?" he said quickly.

She shook her head. "The box was locked. He has the keys."

He felt the sweat prickling out all over his body. He stared at her trying to think of something to say.

"Why do you look at me like that?" she exclaimed angrily. "I cannot help it if he keeps the box locked."

"No, you cannot help it." He knew now that she had not intended to get the revolver. She couldn't be blamed. He couldn't expect her to steal for him. He had asked too much of her. But he had been banking on that revolver of José's. Now, in God's name, what was he going to do?

She rested her hand on his arm. "You are angry with me?"

He shook his head. "Why should I be angry? I should have had the sense to keep my own revolver in my pocket. It's just that I was relying on your getting it. It's my own fault. But, as I told you, I'm not used to this sort of thing."

She laughed. "Ah, you need not worry; I can tell you something. This man does not carry a gun."

"What! How do you know?"

"He was going up the stairs in front of me when I came back just now. His clothes are tight and creased. If he carried a revolver I would have seen the shape of it in his pocket."

"You are sure of this?"

"Of course. I would not tell you if . . ."

"But a *small* gun . . ." He stopped. A nine milli-metre self-loading pistol would *not* be a small gun. It would weigh about two pounds and would be corre-spondingly bulky. It would not be the sort of thing a man would carry about in his pocket if he could leave it in a cabin. If . . .

She was watching his face. "What is it?"

"He'll have left his gun in his cabin," he said slowly.

She looked him in the eyes. "I could see that he does not go to his cabin for a long time."

"How?"

"José will do it."

"José?"

"Be calm. I will not have to tell José anything about you. José will play cards with him this evening."

"Banat would play cards. He is a gambler. But will José ask him?"

"I shall tell José that I saw this man open a wallet with a lot of money in it. José will see that he plays cards. You do not know José."

"You're sure you can do it?"

She squeezed his arm. "Of course. I do not like you to be worried. If you take his gun then you will have nothing at all to fear, eh?"

"No, I shall have nothing at all to fear." He said it almost wonderingly. It seemed so simple. Why hadn't he thought of it before? Ah, but he had not known be-fore that the man did not carry his gun. Take the man's gun away from him and he couldn't shoot. That was logical. And if he couldn't shoot there was nothing to fear. That was logical too. *The essence of all good strategy is simplicity.*

He turned to her. "When can you do this?"

"This evening would be best. José does not like so much to play cards in the afternoon."

"How soon this evening?"

"You must not be impatient. It will be some time after the meal." She hesitated. "It will be better if we are not seen together this afternoon. You do not want him to suspect that we are friends."

"I can play bridge with Kuvetli and the Mathises this afternoon. But how shall I know if it is all right?"

"I will find a way to let you know." She leaned against him. "You are sure that you are not angry with me about José's revolver?"

"Of course I'm not."

"There is no one looking. Kiss me."

"Banking!" Mathis was saying. "What is it but usury? Bankers are money lenders, usurers. But because they lend other people's money or money that does not exist, they have a pretty name. They are still usurers. Once, usury was a mortal sin and an abomination, and to be a usurer was to be a criminal for whom there was a prison cell. To-day the usurers are the gods of the earth and the only mortal sin is to be poor."

"There are so many poor people," said Mr. Kuvetli profoundly. "It is terrible!"

Mathis shrugged impatiently. "There will be more before this war is finished. You may depend upon it. It will be a good thing to be a soldier. Soldiers, at least, will be given food."

"Always," said Madame Mathis, "he talks nonsense. Always, always. But when we get back to France it will be different. His friends will not listen so politely. Banking! What does he know about banking?"

"Ha! That is what the banker likes. Banking is a mystery! It is too difficult for ordinary men to understand." He laughed derisively. "If you make two and two equal five you *must* have a lot of mystery." He turned aggressively to Graham. "The international bankers are the real war criminals. Others do the killing but they sit, calm and collected, in their offices and make money."

"I'm afraid," said Graham, feeling that he ought to say something, "that the only international banker I know is a very harassed man with a duodenal ulcer. He is far from calm. On the contrary, he complains bitterly."

"Precisely," said Mathis triumphantly. "It is the System! I can tell you . . ."

He went on to tell them. Graham picked up his fourth whisky and soda. He had been playing bridge with the Mathises and Mr. Kuvetli for most of the afternoon and he was tired of them. He had seen Josette only once during that time. She had paused by the card-table and nodded to him. He had taken the nod to mean that José had risen to the news that Banat had money in his pocket and that sometime that evening it would be safe to go to Banat's cabin.

The prospect cheered and terrified him alternately. At one moment the plan seemed foolproof. He would go into the cabin, take the gun, return to his own cabin, drop the gun out of the porthole and return to the saloon with a tremendous weight lifted from his shoulders. The next moment, however, doubts would begin to creep in. It was *too* simple. Banat might be insane but he was no fool. A man who earned his living in the way Banat earned his and who yet managed to stay alive and free was not going to be taken in so easily. Supposing he should guess what his victim had in mind, leave José in the middle of the game, and go to his cabin! Supposing he had bribed the steward to keep an eye on his cabin on the grounds that it contained valuables! Supposing . . . ! But what was the alternative? Was he to wait passively while Banat chose the moment to kill him? It was all very well for Haki to talk about a marked man having only to defend himself; but what had he to defend himself with? When the enemy was as close as Banat was, the best defence was attack. Yes, that was it! Anything was better than just waiting. And the plan might well succeed. It was the simple plans of attack that *did* succeed. It would never occur to a man of Banat's conceit to suspect that two could play at the game of stealing guns, that the helpless rabbit might bite back. He'd soon find out his mistake.

Josette and José came in with Banat. José appeared to be making himself amiable.

". . . it is only necessary," Mathis was concluding, "to say one word—Briey! When you have said that you have said all."

Graham drained his glass. "Quite so. Will you all have another drink?"

The Mathis, looking startled, declined sharply; but

Mr. Kuvetli nodded happily.

"Thank you, Mr. Graham. I will."

Mathis stood up, frowning. "It is time that we got ready for dinner. Please excuse us."

They went. Mr. Kuvetli moved his chair over.

"That was very sudden," said Graham. "What's the matter with them?"

"I think," said Mr. Kuvetli carefully, "that they thought you are making joke of them."

"Why on earth should they think that?"

Mr. Kuvetli looked sideways. "You ask them to have to drink three times in five minutes. You ask them once. They say no. You ask them again. They say no again. You ask again. They do not understand English hospitality."

"I see. I'm afraid that I was thinking of something else. I must apologise."

"Please!" Mr. Kuvetli was overcome. "It is not necessary to apologise for hospitality. But"—he glanced hesitantly at the clock—"it is now nearly time for dinner. You allow me later to have this drink you so kindly offer?"

"Yes, of course."

"And you will excuse me please, now?"

"By all means."

When Mr. Kuvetli had gone, Graham stood up. Yes, he'd had just one drink too many on an empty stomach. He went out on deck.

The starlit sky was hung with small smoky clouds. In the distance were the lights of the Italian coast. He stood there for a moment letting the icy wind sting his face. In a minute or two the gong would sound for dinner. He dreaded the approaching meal as a sick man dreads the approach of the surgeon with a probe. He would sit, as he had sat at luncheon, listening to Haller's monologues and to the Beronellis whispering behind their misery, forcing food down his throat to his unwilling stomach, conscious all the time of the man opposite to him—of why he was there and of what he stood for.

He turned round and leaned against a stanchion. With his back to the deck he found himself constantly looking over his shoulder to make sure that he was alone. He felt more at ease with no deck space behind him.

Through one of the saloon portholes he could see Banat with Josette and José. They sat like details in a Hogarth group; José tight-lipped and intent, Josette smiling, Banat saying something that brought his lips forward. The air in there was grey with tobacco smoke and the hard light from the unshaded lamps flattened their features. There was about them all the squalor of a flashlight photograph taken in a bar.

Someone turned the corner at the end of the deck and came towards him. The figure reached the light and he saw that it was Haller. The old man stopped.

"Good evening, Mr. Graham. You look as if you are really enjoying the air. I, as you see, need a scarf and a coat before I can face it."

"It's stuffy inside."

"Yes. I saw you this afternoon very gallantly playing bridge."

"You don't like bridge?"

"One's tastes change." He stared out at the lights. "To

see the land from a ship or to see a ship from the land.
I used to like both. Now I dislike both. When a man
reaches my age he grows, I think, to resent subconsciously
the movement of everything except the respiratory
muscles which keep him alive. Movement is change and
for an old man change means death."

"And the immortal soul?"

Haller sniffed. "Even that which we commonly regard
as immortal dies sooner or later. One day the last Titian
and the last Beethoven quartet will cease to exist. The
canvas and the printed notes may remain if they are carefully preserved but the works themselves will have died
with the last eye and ear accessible to their messages. As
for the immortal soul, that is an eternal truth and the
eternal truths die with the men to whom they were
necessary. The eternal truths of the Ptolemaic system
were as necessary to the mediæval theologians as were
the eternal truths of Kepler to the theologians of the
Reformation and the eternal truths of Darwin to the
nineteenth century materialists. The statement of an
eternal truth is a prayer to lay a ghost—the ghost of primi-
tive man defending himself against what Spengler calls
the 'dark almightiness.'" He turned his head suddenly
as the door of the saloon opened.

It was Josette standing there looking uncertainly from
one to the other of them. At that moment the gong
began to sound for dinner.

"Excuse me," said Haller; "I must see my wife before
dinner. She is still unwell."

"Of course," said Graham hurriedly.

Josette came over to him as Haller went.

"What did he want, that old man?" she whispered.

"He was talking about life and death."

"Ugh! I do not like him. He makes me shudder. But I must not stay. I came only to tell you that it is all right."

"When are they going to play?"

"After dinner." She squeezed his arm. "He is horrible, this man Banat. I would not do this for anyone except you, *chéri*."

"You know I am grateful, Josette. I shall make it up to you."

"Ah, stupid!" She smiled at him fondly. "You must not be so serious."

He hesitated. "Are you sure that you can keep him there?"

"You need not worry. I will keep him. But come back to the *salone* when you have been to the cabin so that I shall know that you have finished. It is understood, *chéri*?"

"Yes, it is understood."

It was after nine o'clock and, for the past half hour, Graham had been sitting near the door of the saloon pretending to read a book.

For the hundredth time his eyes wandered to the opposite corner of the room where Banat was talking to Josette and José. His heart began suddenly to beat faster. José had a deck of cards in his hand. He was grinning at something Banat had said. Then they sat down at the card-table. Josette looked across the room.

Graham waited a moment. Then, when he saw them cutting for the deal, he got slowly to his feet and walked out.

He stood on the landing for a moment, bracing himself for what he had to do. Now that the moment had come he felt better. Two minutes—three at the most—and it would be over. He would have the gun and he would be safe. He had only to keep his head.

He went down the stairs. Cabin number nine was beyond his and in the middle section of the alleyway. There was no one about when he reached the palms. He walked on.

He had decided that any sort of stealth was out of the question. He must walk straight to the cabin, open the door and go in without hesitation. If the worst came to the worst and he was seen as he went in by the steward or anyone else, he could protest that he had thought that number nine was an empty cabin and that he was merely satisfying a curiosity to see what the other cabins were like.

But nobody appeared. He reached the door of number nine, paused for barely a second and then, opening the door softly, went in. A moment later he had shut the door behind him and put up the catch. If, for any reason, the steward should try to get in, he would assume that Banat was there when he found the door fastened.

He looked round. The porthole was closed and the air reeked of attar of roses. It was a two-berth cabin and looked strangely bare. Apart from the scent, there were only two indications that the cabin was occupied: the grey raincoat hanging with the soft hat behind the door and a battered composition suitcase under the lower berth.

He ran his hands over the raincoat. There was nothing in the pockets and he turned his attention to the suitcase.

It was unlocked. He pulled it out and threw back the lid.

The thing was crammed with filthy shirts and underwear. There were, besides, some brightly-coloured silk handkerchiefs, a pair of black shoes without laces, a scent spray and a small jar of ointment. The gun was not there.

He shut the case, pushed it back and opened the washing cabinet-cum-wardrobe. The wardrobe part contained nothing but a pair of dirty socks. On the shelf by the tooth-glass was a grey washcloth, a safety razor, a cake of soap and a bottle of scent with a ground glass stopper.

He was getting worried. He had been so sure that the gun would be there. If what Josette had said were true it *must* be there somewhere.

He looked round for other hiding places. There were the mattresses. He ran his hands along the springs beneath them. Nothing. There was the waste compartment below the washing cabinet. Again nothing. He glanced at his watch. He had been there four minutes. He looked round again desperately. It *must* be in there. But he had looked everywhere. He returned feverishly to the suitcase.

Two minutes later he slowly straightened his back. He knew now that the gun was not in the cabin, that the simple plan had been too simple, that nothing was changed. For a second or two he stood there helplessly, putting off the moment when he must finally admit his failure by leaving the cabin. Then the sound of footsteps in the alleyway nearby jarred him into activity.

The footsteps paused. There was the clank of a bucket being put down. Then the footsteps receded. He eased back the door catch and opened the door. The alleyway was empty. A second later he was walking back the way he had come.

He had reached the foot of the stairs before he allowed himself to think. Then he hesitated. He had told Josette that he would go back to the saloon. But that meant seeing Banat. He must have time to steady his nerves. He turned and walked back to his cabin.

He opened the door, took one step forward, and then stopped dead.

Sitting on the bunk with his legs crossed and a book resting on his knee was Haller.

He was wearing a pair of horn-rimmed reading glasses. He removed them very deliberately and looked up. "I've been waiting for you, Mr. Graham," he said cheerfully.

Graham found his tongue . "I don't . . ." he began.

Haller's other hand came from under the book. In it was a large self-loading pistol.

He held it up. "I think," he said, "that this is what you have been looking for, isn't it?"

CHAPTER EIGHT

GRAHAM LOOKED from the gun to the face of the man who was holding it: the long upper lip, the pale blue eyes, the loose yellowish skin.

"I don't understand," he said, and put out his hand to receive the gun. "How . . . ?" he began and then stopped abruptly. The gun was pointing at him and Haller's forefinger was on the trigger.

Haller shook his head. "No, Mr. Graham. I think I shall keep it. I came for a little talk with you. Supposing you sit down here on the bed and turn sideways so that we can face one another."

Graham strove to conceal the deadly sickness that was stealing over him. He felt that he must be going mad. Amid the flood of questions pouring through his mind there was only one small patch of dry land: Colonel Haki had examined the credentials of all the passengers who had embarked at Istanbul and reported that none of them had booked for the journey less than three days prior to the sailing and that they were all harmless. He clung to it desperately.

"I don't understand," he repeated.

"Of course you don't. If you will sit down I will explain."

"I'll stand."

"Ah, yes. I see. Moral support derived from physical discomfort. Remain standing by all means if it pleases you to do so." He spoke with crisp condescension. This was a new Haller, a slightly younger man. He examined the pistol as if he were seeing it for the first time. "You know, Mr. Graham," he went on thoughtfully, "poor Mavrodopoulos was really very upset by his failure in Istanbul. He is not, as you have probably gathered, very intelligent and, like all stupid people, he blames others for his own mistakes. He complains that you moved." He shrugged tolerantly. "Naturally you moved. He could hardly expect you to stand still while he corrected his aim. I told him so. But he was still angry with you, so when he came aboard I insisted on taking care of his pistol for him. He is young, and these Roumanians are so hotheaded. I did not want anything premature to happen."

"I wonder," said Graham, "if your name happens to be Moeller."

"Dear me!" He raised his eyebrows. "I had no idea that you were so well informed. Colonel Haki must have been in a very talkative mood. Did he know that I was in Istanbul?"

Graham reddened. "I don't think so."

Moeller chuckled. "I thought not. Haki is a clever man. I have a great respect for him. But he is human and, therefore, fallible. Yes, after that fiasco in Gallipoli I thought it advisable to attend to things myself. And then, when everything had been arranged, you were inconsiderate enough to move and spoil Mavrodopolous' shooting. But I bear you no ill will, Mr. Graham. I was irritated at the time, of course. Mavrodopoulos . . ."

"Banat is easier to say."

"Thank you. As I was saying, Banat's failure made more work for me. But now my irritation has passed. Indeed, I am quite enjoying the trip. I like myself as an archæologist. I was a little nervous at first, but as soon as I saw that I had succeeded in boring you I knew that all was well." He held up the book he had been reading. "If you would like a record of my little speeches I can recommend this. It is entitled 'The Sumerian Pantheon' and is by Fritz Haller. His qualifications are given on the title page: ten years with the German Institute in Athens, the period at Oxford, the degrees: it is all here. He seems to be an ardent disciple of Spengler. He quotes the Master a great deal. There is a nostalgic little preface which was most helpful and you will find the piece about eternal truths on page three hundred and forty-one. Naturally I paraphrased a little here and there to suit my own mood. And I drew freely on some of the longer footnotes. You see, the effect I wanted to create was that of an erudite but loveable old bore. I think you will agree that I did well."

"So there *is* a Haller?"

Moeller pursed his lips. "Ah, yes. I was sorry to inconvenience him and his wife, but there was no other way. When I found that you were to leave on this boat I decided that it would be helpful if I travelled with you. Obviously I could not have booked a passage at the last moment without attracting Colonel Haki's attention; I therefore took over Haller's tickets and passport. He and his wife were not pleased. But they are good Germans, and when it was made plain to them that their country's interests must come before their own convenience, they gave no more trouble. In a few days their passport will be returned to them with their own photographs restored to it. My only embarrassment has been the Armenian lady who is doing duty for Frau Professor Haller. She speaks very little German and is virtually a half-wit. I have been forced to keep her out of the way. I had no time to make better arrangements, you see. As it was, the man who found her for me had quite a lot of trouble convincing her that she wasn't being carried off to an Italian *bordello*. Female vanity is sometimes extraordinary." He produced a cigarette-case. "I hope you don't mind my telling you all these little things, Mr. Graham. It's just that I want to be frank with you. I think that an atmosphere of frankness is essential to any business discussion."

"Business?"

"Just so. Now do please sit down and smoke. It will do you good." He held out the cigarette-case. "Your nerves have been a little jumpy to-day, haven't they?"

"Say what you want to say and get out!"

Moeller chuckled. "Yes, certainly a little jumpy!" He looked suddenly solemn. "It is my fault, I'm afraid. You see, Mr. Graham, I could have had this little talk with you before, but I wanted to make sure that you would be in a receptive frame of mind."

Graham leaned against the door. "I think that the best way I can describe my state of mind at the moment is to tell you that I have been seriously considering kicking you in the teeth. I could have done so from here before you could have used your gun."

Moeller raised his eyebrows. "And yet you didn't do it? Was it the thought of my white hairs that stopped you, or was it your fear of the consequences?" He paused. "No answer? You won't mind if I draw my own conclusions, will you?" He settled himself a little more comfortably. "The instinct for self-preservation is a wonderful thing. It is so easy for people to be heroic about laying down their lives for the sake of principles when they do not expect to be called upon to do so. When, however, the smell of danger is in their nostrils they are more practical. They see alternatives not in terms of honour or dishonour, but in terms of greater or lesser evils. I wonder if I could persuade you to see my point of view."

Graham was silent. He was trying to fight down the panic which had seized him. He knew that if he opened his mouth he would shout abuse until his throat ached.

Moeller was fitting a cigarette into a short amber holder as if he had time to waste. Obviously he had not expected any answer to his question. He had the self-contained air of a man who is early for an important appointment. When he finished with the cigarette-holder he looked up. "I like you, Mr. Graham," he said. "I was,

I have admitted, irritated when Banat made such a fool of himself in Istanbul. But now that I know you I am glad that he did so. You behaved gracefully over that awkwardness at the dinner-table the night we sailed. You listened politely to my carefully memorised recitations. You are a clever engineer, and yet you are not aggressive. I should not like to think of your being killed—murdered —by any employee of mine." He lit his cigarette. "And yet, the demands made upon us by our life's needs are so uncompromising. I am compelled to be offensive. I must tell you that, as things stand at present, you will be dead within a few minutes of your landing at Genoa on Saturday morning."

Graham had himself in hand now. He said: "I'm sorry to hear that."

Moeller nodded approval. "I am glad to see you take it so calmly. If I were in your place I should be very frightened. But then, of course"—the pale blue eyes narrowed suddenly—"*I* should know that there was no possible chance of my escaping. Banat, in spite of his lapse in Istanbul, is a formidable young man. And when I consider the fact that ready waiting for me in Genoa there would be reinforcements consisting of several other men quite as experienced as Banat, I should realise that there was not the remotest chance of my being able to reach any sort of sanctuary before the end came. I should be left with only one hope—that they did their work so efficiently that I should know very little about it."

"What do you mean by 'as things stand at present'?"

Moeller smiled triumphantly. "Ah! I am so glad. You have gone straight to the heart of the matter. I mean,

Mr. Graham, that you need not necessarily die. There is an alternative."

"I see. A lesser evil." But his heart leaped in spite of himself.

"Scarcely an evil," Moeller objected. "An alternative and by no means an unpleasant one." He settled himself more comfortably. "I have already said that I liked you, Mr. Graham. Let me add that I dislike the prospect of violence quite as whole-heartedly as you do. I am lily-livered. I admit it freely. I will go out of my way to avoid seeing the results of an automobile accident. So, you see, if there is any way of settling this matter without bloodshed I should be prejudiced in favour of it. And if you are still uncertain of my personal goodwill towards you, let me put the question in another and harder light. The killing would have to be hurried, would consequently subject the killers to additional risks and would, therefore, be expensive. Don't misunderstand me, please. I shall spare no expense if it is necessary. But, naturally enough, I hope it won't be necessary. I can assure you that no one, with the possible exception of yourself, will be more delighted than I am if we can dispose of this whole thing in a friendly way as between business men. I hope you will at least believe that I am sincere in that."

Graham began to get angry. "I don't care a damn whether you're sincere or not."

Moeller looked crestfallen. "No, I suppose you don't. I was forgetting that you have been under some nervous strain. You are naturally interested only in getting home safely to England. That may be possible. It just depends on how calmly and logically you can approach the situation. It is necessary, as you must have gathered, that the completion of the work you are doing should be delayed. Now, if you die before you get back to England, somebody else will be sent to Turkey to do your work over again. I understand that the work as a whole would thus be delayed for six weeks. I also understand that that delay would be sufficient for the purposes of those interested. You might, might you not, conclude from that that the simplest way of dealing with the matter would be to kidnap you in Genoa and keep you under lock and key for the requisite six weeks and then release you, eh?"

"You might."

Moeller shook his head. "But you would be wrong. You would disappear. Your employers and, no doubt, the Turkish Government would make inquiries about you. The Italian police would be informed. The British Foreign Office would address bombastic demands for information to the Italian Government. The Italian Government, conscious that its neutrality was being compromised, would bestir itself. I might find myself in serious difficulties, especially when you were released and could tell your story. It would be most inconvenient for me to be wanted by the Italian police. You see what I mean?"

"Yes, I see."

"The straightforward course is to kill you. There is, however, a third possibility." He paused and then said: "You are a very fortunate man, Mr. Graham."

"What does *that* mean?"

"In times of peace only the fanatical nationalist demands that a man should surrender himself body and soul to the government of the country in which he was born.

Yet, in war time, when men are being killed and there is
emotion in the air, even an intelligent man may be so far
carried away as to talk of his 'duty to his country.' You
are fortunate because you happen to be in a business
which sees these heroics for what they are: the emotional
excesses of the stupid and brutish. 'Love of country!'
There's a curious phrase. Love of a particular patch of
earth? Scarcely. Put a German down in a field in North-
ern France, tell him that it is Hanover, and he cannot
contradict you. Love of fellow-countrymen? Surely
not. A man will like some of them and dislike others.
Love of the country's culture? The men who know most
of their countries' cultures are usually the most intelligent and the least patriotic. Love of the country's government? But governments are usually disliked by the
people they govern. Love of country, we see, is merely
a sloppy mysticism based on ignorance and fear. It has
its uses, of course. When a ruling class wishes a people
to do something which that people does not want to do, it
appeals to patriotism. And, of course, one of the things
that people most dislike is allowing themselves to be killed.
But I must apologise. These are old arguments and I am
sure you are familiar with them."

"Yes, I'm familiar with them."

"I am so relieved. I should not like to think that I had
been wrong in judging you to be a man of intelligence.
And it makes what I have to say so much easier."

"Well, what *have* you got to say?"

Moeller stubbed his cigarette out. "The third possibility, Mr. Graham, is that you might be induced to retire

from business for six weeks of your own free will—that you should take a holiday."

"Are you mad?"

Moeller smiled. "I see your difficulty, believe me. If you simply go into hiding for six weeks, it may be rather awkward to explain matters when you return home. I understand. Hysterical fools might say that in choosing to remain alive instead of choosing to be killed by our friend Banat you did something shameful. The facts that the work would have been delayed in any case and that you were of more use to your country and its allies alive than dead would be ignored. Patriots, in common with other mystics, dislike logical argument. It would be necessary to practise a small deception. Let me tell you how it could be arranged."

"You're wasting your time."

Moeller took no notice. "There are some things, Mr. Graham, which not even patriots can control. One of those things is illness. You have come from Turkey where, thanks to earthquakes and floods, there have been several outbreaks of typhus. What could be more likely than that the moment you get ashore at Genoa a mild attack of typhus should develop? And what then? Well, of course, you will be taken immediately to a private clinic and the doctor there will, at your request, write to your wife and employers in England. Of course, there will be the inevitable delays of war. By the time anyone can get to see you, the crisis will have passed and you will be convalescent: convalescent but much too weak to work or travel. But in six weeks' time you will have re-

covered sufficiently to do both. All will be well again.
How does that appeal to you, Mr. Graham? To me it
seems the only solution satisfactory to both of us."

"I see. You don't have the bother of shooting me. I'm
out of the way for the requisite six weeks and can't tell
tales afterwards without showing myself up. Is that it?"

"That's a very crude way of putting it; but you are
quite right. That *is* it. How do you like the idea? Personally I should find the prospect of six weeks' absolute
peace and quiet in the place I have in mind very attractive. It is quite near Santa Margherita, overlooking the
sea and surrounded by pines. But then, I am old. You
might fret."

He hesitated. "Of course," he went on slowly, "if you
liked the idea, it might be possible to arrange for Señora
Gallindo to share your six weeks' holiday."

Graham reddened. "What on earth do you mean?"

Moeller shrugged. "Come now, Mr. Graham! I am not
short-sighted. If the suggestion really offends you, I apologise humbly. If not . . . I need hardly say that you
would be the only patients there. The medical staff, which
would consist of myself, Banat, and another man, apart
from the servants, would be unobtrusive unless you were
receiving visitors from England. However, that could be
discussed later. Now what do you think?"

Graham steeled himself to make an effort. He said
with deliberate ease: "I think you're bluffing. Hasn't it
occurred to you that I may not be such a fool as you
think? I shall, of course, repeat this conversation to the
Captain. There will be police inquiries when we reach
Genoa. My papers are perfectly genuine. Yours are not.

Nor are Banat's. I have nothing to hide. You have plenty to hide. So has Banat. You're relying on my fear of being killed forcing me to agree to this scheme of yours. It won't. It won't keep my mouth shut either. I admit that I have been badly scared. I have had a very unpleasant twenty-four hours. I suppose that's your way of inducing a receptive frame of mind. Well, it doesn't work with me. I'm worried all right; I should be a fool if I weren't; but I'm not worried out of my senses. You're bluffing, Moeller. That's what I think. Now you can get out."

Moeller did not move. He said, as if he were a surgeon musing over some not entirely unforeseen complication: "Yes, I was afraid you might misunderstand me. A pity." He looked up. "And to whom are you going to take your story in the first place, Mr. Graham? The Purser? The third officer was telling me about your curious behaviour over poor Monsieur Mavrodopoulos. Apparently you have been making wild allegations to the effect that he is a criminal named Banat who wants to kill you. The ship's officers, including the Captain, seem to have enjoyed the joke very much. But even the best of jokes becomes tiresome if it is told too often. There would be a certain unreality about the story that I, too, was a criminal who wanted to kill you. Isn't there a medical name for that sort of delusion? Come now, Mr. Graham! You tell me that you are not a fool. Please do not behave like one. Do you think that I should have approached you in this way if I had thought that you might be able to embarrass me in the way you suggest? I hope not. You are no less foolish when you interpret my reluctance to have you killed as weakness. You may prefer lying dead in a gutter with a bullet in your back to spending six weeks in a villa on the Ligurian Riviera: that is your affair. But please do not deceive yourself: those *are* the inevitable alternatives."

Graham smiled grimly. "And the little homily on patriotism is to still any qualms I might have about accepting the inevitable. I see. Well, I'm sorry, but it doesn't work. I still think you're bluffing. You've bluffed very well. I admit that. You had me worried. I really thought for a moment that I had to choose between possible death and sinking my pride—just like the hero in a melodrama. My real choice was, of course, between using my common sense and letting my stomach do my thinking for me. Well, Mr. Moeller, if that's all you have to say . . ."

Moeller got slowly to his feet. "Yes, Mr. Graham," he said calmly, "that is all I have to say." He seemed to hesitate. Then, very deliberately, he sat down again. "No, Mr. Graham, I have changed my mind. There *is* something else that I should say. It is just possible that on thinking this thing over calmly you may decide that you have been silly and that I may not be as clumsy as you now seem to think. Frankly, I don't expect you to do so. You are pathetically sure of yourself. But in case your stomach should after all take control, I think I should issue a warning."

"Against what?"

Moeller smiled. "One of the many things you don't seem to know is that Colonel Haki considered it advisable to install one of his agents on board to watch over you. I tried hard to interest you in him yesterday, but was unsuccessful. Ihsan Kuvetli is unprepossessing, I agree; but he has the reputation of being a clever little man. If he had not been a patriot, he would have been rich."

"Are you trying to tell me that Kuvetli is a Turkish agent?"

"I am indeed, Mr. Graham!" The pale blue eyes narrowed. "The reason why I approached you this evening instead of to-morrow evening is because I wanted to see you before he made himself known to you. He did not, I think, find out who I was until to-day. He searched my cabin this evening. I think that he must have heard me talking to Banat; the partitions between the cabins are absurdly thin. In any case, I thought it likely that, realizing the danger you were in, he would decide that the time had come to approach you. You see, Mr. Graham, with his experience, he is not likely to make the mistake that you are making. However, he has his duty to do and I have no doubt that he will have evolved some laborious plan for getting you to France in safety. What I want to warn you against is telling him of this suggestion I have made to you. You see, if you should after all come round to my way of thinking, it would be embarrassing for both of us if an agent of the Turkish Government knew of our little deception. We could scarcely expect him to keep silent. You see what I mean, Mr. Graham? If you let Kuvetli into the secret you will destroy the only chance of returning to England alive that remains to you." He smiled faintly. "It's a solemn thought, isn't it?" He got up again and went to the door. "That was all I wanted to say. Good night, Mr. Graham."

Graham watched the door close and then sat down on the bunk. The blood was beating through his head as if he had been running. The time for bluffing was over. He should be deciding what he was going to do. He had to think calmly and clearly.

But he could not think calmly and clearly. He was confused. He became conscious of the vibration and movement of the ship and wondered if he had imagined what had just happened. But there was the depression in the bunk where Moeller had been sitting and the cabin was filled with the smoke from his cigarette. It was Haller who was the creature of imagination.

He was conscious now more of humiliation than of fear. He had become almost used to the tight sensation in his chest, the quick hammering of his heart, the dragging at his stomach, the crawling of his spine which were his body's responses to his predicament. In a queer, horrible way it had been stimulating. He had felt that he was pitting his wits against those of an enemy—a dangerous enemy but an intellectual inferior—with a chance of winning. Now he knew that he had been doing nothing of the kind. The enemy had been laughing up their sleeves at him. It had never even occurred to him to suspect "Haller." He had just sat there politely listening to extracts from a book. Heavens, what a fool the man must think him! He and Banat between them had seen through him as if he were made of glass. Not even his wretched little passages with Josette had escaped their notice. Probably they had seen him kissing her. And as a final measure of their contempt for him, it had been Moeller who had informed him that Mr. Kuvetli was a Turkish agent charged with his protection. Kuvetli! It was funny. Josette would be amused.

He remembered suddenly that he had promised to return to the saloon. She would be getting anxious. And the cabin was stifling. He could think better if he had some air. He got up and put on his overcoat.

José and Banat were still playing cards; José with a peculiar intentness as if he suspected Banat of cheating; Banat coolly and deliberately. Josette was leaning back in her chair smoking. Graham realised with a shock that he had left the room less than half an hour previously. It was amazing what could happen to your mind in so short a time; how the whole atmosphere of a place could change. He found himself noticing things about the saloon which he had not noticed before: a brass plate with the name of the builders of the ship engraved on it, a stain on the carpet, some old magazines stacked in a corner.

He stood there for a moment staring at the brass plate. The Mathis and the Italians were sitting there reading and did not look up. He looked past them and saw Josette turning her head back to watch the game. She had seen him. He went across to the farther door and out on to the shelter deck.

She would follow him soon to find out if he had been successful. He walked slowly along the deck wondering what he would say to her, whether or not to tell her about Moeller and his "alternative." Yes, he would tell her. She would tell him that he was all right, that Moeller was bluffing. But supposing Moeller *weren't* bluffing! "They will do anything to see that it is so. *Anything*, Mr. Graham! Do you understand?" Haki had not talked about bluffing. The wound under the grimy bandage on his hand did not feel like bluffing. And if Moeller wasn't bluffing, what was he, Graham, going to do?

He stopped and stared out at the lights on the coast. They were nearer now; near enough for him to see the movement of the boat in relation to them. It was incredible that this should be happening to him. Impossible! Perhaps, after all, he had been badly wounded in Istanbul and it was all a fantasy born of anæthesia. Perhaps he would become conscious again soon to find himself in a hospital bed. But the teak rail, wet with dew, on which his hand rested was real enough. He gripped it in sudden anger at his own stupidity. He should be thinking, cudgelling his brains, making plans, deciding; doing something instead of standing there mooning. Moeller had left him over five minutes ago and here he was still trying to escape from his senses into a fairyland of hospitals and anæsthetics. What was he going to do about Kuvetli? Should he approach him or wait to be approached? What . . . ?

There were quick footsteps on the deck behind him. It was Josette, her fur coat thrown over her shoulders, her face pale and anxious in the dingy glare of the deck light. She seized his arm. "What has happened? Why were you so long?"

"There was no gun there."

"But there must be. Something has happened. When you walked into the *salone* just now you looked as if you had seen a ghost or were going to be sick. What is it, *chéri*?"

"There was no gun there," he repeated. "I searched carefully."

"You were not seen?"

"No, I wasn't seen."

She sighed with relief. "I was afraid when I saw your face . . ." She broke off. "But don't you see? It is all right. He does not carry a gun. There is no gun in his cabin. He has not got a gun." She laughed. "Perhaps he has pawned it. Ah, do not look so serious, *chéri*. He may get a gun in Genoa, but then it will be too late. Nothing can happen to you. You will be all right." She put on a woebegone expression. "I am the one who is in trouble now."

"You?"

"Your smelly little friend plays cards very well. He is winning money from José. José does not like that. He will have to cheat and cheating puts him in a bad temper. He says that it is bad for his nerves. Really it is that he likes to win because he is a better player." She paused and added suddenly: "Please wait!"

They had reached the end of the deck. She stopped and faced him. "What is the matter, *chéri*? You are not listening to what I am saying. You are thinking of something else." She pouted. "Ah, I know. It is your wife. Now that there is no danger you think of her again."

"No."

"You are sure?"

"Yes, I am sure." He knew now that he did not want to tell her about Moeller. He wanted her to talk to him believing that there was no longer any danger, that nothing could happen to him, that he could walk down the gangway at Genoa without fear. Afraid to create his own illusion, he could live in one of her making. He managed to smile. "You mustn't take any notice of me, Josette. I'm tired. You know, it's a very tiring business searching other people's cabins."

Immediately she was all sympathy. "*Mon pauvre chéri. It is my fault, not yours. I forget how unpleasant things have been for you. Would you like us to go back to the salone and have a little drink?"

He would have done almost anything for a drink but go back to the saloon where he could see Banat. "No. Tell me what we shall do first when we arrive in Paris."

She looked at him quickly, smiling. "If we do not walk we shall get cold." She wriggled into her coat and linked her arm in his. "So we are going to Paris together?"

"Of course! I thought it was all arranged."

"Oh yes, but"—she pressed his arm against her side— "I did not think that you were serious. You see," she went on carefully, "so many men like to talk about what will happen, but they do not always like to remember what they have said. It is not that they do not mean what they say but that they do not always feel the same. You understand me, *chéri*?"

"Yes, I understand."

"I want you to understand," she went on, "because it is very important to me. I am a dancer and must think of my career also." She turned to him impulsively. "But you will think that I am selfish and I would not like you to think that. It is just that I like you very much and do not wish you to do anything simply because you have made a promise. As long as you understand that, it is all right. We will not talk about it." She snapped her fin-

gers. "Look! When we get to Paris we will go straight
to a hotel which I know of near the St. Philippe du Roule
Metro. It is very modern and respectable and if you wish
we can have a bathroom. It is not expensive. Then we
will have champagne cocktails at the Ritz bar. They are
only nine francs. While we have those drinks we can
decide where to eat. I am very tired of Turkish foods
and the sight of ravioli makes me ill. We must have good
French food." She paused and added hesitantly, "I have
never been to the Tour d'Argent."

"You shall."

"You mean it? I shall eat until I am as fat as a pig.
After that we will begin."

"Begin?"

"There are some little places that are still open late in
spite of the police. I will introduce you to a great friend
of mine. She was the *sous-maquecée* of the Moulin Galant
when Le Boulanger had it and before the gangsters came.
You understand *sous-maquecée*?"

"No."

She laughed. "It is very bad of me. I will explain to
you another time. But you will like Suzie. She saved a
lot of money and now she is very respectable. She had a
place in the rue de Liège which was better than Le Jockey
Cabaret in Istanbul. She had to close it when the war
came but she has opened another place in an impasse off
the rue Pigalle and those who are her friends can go there.
She has a great many friends and so she is making money
again. She is quite old and the police do not trouble her.
She shrugs her shoulders at them. Just because there is
this filthy war there is no reason why we should all be

miserable. I have other friends in Paris, too. You will like them when I introduce you. When they know that you are my friend they will be polite. They are very polite and nice when you are introduced by someone who is known in the quarter."

She went on talking about them. Most of them were women (Lucette, Dolly, Sonia, Claudette, Berthe) but there were one or two men (Jojo, Ventura) who were foreigners and had not been mobilised. She spoke of them vaguely but with an enthusiasm half defensive, half real. They might not be rich as Americans understood being rich, but they were people of the world. Each was remarkable in some particular. One was "very intelligent," another had a friend in the Ministry of the Interior, another was going to buy a villa at San Tropez and invite all his friends there for the summer. All were "amusing" and very useful if one wanted "anything special." She did not say what she meant by "anything special" and Graham did not ask her. He did not object to the picture she was painting. The prospect of sitting in the Café Graf buying drinks for *bizness* men and women from the places up the hill seemed to him at that moment infinitely attractive. He would be safe and free; himself again; able to think his own thoughts, to smile without stretching his nerves to breaking point when he did so. It must happen. It was absurd that he should be killed. Moeller was right about one thing at least. He would be more use to his country alive than dead.

Considerably more! Even if the Turkish contract were delayed for six weeks it would still have to be fulfilled. If he were alive at the end of the six weeks he would be able to go on with it; perhaps he might even make up for some of the lost time. He was, after all, the company's chief designer and it would be difficult to replace him in war time. He had been truthful enough when he had told Haki that there were dozens of other men with his qualifications; but he had not thought it necessary to bolster up Haki's argument by explaining that those dozens were made up of Americans, Frenchmen, Germans, Japanese and Czechs as well as Englishmen. Surely the sensible course would be the safe one. He was an engineer, not a professional secret agent. Presumably, a secret agent would have been equal to dealing with men like Moeller and Banat. He, Graham, was not. It was not for him to decide whether or not Moeller was bluffing. His business was to stay alive. Six weeks on the Ligurian Riviera could not do him any harm. It meant lying, of course: lying to Stephanie and to their friends, to his managing director and to the representatives of the Turkish Government. He couldn't tell them the truth. They would think that he ought to have risked his life. It was the sort of thing people did think when they were safe and snug in their arm-chairs. But if he lied, would they believe him? The people at home would; but what about Haki? Haki would smell a rat and ask questions. And Kuvetli? Moeller would have to do something about putting him off. It would be a tricky business; but Moeller would arrange things. Moeller was used to that sort of thing. Moeller. . . .

He stopped with a jerk. For God's sake, what was he thinking? He must be out of his senses! Moeller was an enemy agent. What he, Graham, had been turning over

in his mind was nothing less than treason. And yet. . . .
And yet what? He knew suddenly that something had
snapped in his mind. The idea of doing a deal with an
enemy agent was no longer unthinkable. He could consider Moeller's suggestion on its merits, coolly and calmly.
He was becoming demoralised. He could no longer trust
himself.

Josette was shaking his arm. "What is it, *chéri*? What
is the matter?"

"I've just remembered something," he muttered.

"Ah!" she said angrily, "that is not at all polite. I ask
you if you wish to go on walking. You take no notice.
I ask you again and you stop as if you were ill. You have
not been listening to what I was saying."

He pulled himself together. "Oh yes, I've been listening, but something you said reminded me that if I am to
stop in Paris I shall have to write several important business letters so that I can post them immediately I get
there." He added with a fair assumption of jauntiness:
"I don't want to work while I am in Paris."

"If it is not these *salauds* who tried to kill you, it is
business," she grumbled. But she was apparently molli-
fied.

"I apologise, Josette. It shan't happen again. Are you
sure you are warm? You wouldn't like a drink?" He
wanted to get away now. He knew what he must do and
was impatient to do it before he could begin to think.

But she took his arm again. "No, it is all right. I am not
angry and I am not cold. If we go up on the top deck
you can kiss me to show that we are friends again. Soon

I must go back to José. I said that I would only be a few minutes."

Half an hour later he went down to his cabin, took off his coat and went to look for the steward. He found him busy with a mop and bucket in the lavatories.

"Signore?"

"I promised to lend Signor Kuvetli a book. What is the number of his cabin?"

"Three, signore."

Graham walked back to cabin number three and stood for a moment hesitating. Perhaps he should think again before he did anything decisive, anything for which he might be sorry later. Perhaps it would be better if he left it until the morning. Perhaps . . .

He set his teeth, raised his hand and knocked on the door.

CHAPTER NINE

Mr. Kuvetli opened the door.

He was wearing an old red wool dressing gown over a flannel night-shirt and his fringe of grey hair stood out from the sides of his head in ringlets. He had a book in his hand and looked as if he had been lying in his bunk reading. He stared at Graham blankly for a moment, then his smile returned.

"Mr. Graham! Is very good to see you. What can I do, please?"

At the sight of him, Graham's heart sank. It was to this grubby little man with a stupid smile that he was proposing to commit his safety. But it was too late to turn back now. He said: "I wonder if I could have a talk with you, Mr. Kuvetli."

Mr. Kuvetli blinked a little shiftily. "Talk? Oh, yes. Come in, please."

Graham stepped into the cabin. It was as small as his own and very stuffy.

Mr. Kuvetli smoothed out the blankets on his bunk. "Please take seat."

Graham sat down and opened his mouth to speak, but Mr. Kuvetli forestalled him.

"Cigarette, please, Mr. Graham?"

"Thank you." He took a cigarette. "I had a visit from Herr Professor Haller earlier this evening," he added; and then, remembering that the bulkheads were thin, glanced at them.

Mr. Kuvetli struck a match and held it out. "Herr Professor Haller is very interesting man, eh?" He lit Graham's cigarette and his own and blew the match out. "Cabins on both sides empty," he remarked.

"Then . . ."

"Please," interrupted Mr. Kuvetli, "will you allow me to speak French? My English is not very good, eh? Your French is very good. We understand better each."

"By all means."

"Now, then, we can talk easily." Mr. Kuvetli sat down beside him on the bunk. "Monsieur Graham, I was going to introduce myself to you to-morrow. Now, Monsieur Moeller has saved me the trouble, I think. You know that I am not a tobacco merchant, eh?"

"According to Moeller you are a Turkish agent acting under Colonel Haki's orders. Is that so?"

"Yes, that is so. I will be truthful. I am surprised that you have not discovered me before this. When the Frenchman asked me what firm I belonged to I had to say Pazar and Co., because I had given that name to you. Unfortunately, the firm of Pazar and Co. does not exist. Naturally he was puzzled. I was able to prevent him from asking more questions then, but I expected him to discuss it with you later." The smile had gone and with it the bright-eyed stupidity which, for Graham, had been the tobacco merchant. In its place was a firm determined mouth, and a pair of steady brown eyes which surveyed him with something very like good-humoured contempt.

"He did not discuss it."

"And you did not suspect that I was avoiding his questions?" He shrugged. "One always takes unnecessary precautions. People are so much more trusting than one supposes."

"Why should I suspect?" Graham demanded irritably. "What I cannot understand is why you did not approach me as soon as you knew that Banat was on the ship. I suppose," he added spitefully, "that you *do* know that Banat is on the ship?"

"Yes, I know," said Mr. Kuvetli airily. "I did not approach you for three reasons." He held up podgy fingers. "Colonel Haki instructed me in the first place that your attitude to his efforts to protect you were unsympathetic and that unless it became necessary I would do better to remain unknown to you. Secondly, Colonel Haki has a low opinion of your ability to conceal your feelings and considered that if I wished to keep my true identity secret I had better not tell you of it."

Graham was scarlet. "And what about the third reason?"

"Thirdly," continued Mr. Kuvetli serenely, "I wished to see what Banat and Moeller would do. You tell me that Moeller has talked to you. Excellent. I would like to hear what he had to say."

Graham was angry now. "Before I waste my time doing that," he said coldly, "supposing you show me your credentials. So far I have only Moeller's word and your own that you *are* a Turkish agent. I've already made some silly mistakes on this trip. I don't intend to make any more."

To his surprise, Mr. Kuvetli grinned. "I am pleased to see that you are in such excellent spirits, Monsieur Graham. I was getting a little worried about you this evening. In this sort of situation, whisky does more harm to the nerves than good. Excuse me, please." He turned to his jacket hanging on the hook behind the door and produced from the pocket of it a letter which he handed to Graham. "That was given to me by Colonel Haki to give to you. I think you will find it satisfactory."

Graham looked at it. It was an ordinary letter of introduction written in French on notepaper embossed with the title and address of the Turkish Ministry of the Interior. It was addressed to him personally and signed "Zia Haki." He put it in his pocket. "Yes, Monsieur Kuvetli, it is quite satisfactory. I must apologise for doubting your word."

"It was correct of you to do so," said Mr. Kuvetli primly. "And now, Monsieur, tell me about Moeller. I am afraid Banat's appearance on the ship must have been a shock to you. I felt guilty about keeping you ashore in Athens. But it was for the best. As to Moeller . . ."

Graham looked at him quickly. "Wait a minute! Do you mean to say that you knew Banat was coming aboard? Do you mean that you hung about in Athens asking all those fool questions solely in order to prevent my finding out before we sailed that Banat was on board?"

Mr. Kuvetli looked sheepish. "It was necessary. You must see . . ."

"Of all the damned . . . !" began Graham violently.

"One moment, please," said Mr. Kuvetli sharply. "I have said that it was necessary. At Çanakkale I received a telegram from Colonel Haki saying that Banat had left Turkey, that it was possible that he might try to join the ship at the Piræus and . . ."

"You knew that! And yet . . ."

"Please, Monsieur! I will continue. Colonel Haki added that I was to keep you here on the ship. That was intelligent. On the ship nothing could happen to you. Banat might have been going to the Piræus for the purpose of frightening you on to the land, where very unpleasant things could happen to you. Wait, please! I went to Athens with you partly to see that you were not attacked while you were ashore and partly so that if Banat did join the ship, you would not see him until we had sailed."

"But why, in the name of goodness, didn't Colonel Haki arrest Banat or at least delay him until it was too late for him to reach the ship?"

"Because Banat would certainly have been replaced. We know all about Banat. A strange Monsieur Mavrodopoulos would have been a new problem."

"But you say that Banat's, or, rather, Moeller's idea might have been to scare me off the boat. Banat could not know that I knew him?"

"You told Colonel Haki that Banat was pointed out to you in Le Jockey Cabaret. Banat was watching you then.

He would probably know that you had noticed him. He is not an amateur. You see Colonel Haki's point of view? If they were hoping to drive you on to the land and kill you there, it would be better for them to attempt to do so and fail than for the attempt to be frustrated in time for them to make other arrangements. As it happens, however," he went on cheerfully, "their intention was not to drive you on to the land and my precautions were wasted. Banat did join the ship, but he stayed in his cabin until the pilot had been taken off."

"Precisely!" snarled Graham. "I could have gone ashore, taken a train and been safe in Paris by now."

Mr. Kuvetli considered the criticism for a moment and then slowly shook his head. "I do not think so. You have forgotten Monsieur Moeller. I do not think that he and Banat would have stayed on the boat very long if you had not returned by sailing time."

Graham laughed shortly. "Did you know that then?"

Mr. Kuvetli contemplated dirty fingernails. "I will be very honest, Monsieur Graham. I did not know it. I knew *of* Monsieur Moeller, of course. I was, through an intermediary, once offered a large sum of money to work for him. I had seen a photograph of him. But photographs are mostly useless. I did not recognise him. The fact that he came aboard at Istanbul prevented my suspecting him. Banat's behaviour made me think that I had overlooked something, and when I saw him talking to the Herr Professor I made some inquiries."

"He says that you searched his cabin."

"I did. I found letters addressed to him in Sofia."

"There has," said Graham bitterly, "been quite a lot of

cabin searching. Last night Banat stole my revolver from my suitcase. This evening I went to his cabin and tried to find his gun, the gun he used on me in Istanbul. It was not there. When I returned to my cabin, Moeller was there with Banat's gun."

Mr. Kuvetli had been listening gloomily. "If," he now said, "you will please tell me what Moeller had to say we shall both get to sleep much sooner."

Graham smiled. "You know, Kuvetli, I have had several surprises on this ship. You are the first pleasant one." And then the smile faded. "Moeller came to tell me that unless I agree to delay my return to England for six weeks I shall be murdered within five minutes of my landing in Genoa. He says that apart from Banat, he has other men waiting in Genoa to do the killing."

Mr. Kuvetli did not seem surprised. "And where does he suggest that you should spend the six weeks?"

"In a villa near Santa Margherita. The idea is that I should be certified by a doctor as suffering from typhus and that I should stay in this villa as if it were a clinic. Moeller and Banat would be the medical staff if anyone should come out from England to see me. He proposes, you see, to involve me in the deception so that I cannot tell tales afterwards."

Mr. Kuvetli raised his eyebrows. "And how was I concerned?"

Graham told him.

"And, believing Monsieur Moeller, you decided to ignore his advice and tell me about his suggestion?" Mr. Kuvetli beamed approvingly. "That was very courageous of you, Monsieur."

Graham reddened. "Do you think that I might have agreed?"

Mr. Kuvetli misunderstood. "I think nothing," he said hastily. "But"—he hesitated—"when a person's life is in danger he is not always quite normal. He may do things which he would not do in the ordinary way. He cannot be blamed."

Graham smiled. "I will be frank with you. I came to you now instead of in the morning so that there could be no chance of my thinking things over and deciding to take his advice after all."

"What is important is," said Mr. Kuvetli quietly, "that you *have* in fact come to me. Did you tell him that you were going to do so?"

"No. I told him that I thought he was bluffing."

"And *do* you think that he was?"

"I don't know."

Mr. Kuvetli scratched his armpits thoughtfully. "There are so many things to be considered. And it depends on what you mean by saying that he is bluffing. If you mean that he could not or would not kill you, I think you are wrong. He could and would."

"But how? I have a Consul. What is to prevent my getting into a taxi at the dock and going straight to the Consulate? I could arrange for some sort of protection there."

Mr. Kuvetli lit another cigarette. "Do you know where the British Consulate-General in Genoa is?"

"The taxi-driver would know."

"I can tell you myself. It is at the corner of the Via Ippolito d'Aste. This ship docks at the Ponte San Giorgio in the Vittorio Emanuele basin, several kilometres away from your Consulate. I have travelled this way before and so I know what I am saying. Genoa is a great port. I doubt, Monsieur Graham, whether you would complete one of those kilometres. They will be waiting for you with a car. When you took the taxi they would follow you as far as the Via Francia, then force the taxi on to the pavement and shoot you as you sit there."

"I could telephone to the Consul from the dock."

"Certainly you could. But you would have to go through the Customs shed first. You would then have to wait for the Consul to arrive. *Wait*, Monsieur! Do you understand what that means? Let us suppose that you were to reach the Consul by telephone immediately and convince him that your case was urgent. You would still have to wait at least half an hour for him. Let me tell you that your chances of surviving that half-hour would not be lessened if you spent it drinking prussic acid. To kill an unarmed, unguarded man is never difficult. Among the sheds on the quay it would be simplicity itself. No, I do not think Moeller is bluffing when he says that he can kill you."

"But what about this proposal? He seemed very eager to persuade me to agree."

Mr. Kuvetli fingered the back of his head. "There could be several explanations of that. For instance, it is possible that his intention is to kill you in any case and that he wishes to do so with as little trouble as possible. One cannot deny that it would be easier to kill you on the road to Santa Margherita than on the waterfront at Genoa."

"That's a pleasing idea."

"I am inclined to think that it is the correct one." Mr. Kuvetli frowned. "You see, this proposal of his looks very simple—you are taken ill, there is a forged medical certificate, you get better, you go home. *Voilà!* It is done. But think now of the actuality. You are an Englishman in a hurry to get to England. You land in Genoa. What would you do normally? Take the train for Paris, without a doubt. But what is it necessary to do now? You must, for some mysterious reason, remain in Genoa long enough to discover that you have typhus. Also you must not do what anyone else would do in those circumstances—you must not go to a hospital. You must instead go to a private clinic near Santa Margherita. Is it possible that it would not be thought in England that your behaviour was curious? I think not. Furthermore, typhus is a disease which must be notified to the authorities. That could not be done in this case because there would be no typhus and the medical authorities would soon discover the fact. And supposing your friends discover that your case has not been notified. They might. You are of some importance. The British Consul might be asked to investigate. And then what? No, I cannot see Monsieur Moeller taking such absurd risks. Why should he? It would be easier to kill you."

"He says that he does not like having people killed if he can help it."

Mr. Kuvetli giggled. "He must think you very stupid indeed. Did he tell you what he would do about my presence here?"

"No."

"I am not surprised. For that plan to succeed as he explained it to you, there would be only one thing he could do—kill me. And even when he had killed me I should still embarrass him. Colonel Haki would see to that. I am afraid that Monsieur's proposal is not very honest."

"It sounded convincing. I may say that he was prepared to allow Señora Gallindo to make up the party if I liked to take her along."

Mr. Kuvetli leered: a scurfy faun in a flannel nightshirt. "And did you tell Señora Gallindo that?"

Graham flushed. "She knows nothing of Moeller. I told her about Banat. I'm afraid I gave myself away last night when Banat came into the saloon. She asked me what was wrong and I told her. Anyway," he added defensively but none too truthfully, "I needed her help. It was she who arranged to keep Banat occupied while I searched his cabin."

"By arranging for the good José to play cards with him? Quite so. As to the suggestion that she should accompany you, I think that, if you had accepted it, it would have been withdrawn. It would, no doubt, be explained that difficulties had arisen. Does José know of this business?"

"No. I don't think that she would tell him. She's trustworthy, I think," he added with as much nonchalance as he could muster.

"No woman is trustworthy," gloated Mr. Kuvetli. "But I do not begrudge you your amusements, Monsieur Graham." He moistened his upper lip with the tip of his tongue and grinned. "Señora Gallindo is very attractive."

Graham checked the retort that rose to his lips. "Very," he said tersely. "Meanwhile we have reached the conclusion that I shall be killed if I accept Moeller's proposal and killed if I don't." And then he lost control of himself. "For God's sake, Kuvetli," he burst out in English, "do you think it's pleasant for me to sit here listening to you telling me how easy it would be for these lice to kill me! What am I going to *do*?"

Mr. Kuvetli patted his knee consolingly. "My dear friend, I understand perfectly. I was merely showing you that it would be impossible for you to land in the ordinary way."

"But what other way *can* I land? I'm not invisible."

"I will tell you," said Mr. Kuvetli complacently. "It is very simple. You see, although this ship does not actually reach the quayside for the landing of passengers until nine o'clock on Saturday morning, she arrives off Genoa in the early hours, at about four o'clock. Night pilotage is expensive; accordingly, although she takes on a pilot as soon as it begins to get light, she does not move in until sunrise. The pilot boat . . ."

"If you're suggesting that I leave by the pilot boat, it's impossible."

"For you, yes. For me, no. I am privileged. I have a diplomatic *laisser passer*." He patted his jacket pocket. "By eight o'clock I can be at the Turkish Consulate. Arrangements can then be made for getting you away safely and taking you to the airport. The international train service is not as good as it used to be, and the Paris train does not leave until two o'clock in the afternoon. It is better that you do not remain so long in Genoa. We will charter a plane to take you to Paris immediately."

Graham's heart began to beat faster. An extraordinary feeling of lightness and ease came over him. He wanted to laugh. He said stolidly: "It sounds all right."

"It will be all right, but precautions must be taken to see that it is so. If Monsieur Moeller suspects that there is a chance of your escaping, something unpleasant will happen. Listen carefully, please." He scratched his chest and then held up a forefinger. "First; you must go to Monsieur Moeller to-morrow and tell him that you agree to his suggestion that you should stay in Santa Margherita."

"What!"

"It is the best way to keep him quiet. I leave you to choose your own opportunity. But I will suggest the following: it is possible that he will approach you again, and so perhaps it will be best if you give him time to do so. Wait until late in the evening. If he has not approached you by then, go to him. Do not appear to be too ingenuous, but agree to do what he wants. When you have done that, go to your cabin, lock the door, and remain there. Do not leave your cabin under any circumstances until eight o'clock the following morning. It might be dangerous.

"Now comes the important part of your instructions. At eight o'clock in the morning you must be ready with your baggage. Call the steward, tip him, and tell him to put your baggage in the Customs shed. There must be no mistake at this point. What you have to do is to remain on the ship until I come to tell you that the preparations have been made and that it is safe for you to land. There are difficulties. If you remain in your cabin the steward will make you go ashore with the rest, including Monsieur Moeller and Banat. If you go on deck, the same thing will happen. You must see that you are not forced to go ashore before it is safe for you to do so."

"But how?"

"I am explaining that. What you must do is to leave your cabin and then, taking care that nobody sees you, to go into the nearest unoccupied cabin. You have cabin number five. Go into cabin number four. That is the next cabin to this. Wait there. You will be quite safe. You will have tipped the steward. If he thinks of you again at all it will be to assume that you have gone ashore. If he is asked about you he will certainly not look in unoccupied cabins. Monsieur Moeller and Banat will naturally be looking for you. You will have agreed to go with them. But they will have to go ashore to wait. By that time we shall be there and able to act."

"Act?"

Mr. Kuvetli smiled grimly. "We shall have two men for every one of theirs. I do not think that they will try to stop us. Are you quite clear about what you have to do?"

"Quite clear."

"There is a small matter. Monsieur Moeller will ask you if I have made myself known to you. You will, of course, say yes. He will ask you what I said. You will tell him that I offered to escort you to Paris myself and that when you insisted on going to the British Consul, I threatened you."

"Threatened me!"

"Yes." Mr. Kuvetli was still smiling, but his eyes had narrowed a little. "If your attitude towards me had been different it might have been necessary for me to threaten you."

"What with?" Graham demanded spitefully. "Death? That would have been absurd, wouldn't it?"

Mr. Kuvetli smiled steadily. "No, Monsieur Graham, not death but with the accusation that you had accepted bribes from an enemy agent to sabotage Turkish naval preparations. You see, Monsieur Graham, it is just as important for me that you return to England without delay as it is for Monsieur Moeller that you should not return."

Graham stared at him. "I see. And this is a gentle reminder that the threat still stands if I should allow myself to be persuaded that Moeller's proposal is, after all, acceptable. Is that it?"

His tone was deliberately offensive. Mr. Kuvetli drew himself up. "I am a Turk, Monsieur Graham," he said with dignity, "and I love my country. I fought with the Gazi for Turkey's freedom. Can you imagine that I would let one man endanger the great work we have done? I am ready to give my life for Turkey. Is it strange that I should not hesitate to do less unpleasant things?"

He had struck an attitude. He was ridiculous and yet, for the very reason that his words were at so odd a variance with his appearance, impressive. Graham was disarmed. He grinned. "Not at all strange. You need have no fears. I shall do exactly what you have told me to do. But supposing he wants to know when our meeting took place?"

"You will tell the truth. It is just possible that you were seen to come to my cabin. You can say that I asked you to do so, that I left a note in your cabin. Remember, too, that we must not be seen in private conversation after this. It will be better if we do not have any sort of conversation. In any case there is nothing more to be said. Everything is arranged. There is only one other matter to be considered—Señora Gallindo."

"What about her?"

"She has part of your confidence. What is her attitude?"

"She thinks that everything is all right now." He reddened. "I said that I would travel with her to Paris."

"And after?"

"She believes that I shall spend some time with her there."

"You did not, of course, intend to do so." He had the air of a schoolmaster dealing with a difficult pupil.

Graham hesitated. "No, I suppose I didn't," he said slowly. "To tell you the truth, it has been pleasant to talk of going to Paris. When you're expecting to be killed . . ."

"But now that you are not expecting to be killed it is different, eh?"

"Yes, it's different." Yet was it so different? He was not quite sure.

Mr. Kuvetli stroked his chin. "On the other hand it would be dangerous to tell her that you have changed your mind," he reflected. "She might be indiscreet—or angry, perhaps. Say nothing to her. If she discusses Paris, everything is as it was before. You can explain that you have business to do in Genoa after the ship docks and say that you will meet her on the train. That will prevent her looking for you before she goes ashore. It is understood?"

"Yes. It is understood."

"She is pretty," Mr. Kuvetli went on thoughtfully. "It is a pity that your business is so urgent. However, perhaps you could return to Paris when you have finished your work." He smiled: the schoolmaster promising a sweet for good behaviour.

"I suppose I could. Is there anything else?"

Mr. Kuvetli looked up at him slyly. "No. That is all. Except that I must ask you to continue to look as *distrait* as you have been looking since we left the Piræus. It would be a pity if Monsieur Moeller should suspect anything from your manner."

"My manner? Oh, yes, I see." He stood up and was surprised to find that his knees felt quite weak. He said: "I've often wondered what a condemned man feels like when they tell him that he has been reprieved. Now I know."

Mr. Kuvetli smiled patronisingly. "You feel very well, eh?"

Graham shook his head. "No, Mr. Kuvetli, I don't feel very well. I feel very sick and very tired and I can't stop thinking that there must be a mistake."

"A mistake! There is no mistake. You need not worry. All will be well. Go to bed now, my friend, and in the morning you will feel better. A mistake!"

Mr. Kuvetli laughed.

CHAPTER TEN

As Mr. Kuvetli had prophesied, Graham did feel better in the morning. Sitting up in his bunk drinking his coffee, he felt curiously free and competent. The disease from which he had been suffering was cured. He was himself again: well and normal. He had been a fool to worry at all. He ought to have known that everything would be all right. War or no war, men like him weren't shot in the street. That sort of thing just didn't happen. Only the adolescent minds of the Moellers and the Banats could entertain such possibilities. He had no misgivings. Even his hand was better. In the night the bandage had slipped, taking with it the bloody dressing which had been sticking to the wound. He was able to replace it with a piece of lint and two short strips of adhesive plaster. The change, he felt, was symbolic. Not even the knowledge that in the day before him he had some highly disagreeable things to do, could depress him.

The first thing he had to consider was, of course, his

attitude towards Moeller. As Mr. Kuvetli had pointed out, it was possible that the man would wait until the evening before making any attempt to find out if the line he had put out the previous evening had caught the fish. That meant that he, Graham, would have to sit through two meals with Moeller and Banat without giving himself away. That, certainly, would not be pleasant. He wondered whether it might not be safer to approach Moeller at once. It would, after all, be far more convincing if the victim made the first move. Or would it be less convincing? Should the fish still be struggling on the hook when the line was reeled in? Evidently Mr. Kuvetli thought that it should. Very well. Mr. Kuvetli's instructions should be followed exactly. The questions of how he was going to behave at lunch and dinner could be left to settle themselves when those times came. As for the actual interview with Moeller, he had ideas about making that convincing. Moeller should not have things all his own way. Rather to his surprise, he found that it was the thought of what he had to do about Josette which worried him most.

He was, he told himself, treating her shabbily. She had been kind to him in her way. Indeed, she could not have been kinder. It was no excuse to say that she had behaved badly over that business of José's revolver. It had been unfair of him to ask her to steal for him: José was, after all, her partner. It would not even be possible now for him to give her that handbag with a thousand-franc note in it, unless he left it for her on his way through Paris, and it was always possible that she would not go to the Hotel des Belges. It was no good protesting that she was

out for what she could get. She had made no secret of the
fact and he had tacitly accepted it. He was treating her
shabbily, he told himself again. It was an attempt to
rationalise his feelings about her and it was strangely unsuccessful. He was perplexed.

He did not see her until just before lunch, and then
she was with José.

It was a wretched day. The sky was overcast and there
was an icy north-east wind with a hint of snow in it. He
had spent most of the morning in a corner of the saloon
reading some old copies of *L'Illustration* he found there.
Mr. Kuvetli had seen and looked through him. He had
spoken to no one except the Beronellis, who had given
him a defensive "buon giorno," and the Mathis, who had
returned his greeting with a frigid bow. He had thought
it necessary to explain to the Mathis that his rudeness of
the previous evening had been unintentional and due to
his feeling ill at the time. The explanation had been
accepted by them with some embarrassment and it had
occurred to him that they might have preferred a silent
feud to an apology. The man had been particularly confused as if he were finding himself in some way ridiculous.
They had soon decided that they must go for a walk on
deck. Through the porthole Graham had seen them a few
minutes later walking with Mr. Kuvetli. The only other
person on deck that morning had been Moeller's Armenian demonstrating pathetically, for there was a heavy
swell, that her dislike of the sea was no mere figment of
her "husband's" imagination. Soon after twelve Graham
had collected his hat and coat from his cabin and gone out
for the stroll which he had decided should precede the

drinking of a large whisky and soda.

He was on his way back to the saloon when he encountered Josette and José.

José stopped with an oath and clutched at his curly soft hat which the wind was trying to snatch from his head.

Josette met Graham's eyes and smiled significantly. "José is angry again. Last night he played cards and lost. It was the little Greek, Mavrodopoulos. The attar of roses was too strong for the California Poppy."

"He is no Greek," said José sourly. "He has the accent of a goat as well as the smell. If he is a Greek I will . . ." He said what he would do.

"But he can play cards, *mon cher caïd.*"

"He stopped playing too soon," said José. "You need not worry. I have not finished with him."

"Perhaps he has finished with you."

"He must be a very good player," Graham put in tactfully.

José eyed him distastefully. "And what do you know about it?"

"Nothing," retorted Graham coldly. "For all I know it may be simply that you are a very bad player."

"You would like to play perhaps?"

"I don't think so. Cards bore me."

José sneered. "Ah, yes! There are better things to do, eh?" He sucked his teeth loudly.

"When he is bad-tempered," Josette explained, "he cannot be polite. There is nothing to be done with him. He does not care what people think."

José pursed up his mouth into an expression of saccharine sweetness. " 'He does not care what people think,' " he repeated in a high, derisive falsetto. Then his face relaxed. "What do I care what they think?" he demanded.

"You are ridiculous," said Josette.

"If they do not like it they can stay in the lavabos," José declared aggressively.

"It would be a small price to pay," murmured Graham. Josette giggled. José scowled. "I do not understand." Graham did not see that there was anything to be gained by explaining. He ignored José and said in English: "I was just going to have a drink. Will you come?"

She looked doubtful. "Do you wish to buy José a drink also?"

"Must I?"

"I cannot get rid of him."

José was glowering at them suspiciously. "It is not wise to insult me," he said.

"No one is insulting you, imbecile. Monsieur here asks us to have drinks. Do you want a drink?"

He belched. "I do not care who I drink with if we can get off this filthy deck."

"He is so polite," said Josette.

They had finished their drinks when the gong sounded. Graham soon found that he had been wise to leave the question of his attitude towards Moeller to answer itself. It was "Haller" who appeared in answer to the gong; a Haller who greeted Graham as if nothing had happened and who embarked almost immediately on a long account of the manifestations of An, the Sumerian sky god. Only once did he show himself to be aware of any change in his relationship with Graham. Soon after he began talking, Banat entered and sat down. Moeller paused and glanced across the table at him. Banat stared back sullenly. Moeller turned deliberately to Graham.

"Monsieur Mavrodopoulos," he remarked, "looks as if he has been frustrated in some way, as if he has been told that he may not be able to do something that he wishes to do very badly. Don't you think so, Mr. Graham? I wonder if he is going to be disappointed."

Graham looked up from his plate to meet a level stare. There was no mistaking the question in the pale blue eyes. He knew that Banat, too, was watching him. He said slowly: "It would be a pleasure to disappoint Monsieur Mavrodopoulos."

Moeller smiled and the smile reached his eyes. "So it would. Now let me see. What was I saying? Ah, yes . . ."

That was all; but Graham went on with his meal, knowing that one at least of the day's problems was solved. He would not have to approach Moeller: Moeller would approach him.

But Moeller was evidently in no hurry to do so. The afternoon dragged intolerably. Mr. Kuvetli had said that they were not to have any sort of conversation and Graham deemed it advisable to plead a headache when Mathis suggested a rubber of bridge. His refusal affected the Frenchman peculiarly. There was a troubled reluctance about his acceptance of it, and he looked as if he had been about to say something important and then thought better of it. There was in his eyes the same look of unhappy confusion that Graham had seen in the morning. But Graham wondered about it only for a few seconds. He was not greatly interested in the Mathis.

Moeller, Banat, Josette and José had gone to their cabins immediately after lunch. Signora Beronelli had been induced to make the fourth with the Mathis and Mr. Kuvetli and appeared to be enjoying herself. Her son sat by her watching her jealously. Graham returned in desperation to the magazines. Towards five o'clock, however, the bridge four showed signs of disintegrating and, to avoid being drawn into a conversation with Mr. Kuvetli, Graham went out on deck.

The sun, obscured since the day before, was pouring a red glow through a thinning of the clouds just above the horizon. To the east the long, low strip of coast which had been visible earlier was already enveloped in a slate grey dusk and the lights of a town had begun to twinkle. The clouds were moving quickly as for the gathering of a storm and heavy drops of rain began to slant in on to the deck. He moved backwards out of the rain and found Mathis at his elbow. The Frenchman nodded.

"Was it a good game?" Graham asked.

"Quite good. Madame Beronelli and I lost. She is enthusiastic, but inefficient."

"Then, except for the enthusiasm, my absence made no difference."

Mathis smiled a little nervously. "I hope that your headache is better."

"Much better, thank you."

It had begun to rain in earnest now. Mathis stared out gloomily into the gathering darkness. "Filthy!" he commented.

"Yes."

There was a pause. Then:

"I was afraid," said Mathis suddenly, "that you did not wish to play with us. I could not blame you if such were the case. This morning you were good enough to make an apology. The true apology was due from me to you."

He was not looking at Graham. "I am quite sure . . ." Graham began to mumble, but Mathis went on as if he were addressing the seagulls following the ship. "I do not always remember," he said bitterly, "that what to some people is good or bad is to others simply boring. My wife has led me to put too much faith in the power of words."

"I'm afraid I don't understand."

Mathis turned his head and smiled wryly. "Do you know the word *encotillonné*?"

"No."

"A man who is governed by his wife is *encotillonné*."

"In English we say 'hen-pecked.'"

"Ah, yes?" Obviously he did not care what was said in English. "I must tell you a joke about it. Once I was *encotillonné*. Oh, but very badly! Does that surprise you?"

"It does." Graham saw that the man was dramatising himself, and was curious.

"My wife used to have a very great temper. She still has it, I think, but now I do not see it. But for the first ten years of our marriage it was terrible. I had a small business. Trade was very bad and I became bankrupt. It was not my fault, but she always pretended that it was. Has your wife a bad temper, Monsieur?"

"No. Very good."

"You are lucky. For years I lived in misery. And then one day I made a great discovery. There was a socialist

meeting in our town and I went to it. I was, you must
understand, a Royalist. My family had no money, but
they had a title which they would have liked to use without their neighbours sniggering. I was of my family. I
went to this meeting because I was curious. The speaker
was good, and he spoke about Briey. That interested me
because I had been at Verdun. A week later we were with
some friends in the café and I repeated what I had heard.
My wife laughed in a curious way. Then when I got
home I made my great discovery. I found that my wife
was a snob and more stupid than I had dreamed. She said
that I had humiliated her by saying such things as if I
believed them. All her friends were respectable people.
I must not speak as if I were a workman. She cried. I
knew then that I was free. I had a weapon that I could
use against her. I used it. If she displeased me I became
a socialist. To the smug little tradesmen whose wives
were her friends I would preach the abolition of profit
and the family. I bought books and pamphlets to make
my arguments more damaging. My wife became very
docile. She would cook things that I liked so that I would
not disgrace her." He paused.

"You mean that you don't believe all these things you
say about Briey and banking and capitalism?" demanded
Graham.

Mathis smiled faintly. "That is the joke about which I
told you. For a time I was free. I could command my
wife and I became more fond of her. I was a manager
in a big factory. And then a terrible thing happened. I
found that I had begun to believe these things I said. The
books I read showed me that I had found a truth. I, a

Royalist by instinct, became a socialist by conviction. Worse, I became a socialist martyr. There was a strike in the factory and I, a manager, supported the strikers. I did not belong to a union. Naturally! And so I was dismissed. It was ridiculous." He shrugged. "So here I am! I have become a man in my home at the price of becoming a bore outside it. It is funny, is it not?"

Graham smiled. He had decided that he liked Monsieur Mathis. He said: "It would be funny if it were wholly true. But I can assure you that it was not because I was bored that I did not listen to you last night."

"You are very polite," began Mathis dubiously; "but . . ."

"Oh, there is no question of politeness. You see, I work for an armaments manufacturer, and so I have been more than interested in what you have had to say. On some points I find myself in agreement with you."

A change came over the Frenchman's face. He flushed slightly; a small delighted smile hovered round his lips; for the first time Graham saw the tense frown relax. "On which points do you *not* agree?" he demanded eagerly.

At that moment Graham realised that, whatever else had happened to him on the *Sestri Levante,* he had made at least one friend.

They were still arguing when Josette came out on deck. Unwillingly, Mathis interrupted what he was saying to acknowledge her presence.

"*Madame.*"

She wrinkled her nose at them. "What are you discussing? It must be very important that you have to stand in the rain to talk about it."

"We were talking politics."

"No, no!" said Mathis quickly. "Not politics, economics! Politics are the effect. We were talking about causes. But you are right. This rain is filthy. If you will excuse me, please, I will see what has happened to my wife." He winked at Graham. "If she suspects that I am making propaganda she will not be able to sleep to-night."

With a smile and a nod he went. Josette looked after him. "He is nice, that man. Why does he marry such a woman?"

"He is very fond of her."

"In the way that you are fond of me?"

"Perhaps not. Would you rather we went in?"

"No. I came out for some air. It will not be so wet round on the other side of the deck."

They began to walk round to the other side. It was dark now and the deck lights had been put on.

She took his arm. "Do you realise that to-day we have not really seen each other until now? No! Of course you do not realise it! You have been amusing yourself with politics. It does not matter that I am worried."

"Worried? What about?"

"This man who wants to kill you, imbecile! You do not tell me what you are going to do at Genoa."

He shrugged. "I've taken your advice. I'm not troubling about him."

"But you will go to the British Consul?"

"Yes." The moment had come when he must do some really steady lying. "I shall go straight there. Afterwards I shall have to see one or two people on business. The train does not leave until two o'clock in the afternoon, so

I think that I shall have time. We can meet on the train."

She sighed. "So much business! But I shall see you for lunch, eh?"

"I'm afraid it's unlikely. If we did arrange to meet I might not be able to keep the appointment. It'll be best if we meet on the train."

She turned her head a little sharply. "You are telling me the truth? You are not saying this because you have changed your mind?"

"My dear Josette!" He had opened his mouth to explain again that he had business to attend to, but had stopped himself in time. He must not protest too much.

She pressed his arm. "I did not mean to be disagreeable, *chéri*. It is only that I wish to be sure. We will meet at the train if you wish it. We can have a drink together at Torino. We reach there at four and stop for half an hour. It is because of the coaches from Milano. There are some nice places to drink in Torino. After the ship here it will be wonderful."

"It'll be splendid. What about José?"

"Ah, it does not matter about him. Let him drink by himself. After the way he was rude to you this morning, I do not care what José does. Tell me about the letters you are writing. Are they all finished?"

"I shall finish them this evening."

"And after that, no more work?"

"After that, no more work." He felt that he could not stand much more of this. He said: "You'll get cold if we stay out here much longer. Shall we go inside?"

She stopped and withdrew her arm from his so that he could kiss her. Her back was taut as she strained her body against his. Seconds later she drew away from him, laughing. "I must remember," she said, "not to say 'whisky-soda,' but 'whisky and soda' now. That is very important, eh?"

"Very important."

She squeezed his arm. "You are nice. I like you very much, *chéri.*"

They began to walk back towards the saloon. He was grateful for the dimness of the lights.

He did not have long to wait for Moeller. The German agent had been in the habit of leaving the table and going to his cabin as soon as a meal was finished. To-night, however, Banat was the first to go, evidently by arrangement; and the monologue continued until the Beronellis had followed him. It was an account of comparisons made between the Sumero-Babylonian liturgies and the ritual forms of certain Mesopotamian fertility cults and it was with unmistakable triumph that he at last brought it to an end. "You must admit, Mr. Graham," he added, lowering his voice, "that I have done extremely well to remember so much. Naturally, I made a few mistakes, and a good deal was lost, I have no doubt, in my translation. The author would probably fail to recognize it. But to the uninitiated I should say it would be most convincing."

"I have been wondering why you have taken so much trouble. You might have been talking Chinese for all the Beronellis knew or cared."

Moeller looked pained. "I was not talking for the Beronellis, but for my own private satisfaction. How stupid it is to say that the memory fails with the approach of old age. Would you think that I am sixty-six?"

"I'm not interested in your age."

"No, of course not. Perhaps we could have a private talk. I suggest that we take a walk together on deck. It is raining, but a little rain will not hurt us."

"My coat is on the chair over there."

"Then I will meet you on the top deck in a few minutes' time."

Graham was waiting at the head of the companionway when Moeller came up. They moved into the lee of one of the lifeboats.

Moeller came straight to the point.

"I gather that you have seen Kuvetli."

"I have," said Graham grimly.

"Well?"

"I have decided to take your advice."

"At Kuvetli's suggestion?"

This, Graham reflected, was not going to be as easy as he had thought. He answered: "At my own. I was not impressed by him. Frankly, I was amazed. That the Turkish Government should have put such a fool of a man on the job seems to me incredible."

"What makes you think he is a fool?"

"He seems to think that you are making some attempt to bribe me and that I am inclined to accept the money. He threatened to expose me to the British Government. When I suggested that I might be in some personal danger he seemed to think that I was trying to trick him in some stupid way. If that's your idea of a clever man, I'm sorry for you."

"Perhaps he is not used to dealing with the English

brand of self-esteem," Moeller retorted acidly. "When did this meeting take place?"

"Last night, soon after I saw you."

"And did he mention me by name?"

"Yes. He warned me against you."

"And how did you treat the warning?"

"I said that I would report his behaviour to Colonel Haki. He did not, I must say, seem to care. But if I had any idea of securing his protection, I gave it up. I don't trust him. Besides, I don't see why I should risk my life for people who treat me as if I were some sort of criminal."

He paused. He could not see Moeller's face in the darkness but he felt that the man was satisfied.

"And so you've decided to accept my suggestion?"

"Yes, I have. But," Graham went on, "before we go any farther, there are one or two things I want to get clear."

"Well?"

"In the first place, there is this man Kuvetli. He's a fool, as I've said, but he'll have to be put off the scent somehow."

"You need have no fears." Graham thought he detected a note of contempt in the smooth heavy voice. "Kuvetli will cause no trouble. It will be easy to give him the slip in Genoa. The next thing he will hear of you is that you are suffering from typhus. He will be unable to prove anything to the contrary."

Graham was relieved. Obviously, Moeller thought him a fool. He said doubtfully: "Yes, I see. That's all right, but what about this typhus? If I'm going to be taken ill I've got to be taken ill properly. If I were really taken ill

I should probably be on the train when it happened."

Moeller sighed. "I see that you've been thinking very seriously, Mr. Graham. Let me explain. If you were really infected with typhus you would already be feeling unwell. There is an incubation period of a week or ten days. You would not, of course, know what was the matter with you. By to-morrow you would be feeling worse. It would be logical for you to shrink from spending the night in a train. You would probably go to an hotel for the night. Then, in the morning, when your temperature began to rise and the characteristics of the disease became apparent, you would be removed to a clinic."

"Then we shall go to an hotel to-morrow?"

"Exactly. There will be a car waiting for us. But I advise you to leave the arrangements to me, Mr. Graham. Remember, I am just as interested as you are in seeing that nobody's suspicions are aroused."

Graham affected to ponder this. "All right then," he said at last. "I'll leave it to you. I don't want to be fussy, but you can understand that I don't want to have any trouble when I get home."

There was a silence and for a moment he thought that he had overacted. Then Moeller said slowly: "You have no reason to worry. We shall be waiting for you outside the Customs shed. As long as you do not attempt to do anything foolish—you might, for example, decide to change your mind about your holiday—everything will go smoothly. I can assure you that you will have no trouble when you get home."

"As long as that's understood."

"Is there anything else you want to say?"

"No. Good night."

"Good night, Mr. Graham. Until to-morrow."

Graham waited until Moeller had reached the deck below. Then he drew a deep breath. It was over. He was safe. All he had to do now was to go to his cabin, get a good night's sleep and wait for Mr. Kuvetli in cabin number four. He felt suddenly very tired. His body was aching as if he had been working too hard. He made his way down to his cabin. It was as he passed the landing door of the saloon that he saw Josette.

She was sitting on one of the *banquettes* watching José and Banat playing cards. Her hands were on the edge of the seat and she was leaning forward, her lips parted slightly, her hair falling across her cheeks. There was something about the pose that reminded him of the moment, years ago it seemed, when he had followed Kopeikin into her dressing-room at Le Jockey Cabaret. He half expected her to raise her head and turn towards him, smiling.

He realized suddenly that he was seeing her for the last time, that before another day had passed he would be for her merely a disagreeable memory, someone who had treated her badly. The realization was sharp and strangely painful. He told himself that he was being absurd, that it had always been impossible for him to stay with her in Paris and that he had known it all along. Why should the leave-taking trouble him now? And yet it did trouble him. A phrase came into his head: "to part is to die a little." He knew suddenly that it was not Josette of whom he was taking his leave, but of something of himself. In the back streets of his mind a door was slowly closing for the last time. She had complained that for him she was just a part of the journey from Istanbul to London. There was more to it than that. She was part of the world beyond the door: the world into which he had stepped when Banat had fired those three shots at him in the Adler-Palace: the world in which you recognised the ape beneath the velvet. Now he was on his way back to his own world; to his house and his car and the friendly, agreeable woman he called his wife. It would be exactly the same as when he had left it. Nothing would be changed in that world; nothing, except himself.

He went on down to his cabin.

He slept fitfully. Once he awoke with a start, believing that someone was opening the door of his cabin. Then he remembered that the door was bolted and concluded that he had been dreaming. When next he awoke, the engines had stopped and the ship was no longer rolling. He switched on the light and saw that the time was a quarter past four. They had arrived at the entrance to Genoa harbour. After a while he heard the chugging of a small boat and a fainter clatter from the deck above. There were voices too. He tried to distinguish Mr. Kuvetli's among them, but they were too muffled. He dozed.

He had told the steward to bring coffee at seven. Towards six, however, he decided that it was useless to try to sleep any more. He was already dressed when the steward arrived.

He drank his coffee, put the remainder of his things

in his case and sat down to wait. Mr. Kuvetli had told him to go into the empty cabin at eight o'clock. He had promised himself that he would obey Mr. Kuvetli's instructions to the letter. He listened to the Mathis arguing over their packing.

At about a quarter to eight the ship began to move in. Another five minutes and he rang for the steward. By five to eight the steward had been, received with barely concealed surprise fifty lire, and gone, taking the suitcase with him. Graham waited another minute and then opened the door.

The alleyway was empty. He walked along slowly to number four, stopped as if he had forgotten something, and half turned. The coast was still clear. He opened the door, stepped quickly into the cabin, shut the door, and turned round.

The next moment he almost fainted.

Lying across the floor with his legs under the lower berth and his head covered with blood, was Mr. Kuvetli.

CHAPTER ELEVEN

MOST OF THE BLEEDING seemed to have been caused by a scalp wound on the back of the head; but there was another wound, which had bled comparatively little and which looked as if it had been made with a knife, low on the left side of the neck. The movements of the ship had sent the slowly congealing blood trickling to and fro in a madman's scrawl across the linoleum. The face was the colour of dirty clay. Mr. Kuvetli was clearly dead.

Graham clenched his teeth to prevent himself retching and held on to the washing cabinet for support. His first thought was that he must not be sick, that he must pull himself together before he called for help. He did not realise immediately the implications of what had happened. So that he should not look down again he had kept his eyes fixed on the porthole and it was the sight of the funnel of a ship lying beyond a long concrete jetty that reminded him that they were going into harbour. In less than an hour the gangways would be down. And Mr.

Kuvetli had not reached the Turkish Consulate.

The shock of the realisation brought him to his senses. He looked down.

It was Banat's work without a doubt. The little Turk had probably been stunned in his own cabin or in the alleyway outside it, dragged out of sight into this, the nearest empty cabin, and butchered while he was still insensible. Moeller had decided to dispose of a possible threat to the smooth working of his arrangements for dealing with the principal victim. Graham remembered the noise which had awakened him in the night. It might have come from the next cabin. "Do not leave your cabin under any circumstances until eight o'clock the following morning. It might be dangerous." Mr. Kuvetli had failed to take his own advice and it *had* been dangerous. He had declared himself ready to die for his country and he had so died. There he was, his chubby fists clenched pitifully, his fringe of grey hair matted with his blood and the mouth which had smiled so much half open and inanimate.

Someone walked along the alleyway outside and Graham jerked his head up. The sound and the movement seemed to clear his brain. He began to think quickly and coolly.

The way the blood had congealed showed that Mr. Kuvetli must have been killed before the ship had stopped. Long before! Before he had made his request for permission to leave by the pilot boat. If he had made the request, a thorough search for him would have been made when the boat came alongside and he would have been found. He had not yet been found. He was not travelling with an ordinary passport but with a diplomatic *laisser passer* and so had not had to surrender his papers to the Purser. That meant that unless the Purser checked off the passenger list with the passport control officer at Genoa—and Graham knew from past experience that they did not always bother to do that at Italian ports—the fact that Mr. Kuvetli did not land would not be noticed. Moeller and Banat had probably counted on the fact. And if the dead man's baggage had been packed, the steward would put it in the Customs shed with the rest and assume that its owner was lying low to avoid having to give a tip. It might be hours, days even, before the body were discovered if he, Graham, did not call anyone.

His lips tightened. He became conscious of a slow cold rage mounting in his brain, stifling his sense of self-preservation. If he did call someone he could accuse Moeller and Banat; but would he be able to bring the crime home to them? His accusation by itself would carry no weight. It might well be suggested that the accusation was a ruse to conceal his own guilt. The Purser, for one, would be glad to support that theory. The fact that the two accused were travelling with false passports could, no doubt, be proved, but that alone would take time. In any case, the Italian police would be amply justified in refusing him permission to leave for England. Mr. Kuvetli had died in trying to make it possible for him to reach England safely and in time to fulfil a contract. That Mr. Kuvetli's dead body should become the very means of preventing the fulfilment of that contract was stupid and grotesque; but if he, Graham, wanted to be sure of saving his own skin, that was what must happen. It was strangely unthinkable. For him, standing there above the dead body of the man whom Moeller had described as a patriot, there seemed to be only one thing of importance in the world—that Mr. Kuvetli's death should be neither stupid nor grotesque, that it should be useless only to the men who had murdered him.

But if he were not going to raise the alarm and wait for the police, what was he going to do?

Supposing Moeller had planned this. Supposing he or Banat had overheard Mr. Kuvetli's instructions to him and, believing that he was sufficiently intimidated to do anything to save himself, had thought of this way of delaying his return. Or they might be preparing to "discover" him with the body and so incriminate him. But no: both those suppositions were absurd. If they had known of Mr. Kuvetli's plan they would have let the Turk go ashore by the pilot boat. It would have been his, Graham's, body that would have been found and the finder would have been Mr. Kuvetli. Obviously, then, Moeller could neither know of the plan nor suspect that the murder would be discovered. An hour from now he would be standing with Banat and the gunmen who were to meet him, waiting for the victim to walk unsuspectingly . . .

But the victim would not be unsuspecting. There was a very slender chance . . .

He turned and, grasping the handle of the door, began to turn it gently. He knew that if he thought twice about what he had decided to do he would change his mind. He must commit himself before he had time to think.

He opened the door a fraction of an inch. There was no one in the alleyway. A moment later, he was out of the cabin and the door of it was shut behind him. He hesitated barely a second. He knew that he must keep moving. Five steps brought him to cabin number three. He went in.

Mr. Kuvetli's luggage consisted of one old-fashioned valise. It was standing strapped up in the middle of the floor, and perched on one of the straps was a twenty lire piece. Graham picked up the coin and held it to his nose. The smell of attar of roses was quite distinct. He looked in the wardrobe and behind the door for Mr. Kuvetli's overcoat and hat, failed to find them, and concluded that they had been disposed of through the porthole. Banat had thought of everything.

He put the valise up on the berth and opened it. Most of the things on top had obviously been stuffed in anyhow by Banat, but lower down the packing had been done very neatly. The only thing of any interest to Graham, however, was a box of pistol ammunition. Of the pistol which fired them there was no sign.

Graham put the ammunition in his pocket and shut the valise again. He was undecided as to what he should do with it. Banat had obviously counted on its being taken to the Customs shed by the steward, who would pocket the twenty lire and forget about Mr. Kuvetli. That would be all right from Banat's point of view. By the time the people in the Customs shed started asking questions about an unclaimed valise, Monsieur Mavrodopoulos would be non-existent. Graham, however, had every intention of remaining in existence if he could possibly do so. Moreover, he intended—with the same proviso —to use his passport to cross the Italian frontier into France. The moment Mr. Kuvetli's body was found the rest of the passengers would be sought for questioning by the police. There was only one thing for it: Mr. Kuvetli's valise would have to be hidden.

He opened the washing cabinet, put the twenty lire piece on the corner by the bowl, and went to the door. The coast was still clear. He opened the door, picked up the valise, and lugged it along the alleyway to cabin number four. Another second or two and he was inside with the door shut again.

He was sweating now. He wiped his hands and forehead on his handkerchief and then remembered that his fingerprints would be on the hard leather handle of the valise as well as on the door handle and washing cabinet. He went over these objects with his handkerchief and then turned his attention to the body.

Obviously the gun was not in the hip pocket. He went down on one knee beside the body. He felt himself beginning to retch again and took a deep breath. Then he leaned across, gripped the right shoulder with one hand and the right side of the trousers with the other and pulled. The body rolled on to its side. One foot slid over the other and kicked the floor. Graham stood up quickly. In a moment or two, however, he had himself in hand sufficiently to bend down and pull the jacket open. There was a leather holster under the left arm but the gun was not in it.

He was not unduly disappointed. The possession of the gun would have made him feel better but he had not been counting on finding it. A gun was valuable. Banat would naturally take it. Graham felt in the jacket pocket. It was empty. Banat had evidently taken Mr. Kuvetli's money and *laisser passer* as well.

He got up. There was nothing more to be done there. He put on a glove, cautiously let himself out and walked along to cabin number six. He knocked. There was a quick movement from within and Madame Mathis opened the door.

The frown with which she had prepared to meet the steward faded when she saw Graham. She gave him a startled "good morning."

"Good morning, Madame. May I speak to your husband for a moment?"

Mathis poked his head over her shoulder. "Hullo! Good morning! Are you ready so soon?"

"Can I speak to you for a moment?"

"Of course!" He came out in his shirt sleeves and grinning cheerfully. "I am important only to myself. I am easy to approach."

"Would you mind coming into my cabin for a moment?"

Mathis glanced at him curiously. "You look very serious, my friend. Yes, of course I will come." He turned to his wife. "I will be back in a minute, *chérie*."

Inside the cabin, Graham shut the door, bolted it and turned to meet Mathis' puzzled frown.

"I need your help," he said in a low voice. "No, I don't want to borrow money. I want you to take a message for me."

"If it is possible, of course."

"It will be necessary to talk very quietly," Graham went on. "I do not want to alarm your wife unnecessarily and the partitions are very thin."

Fortunately, Mathis missed the full implications of this statement. He nodded. "I am listening."

"I told you that I was employed by an armaments manufacturer. It is true. But in a sense I am also, at the moment, in the joint services of the British and Turkish Governments. When I get off this ship this morning, an attempt is going to be made by German agents to kill me."

"This is true?" He was incredulous and suspicious.

"I am afraid it is. It would not amuse me to invent it."

"Excuse me, I . . ."

"That's all right. What I want you to do is to go to the Turkish Consulate in Genoa, ask for the Consul and give him a message from me. Will you do that?"

Mathis stared hard at him for a moment. Then he nodded. "Very well. I will do it. What is the message?"

"I should like to impress upon you first that this is a highly confidential message. Is that understood?"

"I can keep my mouth shut when I choose."

"I know I can rely on you. Will you write the message down? Here is a pencil and some paper. You would not be able to read my writing. Are you ready?"

"Yes."

"This is it: 'Inform Colonel Haki, Istanbul, that agent I.K. is dead, but do not inform the police. I am forced to accompany German agents, Moeller and Banat, travelling with passports of Fritz Haller and Mavrodopoulos. I . . .'"

Mathis's jaw dropped and he let out an exclamation. "Is it possible!"

"Unfortunately, it is."

"Then it was not seasickness that you had!"

"No. Shall I go on with the message?"

Mathis swallowed. "Yes. Yes. I did not realise. . . . Please."

" 'I shall attempt to escape and reach you, but in the event of my death please inform British Consul that these men are responsible.' " It was, he felt, melodramatic; but it was no more than he wished to say. He felt sorry for Mathis.

The Frenchman was staring at him with horror in his eyes. "Is it not possible," he whispered. "Why . . . ?"

"I should like to explain but I am afraid that I can't. The point is, will you deliver the message for me?"

"Of course. But is there nothing else that I can do? These German agents—why can you not have them arrested?"

"For various reasons. The best way you can help me is to take this message for me."

The Frenchman stuck out his jaw aggressively. "It is ridiculous!" he burst out and then lowered his voice to a fierce whisper. "Discretion is necessary. I understand that. You are of the British secret service. One does not confide these things but I am not a fool. Very well! Why do we not together shoot down these filthy Bosches and escape? I have my revolver and together. . . ."

Graham jumped. "Did you say that you had a revolver —here?"

Mathis looked defiant. "Certainly I have a revolver. Why not? In Turkey . . ."

Graham seized his arm. "Then you can do something more to help me."

Mathis scowled impatiently. "What is that?"

"Let me buy your revolver from you."

"You mean you are unarmed?"

"My own revolver was stolen. How much will you take for yours?"

"But. . . ."

"It will be more use to me than to you."

Mathis drew himself up. "I will not sell it to you."

"But. . . ."

"I will give it to you. Here. . . ." He pulled a small nickel-plated revolver out of his hip pocket and thrust it in Graham's hand. "No, please. It is nothing. I would like to do more."

Graham thanked his stars for the impulse which had led him to apologize to the Mathises the previous day. "You have done more than enough."

"Nothing! It is loaded, see? Here is the safety catch. There is a light pull on the trigger. You do not have to be a Hercules. Keep your arm straight when you fire . . . but I do not have to tell you."

"I am grateful, Mathis. And you will go to the Turkish Consul as soon as you land."

"It is understood." He held out his hand. "I wish you luck, my friend," he said with emotion. "If you are sure that there is nothing else that I can do. . . ."

"I am sure."

A moment later Mathis had gone. Graham waited. He heard the Frenchman go into the next cabin and Madame Mathis' sharp voice.

"Well?"

"So you cannot mind your own business, eh? He is broke and I have lent him two hundred francs."

"Imbecile! You will not touch it again."

"You think not? Let me tell you he has given me a cheque."

"I detest cheques."

"I am not drunk. It is on an Istanbul bank. As soon as we arrive I shall go to the Turkish Consulate and see that the cheque is a good one."

"A lot they will know—or care!"

"Enough! I know what I am doing. Are you ready? No! Then . . ."

Graham breathed a sigh of relief and examined the revolver. It was smaller than Kopeikin's and of Belgian manufacture. He worked the safety catch and fingered the trigger. It was a handy little weapon and looked as if it had been carefully used. He looked about him for a place to put it. It must not be visible from the outside yet he must be able to get at it quickly. He decided eventually on his top left hand waistcoat pocket. The barrel, breach and half the trigger guard just fitted in. When he buttoned his jacket the butt was hidden while the lapels set in a way that concealed the bulge. What was more, he could, by touching his tie, bring his fingers within two inches of the butt. He was ready.

He dropped Mr. Kuvetli's box of ammunition through the porthole and went up on deck.

They were in the harbour now and moving across to the west side. Towards the sea the sky was clear but a mist hung over the heights above the town, obscuring the sun and making the white amphitheatrical mass of buildings seem cold and desolate.

The only other person on deck was Banat. He was standing gazing out at the shipping with the absorbed interest of a small boy. It was difficult to realise that, at some moment in the last ten hours, this pale creature had come out of cabin number four with a knife which he had just driven into Mr. Kuvetli's neck; that in his pocket at that moment were Mr. Kuvetli's papers, Mr. Kuvetli's money and Mr. Kuvetli's pistol; that he intended to commit within the next few hours yet another murder. His very insignificance was horrible. It lent a false air of normality to the situation. Had Graham not been so acutely alive to the danger he was in, he would have been tempted to believe that the memory of what he had seen in cabin number four was the memory not of a real experience, but of something conceived in a dream.

He was no longer conscious of any fear. His body was tingling in a curious way; he was short of breath, and every now and again a wave of nausea would rise up from the pit of his stomach; but his brain seemed to have lost touch with his body. His thoughts arranged themselves with a quick efficiency that surprised him. He knew that short of abandoning all hope of reaching England in time to fulfil the Turkish contract by the specified date, his only chance of getting out of Italy alive lay in his beating Moeller at Moeller's own game. Mr. Kuvetli had made it clear that Moeller's "alternative"

was a trick devised with the sole object of transfer-
ring the scene of the killing to a less public place than
a main street of Genoa. In other words, he was to be
"taken for a ride." In a very short time now, Moeller,
Banat and some others would be waiting with a car outside the Customs shed ready, if necessary, to shoot him
down there and then. If, however, he were considerate
enough to step into the car they would take him away
to some quiet place on the Santa Margherita road and
shoot him there. There was just one weak spot in
their plan. They thought that if he were to get into
the car he would do so believing that he was to be driven
to a hotel in order to make an elaborate show of falling
ill. They were mistaken; and in their being mistaken
they presented him with the beginnings of a way out.
If he acted quickly and boldly he might be able to get
through.

They would not, he reasoned, be likely to tell him
as soon as he got in the car what they were going to do.
The fiction about the hotel and the clinic near Santa
Margherita would be maintained until the last moment.
From their point of view, it would be much easier to
drive through the narrow streets of Genoa with a man
who thought he was going to have six weeks' holiday than
with a man who had to be forcibly prevented from
attracting the attention of passers-by. They would be
inclined to humour him. They might even let him
register at a hotel. In any case, it was unlikely that the
car would go right through the city without being held
up once by the traffic. His chances of escape lay in his
being able to take them by surprise. Let him once get

free in a crowded street, and they would have great difficulty in catching him. His objective, then, would be the Turkish Consulate. He had chosen the Turkish Consulate rather than his own, for the simple reason that with the Turks he would have to do less explaining. A reference to Colonel Haki would simplify matters considerably.

The ship was approaching the berth now, and men were standing on the quay ready to catch the lines. Banat had not seen him, but now Josette and José came out on deck. He moved quickly round to the other side. Josette was the last person he wanted to talk to at that moment. She might suggest that they share a taxi to the centre of the city. He would have to explain why he was leaving the quay in a private car with Moeller and Banat. There might be all sorts of other difficulties. At that moment he came face to face with Moeller.

The old man nodded affably. "Good morning, Mr. Graham. I was hoping to see you. It will be pleasant to get ashore again, won't it?"

"I hope so."

Moeller's expression changed slightly. "Are you ready?"

"Quite." He looked concerned. "I haven't seen Kuvetli this morning. I hope everything is going to be all right."

Moeller's eyes did not flicker. "You need not worry, Mr. Graham." Then he smiled tolerantly. "As I told you last night, you can safely leave everything to me. Kuvetli will not worry us. If necessary," he went on blandly, "I shall use force."

"I hope that won't be necessary."

"And so do I, Mr. Graham! So do I!" He lowered his voice confidentially. "But while we are on the subject of the use of force, may I suggest that you are not in too much of a hurry to land? You see, should you happen to land before Banat and I have time to explain the new situation to those who are waiting, an accident might happen. You are so obviously an Englishman. They would have no difficulty in identifying you."

"I had already thought of that."

"Splendid! I am so glad that you are entering into the spirit of the arrangements." He turned his head. "Ah, we are alongside. I shall see you again in a few minutes, then." His eyes narrowed. "You won't make me feel that my confidence has been misplaced, will you, Mr. Graham?"

"I shall be there."

"I am sure that I can count on you."

Graham went into the deserted saloon. Through one of the port-holes he could see that a section of the deck had been roped off. The Mathis and the Beronellis had already joined Josette, José and Banat and, as he watched, Moeller came up with his "wife." Josette was looking round as if she were expecting someone, and Graham guessed that his absence was puzzling her. It was going to be difficult to avoid an encounter with her. She might even wait for him in the Customs shed. He would have to forestall that.

He waited until the gangway had been hoisted into position and the passengers, headed by the Mathis, were beginning to troop down it, then went out and brought up the rear of the procession immediately behind Josette. She half turned her head and saw him.

"Ah! I have been wondering where you were. What have you been doing?"

"Packing."

"So long! But you are here now. I thought that perhaps we could drive together and leave our luggage in the *consigne* at the station. It will save a taxi."

"I'm afraid I shall keep you waiting. I have some things to declare. Besides, I must go to the Consulate first. I think that we had better keep to our arrangement to meet at the train."

She sighed. "You are so difficult. Very well, we will meet at the train. But do not be late."

"I won't."

"And be careful of the little *salop* with the perfume."

"The police will take care of him."

They had reached the passport control at the entrance to the Customs shed and José, who had walked on ahead, was waiting as if the seconds were costing him money. She pressed Graham's hand hurriedly. *"Alors, chéri! A tout à l'heure."*

Graham got his passport and slowly followed them through to the Customs shed. There was only one Customs officer. As Graham approached he disposed of Josette and José, and turned to the Beronelli's mountainous bundles. To his relief, Graham had to wait. While he was waiting he opened his case and transferred some papers that he needed to his pocket; but several more minutes passed before he was able to show his transit *visa*, have his suit-case chalked and give it to a porter. By

the time he had made his way through the group of
mourning relatives which had surrounded the Beronellis,
Josette and José had gone.

Then he saw Moeller and Banat.

They were standing beside a big American sedan drawn
up beyond the taxis. There were two other men on the
far side of the car: one was tall and thin and wore a
mackintosh and a workman's cap, the other was a very
dark heavy-jowled man with a grey belted ulster and a
soft hat which he wore without a dent in it. A fifth and
younger man sat at the wheel of the car.

His heart thumping, Graham beckoned to the porter,
who was making for the taxis, and walked towards them.

Moeller nodded as he came up. "Good! Your luggage? Ah, yes." He nodded to the tall man, who came
round, took the case from the porter, and put it in the
luggage boot at the back.

Graham tipped the porter and got in the car. Moeller
followed him and sat beside him. The tall man got in
beside the driver. Banat and the man in the ulster sat
on the pull-down seats facing Graham and Moeller.
Banat's face was expressionless. The man in the ulster
avoided Graham's eyes and looked out of the window.

The car started. Almost immediately, Banat took out
his pistol and snapped the safety catch.

Graham turned to Moeller. "Is that necessary?" he
demanded. "I'm not going to escape."

Moeller shrugged. "As you please." He said something to Banat who grinned, snapped the safety catch
again and put the gun back in his pocket.

The car swung into the cobbled road leading to the dock gates.

"Which hotel are we going to?" Graham inquired.

Moeller turned his head slightly. "I have not yet made up my mind. We can leave that question until later. We shall drive out to Santa Margherita first."

"But . . ."

"There are not 'buts.' I am making the arrangements." He did not bother to turn his head this time.

"What about Kuvetli?"

"He left by the pilot boat early this morning."

"Then what's happened to him?"

"He is probably writing a report to Colonel Haki. I advise you to forget about him."

Graham was silent. He had asked about Mr. Kuvetli with the sole object of concealing the fact that he was badly frightened. He had been in the car less than two minutes, and already the odds against him had lengthened considerably.

The car bumped over the cobbles to the dock gates, and Graham braced himself for the sharp right turn that would take them towards the town and the Santa Margherita road. The next moment he lurched sideways in his seat as the car swerved to the left. Banat whipped out his gun.

Graham slowly regained his position. "I'm sorry," he said. "I thought we turned right for Santa Margherita."

There was no reply. He sat back in his corner trying to keep his face expressionless. He had assumed quite unwarrantably that it would be through Genoa itself, and on to the Santa Margherita road that he would be taken for his "ride." All his hopes had been based on the assumption. He had taken too much for granted.

He glanced at Moeller. The German agent was sitting back with his eyes closed: an old man whose work for the day was done. The rest of the day was Banat's. Graham knew that the small deep-set eyes were feeling for his, and that the long-suffering mouth was grinning. Banat was going to enjoy his work. The other man was still looking out of the window. He had not uttered a sound.

They reached a fork and turned to the right along a secondary road with a direction sign for Novi-Torimo. They were going north. The road was straight and lined with dusty plane trees. Beyond the trees there were rows of grim-looking houses and a factory or two. Soon, however, the road began to rise and twist, and the houses and factories were left behind. They were getting into the country.

Graham knew that unless some wholly unexpected way of escape presented itself, his chances of surviving the next hour were now practically non-existent. Presently the car would stop. Then he would be taken out and shot as methodically and efficiently as if he had been condemned by a court martial. The blood was thundering in his head, and his breathing was quick and shallow. He tried to breathe slowly and deeply, but the muscles in his chest seemed incapable of making the effort. He went on trying. He knew that if he surrendered himself to fear now, if he let himself go, he would be lost, whatever happened. He must not be frightened. Death, he told himself, would not be so bad. A moment of astonishment, and it would be over. He had to die sooner or later, and a bullet through the base of the skull now would be better than months of illness when he was old. Forty years was not a bad lifetime to have lived. There were many young men in Europe at that moment who would regard the attainment of such an age as an enviable achievement. To suppose that the lopping off of thirty years or so from a normal span of life was a disaster was to pretend to an importance which no man possessed. Living wasn't even so very pleasant. Mostly it was a matter of getting from the cradle to the grave with the least possible discomfort; of satisfying the body's needs, and of slowing down the process of its decay. Why make such a fuss about abandoning so dreary a business? Why, indeed! And yet you did make a fuss . . .

He became conscious of the revolver pressing against his chest. Supposing they decided to search him! But no, they wouldn't do that. They'd taken one revolver from him, and another from Mr. Kuvetli. They would scarcely suspect that there was a third. There were five other men in the car, and four of them at least were armed. He had six rounds in the revolver. He might be able to fire two of them before he himself were hit. If he waited until Banat's attention had wandered he might get off three or even four of them. If he were going to be killed, he'd see that the killing was as expensive as possible. He got a cigarette out of his pocket and then, putting his hand inside his jacket as if he were looking for a match, snicked off the safety catch. For a moment he considered drawing the revolver there and then, and trusting to luck and the driver's swerving to survive Banat's first shot; but the gun in Banat's hand was steady. Besides, there was always a chance that something unexpected might happen to create a better opportunity. For instance, the driver might take a corner too fast and wreck the car.

But the car purred steadily on. The windows were tightly shut, and Banat's attar of roses began to scent the air inside. The man in the ulster was becoming drowsy. Once or twice he yawned. Then, obviously to give himself something to do, he brought out a heavy German pistol and examined the magazine. As he replaced it, his dull pouched eyes rested for a moment on Graham. He looked away again indifferently, like a passenger in a train with the stranger opposite to him.

They had been driving for about twenty-five minutes. They passed through a small straggling village with a single fly-blown-looking café with a petrol pump outside it, and two or three shops, and began to climb. Graham was vaguely aware that the fields and farmlands which had flanked the road till then were giving way to clumps of trees and uncultivable slopes, and guessed that they were getting into the hills to the north of Genoa and west of the railway pass above Pontedecimo. Suddenly the car swung left down a small side road between trees, and began to crawl in low gear up a long twisting hill cut in the side of a wooded slope.

There was a movement by his side. He turned quickly, the blood rushing up into his head, and met Moeller's eyes.

Moeller nodded. "Yes, Mr. Graham, this is just about as far as you are going."

"But the hotel . . . ?" Graham began to stammer.

The pale eyes did not flicker. "I am afraid, Mr. Graham, that you must be very simple. Or can it be that you think that I am simple?" He shrugged. "No doubt it is unimportant. But I have a request to make. As you have already caused me so much trouble, discomfort and expense, would it be asking too much of you to suggest that you do not cause me any more? When we stop and you are asked to get out, please do so without argument or physical protest. If you cannot consider your own dignity at such a time, please think of the cushions of the car."

He turned abruptly and nodded to the man in the ulster who tapped on the window behind him. The car jerked to a standstill, and the man in the ulster half rose and put his hand down on the latch which opened the door beside him. At the same moment Moeller said something to Banat. Banat grinned.

In that second Graham acted. His last wretched little bluff had been called. They were going to kill him, and did not care whether he knew it or not. They were anxious only that his blood should not soil the cushions he was sitting on. A sudden blind fury seized him. His self-control, racked out until every nerve in his body was quivering, suddenly went. Before he knew what he was doing, he had pulled out Mathis's revolver and fired it full in Banat's face.

Even as the din of the shot thudded through his head, he saw something horrible happen to the face. Then he flung himself forward.

The man in the ulster had the door open about an inch

when Graham's weight hit him. He lost his balance, and hurtled backwards through the door. A fraction of a second later he hit the road with Graham on top of him.

Half stunned by the impact, Graham rolled clear and scrambled for cover behind the car. It could, he knew, last only a second or two now. The man in the ulster was knocked out; but the other two, shouting at the tops of their voices, had their doors open, and Moeller would not be long in picking up Banat's gun. He might be able to get in one more shot. Moeller, perhaps . . .

At that moment chance took a hand. Graham realised that he was crouching only a foot or so away from the car's tank, and with some wild notion of hindering the pursuit should he succeed in getting clear, he raised the revolver and fired again.

The muzzle of the revolver had been practically touching the tank when he pulled the trigger, and the sheet of flame which roared up sent him staggering back out of cover. Shots crashed out, and a bullet whipped by his head. Panic seized him. He turned and dashed for the trees, and the slope shelving away from the edge of the road. He heard two more shots, then something struck him violently in the back, and a sheet of light flashed between his eyes and his brain.

He could not have been unconscious for more than a minute. When he came to he was lying face downwards on the surface of dead pine needles on the slope below the level of the road.

Dagger-like pains were shooting through his head. For a moment or two he did not try to move. Then he opened his eyes again and his gaze, wandering inch by inch away from him, encountered Mathis' revolver. Instinctively he stretched out his hand to take it. His body throbbed agonisingly, but his fingers gripped the revolver. He waited for a second or two. Then, very slowly, he drew his knees up under him, raised himself on his hands and began to crawl back to the road.

The blast of the exploding tank had scattered fragments of ripped panelling and smouldering leather all over the road. Lying on his side amid this wreckage was the man in the workman's cap. The mackintosh down his left side hung in charred shreds. What was left of the car itself was a mass of shimmering incandescence, and the steel skeleton buckling like paper in the terrific heat was only just visible. Farther up the road the driver was standing with his hands to his face, swaying as if he were drunk. The sickening stench of burning flesh hung in the air. There was no sign of Moeller.

Graham crawled back down the slope for a few yards, got painfully to his feet and stumbled away, down through the trees towards the lower road.

CHAPTER TWELVE

IT WAS AFTER MIDDAY before he reached the café in the village and a telephone. By the time a car from the Turkish Consulate arrived, he had had a wash and fortified himself with brandy.

The Consul was a lean, business-like man, who spoke English as if he had been to England. He listened intently to what Graham had to say before he said much himself. When Graham had finished, however, the Consul squirted some more soda water into his vermouth, leaned back in his chair and whistled through his teeth.

"Is that all?" he inquired.

"Isn't it enough?"

"More than enough." The Consul grinned apologetically. "I will tell you, Mr. Graham, that when I received your message this morning, I telegraphed immediately to Colonel Haki, reporting that you were very likely dead. Allow me to congratulate you."

"Thank you. I was lucky." He spoke automatically.

There seemed to be something strangely fatuous about congratulations on being alive. He said: "Kuvetli told me the other night that he had fought for the Gazi and that he was ready to give his life for Turkey. You don't, somehow, expect people who say that sort of thing to be taken up on it so quickly."

"That is true. It is very sad," said the Consul. He was obviously itching to get to business. "Meanwhile," he continued adroitly, "we must see that no time is lost. Every minute increases the danger of his body being found before you are out of the country. The authorities are not very well disposed towards us at the moment, and if he were found before you had left, I doubt if we could prevent your being detained for at least some days."

"What about the car?"

"We can leave the driver to explain that. If, as you say, your suit-case was destroyed in the fire, there is nothing to connect you with the accident. Are you feeling well enough to travel?"

"Yes. I'm bruised a bit and I still feel damnably shaky, but I'll get over that."

"Good. Then, all things considered, it will be as well if you travel immediately."

"Kuvetli said something about a 'plane."

"A 'plane? Ah! May I see your passport, please?"

Graham handed it over. The Consul flicked over the pages, shut the passport with a snap and returned it. "Your transit visa," he said, "specifies that you are entering Italy at Genoa and leaving it at Bardonecchia. If you are particularly anxious to go by air we can get the visa amended, but that will take an hour or so. Also you will have to return to Genoa. Also, in case Kuvetli is found within the next few hours, it is better not to bring yourself to the notice of the police with a change of arrangements." He glanced at his watch. "There is a train to Paris which leaves Genoa at two o'clock. It stops at Asti soon after three. I recommend that you get on it there. I can drive you to Asti in my car."

"I think some food would do me good."

"My dear Mr. Graham! How stupid of me! Some food. Of course! We can stop at Novi. You will be my guest. And if there is any champagne to be had we shall have it. There is nothing like champagne when one is depressed."

Graham felt suddenly a little light-headed. He laughed.

The Consul raised his eyebrows.

"I'm sorry," Graham apologised. "You must excuse me. You see, it is rather funny. I had an appointment to meet someone on the two o'clock train. She'll be rather surprised to see me."

He became conscious of someone shaking his arm and opened his eyes.

"Bardonecchia, signore. Your passport, please."

He looked up at the wagon-lit attendant bending over him and realised that he had been asleep since the train had left Asti. In the doorway, partly silhouetted against the gathering darkness outside, were two men in the uniform of the Italian railway police.

He sat up with a jerk, fumbling in his pocket. "My passport? Yes, of course."

One of the men looked at the passport, nodded and dabbed at it with a rubber stamp.

"*Grazie, signore*. Have you any Italian bank-notes?"

"No."

Graham put his passport back in his pocket, the attendant switched the light off again, and the door closed. That was that.

He yawned miserably. He was stiff and shivering. He stood up to put his overcoat on and saw that the station was deep in snow. He had been a fool to go to sleep like that. It would be unpleasant to arrive home with pneumonia. But he was past the Italian passport control. He turned the heating on and sat down to smoke a cigarette. It must have been that heavy lunch and the wine. It . . . And then he remembered suddenly that he had done nothing about Josette. Mathis would be on the train, too.

The train started with a jerk and began to rumble on towards Modane.

He rang the bell and the attendant came.

"Signore?"

"Is there going to be a restaurant car when we get over the frontier?"

"No, signore." He shrugged. "The war."

Graham gave him some money. "I want a bottle of beer and some sandwiches. Can you get them at Modane?"

The attendant looked at the money. "Easily, signore."

"Where are the third-class coaches?"

"In the front of the train, signore."

The attendant went. Graham smoked his cigarette and decided to wait until the train had left Modane before he went in search of Josette.

The stop at Modane seemed interminable. At last, however, the French passport officials finished their work and the train began to move again.

Graham went out into the corridor.

Except for the dim blue safety lights, the train was in darkness now. He made his way slowly towards the third-class coaches. There were only two of them, and he had no difficulty in finding Josette and José. They were in a compartment by themselves.

She turned her head as he slid the door open and peered at him uncertainly. Then, as he moved forward into the blue glow from the ceiling of the compartment, she started up with a cry.

"But what has happened?" she demanded. "Where have you been? We waited, José and I, until the last moment, but you did not come as you had promised. We waited. José will tell you how we waited. Tell me what happened."

"I missed the train at Genoa. I had a long drive to catch it up."

"You drove to Bardonecchia! It is not possible!"

"No. To Asti."

There was a silence. They had been speaking in French. Now José gave a short laugh and, sitting back in his corner, began to pick his teeth with his thumb-nail.

Josette dropped the cigarette she had been smoking on to the floor and trod on it. "You got on the train at Asti," she remarked lightly, "and you wait until now before you come to see me? It is very polite." She paused

and then added slowly: "But you will not keep me waiting like that in Paris, will you, *chéri?*"

He hesitated.

"Will you, *chéri?*" There was an edge to her voice
now.

He said: "I'd like to talk to you alone, Josette."

She stared at him. Her face in that dim, ghastly light
was expressionless. Then she moved towards the door.
"I think," she said, "that it will be better if you have a
little talk with José."

"José? What's José got to do with it? You're the
person I want to talk to."

"No, *chéri.* You have a little talk with José. I am not
very good at business. I do not like it. You understand?"

"Not in the least." He was speaking the truth.

"No? José will explain. I will come back in a minute.
You talk to José now, *chéri.*"

"But . . ."

She stepped into the corridor and slid the door to
behind her. He went to open it again.

"She will come back," said José; "why don't you sit
down and wait?"

Graham sat down slowly. He was puzzled. Still picking his teeth, José glanced across the compartment. "You
don't understand, eh?"

"I don't even know what I'm supposed to understand."

José peered at his thumbnail, licked it, and went to
work again on an eye tooth. "You like Josette, eh?"

"Of course. But . . ."

"She is very pretty, but she has no sense. She is a

woman. She does not understand business. That is why I, her husband, always look after the business. We are partners. Do you understand that?"

"It's simple enough. What about it?"

"I have an interest in Josette. That is all."

Graham considered him for a moment. He was beginning to understand only too well. He said: "Say exactly what you mean, will you?"

With the air of making a decision, José abandoned his teeth and twisted on his seat so that he was facing Graham. "You are a business man, eh?" he said briskly. "You do not expect something for nothing. Very well. I am her manager and I do not give anything for nothing. You want to amuse yourself in Paris, eh? Josette is a very nice girl and very amusing for a gentleman. She is a nice dancer, too. Together we earn at least two thousand francs a week in a nice place. Two thousand francs a week. That is something, eh?"

Memories were flooding into Graham's mind: of the Arab girl, Maria, saying, "She has many lovers"; of Kopeikin saying, "José? He does well for himself"; of Josette herself saying of José that he was jealous of her only when she neglected business for pleasure; of innumerable little phrases and attitudes. "Well?" he said coldly.

José shrugged. "If you are amusing yourself, we cannot earn our two thousand francs a week by dancing. So, you see, we must get it from somewhere else." In the semi-darkness, Graham could see a small smile twist the black line of José's mouth. "Two thousand francs a week. It is reasonable, eh?"

It was the voice of the philosopher of the apes in velvet. *"Mon cher caïd"* was justifying his existence. Graham nodded. "Quite reasonable."

"Then we can settle it now, eh?" José went on briskly. "You are experienced, eh? You know that it is the custom." He grinned and then quoted: " *'Chéri, avant que je t'aime t'oublieras pas mon petit cadeau.'* "

"I see. And who do I pay? You or Josette?"

"You can pay it to Josette if you like, but that would not be very *chic*, eh? I will see you once a week." He leaned forward and patted Graham's knee. "It is serious, eh? You will be a good boy? If you were, for example, to begin now. . . ."

Graham stood up. He was surprised at his own calmness. "I think," he said, "that I should like to give the money to Josette herself."

"You don't trust me, eh?"

"Of course I trust you. Will you find Josette?"

José hesitated, then, with a shrug, got up and went out into the corridor. A moment later he returned with Josette. She was smiling a little nervously.

"You have finished talking to José, *chéri?*"

Graham nodded pleasantly. "Yes. But, as I told you, it was you I really wanted to talk to. I wanted to explain that I shall have to go straight back to England after all."

She stared at him blankly for a moment; then he saw her lips drawing in viciously over her teeth. She turned suddenly on José.

"You dirty Spanish fool!" She almost spat the words at him. "What do you think I keep you for? Your dancing?"

José's eyes glittered dangerously. He slid the door to behind him. "Now," he said, "we will see. You shall not speak to me so or I shall break your teeth."

"*Salaud!* I shall speak to you as I like." She was standing quite still, but her right hand moved an inch or two. Something glittered faintly. She had slipped the diamanté bracelet she was wearing over her knuckles.

Graham had seen enough violence for one day. He said quickly: "Just a moment. José is not to blame. He explained matters very tactfully and politely. I came, as I said, to tell you that I have to go straight back to England. I was also going to ask you to accept a small present. It was this." He drew out his wallet, produced a ten-pound note, and held it near the light.

She glanced at the note and then stared at him sullenly. "Well?"

"José made it clear that two thousand francs was the amount I owed. This note is only worth just over seventeen hundred and fifty. So, I am adding another two hundred and fifty francs." He took the French notes out of his wallet, folded them up in the larger note and held them out.

She snatched them from him. "And what do you expect to get for this?" she demanded spitefully.

"Nothing. It's been pleasant being able to talk to you." He slid the door open. "Good-bye, Josette."

She shrugged her shoulders, stuffed the money into the pocket of her fur coat and sat down again in her corner. "Good-bye. It is not my fault if you are stupid."

José laughed. "If you should think of changing your mind, Monsieur," he began mincingly, "we . . ."

Graham shut the door and walked away along the corridor. His one desire was to get back to his own compartment. He did not notice Mathis until he had almost bumped into him.

The Frenchman drew back to let him pass. Then, with a gasp, he leaned forward.

"Monsieur Graham! Is it possible?"

"I was looking for you," said Graham.

"My dear friend. I am so glad. I was wondering. . . . I was afraid. . . ."

"I caught the train at Asti." He pulled the revolver from his pocket. "I wanted to return this to you with my thanks. I'm afraid that I haven't had time to clean it. It has been fired twice."

"Twice!" Mathis' eyes widened. "You killed them both?"

"One of them. The other died in a road accident."

"A road accident!" Mathis chuckled. "That is a new way to kill them!" He looked at the revolver affectionately. "Perhaps I will not clean it. Perhaps I will keep it as it is as a souvenir." He glanced up. "It was all right, that message I delivered?"

"Quite all right, and thank you again." He hesitated. "There's no restaurant car on the train. I have some sandwiches in my compartment. If you and your wife would like to join me. . . ."

"You are kind, but no thank you. We get off at Aix. It will not be long now. My family lives there. It will be strange to see them after so long. They . . ."

The door of the compartment behind him opened and Madame Mathis peered into the corridor. "Ah, there you are!" She recognised Graham and nodded disapprovingly.

"What is it, *chérie*?"

"The window. You open it, and go out to smoke. I am left to freeze."

"Then you may shut it, *chérie*."

"Imbecile! It is too stiff."

Mathis sighed wearily and held out his hand. "Goodbye, my friend. I shall be discreet. You may depend upon it."

"Discreet?" demanded Madame Mathis suspiciously. "What is there to be discreet about?"

"Ah, you may ask!" He winked at Graham. "Monsieur and I have made a plot to blow up the Bank of France, seize the Chamber of Deputies, shoot the two hundred families and set up a Communist government."

She looked round apprehensively. "You should not say such things, even for a joke."

"A joke!" He scowled at her malevolently. "You will see if it is a joke or not when we drag these capitalist reptiles from their great houses and cut them to pieces with machine-guns."

"Robert! If someone should hear you say such things . . ."

"Let them hear!"

"I only asked you to shut the window, Robert. If it had not been so stiff I would have done it myself. I . . ."

The door closed behind them.

Graham stood for a moment looking out of the window at the distant searchlights: grey smudges moving restlessly among the clouds low down on the horizon.

It was not, he reflected, unlike the skyline that he could see from his bedroom window when there were German planes about over the North Sea.

He turned and made his way back to his beer and sandwiches.

The Light of Day

Chapter

I

It came down to this: if I had not been arrested by the Turkish police, I would have been arrested by the Greek police. I had no choice but to do as this man Harper told me. He was entirely responsible for what happened to me.

I thought he was an American. He looked like an American—tall, with the loose, light suit, the narrow tie and button-down collar, the smooth, old-young, young-old face and the crew cut. He spoke like an American, too; or at least like a German who has lived in America for a long time. Of course, I now know that he is not an American, but he certainly gave that impression. His luggage, for instance, was definitely American; plastic leather and imitation gold locks. I know American luggage when I see it. I didn't see his passport.

He arrived at the Athens airport on a plane from Vienna. He could have come from New York or London or Frankfurt or Moscow and arrived by that plane—or just from Vienna. It was impossible to tell. There were no hotel labels on the luggage. I just assumed that he came from New York. It was a mistake anyone might have made.

This will not do. I can already hear myself protesting too much, as if I had something to be ashamed of; but I am simply trying to explain what happened, to be completely frank and open.

I really did not suspect that he was not what he seemed. Naturally, I approached him at the airport. The car-hire business is only a temporary sideline with me, of course—I am a journalist by profession—but Nicki had been complaining about needing more new clothes, and the rent was due on the flat that week. I needed money, and this man looked as if he had some. Is it a crime to earn money? The way some people go on you would think it was. The law is the law and I am certainly not complaining, but what I can't stand is all the humbug and hypocrisy. If a man goes to the red-light district on his own, nobody says anything. But if he wants to do another chap, a friend or an acquaintance, a good turn by showing him the way to the best house, everyone starts screaming blue murder. I have no patience with it. If there is one thing I pride myself on it is my common sense—that and my sense of humor.

My correct name is Arthur Simpson.

No! I said I would be completely frank and open and I am going to be. My correct *full* name is Arthur Abdel Simpson. The Abdel is because my mother was Egyptian. In fact, I was born in Cairo. But my father was a British officer, a regular, and I myself am British to the core. Even my background is typically British.

My father rose from the ranks. He was a Regimental Sergeant Major in the Buffs when I was born; but in 1916 he was commissioned as a Lieutenant Quartermaster in the Army Service Corps. We were living in officers' married quarters in Ismailia when he was killed a year later. I was too young at the time to be told the details. I thought, naturally, that he must have been killed by the Turks; but Mum told me later that he had been run over by an army lorry as he was walking home one night from the officers' mess.

Mum had his pension, of course, but someone told her to write to the Army Benevolent Association for the Sons of Fallen Officers, and they got me into the British school in Cairo. She still kept on writing to them about me, though. When I was nine, they said that if there were some relative in England I could live with, they would pay for my schooling there. There was a married sister of father's living at Hither Green in South-East London. When the Benevolent Association said that they would pay twelve-and-six a week for my keep, she agreed to have me. This was a great relief to Mum because it meant that she could marry Mr. Hafiz, who had never liked me after the day I caught them in bed together and told the Imam about it. Mr. Hafiz was in the restaurant business and was as fat as a pig. It was disgusting for a man of his age to be in bed with Mum.

I went to England on an army troop ship in care of the sick-bay matron. I was glad to go. I have never liked being where I am not wanted. Most of the men in the sick bay were V.D. cases, and I used to listen to them talking. I picked up quite a lot of useful information, before the matron, who was (there is no other word) an old bitch, found out about it and handed me over to the P.T. instructor for the rest of the voyage. My aunt in Hither Green was a bitch, too, but I was wanted there all right. She was married to a bookkeeper who spent half his time out of work. My twelve-and-six a week came in very handy. She didn't dare get too bitchy. Every so often, a man from the Benevolent Association would come down to see how I was getting on. If I had told him the tale they would have taken me away. Like most boys of that age, I suppose I was what is known nowadays as "a bit of a handful."

The school was on the Lewisham side of Blackheath and had a big board outside with gold lettering on it:

CORAM'S GRAMMAR SCHOOL
For the Sons of Gentlemen
FOUNDED 1781

On top of the board there was the school coat of arms and motto, *Mens aequa in arduis.* The Latin master said it was from Horace; but the English master liked to translate it in Kipling's words: "If you can keep your head when all about you are losing theirs . . . you'll be a Man, my son!"

It was not exactly a public school like Eton or Winchester; there were no boarders, we were all day boys; but it was run on the same lines. Your parents, or (as in my case) guardian, had to pay to send you there. There were a few scholarship boys from the local council schools—I think we had to have them because of the Board of Education subsidy—but never more than twenty or so in the whole school. In 1920 a new Head was appointed. His name was Brush and we nicknamed him "The Bristle." He'd been a master at a big public school and so he knew how things should be done. He made a lot of changes. After he came, we played rugger instead of soccer, sat in forms instead of in classes, and were taught how to speak like gentlemen. One or two of the older masters got the sack, which was a good thing; and The Bristle made all the masters wear their university gowns at prayers in the morning. As he said, Coram's was a school with a good tradition, and although we might not be as old as Eton or Winchester, we were a good deal older than Brighton or Clifton. All the swotting in the world was no good if you didn't have character and tradition. He made us stop reading trash like the *Gem* and *Magnet* and turn to worthwhile books by authors like Stevenson and Talbot Baines Reed.

I was too young when my father was killed to have known him well; but one or two of his pet sayings have always remained in my memory; perhaps because I heard him repeat them so often to Mum or to his army friends. One, I remember, was "Never volunteer for anything," and another was "Bullshit baffles brains."

Hardly the guiding principles of an officer and a gentleman, you say? Well, I am not so sure about that; but I won't argue. I can only say that they were the guiding principles of a practical, professional soldier, and that at Coram's they worked. For example, I found out very early on that nothing annoyed the masters more than untidy handwriting. With some of them, in fact, the wrong answer to a question neatly written would get almost as many marks as the right answer badly written or covered with smears and blots. I have always written very neatly. Again, when a master asked something and then said "Hands up who knows," you could always put your hand up even if you did not know, as long as you let the eager beavers put their hands up first, and as long as you smiled. Smiling—pleasantly, I mean, not grinning or smirking—was very important at all times. The masters did not bother about you so much if you looked as if you had a clear conscience.

I got on fairly well with the other chaps. Because I had been born in Egypt, of course, they called me "Wog," but, as I was fair-haired like my father, I did not mind that. My voice broke quite early, when I was twelve. After a while, I started going up to Hilly Fields at night with a fifth-former named Jones iv, who was fifteen, and we used to pick up girls—"square-pushing," as they say in the army. I soon found that some of the girls didn't mind a bit if you put your hand up their skirts, and even did a bit more. Sometimes we would stay out late. That meant that I used to have to get up early and do my homework, or make my aunt write an excuse note for me to take to school saying that I had been sent to bed after tea with a feverish headache. If the worse came to the worst, I could always crib from a boy named Reese and do the written work in the lavatory. He had very bad acne and never minded if you cribbed from him; in fact I think he liked it. But you had to be careful. He was one of the bookworms and usually got everything right. If you cribbed from him word for word you risked getting full marks. With me, that would make the master suspicious. I got ten out of ten for a chemistry paper once, and the master caned me for cheating. I had never really liked the man and I got my revenge later by pouring a test tube of sulphuric acid (conc.) over the saddle of his bicycle; but I have always remembered the lesson that incident taught me. Never try to pretend that you're better than you are. I think I can fairly say that I never have.

Of course, an English public-school education is mainly designed to build character, to give a boy a sense of fair play and sound values, teach him to take the rough with the smooth, and make him look and sound like a gentleman.

Coram's at least did those things for me; and, looking back, I suppose that I should be grateful. I can't say that I enjoyed the process though. Fighting, for instance: that was supposed to be very manly, and if you did not enjoy it they called you "cowardy custard." I don't think it is cowardly not to want someone to hit you with his fist and make your nose bleed. The trouble was that when I used to hit back I always sprained my thumb or grazed my knuckles. In the end, I found the best way to hit back was with a satchel, especially if you had a pen or the sharp edge of a ruler sticking out through the flap; but I have always disliked violence of any kind.

Almost as much as I dislike injustice. My last term at Coram's, which I should have been able to enjoy because it *was* the last, was completely spoiled.

Jones iv was responsible for that. He had left school by

then, and was working for his father, who owned a garage, but I still went up to Hilly Fields with him sometimes. One evening he showed me a long poem typed out on four foolscap pages. A customer at the garage had given it to him. It was called *The Enchantment* and was supposed to have been written by Lord Byron. It began:

> *Upon one dark and sultry day,*
> *As on my garret bed I lay,*
> *My thoughts, for I was dreaming half,*
> *Were broken by a silvery laugh,*
> *Which fell upon my startled ear,*
> *Full loud and clear and very near.*

Well, it turned out that the laugh was coming through a hole in the wall behind his bed, so he looked through the hole.

> *A youth and maid were in the room,*
> *And each in youth's most beauteous bloom.*

It then went on to describe what the youth and maid did together for the next half hour—very poetically, of course, but in detail. It was really hot stuff.

I made copies and let some of the chaps at school read it. Then I charged them fourpence a time to be allowed to copy it out for themselves. I was making quite a lot of money, when some fourth-form boy left a copy in the pocket of his cricket blazer and his mother found it. Her husband sent it with a letter of complaint to The Bristle. He began questioning the boys one by one to find out who had started it, and, of course, he eventually got back to me. I said I had been given it by a boy who had left the term be-fore—The Bristle couldn't touch *him*—but I don't think he believed me. He sat tapping his desk with his pencil and saying "filthy smut" over and over again. He looked very red in the face, almost as if he were embarrassed. I remember wondering if he could be a bit "queer." Finally, he said that as it was my last term he would not expel me, but that I was not to associate with any of the younger boys for the rest of my time there. He did not cane me or write to the Benevolent Association, which was a relief. But it was a bad experience all the same and I was quite upset. In fact, I think that was the reason I failed my matriculation.

At Coram's they made a fetish out of passing your matric. Apparently, you couldn't get a respectable job in a bank or an insurance company without it. I did not want a job in a bank or an insurance company—Mr. Hafiz had died and Mum wanted me to go back and learn the restaurant business—but it was a disappointment all the same. I think that if The Bristle had been more broad-minded and understanding, not made me feel as if I had committed some sort of crime, things would have been different. I was a sensitive boy and I felt that Coram's had somehow let me down. That was the reason I never applied to join the Old Coramians Club.

Now, of course, I can look back on the whole thing and smile about it. The point I am making is that persons in authority—headmasters, police officials—can do a great deal of damage simply by failing to understand the other fellow's point of view.

How could I have possibly known what kind of man this Harper was?

As I explained, I had simply driven out to the Athens airport looking for business. I spotted this man going through customs and saw that he was carrying his ticket in an American Express folder. I gave one of the porters two drachmas to get me the man's name from his customs declaration. Then I had one of the uniformed airline girls give him my card and the message: "Car waiting outside for Mr. Harper."

It is a trick I have used lots of times and it has almost always worked. Not many Americans or British speak demotic Greek; and by the time they have been through the airport customs, especially in the hot weather, and been jostled by the porters and elbowed right and left, they are only too ready to go with someone who can understand what they're talking about and take care of the tipping. That day it was really very hot and humid.

As he came through the exit from the customs I went up to him.

"This way, Mr. Harper."

He stopped and looked me over. I gave him a helpful smile, which he did not return.

"Wait a minute," he said curtly. "I didn't order any car."

I looked puzzled. "The American Express sent me, sir. They said you wanted an English-speaking driver."

He stared at me again, then shrugged. "Well, okay. I'm going to the Hotel Grande-Bretagne."

"Certainly, sir. Is this all your luggage?"

Soon after we turned off the coast road by Glyphada he began to ask questions. Was I British? I side-stepped that one as usual. Was the car my own? They always want to know that. It is my own car, as it happens, and I have two speeches about it. The car itself is a 1954 Plymouth. With an American I brag about how many thousands of miles it has done without any trouble. For the Britishers I have a stiff-upper-lip line about part-exchanging it, as soon as I can save enough extra cash, for an Austin Princess, or an old Rolls-Royce, or some other real quality car. Why shouldn't people be told what they want to hear?

This Harper man seemed much like the rest. He listened and grunted occasionally as I told him the tale. When you know that you are beginning to bore them, you usually know that everything is going to be all right. Then, you stop. He did not ask how I happened to live and work in Greece, as they usually do. I thought that would probably come later; that is, if there were going to be a later with him. I had to find out.

"Are you in Athens on business, sir?"

"Could be."

His tone as good as told me to mind my own business, but I pretended not to notice. "I ask, sir," I went on, "because if you should need a car and driver while you are here I could arrange to place myself at your disposal."

"Yes?"

It wasn't exactly encouraging, but I told him the daily rate and the various trips we could take if he wanted to do some sight-seeing—Delphi and the rest.

"I'll think about it," he said. "What's your name?"

I handed him one of my cards over my shoulder and watched him in the driving mirror while he read it. Then he slipped it into his pocket.

"Are you married, Arthur?"

The question took me by surprise. They don't usually want to know about your private life. I told him about my first wife and how she had been killed by a bomb in the Suez troubles in 1956. I did not mention Nicki. I don't know why; perhaps because I did not want to think about her just then.

"You did say you were British, didn't you?" he asked.

"My father was British, sir, and I was educated in England." I said it a little distantly. I dislike being cross-examined in that sort of way. But he persisted just the same.

"Well, what nationality *are* you?"

"I have an Egyptian passport." That was perfectly true, although it was none of his business.

"Was your wife Egyptian?"

"No, French."

"Did you have any children?"

"Unfortunately no, sir." I was definitely cold now.

"I see."

He sat back staring out of the window, and I had the feeling that he had suddenly put me out of his mind altogether. I thought about Annette and how used I had become to saying that she had been killed by a bomb. I was almost beginning to believe it myself. As I stopped for the traffic lights in Omonias Square, I wondered what had happened to her, and if the gallant gentlemen she had preferred to me had ever managed to give her the children she had said she wanted. I am not one to bear a grudge, but I could not help hoping that she believed now that the sterility had been hers not mine.

I pulled up at the Grande-Bretagne. While the porters were getting the bags out of the car Harper turned to me.

"Okay, Arthur, it's a deal. I expect to be here three or four days."

I was surprised and relieved. "Thank you, sir. Would you like to go to Delphi tomorrow? On the weekends it gets very crowded with tourists."

"We'll talk about that later." He stared at me for a moment and smiled slightly. "Tonight I think I feel like going out on the town. You know some good places?"

As he said it there was just the suggestion of a wink. I am sure of that.

I smiled discreetly. "I certainly do, sir."

"I thought you might. Pick me up at nine o'clock. All right?"

"Nine o'clock, sir. I will have the concierge telephone to your room that I am here."

It was four-thirty then. I drove to my flat, parked the car in the courtyard, and went up.

Nicki was out, of course. She usually spent the afternoon with friends—or said she did. I did not know who the friends were and I never asked too many questions. I did not want her to lie to me, and, if she had picked up a lover at the Club, I did not want to know about it. When a middle-aged man marries an attractive girl half his age, he has to accept certain possibilities philosophically. The clothes she had changed out of were lying all over the bed and she had spilled some scent, so that the place smelled more strongly of her than usual.

There was a letter for me from a British travel magazine I had written to. They wanted me to submit samples of my work for their consideration. I tore the letter up. Practically thirty years in the magazine game and they treat you like an amateur! Send samples of your work, and the next thing you know is that they've stolen all your ideas without paying you a penny-piece. It has happened to me again and again, and I am not being caught that way any more. If they want me to write for them, let them say so with a firm offer of cash on delivery, plus expenses in advance.

I made a few telephone calls to make sure that Harper's evening out would go smoothly, and then went down to the café for a drink or two. When I got back Nicki was there, changing again to go to work at the Club.

It was no wish of mine that she should go on working after our marriage. She chose to do so herself. I suppose some men would be jealous at the idea of their wives belly dancing with practically no clothes on in front of other men; but I am not narrow-minded in that way. If she chooses to earn a little extra pocket money for herself, that is her affair.

While she dressed, I told her about Harper and made a joke about all his questions. She did not smile.

"He does not sound easy, papa," she said. When she calls me "papa" like that it means that she is in a friendly mood with me.

"He has money to spend."

"How do you know?"

"I telephoned the hotel and asked for him in Room 230.

The operator corrected me and so I got his real room number. I know it. It is a big air-conditioned suite."

She looked at me with a slight smile and sighed. "You do so much enjoy it, don't you?"

"Enjoy what?"

"Finding out about people."

"That is my newspaper training, *chérie*, my nose for news."

She looked at me doubtfully, and I wished I had given a different answer. It has always been difficult for me to explain to her why certain doors are now closed to me. Reopening old wounds is senseless as well as painful.

She shrugged and went on with her dressing. "Will you bring him to the Club?"

"I think so."

I poured her a glass of wine and one for myself. She drank hers while she finished dressing and then went out. She patted my cheek as she went, but did not kiss me. The "papa" mood was over. "One day," I thought, "she will go out and not come back."

But I am never one to mope. If that happened, I decided, then good riddance to bad rubbish. I poured myself another glass of wine, smoked a cigarette, and worked out a tactful way of finding out what sort of business Harper was in. I think I must have sensed that there was something not quite right about him.

At five to nine I found a parking place on Venizelos Avenue just round the corner from the Grande-Bretagne, and went to let Harper know that I was waiting.

He came down after ten minutes and I took him round the corner to the car. I explained that it was difficult for private cars to park in front of the hotel.

He said, rather disagreeably I thought: "Who cares?"

I wondered if he had been drinking. Quite a lot of tourists who, in their own countries, are used to dining early in the evening, start drinking *ouzo* to pass the time. By ten o'clock, when most Athenians begin to think about dinner, the tourists are sometimes too tight to care what they say or do. Harper, however, was all too sober. I soon found that out.

When we reached the car I opened the rear door for him to get in. Ignoring me, he opened the other door and got into the front passenger seat. Very democratic. Only I happen to prefer my passengers in the back seat where I can keep my eye on them through the mirror.

I went round and got into the driver's seat.

"Well, Arthur," he asked, "where are you taking me?"

"Dinner first, sir?"

"How about some sea food?"

"I'll take you to the best, sir."

I drove him out to the yacht harbor at Tourcolimano. One of the restaurants there gives me a good commission. The waterfront is really very picturesque, and he nodded approvingly as he looked around. Then, I took him into the restaurant and introduced him to the cook. When he had chosen his food and a bottle of dry Patras wine he looked at me.

"You eaten yet, Arthur?"

"Oh, I will have something in the kitchen, sir." That way my dinner would go on his bill without his knowing it, as well as my commission.

"You come and eat with me."

"It is not necessary, sir."

"Who said it was? I asked you to eat with me."

"Thank you, sir. I would like to."

More democracy. We sat at a table on the terrace by the water's edge and he began to ask me about the yachts anchored in the harbor. Which were privately owned, which were for charter? What were charter rates like?

I happened to know about one of the charter yachts, an

eighteen-meter ketch with twin diesels, and told him the rate—one hundred and forty dollars U.S. per day, including a crew of two, fuel for eight hours' steaming a day, and everything except charterer's and passengers' food. The real rate was a hundred and thirty, but I thought that, if by any chance he was serious, I could get the difference as commission from the broker. I also wanted to see how he felt about that kind of money; whether he would laugh as an ordinary salaried man would, or begin asking about the number of persons it would sleep. He just nodded, and then asked about fast, sea-going motorboats without crew.

In the light of what happened I think that point is specially significant.

I said that I would find out. He asked me about the yacht brokers. I gave him the name of the one I knew personally, and told him the rest were no good. I also said that I did not think that the owners of the bigger boats liked chartering them without their own crewmen on board. He did not comment on that. Later, he asked me if I knew whether yacht charter parties out of Tourcolimano or the Piraeus covered Greek waters only, or whether you could "go foreign," say across the Adriatic to Italy. Significant again. I told him I did not know, which was true.

When the bill came, he asked if he could change an American Express traveler's check for fifty dollars. That was more to the point. I told him that he could, and he tore the fifty-dollar check out of a book of ten. It was the best thing I had seen that day.

Just before eleven o'clock we left, and I drove him to the Club.

The Club is practically a copy of the Lido night club in Paris, only smaller. I introduced him to John, who owns the place, and tried to leave him there for a while. He was still absolutely sober, and I thought that if he were by himself he would drink more; but it was no good. I had to go in and sit and drink with him. He was as possessive as a woman. I was puzzled. If I had been a fresh-looking young man instead of, well, frankly, a potbellied journalist, I would have understood it—not approved, of course, but understood. But he was at least ten or fifteen years younger than me.

They have candles on the tables at the Club and you can see faces. When the floor show came on, I watched him watch it. He looked at the girls, Nicki among them, as if they were flies on the other side of a window. I asked him how he liked the third from the left—that was Nicki.

"Legs too short," he said. "I like them with longer legs. Is that the one you had in mind?"

"In mind? I don't understand, sir." I was beginning to dislike him intensely.

He eyed me. "Shove it," he said unpleasantly.

We were drinking Greek brandy. He reached for the bottle and poured himself another. I could see the muscles in his jaw twitching as if with anger. Evidently something I had said, or which he thought I had said, had annoyed him. It was on the tip of my tongue to mention that Nicki was my wife, but I didn't. I remembered, just in time, that I had only told him about Annette, and about her being killed by a bomb.

He drank the brandy down quickly and told me to get the bill.

"You don't like it here, sir?"

"What more is there to see? Do they start stripping later?"

I smiled. It is the only possible response to that sort of boorishness. In any case, I had no objection to speeding up my program for the evening.

"There is another place," I said.

"Like this?"

"The entertainment, sir, is a little more individual and private." I picked the words carefully.

"You mean a cat house?"

"I wouldn't put it quite like that, sir."

He smirked. "I'll bet you wouldn't. How about 'maison de rendezvous'? Does that cover it?"

"Madame Irma's is very discreet and everything is in the best of taste, sir."

He shook with amusement. "Know something, Arthur?" he said. "If you shaved a bit closer and had yourself a good haircut, you could hire out as a butler any time."

From his expression I could not tell whether he was being deliberately insulting or making a clumsy joke. It seemed advisable to assume the latter.

"Is that what Americans call 'ribbing,' sir?" I asked politely.

This seemed to amuse him even more. He chuckled fatuously. "Okay, Arthur," he said at last, "okay. We'll play it your way. Let's go to see your Madame Irma."

I didn't like the "your Madame Irma" way of putting it, but I pretended not to notice.

Irma has a very nice house standing in its own grounds just off the road out to Kephisia. She never has more than six girls at any one time and changes them every few months. Her prices are high, of course, but everything is very well arranged. Clients enter and leave by different doors to avoid embarrassing encounters. The only persons the client sees are Irma herself, Kira, the manageress who takes care of the financial side, and, naturally, the lady of his choice.

Harper seemed to be impressed. I say "seemed" because he was very polite to Irma when I introduced them, and complimented her on the decorations. Irma is not unattractive herself and likes presentable-looking clients. As I had expected, there was no nonsense about my joining him at *that* table. As soon as Irma offered him a drink, he glanced at me and made a gesture of dismissal.

"See you later," he said.

I was sure then that everything was all right. I went in to Kira's room to collect my commission and tell her how much money he had on him. It was after midnight then. I said that I had had no dinner and would go and get some. She told me that they were not particularly busy that night and that there need be no hurry.

I drove immediately to the Grande-Bretagne, parked the car at the side, walked round to the bar, and went in and ordered a drink. If anyone happened to notice me and re- member later, I had a simple explanation for being there.

I finished the drink, gave the waiter a good tip, and walked through across the foyer to the lifts. They are fully automatic; you work them yourself with push buttons. I went up to the third floor.

Harper's suite was on the inner court, away from the noise of Syntagmaios Square, and the doors to it were out of sight of the landing. The floor servants had gone off duty for the night. It was all quite easy. As usual, I had my pass key hidden inside an old change purse; but, as usual, I did not need it. Quite a number of the sitting-room doors to suites in the older part of the hotel can be opened from outside without a key, unless they have been specially locked, that is; it makes it easier for room-service waiters carrying trays. Often the maid who turns down the beds last thing can't be bothered to lock up after her. Why should she? The Greeks are a particularly honest people and they trust one another.

His luggage was all in the bedroom. I had already han- dled it once that day, stowing it in the car at the airport, so I did not have to worry about leaving fingerprints.

I went to his briefcase first. There were a lot of business papers in it—something to do with a Swiss company named Tekelek, who made accounting machines—I did not pay much attention to them. There was also a wallet with money in it—Swiss francs, American dollars, and West German marks—together with the yellow number slips of over two thousand dollars' worth of traveler's checks. The number slips are for record purposes in case the checks are lost and you want to stop payment on them. I left the money where it was and took the slips. The checks themselves I found in the side pocket of a suitcase. There were thirty-five of them, each for fifty dollars. His first name was Walter, middle initial K.

In my experience, most people are extraordinarily careless about the way they look after traveler's checks. Just because their counter-signature is required before a check can be cashed, they assume that only they can negotiate it. Yet anyone with eyes in his head can copy the original signature. No particular skill is required; haste, heat, a different pen, a counter of an awkward height, writing standing up instead of sitting—a dozen things can account for small variations in the second signature. It is not going to be examined by a handwriting expert, not at the time that it is cashed anyway; and usually it is only at banks that the cashier asks to see a passport.

Another thing: if you have ordinary money in your pocket, you usually know, at least approximately, how much you have. Every time you pay for something, you receive a reminder; you can see and feel what you have. Not so with traveler's checks. What you see, if and when you look, is a blue folder with checks inside. How often do you count the checks to make sure that they are all there? Supposing someone were to remove the *bottom* check in a folder. When would you find out that it had gone? A hundred to one it would not be until you had used up all the checks which had been on top of it. Therefore, you would not know exactly *when* it had been taken; and, if you had been doing any traveling, you probably would not even know *where*. If you did not know when or where, how could you possibly guess *who*? In any case you would be too late to stop its being cashed.

People who leave traveler's checks about *deserve* to lose them.

I took just six checks, the bottom ones from the folder. That made three hundred dollars, and left him fifteen hundred or so. It is a mistake, I always think, to be greedy; but unfortunately I hesitated. For a moment I wondered if he would miss them all that much sooner if I took two more.

So I was standing there like a fool, with the checks right in my hands, when Harper walked into the room.

Chapter

2

I was in the bedroom and he came through from the sitting room. All the same he must have opened the outer door very quietly indeed, or I would certainly have heard the latch. I think he expected to find me there. In that case, the whole thing was just a cunningly planned trap.

I was standing at the foot of one of the beds, so I couldn't move away from him. For a moment he just stood there grinning at me, as if he were enjoying himself.

"Well now, Arthur," he said, "you ought to have waited for me, oughtn't you?"

"I was going back." It was a stupid thing to say, I suppose; but almost anything I had said would have sounded stupid at that point.

And then, suddenly, he hit me across the face with the back of his hand.

It was like being kicked. My glasses fell off and I lurched back against the bed. As I raised my arms to protect myself he hit me again with the other hand. When I started to fall to my knees, he dragged me up and kept on hitting me. He was like a savage.

I fell down again and this time he let me be. My ears were singing, my head felt like bursting, and I could not see properly. My nose began to bleed. I got my handkerchief out to stop the blood from getting all over my clothes, and felt about among the checks lying on the carpet for my glasses. I found them eventually. They were bent a bit but not broken. When I put them on, I saw the soles of his shoes about a yard from my face.

He was sitting in the armchair, leaning back, watching me.

"Get up," he said, "and watch that blood. Keep it off the rug."

As I got to my feet, he stood up quickly himself. I thought he was going to start hitting me again. Instead, he caught hold of one lapel of my jacket.

"Do you have a gun?"

I shook my head.

He slapped my pockets, to make sure, I suppose, then shoved me away.

"There are some tissues in the bathroom," he said. "Go clean your face. But leave the door open."

I did as I was told. There was a window in the bathroom; but even if it had been possible to escape that way without breaking my neck, I don't suppose I would have tried it. He would have heard me. Besides, where could I have escaped to? All he would have had to do was call down to the night concierge, and the police would have been there in five minutes. The fact that he had not called down already was at least something. Perhaps, as a foreigner, he did not want to get involved as a witness in a court case. After all, he had not actually lost anything; and if I were to eat enough humble pie, perhaps even cry a bit, he might decide to forget the whole thing; especially after the brutal way in which he had attacked me. That was my reasoning. I should have known better. You cannot expect common decency from a man like Harper.

When I came out of the bathroom, I saw that he had picked up the check folder and was putting it back in the suitcase. The checks I had torn out, however, were lying on the bed. He gathered them up and motioned me towards the sitting room.

"In there."

As I went in, he moved past me to the door and bolted it.

There was a marble-topped commode against the side wall. On the commode was a tray with an ice bucket, a bottle of brandy, and some glasses. He picked up a glass, then looked at me.

"Sit down right there," he said.

The chair he motioned to was by a writing table under the window. I obeyed orders; there did not seem to be anything else to do. My nose was still bleeding, and I had a headache.

He slopped some brandy into the glass and put it on the table beside me. For a moment or two I felt encouraged. If you are going to have a man arrested you don't sit him down first and give him a drink. Perhaps it was just going to be a man-to-man chat in which I told him a hard-luck story and said how sorry I was, while he got dewy-eyed over his own magnanimity and decided to give me another chance.

That one did not last long.

He poured himself a drink and then glanced across at me as he put ice in the glass.

"First time you've been caught at it, Arthur?"

I blew my nose a little to keep the blood running before I answered. "It's the first time I've ever been tempted, sir.

I don't know what came over me. Perhaps it was the brandy I had with you. I'm not really used to it."

He turned and stared at me. All at once his face was neither old-young nor young-old. It was white and pinched and his mouth worked in an odd way. I have seen faces go like that before and I braced myself. There was a metal lamp on the writing table beside me. I wondered if I could possibly hit him with it before he got to me.

But he did not move. His eyes flickered towards the bedroom and then back to me.

"You'd better get something straight, Arthur," he said slowly. "That was just a little roughing up you had in there. If I really start giving you a going over, you'll leave here on a stretcher. Nobody's going to mind about that except you. I came back and caught you stealing. You tried to strong-arm your way out of it and I had to defend myself. That's how it'll be. So cut out the bull, and the lies. Right?"

"I'm sorry, sir."

"Empty your pockets. On this table here."

I did as I was told.

He looked at everything, my driving license, my *permis de séjour,* and he touched everything. Finally, of course, he found the pass key in the change purse. I had sawn off the shank of it and cut a slot in the end so that I could use a small coin to turn it, but it was still over two inches long, and heavy. The weight gave it away. He looked at it curiously.

"You make this?"

"Not the key part. I just cut it down." There seemed no point in trying to lie about that.

He nodded. "That's better. Okay, we'll start over. We know you're a two-bit ponce and we know you heist traveler's checks from hotel rooms when you get the chance. Do you write the counter-signature yourself?"

"Yes."

"So that's forgery. Now, I'm asking again. Have you ever been caught before?"

"No, sir."

"Sure?"

"Yes."

"Do you have any sort of police record?"

"Here in Athens?"

"We'll start with Athens."

I hesitated. "Well, not exactly a police record. Do you mean traffic offenses?"

"You know what I mean. Quit stalling."

I sneezed, quite unintentionally, and my nose began bleeding again. He sighed impatiently and threw me a bunch of paper napkins from the drink tray.

"I had you pretty well figured out at the airport," he went on; "but I didn't think you'd be quite so stupid. Why did you have to tell that Kira dame that you'd had no dinner?"

I shrugged helplessly. "So that I could come here."

"Why didn't you tell her you'd gone to gas up the car? I just might have bought that one."

"It didn't seem important. Why should you suspect me?"

He laughed. "Oh brother! I know what that car you have sells for here, and I know that gasoline costs sixty cents a gallon. At the rates you charge you couldn't break even. Okay, you get your payoffs—the restaurant, the clip joint, the cat house—but they can't amount to much, so there must be something else. Kira doesn't know what it is, but she knows there's something because you've cashed quite a few traveler's checks through her."

"She told you that?" This really upset me; the least one can expect from a brothel keeper is discretion.

"Why shouldn't she tell me? You didn't tell her they were stolen, did you?" He drank his brandy down. "I don't happen to like paying for sex, but I wanted to find out a bit more about you. I did. When they realized that I wasn't going to leave without paying, they were both real friendly. Called me a cab and everything. Now, supposing *you* start talking."

I took a sip of brandy. "Very well. I have had three convictions."

"What for?"

"The charge in each case was representing myself as an official guide. In fact, all I did was to try to save one or two clients from those boring archaeological set speeches. The official guides have to learn them by heart before they can pass the examination. Tourists like to know what they are looking at, but they do not want to be bored."

"What happened? Did you go to jail?"

"Of course not. I was fined."

He nodded approvingly. "That was what Irma thought. Now you just keep on playing it straight like that and maybe we can keep the police out of this. Have you ever been jailed anywhere, to serve time, I mean?"

"I do not see why I should . . ."

"Okay, skip it," he broke in. "What about Turkey?"

"Turkey? Why do you ask?"

"Have you been there?"

"Yes."

"Any police record there?"

"I was fined in Istanbul for showing some people round a museum."

"Which museum?"

"The Topkapi."

"Were you posing as an official guide that time?"

"Guides must be licensed there. I did not have a license."

"Have you ever driven from here to Istanbul?"

"Is that a criminal offense?"

"Just answer. Have you?"

"Occasionally. Some tourists like to travel by road. Why?"

He did not answer. Instead, he took an envelope from the writing desk and began to scribble something in pencil. I desperately needed a cigarette, but was afraid to light one in case it might look as if I were no longer worried. I *was* worried, and confused, too; but I wanted to be sure I looked that way. I drank the brandy instead.

He finished his scribbling at last and looked up. "All right, Arthur. There's a pad of plain paper there and a pen. I'm going to dictate. You start writing. No, don't give me any arguments. Just do as I tell you."

I was hopelessly bewildered now. I picked up the pen.

"Ready?"

"Yes."

"Head it: *To the Chief of Police, Athens.* Got that? Now go on. *I, Arthur A. Simpson, of*—put in your address—*do hereby confess that on June fifteenth, using an illegal pass key, I entered the suite of Mr. Walter K. Harper in the Hotel Grande-Bretagne and stole American Express traveler's checks to the value of three hundred dollars. The numbers of the checks were* . . ."

As he felt in his pocket for the loose checks, I started to protest.

"Mr. Harper, I can't possibly write this. It would convict me. I couldn't defend myself."

"Would you sooner defend yourself right now? If so, I can call the police, and you can explain about that pass key." He paused and then went on more patiently. "Look, dad, maybe you and I will be the only ones who will ever read it. Maybe in a week's time it won't even exist. I'm just giving you a chance to get off the hook. Why don't you take it and be thankful?"

"What do I have to do for it?"

"We'll get to that later. Just you keep writing. *The numbers of the checks were P89.664.572 through P89.664.577, all in fifty-dollar units. I intended to forge Mr. Harper's signature on them so that I could cash them illegally. I have stolen, forged, and cashed other checks in that way.* Shut up and keep writing! *But now I find I cannot go through with it. Because of Mr. Harper's great kindness to me during his visit to Athens, and his Christian charity, I feel that I cannot rob him. I am, therefore, sending the checks I stole from him back with this letter. By taking this decision, I feel that I have come out of the darkness into the light of day. I know now that, as a sinner of the worst type, my only chance is to make restitution, to confess everything, and to pay the penalties the law demands. Only in this way can I hope for salvation in the world to come.* Now sign it."

I signed it.

"Now date it a week from today. No, better make it the twenty-third."

I dated it.

"Give it to me."

I gave it to him and he read it through twice. Then he looked at me and grinned.

"Not talking any more, Arthur?"

"I wrote down what you dictated."

"Sure. And now you're trying to figure out what would happen if I sent it to the police."

I shrugged.

"All right, I'll tell you what would happen. First they'd think you were a nut. They'd probably think that I was some kind of a nut, too, but they wouldn't be interested in me. I wouldn't be around anyway. On the other hand, they couldn't ignore the whole thing, because of the checks. Three hundred dollars! They'd have to take that seriously. So they'd start by getting on to the American Express and finding out about all the check forgeries that have been traced back to accounts in Athens banks. Then they'd pull you in and grill you. What would you do, Arthur? Tell them about me and what really happened? You'd be silly to do that, wouldn't you? They'd throw the book at you. No, you're too smart for that. You'd go along with the reformation jazz. That way, you'd have a real defense—voluntary confession, restitution, sincere repentance. I'll bet you'd get away with just a nominal sentence, maybe no more than a year."

"Thank you."

He grinned again. "Don't you worry, Arthur. You're not going to do any time at all." He waved the paper I had written and the checks. "This is just a little insurance." He picked up the brandy bottle and refilled my glass. "You see, a friend of mine is going to trust you with something valuable."

"What?"

"A car. You're going to drive it to Istanbul. You'll be paid a hundred bucks and expenses. That's all there is to it."

I managed to smile. "If that's all there is to it, I don't see why you have to blackmail me. I would gladly do the job every week for that money."

He looked pained. "Who said anything about blackmail? I said insurance. This is a seven-thousand-dollar Lincoln, Arthur. Do you know what it's worth now in Turkey?"

"Fourteen thousand."

"Well then, isn't it obvious? Supposing you drove it into the first garage you came to and sold it."

"It wouldn't be so easy."

"Arthur, you took a hell of a risk tonight for just three hundred dollars. For fourteen thousand you'd do pretty well anything, now wouldn't you? Be your age! As it is, I don't have to worry, and my friend doesn't have to worry. As soon as I know the car's delivered, this little confession'll be torn up and the checks'll go back in my pocket."

I was silent. I didn't believe a word he was saying and he knew it. He didn't care. He was watching me, enjoying himself. "All right," I said finally; "but there are just one or two questions I'd like to ask."

He nodded. "Sure there are. Only that's the one condition there is on the job, Arthur—no questions."

I would have been surprised if he said anything else. "Very well. When do I start?"

"Tomorrow. How long does it take to drive to Salonika?"

"About six or seven hours."

"Let's see. Tomorrow's Tuesday. If you start about noon you can spend the night there. Then Wednesday night in Edirne. You should make Istanbul Thursday afternoon. That'll be okay." He thought for a moment. "I'll tell you what you do. In the morning, you pack an overnight bag and come here by cab or streetcar. Be downstairs at ten."

"Where do I pick up the car?"

"I'll show you in the morning."

"Whatever you say."

He unbolted the door. "Good deal. Now take your junk and beat it. I have to get some sleep."

I put my belongings back in my pockets and went to the door.

"Hey!"

As I turned, something hit me in the chest and then fell at my feet.

"You've forgotten your pass key," he said.

I picked it up and left. I didn't say good night or anything. He didn't notice. He was finishing his drink.

The worst thing at school was being caned. There was a ritual about it. The master who had lost his temper with you would stop ranting, or, if it was one of the quiet ones, stop clenching his teeth, and say: "Take a note to the Headmaster." That meant you were for it. The note was always the same, *Request permission to punish*, followed by his initials; but he would always fold it twice before he gave it to you. You were not supposed to read it. I don't know why;

perhaps because they didn't like having to ask for permission.

Well, then you had to go and find The Bristle. Sometimes, of course, he would be in his study; but more often he would be taking the sixth form in trigonometry or Latin. That meant you had to go in and stand there until he decided to notice you. You would have to wait five or ten minutes sometimes; it depended on the mood he was in. He was a tall, thick man with a lot of black hair on the backs of his hands, and a purple face. He spoke very fast while he was teaching, and after a while little flecks of white stuff would gather at the corners of his mouth. When he was in a good mood, he would break off almost as soon as you came in and start making jokes. "Ah, the good Simpson, or perhaps we should say the insufficiently good Simpson, what can we do for you?" Whatever he said, the sixth form always rocked with laughter, because the more they laughed, the longer he would go on wasting time. "And how have you transgressed, Simpson, how have you transgressed? Please tell us." You always had to say what you'd done or not done—bad homework, lying, flicking ink pellets—and you had to be truthful, in case he asked the master later. When he had made some more jokes, he initialed the note and you went. Before that *Enchantment* business I think he rather liked me, because I pretended not to be able to help laughing at his jokes even though I was going to be caned. When he was in a bad mood he used to call you "sir," which I always thought a bit stupid. "Well, sir, what is this for? Cribbing under the desk? A pauper spirit, sir, a pauper spirit! Work, for the night cometh! Now get out and stop wasting my time."

When you returned to the form room you gave the master the initialed note. Then, he took his gown off, so that his arms were free, and got the cane out of his desk. The canes were all the same, about thirty inches long and quite thick.

Some masters would take you outside into the coat lobby to do it, but others would do it in front of the form. You had to bend down and touch your toes and then he would hit you as hard as he could, as if he were trying to break the cane. It felt like a hot iron across your backside, and if he happened to hit twice in exactly the same place, like a heavy club with spikes on it. The great thing was not to cry or make a fuss. I remember a boy once who wet himself after it and had to be sent home; and there was another one who came back into the room and threw up, so that the master had to send for the school porter to clean up the mess. (They always sent for the porter when a boy threw up, and he always said the same thing when he came in with his bucket and mop—"Is *this* all?"—as if he were disappointed it wasn't blood.) Most boys, though, when they were caned, just got very red in the face and tried to walk back to their places as if nothing had happened. It wasn't pride; it was the only way to get any sympathy. When a boy cried you didn't feel sorry for him, merely embarrassed because he was so sorry for himself, and resentful because the master would feel that he had done something effective. One of the most valuable things I learned at Coram's was how to hate; and it was the cane that taught me. I never forgot and never began to forgive a caning until I had somehow evened the score with the master who had given it to me. If he were married, I would write an anonymous letter to his wife saying that he was a sodomite and that he had been trying to interfere with young boys. If he were a bachelor, I would send it as a warning to one of the other boys' parents. Mostly I never heard what happened, of course; but on at least two occasions I heard that the parents had questioned their boys and then forwarded my letters to The Bristle. I never told anyone, because I did not want the others copying my idea; and as I was very good at disguising my writing, the masters never knew for certain who had done it. Just as long as they had a suspicion they could not prove, I was satisfied. It meant that they knew I could hit back, that I was a good friend but a bad enemy.

My attitude to Harper was the same. He had given me a "caning"; but instead of wallowing in self-pity, as any other man in my position might have done, I began to think of ways in which I could hit back.

Obviously, there was nothing much I could do while he had that "confession"; but I knew one thing—he was a crook. I didn't know yet what kind of a crook—although I had some ideas—but I would find out for certain sooner or later. Then, when it was safe to do so, I would expose him to the police.

Nicki was in bed when I got back to the flat. I had hoped that she would be asleep, because one side of my face was very red where he had hit me and I didn't want to have to do any explaining; but she had the light on and was reading some French fashion magazine.

"Hullo, papa," she said.

I said hullo back and went to the bathroom to get rid of the handkerchief with all the blood on it. Then I went in and began to get undressed.

"You didn't stay long at the Club," she said.

"He wanted to go on to Irma's."

She did not like that, of course. "Did you find out any more about him?"

"He is a businessman—accounting machines, I think. He has a friend who owns a Lincoln. He wants me to drive it to Istanbul for him. I start tomorrow. He's paying quite well—a hundred dollars American.

She sat up at that. "That's very good, isn't it?" And then, inevitably, she saw my face. "What have you done to yourself?"

"I had a bit of an accident. Some fool in a Simca. I had to stop suddenly."

"Did the police come?"

She had a tiresome habit of assuming that, just because I was once accused (falsely) of causing an accident through driving while drunk, every little traffic accident in which I am involved is going to result in my being prosecuted by the police.

"It wasn't important," I said. I turned away to hang up my suit.

"Will you be long away?" She sounded as if she had accepted the accident.

"Two or three days. I shall come back suddenly by air and surprise you with a lover."

I thought that would amuse her, but she did not even smile. I got into bed beside her and she put the light out. After a few moments she said: "Why does a man like Mr. Harper want to go to a house?"

"Probably because he is impotent anywhere else."

She was silent for a time. Then she put up a hand and touched my face.

"What really happened, papa?"

I considered telling her; but that would have meant admitting openly that I had lied about the accident, so I did not answer. After a while, she turned away from me and went to sleep.

She was still asleep, or pretending to be, when I left in the morning.

Harper kept me waiting ten minutes; just long enough for me to remember that I had forgotten to disconnect the battery on my car. It did not hold its charge very well anyway, and the electric clock would have run it down by the time I returned. I was wondering if I would have time to telephone Nicki and tell her to ask the concierge to disconnect the battery, when Harper came down.

"All set?" he asked.

"Yes."

"We'll get a cab."

He told the driver to go to Stele Street out in the Piraeus.

As soon as we were on the way, he opened the briefcase and took out a large envelope. It had not been there the night before; of that I am certain. He gave it to me.

"There's everything you'll need there," he said; "*carnet de tourisme* for the car, insurance Green Card, a thousand Greek drachma, a hundred Turkish lira, and fifty American dollars for emergencies. The *carnet* has been countersigned authorizing you to take it through customs, but you'd better check everything out yourself."

I did so. The *carnet* showed that the car was registered in Zurich, and that the owner, or at any rate the person in legal charge of it, was a Fräulein Elizabeth Lipp. Her address was Hotel Excelsior, Laufen, Zurich.

"Is Miss Lipp your friend?" I asked.

"That's right."

"Are we going to meet her now?"

"No, but maybe you'll meet her in Istanbul. If the customs should ask, tell them she doesn't like eight-hundred-and-fifty-mile drives, and preferred to go to Istanbul by boat."

"Is she a tourist?"

"What else? She's the daughter of a business associate of mine. I'm just doing him a favor. And by the way, if she wants you to drive her around in Turkey you'll be able to pick up some extra dough. Maybe she'll want you to drive the car back here later. I don't know yet what her future plans are."

"I see." For someone who had told me that I wasn't to ask questions, he was being curiously outgoing. "Where do I deliver the car in Istanbul?"

"You don't. You go to the Park Hotel. There'll be a room reservation for you there. Just check in on Thursday and wait for instructions."

"Very well. When do I get that letter I signed?"

"When you're paid off at the end of the job."

Stele Street was down at the docks. By an odd coincidence there happened to be a ship of the Denizyollari Line berthed right opposite; and it was taking on a car through one of the side entry ports. I could not help glancing at Harper to see if he had noticed; but if he had he gave no sign of the fact. I made no comment. If he were simply ignorant, I was not going to enlighten him. If he still really thought that I was foolish enough to believe his version of Fräulein Lipp's travel needs and arrangements, so much the better. I could look after myself. Or so I thought.

There was a garage halfway along the street, with an old Michelin tire sign above it. He told the cab driver to stop there and wait. We got out and went towards the office. There was a man inside, and when he saw Harper through the window he came out. He was thin and dark and wore a greasy blue suit. I did not hear Harper address him by any name, but they appeared to know one another quite well. Unfortunately, they spoke together in German, which is a language I have never learned.

After a moment or two, the man led the way through a small repair shop and across a scrap yard to a row of lock-up garages. He opened one of them and there was the Lincoln. It was a gray four-door Continental, and looked to me about a year old. The man handed Harper the keys. He got in, started up, and drove it out of the garage into the yard. The car seemed a mile long. Harper got out.

"Okay," he said. "She's all gassed up and everything. You can start rolling."

"Very well." I put my bag on the back seat. "I would just like to make a phone call first."

He was instantly wary. "Who to?"

"The concierge at my apartment. I want to let him know that I may be away longer than I said, and ask him to disconnect the battery on my car."

He hesitated, then nodded. "Okay. You can do it from the office." He said something to the man in the blue suit and we all went back inside.

Nicki answered the telephone and I told her about the battery. When she started to complain that I had not wakened her to say good-by, I hung up. I had spoken in Greek, but Harper had been listening.

"That was a woman's voice," he said.

"The concierge's wife. Is there anything wrong?"

He said something to the man in the blue suit of which I understood one word, *Adressat*. I guessed that he had wanted to know if I had given the address of the garage. The man shook his head.

Harper looked at me. "No, nothing wrong. But just remember you're working for me now."

"Will I see you in Istanbul or back here?"

"You'll find out. Now get going."

I spent a minute or two making sure that I knew where all the controls were, while Harper and the other man stood watching. Then I drove off and headed back towards Athens and the Thebes-Larissa-Salonika road.

After about half a mile I noticed that the taxi we had used on the drive out there was behind me. I was driving slowly, getting used to the feel of the car, and the taxi would normally have passed me; but it stayed behind. Harper was seeing me on my way.

About five miles beyond Athens I saw the taxi pull off the road and start to turn around. I was on my own. I drove on for another forty minutes or so, until I reached the first of the cotton fields, then turned off down a side road and stopped in the shade of some acacias.

I spent a good half hour searching that car. First I looked in the obvious places: in the back of the spare-wheel compartment, under the seat cushions, up behind the dashboard. Then I took off all the hub caps. It's surprising how big the cavities are behind some of them, especially on

American cars. I knew of a man who had regularly smuggled nearly two kilos of heroin a time that way. These had nothing in them, however. So I tried the tank, poking about with a long twig to see if any sort of a compartment had been built into or onto it; that has been done, too. Again I drew a blank. I would have liked to crawl underneath to see if any new welding had been done, but there was not enough clearance. I decided to put the car into a garage greasing bay in Salonika and examine the underside from below. Meanwhile, there was an air-conditioner in the car, so I unscrewed the cover and had a look inside that. Another blank.

The trouble was that I did not have the slightest idea what I was looking for—jewelry, drugs, gold, or currency. I just felt that there must be something. After a bit, I gave up searching and sat and smoked a cigarette while I tried to work out what would be worth smuggling into Turkey from Greece. I could not think of anything. I got the *carnet* out and checked the car's route. It had come from Switzerland, via Italy and the Brindisi ferry, to Patras. The counterfoils showed that Fräulein Lipp had been with the car herself then. She, at least, *did* know about ferrying cars by sea. However, that only made the whole thing more mysterious.

And then I remembered something. Harper had spoken of the possibility of a *return* journey, of my being wanted to drive the car back from Istanbul to Athens. Supposing *that* was the real point of the whole thing. I drive from Greece into Turkey. Everything is perfectly open and aboveboard. Both Greek and Turkish customs would see and remember car and chauffeur. Some days later, the same car and chauffeur return. "How was Istanbul, friend? Is your stomach still with you? Anything to declare? No fat-tailed sheep hidden in the back? Pass, friend, pass." And then the car goes back to the garage in the Piraeus, for the man in the blue suit to recover the packages of heroin con-

cealed along the inner recesses of the chassis members, under the wheel arches of the body, and inside the cowling
beside the automatic transmission. Unless, that is, there is a
Macedonian son of a bitch on the Greek side who's out to
win himself a medal. In that event, what you get is the
strange case of the respectable Swiss lady's disreputable
chauffeur who gets caught smuggling heroin; and Yours
Truly is up the creek.

All I could do was play it by ear.

I got the Lincoln back on the road again and drove on. I
reached Salonika soon after six that evening. Just to be on
the safe side, I pulled into a big garage and gave the boy a
couple of drachmas to put the car up on the hydraulic
lift. I said I was looking for a rattle. There were no signs of
new welding. I was not surprised. By then I had pretty
well made up my mind that it would be the return journey
that mattered.

I found a small comfortable hotel, treated myself to a
good dinner and a bottle of wine at Harper's expense, and
went to bed early. I made an early start the following morning, too. It is an eight-hour run from Salonika across Thrace
to the Turkish frontier near Edirne (Adrianople, as it used
to be called), and if you arrive late, you sometimes find
that the road-traffic customs post has closed for the night.

I arrived at about four-thirty and went through the Greek
control without difficulty. At Karaagac, on the Turkish side,
I had to wait while they cleared some farm trucks ahead
of me. After about twenty minutes, however, I was able to
drive up to the barrier. When I went into the customs post
with the *carnet* and my other papers, the place was practically empty.

Naturally, I was more concerned about the car than with
myself, so I simply left my passport and currency declaration with the security man, and went straight over to the
customs desk to hand in the *carnet*.

Everything seemed to be going all right. A customs inspector went out to the car with me, looked in my bag, and merely glanced in the car. He was bored and looking forward to his supper.

"*Tourisme?*" he asked.

"Yes."

We went back inside and he proceeded to stamp and validate the *carnet* for the car's entry, and tear out his part of the counterfoil. He was just folding the *carnet* and handing it back when I felt a sharp tap on my shoulder.

It was the security man. He had my passport in his hand. I went to take it, but he shook his head and began waving it under my nose and saying something in Turkish.

I speak Egyptian Arabic and there are many Arabic words in Turkish; but the Turks pronounce them in a funny way and use a lot of Persian and old Turkish words mixed up with them. I shrugged helplessly. Then he said it in French and I understood.

My passport was three months out of date.

I knew at once how it had happened. Earlier in the year I had had some differences with the Egyptian consular people (or "United Arab Republic," as they preferred to call themselves) and had allowed the whole question of my passport to slide. In fact, I had made up my mind to tell the Egyptians what they could do with their passport, and approach the British with a view to reclaiming my United Kingdom citizenship, to which, I want to make it clear, I am perfectly entitled. The thing was that, being so busy, I had just not bothered to fill in all the necessary forms. My Greek *permis de séjour* was in order, and that was all I normally needed in the way of papers. Frankly, I find all this paper regimentation we have to go through nowadays extremely boring. Naturally, with all the anxiety I had had over Harper, I had not thought to look at the date on my passport. If I had known that it was out of date, obviously

I would have taken more trouble with the security man, kept him in conversation while he was doing the stamping or something like that. I have never had any bother like that before.

As it was, the whole thing became utterly disastrous; certainly through no fault of mine. The security man refused to stamp the passport. He said that I had to drive back to Salonika and have the passport renewed by the Egyptian vice-consul there before I could be admitted.

That would have been impossible as it happened; but I did not even have to try to explain why. The customs inspector chimed in at that point, waving the *carnet* and shouting that the car *had* been admitted and was now legally in Turkey. As *I* had *not* been admitted and was *not*, therefore, legally in Turkey, how was I, *legally*, to take the car out again? What did it matter if the passport was out of date? It was only a matter of three months. Why did he not just stamp the passport, admit me, and forget about it?

At least that was what I think he said. They had lapsed into Turkish now and were bawling at one another as if I did not exist. If I could have got the security man alone, I would have tried to bribe him; but with the other one there it was too dangerous. Finally, they both went off to see some superior officer and left me standing there, without *carnet* or passport, but with, I admit it frankly, a bad case of the jitters. Really, my only hope at that point was that they would do what the customs inspector wanted and overlook the date on the passport.

With any luck, that might have happened. I say "with any luck," although things would still have been awkward even if they had let me through. I would have had somehow to buy an Egyptian consular stamp in Istanbul and forge the renewal in the passport—not easy. Or I would have had to have gone to the British Consulate-General, re-

ported a lost British passport, and tried to winkle a temporary travel document out of them before they had had time
to check up—not easy either. But at least those would have
been the sort of difficulties a man in my anomalous position would understand and could cope with. The difficulties that, in fact, I did have to face were quite outside anything I had ever before experienced.

I stood there in the customs shed for about ten minutes,
watched by an armed guard on the door who looked as if
he would have liked nothing better than an excuse for
shooting me. I pretended not to notice him; but his presence did not improve matters. In fact, I was beginning to
get an attack of my indigestion.

After a while, the security man came back and beckoned
to me. I went with him, along a passage with a small bar-
rack room off it, to a door at the end.

"What now?" I asked in French.

"You must see the Commandant of the post."

He knocked at the door and ushered me in.

Inside was a small bare office with some hard chairs and
a green baize trestle table in the center. The customs inspector stood beside the table. Seated at it was a man of
about my own age with a lined, sallow face. He wore some
sort of officer's uniform. I think he belonged to the military
security police. He had the *carnet* and my passport on the
table in front of him.

He looked up at me disagreeably. "This is your passport?" He spoke good French.

"Yes, sir. And I can only say that I regret extremely that
I did not notice that it was not renewed."

"You have caused a lot of trouble."

"I realize that, sir. I must explain, however, that it was
only on Monday evening that I was asked to make this
journey. I left early yesterday morning. I was in a hurry. I
did not think to check my papers."

He looked down at the passport. "It says here that your occupation is that of journalist. You told the customs inspector that you were a chauffeur."

So he had an inquiring mind; my heart sank.

"I am acting as a chauffeur, sir. I was, I *am* a journalist, but one must live and things are not always easy in that profession."

"So now you are a chauffeur, and the passport is incorrect in yet another particular, eh?" It was a very unfair way of putting it, but I thought it as well to let him have his moment.

"One's fortunes change, sir. In Athens I have my own car, which I drive for hire."

He peered, frowning, at the *carnet*. "This car here is the property of Elizabeth Lipp. Is she your employer?"

"Temporarily, sir."

"Where is she?"

"In Istanbul, I believe, sir."

"You do not know?"

"Her agent engaged me, sir—to drive her car to Istanbul, where she is going as a tourist. She prefers to make the journey to Istanbul by sea."

There was an unpleasant pause. He looked through the *carnet* again and then up at me abruptly.

"What nationality is this woman?"

"I don't know, sir."

"What age? What sort of woman?"

"I have never seen her, sir. Her agent arranged everything."

"And she is going from Athens to Istanbul by sea, which takes twenty-four hours, but she sends her car fourteen hundred kilometers and three days by road. If she wants the car in Istanbul, why didn't she take the car on the boat with her? It is simple enough and costs practically nothing."

I was only too well aware of it. I shrugged. "I was paid

to drive, sir, and well paid. It was not for me to question the lady's plans."

He considered me for a moment, then drew a sheet of paper towards him and scribbled a few words. He handed the result to the customs inspector, who read, nodded, and went out quickly.

The Commandant seemed to relax. "You say you know nothing about the woman who owns the car," he said. "Tell me about her agent. Is it a travel bureau?"

"No, sir, a man, an American, a friend of Fräulein Lipp's father he said."

"What's his name? Where is he?"

I told him everything I knew about Harper, and the nature of my relationship with him. I did not mention the disagreement over the traveler's checks. That could have been of no interest to him.

He listened in silence, nodding occasionally. By the time I had finished, his manner had changed considerably. His expression had become almost amiable.

"Have you driven this way before?" he asked.

"Several times, sir."

"With tourists?"

"Yes, sir."

"Ever without tourists?"

"No, sir. They like to visit Olympus, Salonika, and Alexandropolis on their way to Istanbul."

"Then did you not think this proposal of Mr. Harper's strange?"

I permitted myself to smile. "*Monsieur le Commandant*," I said, "I thought it so strange that there could be only two possible reasons for it. The first was that Mr. Harper was so much concerned to impress the daughter of a valuable business associate with his *savoir-faire* that he neglected to ask anyone's advice before he made his arrangements."

"And the second?"

"That he knew that uncrated cars carried in Denizyollari ships to Istanbul must be accompanied by the owner as a passenger, and that he did not wish to be present when the car was inspected by customs for fear that something might be discovered in the car that should not be there."

"I see." He smiled slightly. "But *you* had no such fear."

We were getting cozier by the minute. *"Monsieur le Commandant,"* I said, "I may be a trifle careless about having my passport renewed, but I am not a fool. The moment I left Athens yesterday, I stopped and searched the car thoroughly, underneath as well as on top, the wheels, everywhere."

There was a knock on the door and the customs inspector came back. He put a sheet of paper down in front of the Commandant. The Commandant read it and his face suddenly tightened. He looked up again at me.

"You say you searched everywhere in the car?"

"Yes, sir. Everywhere."

"Did you search inside the doors?"

"Well, no, sir. They are sealed. I would have damaged . . ."

He said something quickly in Turkish. Suddenly the security man locked an arm round my neck and ran his free hand over my pockets. Then he shoved me down violently onto a chair.

I stared at the Commandant dumbly.

"Inside the doors there are"—he referred to the paper in his hand—"twelve tear-gas grenades, twelve concussion grenades, twelve smoke grenades, six gas respirators, six Parabellum pistols, and one hundred and twenty rounds of nine-millimeter pistol ammunition." He put the paper down and stood up. "You are under arrest."

Chapter

3

The post had no facilities for housing prisoners, and I was put in the lavatory under guard while the Commandant reported my arrest to headquarters and awaited orders. The lavatory was only a few yards from his office, and during the next twenty minutes the telephone there rang four times. I could hear the rumble of his voice when he answered. The tone of it became more respectful with each call.

I was uncertain whether I should allow myself to be encouraged by this or not. Police behavior is always difficult to anticipate, even when you know a country well. Sometimes Higher Authority is more responsive to a reasonable explanation of the misunderstanding, and more disposed to accept a dignified expression of regret for inconvenience caused, than some self-important or sadistic minor official who is out to make the most of the occasion. On the other hand, the Higher Authority has more power to abuse, and, if it comes to the simple matter of a bribe, bigger ideas about his nuisance value. I must admit, though, that what I was mainly concerned about at that point was the kind of physical treatment I would receive. Of course, every police authority, high or low, considers its behavior "correct" on all occasions; but in my experience (although I have only really been arrested ten or twelve times in my whole life) the word "correct" can mean almost anything from hot meals brought in from a nearby restaurant and plenty of cigarettes, to tight-handcuffing in the cell and a knee in the groin if you dare to complain. My previous encounters with the Turkish police had been uncomfortable only in the sense that they had been inconvenient and humiliating; but then, the matters in dispute had been of a more or less technical nature. I had to face the fact that "being in possession of arms, explosives, and other offensive weapons, attempting to smuggle them into the Turkish Republic, carrying concealed firearms and illegal entry without valid identification papers," were rather more serious charges. My complete and absolute innocence of them would take time to establish, and a lot of quite unpleasant things could happen in the interim.

The possibility that my innocence might *not* be established was something that, realist though I am, I was not just then prepared to contemplate.

After the fourth telephone call, the Commandant came out of his office, gave some orders to the security man who had been waiting in the passage, and then came into the lavatory.

"You are being sent at once to the garrison jail in Edirne," he said.

"And the car I was driving, sir?"

He hesitated. "I have no orders about that yet. No doubt it will be wanted as evidence."

Direct communication with Higher Authority seemed to have sapped a little of his earlier self-confidence. I decided to have one more shot at bluffing my way out. "I must remind you, sir," I said loudly, "that I have already protested formally to you against my detention here. I repeat that protest. The car and its contents are within your legal jurisdiction. I am not. I was refused entry because my papers were not in order. Therefore, legally, I was not in Turkey and should have been at once returned to the Greek side of the border. In Greece, I have a *permis de séjour* which *is* in order. I think that when your superiors learn these facts, you will find that you have a lot to answer for."

It was quite well said. Unfortunately, it seemed to amuse him.

"So you are a lawyer, as well as a journalist, a chauffeur, and an arms smuggler."

"I am simply warning you."

His smile faded. "Then let me give you a word of warning, too. In Edirne you will not be dealing with the ordinary police authorities. It is considered that there may be political aspects to your case and it has been placed under the jurisdiction of the Second Section, the *Ikinci Büro*."

"Political aspects? What political aspects?" I tried, not very successfully, to sound angry instead of alarmed.

"That is not for me to say. I merely warn you. The Director, Second Section, is General Haki. It will be his men who will interrogate you. You will certainly end by cooperating with them. You would be well advised to begin by doing so. Their patience, I hear, is quite limited. That is all."

He went. A moment or two later the security man came in.

I was driven to the garrison jail in a covered jeep with my right wrist handcuffed to a grab rail, and an escort of two soldiers. The jail was an old stone building on the outskirts of the town. It had a walled courtyard, and there were expanded metal screens as well as bars over the windows.

One of the soldiers, an N.C.O., reported to the guard on the inner gate, and after a few moments two men in a different sort of uniform came out through a smaller side door. One of them had a paper which he handed to the N.C.O. I gathered that it was a receipt for me. The N.C.O. immediately unlocked the handcuffs and waved me out of the jeep. The new escort-in-charge prodded me towards the side door.

"*Girmek, girmek!*" he said sharply.

All jails seem to smell of disinfectants, urine, sweat, and leather. This was no exception. I went up some wooden stairs to a steel gate, which was opened by a man with a long chain of keys from the inside. Beyond it and to the right was a sort of reception room with a man at a desk and two cubicles at the back. The guard shoved me up to the desk and rapped out an order. I said in French that I didn't understand. The man at the desk said: "*Vide les poches.*"

I did as I was told. They had taken all my papers and keys from me at the frontier post. All I had left in my pockets was my money, my watch, a packet of cigarettes, and matches. The desk man gave me back the watch and the cigarettes, and put the money and the matches into an envelope. A man in a grubby white coat now arrived and went into one of the cubicles. He was carrying a thin yellow file folder. After a moment or two he called out an order and I was sent in to him.

The cubicle contained a small table and a chair and a covered bucket. In one corner there was a washbasin, and on the wall a white metal cabinet. The white-coated man was at the table preparing an inking plate of the kind used for fingerprinting. He glanced up at me and said in French: "Take your clothes off."

People who run jails are all the same. When I was naked, he searched the inside of the clothes and the shoes. Next he looked in my mouth and ears with a flashlight. Then he took a rubber glove and a jar of petroleum jelly from the wall cabinet and searched my rectum. I have always deeply resented that indignity. Finally he took my fingerprints. He was very businesslike about it all; he even gave me a piece of toilet paper to wipe the ink off my hands before he told me to dress and go into the next cubicle. In there, was a camera, set up with photofloods and a fixed focus bar. When I had been photographed, I was taken along some corridors to a green wooden door with the word ISTIFHAM lettered on it in white paint. *Istifham* is a Turkish word I know; it means "interrogation."

There was only one small screened and barred window in the room; the sun was beginning to set and it was already quite dark in there. As I went in, one of the guards followed me and switched on the light. His friend shut and locked the door from the outside. The guard who was to stay with me sat down on a bench against the wall and yawned noisily.

The room was about eighteen feet square. Off one corner there was a washroom with no door on it. Apart from the bench, the furniture consisted of a solid-looking table bolted to the floor and half a dozen chairs. On the wall was a telephone and a framed lithograph of Kemal Atatürk. The floor was covered with worn brown linoleum.

I got out my cigarettes and offered one to the guard. He shook his head and looked contemptuous, as if I had offered him an inadequate bribe. I shrugged and, putting the cigarette in my own mouth, made signs that I wanted a light. He shook his head again. I put the cigarette away and sat down at the table. I had to assume that at any moment now a representative of the Second Section would arrive and start questioning me. What I needed, very badly, was something to tell him.

It is always the same with interrogation. I remember my father trying to explain it to Mum one night, just before

he was killed. It's no good for a soldier who is up on a charge
before his C.O. just telling the truth; he has to have something more, something fancy to go with it. If he got back
to barracks half an hour after lights-out just because he'd
had too much beer and missed the last bus, who cares about
him? He's simply a careless bloody fool—seven days con-
fined to barracks, next case. But if, when he's asked if he
has anything to say, he can tell the tale so that the C.O.
gets a bit of fun out of hearing it, things are different. He
may be only admonished. My father said that there was a
corporal in his old regiment who was so good at making up
yarns for the orderly room that he used to sell them for
half-a-crown apiece. They were known as "well-sirs." My
father bought a well-sir once when he was "crimed" for
overstaying an evening pass. It went like this:

*Well, sir, I was proceeding back along Cantonment Road
towards the barracks in good time for lights-out and in a
soldierly manner. Then, sir, just as I was passing the shopping arcade by Ordnance Avenue, I heard a woman
scream.* Pause. *Well, sir, I stopped to listen and heard her
scream again. There were also some confused cries. The
sound was coming from one of the shops in the arcade, so
I went to investigate.* Pause again, then go on slowly. *Well,
sir, what I found was one of these Wogs—beg pardon, sir,
a native—molesting a white woman in a doorway. I could
see she was a lady, sir.* Let that sink in a bit. *Well, sir, the
moment this lady saw me, she appealed to me for help. She
said she'd been on her way home to her mother's house,
which was over on the other side of Artillery Park, when
this native had attempted to—well, interfere with her. I
told him to clear out. In reply, sir, he became abusive, calling me some very dirty names in his own lingo and using
insulting language about the Regiment.* Take a deep breath.
*Well, sir, for the lady's sake I managed to hold on to my
temper. As a matter of fact, sir, I think the man must have*

*been drunk or under the influence of drugs. He had sense
enough to keep his distance, but the moment I escorted the
lady out of the arcade I realized that he was following us.
Just waiting for a chance to molest her again, sir. She knew
it, too. I've never seen a lady more frightened, sir. When
she appealed to me to escort her to her mother's house, sir,
I realized that it would make me late. But if I'd just gone
on my way and something terrible had happened to her,
I'd have never forgiven myself, sir.* Stiffen up and look without blinking at the wall space over the C.O.'s head. *No excuse to offer, sir, I'll take my medicine.* C.O. can't think of
anything to say except: "Don't let it happen again."
Charge dismissed.

The only trouble is that, in the army, unless you are always making a damned nuisance of yourself, they would
sooner give you the benefit of the doubt than not, because
it's easier for them that way. Besides, they know that even
if you *have* made the whole thing up, at least they've had
you sweating over it. The police are much more difficult.
They don't *want* you to have the benefit of any doubt. They
want to start checking and double-checking your story, and
getting witnesses and evidence, so that there *is* no doubt.
"What was the lady's name? Describe her. Exactly where
was the house to which you escorted her? Was her mother
in fact there? Did you see her? It takes twenty-two minutes
to walk from the shopping arcade to the other side of Artillery Park, and a further thirty minutes to walk from there
to the barracks. That makes fifty-two minutes. But you
were two hours late getting in. Where did you spend the
other hour and eight minutes? We have a witness who says
that he saw you . . ." And so on. You can't buy well-sirs
good enough for the police for half-a-crown. Intelligence
people are even worse. Nine times out of ten they don't
even have to worry about building up a case against you to

go into court. *They* are the court—judge, jury, and prosecutor, all in one.

I did not know anything about this "Second Section" which the Commandant had mentioned; but it was not hard to guess what it was. The Turks have always been great borrowers of French words and phrases. The *Ikinci Büro* sounded to me like the Turkish counterpart of the *Deuxième Bureau.* I wasn't far wrong.

I think that if I were asked to single out one specific group of men, one type, one category, as being the most suspicious, unbelieving, unreasonable, petty, inhuman, sadistic, double-crossing set of bastards in any language, I would say without any hesitation: "the people who run counter-espionage departments." With them, it is no use having just one story; and especially not a true story; they automatically disbelieve that. What you must have is a series of stories, so that when they knock the first one down you can bring out the second, and then, when they scrub that out, come up with a third. That way they think they are making progress and keep their hands off you, while you gradually find out the story they really want you to tell.

My position at Edirne was hopeless from the start. If I had known what was hidden in the car *before* the post Commandant had started questioning me, I wouldn't have told him about Harper. I would have pretended to be stupid, or just refused to say anything. Then, later, when I had finally broken down and "told all," they would have believed at least some of what I had said. As it was, I had told a story that happened to be true, but sounded as if I thought they were half-witted. You can imagine how I felt as I waited. With no room at all for maneuver, I knew that I must be in for a bad time.

The sun went down and the window turned black. It was very quiet. I could hear no sounds at all from other parts of the jail. Presumably, things were arranged so that there they could hear no sounds made in the interrogation room— screams, etc. When I had been there two hours, there were footsteps in the corridor outside, the door was unlocked, and a new guard came in with a tin bowl of mutton soup and a hunk of bread. He put these on the table in front of me, then nodded to his friend, who went out and relocked the door. The new man took his place on the bench.

There was no spoon. I dipped a piece of bread in the soup and tasted it. It was lukewarm and full of congealed fat. Even without my indigestion I could not have eaten it. Now, the smell alone made me want to throw up.

I looked at the guard. "*Su?*" I asked.

He motioned to the washroom. Evidently, if I wanted water I would have to drink from the tap. I did not relish the idea. Indigestion was bad enough; I did not want dys- entery, too. I made myself eat some of the bread and then took out my cigarettes again in the hope that the new man might be ready to give me a match. He shook his head. I pointed to a plastic ash tray on the table to remind him that smoking was not necessarily prohibited. He still shook his head.

A little before nine, a twin-engined plane flew over the jail and then circled as if on a landing pattern. The sound seemed to mean something to the guard. He looked at his watch, and then absently ran his hand down the front of his tunic as if to make sure that the buttons were all done up.

More to break the interminable silence in the room than because I wanted to know, I asked: "Is there a big airport at Edirne?"

I spoke in French, but it meant nothing to him. I made signs, which he misunderstood.

"*Askeri ucak,*" he said briefly.

An army plane. That concluded that conversation; but I

noticed that he kept glancing at his watch now. Probably, I thought, it was time for his relief and he was becoming impatient.

Twenty minutes later there was the distant sound of a car door slamming. The guard heard it, too, and promptly stood up. I stared at him and he glowered back.

"*Hazirol!*" he snapped, and then exasperatedly: "*Debout! Debout!*"

I stood up. I could hear approaching footsteps and voices now. Then the door was unlocked and flung open.

For a moment nothing more happened, except that someone in the corridor, whom I could not see, went on speaking. He had a harsh, peremptory voice which seemed to be giving orders that another voice kept acknowledging deferentially—"*Evet, evet efendim, derhal.*" Then the orders ceased and the man who had been giving them came into the room.

He was about thirty-five, I would think, perhaps younger, tall and quite slim. There were high cheekbones, gray eyes, and short brown hair. He was handsome, I suppose, in a thin-lipped sort of way. He was wearing a dark civilian suit that looked as if it had been cut by a good Roman tailor, and a dark-gray silk tie. He looked as if he had just come from a diplomatic corps cocktail party; and for all I know he may have done so. On his right wrist there was a gold identity bracelet. The hand below it was holding a large manila envelope.

He examined me bleakly for a moment, then nodded. "I am Major Tufan, Deputy Director, Second Section."

"Good evening, sir."

He glanced at the guard, who was staring at him round-eyed, and suddenly snapped out an order: "*Defol!*"

The guard nearly fell over himself getting out of the room.

As soon as the door closed, the major pulled a chair up

to the table and sat down. Then he waved me back to my seat by the bread.

"Sit down, Simpson. I believe that you speak French easily, but not Turkish."

"Yes, sir."

"Then we will speak in French instead of English. That will be easier for me."

I answered in French. "As you wish, sir."

He took cigarettes and matches from his pocket and tossed them on the table in front of me. "You may smoke."

"Thank you."

I was glad of the concession, though not in the least reassured by it. When a policeman gives you a cigarette it is usually the first move in one of those "let's see if we can't talk sensibly as man to man" games in which he provides the rope and you hang yourself. I lit a cigarette and waited for the next move.

He seemed in no hurry to make it. He had opened the envelope and taken from it a file of papers which he was searching through and rearranging, as if he had just dropped them all and was trying to get them back into the right order.

There was a knock at the door. He took no notice. After a moment or two, the door opened and a guard came in with a bottle of *raki* and two glasses. Tufan motioned to him to put them on the table, and then noticed the soup.

"Do you want any more of that?" he asked.

"No thank you, sir."

He said something to the guard, who took the soup and bread away and locked the door again.

Tufan rested the file on his knees and poured himself a glass of *raki*. "The flight from Istanbul was anything but smooth," he said; "we are still using piston-engined planes on these short runs." He swallowed the drink as if he were washing down a pill, and pushed the bottle an inch or two in my direction. "You'd better have a drink, Simpson. It may make you feel better."

"And also make me more talkative, sir?" I thought the light touch might make him think that I was not afraid.

He looked up and his gray eyes met mine. "I hope not," he said coldly; "I have no time to waste." He shut the file with a snap and put it on the table in front of him.

"Now then," he went on, "let us examine your position. First, the offenses with which you are charged render you liable upon conviction to terms of imprisonment of at least twenty years. Depending on the degree of your involvement in the political aspects of this affair, we might even consider pressing for a death sentence."

"But I am not involved at all, Major, I assure you. I am a victim of circumstances—an innocent victim." Of course, he could have been bluffing about the death sentence, but I could not be sure. There was that phrase "political aspects" again. I had read that they had been hanging members of the former government for political crimes. I wished now that I had taken the drink when he had offered it. Now, my hands were shaking, and I knew that, if I reached for the bottle and glass, he would see that they were.

Apparently, however, he did not have to see them; he knew what he was doing to me, and wanted me to know that he knew. Quite casually, he picked up the bottle, poured me half a glass of *raki*, and pushed it across to me.

"We will talk about the extent of your involvement in a minute," he said. "First, let us consider the matter of your passport."

"It is out of date. I admit that. But it was a mere oversight. If the post Commandant had behaved correctly I would have been sent back to the Greek post."

He shrugged impatiently. "Let us be clear about this. You had already committed serious criminal offenses on Turkish soil. Would you expect to escape the consequences because your papers are not in order? You know better. You also know that your passport was not invalid through any oversight. The Egyptian government had refused to renew it. In fact, they revoked your citizenship two years ago on the grounds that you made false statements on your naturalization papers." He glanced in the file. "You stated that you had never been convicted of a criminal offense and that you had never served a prison sentence. Both statements were lies."

This was such an unfair distortion of the facts that I could only assume that he had got it from the Egyptians. I said: "I have been fighting that decision."

"And also using a passport to which you were not entitled and had failed to surrender."

"My case was still *sub judice.* Anyway, I have already applied for restoration of my British citizenship, to which I am entitled as the son of a serving British officer. In fact, I *am* British."

"The British don't take that view. After what happened you can scarcely blame them."

"Under the provisions of the British Nationality Act of 1948 I remain British unless I have specifically renounced that nationality. I have never formally renounced it."

"That is unimportant. We are talking about your case here and the extent of your involvement. The point I wish to make is that our action in your case is not going to be governed in any way by the fact that you are a foreigner. No consul is going to intercede on your behalf. You have none. You are stateless. The only person who can help you is my Director." He paused. "But he will have to be persuaded. You understand me?"

"I have no money."

It seemed a perfectly sensible reply to me, but for some reason it appeared to irritate him. His eyes narrowed and for a moment I thought he was going to throw the glass he was holding in my face. Then he sighed. "You are over fifty," he said, "yet you have learned nothing. You still see other men in your own absurd image. Do you really believe that I could be bought, or that, if I could be, a man like you could ever do the buying?"

It was on the tip of my tongue to retort that that would depend on the price he was asking; but if he wanted to take this high-and-mighty attitude, there was no sense in arguing. Obviously, I had touched him in a sensitive area.

He lit a cigarette as if he were consciously putting aside his irritation. I took the opportunity to drink some of the *raki*.

"Very well." He was all business again. "You understand your position, which is that you have no position. We come now to the story you told to the post Commandant before your arrest."

"Every word I told the Commandant was the truth."

He opened the file. "On the face of it that seems highly unlikely. Let us see. You stated that you were asked by this American, Harper, to drive a car belonging to a Fräulein Lipp from Athens to Istanbul. You were to be paid one hundred dollars. You agreed. Am I right?"

"Quite right."

"You agreed, even though the passport in your possession was not in order?"

"I did not realize it was out of date. It has been months since I used it. The whole thing was arranged within a few hours. I scarcely had time to pack a bag. People are using out-of-date passports all the time. Ask anyone at any international airline. They will tell you. That is why they always check passengers' passports when they weigh their baggage. They do not want difficulties at the other end. I had nobody to check. The Greek control scarcely looked at the passport. I was leaving the country. They were not interested."

I knew I was on safe ground here, and I spoke with feeling.

He thought for a moment, then nodded. "It is possible, and, of course, you had good reason not to think too much about the date on your passport. The Egyptians were not going to renew it anyway. That explanation is acceptable, I think. We will go on." He referred again to the file. "You told the Commandant that you suspected this man Harper of being a narcotics smuggler."

"I did."

"To the extent of searching the car after you left Athens."

"Yes."

"Yet you still agreed to make the journey."

"I was being paid one hundred dollars."

"That was the only reason?"

"Yes."

He shook his head. "It really will not do."

"I am telling you the truth."

He took a clip of papers from the file. "Your history does not inspire confidence."

"Give a dog a bad name."

"You seem to have earned one. Our dossier on you begins in fifty-seven. You were arrested on various charges and fined on a minor count. The rest were abandoned by the police for lack of evidence."

"They should never have been brought in the first place."

He ignored this. "We did, however, ask Interpol if they knew anything about you. It seemed they knew a lot. Apparently you were once in the restaurant business."

"My mother owned a restaurant in Cairo. Is that an offense?"

"Fraud is an offense. Your mother was *part* owner of a restaurant. When she died, you sold it to a buyer who believed that you now owned all of it. In fact, there were two other shareholders. The buyer charged you with fraud, but withdrew his complaint when the police allowed you to regularize the transaction."

"I didn't know of the existence of these other shareholders. My mother had never told me that she had sold the shares." This was perfectly true. Mum was entirely responsible for the trouble I got into over that.

"In 1931 you bought a partnership in a small publishing business in Cairo. Outwardly it concerned itself with distributing foreign magazines and periodicals. Its real business was the production of pornography for the Spanish- and English-speaking markets. And that became *your* real business."

"That is absolutely untrue."

"The information was supplied through Interpol in fifty-four by Scotland Yard. It was given in response to an inquiry by the New York police. Scotland Yard must have known about you for a long time."

I knew it would do no good for me to become angry. "I have edited and sometimes written for a number of magazines of a literary nature over the years," I said quietly. "Sometimes they may have been a little daring in their approach and have been banned by various censoring authorities. But I would remind you that books like *Ulysses* and *Lady Chatterley's Lover*, which were once described by those same authorities as pornographic or obscene, are now accepted as literary works of art and published quite openly."

He looked at his papers again. "In January fifty-five you were arrested in London. In your possession were samples of the various obscene and pornographic periodicals which you had been attempting to sell in bulk. Among them was a book called *Gents Only* and a monthly magazine called *Enchantment*. All were produced by your Egyptian company. You were charged under the British law governing such publications, and also with smuggling them. At your trial you said nothing about their being literary works of art. You pleaded guilty and were sentenced to twelve months' imprisonment."

"That was a travesty of justice."

"Then why did you plead guilty?"

"Because my lawyer advised me to." In fact, the C.I.D. Inspector had tricked me into it. He had as good as promised me that if I pleaded guilty I would get off with a fine.

He stared at me thoughtfully for a moment, then shut the file. "You must be a very stupid man, Simpson. You say to me: 'I am telling you the truth,' and yet when I try to test that statement all I hear from you is whining and protestation. I am not interested in how you explain away the past, or in any illusions about yourself that you may wish to preserve. If you cannot even tell the truth when there is nothing to be gained by lying, then I can believe nothing you tell me. You were caught by the British smuggling pornography and trying to peddle it. Why not admit it? Then, when you tell me that you did not know that you were smuggling arms and ammunition this afternoon, I might at least think: 'This man is a petty criminal, but it is remotely possible that for once he is being truthful.' As it is, I can only assume that you are lying and that I must get the truth from you in some other way."

I admit that "some other way" gave me a jolt. After all, five minutes earlier he had been pouring me a glass of *raki*. He meant to put the fear of God into me, of course, and make me panic. Unfortunately, and only because I was tired, upset, and suffering from indigestion, he succeeded.

"I am telling you the truth, sir." I could hear my own voice cracking and quavering but could do nothing to control it. "I swear to God I am telling you the truth. My only wish is to tell you all I can, to bring everything out of the darkness into the light of day."

He stared at me curiously; and then, as I realized what I had said, I felt myself reddening. It was awful. I had used those absurd words Harper had made me write in that confession about the checks.

A sour smile touched his lips for an instant. "Ah yes," he said. "I was forgetting that you have been a journalist. We will try once more then. Just remember that I do not want speeches in mitigation, only plain statements."

"Of course." I was too confused to think straight now.

"Why did you go to London in fifty-five? You must have known that Scotland Yard knew all about you."

"How could I know? I hadn't been in England for years."

"Where were you during the war?"

"In Cairo doing war work."

"What work?"

"I was an interpreter."

"Why did you go to London?"

I cleared my throat and took a sip of *raki*.

"Answer me!"

"I was going to answer, sir." There was nothing else for it. "The British distributor of our publications suddenly ceased making payments and we could get no replies from him to our letters. I went to England to investigate, and found his offices closed. I assumed that he had gone out of business, and began to look for another distributor. The man I eventually discussed the possibility with turned out to be a Scotland Yard detective. We used to send our shipments to Liverpool in cotton bales. It seems that the customs had discovered this and informed the police. Our distributor had been arrested and sent to prison. The police had kept it out of the papers somehow. I just walked into a trap."

"Better, much better," he said. He looked almost amused. "Naturally, though, you felt bitter towards the British authorities."

I should have remembered something he had let drop earlier, but I was still confused. I tried to head him off.

"I was bitter at the time, of course, sir. I did not think I had had a fair trial. But afterwards I realized that the police had their job to do"—I thought that would appeal to him —"and that they weren't responsible for making the laws. So I tried to be a model prisoner. I think I was. Anyway, I received the maximum remission for good behavior. I certainly couldn't complain of the treatment I had in Maidstone. In fact, the Governor shook hands with me when I left and wished me well."

"And then you returned to Egypt?"

"As soon as my probationary period was up, yes. I went back to Cairo, sir."

"Where you proceeded to denounce a British businessman named Colby Evans to the Egyptian authorities as a British secret agent."

It was like a slap in the face, but I managed to keep my head this time. "Not immediately, sir. That was later, during the Suez crisis."

"Why did you do it?"

I didn't know what to say. How could I explain to a man like that that I had to pay back the caning they had given me. I said nothing.

"Was it because you needed to prove somehow to the Egyptian authorities that you were anti-British, or because you didn't like the man, or because you were sincerely anti-British?"

It was all three, I suppose; I am not really sure. I answered almost without thinking.

"My mother was Egyptian. My wife was killed by a British bomb in the attack they made on us. Why shouldn't I feel sincerely anti-British?"

It was probably the best answer I had given so far; it sounded true, even though it wasn't quite.

"Did you really believe this man was an agent?"

"Yes, sir."

"And then you applied for Egyptian citizenship."

"Yes, sir."

"You stayed in Egypt until fifty-eight. Was that when they finally decided that Evans had *not* been a British agent after all and released him?"

"He was convicted at his trial. His release was an act of clemency."

"But the Egyptians did start to investigate you at that time." It was a statement.

"I suppose so."

"I see." He refilled my glass. "I think we are beginning to understand one another, Simpson. You now realize that it is neither my business nor my inclination to make moral judgments. I, on the other hand, am beginning to see how your mind works in the areas we are discussing—what holds the pieces together. So now let us go back to your story about Mr. Harper and Fräulein Lipp." He glanced again at the file. "You see, for a man of your experience it is quite incredible. You suspect that Harper may be using you for some illegal purpose which will be highly profitable to him, yet you do as he asks for a mere hundred dollars."

"It was the return journey I was thinking of, sir. I thought that when he realized that I had guessed what he was up to, he would have to pay me to take the risk."

He sat back, smiling. "But you had accepted the hundred dollars *before* that possibility had occurred to you. You would not have searched the car outside Athens otherwise. You see the difficulty?"

I did. What I didn't see was the way out of it.

He lit another cigarette. "Come now, Simpson, you were emerging very sensibly from the darkness a few minutes ago. Why not continue? Either your whole story is a lie, or you have left something of importance out. Which is it? I am going to find out anyway. It will be easier for both of us if you just tell me now."

I know when I am beaten. I drank some more *raki*. "All right. I had no more choice with him than I have with you. He was blackmailing me."

"How?"

"Have you got an extradition treaty with Greece?"

"Never mind about that. I am not the police."

So I had to tell him about the traveler's checks after all.

When I had finished, he nodded. "I see" was all he said. After a moment, he got up and went to the door. It opened the instant he knocked on it. He began to give orders.

I was quite sure that he had finished with me and was telling the guards to take me away to a cell, so I swallowed the rest of the *raki* in my glass and put the matches in my pocket on the off chance that I might get away with them.

I was wrong about the cell. When he had finished speaking, he shut the door and came back.

"I have sent for some eatable food," he said.

He did not stop at the table, but went across to the telephone. I lighted a cigarette and returned the matches to the table. I don't think he noticed. He was asking for an Istanbul number and making a lot of important-sounding noise about it. Then he hung up and came back to the table.

"Now tell me everything you remember about this man Harper," he said.

I started to tell him the whole story again from the beginning, but he wanted details now.

"You say that he spoke like a German who has lived in America for some years. When did you reach that conclusion? After you heard him speak German to the man at the garage?"

"No. Hearing him speak German only confirmed the impression I had had."

"If you were to hear me speak German fluently could you tell whether it was my mother tongue or not?"

"No."

"How did he pronounce the English word 'later,' for example?"

I tried to tell him.

"You know, the German 'l' is more frontal than that," he said; "but in Turkish, before certain vowels, the 'l' is like the English consonant you were pronouncing. If you were told that this man had a Turkish background, would you disbelieve it?"

"Not if I were told it was true perhaps. But is Harper a Turkish name?"

"Is it a German one?"

"It could be an anglicization of Hipper."

"It could also be an anglicization of Harbak." He shrugged. "It could also be an alias. It most probably is. All I am trying to discover is if the man could be Turkish."

"Because of the political aspects you mentioned?"

"Obviously. Tear-gas grenades, concussion grenades, smoke grenades, six pistols, six times twenty rounds of ammunition. Six determined men equipped with that material making a surprise attack on some important person or group of persons could accomplish a great deal. There are still many supporters of the former regime. They do not like the army's firm hands."

I refrained from telling him that I wasn't so very fond of those firm hands myself.

"But, of course," he went on, "we keep our eyes on them. If they wished to attempt anything they would need help from outside. You say he had Swiss francs and West German marks as well as dollars?"

"Yes."

"Naturally it is possible that what we have here is only one small corner of a much larger plan. If so, there is a lot of money behind it. This man Harper went to a great deal of trouble and expense to get that material through. Perhaps . . ."

The telephone rang and he broke off to answer it. His call to Istanbul had come through. I understood about one word in ten of his side of the conversation. He was reporting to his boss; that much was easily gathered. My name was mentioned several times. After that he mostly listened, just putting in an occasional *evet* to show that he was getting the point. I could hear the faint quacking of the voice at the other end of the line. Finally it stopped. Tufan asked a question and received a brief reply. That was all. Tufan made a respectful sound, then hung up and looked across at me.

"Bad news for you, Simpson," he said. "The Director does not feel disposed to help you in any way. He regards the charges against you as too serious."

"I'm sorry." There seemed nothing more to say. I downed another *raki* to try to settle my stomach.

"He considers that you have not been sufficiently helpful to us. I was unable to persuade him."

"I've told you everything I know."

"It is not enough. What we need to know is more about this man Harper, who his associates and contacts are, who this Fräulein Lipp is, where the arms and ammunition are going, how they are to be used. If you could supply that information or help to supply it, of course, your case might be reconsidered."

"The only way I could possibly get information like that would be to drive on to Istanbul tomorrow as if nothing had happened, go to the Park Hotel, and wait for somebody to contact me as arranged. Is that what you're telling me I have to do?"

He sat down facing me. "It is what we might tell you to do, if we thought that we could trust you. My Director is doubtful. Naturally, he is thinking of your past record."

"What has that to do with it?"

"Isn't it obvious? Supposing you warn these people that the car was searched. Perhaps they would reward you."

"Reward me?" I laughed loudly; I think I must have been getting a bit tight. "Reward me for telling them that they are under surveillance? Are you serious? You were talking about a group of men determined enough to risk their lives. At the moment, the only contact I can identify is Harper. He may or may not be in Istanbul. Supposing he's not. Someone has to contact me to get at the car. What do I do? Whisper 'Fly, all is discovered' into his ear, and expect him to tip me before he leaves? Or do I wait until I've made a few more contacts before I tell them the good news, so that they can pass the hat round? Don't be ridiculous! They'd know at once that they wouldn't get far, because you'd pick me up again and make me talk. Reward? I'd be lucky if they let me stay alive."

He smiled. "The Director wondered if you would have the sense to see that."

But I was too annoyed by what I thought was his stupidity to grasp the implication of what he had said. I went on in English. I didn't care any more whether he understood me or not. I said: "In any case, what have *you* got to lose? If I don't turn up in Istanbul tomorrow, they'll know that something's gone wrong, and all you'll have is a couple of names that don't mean anything to you, and a secondhand Lincoln. You'll have me, too, of course, but you already know all I know about this, and you're going to look damn silly standing up in court trying to prove that I was going to carry out a one-man *coup d'état*. Your bloody Director may be one of these fine, upstanding, crap-packed bastards who thinks that everybody who doesn't smell to high heaven of sweetness and roses isn't worth a second thought, but if his brain isn't where his arse ought to be he must know he's got to trust me. He has no bloody alternative."

Tufan nodded calmly and moved the *raki* bottle just out of my reach. "Those were more or less the Director's own words," he said.

Chapter

4

I woke up the next morning with a hangover; and not just because of the *raki*. Nervous strain always has that effect on me. It was a wonder that I had been able to sleep at all.

The "eatable food" that Tufan had ordered had turned out to be yoghurt (which I detest) and some sort of sheep's milk cheese. I had just eaten some more bread while Tufan made telephone calls.

The Lincoln had been left out at the Karaagac customs post, which was closed for the night. He had had to get the Commandant out of bed to open the place up, and arrange for an army driver to take the car to the garrison repair shop. The grenades and arms, and my bag, had been removed to the local army H.Q. for examination. That meant that more people, including the customs inspector who had searched the car, had then had to be rounded up so that the stuff could be put back inside the doors again exactly as it had been found.

Even with all the authority he had, it had taken an hour just to organize the work. Then the question of a hotel room for me had come up. I was so exhausted by then that I would not have minded sleeping in a cell. I had told him so; but, of course, it had not been my comfort he had been thinking about. I had had to listen to a lecture. Supposing Harper asked me where I had spent the night; supposing this, supposing that. An agent sometimes had to take risks, but he should never take unnecessary ones; to be caught out through carelessness over trifles was unforgivable; and so on and so on. That had been the first time he had referred to me as an "agent." It had given me an uncomfortable feeling.

He had told me to meet him outside a new apartment building near the hotel at nine o'clock. He was already there when I arrived. His clothes were still quite neat, but he hadn't shaved and his eyes were puffy. He looked as if he had been up all night. Without even saying "good morning" he motioned to me to follow him, and led the way down a ramp to a small garage in the basement of the building.

The Lincoln was there and looking very clean.

"I had it washed," he said. "It had too many finger marks on it. It'll be dusty again by the time you get to Istanbul. You had better look at the doors."

I had warned him to be careful about the interior door panels. They were leather and had been quite clean when I had taken the car over in Athens. If some clumsy lout of an army fitter had made scratches or marks when replacing them, Harper would be bound to notice.

I could see nothing wrong, however. If I had not been told, I would not have known that the panels had ever been taken off.

"It's all inside there, just as it was before?" I asked.

"The customs inspector says so. All the objects were

taped out of the way of the window glasses against the metal. Photographs were taken before they were removed."

He had a set of prints in his pocket and he showed them to me. They didn't convey much. They looked like pictures of hibernating bats.

"Have you any idea where the stuff was bought?" I asked.

"A good question. The pistols and ammunition are German, of course. The grenades, all kinds, are French. That doesn't help us much. We do know that the packing was done in Greece."

"How?"

"It was padded with newspapers to stop any rattling. There are bits of Athens papers dated a week ago." He took a sealed envelope from the front seat of the car and opened it up. "These are the things that were taken from you at the frontier post," he said. "You had better put them back in your pockets now and I will keep the envelope. I have had a special tourist visa stamped in the passport validating it as a travel document within Turkey for one month. That is in case the hotel clerk should notice the expiry date, or if you are stopped by the traffic police for any reason. If Harper or any one else should happen to see it, you will simply say that the security control made no difficulties when you promised to get the passport renewed in Istanbul. The *carnet* is in order, of course, and there are your other personal papers." He handed them to me, then tore the envelope in four and put the pieces in his pocket.

"Now," he went on, "as to your orders. You know the information we want. First, the names and addresses of all contacts, their descriptions, what they say and do. Secondly, you will attempt, by keeping your ears and eyes open, to discover where and how these arms are to be used. In that connection you will take particular note of any place names mentioned, no matter in what context. Buildings or particular areas, too. Do you understand that?"

"I understand. How do I report?"

"I am coming to that. First, from the moment you leave here you will be under surveillance. The persons allocated to this duty will be changed frequently, but if you should happen to recognize any of them you will pretend not to. Only in an emergency, or in a case of extreme urgency, will you approach them. In that event they will help you if you say my name. You will report normally by telephone, but not from a telephone that goes through a private switchboard. Certainly not from the telephone in a hotel room. Use café telephones. Unless, for physical or security reasons, it is impossible, you will report at ten every night, or at eight the following morning if you have missed the ten o'clock call." He took a box of matches from his pocket. "The number is written here underneath the matches. As soon as you are certain that you will not forget it, throw the box away. If you want to communicate other than at the daily report times, a duty officer will pass your call or give you another number at which I can be reached. Is that all clear?"

"Yes." I took the matches and looked at the number.

"Just one more thing," he said. "The Director is not an amiable or kindly man. You will keep faith with us because it would not be in your interests to do otherwise. He knows that, of course. But, for him, stupidity or clumsiness in carrying out orders are just as unacceptable as bad faith and have the same consequences. I would strongly advise you to be successful. That is all, I think, unless you have any questions."

"No. No questions."

With a nod, he turned away and walked up the ramp to the street. I put my bag in the back of the car again. Ten minutes later I was clear of Edirne and on the Istanbul road.

After a few miles I identified the surveillance car as a sand-colored Peugeot two or three hundred yards behind me. It kept that distance, more or less, even when trucks or other cars got between us, or going through towns. It never closed up enough for me to see the driver clearly. When I stopped at Corlu for lunch he did not overtake me. I did not see the Peugeot while I was there.

The restaurant was a café with a few shaky tables under a small vine-covered terrace outside. I had a glass or two of *raki* and some stuffed peppers. My stomach began to feel a bit better. I sat there for over an hour. I would have liked to stay longer. There were moments like that at school, too; when one bad time has ended and the next has not yet begun. There can be days of it also, the days when one is on remand awaiting trial—not innocent, not guilty, not responsible, out of the game. I often wish that I could have an operation—not a painful or serious one, of course—just so as to be convalescent for a while after it.

The Peugeot picked me up again three minutes after I left Corlu. I stopped again only once, for petrol. I reached Istanbul soon after four.

I put the Lincoln in a garage just off Taxim Square and walked to the hotel carrying my bag.

The Park Hotel is built against the side of a hill overlooking the Bosphorus. It is the only hotel that I know of which has the foyer at the top, so that the lift takes you down to your room instead of up. My room was quite a long way down and on a corner overlooking a street with a café in it. The café had a gramophone and an inexhaustible supply of Turkish *caz* records. Almost level with the window and about fifty yards away was the top of a minaret belonging to a mosque lower down the hill. It had loudspeakers in it to amplify the voice of the muezzin, and his call to prayer was deafening. When Harper had made the reservation, he had obviously asked for the cheapest room in the hotel.

I changed into a clean shirt and sat down to wait.

At six o'clock the telephone rang.

"Monsieur Simpson?" It was a man's voice with a condescending lilt to it and an unidentifiable accent. He wasn't an Englishman or an American.

"This is Simpson," I answered.

"Miss Lipp's car is all right? You have had no accidents or trouble on the journey from Athens?"

"No. The car is fine."

"Good. Miss Lipp has a pressing engagement. This is what you are to do. You know the Hilton Hotel?"

"Yes."

"Drive the car to the Hilton at once and put it in the car park opposite the entrance to the hotel and behind the Kervansaray night club. Leave the *carnet* and insurance papers in the glove compartment and the ignition key beside the driver's seat on the floor. Is it understood?"

"It is understood, yes. But who is that speaking?"

"A friend of Miss Lipp. The car should be there in ten minutes." He rang off abruptly as if my question had been impertinent.

I sat there wondering what I ought to do. I was certainly not going to do as he had told me. The only hope I had of my making any sort of contact with the people Tufan was interested in was through the car. If I just let it go like that I would be helpless. Even without Tufan's orders to carry out I would have refused. Harper had said that I would be paid and get my letter back when the job was done. He, or someone in his behalf, would have to fulfill those conditions before I surrendered control of the car. He must have known that, too. After what had happened in Athens he could scarcely have expected me to trust to his good nature.

And what had happened to all that talk of driving for Miss Lipp while she was in Turkey?

I hid the *carnet* under some shelf lining paper on top of the wardrobe and went out. It took me about ten minutes to walk to the Hilton.

I approached the car park briskly, swinging my keys in my hand as if I were going to pick up a car already there. I guessed that either the man who had telephoned or someone acting on his instructions would be waiting for the Lincoln to arrive, all ready to drive it away the instant I had gone. In Istanbul, it is unwise to leave even the poorest car unlocked and unattended for very long.

I spotted him almost immediately. He was standing at the outer end of the Hilton driveway smoking a cigarette and staring into the middle distance, as if he were trying to decide whether to go straight home to his wife or visit his girl friend first. Remembering that I would have to give Tufan his description, I took very careful note of him. He was about forty-five and thickset, with a barrel chest and a mop of crinkly gray hair above a brown puffy face. The eyes were brown, too. He was wearing a thin light-gray suit, yellow socks, and plaited leather sandals. Height about five ten, I thought.

I walked through the car park to make sure that there were no other possibilities there, then came out the other side and walked back along the street for another glimpse of him.

He was looking at his watch. The car should have been there by then if I were following instructions.

I walked straight back to the Park Hotel. As I unlocked the door to my room I could hear the telephone inside ringing.

It was the same voice again, but peremptory now.

"Simpson? I understand that the car is not yet delivered. What are you doing?"

"Who is that speaking?"

"The friend of Miss Lipp. Answer my question, please. Where is the car?"

"The car is quite safe and will remain so."

"What are you talking about?"

"The *carnet* is in the hotel strong-room and the car is garaged. It will remain that way until I hand it over to Mr. Harper or someone holding credentials from Mr. Harper."

"The car is the property of Miss Lipp."

"The *carnet* is in the name of Miss Lipp," I answered; "but the car was placed in my care by Mr. Harper. I am responsible for it. I don't know Miss Lipp except by name. I don't know you *even* by name. You see the difficulty?"

"Wait."

I heard him start to say something to someone with him: "*Il dit que . . .*" And then he clamped a hand over the telephone.

I waited. After a few moments he spoke again. "I will come to your hotel. Remain there." Without waiting for my agreement, he hung up.

I went upstairs to the foyer and told the desk clerk that I would be out on the terrace if I were wanted. The terrace was crowded, but I eventually managed to find a table and order a drink. I was quite prepared to make the contact; but I had not liked the sound of the man on the telephone, and preferred to encounter him in a public place rather than in the privacy of my room.

I had left my name with the head waiter, and after about twenty minutes I saw him pointing me out to a tall, cadaverous man with a narrow, bald head and large projecting ears. The man came over. He was wearing a cream-and-brown-striped sports shirt and tan linen slacks. He had a long, petulant upper lip and a mouth that drooped at the corners.

"Simpson?"

"Yes."

He sat down facing me. Brown eyes, one gold tooth left side lower jaw, gold-and-onyx signet ring on little finger of left hand; I made mental notes.

"Who are you?" I asked.

"My name is Fischer."

"Will you have a drink, Mr. Fischer?"

"No. I wish to clear this misunderstanding relative to Miss Lipp's car."

"There is no misunderstanding in my mind, Mr. Fischer," I answered. "My orders from Mr. Harper were quite explicit."

"Your orders were to await orders at the hotel," he snapped. "You have not complied with them."

I looked respectfully apologetic. "I am not doubting that you have a perfect right to give those orders, Mr. Fischer, but I assumed, naturally, that Mr. Harper would be here, or if not here in person, that he would have given a written authorization. That is a very valuable car and I . . ."

"Yes, yes." He broke in impatiently. "I understand. The point is that Mr. Harper has been delayed until tomorrow afternoon and Miss Lipp wishes her car at once."

"I'm sorry."

He leaned across the table towards me and I caught a whiff of after-shave lotion. "Mr. Harper would not be pleased that you put Miss Lipp to the trouble of coming to Istanbul herself to claim her car," he said menacingly.

"I thought Miss Lipp *was* in Istanbul."

"She is at the villa," he said shortly. "Now we will have no more of this nonsense, please. You and I will go and get the car immediately."

"If you have Mr. Harper's written authority, of course."

"I have Mr. Harper's authority."

"May I see it, sir?"

"That is not necessary."

"I'm afraid that is for me to decide."

He sat back breathing deeply. "I will give you one more chance," he said after a pause. "Either you hand over the car immediately or steps will be taken to *compel* you to do so."

As he said the word "compel," his right hand came out and deliberately flicked the drink in front of me into my lap.

At that moment something happened to me. I had been through an awful twenty-four hours, of course; but I don't think it was only that. I suddenly felt as if my whole life had been spent trying to defend myself against people compelling me to do this or that, and always succeeding because they had all the power on their side; and then, just as suddenly, I realized that for once the power was mine; for once I wasn't on my own.

I picked up the glass, set it back on the table, and dabbed at my trousers with my handkerchief. He watched me intently, like a boxer waiting for the other man to get to his feet after a knockdown, ready to move in for the kill.

I called the waiter over. "If this gentleman wished to make a report about a missing car to the police, where should he go?"

"There is a police post in Taxim Square, sir."

"Thank you. I spilled my drink. Wipe the table and bring me another, please."

As the waiter got busy with his cloth, I looked across at Fischer. "We could go there together," I said. "Or, if you would prefer it, I could go alone and explain the situation. Of course, I expect the police would want to get in touch with you. Where should I tell them to find you?"

The waiter had finished wiping the table and was moving away. Fischer was staring at me uncertainly.

"What are you talking about?" he said. "Who said anything about the police?"

"You were talking of compelling me to hand over the car to you. Only the police could make me do that." I paused. "Unless, that is, you had some other sort of compulsion in mind. In that case, perhaps I should go to the police anyway."

He did not know what to say to that. He just stared. It was all I could do not to smile. It was quite obvious that he knew perfectly well what was hidden in the car, and that the very last thing he wanted was the police taking an interest in it. Now he had to make sure that I didn't go to them.

"There is no need for that," he said finally.

"I'm not so sure." The waiter brought me the drink and I motioned to Fischer. "This gentleman will pay."

Fischer hesitated, then threw some money on the table and stood up. He was doing his best to regain control of the situation by trying to look insulted.

"Very well," he said stiffly, "we shall have to wait for Mr. Harper's arrival. It is very inconvenient and I shall report your insubordinate behavior to him. He will not employ you again."

And then, of course, I had to go too far. "When he knows how careless you can be, maybe he won't have much use for you either."

It was a silly thing to say, because it implied that I knew that the situation was not what it appeared on the surface, and I wasn't supposed to know.

His eyes narrowed. "What did Harper tell you about me?"

"Until tonight I didn't even know you existed. What should he have told me?"

Without answering he turned and went.

I finished my drink slowly and planned my movements for the evening. It would be best, I thought, to dine in the hotel. Apart from the fact that the cost of the meal would go on the bill, which Harper would be paying, I wasn't too keen on going out just then. Fischer had seemed to accept the situation; but there was just a chance that he might change his mind and decide to get rough after all. Tufan's men would be covering me, presumably, but I didn't know what their orders were. If someone were to beat me up, it wouldn't be much consolation to know that they were standing by taking notes. It was certainly better to stay in. The only problem was the ten o'clock telephone report. I had already noticed that the public telephones in the foyer were handled by an operator who put the calls through the hotel switchboard, so I would have to risk going out later. Unless, that is, I missed the ten o'clock call and left it until the morning at eight. The only trouble was that I would then have to explain to Tufan why I had done so, and I did not want to have to explain that I was afraid of anything that Fischer might do. My trousers were still damp where he had upset the drink over me, and I was still remembering how good it had felt to make him climb down and do what I wanted. I could not expect Tufan to realize how success-fully I had handled Fischer if I had to start by admitting that I had been too nervous to leave the hotel afterwards.

All I could do was to minimize the risk. The nearest café I knew of was the one on the side street below my room. With so many lighted hotel windows above, the street would not be too dark for safety. The telephone would probably be on the bar, but with any luck the noise of the music would compensate for the lack of privacy. Anyway, it would have to do.

By the time I had finished dinner I was feeling so tired that I could hardly keep my eyes open. I went back to the terrace and drank brandy until it was time for the call.

As I walked from the hotel entrance to the road I had to get out of the way of a taxi and was able to glance over my

shoulder casually as if to make sure that it was safe to walk
on. There was a man in a chauffeur's cap about twenty yards
behind me.

Because of the contours of the hill and the way the street
twisted and turned, it took me longer than I had expected
to get to the café. The man in the chauffeur's cap stayed behind me. I listened carefully to his footsteps. If he had
started to close in, I would have made a dash for the café;
but he kept his distance, so I assumed that he was one of
Tufan's men. All the same it was not a very pleasant walk.

The telephone was on the wall behind the bar. There
was no coin box and you had to ask the proprietor to get the
number so that he knew what to charge you. He couldn't
speak anything but Turkish, so I wrote the number down
and made signs. The noise of the music wasn't as bad inside
the place as it sounded from my room, but it was loud
enough.

Tufan answered immediately and characteristically.

"You are late."

"I'm sorry. You told me not to call through the hotel
switchboard. I am in a café."

"You went to the Hilton Hotel just after six. Why?
Make your report."

I told him what had happened. I had to repeat the descriptions of the man at the Hilton car park and of Fischer
so that he could write them down. My report on the meeting with Fischer seemed to amuse him at first. I don't know
why. I had not expected any thanks, but I felt that I had
earned at least a grunt of approval for my quick thinking.
Instead, he made me repeat the conversation and then began harping on Fischer's reference to a villa outside Istanbul
and asking a lot of questions for which I had no answers. It
was very irritating; although, of course, I didn't say so. I just
asked if he had any additional orders for me.

"No, but I have some information. Harper and the Lipp woman have reservations on an Olympic Airways plane from Athens tomorrow afternoon. It arrives at four. The earliest you will hear from him probably will be an hour after that."

"Supposing he gives me the same orders as Fischer—to hand over the car with its papers—what do I do?"

"Ask for your wages and the letter you wrote."

"Supposing he gives them to me."

"Then you must give up the car, but forget to bring the *carnet* and the insurance papers. Or remind him of his promise that you could work for Miss Lipp. Be persistent. Use your intelligence. Imagine that he is an ordinary tourist whom you are trying to cheat. Now, if there is nothing more, you can go to bed. Report to me again tomorrow night."

"One moment, sir. There is something." I had had an idea.

"What is it?"

"There is something that you could do, sir. If, before I speak to Harper, I could have a license as an official guide with tomorrow's date on it, it might help."

"How?"

"It would show that in the expectation of driving Miss Lipp on her tour, I had gone to the trouble and expense of obtaining the license. It would look as if I had taken him seriously. If he or she really wanted a driver for the car it might make a difference."

He did not answer immediately. Then he said: "Good, very good."

"Thank you, sir."

"You see, Simpson, when you apply your intelligence to carrying out orders instead of seeing only the difficulties, you become effective." It was just like The Bristle in one of his good moods. "You remember, of course," he went on, "that, as a foreigner, you could not hold a guide's license. Do you think Harper might know that?"

"I'm almost sure he doesn't. If he does, I can say that I bribed someone to get it. He would believe me."

"I would believe you myself, Simpson." He chuckled fatuously, enchanted by his own joke. "Very well, you shall have it by noon, delivered to the hotel."

"You will need a photograph of me for it."

"We have one. Don't tell me you have forgotten so soon. And a word of caution. You know only a few words of Turkish. Don't attract attention to yourself so that you are asked to show the license. It might cause trouble with museum guards. You understand?"

"I understand."

He hung up. I paid the proprietor for the call and left.

Outside, the man in the chauffeur's cap was waiting up the street. He walked ahead of me back to the hotel. I suppose he knew why I had been to the café.

There was a guide to Istanbul on sale at the concierge's desk. I bought one with the idea of brushing up on my knowledge of the Places of Interest and how to get to them. On my way down to my room I had to laugh to myself. "Never volunteer for anything," my father had said. Well, I hadn't exactly volunteered for what I was doing now, but it seemed to me that I was suddenly getting bloody conscientious about it.

I spent most of the following morning in bed. Just before noon I got dressed and went up to the foyer to see if Tufan had remembered about the guide's license. He had; it was in a sealed Ministry of Tourism envelope in my mailbox.

For a few minutes I felt quite good about that. It showed, I thought, that Tufan kept his promises and that I could rely on him to back me. Then I realized that there was another way of looking at it. I had asked for a license and I had promptly received one; Tufan expected results and wasn't giving me the smallest excuse for not getting them.

I had made up my mind not to have any drinks that day so as to keep a clear head for Harper; but now I changed my mind. You can't have a clear head when there's a sword hanging over it. I was careful though and only had three or four *rakis*. I felt much better for them, and after lunch I went down to my room to take a nap.

I must have needed it badly, for I was still asleep when the phone rang at five. I almost fell off the bed in my haste to pick it up, and the start that it gave me made my head ache.

"Arthur?" It was Harper's voice.

"Yes."

"You know who this is?"

"Yes."

"Car okay?"

"Yes."

"Then what have you been stalling for?"

"I haven't been stalling."

"Fischer says you refused to deliver the car."

"You told me to wait for *your* instructions, so I waited. You didn't tell me to hand the car over to a perfect stranger without any proof of his authority . . ."

"All right, all right, skip it! Where is the car?"

"In a garage near here."

"Do you know where Sariyer is?"

"Yes."

"Get the car right away and hit the Sariyer road. When you get to Yeniköy look at your mileage reading, then drive on towards Sariyer for exactly four more miles. On your right you'll come to a small pier with some boats tied up alongside it. On the left of the road opposite the pier you'll see a driveway entrance belonging to a villa. The name of the villa is Sardunya. Have you got that?"

"Yes."

"You should be here in about forty minutes. Right?"

"I will leave now."

Sariyer is a small fishing port at the other end of the Bosphorus where it widens out to the Black Sea, and the road to it from Istanbul runs along the European shore. I wondered if I should try to contact Tufan before I left and report the address I had been given, then decided against it. Almost certainly, he had had Harper followed from the airport, and in any case I would be followed to the villa. There would be no point in reporting.

I went to the garage, paid the bill, and got the car. The early-evening traffic was heavy and it took me twenty minutes to get out of the city. It was a quarter to six when I reached Yeniköy. The same Peugeot which had followed me down from Edirne was following me again. I slowed for a moment to check the mileage and then pushed on.

The villas of the Bosphorus vary from small waterfront holiday places, with window boxes and little boathouses, to things like palaces. Quite a lot of them *were* palaces once; and before the capital was moved from Istanbul to Ankara the diplomatic corps used to have summer embassy buildings out along the Bosphorus, where there are cool Black Sea breezes even when the city is sweltering. The Kösk Sardunya looked as if it had started out in some such way.

The entrance to the drive was flanked by huge stone pillars with wrought-iron gates. The drive itself was several hundred yards long and wound up the hillside through an avenue of big trees which also served to screen the place from the road below. Finally, it left the trees and swept into the gravel courtyard in front of the villa.

It was one of those white stucco wedding-cake buildings of the kind you see in the older parts of Nice and Monte Carlo. Some French or Italian architect must have been imported around the turn of the century to do the job. It had everything—a terrace with pillars and balustrades, balconies, marble steps up to the front portico, a fountain in the courtyard, statuary, a wonderful view out over the Bosphorus—and it was huge. It was also run down. The stucco was peeling in places and some of the cornice moldings had crumbled or broken away. The fountain basin had no water in it. The courtyard was fringed with weeds.

As I drove in, I saw Fischer get up from a chair on the terrace and go through a french window into the house. So I just pulled up at the foot of the marble steps and waited. After a moment or two, Harper appeared under the portico and I got out of the car. He came down the steps.

"What took you so long?"

"They had to make out a bill at the garage, and then there was the evening traffic."

"Well . . ." He broke off as he noticed me looking past him and over his shoulder.

A woman was coming down the steps.

He smiled slightly. "Ah yes. I was forgetting. You haven't met your employer. Honey, this is Arthur Simpson. Arthur, this is Miss Lipp."

Chapter

5

Some men can make a good guess at a woman's age just by looking at her face and figure. I never can. I think that this may be because, in spite of Mum, I fundamentally respect women. Yes, it must be that. If she is very attractive, but obviously not a young girl, I always think of twenty-eight. If she has let herself go a bit, but is obviously not elderly, I think of forty-five. For some reason I never think of any ages in between those—or outside them, for that matter—except my own, that is.

Miss Lipp made me think of twenty-eight. In fact she was thirty-six; but I only found that out later. She looked twenty-eight to me. She was tall with short brownish-blond hair, and the kind of figure that you have to notice, no matter what dress covers it. She also had the sort of eyes, insolent, sleepy, and amused, and the full good-humored mouth which tell you that she knows you can't help watching the way her body moves, and that she doesn't give a damn whether you do so or not; watching is not going to get you anywhere anyway. She wasn't wearing a dress that first time; just white slacks and sandals, and a loose white shirt. Her complexion was golden brown and the only make-up she was wearing was lipstick. Obviously, she had just bathed and changed.

She nodded to me. "Hullo. No trouble with the car?" She had the same combination of accents as Harper.

"No, madam."

"That's good." She did not seem surprised.

Fischer was coming down the steps behind her. Harper glanced at him.

"Okay, Hans, you'd better run Arthur into Sariyer." To me he said: "You can take the ferryboat back to town. Are the *carnet* and Green Card in the glove compartment?"

"Of course not. They are in the hotel safe."

"I told you to put them in the glove compartment," said Fischer angrily.

I kept my eyes on Harper. "*You* didn't tell me," I said; "and you didn't tell me to take orders from your servant."

Fischer swore angrily in German, and Miss Lipp burst out laughing.

"But isn't he a servant?" I asked blandly; "he behaved like one, though not a very good one, perhaps."

Harper raised a repressive hand. "Okay, Arthur, you can cut that out. Mr. Fischer is a guest here and he only meant to be helpful. I'll arrange to have the documents picked up from you tomorrow before you leave. You'll get paid off when you hand them over."

My stomach heaved. "But I understood, sir, that I was to act as Miss Lipp's driver while she is in Turkey."

"That's okay, Arthur. I'll hire someone locally."

"I can drive the car," said Fischer impatiently.

Harper and Miss Lipp both turned on him. Harper said something sharply in German and she added in English: "Besides, you don't know the roads."

"And I do know the roads, madam." I was trying hard to make my inner panic come out sounding like respectful indignation. "Only today I went to the trouble and expense of obtaining an official guide's license so that I could do the job without inconvenience to you. I was a guide in Istanbul before." I turned to Harper and thrust the license under his nose. "Look, sir!"

He frowned at it and me incredulously. "You mean you really *want* the job?" he demanded. "I thought all you wanted was this." He took my letter out of his pocket.

"Certainly, I want that, sir." It was all I could do to stop myself from reaching out for it. "But you are also paying me a hundred dollars for three or four days' work." I did my best to produce a grin. "As I told you in Athens, sir, for that money I do not have to be persuaded to work."

He glanced at her and she answered, with a shrug, in German. I understood the last three words: ". . . man English speaks."

His eyes came to me again. "You know, Arthur," he said thoughtfully, "you've changed. You could be off the hook if you wanted, but now you don't want to be off. Why?"

This was just answerable. I looked at the letter in his hand. "You didn't send that. I was afraid all the time that you'd sent it anyway, out of spite."

"Even though it would have cost me three hundred dollars?"

"It wouldn't have cost you anything. The checks would have been returned to you eventually."

"That's true." He nodded. "Not bad, Arthur. Now tell me what you meant when you told Mr. Fischer that he'd been careless. What did you think he'd been careless about?"

They were all three waiting for my answer to that. The men's suspicion of me was in the air and Miss Lipp had smelled it as well. What was more, she didn't look in the least puzzled by what Harper was saying. Whatever the game was, they were all in it.

I did the best I could. "Why? Because of the way he'd behaved, of course. Because he *had* been careless. Oh, he knew your name all right and he knew enough to get in touch with me, but I knew he couldn't be acting on your orders."

"How did you know?"

I pointed to the letter. "Because of that. You'd told me it was your insurance. You'd know I wouldn't turn the car over to a complete stranger without getting my letter back. He didn't even mention it."

Harper looked at Fischer. "You see?"

"I was only trying to save time," said Fischer angrily. "I have said so. This does not explain why he used that word."

"No, it doesn't," I said. The only way was to bull it through. "But this does. When he started threatening me I offered to go with him to the police and settle the matter. I've never seen anyone back down so fast in my life."

"That is a lie!" Fischer shouted; but he wasn't so sure of himself now.

I looked at Harper. "Anyone who pulls that sort of bluff without knowing what to do when it's called, is careless to my way of thinking. If Mr. Fischer had been a dishonest servant instead of your helpful guest, you'd have said I'd been pretty careless to let him get away with a fourteen-thousand-dollar car. I'd be lucky if that was all you said."

There was a brief silence, then Harper nodded. "Well, Arthur, I guess Mr. Fischer won't mind accepting your apology. Let's say it was a misunderstanding."

Fischer shrugged.

Just what Harper thought I was making of the situation I cannot imagine. Even if I hadn't known what was hidden in the car, I would have realized by now that there was something really fishy going on. Miss Lipp, in Turkey for a little ten-day tourist trip with a Lincoln and a villa the size of the Taj Mahal, was sufficiently improbable. The she-nanigans over the delivery of the car had been positively grotesque.

However, it was soon apparent that nothing I might think or suspect was going to give Harper any sleepless nights.

"All right, Arthur," he said, "you've gotten yourself a deal. A hundred a week. You still have that fifty dollars I gave you?"

"Yes, sir."

"Will that take care of the bill at the Park?"

"I think so."

"Right. Here's the hundred you have coming for the trip down. Go back to town now. In the morning check out of the hotel. Then take a ferryboat back to Sariyer pier so that you get there around eleven. Someone will meet you. We'll find a room for you here."

"Thank you, sir, but I can find a room in a hotel."

"There isn't a hotel nearer than Sariyer, and that's too far away. You'd have to use the car to get to and fro, and it'd always be there when we wanted it here. Besides, we've got plenty of rooms."

"Very well, sir. May I have my letter?"

He put it back in his pocket. "Sure. When you're paid off at the end of the job. That was the deal, remember?"

"I remember," I said grimly.

Of course, he thought that, by still holding the letter over me, he was making sure that I toed the line, and that, if I happened to see or hear anything that I shouldn't, I would be too scared to do anything but keep my mouth shut about it. The fact that he wasn't being as clever as he thought was no consolation to me. I wanted to get back to Athens and Nicki, but I wanted that letter first.

"You will drive," said Fischer.

I said "Good night, madam," to Miss Lipp, but she didn't seem to hear. She was already walking back up the steps with Harper.

Fischer got into the back seat. I thought at first that he merely intended, in a petty way, to show me who was boss; but, as I drove back down to the road, I saw him looking over the door panels. He was obviously still suspicious. I thanked my stars that the packing had been carefully done. It was almost comforting to see the sand-colored Peugeot in the driving mirror.

He didn't say anything to me on the way. In Sariyer, I stopped at the pier approach and turned the car for him. Then I got out and opened the door as if he were royalty. I'd hoped it would make him feel a bit silly, but it didn't seem to. Without a word he got in behind the wheel, gave me a black look, and tore off back along the coast road like a maniac.

The Peugeot had stopped and turned about a hundred yards back, and a man was scrambling out of its front passenger seat. He slammed the door and the Peugeot shot away after the Lincoln. There was a ferryboat already at the pier, and I did not wait to see if the man who had got out followed me. I suppose he did.

I was back at the Kabatas ferry pier soon after eight and shared a *dolmus* cab going up to Taxim Square. Then I walked down to the hotel and had a drink or two.

I needed them. I had managed to do what Tufan wanted, up to a point. I was in touch with Harper and would for the moment remain so. On the other hand, by agreeing to stay at the villa I had put myself virtually *out* of touch with Tufan; at least as far as regular contact was concerned. There was no way of knowing what life at the villa was going to be like, nor what would be expected of me there. It might be easy for me to get out to a safe telephone, or it might be quite difficult. If I were seen telephoning, Harper would immediately get suspicious. Who did I know in Istanbul? What was the number? Call it again. And so on. Yet I didn't see how I could have refused to stay there. If I had argued the point any further, Harper might have changed his mind about keeping me on. Tufan couldn't have it both ways; and I made up my mind to tell him so if he started moaning at me.

I had some dinner and went down to the café beside the hotel. A man with a porter's harness on his back followed me this time.

Tufan did not moan at me as a matter of fact; but when I had finished my report he was silent for so long that I thought he'd hung up. I said: "Hullo."

"I was thinking," he said; "it will be necessary for us to meet tonight. Are you in the café in the street by the hotel?"

"Yes."

"Wait five minutes, then go up to the hotel and walk along the street past it for about a hundred yards. You will see a small brown car parked there."

"The Peugeot that's been following me?"

"Yes. Open the door and get in beside the driver. He will know where to take you. Is that clear?"

"Yes."

I paid for the telephone call and bought a drink. When the five minutes were up I left.

As I approached the Peugeot, the driver leaned across and pushed open the door for me to get in. Then he drove off past the hotel and down the hill towards the Necati Bey Avenue.

He was a young, plump, dark man. The car smelled of cigarettes, hair oil, and stale food. In his job, I suppose, he had to eat most of his meals sitting in the car. There was a V.H.F. two-way taxi radio fitted under the dash, and every now and again Turkish voices would squawk through the loudspeaker. He appeared not to be listening to them. After a minute or so he began to talk to me in French.

"Did you like driving the Lincoln?" he asked.

"Yes, it's a good car."

"But too big and long. I saw the trouble you had in the narrow streets this afternoon."

"It's very fast though. Were you able to keep up with him when he drove back to the villa?"

"Oh, he stopped about a kilometer up the road and began looking at the doors. Did they rattle?"

"Not that I noticed. Did he stop long?"

"A minute or two. After that he did not go so fast. But this little . . ."

He broke off and picked up a microphone as a fresh lot of squawks came over the radio.

"*Evet, effendi, evet*," he answered, then put the microphone back. "But this little machine can show those big ones a thing or two. On a narrow hill with corners I can leave them standing."

He had turned onto the Avenue and we were running parallel to the shore.

"Where are we going?" I asked.

"I am not permitted to answer questions."

We were passing the state entrance to the Dolmabahçe Palace now.

It was built in the last century when the Sultans gave up wearing robes and turbans and took to black frock coats and the fez. From the sea it looks like a lakeside grand hotel imported from Switzerland; but from the road, because of the very high stone wall enclosing the grounds, it looks like a prison. There is about half a mile of this wall running along the right-hand side of the road, and just to look up at it gave me an uncomfortable feeling. It reminded me of the yard at Maidstone.

Then I saw a light high up on the wall ahead, and the driver began to slow down.

"What are we stopping here for?" I asked.

He did not answer.

The light came from a reflector flood and the beam of it shone down vertically onto an armed sentry. Behind him was a pair of huge iron-bound wooden gates. One of them was half open.

The car stopped just short of the gates and the driver opened his door.

"We get out," he said.

I joined him on the roadway and he led the way up to the gates. He said something to the sentry, who motioned us on. We went through the gap between the gates and turned left. There was a light burning in what I assumed was the guard room. He led the way up a low flight of steps to the door. Inside was a bare room with a table and chair. A young lieutenant—I suppose he was orderly officer of the day—sat on the table talking to the sergeant of the guard, who was standing. As we came in, the officer stood up, too, and said something to the driver.

He turned to me. "You have a guide's license," he said. "You are to show it to this officer."

I did so. He handed it back to me, picked up a flashlight, and said in French: "Follow me, please."

The driver stayed behind with the sergeant of the guard. I followed the lieutenant down the steps again and across some uneven cobblestones to a narrow roadway running along the side of a building which seemed to be a barracks. The windows showed lights and I could hear the sound of voices and a radio playing *caz*. There were light posts at intervals, and, although the surface of the road was broken in places, it was just possible to see where one was walking. Then we went through a high archway out of the barracks area into some sort of garden. Here it was very dark. There

was some moonlight and I could see parts of the white
bulk of the palace looming to the left of us, but trees
shadowed the ground. The lieutenant switched on his flashlight and told me to be careful where I walked. It was necessary advice. Restoration work seemed to be in progress.
There were loose flagstones and masonry rubble everywhere. Finally, however, we came to a solidly paved walk.
Ahead was a doorway and, beside it, a lighted window.

The lieutenant opened the door and went in. The light
came from a janitor's room just inside, and, as the lieutenant entered, a man in a drab blue uniform came out. He
had some keys in his hand. The lieutenant said something
to him. The janitor answered briefly, and then, with a curious glance at me, led the way across a hall and up a staircase, switching on lights as he went. At the landing he
turned off down a long corridor with a lot of closed doors
along one side and grilled, uncurtained windows on the
other. There was carpet on the floor with a narrow drugget
along the middle to save wear.

From the proportions of the staircase and the height of
the ceilings it was obvious that we were in a large building;
but there was nothing noticeably palatial about that part
of it. We might have been in a provincial town hall. The
walls were covered with dingy oil paintings. There seemed
to be hundreds of them, mostly landscapes with cattle or
battle scenes, and all with the same yellowy-brown varnish
color. I don't know anything about paintings. I suppose
they must have been valuable or they would not have been
in a palace; but I found them depressing, like the smell of
mothballs.

There was a pair of heavy metal doors at the end of that
corridor, and beyond it more corridors and more paintings.

"We are in what used to be the palace harem now," the
lieutenant said impressively. "The steel doors guarded it.
Each woman had her own suite of rooms. Now certain im-

portant government departments have their offices here."

I was about to say: "Ah, taken over by the eunuchs, you mean," but thought better of it. He did not look as if he cared for jokes. Besides, I had had a long day and was feeling tired. We went on through another lot of steel doors. I was resigned to more corridors, when the janitor stopped and unlocked the door of one of the rooms. The lieutenant turned on the lights and motioned me in.

It was not much larger than my room at the Park, but probably the height of the ceiling and the heavy red-and-gold curtains over the window made it seem smaller. The walls were hung with patterned red silk and several large paintings. There was a parquet floor and a white marble fireplace. A dozen gilt armchairs stood around the walls, as if the room had just been cleared for dancing. The office desk and chairs standing in the center looked like a party of badly dressed gate crashers.

"You may sit down and you may smoke," the lieutenant said; "but please be careful if you smoke to put out your cigarettes in the fireplace."

The janitor left, shutting the door behind him. The lieutenant sat down at the desk and began to use the telephone.

The paintings in the room were, with one exception, of the kind I had seen in the corridors, only bigger. On one wall was a Dutch fishing boat in a storm; facing it, alongside a most un-Turkish group of nymphs bathing in a woodland stream, was a Russian cavalry charge. The painting over the fireplace, however, was undoubtedly Turkish. It showed a bearded man in a frock coat and fez facing three other bearded men who were looking at him as if he had B.O. or had said something disgusting. Two of the group wore glittering uniforms.

When the lieutenant had finished telephoning, I asked him what the painting was about.

"That is the leaders of the nation demanding the abdication of Sultan Abdul Hamid the Second."

"Isn't that rather a strange picture to have in a Sultan's palace?"

"Not in this palace. A greater man than any of the Sultans died here, greater even than Suleiman." He gave me a hard, challenging look, daring me to deny it.

I agreed hastily. He went into a long rambling account of the iniquities of the Bayar-Menderes government and of the reasons why it had been necessary for the army to clean out that rats' nest and form the Committee of National Union. Over the need to shoot down without mercy all who were trying to wreck the Committee's work, especially those members of the Democratic party who had escaped justice at the army's hands, he became so vehement that he was still haranguing me when Major Tufan walked into the room.

I felt almost sorry for the lieutenant. He snapped to attention, mumbling apologies like a litany. Tufan had been impressive enough in civilian clothes; in uniform and with a pistol on his belt he looked as if he were on his way to take charge of a firing squad—and looking forward keenly to the job. He listened to the lieutenant for about five seconds, then dismissed him with a flick of a hand.

As the door closed on the lieutenant, Tufan appeared to notice me. "Do you know that President Kemal Atatürk died in this palace?" he asked.

"I gathered so from the lieutenant."

"It was in 1938. The Director was much with him before the end and the President talked freely. One thing he said the Director has always remembered. 'If I can live another fifteen years, I can make Turkey a democracy. If I die sooner, it will take three generations.' That young officer probably represents the type of difficulty he had in mind." He put his

briefcase on the desk and sat down. "Now, as to your difficulties. We have both had time to think. What do you
propose?"

"Until I know what it's going to be like at the villa, I
don't see how I can propose anything."

"As you are their chauffeur, it will obviously be necessary
for you to attend to the fueling of the car. There is a garage
outside Sariyer that you could go to. It has a telephone."

"I had thought of that, but it may not be reliable. It depends on how much the car is used. For example, if I only
drive into Istanbul and back, I can't pretend to need petrol
immediately. That car takes over a hundred liters. If I were
always going to the garage at a fixed time to fill up no matter what mileage I had driven, they would become suspicious."

"We can dispense with the fixed time. I have arranged
for a twenty-four-hour watch. And even if you foresee future difficulties, you should be able to make one single call
to report on them. After that, if necessary, we will use a different method. It will entail more risk for you, but that
cannot be avoided. You will have to write your reports.
Then you will put the report inside an empty cigarette
packet. The person following you at the time—I have arranged to have the car changed every day—will then pick
the reports up."

"You mean you expect me to throw them out of the window and hope they won't notice?"

"Of course not. You will drop them whenever you find a
suitable moment when you have stopped and are outside
the car."

I thought it over; that part of it might not be so bad. I
would just have to make sure that I had plenty of cigarette
packets. What I did not like was having to write out the
reports. I said so.

"There is a slight risk, I agree," he said; "but you will

have to take it. Remember, they will only search you if you have given them reason to suspect you. You must be careful not to."

"I still have to write the reports."

"You can do that in the toilet. I do not imagine you will be observed there. Now, as to our communicating information and orders to you." He opened his briefcase and took out a small portable transistor radio of the type I had seen German tourists carrying. "You will carry this in your bag. If it should be seen, or you should be heard using it, you will say that it was given to you by a German client. Normally it receives only standard broadcast frequencies, but this one has been modified. I will show you." he slipped it out of the carrying case, took the back off, and pointed to a small switch just by the battery compartment. "If you operate that switch it will receive V.H.F. transmissions on a fixed frequency from up to half a mile away. The transmissions will be made to you from a surveillance car. It is a system we have tried out, and, providing there are no large obstacles such as buildings between the two points, it works. Your listening times will be seven in the morning and eleven at night. Is that clear? For security it will be better if you use the earphone attachment."

"I see. You say it has been modified. Does that mean that it won't receive ordinary broadcasts? Because if so I couldn't explain it . . ."

"It will work normally unless you move this switch." He replaced the back. "Now then, I have some information for you. Both Harper and Miss Lipp are traveling on Swiss passports. We had no time at the airport to discover, without arousing suspicion, if the passports were genuine or not. The relevant particulars are as follows: Walter Karl Harper, aged thirty-eight, described as an engineer, place of birth Berne, and Elizabeth Maria Lipp, aged thirty-six, described as a student, place of birth Schaffhausen."

"A student?"

"Anyone can be described as a student. It is meaningless. Now, as to the Kösk Sardunya." He referred to a paper in the briefcase. "It is the property of the widow of a former minister in the government of President Inönü. She is nearly eighty now and has for some years lived quietly with her daughter in Izmir. She has from time to time tried to sell Sardunya, but nobody has wished to buy at the price she asks. For the past two years, she has leased it furnished to a NATO naval mission which had business in the zone. The mission's work ended at the beginning of the year. Her agent here in Istanbul was unable to find another tenant until three months ago. Then he received an inquiry from an Austrian named Fischer—yes, exactly—who was staying at the Hilton Hotel. Fischer's other names are Hans Andreas, and he gave an address in Vienna. He wanted a furnished villa for two months, not a particular villa, but one in that neighborhood and near to the shore. He was willing to pay well for a short lease, and gave a deposit in Swiss francs. On the lease, which is in his name, his occupation is given as manufacturer. He arrived three weeks ago, when the lease began, and has not registered with the police. We have not yet traced the record of his entry, so we do not have all passport particulars about him."

"What is he a manufacturer of?"

"We do not know. We have sent an inquiry to Interpol, but I expect a negative reply. We received negative replies on both Harper and Lipp. That increases the probability that they are politicals."

"Or that they are using aliases."

"Perhaps. Now, the other personnel at the villa. There are a husband and wife who live over what was the stabling. Their name is Hamul and they are old servants who have been there for some years as caretakers and who do cleaning work. Then there is the cook. Through the owner's agent,

Fischer requested a cook with experience of Italian cooking. The agent found a Turkish Cypriot named Geven who had worked in Italy. The police here have had trouble with him. He is a good cook, but he gets drunk and attacks people. He served a short prison sentence for wounding a waiter. It is believed that the agent did not know this when he recommended the man to Fischer."

"Is there anything against the couple?"

"No. They are honest enough." He put his papers away. "That is all we know so far, but, as you see, the shape of a conspiracy begins to unfold. One person goes ahead to establish a base of operations, a second person arranges for the purchase of weapons, a third arrives with the means of transporting them and a prepared cover story. Probably, the real leaders have not yet arrived. When they do, it will be your duty to report the fact. Meanwhile, your orders are, specifically, first to ascertain whether the weapons have been removed from the car or not, and secondly, if they have been removed, where they are cached. The first will be easy, the second may be difficult."

"If not impossible."

He shrugged. "Well, you must run no risks at this stage. Thirdly, you will continue to listen for any mention of names—names of persons or places—and report movements. Finally, you will listen particularly for any political content in their conversation. The smallest hint may be of importance in that connection. That is all, I think. Have you any questions?"

"Dozens," I said; "only I don't know what they are at the moment."

I could see he hadn't liked that at once. It was a bit cheeky, I suppose; but I was really tired of him.

He pursed his lips at me. "The Director is very pleased with you so far, Simpson," he said. "He even spoke of the possibility of helping you in some way beyond the withdrawal of the charges against you, perhaps in connection with your papers, if your co-operation brought about a successful disposal of this matter. It is your chance. Why don't you take it?"

This boy could do better. He should be encouraged to adopt a more positive attitude towards his schoolwork. Athletics: *Fair.* Punctuality: *Fair.* Conduct: *Has left much to be desired this term.* Signed: *G. D. Brush, M.A. (Oxon.),* Headmaster.

I did my best. "What do you mean by 'political context'?" I asked. "Do you mean, are they in favor of democratic ideals? Or against a military dictatorship?—that's what some people call your government, isn't it? Do they talk about capitalist oppression or Soviet domination or the welfare of mankind? Things like that? Because, if so, I can tell you now that the only section of mankind that Harper is interested in is the bit represented by himself."

"That could be said of a great many political conspirators. Obviously, what we are concerned with is their attitudes to the political situation here, where the army acts at present as a trustee for the Republic." He said that stiffly; he hadn't liked the bit about military dictatorship either. "As I have said, Harper may be merely a hired operative, but we cannot say yet. Remember, there are six pistols and ammunition for six."

"That's another thing I don't understand, sir. I know that there are all those grenades, too—but *pistols*? Is that enough for a *coup d'état*. If they were machine guns now . . ."

"My dear Simpson, the head of a secret political organization in Belgrade once handed out four pistols to four rather stupid students. In the event, only one was used, but it was used to assassinate the Archduke Ferdinand of Austria and it started a European war. Pistols can be carried in the pocket. Machine guns cannot."

"You think these people are out to assassinate some-body?"

"That is for you to help us discover. Have you any more questions?"

"Is there any information yet about this business-machine company, Tekelek? Harper seemed to be using it as a cover."

"We are still awaiting word from Switzerland. If it is of interest I will let you know."

He handed me the portable radio; then, as I got up to go, he went to the door and gave an order to the lieutenant waiting outside about taking me back to the gate. I had started to move when he had an afterthought and stopped me.

"One more thing," he said, "I do not wish you to take foolish risks, but I do wish you to feel confidence in your-self if you are obliged to take necessary ones. Some men have more confidence in themselves if they are armed."

I couldn't help glancing at the polished pistol holster on his belt. He smiled thinly. "This pistol is part of an officer's uniform. You may borrow it if you wish. You could put it in your bag with the radio."

I shook my head. "No, thank you. It wouldn't make me feel better. Worse, more likely. I'd be wondering how to explain it away if anyone happened to see it."

"You are probably wise. Very well, that is all."

Of course, I hadn't the slightest intention of taking any sort of risk if I could help it. All I intended to do was to go through the motions of co-operating so as to keep Tufan happy, and somehow get my letter back from Harper before Tufan's people pulled him in. Of course, I was quite cer-tain that he was going to be pulled in. He *had* to be!

Tufan stayed behind telephoning. As I went back along the corridors with the lieutenant, I saw him glancing at me, wondering if it were better to make polite conversation with someone who seemed on such good terms with the powerful Major Tufan, or to say nothing and keep his nose clean. In the end, all he said was a courteous good night.

The Peugeot was still outside. The driver glanced at the radio I was carrying. I wondered if he knew about the modification, but he made no comment on it. We drove back to the hotel in silence. I thanked him and he nodded amiably, patting the wheel of his car. "Better on the narrow roads," he said.

The terrace was closed. I went to the bar for a drink. I had to get the taste of the Dolmabahçe out of my mouth.

"Conspiracy," Tufan had said. Well, that much I was prepared to concede. The whole Harper-Lipp-Fischer setup was obviously a cover for something; but all this cloak-and-dagger stuff about *coups d'état* and assassination plots I really couldn't swallow. Even sitting in the palace with a painting about a Sultan being deposed staring down from the wall, it had bothered me. Sitting in a hotel bar with a glass of brandy—well, frankly I didn't believe a bloody word of it. The point was that I knew the people concerned —or, anyway, I had met them—and Tufan didn't know and hadn't met any of them. "Political context," for heaven's sake! Suddenly Major Tufan appeared in my mind's eye not as a man in charge of a firing squad, but as a military old maid always looking for secret agents and assassins under her bed—a typical counter-espionage man in fact.

For a moment or two I almost enjoyed myself. Then I remembered the doors of the car and the arms and the respirators and the grenades, and went back to zero.

If it hadn't been for those things, I thought, I could have made two good guesses about the Harper setup, and one of them would certainly have been right. My first guess would have been narcotics. Turkey is an opium-producing country. If you had the necessary technical personnel— Fischer, the "manufacturer," Lipp, the "student"—all you would need would be a quiet, secluded place like the Kösk Sardunya in which to set up a small processing plant to make heroin, and an organizer—Harper, of course—to handle distribution and sales.

My second guess would have been some de luxe variation of the old badger game. It begins in the romantic villa on the Bosphorus graced by the beautiful, blue-blooded Princess Lipp, whose family once owned vast estates in Rumania, her faithful servitor Andreas (Fischer), and a multimillionaire sucker enslaved by the lady's beauty. Then, just as the millionaire is preparing to dip his wick, in comes the mad, bad, dangerous husband Prince (Harper) Lipp, who threatens to spread the whole story (with pictures, no doubt) over the front pages of every newspaper from Istanbul to Los Angeles, *unless* . . . The millionaire can't wait to pay up and get out. Curtain.

On the whole, though, I would have made narcotics the first choice. Not that I didn't see Harper as a con man, or in the role of blackmailer (I knew all too well that he could play that), but the cost and extent of the preparatory work suggested that big profits were expected. Unless the supply of gullible millionaires had suddenly increased in the Istanbul area, it seemed more likely that the expectation was based on the promise of a successful narcotics operation.

It seemed to me so obviously the right answer that I began to think again about the grenades and pistols. Supposing they did fit into the narcotics picture after all; but in a subsidiary sort of way. Supposing they had no direct relationship with Harper, but had been carried for someone *outside* the villa group—someone Turkish with political intentions of the kind in which Tufan was interested. The narcotics picture had to include a supplier of illicit raw opium. Almost certainly that supplier would be Turkish. Why shouldn't the price for his illicit opium have included a small shipment of illicit arms? No reason at all. Or the delivery of the arms might merely have been one of those little gestures of goodwill with which businessmen sometimes like to sweeten their contractual relationships. "I'm bringing a car in anyway. Why not let me take care of that other little matter for you? Just give me a letter to your man in Athens."

There was only one thing that I could see that was not quite right about it—the time factor. The villa had been taken on a short lease. The car had been imported on a tourist *carnet*. I didn't know how long it took to set up a laboratory and process enough heroin to make a killing in the dope market; but, on the face of it, two months seemed a bit short. I decided in the end that, for safety, they might well want to avoid remaining for too long in any one place and intended to keep the laboratory on the move.

I think I knew, secretly, that it wasn't a highly convincing explanation; but, at that moment, it was the best that I could think of, and until a better one occurred to me I was prepared to be uncritical. I liked my arms-for-opium theory. At least it held out a promise of release. When Tufan realized that, as far as the arms were concerned, Harper was only an intermediary, his interest must shift from the villa group to someone somewhere else. My usefulness would be at an end. Harper would accept my resignation with a shrug, return my letter, and pay me off. Tufan's delighted Director would help me over my papers. A few hours later I would be back in Athens, safe and sound.

I remembered that I hadn't yet written to Nicki. Before I went to bed, I bought a postcard from the concierge and wrote a few lines. *Still on Lincoln job. Money good. Should last a few more days. Home mid-week latest. Be good. Love, Papa.*

I didn't put the villa address, because that would have made her curious. I didn't want to have to answer a lot of questions when I got back. Even when I've had a good time,

I don't like having to talk about it. Good or bad, what's over's done with. Anyway, there was no point really in giving an address. I knew she wouldn't write back to me.

The following morning I went out early, bought a dozen packets of cigarettes, and then looked for a shop which sold tools. If I were to make sure that the stuff had been removed from the car doors, I would have to look inside at least one of them. The only trouble was that the screws which fastened the leather panels had Phillips heads. If I tried to use an ordinary screwdriver on them, there would be a risk of making marks or possibly scratching the leather.

I could not find a tool shop, so, in the end, I went to the garage off Taxim Square, where they knew me, and persuaded the mechanic there to sell me a Phillips. Then I went back to the hotel, paid my bill, and took a taxi to the ferry pier. There was no sign of the Peugeot following.

A ferryboat came in almost immediately and I knew that I was going to be early at Sariyer. In fact, I was twenty minutes early, so I was all the more surprised to see the Lincoln coming along the road as the boat edged in to the pier.

Miss Lipp was driving.

Chapter

6

As I came off the pier, she got out of the car. She was wearing a light yellow cotton dress that did even less to obscure the shape of her body than the slacks and shirt I had seen her in the day before. She had the keys of the car in her hand, and, as I came up, she handed them to me with a friendly smile.

"Good morning, Arthur."

"Good morning, madam. It's good of you to meet me."

"I want to do some sightseeing. Why don't you put your bag in the trunk for now, then we won't have to stop off at the villa."

"Whatever you say, madam." I put my bag down and went to hold the rear door open for her, but she was already walking round to the front passenger seat, so I had to scuttle round to get to that door ahead of her.

When she was installed, I hurriedly put my bag in the luggage compartment and got into the driver's seat. I was sweating slightly, not only because it was a warm day but also because I was flustered. I had expected Fischer to meet me with the car; I had expected to go straight to the villa, to be told where I would sleep, to be given a moment to orient myself, a chance to think and time to plan. Instead, I was on my own with Miss Lipp, sitting where she had been sitting until a few moments ago, and smelling the scent she used. My hand shook a little as I put the ignition key in, and I felt I had to say something to cover my nerves.

"Isn't Mr. Harper joining you, madam?"

"He had some business to attend to." She was lighting a cigarette. "And by the way, Arthur," she went on, "don't call me madam. If you have to call me something, the name's Lipp. Now, tell me what you have on the tour menu."

"Is this your first time in Turkey, Miss Lipp?"

"First in a long time. All I remember from before is mosques. I don't think I want to see any more mosques."

"But you would like to begin with Istanbul?"

"Oh yes."

"Did you see the Seraglio?"

"Is that the old palace where the Sultans' harem used to be?"

"That's it." I smiled inwardly. When I had been a guide in Istanbul before, it had been the same. Every woman tourist was always interested in the harem. Miss Lipp, I thought to myself, was no different.

"All right," she said, "let's go see the Seraglio."

I was regaining my composure now. "If I may make a suggestion."

"Go ahead."

"The Seraglio is organized as a museum now. If we go straight there we shall arrive before it opens. I suggest that I drive you first to the famous Pierre Loti café, which is high up on a hill just outside the city. There, you could have a light lunch in pleasant surroundings and I could take you to the Seraglio afterwards."

"What time would we get there?"

"We can be there soon after one o'clock."

"Okay, but I don't want to be later."

That struck me as rather odd, but I paid no attention. You do get the occasional tourist who wants to do everything by the clock. She just had not impressed me as being of that type.

I started up and drove back along the coast road. I looked for the Peugeot, but it wasn't there that day. Instead, there was a gray Opel with three men in it. When we got to the old castle at Rumelihisari, I stopped and told her about the blockade of Constantinople by Sultan Mehmet Fatih in 1453, and how he had stretched a great chain boom across the Bosphorus there to cut off the city. I didn't tell her that it was possible to go up to the main keep of the castle because I didn't want to exhaust myself climbing up all those paths and stairs; but she didn't seem very interested anyway, so, in the end, I cut the patter short and pushed on. After a while, it became pretty obvious that she wasn't really much interested in anything in the way of ordinary sightseeing. At least that was how it seemed at the time. I don't think she was bored, but when I pointed places out to her, she only nodded. She asked no questions.

It was different at the café. She made me sit with her at a table outside under a tree and order *raki* for us both; then she began asking questions by the dozen; not about Pierre Loti, the Turkophile Frenchman, but about the Seraglio.

I did my best to explain. To most people, the word "palace" means a single very big building planned to house a monarch. Of course, there are usually a few smaller buildings around it, but the big building is The Palace. Although the word "Seraglio" really means "palace," it isn't at all like one. It is an oval-shaped walled area over two miles in circumference, standing on top of the hill above Seraglio Point at the entrance to the Bosphorus; and it is a city within a city. Originally, or at least from the time of Suleiman the Magnificent until the mid-nineteenth century, the whole central government, ministers and high civil servants as well as the Sultan of the time, lived and worked in it. There were household troops and a cadet school as well as the Sultan's harem inside the walls. The population was generally over five thousand, and there was always new building going on. One reason for this was a custom of the Ottomans. When a new Sultan came to the throne, he naturally inherited all the wealth and property accumulated by his father; but he could not take the personalized property for his own personal use without losing face. Consequently, all the old regalia had to be stored away and new pieces made, a new summer palace had to be built and, of course, new private apartments inside the Seraglio, and a new mosque. As I say, this went on well into the nineteenth century. So the Seraglio today is a vast rabbit warren of reception rooms, private apartments, pavilions, mosques, libraries, gateways, armories, barracks, and so on, interspersed by a few open courtyards and gardens. There are no big buildings in the "palace" sense. The two biggest single structures happen to be the kitchens and the stables.

Although the guidebooks try to explain all this, most tourists don't seem to understand it. They think "Seraglio" means "harem" anyway and all they are interested in apart from that is the "Golden Road," the passage that the chosen girls went along to get from the harem to the Sultan's bed. The harem area isn't open to the public as a matter of fact; but I always used to take the tourists I had through the Mustafa Pasha pavilion at the back and tell them that that was part of the harem. They never knew the difference, and it was something they could tell their friends.

Miss Lipp soon got the idea, though. I found that she
knew something about Turkish history; for instance, who
the Janissaries had been. For someone who, only an hour or
so earlier, had been asking if the Seraglio was the old
palace, that was a little surprising. At the time, I suppose, I
was too busy trying to answer her other questions to pay
much attention. I had shown her the guidebook plan and
she was going through all the buildings marked on it.

"The White Eunuchs' quarters along here, are they
open?"

"Only these rooms near the Gate of Felicity in the middle."

"The Baths of Selim the Second, can we see them?"

"That is part of the museum now. There is a collection of
glass and silverware there, I think."

"What about the Hall of the Pantry?"

"I think that building has the administration offices in it
now."

Some of the questions I couldn't answer at all, even
vaguely, but she still kept on. Finally, she broke off, swallowed her second *raki* at a gulp, and looked across at me.

"Are you hungry, Arthur?"

"Hungry? No, Miss Lipp, not particularly."

"Why don't we go to the palace right now then?"

"Certainly, if you wish."

"Okay. You take care of the check here. We'll settle
later."

I saw the eyes of one or two men sitting in the café follow her as she went back to the car, and I noticed them
glancing at me as I paid for the drinks. Obviously they were
wondering what the relationship was—father, uncle, or
what? It was oddly embarrassing. The trouble was, of
course, that I didn't know what to make of Miss Lipp and
couldn't decide what sort of attitude to adopt towards her.
To add to the confusion, a remark Harper had made at the

Club in Athens, about Nicki's legs being too short, kept coming into my mind. Miss Lipp's legs were particularly long, and, for some reason, that was irritating as well as exciting; exciting because I couldn't help wondering what difference long legs would make in bed; irritating because I knew damn well that I wasn't going to be given the chance to find out.

I drove her to the Seraglio and parked in what used to be the Courtyard of the Janissaries, just outside the Ortakapi Gate by the executioner's block. As it was so early, there were only two or three other cars besides the Lincoln. I was glad of that because I was able to get off my piece about the gate without being overheard by official guides with other parties. The last thing I wanted at that moment was to have my guide's license asked for and challenged.

The Ortakapi Gate is a good introduction to the "feel" of the Seraglio. "It was here at this gate that the Sultans used to stand to watch the weekly executions. The Sultan stood just there. You see the block where the beheading was done. Now, see that little fountain built in the wall there? That was for the executioner to wash the blood off himself when he had finished. He was also the Chief Gardener. By the way, this was known as the Gate of Salvation. Rather ironic, don't you think? Of course, only high palace dignitaries who had offended the Sultan were beheaded here. When princes of the royal house were executed—for instance, when a new Sultan had all his younger brothers killed off to prevent arguments about the succession—their blood could not be shed, so they were strangled with a silk cord. Women who had offended were treated in a different way. They were tied up in weighted sacks and dropped into the Bosphorus. Shall we go inside now?"

Until Miss Lipp, I had never known it to fail.

She gave me a blank stare. "Is any of that true, Arthur?"

"Every word of it." It *is* true, too.

"How do you know?"

"Those are historic facts, Miss Lipp." I had another go. "In fact, one of the Sultans got bored with his whole harem and had them all dumped into the Bosphorus. There was a shipwreck off Seraglio Point soon after, and a diver was sent down. What he saw there almost scared him to death. There were all those weighted sacks standing in a row on the bottom and swaying to and fro with the current."

"Which Sultan?"

Naturally, I thought it was safe to guess. "It was Murad the Second."

"It was Sultan Ibrahim," she said. "No offense, Arthur, but I think we'd better hire a guide."

"Whatever you say, Miss Lipp."

I tried to look as if I thought it a good idea, but I was really quite angry. If she had asked me right out whether I was a historical expert on the Seraglio, I would have told her, quite frankly, that I was not. It was the underhand way in which she had set out to trap me that I didn't like.

We went through the gate, and I paid for our admissions and selected an English-speaking guide. He was solemn and pedantic, of course, and told her all the things I had already explained all over again; but she did not seem to mind. From the way she bombarded him with questions you would have thought she was going to write a book about the place. Of course, that flattered him. He had a grin like an ape.

Personally, I find the Seraglio rather depressing. In Greece, the old buildings, even when they are in ruins and nothing much has been done in the way of restoration, always seem to have a clean, washed look about them. The Seraglio is stained, greasy, and dilapidated. Even the trees and shrubs in the main courtyards are neglected, and the so-called Tulip Garden is nothing but a scrubby patch of dirt.

As far as Miss Lipp was concerned though, the place might have been Versailles. She went everywhere, through the kitchens, through the museum rooms, the exhibition of saddles, this kiosk, that pavilion, laughing at the guide's standard jokes and scuffing her shoes on the broken paving stones. If I had known what was going on in her mind, of course, I would have felt differently; but as it was, I became bored. After a bit, I gave up following them everywhere and just took the short cuts.

I was looking forward to a sit-down by the Gate of the Fountain while they "did" the textiles exhibition, when she called me over.

"Arthur, how long will it take us to get to the airport from here?"

I was so surprised that I must have looked at her a bit blankly. "The airport?"

She put on a slight heaven-give-me-patience look. "Yes, Arthur, the airport. Where the planes arrive. How long from here?"

The guide, who hadn't been asked, said: "Forty minutes, *madame.*"

"Better allow forty-five, Miss Lipp," I said, ignoring him.

She looked at her watch. "The plane gets in at four," she said. "I tell you what, Arthur. You go get yourself a sandwich or something. I'll meet you where you parked the car in an hour. Right?"

"As you wish, Miss Lipp. Are we meeting someone at the airport?"

"If that's all right with you." Her tone was curt.

"I only meant that if I knew the line and flight number I could check if the plane is going to be on time."

"So you could, Arthur. I didn't think of that. It's Air France from Geneva."

I was in the sunshine of her smile again, the bitch.

There was a restaurant of sorts near the Blue Mosque,

and when I had ordered some food I telephoned Tufan.

He listened to my report without comment until I had finished. "Very well," he said then, "I will see that the passports of the Geneva passengers are particularly noted. Is that all?"

"No." I started to tell him my theory about the drug operation and its necessary link with a raw-opium supplier, but almost at once he began interrupting.

"Have you new facts to support this?"

"It fits the information we have."

"Any imbecile could think of ways of interpreting the information we have. It is the information we do not have that I am interested in. Your business is to get it, and that is all you should be thinking about."

"Nevertheless . . ."

"You are wasting time. Report by telephone, or as otherwise arranged, and remember your listening times. Now, if that is all, I have arrangements to make."

The military mind at work! Whether he was right or wrong (and, as it happens, he was both right *and* wrong) made no difference. It was the arrogance of the man I couldn't stand.

I ate a disgusting meal of lukewarm mutton stew and went back to the car. I was angry with myself, too.

I have to admit it; what had really exasperated me was not so much Tufan's anxiety-bred offensiveness as my own realization that the train of thought which had seemed so logical and reasonable the previous night, was not looking as logical and reasonable in the morning. My conception of the "student" Miss Lipp as a laboratory technician was troublesome enough; but speaking again with Tufan had reminded me that the villa, which I had so blithely endowed with a clandestine heroin-manufacturing plant, also housed an elderly married couple and a cook. So that, in addition to the time-factor improbability, I now had to accept another: either the plant was to be so small that the servants would not notice it or Harper counted on buying their discretion.

Then, in sheer desperation, I did something rather silly. I felt that I had to know if the grenades and pistols were still in the car. If they had been taken out, at least one bit of my theory was still just tenable. I could assume that they had been delivered or were in process of delivery to the person who wanted them.

I had about twenty minutes to spare before Miss Lipp came out of the Seraglio; but in case she was early I drove the car to the other end of the courtyard under some trees opposite the Church of St. Irene. Then I got the Phillips screwdriver out of my bag and went to work on the door by the driver's seat.

I wasn't worried about anyone seeing me. After all, I was only carrying out Tufan's orders. The men in the Opel wouldn't interfere; and if some cab driver became inquisitive, I could always pretend that I was having trouble with a door lock. All that mattered was the time, because I had to do it carefully to avoid making marks.

I loosened all the screws carefully first, and then began to remove them. It seemed to take an age. And then a horrible thing happened. Just as I was taking out the last screw but one, I happened to glance up and saw Miss Lipp with the guide walking across the courtyard from the alleyway leading to the Archaeological Museum.

I knew at once that she had seen the car because she was walking straight towards it. She was about two hundred yards away, and on the opposite side of the car to the door I had been working on, but I knew that I couldn't get even one of the screws back in time. Besides, I was not in the place she had told me to be. There was only one thing I could do: stuff the screws and screw driver into my pocket, start the car, drive around the courtyard to meet her, and hope to God the two loose screws would hold the panel in place when I opened the door to get out.

I had one piece of luck. The guide practically fell over himself opening her door for her, so I didn't have to open the one on my side. I was able to get my apology in at the same time.

"I'm so sorry, Miss Lipp. I thought you might be visiting the St. Irene Church and I wanted to save you the walk back."

That got by all right because she couldn't thank the guide and answer me at the same time. The guide was an unexpected help, too, as he immediately asked her if she would like to see the church, "pure Byzantine, built in the reign of Justinian, and of great historical interest."

"I'll leave that for another time," she said.

"But you will be here tomorrow, *madame*, when the Treasury Museum is on view?"

"Well, maybe."

"Otherwise, it must be Thursday, *madame*. That part and the pictures are on view only two days in the week, when all the other rooms are closed." He was obviously panting for her to come again. I wondered how much she had tipped him.

"I'll try and make it tomorrow. Thank you again." She gave him the smile. To me, she said: "Let's go."

I drove off. As soon as we got onto the cobbles the panel started to vibrate. I immediately pressed my knee against it and the vibration stopped; but I was really scared now. I didn't think that she would notice that the screws were out; but Fischer or Harper certainly would; and there was this unknown we were going to meet. I knew that I had somehow to replace the screws while the car was at the airport.

"Is the plane on time?" she asked.

A donkey cart came rattling out of a side street at that moment, and I made a big thing of braking and swerving out of its way. I didn't have to pretend that the cart had shaken me up. I was shaken up all right. My call to Tufan and the argument with him had made me forget completely about calling the airline. I did the best I could.

"They didn't know of any delay," I said; "but the plane was making an intermediate stop. Would you like me to check again?"

"No, it's not worth it now."

"Did you enjoy the Seraglio, Miss Lipp?" I thought if I kept talking it might quieten my stomach down a bit.

"It was interesting."

"The Treasury is worth seeing, too. Everything the Sultans used was covered with jewels. Of course, a great many of the things were gifts from kings and emperors who wanted to impress the Sultans with their greatness. Even Queen Victoria sent things."

"I know." She chuckled. "Clocks and cut glass."

"But some of the things are really incredible, Miss Lipp. There are coffee cups sculptured out of solid amethyst, and, you know, the largest emerald in the world is there on the canopy of one of the thrones. They even did mosaic work with rubies and emeralds instead of marble." I went on to tell her about the gem-encrusted baldrics. I gave her the full treatment. In my experience every normal woman likes talking about jewels. But she didn't seem much interested.

"Well," she said, "they can't be worth much."

"All those hundreds and thousands of jewels, Miss Lipp!" My leg was getting stiff trying to stop the panel from vibrating. I wriggled surreptitiously into a new position.

She shrugged. "The guide told me that the reason they have to close some rooms on the days they open up the others is because they're understaffed. The reason they're understaffed is because the government hasn't the money to spend. That's why the place is so shabby, too. Pretty well all of the money they have for restoration goes into the older, the Byzantine buildings. Besides, if all those stones were real gems they'd be in a strong-room, not a museum. You know, Arthur, quite a lot of these old baubles turn out in the end to be just obsidian and garnet."

"Oh, these are real gems, Miss Lipp."

"What's the biggest emerald in the world look like, Arthur?"

"Well, it's pear-shaped, and about the size of a pear, too."

"Smooth or cut?"

"Smooth."

"Couldn't it be green tourmaline?"

"Well, I suppose I don't know really, Miss Lipp. I'm not an expert."

"Do you care *which* it is?"

I was getting bored with this. "Not much, Miss Lipp," I answered. "It just makes a more interesting story if it's an emerald."

She smiled. "It makes a more amusing story if it's not. Have you ever been to the mysterious East?"

"No, Miss Lipp."

"But you've seen pictures. Do you know what makes those tall pagodas glitter so beautifully in the moonlight?"

"No, Miss Lipp."

"They're covered with little pieces of broken bottle glass. And the famous emerald Buddha in Bangkok isn't emerald at all, it's carved from a block of ordinary green jasper."

"Little-known facts," I thought. "Why don't you send it in to *Reader's Digest?*" I didn't say it though.

She took a cigarette from the gold case in her bag and I fumbled in my pocket for matches; but she had a gold lighter, too, and didn't notice the matches I held out to her. "Have you always done this sort of work?" she asked suddenly.

"Driving? No, Miss Lipp. Most of my life I have been a

journalist. That was in Egypt. When the Nasser crowd took over, things became impossible. It was a matter of starting again." Simple, straightforward—a man who has suffered the slings and arrows of outrageous fortune but wasn't looking for anyone's shoulder to weep on.

"I was thinking about the traveler's checks," she said. "Is that what you meant by 'starting again'?"

"I'm sorry Mr. Harper had to tell you about that." It was no surprise, of course, that Harper had told her; but with so many other things on my mind—driving, keeping the door panel from rattling, cramp in my leg and wondering how the hell I was going to replace the screws—all I could think of was that obvious reply.

"Did you think he wouldn't tell me?" she went on.

"I didn't think about it either way, Miss Lipp."

"But since he did tell me and since you're driving this car, that must mean that I don't mind too much about things like that, mustn't it?"

For one idiotic moment I wondered if she were making some sort of pass at me; but it was a brief moment.

"I suppose so," I answered.

"And that Mr. Harper doesn't mind either?"

"Yes."

"And that, in fact, we're all very sensible, tolerant persons?"

I couldn't help glancing at her. She was watching me in her amused, considering way, but there was nothing sleepy about her eyes now. They were steadily intent.

And then I got the message. I was being sounded, either to discover what I had made of the setup and if they had left any shirt-tails showing, or to find out if I could be trusted in some particular way. I knew that how I answered would be very important indeed to me; but I didn't know what to say. It was no use pretending to be stupid any more, or trying to avoid the issue. A test was being applied.

If I failed it, I was out—out with Harper, out with Tufan and his Director, out with the Turkish customs, and, in all probability, out with the Greek police as well.

I felt my face getting red and knew that she would notice. That decided me. People get red when they feel guilty or nervous; but they also get red when they are angry. In order not to seem nervous or guilty, all I could do was to seem angry.

"Including Mr. Fischer?" I asked.

"What about Mr. Fischer?"

"Is he sensible, too, Miss Lipp?"

"Does that matter?"

I glanced at her again. "If my personal safety—safety from some sort of bad luck, let us say—depended on Fischer's being sensible, I'd be quite worried."

"Because he upset a drink over you?"

"Ah, he told you that, did he? No, that was only stupid. I'd be worried because he was careless, because he gave himself away."

"Only himself?" There was quite an edge to her voice now. I knew that I had gone far enough.

"What else is there to give away, Miss Lipp?" *I am wary but not treacherous, Miss Lipp. I watch my own interests, Miss Lipp, but I know how to be discreet, too, no matter how phony the setup looks.*

"What indeed?" she said shortly.

She said no more. The test was over. I did not know whether I had passed or not; but there was nothing more that I could do, and I was glad of the relief. I hoped she would not notice that I was sweating.

We arrived at the airport ten minutes before the plane was due. She got out and went into the arrivals section, leaving me to find a place to park. I quickly did the two loose screws up before I went to join her.

She was at the Air France counter.

"Fifteen minutes to wait," she said.

"And at least another fifteen before they get through customs," I reminded her. "Miss Lipp, you have had no lunch. The café here is quite clean. Why not wait there and have some cakes and tea? I will keep a check on the plane and arrange for a porter to be ready. When the passengers are in customs I will let you know."

She hesitated, then, to my relief, nodded. "All right, you do that."

"May I ask who it is that we are meeting?"

"Mr. Miller."

"I will take care of everything."

I showed her where the café was, hung around long enough to make sure that she was going to stay there, and then hurried back to the car.

I was sweating so much by this time that my fingers kept slipping on the screwdriver. In fact, I did what I had been trying hard to avoid doing and scratched the leather; but it couldn't be helped. I rubbed some spit on the place and hoped for the best. The Opel was parked about a dozen yards away and I could see the men in it watching me. They probably thought I'd gone mad.

When the last screw was in place, I put the screwdriver back in my bag and went inside again to the Air France counter. The plane was just landing. I found a porter, gave him five lira, and told him about Mr. Miller. Then I went to the men's room and tried to stop myself from sweating by running cold water over my wrists. It helped a little. I cleaned myself up and went back to the café.

"The passengers are beginning to come through now, Miss Lipp."

She picked up her bag. "Take care of the check will you, Arthur?"

It took me a minute or two to get the waiter's attention, so I missed the meeting between Miss Lipp and Mr. Miller. They were already on the way out to the car when I saw them. The porter was carrying two pieces of luggage, one suitcase and one smaller bag. I went ahead and got the luggage compartment open.

Mr. Miller was about sixty with a long neck and nose, lined gray cheeks, and a bald head with brown blotches on the skin. The backs of his hands had blotches, too. He was very thin and his light tussore suit flapped as he walked as if it had been made for someone with more flesh to cover. He had rimless glasses, pale lips, a toothy smile, and that fixed stare ahead which says: "You'll have to get out of my way, I'm afraid, because I haven't the time to get out of yours."

As they came up to the car Miss Lipp said: "This is Arthur Simpson, who's driving for us, Leo."

Before I could even say "good afternoon" he had handed me the raincoat he had been carrying over his arm. "Good, good," he said, and climbed into the back seat. She smiled slightly as she got in after him, though not at me, to herself.

The coat smelled of lavender water. I put it with the luggage, tipped the porter again, and got into the driver's seat.

"To the villa, Miss Lipp?" I asked.

"Yes, Arthur."

"Wait a minute." It was Miller. "Where is my coat?"

"With your luggage, sir."

"It will get dirty in there. It should be on a seat in here."

"Yes, sir."

I got out again and retrieved the coat.

"What a fuss you make, Leo," I heard her say. "The car's quite clean."

"The baggage in there is not clean. It has been in the belly of a plane with other baggage. It has been on the floor and table of the customs place. It has been handled by the man who searched it, handled again by the porter. Nothing is clean." His accent had no American inflections, and he couldn't pronounce his *th*'s. I thought he might be French.

I draped the coat over the back of the seat in front of him. "Will that be all right, sir?"

"Yes, of course," he said impatiently.

That type is always the same. *They* make the difficulties and then behave as if *you're* the one who's being the nuisance.

"Let's go, Arthur," said Miss Lipp. Her tone was non-committal. I couldn't tell whether she found him tiresome or not. I watched them in the driving mirror.

As soon as we were clear of the airport, he settled back and looked her over in a fatherly way.

"Well, my dear, you're looking healthy. How are Karl and Giulio?"

"Karl's fine. Giulio we haven't seen yet. He's with the boat. Karl was thinking of going over there tomorrow."

"Have you anything planned for then?"

"We thought you might like to do a little sightseeing. That is unless you're tired."

"You are more considerate than a daughter, my dear." The teeth leered at her and the pale eyes behind the rimless glasses flickered towards my back.

I had already realized that this was a conversation conducted solely for my benefit, but now I saw her face stiffen. She knew that I was listening hard and was afraid that he was overdoing it.

"You must persuade Arthur to show you around the Seraglio Palace," she said. "He is quite an authority on it. Isn't that right, Arthur?"

That was as good as telling me that the old fool would believe any cock-and-bull story I cared to tell him. On the other hand, it must be telling him something, too; perhaps warning him that the driver wasn't such a fool as he looked. I had to be careful.

"I would be happy to show Mr. Miller what there is to see," I said.

"Well, we must certainly think about that," he replied; "certainly, we must think about it."

He glanced at her to see if he had said the right thing. A sentence of my father's came into my mind. "One moment they're all full of piss and wind and the next moment . . ." At that point he would make a raspberry sound with his tongue. Vulgar, of course, but there was never any doubt about the kind of man he meant.

Mr. Miller kept quiet after that. Once or twice she pointed out places of interest, in the manner of a hostess with a newly arrived guest; but the only thing he asked about was the tap water at the villa. Was it safe to drink or was there bottled water available? There was bottled water, she told him. He nodded, as if that had confirmed his worst fears, and said that he had brought plenty of Entero Vioform for intestinal prophylaxis.

We reached the villa a little after five. Miss Lipp told me to sound the horn as I went up the drive.

The reception committee consisted of Harper and Fischer. Hovering in the background, ready to carry luggage, was an old man wearing an apron whom I took to be Hamul, the resident caretaker.

Tufan had said that Fischer was the lessee of the villa but there was no doubt who was the real host there. All Fischer received from the incoming guest was a nod of recognition. Harper got a smile and an "Ah, my dear Karl." They shook hands with businesslike cordiality, and then Harper, Miller, and Miss Lipp went straight into the house. To Fischer were left the menial tasks of telling Hamul where Miller's bags were to go, and of showing me where to put the car and where I was to sleep.

At the back of the villa there was a walled stable yard. Part of the stabling had been converted into a garage with room for two cars. It was empty except for a Lambretta motor scooter.

"The Lambretta belongs to the cook," Fischer said; "see that he does not steal gasoline from the car."

I followed him across the yard to the rear entrance of the house.

Inside, I had a brief glimpse of the polished wood flooring of a passage beyond the small tiled hallway, before he led the way up a narrow staircase to the top floor. All too obviously we were in the old servants' quarters. There were six small attic cubicles with bare wood floors, bare wood partition walls, and a single skylight in the roof for all of them. The sanitary arrangements consisted of an earthenware sink with a water tap on the wall at the head of the stairs. It was stiflingly hot under the low roof and there were dust and cobwebs everywhere. Two of the cubicles showed signs of having been swept out recently. Each contained an iron bedstead with a mattress and gray blankets. In one, there was a battered composition-leather suitcase. Fischer showed me to the other.

"You will sleep here," he said. "The chef has the next bed. You will eat your meals with him in the kitchen."

"Where is the toilet?"

"There is a *pissoir* across the yard in the stables."

"And the bathroom?"

He waved his hand towards the sink. He was watching my face and enjoying himself just a bit too obviously. I guessed that this had been his own wonderful idea of a punishment for the crime of calling him a servant, and that Harper probably did not know of it. In any case, I had to protest. Without some privacy, especially at night, I could neither use the radio nor write reports.

I had put my bag down on the floor to rest my arm. Now

I picked it up and started to walk back the way we had come.

"Where are you going?"

"To tell Mr. Harper that I'm not sleeping here."

"Why not? If it is good enough for the chef it is good enough for you, a driver."

"It will not be good enough for Miss Lipp if I smell because I am unable to take a bath."

"What did you expect—the royal apartment?"

"I can still find a hotel room in Sariyer. Or you can get another driver."

I felt fairly safe in saying that. If he were to call my bluff I could always back down; but I thought it more likely that I had already called his. The very fact that he was arguing with me suggested weakness.

He glared at me for a moment, then walked to the stairs.

"Put the car away," he said. "It will be decided later what is to be done with you."

I followed him down the stairs. At the foot of them, he turned off left into the house. I went out to the yard, left my bag in the garage, and walked back to the car. When I had put it away, I went into the house and set about finding the kitchen. It wasn't difficult. The passage which I had glimpsed from the back entrance ran along the whole length of the house, with a servants' stairway leading to the bedroom floor, and, on the right, a series of doors which presumably gave the servants access to the various reception rooms in front. There was a smell of garlic-laden cooking. I followed the smell.

The kitchen was a big stone-floored room on the left of the passage. It had an old charcoal range along the rear wall with three battered flues over it, and a heavy pinewood table with benches in the middle. The table was cluttered with cooking debris and bottles, and scarred from years of use as a chopping block. Empty butcher's hooks hung from the beams. There was a barrel on a trestle, and beside it a sinister-looking zinc icebox. A doorway to one side gave on to what appeared to be a scullery. A short man in a dirty blue denim smock stood by the range stirring an iron pot. This was Geven, the cook. As I came in he looked up and stared.

He was a dark, moon-faced, middle-aged man with an upturned nose and large nostrils. The mouth was wide and full with a lower lip that quivered much of the time as if he were on the verge of tears. The thick, narrow chest merged into a high paunch. He had a three-day growth of beard, which was hardly surprising in view of the fact that he had nowhere to shave.

I remembered that he was a Cypriot and spoke to him in English. "Good evening. I am the chauffeur, Simpson. Mr. Geven?"

"Geven, yes." He stopped stirring and we shook hands. His hands were filthy and it occurred to me that Mr. Miller was probably going to need his Entero Vioform. "A drink, eh?" he said.

"Thanks."

He pulled a glass out of a bowl of dirty water by the sink, shook it once, and poured some *konyak* from an already opened bottle on the table. He also refilled his own half-empty glass, which was conveniently to hand.

"Here's cheers!" he said, and swallowed thirstily. A sentence of Tufan's came into my mind—"He gets drunk and attacks people." I had not thought to ask what sort of people he usually attacked, the person with whom he was drinking or some casual bystander.

"Are you British?" he asked.

"Yes."

"How you know I speak English?"

An awkward question. "I didn't know, but I don't speak Turkish."

He nodded, apparently satisfied. "You worked for these people before?"

"A little. I drove the car from Athens. Normally, I work there with my own car."

"Driving tourists?"

"Yes."

"Are these people tourists?" His tone was heavily ironical.

"I don't know. They say so."

"Ah!" He winked knowingly and went back to his stirring again. "Are you by the week?"

"Paid you mean? Yes."

"You had some money from them?"

"For the trip from Athens."

"Who paid? The Fischer man?"

"The Harper man. You don't think they really are tourists?"

He made a face and rocked his head from side to side as if the question were too silly to need an answer.

"What are they, then?"

He shrugged. "Spies, Russia spies. Everyone know— Hamul and his wife, the fishermen down below, everyone. You want something to eat?"

"That smells good."

"It *is* good. It is for us. Hamul's wife cooks for him in their room before they come to wait table in the dining room. Then, I cook for the spies. Maybe, if I feel like it, I give them what is left after we eat, but the best is for us. Get two dishes, from the shelf there."

It was a chicken and vegetable soup and was the first thing I had eaten with any pleasure for days. Of course, I knew that I would have trouble with the garlic later; but, with my stomach knotted up by nerves the way it was, I would have had trouble with anything. Geven did not eat

much. He went on drinking brandy; but he smiled approvingly when I took a second helping of the soup.

"Always I like the British," he said. "Even when you are
backing the Greeks in Cyprus against us, I like the British.
It is good you are here. A man does not like drinking alone.
We can take a bottle upstairs with us every night." He
smiled wetly at the prospect.

I returned the smile. It was not the moment, I felt, to
tell him that I hoped not to be sharing the servants' quarters
with him.

And then Fischer had to come in.

He looked at the brandy bottle disapprovingly, and then
at me. "I will show you your room," he said.

Geven held up an unsteadily protesting hand. "*Effendi*,
let him finish his dinner. I will show him where to sleep."

It was Fischer's opportunity. "Ah no, chef," he said; "he
thinks himself too good to sleep with you." He nodded to
me. "Come."

Geven's lower lip quivered so violently that I was sure he
was about to burst into tears; but his hand also went to
the bottle as if he were about to throw it at me. It was possible, I thought, that he might be going to do both things.

I whispered hurriedly: "Harper's orders, nothing to do
with me," and got out out of the room as quickly as I could.

Fischer was already at the staircase in the passage.

"You will use these stairs," he said; "not those in the
front of the house."

The room to which he now showed me was at the side of
the house on the bedroom floor. He pointed to the door
of it.

"There is the room," he said, and then pointed to another
door along the corridor; "and there is a bathroom. The car
will be wanted in the morning at eleven." With that he left,
turning off the lights in the corridor as he went.

When he had gone, I turned the lights on again. The corridor had cream lincrusta dadoes with flowered wallpaper above. I had a look at the bathroom. It was a most peculiar shape and had obviously been installed, as an afterthought, in a disused storage closet. There was no window. The plumbing fixtures were German, *circa* 1905. Only the cold-water taps worked.

The bedroom wasn't too bad. It had a pair of french windows, a brass bedstead, a chest of drawers, and a big wardrobe. There was also a deal table with an ancient hand-operated sewing machine on it. At the time when women guests in big houses always brought their lady's maids with them to stay, the room had probably been given to one of the visiting maids.

There was a mattress on the bed, but no sheets or blankets. I knew it would be unwise to complain again. Before I got my bag from the garage, I went back up to the servants' quarters and took the blankets from the cubicle which Fischer had allocated to me. Then I returned to the room. The car radio transmission wasn't due until eleven; I had time to kill. I began by searching the room.

I always like looking inside other people's drawers and cupboards. You can find strange things. I remember once, when I was at Coram's, my aunt had pleurisy and the District Nurse said that I would have to be boarded out for a month. Some people with an old house off the Lewisham High Road took me in. The house had thick laurel bushes all round it and big chestnut trees that made it very dark. I hated going past the laurel bushes at night, because at that time I believed (in the way a boy does) that a madman with a German bayonet was always lying in wait ready to pounce on me from behind and murder me. But inside the house it was all right. There was a smell of Lifebuoy soap and furniture polish. The people had had a son who had been killed on the Somme, and they gave me his room. I found all sorts of things in the cupboard. There was a stamp collection, for instance. I had never collected stamps, but a lot of chaps at school did and I took one or two of the stamps and sold them. After all, he was dead, so he didn't need them. The thing I liked most though was his collection of minerals. It was in a flat wooden case divided up into squares with a different piece of mineral in each one and labels saying what they were—graphite, galena, mica, quartz, iron pyrites, chalcocite, fluorite, wolfram, and so on. There were exactly sixty-four squares and exactly sixty-four pieces of mineral, so at first I couldn't see how to keep any of them for myself because the empty square would have shown that something was missing. I did take one or two of them to school to show the chemistry master and try to get in his good books; but he only got suspicious and asked me where I had found them. I had to tell him that an uncle had lent them to me before he would let me have them back. After that, I just kept them in the box and looked at them; until I went back to my aunt's that is, when I took the iron pyrites because it looked as if it had gold in it. I left a small piece of coal in the square instead. I don't think they ever noticed. I kept that piece of iron pyrites for years. "Fool's gold" some people call it.

All I found in the room at Sardunya was an old Russian calendar made of cardboard in the shape of an icon. There was a dark-brown picture of Christ on it. I don't read Russian, so I couldn't make out the date. It wasn't worth taking.

I had the windows wide open. It was so quiet up there that I could hear the diesels of a ship chugging upstream against the Black Sea current towards the boom across the narrows above Sariyer. Until about eight-thirty there was a faint murmur of voices from the terrace in front. Then they went in to dinner. Some time after nine, I became restless. After all, nobody had told me to stay in my room. I decided to go for a stroll.

Just to be on the safe side, in case anyone took it into his head to go through my things, I hid the radio on top of the wardrobe. Then I went down, out through the rear door, and skirted the front courtyard to the drive.

It was so dark there under the trees that I couldn't really see where I was going, and after I had gone a hundred yards or so I turned back. Miss Lipp, Harper, Miller, and Fischer were coming out onto the terrace again when I reached the courtyard, and Hamul was lighting candles on the tables.

Along the side of the courtyard it was quite dark, and the weeds made it easy to move quietly over the gravel. At the entrance to the stable yard I stopped by the wall to see if I could hear anything they said.

I must have waited there for twenty minutes or more before I heard anything but an indistinct mumble. Then, one of the men laughed loudly—Miller it was—and I heard him saying seven words as if they were the climax of a joke.

"Let the dogs be fed and clothed!" he cackled, and then repeated it. "Let the dogs be fed and clothed!"

The others laughed with him, and then the mumbling began again. I went on in and up to my room.

I made the bed as comfortable as I could with the blankets, and then shaved to save myself the trouble of doing so in the morning.

Just before eleven, I took the radio out of its case, opened the back, and turned the small switch. All I got was a hissing sound. I waited. I did not trouble to use the earphone, because I did not see any reason to then. I had not even shut the windows.

On the stroke of eleven, the set made a harsh clacking noise. A moment later, a voice crackled through the tiny loudspeaker at such a high volume level that I could feel the whole set vibrating in my hands. I tried to turn the thing down, but, with the V.H.F. on, the control seemed to have no effect. All I could do was stuff the set under the blankets.

Even there it seemed like a public-address system. I scrambled to the windows and shut them. The loudspeaker began repeating its message.

Attention period report. Attention period report. New arrival is Leopold Axel Miller. Belgian passport gives following data: Age sixty-three, described as importer, place of birth Antwerp. Data now also received concerning Tekelek S.A., a Swiss corporation registered in Berne. Nominal capital fifty thousand Swiss francs. Directors are K. W. Hoffman, R. E. Kohner, G. D. Bernadi, and L. A. Mathis, all of whom are believed to have personal numbered and secret accounts at Banque Crédit Suisse, Zurich. Business of Tekelek said to be sale of electronic accounting machines manufactured in West Germany. Urgent you report progress. Attention period report . . .

I fumbled under the blankets, turned the V.H.F. switch off, and replaced the back on the set. Then I tuned in a Turkish station in case anyone had heard the noise and came to investigate.

Nobody did.

"Urgent you report progress."

I had a cigarette packet with two cigarettes left in it. I lit one, put the other in my pocket, and went to the bathroom for a piece of toilet paper.

When I returned I locked the door and sat down to write my progress report. It was quite short.

Cook, caretaker, and local fishermen all believe suspects to be Russian spies.

I folded the toilet paper, put it inside the cigarette packet, crumpled the packet, and put the result in my pocket ready for disposal in the morning.

I felt I had done my duty for that day.

Chapter

7

I woke up very early in the morning and with that nasty sick feeling that I used to have when it was a school day and I hadn't done my homework properly the night before.

I got the cigarette packet out of my pocket and had another look at my toilet-paper report. It really was not good enough. Unless I could think of something else to say, Tufan would think that I was trying to be funny. I went and had an extremely uncomfortable cold bath, collected some more sheets of toilet paper, and started again.

Period report heard. Attempts to check door contents frustrated. Will try again today, I wrote.

I thought about the "today." Fischer had ordered the car for eleven o'clock. With that instruction to rely upon, it would be perfectly natural for me to go and fill up the car with petrol without asking anyone's permission; and, as long as I didn't keep them waiting, I could take my time about it. If, when I got back, they objected to my having taken the car out by myself or wanted to know why I had been so long, I could say that I had been to buy razor blades or something, and be the injured innocent.

It was six forty-five by then and in a few minutes I would have to get ready for the seven o'clock radio contact. Two other things occurred to me that I might add to my report.

Will telephone you from garage after inspection if time and circumstances allow, or will add to this report. During conversation Lipp–Miller yesterday name "Giulio" was mentioned in connection with a boat. No other details.

Then I added the bit about the Russian spies. It didn't look quite so bald and stupid now.

I hid the report under the lining paper of one of the drawers, shut the french windows tight, and got the radio ready with the earphone attachment plugged in. Promptly at seven the car began transmitting.

Attention period report. Attention period report. Advice received from Swiss source that no passports have been legally issued to Harper and Lipp. In view Miller contact and Tekelek papers with Harper, possibility must be considered that correct names of Harper and Lipp are Hoffman and Kohner or vice versa. Miller may be Mathis. Imperative you report progress.

As the voice began repeating I switched off. When I had packed the set away, I got the report out and added five words.

Hoffman, Kohner, and Mathis names noted.

At least, I ought to get an "E" for Effort. I put the new report in the cigarette packet, burned the earlier one, and started to get dressed. As I did so, I heard the Lambretta start up and then go whining off down the drive. About twenty minutes later, I heard the sound of it returning. I looked out of the window and saw it disappearing into the stable yard with a bundle of partially wrapped loaves strapped to the rear seat.

Geven was back in the kitchen when I went down. He gave me a sullen look and did not answer when I said "good morning." He was probably hung over as well as disgusted with me; but he looked such a mess anyway that it was hard to tell.

There was a pot of coffee on the range and I looked from it to him inquiringly. He shrugged, so I got a cup and helped myself. He was slicing the bread by hacking at it with a heavy chopping knife. From the neat way the slices fell I knew that the chopping knife was as sharp as a razor. As I had no desire to lose any fingers, I waited until he had put it aside before taking a piece of bread.

The coffee did not taste much like coffee, but the bread was good. I considered attempting to heal the breach by offering him the use of my bathroom; but I only had one towel and the thought of what it would look like by the time he had finished with it kept me silent. Instead, I offered him a cigarette.

He took it and motioned to a basket of apricots on the table. I don't like apricots, but it seemed as well to accept the offer. Soon he began to mutter about the breakfasts which had to be served, each on a separate tray to the four "lords and ladies" above. I offered to lay the trays and, although he waved away the offer, friendly relations seemed to be re-established. After a while, Mr. and Mrs. Hamul arrived and were introduced. Mrs. Hamul was a small, stout, sad-looking old woman with the black dress and head scarf of the conservative Turkish matron. As neither she nor her husband spoke a word of anything but Turkish, the formalities were brief. I lingered there, though, and had another piece of bread. The best time to leave without attracting attention, I had decided, would be while Harper and the rest were having their breakfasts.

As soon as the trays started going up, I told Geven that I had to buy petrol and asked if there was anything I could get for him while I was in town. At once he wanted to come with me. I got out of that by saying that I had to go immediately in order to be back at the time for which the car had been ordered. I left him, sulking, picked up the Phillips screwdriver from my room, and went to the garage.

The Lincoln was a quiet car, and I knew that all they would probably hear of my going would be the sound of the tires on the gravel of the courtyard; but I was so afraid of Harper or Fischer suddenly appearing on one of the bedroom balconies and yelling at me to stop, that in my haste to reach the drive I almost hit the basin of the fountain. As I went on down the drive I broke into a sweat and my legs felt weak and peculiar. I wanted to stop and be sick. That may sound very stupid; but when you are like I am, the bad things that *nearly* happen are just as hard, in a way, as the bad things that actually do happen. They are certainly no easier to forget. I always envied those characters in *Alice* who only felt pain before they were hurt. I seem to feel things before, during, and after as well; nothing ever goes completely away. I have often thought of killing myself, so that I wouldn't have to think or feel or remember any more, so that I could rest; but then I have always started worrying in case this afterlife they preach about really exists. It might turn out to be even bloodier than the old one.

The Peugeot was back on duty again. I drove towards Sariyer for about half a mile, and then turned left onto one of the roads leading up to the forest. It was Sunday morning and families from Istanbul would soon be arriving at the municipal picnic grounds to spend the day; but at that early hour the car-parking areas were still fairly empty, and I had no difficulty in finding a secluded place under the trees.

I decided to try the same door again. I had scratched the leather on it once already; but if I were very careful it need not be scratched again. In any case, as long as I drove the car, scratches would be less noticeable on that door than on the others. The earlier attempt had taught me something, too. If I removed all the screws on the hinge side of the door first and only loosened the others, I thought it might be possible to ease the panel back enough to see inside the door without taking the whole panel and electric window mechanism completely away.

It took me twenty minutes to find out that I was right about the panel, and a further five seconds to learn that I had been completely wrong about the stuff having been removed. There it still was, just as I had seen it in the photographs Tufan had shown me at Edirne. In this particular door there were twelve small, paper-wrapped cylinders— probably grenades.

I screwed the panel back into place, and then sat there for a while thinking. The Peugeot was parked about a hundred yards away—I could see it in the mirror—and I very nearly got out and walked back to tell the driver what I had found. I wanted badly to talk to someone. Then I pulled myself together. There was no point in talking to someone who wouldn't, or couldn't, usefully talk back. The sensible thing would be to obey orders.

I took my report out of the cigarette packet and added to it.

9:20 a.m. inspected interior front door driver's side. Material still in place as per photo. In view of time absent from villa and inability to add to this report, will not telephone from garage now.

I replaced the toilet paper in the packet, tossed it out of the window, and drove back onto the road. I waited just long enough to see a man from the Peugeot pick up the report, then I drove into Sariyer and filled the tank. I arrived back at the villa just before ten.

I half expected to find an angry Fischer pacing the courtyard and demanding to know where the hell I'd been. There was nobody. I drove the car into the stable yard, emptied the ash trays, brushed the floor carpeting, and ran a duster over the body. The Phillips screwdriver in my pocket worried me. Now that I knew that the stuff was still in the car, it seemed an incriminating thing to have. I certainly did not want to put it back in my room. It might be needed again, so I could not throw it away. In the end, I hid it inside the cover of an old tire hanging on the wall of the garage. Then I went and tidied myself up. Shortly before eleven o'clock I drove the car round to the marble steps in the front courtyard.

After about ten minutes Harper came out. He was wearing a blue sports shirt with blue slacks, and he had a map in his hand. He nodded in response to my greeting.

"Are we all right for gas, Arthur?"

"I filled it this morning, sir."

"Oh, you did." He looked agreeably surprised. "Well, do you know a place called Pendik?"

"I've heard the name. On the other side somewhere, isn't it? There's supposed to be a good restaurant there, I think."

"That's the place. On the Sea of Marmara." He spread the map out and pointed to the place. From Uskudar, on the Asian side of the Bosphorus, it was twenty-odd miles south along the coast. "How long will it take us to get there?"

"If we have luck with the car ferry about an hour and a half from here, sir."

"And if we don't have luck?"

"Perhaps ten or twenty minutes more."

"All right. Here's what we do. First, we go into town and drop Miss Lipp and Mr. Miller off at the Hilton Hotel. Then, you drive Mr. Fischer and me to Pendik. We'll be there a couple of hours. On the way back we stop off at the Hilton to pick the others up. Clear?"

"Yes, sir."

"Who paid for the gas?"

"I did, sir. I still have some of the Turkish money you gave me. I have the garage receipt here."

He waved it aside. "Do you have any money left?"

"Only a few lira now."

He gave me two fifty-lira notes. "That's for expenses. You picked up a couple of checks for Miss Lipp, too. Take the money out of that."

"Very well, sir."

"And, Arthur—stop needling Mr. Fischer, will you?"

"I rather thought that he intended to needle me, sir."

"You got the room and bathroom you asked for, didn't you?"

"Yes, sir."

"Well then, cut it out."

I started to point out that since I had been shown to the room the previous night I had not even set eyes on Fischer, much less "needled" him, but he was already walking back to the house.

They all came out five minutes later. Miss Lipp was in white linen; Miller, draped with camera and lens attachment case, looked very much the tourist; Fischer, in *maillot*, white jeans, and sandals, looked like an elderly beach boy from Antibes.

Harper sat in front with me. The others got into the back. Nobody talked on the way into Istanbul. Even at the time, I didn't feel that it was my presence there that kept them silent. They all had the self-contained air of persons on the way to an important business conference who have already explored every conceivable aspect of the negotiations that lie ahead, and can only wait now to learn what the other side's attitude is going to be. Yet, two of them seemed headed for a sightseeing tour, and the others for a seaside lunch. It was all rather odd. However, the Peugeot was following and, presumably, those in it would be able to cope with the situation when the party split up. There was nothing more I could do.

Miss Lipp and Miller got out at the door of the Hilton. A tourist bus blocked the driveway long enough for me to see that they went inside the hotel, and that a man from the Peugeot went in after them. The narcotics operation suddenly made sense again. The raw-opium supplier would be waiting in his room with samples which Miller, the skilled chemist, would proceed to test and evaluate. Later, if the samples proved satisfactory, and *only* if they did, Harper would consummate the deal. In the meantime, a good lunch seemed to be in order.

We had to wait a few minutes for the car ferry to Uskudar. From the ferry pier it is easy to see across the water the military barracks which became Florence Nightingale's hospital during the Crimean War. Just for the sake of something to say, I pointed it out to Harper.

"What about it?" he said rudely.

"Nothing, sir. It's just that that was Florence Nightingale's hospital. Scutari the place was called then."

"Look, Arthur, we know you have a guide's license, but don't take it too seriously, huh?"

Fischer laughed.

"I thought you might be interested, sir."

"All we're interested in is getting to Pendik. Where's this goddam ferry you talked about?"

I didn't trouble to answer that. The ferryboat was just coming in to the pier, and he was merely being offensive—for Fischer's benefit, I suspected. I wondered what they would have said if I had told them what the sand-colored Peugeot just behind us in the line of cars was there for, and whose orders its driver was obeying. The thought kept me amused for quite a while.

From Uskudar I took the Ankara road, which is wide and fast, and drove for about eighteen miles before I came to the secondary road which led off on the right to Pendik. We arrived there just before one o'clock.

It proved to be a small fishing port in the shelter of a headland. There were several yachts anchored in the harbor. Two wooden piers jutted out from the road which ran parallel to the foreshore; one had a restaurant built on it, the other served the smaller boats and dinghies as a landing stage. The place swarmed with children.

I was edging my way along the narrow road towards the restaurant when Harper told me to stop.

We were level with the landing stage and a man was approaching the road along it. He was wearing a yachting cap now, but I recognized him. It was the man who had been waiting at the Hilton car park on the night I had arrived in Istanbul.

He had obviously recognized the car and raised his hand in greeting as Harper and Fischer got out.

"Park the car and get yourself something to eat," Harper said to me. "Meet us back here in an hour."

"Very good, sir."

The man in the yachting cap had reached the road and I heard Harper's greeting as the three met.

"Hi, Giulio. *Sta bene?*"

And then they were walking back along the landing stage. In the driving mirror, I could see a man from the Peugeot sauntering down to the quayside to see what happened next.

At the end of the landing stage they climbed into an outboard dinghy. Giulio started it up and they shot away towards a group of yachts anchored about two hundred yards out. They went alongside a sixty-foot cabin cruiser with a squat funnel. The hull was black, the upper works white, and the funnel had a single band of yellow round it. A Turkish flag drooped from the staff at the stern. There was a small gangway down, and a deck hand with a boat hook to hold the dinghy as the three went on board. It was too far away for me to see the name on the hull.

I parked the car and went into the restaurant. The place was fairly full, but I managed to get a table near a window from which I could keep an eye on the cruiser. I asked the headwaiter about her and learned her name, *Bulut,* and the fact that she was on charter to a wealthy Italian gentleman, Signor Giulio, who could eat two whole lobsters at a sitting.

I did not pursue my inquiries; Tufan's men would doubtless get what information was to be had from the local police. At least I knew now what Giulio looked like, and where the boat which Miss Lipp had mentioned to Miller was based. I could also guess that Giulio was no more the true charterer of the *Bulut* than was Fischer the true lessee of the Kösk Sardunya. Wealthy Italian gentlemen with yachts do not lurk in the Istanbul Hilton car park waiting to drive away cars stuffed with contraband arms; they employ underlings to do such things.

Just as my grilled swordfish cutlet arrived, I saw that the *Bulut* was moving. A minute or two later, her bow anchor came out of the water and there was a swirl of white at her stern. The dinghy had been left moored to a buoy. The only people on the deck of the cabin cruiser were the two hands at the winches. She headed out across the bay towards an offshore island just visible in the distant haze. I wondered whether the Peugeot men would commandeer a motorboat and follow; but no other boat of any kind left the harbor. After about an hour, the *Bulut* returned and anchored in the same place as before. I paid my bill and went to the car.

Giulio brought Harper and Fischer back to the landing stage in the dinghy, but did not land with them. There was an exchange of farewells that I could see but not hear, and then they walked ashore to the car. Harper was carrying a flat cardboard box about two feet long by six inches wide. It was roughly tied with string.

"Okay, Arthur," he said as he got into the car. "Back to the Hilton."

"Very good, sir."

As I drove off he glanced back at the piers.

"Where did you lunch?" he asked. "That restaurant there?"

"Yes, sir."

"Good food?"

"Excellent, sir."

He grinned over his shoulder at Fischer. "Trust Giulio!"

"Our man Geven can cook well," said Fischer defensively, "and I intend to prove it to you."

"He's a lush," Harper said shortly.

"He cooked a *castradina* before you arrived which would have made you think that you were in the Quadri." Fischer was getting worked up now and leaning forward over the back of the front seat. His breath smelled of garlic and wine.

I could not resist the opportunity. "If you don't mind my saying so, sir," I said to Harper, "I think Mr. Fischer is right. Geven is an excellent cook. The chicken soup he gave me last night was perfect."

"What soup?" Fischer demanded. "We did not get soup."

"He was upset," I said. "You remember, Mr. Fischer, that you told him that he was not good enough to have a bathroom. He was upset. I think he threw away the soup he had made."

"I told him no such a thing!" Fischer was becoming shrill.

"Wait a minute," said Harper. "The cook doesn't have a *bathroom*?"

"He has the whole of the servants' rooms for himself," Fischer said.

"But no bathroom?"

"There is no bathroom there."

"What are you trying to do, Hans—poison us?"

Fischer flung himself against the back seat with a force that made the car lurch. "I am tired," he declared loudly, "of trying to arrange every matter as it should be arranged and then to receive nothing but criticism. I will not so to be accused, thus . . ." His English broke down completely and he went into German.

Harper answered him briefly in the same language. I don't know what he said, but it shut Fischer up. Harper lit a cigarette. After a moment or two he said: "You're a stupid crook, aren't you, Arthur?"

"Sir?"

"If you were a smart one, all you'd be thinking about would be how much dough you could screw out of this deal without getting your fingers caught in the till. But not you. That miserable little ego of yours had to have its kicks, too, doesn't it?"

"I don't understand, sir."

"Yes you do. I don't like stupid people around me. They make me nervous. I warned you once before. I'm not warning you again. Next time you see a chance of getting cute, you forget it, quick; because if you don't, that ego's liable to get damaged permanently."

It seemed wiser to say nothing.

"You're not still saying that you don't understand, Arthur?" He flicked my knee viciously with the back of his hand. The pain startled me and I swerved. He flicked me again. "Watch where you're going. What's the matter? Can't you talk while you're driving, or has the cat got your tongue?"

"I understand, sir."

"That's better. Now you apologize, like a little Egyptian gentleman, to Mr. Fischer."

"I'm very sorry, sir."

Fischer, appeased, signified his forgiveness with a short laugh.

The ferry from Uskudar was crowded with returning Sunday motorists and it took half an hour to get on a boat. Miss Lipp and Miller were waiting at the hotel entrance when I pulled up. Miller gave a wolfish grin and, as usual, leaped into the car ahead of Miss Lipp.

"You took your time," he said to no one in particular.

"The ferry was crowded," Harper replied. "Did you have a good afternoon?"

It was Miss Lipp who answered him. "Let the dogs be fed and clothed," she said. It was the same sentence that I had heard Miller cackling over the previous night, and I wondered idly what it could mean.

Harper nodded to her. "Let's get back to the villa, Arthur," he said.

None of them uttered a word on the drive back. I sensed a feeling of tension between them, and wondered who was waiting to report to whom. As they got out of the car, Harper picked the cardboard box up off the floor and turned to me.

"That's it for today, Arthur."

"What time tomorrow, sir?"

"I'll let you know."

"The car is very dusty, sir, and there is no proper hose here. I would like to get it washed at a garage."

"You do that." He could not have cared less what I did.

I drove into Sariyer and found a garage where they would wash the car. I left it there and went to a café. I had a drink before I telephoned Tufan.

The written report of the morning had been supplemented by reports from the surveillance squad and he had more to tell me than I had to tell him. Giulio's other name was Corzo, and his Swiss passport gave his occupation as "industrial designer." His age was forty-five and his place of birth Lugano. The cabin cruiser had been chartered a week earlier, for one month, through a yacht broker in

Antalya. The crew of three were local men of good reputation. As for Miss Lipp and Miller, they had lunched in the Hilton grill room, then hired a car. They had spent forty-five minutes sightseeing and returned to the Hilton, where Miss Lipp had visited the hairdresser. She had had a shampoo and set. Miller had passed the time reading French newspapers on the terrace.

"Then it must have been the meeting with Giulio they wanted to hear about," I said.

"What do you mean?"

I told him of the feeling I had had on the way back that they had been impatient for a chance to talk privately.

"Then why are you not at the villa? Go back there immediately."

"If they wish to have private talk there is nothing I can do to overhear it. Their part of the house on the ground floor is separate. I have not even seen those rooms."

"Are there no windows?"

"Giving on to their private terrace, yes. I could have no excuse for being even near it, let alone on it."

"Then do without an excuse."

"You told me to take no risks."

"No *unnecessary* risks. An important discussion justifies risk."

"I don't *know* that it is important. I just had a feeling. I don't know that it's a discussion either. Harper may just have wanted to pass on a piece of private information he had received from Giulio to the others. The whole thing could have been over in a minute."

"The meeting at Pendik was obviously important. We must know why. So far all you have learned is gossip from a fool of a cook. What do these people with arms and ammunition hidden in their car and false passports discuss when they are alone? What do they say? It is for you to find out."

"I can tell you one thing they say—'Let the dogs be fed and clothed.' I overheard it first last night. It seemed to be some sort of private joke."

He was silent for a moment and I waited for another angry outburst. None came. Instead he said thoughtfully: "That is quite an interesting joke."

"What does it mean?"

"When one of the old Sultans was preparing to receive a certain class of persons, he would always keep them waiting a long time, perhaps a whole day. Then, when he thought that they had been sufficiently humbled, he would give that order—'Let the dogs be fed and clothed.' After that, they would be admitted to the chamber of the Grand Vizier, given food, and robed in caftans."

"What class of persons?"

"The ambassadors of foreign powers." He paused. Obviously, he was still thinking about it. Then he dismissed me curtly. "You have your orders. Report as arranged."

I went and got the car. The man at the garage who had the key to the petrol pump had gone home, and there was only the old man who had washed the car waiting for me. I wasn't too pleased about that, as it meant that I would have to fill the tank in the morning. Opportunities for making telephone reports to Tufan did not seem particularly desirable at that moment.

When I got back to the villa it was almost dark and the lights were on in the terrace rooms. I put the car away and went to the kitchen.

Geven was in a jovial mood. Fischer had moved him to a bedroom near mine and told him to share my bathroom. Whether this was due to spite on Fischer's part or a shortage of bathrooms, I couldn't tell. Geven, through some obscure reasoning process of his own, had decided that the whole thing had been my idea. In a way, I suppose, he was right; but there was nothing to be done about it. I took a

tumbler of brandy from him and beamed like an idiot as if
I had earned every drop. He had cooked a spaghetti Bo-
lognese for the kitchen. The spies were having canned soup
and a shish kebab made with mutton which, he proudly as-
sured me, was as tough as new leather. The spaghetti was
really good. I had a double helping of it. As soon as the
Hamuls arrived, I got away, giving as an excuse that I had
work to do on the car. I went out to the yard.

The terrace ran along the front and right side of the
house; I had noticed a door in the wall beside the garage.
There was an orchard of fig trees beyond and I thought it
possible that the side terrace might be accessible from
there.

The door had no lock, only a latch, but the old hinges
were rusty and I used the dip stick from the car to run some
oil into them before I attempted to open it. It swung inward silently and I shut it behind me. I waited then, not
only so that my eyes would get used to the dark but because
the spies had not yet gone into dinner. I could hear their
voices faintly. I knew that Tufan would have wanted me to
go closer and hear what they were saying; but I didn't. The
ground was uneven and I would have to feel my way towards the terrace balustrade. I preferred to do that while
they were well away from the terrace and trying to get
their teeth into Geven's shish kebab.

After fifteen or twenty minutes, dinner was served and
I edged forward slowly to the terrace. As soon as I reached
it and was able to see through the balustrade, I realized
that it would be impossible for me to get close enough to
the windows of the room they had been using to hear anything. There was too much light coming from them. I suppose one of these daredevil agents you hear about would
have concealed himself in the shadows; but that looked
too risky for me. Getting to the shadows would have been
easy enough; but if Harper and Co. decided to sit outside,

as they had done the night before, there would have been no way of getting back without being seen.

I walked on through the orchard until I came to the outer edge of the front courtyard. This was the side which over-looked the Bosphorus and there were no trees to obstruct the view. A low stone balustrade ran along the edge with a statue on a plinth at each end. The first of these statues was over thirty feet from the corner of the terrace, but it was the nearest I could get and still remain in cover. The top of the plinth was chest-high. Using the balustrade as a steppingstone, it wasn't difficult to climb up. The statue, a larger than life-size Vestal virgin with bird-droppings all over her, seemed quite steady, and I was able to hold on to her draperies. From the plinth I could see over the terrace balustrading and through the windows of the corner draw-ing room. It was not much, but it was something. If they did decide to come out onto the terrace, I might even catch a word or two of what they said.

After about twenty minutes, they came back into the room. The bits of it that I could see contained an old leather-topped library table, part of a faded green settee, part of a wall mirror, a low round table, and one or two gilt chairs. The only person I could actually see at first was Miller, who took a corner of the settee; but he was talking nineteen to the dozen and waving his hands about, so he obviously wasn't alone. Then Mrs. Hamul came in with a coffee tray, which she put on the round table, and I saw bits of the others as they helped themselves. Somebody gave Miller a glass of brandy, which he drank as if he needed it; he could have been trying to wash away the taste of his din-ner. After a bit, he stopped talking and appeared to be lis-tening, his head moving slightly as he shifted his attention from one speaker to another. Then, there was a flash of white in the mirror and his head turned. For a moment, I saw Miss Lipp. She had changed into a green dress, though;

the white belonged to a large sheet of paper. Almost immediately it disappeared from view. Miller's head lifted as he began to listen to someone who was standing up. A minute or so went by, and then the paper reappeared, as if put aside, on the library table. I could see now that it was a map. At that distance and at that angle it was impossible to tell what it was a map of, but it looked to me like a roughly triangular island. I was still staring at it when Harper moved in and folded it into four.

After that, nothing seemed to happen until, suddenly, Harper and Miss Lipp came out onto the terrace from a window much farther away and walked down the marble steps. There was nothing purposeful about their movements —they were obviously just going for a stroll—but I thought it as well to get out of the way. If they were going to admire the view from the balustrade, I would be in an awkward spot.

I got down from the plinth and moved back into the shelter of the fig trees. Sure enough, they made their way round to the balustrade. When they turned to go back I was only twenty-five feet away from them. I heard a snatch of conversation.

". . . if I took over?" That was Miss Lipp.

"He was Leo's idea," he answered. "Let Leo take care of him. After tomorrow, he doesn't matter too much anyway. Even Arthur could do the rest of that job."

She laughed. "The indignant sheep? With his breath you wouldn't even need the grenades, I guess. You'd get a mass surrender."

He laughed.

She said: "When does Giulio's man arrive?"

"Sometime today. I didn't wait. Giulio knows . . ."

I heard no more.

As soon as they were well clear, I went back through the orchard to the yard, and then up to my room. I locked the door. Geven would be free of the kitchen at any moment, and I did not want to be bothered with him.

I had to think about what they had said and it was hard to do so, because all I could think about was her laugh and the words she had used about me. I felt sick. There was another time when it had been like that, too. Jones iv and I had gone up to Hilly Fields to meet a couple of girls we knew. One of them was named Muriel, the other was Madge. Madge didn't turn up because, so Muriel said, she had a cold. So there were just the three of us. Muriel was really Jones' girl, so I was more or less out of it. I tried to pick up another girl, but that was more difficult when you were alone and I didn't have any luck. After a while, I gave up and went back to where I had left the other two necking on a seat under the trees. I thought I'd come up quietly and give them a surprise. That is how I overheard it. She was saying that she had to get home early, for some reason or other, and he was asking her about Saturday night.

"With Arthur, too?" she said.

"I suppose so."

"Well, Madge won't come."

"She'll be over her cold by then."

"She hasn't got a cold. She just didn't want to come. She says Arthur's a little twerp and gives her the creeps."

I went away and they didn't know that I'd heard. Then I was sick behind the bushes. I hated that girl Madge so much that it was like a pain.

Geven came up and I heard him go into the bathroom. A little while afterwards he came out and knocked on my door. I had taken the precaution of switching off the light so that it wouldn't show under the door and he would think that I was asleep. He knocked again. After a few moments I heard him muttering to himself. Then he went away.

I nearly changed my mind and called him in. I could have done with a drink just then, and someone to talk to. But then I thought of how dirty he was and how the stink of his body would stay in the room—the "perfume of the great unwashed," as my father would have said. Besides, I couldn't be sure of getting rid of him when I wanted to, and I had the eleven o'clock radio call to take.

It came at last.

Attention period report. Attention period report. Passenger for yacht Bulut *arrived Pendik seventeen hundred hours today. Name Enrico, other names unknown so far. Description: short, stocky, black hair, brown eyes, age about thirty-five. Casual observation of subject and hand luggage suggests workman rather than guest of charterer Corzo. Are you able to identify this man? Important that written notes of all conversations, with particular care as to political content, should be made. Essential you report progress. Repeat. Essential.*

The outside of the body can be washed of sweat and grease; but inside there are processes which produce other substances. Some of these smell. How do you wash away the smells of the inside of the body?

Chapter

8

The morning call was a repetition of that of the previous night, and made no more sense at 7 a.m. than it had at 11. I got up and went to the bathroom. Luckily, I had had the sense to remove my towel to my bedroom; but Geven had left a filthy mess. There was gray scum in the bath and shaving soap in the basin. Patience was necessary in order to flush the toilet successfully, and he had given up too soon.

Shaved, he looked more bleary-eyed than he had with the three-day growth, but his mood was one of jovial aggression. Fischer's complaints about the shish kebab, it seemed, had been loud and insolent. But the reprisal had already been planned—the spies' dinner that night would be boiled mutton in yoghurt *à la Turque*. Fischer would learn to his cost who was master in the kitchen; and if he didn't like the knowledge, well then, the spies could go on eating pig swill or find themselves another chef.

I had breakfast, got the car out, and drove to the garage for petrol.

Tufan answered promptly. I made my report about the overheard conversation first, editing only slightly. "If I took over. He was Leo's idea, let Leo take care of him. After tomorrow he doesn't matter too much anyway. Grenades . . . mass surrender."

He made me repeat it slowly. When he started to complain that there wasn't more of it, I told him about the map. I had guessed that this would excite his interest, and it did.

"You say it looked like a map of an island?"

"I thought so. The shape was roughly triangular."

"Was it a colored map?"

"No, black and white."

"Then it could have been a marine chart?"

"I suppose so."

He said thoughtfully: "A boat, the chart of an island, grenades, respirators, guns, surrender . . ."

"And something that Fischer is to do today," I reminded him.

He ignored the interruption. "You are sure this island had a triangular shape?"

"I thought so, but the map wasn't absolutely flat. It was hard to see. It could have been a design for a swimming pool."

He ignored the frivolity. "Could it have been kidney-shaped?"

"Perhaps. Would that mean something?"

"That is the shape of the island of Yassiada, where certain political prisoners are held awaiting trial. It is only fifteen kilometers from Pendik. Have you heard the name Yassiada mentioned?"

"No."

"Or Imrali?"

"No. Is that an island, too?"

"It is a town on an island sixty kilometers from Pendik. It is also the place where Menderes was hanged."

"How is that island shaped?"

"Like the head of a dog. I must have another report from you this evening without fail, even if it is only negative."

"I will do what I can."

"Above all, you must search for this chart."

"How can I?"

"You can search at night. In any case you must obtain a closer look at it."

"I don't see how I can do that. Even if they bring it out again, I won't be able to get any closer."

"With binoculars you could."

"I have no binoculars."

"On the way back to the villa, stop on the road. The Opel is on surveillance duty today. An agent from the car will give you binoculars."

"Supposing Harper sees them. How do I explain them?"

"Do not let him see them. I expect a report tonight. If necessary you will make direct contact with the surveillance personnel. Is that clear?" He hung up.

I drove back towards the villa. Just outside Sariyer on the coast road I pulled up. The Opel stopped a hundred yards behind me. After a minute or two, a man got out of it and walked towards the Lincoln. He was carrying a leather binocular case. He handed it to me without a word and went back to the Opel.

I put the binoculars on the seat and drove on. They were too big to put in my pocket. I would either have to smuggle them up to my room somehow, or hide them in the garage. I was annoyed with myself. I should have known better. Any sort of map is catnip to intelligence people. I should have kept quiet about it.

Even without the binoculars, though, I would have been irritated, and I did have sense enough to realize that. The binoculars were only a nusiance. It was really the conclusion he had come to that bothered me.

What he'd wanted to see all along, and, quite evidently, what he now *did* see, was yet another conspiracy against the Committee of National Union, yet another coup in preparation. The last attempt to overthrow the Committee had been made by a group of dissident army officers *inside* the country. What more likely than that the next attempt would be made with the help of money and hired terrorists from *outside* the country? What more likely than that it would begin with a daring rescue of officer prisoners awaiting trial? As he had said: "A boat, the chart of an island, grenades, respirators, guns, surrender." It all added up so neatly.

The trouble was, as it had been all along, that he didn't know the people concerned. I did. I knew how vile they were, too. In fact, there was nothing I wanted more at that moment than to see them get hell. But they just didn't strike me as the sort of people who would be hired terrorists. I could not have said why. If he had countered by asking me what sort of people *were* hired terrorists and how many I had met, I would have had no sensible answer. All I could have said would have been: "These people wouldn't take that kind of risk."

When I got back to the villa, Fischer was standing on the terrace at the top of the steps. He motioned to me to pull up there. As he came down the steps, I remembered, just in time, to shove the binoculars onto the floor by my feet.

"You will not be wanted today, Simpson," he said. "We are going on a private excursion. I will drive the car."

"Very good, sir. It is full of petrol, but I was going to dust it." I was all smiles above, and all binoculars below.

"Very well." He waved me off in his highhanded way. "The car must be here in half an hour."

"Yes, sir."

I drove round the courtyard into the garage, and hid the binoculars behind an empty oil drum before I gave the car a flick-over with a wet duster.

Just before ten I drove it to the courtyard and left it there with the ignition key in. Then, I went back to the yard, through the door into the orchard, and found a place from which I could see the car without being seen. When they went out, I wanted to make sure that they had all gone—Fischer, Harper, Miss Lipp, and Miller.

After forty minutes or so, all four came out and got into the car. As soon as they had gone, I went to the kitchen. Geven was there chopping meat and sipping brandy. I had a drink myself and let him talk for a while before asking whether they were expected back for lunch. They were not. He would make an omelet *pour le personnel*.

I went upstairs to the bedroom floor. At the head of the back stairs the corridor ran left and right, parallel to the rear wall of the villa. If you turned right, you came to my room and Geven's, among others; if you turned left, you were faced by a pair of double doors. Beyond them were the master bedrooms and guest suites.

The double doors were half open when I went up. Through the opening, I caught a glimpse of a wickerwork trolley full of dirty linen, and of old Hamul working on the floor of the corridor with a carpet sweeper. Mrs. Hamul was presumably changing the sheets on the beds.

I went to my room, waited an hour, and then strolled back along the corridor.

The door was still open and the Hamuls were still messing about in the bedrooms. I went down to the kitchen and had another drink with Geven. He was busy with the stewpot and another hour went by before he decided to make the omelet. I heard the Hamuls come down at about the same time and go through to the laundry. As soon as I had finished eating, I told Geven that I was going to have a sleep and went upstairs again.

First, I locked my room from the outside in case he looked in to see if I were there; then I went through the double doors and shut them behind me.

What I was looking for was the map, and it was difficult to know where to start. There were about eighteen rooms there, and they were of all shapes and sizes. Some were bedrooms, some sitting rooms; some were so sparsely furnished that it was hard to tell what they had been. Where there was furniture, it was all in the same bilious-looking French-hotel style. The only things not in short supply were mirrors and chandeliers; every room had those.

I identified Miller's room first, because his suitcase was open on the bed, then Fischer's because of the shirts in one of the drawers. I found no map in either room. Miss Lipp's suite was over the center portico, with Harper's next to it on the corner. There was a connecting door. I looked through all the drawers and cupboards, I looked inside the suitcases, I looked above and below every piece of furniture. The only maps I found were in a copy of *Europa Touring* that was on Miss Lipp's writing desk, along with some Italian paperback novels.

Beyond Harper's suite, and on the side of the building overlooking the orchard, there was a room that had been fitted up as a studio. Architect's drawers had been built along one wall. It seemed a good place to look for a large flat map, and I was carefully going through every drawer when I heard the sound of car doors slamming.

I scrambled through Harper's bedroom, which had windows onto the courtyard, and saw the roof of the Lincoln in front of the portico. Then I panicked. I missed the door which led to the passage and got into his bathroom instead. By the time I had found the right door, I could hear

Fischer's voice from the stairs. It was hopeless to try to dodge round through the rooms. I didn't know the way well enough. All I could do was retreat back through Harper's bedroom into the studio and shut the door. From there, there was no other way out, except through the window; but it was the only hiding place I could find.

I heard him come into the room, then a clink of money, then a sort of slap. He was emptying his pockets onto the table. The door didn't latch properly and I could hear every move he made. I knew that he would hear any move I made, too. I froze there.

"My God, that city's worse than New York in August," he said.

I heard Miss Lipp answer him. The door connecting the suites, which I had shut, must have been opened by her.

"I wonder if Hamul fixed that water. Undo me, will you, *Liebchen?*"

He moved away. I tiptoed over to the studio window and looked out. There was a small balcony outside and, a few feet below, the roof of the terrace. If I could get down there, I thought it might be possible to reach the orchard without breaking my neck. The trouble was that I would have to open the french window to get to the balcony. It had one of those long double bolts that you work by twisting a handle in the center. They can make a clattering noise when they spring open, and this one looked as if it would. I went back to the door.

It sounded as if they were in his sitting room. I heard her give a soft chuckle.

"Too many clothes on," she said.

He came back into the bedroom and, then, after a moment or two, went into the bathroom. Water began to run. I went to the window again and gingerly tried the handle. It moved easily enough. The bottom bolt slid out and the door sprang inward with a slight thud; but then I saw that one side of the connecting link was broken and that the top bolt hadn't moved. I tried to pull it down by hand, but it was too stiff. I would have to push it down through the slot at the top. I put a chair against the window and looked about for something metal I could use to push with.

The noise of running water from the bathroom stopped, and I stood still again. I tried to think what I had in my pockets that might move the bolt; a key perhaps.

"I will have to do something about my tan when we get back," said Miss Lipp. She was in the next room now.

"It's holding up."

"Your hair's wet."

Silence, then a deep sigh from her and the bed creaked.

For about two minutes I clung to the hope that they were going to have a siesta. Then movements began. After a while I could hear their breathing and it wasn't the breathing of sleep. More minutes went by and there were other sounds. Then, the beast with two backs was at work, and soon it was making its usual noises, panting and grunting and moaning, while I stood there like a half-wit, picturing her long legs and slim thighs and wondering how on earth I was going to get out of there without anybody seeing me. I was sweating so much that it was running into my eyes and misting my glasses. I couldn't have seen to get the bolt open just then, even if I had dared to try.

They seemed to go on interminably; but the noisy finales arrived at last. I waited, hopefully, for them to go to their bathrooms; but they didn't. There was just a long silence, until I heard him say: "Here," and a lighter clicked. Another silence, until he broke it.

"Where shall we eat tonight?"

"Les Baux. I will have the *feuilleté de ris de veau*. You?"

"Avallon, Moulin des Ruats, the *coq au vin*."

"With the Cuvée du Docteur?"

"Of course. Though right now, frankly, I'd settle for a ham sandwich and a glass of beer."

"It's not for long, *Liebchen*. I wonder who told Hans that this man could cook."

"He can cook all right, but he's one of those lushes who has to be wooed. If he isn't, he gets into a white rage and says 'The hell with you.' Hans doesn't know how to handle him. I'll bet Arthur eats better than we do. In fact, I know damn well he does. Where's the ash tray?"

"Here." She giggled. "Careful!"

"*Merde, alors!*"

"That is not the place for an ash tray."

Soon it began all over again. Eventually, when they were exhausted, they did have the decency to go to the bathrooms. While the water was running, I got up onto the chair and worked on the bolt with my room key. By the time he had finished in the bathroom, I had the window unlatched. I had to wait then until they were asleep; though it was not until I heard her voice again that I knew that she had returned to his bed.

"*Liebchen*," she said drowsily.

"What is it?" He was half asleep, too.

"Be careful, please, tomorrow."

"*Entendu*."

There was the sound of a kiss. I looked at my watch. It was twenty past three. I gave them ten minutes, then carefully edged over to the window and pulled one side open. I did it very slowly because there was a slight breeze outside and I did not want the draft to open the bedroom door while I was still there. Then I edged my way out onto the balcony.

It was a four-foot drop to the roof of the terrace and I made scarcely any noise getting down. I had more trouble at the end of the terrace. I am really not built for climbing, and I tried to use the trelliswork as a stepladder. It gave way, and I slithered to the ground clutching at the branches of an espaliered peach tree.

I managed to get to my room without anyone seeing the mess I was in. When I had cleaned up and changed my shirt, I went down to the car and put it away in the garage.

If I had noticed then that the door panels had been taken off, things would have turned out very differently for Harper, Lipp, and Miller; but I didn't notice. It didn't even occur to me to look at them. I was still too flustered to do anything except try to behave naturally. Garaging the car was just a way of showing myself outside and on the job.

I went back into the kitchen. There was nobody there. I found a bottle of Geven's brandy and had a drink and a cigarette. When I was quite calm again, I went out and walked down the drive to the road.

The Opel was parked near the fishing-boat pier. I strolled across to it and saw the men inside watching me. As I passed, I said: "Tufan."

When I had gone on a few paces I heard a car door open. A moment or so later a man fell in step beside me.

"What is it?" He was a dark, hard-eyed police type in an oatmeal-colored shirt with buttoned pockets. He spoke in French.

"Something dangerous is to be attempted tomorrow," I said. "I do not know what. I overheard part of a conversation. Major Tufan should be informed."

"Very well. Why did you not drive today?"

"They told me I wasn't needed. Where did they go?"

"To Istanbul, Beyoglu. They drove to a garage by the Spanish Consulate. It is a garage that has spare parts for American cars. The driver, Fischer, remained there with the car for ten minutes. The other two men and the woman walked to the Divan Hotel. They had lunch there. Fischer joined them there and also had lunch. Then they walked back to the garage, picked up the car, and returned here. Major Tufan says that you are to report on a chart later."

"If I can. Tell him I made a search of the bedrooms while they were out, but could not find the chart. I will try to search the living rooms tonight. It may be quite late before I can report. Will you be here?"

"Someone will be."

"All right."

As we turned and walked back towards the Opel, I crossed the road and re-entered the drive. I had something to think about now. From what I had overheard in the courtyard the night before, I knew that Fischer had some special task to perform that day. Had he already performed it, or was it yet to be performed? Driving the car into Istanbul so that he and the others could have some eatable food didn't seem very special. On the other hand, it was odd that I should have been told to stay behind, and odd about that visit to the garage. There was nothing wrong with the car and it needed no spare parts. And why had Fischer not walked to the Divan with the other three? Why had he stayed behind?

It is obvious that I should have thought of the car doors first. I didn't do so for a very simple reason: I knew from personal experience how long it took to remove and replace one panel, and Fischer had not been at the garage long enough to empty one door, let alone four. The possibility that his function might have been to give orders instead of doing the actual work didn't occur to me, *then*. And, I may say, it didn't occur to Tufan *at all*. If it had, I should have been spared a ghastly experience.

Anyway, when I went back through the yard to take a look at the car, my mind was on spare parts. I looked in the luggage compartment first to see if anything had been stowed away there; then I examined the engine. You can usually tell by the smudges and oil smears when work has been done on an engine. I drew a blank, of course. It wasn't until I opened the door to see if anything had been left in the glove compartment that I saw the scratches.

Whoever had taken the panels off had made the very mistake I had been so careful to avoid; he had used an ordinary screwdriver on the Phillips heads. There were scratches and bright marks on the metal as well as cuts in the leather where the tool had slipped. Of course, nobody would have noticed them on a casual inspection, but I was so conscious of the panels and what I had seen behind them that the slightest mark stood out. I went over all four and knew at once that they had all been taken off and replaced. I also knew, from the different feel of the doors when I swung them on their hinges, that the heavy things which had been concealed inside were no longer there. Presumably, they had been removed in the garage near the Spanish Consulate. Where they were at that moment was anybody's guess.

I wondered whether I should go down to the road again immediately and report to the surveillance car, or wait until I reported later about the map. I decided to wait. If the stuff was still in the garage, it would probably still be there in the morning. If, as seemed more likely, it had already been moved somewhere else, then the damage was done and two or three hours would make no difference. Anyway, I didn't *want* to go back down to the road. I felt that I had run enough risks for one day already; and I still had to go looking for that damned map. I think I did the sensible thing. I can't stand people who are wise after the event, but it must be obvious now that it was Tufan who made the real mistakes, not me.

The trouble with Geven began while we were in the kitchen eating our dinner; or, rather, while I was eating and he was putting away more brandy. It was about seven o'clock, and he had been drinking steadily since six. In that hour he must have had nearly a third of a bottle. He wasn't yet quite drunk; but he was certainly far from sober.

He had made a perfectly delicious *risotto* with finely chopped chicken livers and pimientos in it. I was on my second helping and trying to persuade him to eat what he had on his plate, when Fischer came in.

"Geven!"

Geven looked up and gave him his wet smile. "*Vive la compagnie*," he said convivially, and reached for a dirty glass. "*Un petit verre, monsieur?*"

Fischer ignored the invitation. "I wish to know what you are preparing for dinner tonight," he said.

"It is prepared." Geven gave him a dismissive wave of his hand and turned to me again.

"Then you can tell me what it is." At that moment Fischer caught sight of my plate. "Ah, I see. A *risotto*, eh?"

Geven's lip quivered. "That is for us servants. For the master and his guests there is a more important dish in the manner of the country."

"What dish?"

"You would not understand."

"I wish to know."

Geven answered in Turkish. I understood one word of what he said: *kuzu*, baby lamb.

To my surprise, and to Geven's, too, I think, Fischer answered in the same language.

Geven stood up and shouted something.

Fischer shouted back, and then walked from the room before Geven had time to answer.

Geven sat down again, his lower lip quivering so violently that, when he tried to drain his glass, most of the brandy ran down his chin. He refilled the glass and glowered at me.

"*Pislik!*" he said. "*Domuz!*"

Those are rude words in Turkish. I gathered that they

were meant for Fischer, so I said nothing and got on with my food.

He refilled my glass and shoved it towards me. "A toast," he said.

"All right."

"There'll be no promotion this side of the ocean, so drink up, my lads, bless 'em all!"

Only he didn't say "bless." I had forgotten that he had been educated in Cyprus when it was under British rule.

"Drink!"

I drank. "Bless 'em all."

He began to sing. "Bless all the sergeants and W.O. ones, bless all the corporals and their bleeding sons! Drink!"

I sipped. "Bless 'em all."

He drained the glass again and leaned across the chopping table breathing heavily. "I tell you," he said menacingly; "if that bastard says one more word, I kill him."

"He's just a fool."

"You defend him?" The lower lip quivered.

"No, no. But is he *worth* killing?"

He poured himself another drink. Both lips were working now, as if he had brought another thought agency into play in order to grapple with the unfamiliar dilemma my question had created.

The Hamuls arrived just then to prepare for the service of the evening meal, and I saw the old man's eyes take in the situation. He began talking to Geven. He spoke a country dialect and I couldn't even get the drift of what he was saying; but it seemed to improve matters a little. Geven grinned occasionally and even laughed once. However, he still went on drinking, and, when I tried to slip away to my room, there was a sudden flare of temper.

"Where you go?"

"You have work to do here. I am in the way."

"You sit down. You are my guest in the kitchen. You drink nothing. Why?"

I had a whole tumblerful of brandy in front of me by now. I took another sip.

"Drink!"

I drank and tried to look as if I were enjoying myself. When he wasn't looking, I managed to tip half the brandy in my glass down the sink. It didn't do much good. As soon as he noticed the half-empty glass, he filled it up again.

Dinner had been ordered for eight-thirty, and by then he was weaving. It was Mrs. Hamul who did the dishing up. He leaned against the range, glass in hand, smiling benignly on her while she ladled the loathsome contents of the stewpot onto the service platters. Dinner was finally served.

"Bless 'em all!"

"Bless 'em all!"

"Drink!"

At that moment there was an indistinct shout from the direction of the dining room. Then a door along the passage was flung open, and there were quick footsteps. I heard Miss Lipp call out: "Hans!" Then Fischer came into the kitchen. He was carrying a plateful of food.

As Geven turned unsteadily to confront him, Fischer yelled something in Turkish and then flung the plate straight at his head.

The plate hit Geven on the shoulder and then crashed to the floor; but quite a lot of food went onto his face. Gravy ran down his smock.

Fischer was still shouting. Geven stared at him stupidly. Then, as Fischer flung a final insult and turned to go, a most peculiar expression came over Geven's face. It was almost like a wide-eyed smile. "*Monsieur est servi,*" he said. At the same instant, I saw his hand dart out for the chopping knife.

I shouted a warning to Fischer, but he was already out in the passage. Geven was after him in a flash. By the time I got through the door, Fischer was already backing away and yelling for help. There was blood streaming from a gash on his face and he had his hands up trying to protect himself. Geven was hacking and slashing at him like a madman.

As I ran forward and clung onto the arm wielding the chopping knife, Harper came into the passage from the dining room.

"*Senden illâllah!*" bawled Geven.

Then Harper hit him in the side of the neck and he went down like an empty sack.

Fischer's arms and hands were pouring blood now, and he stood there looking down at them as if they did not belong to him.

Harper glanced at me. "Get the car around, quick."

I stopped the car at the foot of the steps and went in through the front of the house. It did not seem to be a moment for standing on ceremony.

Fischer was sitting in a marble-floored washroom just off the main hall. Harper and Miss Lipp were wrapping his hands and arms in towels; Miller was trying to stanch the face wound. The Hamuls were running round in circles.

Harper saw me and motioned to Hamul. "Ask the old guy where the nearest doctor is. Not a hospital, a private doctor."

"I will ask him," muttered Fischer. His face was a dirty gray.

I caught Hamul's arm and shoved him forward.

There were two doctors in Sariyer, he said, but the nearest was outside Bülyükdere in the other direction. He would come to the villa if called by telephone.

Harper shook his head when Fischer told him this. "We'll go to *him*," he said. "We'll give him five hundred lira and tell him you tripped over an electric fan. That should fix it." He looked at Miss Lipp. "You and Leo had better stay here, honey. The fewer, the better."

She nodded.

"I don't know the way to this doctor's house," I said. "May we take Hamul as a guide?"

"Okay."

Harper sat in the back with Fischer and a supply of fresh towels; Hamul came in front with me.

The doctor's house was two miles along the coast road. When we got there, Fischer told Hamul to wait outside in the car with me; so it was not possible for me to walk back and tell the men in the Opel what was going on. Presumably, they would find out from the doctor later on. Hamul fingered the leather of the seat for a while, then curled up on it and went to sleep. I tried to see if I could get out without waking him, but the sound of the door opening made him sit up instantly. After that, I just sat there and smoked. I suppose that I should have written a cigarette packet message about the car doors and dropped it then—Hamul wouldn't have noticed that—but at that point I still thought that I was going to be able to make a verbal report later.

They were inside well over an hour. When he came out, Fischer didn't look too bad at first sight. The cut on his face had a lint dressing neatly taped over it, and his left arm was resting in a small sling of the kind that suggests comfort for a minor sprain rather than a serious injury. But when he got closer I could see that both his hands and forearms were quite extensively bandaged, and that the left hand was cupped round a thick pad taped so as to immobilize the fingers. I got out and opened the door for him. He smelled of disinfectant and surgical spirit.

He and Harper got in without a word, and remained silent on the way back to the villa.

Miller and Miss Lipp were waiting on the terrace. As I

pulled up into the courtyard, they came down the steps. I opened the door for Fischer. He got out and walked past them into the house. Still, nothing was said. Hamul was already making for his own quarters at the back. Miller and Miss Lipp came up to Harper.

"How is he?" Miller asked. There was nothing solicitous about the question. It was a grim request for information.

"The left hand has seven stitches on one cut, four on another, more stitches on the arm. The right forearm has seven stitches. The other cuts weren't so deep. The doctor was able to tape those up. He gave him some shots and a sedative." His eyes went to Miss Lipp. "Where's the cook?"

"Gone," she said. "When he woke up, he asked if he could go to his room. We let him. He just packed his things and went off on that scooter of his. We didn't try to stop him."

He nodded.

"But about Fischer . . ." Miller began, his teeth showing as if he wanted to eat someone.

Harper broke in firmly. "Let's go inside, Leo." He turned to me. "You can put the car away for now, Arthur, but I may want it again later to drive to Pendik, so you stick around. Make yourself some coffee in the kitchen, then I'll know where to find you."

"Very good, sir."

When I got to the kitchen I found that someone, Mrs. Hamul no doubt, had washed the dishes and cleaned the place up. The charcoal fires on the range were not quite dead, but I made no attempt to revive one. I found a bottle of red wine and opened that.

I was getting anxious. It was nearly ten-thirty and the radio call was due at eleven; but I didn't so much mind missing another *Essential you report progress*; it was the undelivered report on the car doors that bothered me. Obviously, Fischer's getting hurt had thrown some sort of wrench into the works and changes of plan were being made. If those changes meant that I was going to be up all night driving Harper to Pendik and back, I would have to deliver the message via a cigarette packet after all. I went into the scullery, in case Harper should suddenly come into the kitchen, and wrote the message—*Car doors now empty, check garage near Spanish Consulate*—on a piece of paper torn off a shelf lining. I felt better when I had done that. My other assignment for the night, the search for the mysterious map, didn't worry me at all. In fact, though it may seem funny now, at that point in the proceedings I had completely forgotten about it.

It was after eleven-thirty and I had finished the last of the wine, when there was the sound of a door opening and Harper came through from the dining room. I got to my feet.

"Sorry to keep you up this late, Arthur," he said; "but Mr. Miller and I are having a friendly argument, and we want you to help us decide who's right. Come in."

I followed him through the dining room, and along a passage to the room in which I had seen them the previous night.

It was L-shaped and even bigger than I had thought. When I had looked through the windows, all I had seen had been the short arm of the L. The long arm went all the way to the main entrance hall. There was a low platform with a concert-size grand piano on it. The room looked as if it had been used at some time for "musical soirées."

Miss Lipp and Miller were sitting at the library desk. Fischer was in the background, sitting in an armchair with his head thrown back so that he stared at the ceiling. I thought for a moment that he had passed out, but as I came in he slowly raised his head and stared at me. He looked terrible.

"Sit down, Arthur." Harper motioned me to a chair facing Miller.

I sat down. Miss Lipp was watching Miller. Miller was watching me through his rimless glasses. The toothy smile was there as ever, but it was the most unamused smile I have ever seen; it was more like a grimace.

Harper leaned against the back of the settee.

"It's really two problems, Arthur," he said. "Tell me this. How long does it take to get to Pendik at this time of night? The same as during the day?"

"Less, perhaps; but it would depend on the ferry to Uskudar."

"How often does that run at night?"

"Every hour, sir."

"So if we missed one it could take us well over two hours?"

"Yes."

He looked at Miller. "Two hours to Pendik, two hours to persuade Giulio, two more hours to persuade Enrico . . ."

"If he would be persuaded," Miss Lipp put in.

Harper nodded. "Of course. And then two hours back. Not a very restful night, Leo."

"Then postpone," Miller snapped.

Harper shook his head. "The overheads, Leo. If we postpone, it means abandon. What will our friends say to that?"

"It is not their necks." Miller looked resentfully at Fischer. "If you had not . . ." he began, but Harper cut him off sharply.

"We've been over all that, Leo. Now, why don't you at least give it a whirl?"

Miller shrugged.

Harper looked at me. "We want to make an experiment, Arthur. Do you mind going over there and standing against the wall with your back against it?"

"Over here?"

"That's right. Your back touching the wall." He went over to Fischer, picked up a length of thick cord which was lying across the bandaged hands, and threw one end of it to me. I saw that the other end was attached to a leg of the settee. "Now here's what it is, Arthur," he went on; "I've told Mr. Miller that you can pull that settee six feet towards you just with the strength of your arms. Of course, your back's leaning against the wall, so you can't use your weight to help you. It has to be just your arms. Mr. Miller says you can't do it, and he's got a hundred-dollar bill that says he's right. I've got one that says he's wrong. If he wins, I pay. If I win, you and I split fifty-fifty. How about it?"

"I'll try," I said.

"Very well, begin," said Miller. "Your shoulders against the wall, your heels not more than ten centimeters from it and together." He moved over so that he could see that I didn't cheat.

I have always detested that kind of parlor trick; in fact, I dislike any sort of trial of physical strength. They always remind me of a lot of boys I once saw in the school lavatories. They were standing in a row seeing who could urinate the farthest. Suddenly they started laughing and then began to aim at each other. I happened to get in the way and it was very unpleasant. In my opinion, rugger is the same kind of thing—just childish, smelly, homosexual horseplay. I always got out of it whenever I could. Today, any sort of exercise brings on my indigestion immediately.

Frankly, then, I didn't think that there was the slightest chance of my being able to pull that heavy settee one foot, much less six. I am not particularly strong in the arms anyway. Why should I be? I have enough strength to lift a suitcase and drive a car; what more do I want?

"Go on," said Miller. "Pull with all your strength!"

I should have done as he said and fallen flat on my face.

Then, Harper would have lost a hundred dollars, and I should have been spared the ordeal. But Miss Lipp had to interfere.

"Just a minute, Arthur," she said; "I tried this and I couldn't do it. But you're a man with a good pair of shoulders on you, and I think you *can* do it."

Even if I had never heard her use the phrase "indignant sheep" about me, I would have known this heavy-handed guile for what it was. I do *not* have a good pair of shoulders on me. I have narrow, sloping ones. Women who think they can get away with that childish sort of flattery make me sick. I was really annoyed. Unfortunately, that made me go red. She smiled. I suppose she thought I was blushing because of her bloody compliment.

"I'm not much good at this sort of game," I said.

"The thing is to pull on the cord steadily, Arthur. Don't jerk it. Pull steadily, and when it starts moving, keep pulling steadily hand over hand. It's an easy fifty dollars. I *know* you can do it."

I was getting really browned off with her now. "All right, you bitch," I thought to myself; "I'll show you!" So I did the exact opposite of what she'd said. I jerked on the cord as hard as I could.

The settee moved a few inches; but, of course, what I'd done by jerking it, was to get the feet out of the dents they'd made for themselves in the thick carpet. After that, I just kept on pulling and it slid some more. As it got nearer it became easier because I was pulling up as well as along.

Harper looked at Miller. "What about it, Leo?"

Miller felt my arms and shoulders as if he were buying a horse. "He is flabby, out of condition," he said sourly.

"But he did the trick," Harper reminded him.

Miller spread out his hands as if to abandon the argument.

Harper took a note from his wallet. "Here, Arthur," he

said, "fifty dollars." He paused and then went on quietly:
"How would you like to earn two thousand?"

I stared at him.

"Sit down," he said.

I sat down and was glad to do so. My legs were trembling.
With two thousand dollars I could buy a Central American
passport that would be good for years; and it would be a real
passport, too. I know, because I have looked into such matters. As long as you don't actually go to the country concerned, there's no trouble at all. You just buy the passport.
That's the way their consuls abroad line their pockets. Of
course, I knew it was all a pipe dream. Even if I did whatever it was they wanted, Harper wasn't going to be in a position to pay me, because the chances were that Tufan would
have him in jail by then. Still, it was a good dream.

"I'd like that very much," I said.

They were all watching me intently now.

"Don't you want to know what you have to do for it?"
Harper asked.

I wasn't going to let him walk all over me. I sat back.
"What Mr. Fischer was going to do, I suppose," I answered;
"that is, if he hadn't that little accident this evening."

Miss Lipp laughed. "I told you Arthur wasn't as simple as
he looks," she said.

"What else do you know, Arthur?" This was Harper
again.

"Only what Miss Lipp told me, sir—that you are all very
sensible, tolerant persons, who are very broad-minded about
things that the law doesn't always approve of, but who
don't like taking risks."

"I told you all that, Arthur?" She pretended to be surprised.

"It was what I gathered, Miss Lipp."

Harper smiled. "All right, Arthur," he said; "suppose we
just leave it there. We have a deal."

"I think I'm entitled to know a little more than that."

"And you will, Arthur. We'll be leaving here tomorrow afternoon around three, bags packed and everything because we won't be coming back. Before we go you'll have a complete briefing. And don't worry. All you have to do is just pull on a rope at the right place and time. Everything else is taken care of."

"Is this a police matter?"

"It would be if they knew about it, but they don't. I told you, you don't have to worry. Believe me, you've taken bigger risks in Athens for a lot less than two thousand."

"On that subject, sir, I think I am now entitled to have my letter back."

Harper looked questioningly at Miller and Fischer. The latter began to talk in German. He spoke slowly and wearily now, and I guessed that the sedative had taken effect, but his attitude was clear enough. So was Miller's. Harper turned to me and shook his head regretfully.

"I'm sorry, Arthur, that'll have to wait. In fact, my friends seem to feel that you may be quite a security risk for the next twelve hours or so."

"I don't understand."

"Sure you do." He grinned. "I'll bet the idea's been churning around in that cute little brain of yours for the last five minutes. 'If two hands on a rope are worth two thousand dollars to these people, what would a tip-off be worth to the police?' "

"I assure you . . ."

"Of course you do, Arthur. I was only kidding." His tone was quite friendly. "But you see the problem. We like to feel safe. Even that letter doesn't mean much here. Do you have the car keys?"

"Yes."

"Let me have them."

I handed them to him.

"You see we wouldn't want you to have second thoughts and maybe walk out on us," he explained.

"And we would not like him to use the telephone," said Miller.

"That's right." Harper thought for a moment. "Hans is going to need help undressing," he said; "and the doctor's given him another antibiotic he has to take. I think it would be best if we made up an extra bed in his room and Arthur slept there."

"So that he can kill me when I am helpless and get out by the window?" Fischer demanded thickly.

"Oh, I don't think Arthur would do that. Would you, Arthur?"

"Of course not."

"That's right. But we don't want Hans to be worrying, do we? The doctor says he really needs to sleep. And you should have a good night's sleep, too, Arthur. You won't get any tomorrow night. You wouldn't mind taking a couple of good strong sleeping pills, would you? Or maybe even three?"

I hesitated.

"Oh, they won't hurt you, Arthur." Miss Lipp gave me a fond smile. "I'll tell you what. If you'll be a good boy and take your pills, I'll take one, too. We'll all need our sleep tomorrow."

What could I say?

Chapter

9

My head felt as if it had been stuffed with steel wool. There was even a metallic taste in my mouth. It took me some time to remember where I was. I could hear a loud buzzing noise. When, at last, I managed to open my eyes, I saw Fischer. The buzzing came from an electric shaver which he was holding, awkwardly, in his right hand.

My bed consisted of a mattress on the floor and the blankets from my old room. I rolled off the mattress and got to my feet unsteadily. Fischer gave me a disagreeable look.

"You snore like a pig," he said.

He had a shirt and slacks on, I was glad to see; Harper or Miller must have helped him. Undressing him, the night before, had been an unpleasant task. It had meant touching him, and I hate touching anyone I dislike—another man especially.

"What's the time?" I asked.

They had taken everything from me after they had made me swallow the sleeping pills, even my watch. All I had been allowed had been my pajama coat.

"About eleven," he answered. "Your clothes have been put in there." He indicated a door.

I went through and found myself in one of the partly furnished rooms I had seen the day before. My things were piled on a brown cut-velvet chaise longue. I disposed of a minor anxiety first. The cigarette packet with the message inside it was still in my hip pocket and apparently undetected. I left it where it was. With any luck, I thought, I might be able to add to it. My papers were there. The radio was in its case.

From the bedroom Fischer said: "I have finished with this bathroom. You may use it."

"I think I will go and get some coffee first."

"Then bring all your papers and money in here."

There was no point in arguing. I did as he said, put some trousers on, and found my way downstairs to the kitchen.

Mrs. Hamul was there. The sight of the hired driver unshaven and wearing a pajama jacket at eleven in the morning must have seemed odd to her. She looked at me as if I were raving mad. I asked her for coffee. She gave me tea, and some of the previous day's bread toasted. The tea wasn't bad. My head began to clear. As I ate the toast, I wondered if I could muster enough Turkish to persuade her or her husband to take a message to the surveillance people on the road. Then Miss Lipp came in, well groomed and very chic in white and yellow stripes.

"Good morning, Arthur. How do you feel?"

"Good morning, Miss Lipp. I feel terrible, thank you."

"Yes, you look it, but I expect you'll feel better when you've cleaned up a bit. What's the Turkish for 'eggs'?"

"*Yumurta*, I think."

Mrs. Hamul heard the word and they began a sign-language conversation about eggs. I went back upstairs.

Miller was helping Fischer to pack. I slipped the empty cigarette packet and a pencil into my shaving kit and went into the bathroom. There was a lock on the door. While my bath was running, I added to the message I had written the previous night. *Am forced replace injured Fischer and closely watched. Event planned for tonight. Details unknown. Miller may be key person.*

The bedroom was empty when I returned to it. I dressed, packed my bag, and went back down to the kitchen.

Miss Lipp was supervising the Hamuls' preparations for lunch. She looked up as I came in.

"The others are out on the terrace, Arthur," she said. "Why don't you go out there and get yourself a drink?"

"Very well."

I went through the dining room into the main hall. There, I hesitated. I was still trying to think of a way of getting down to the road and back without their knowing. As they were on the terrace, it was, of course, hopeless to attempt to cross the courtyard. I would have to find some way round the back and down through the trees. But that might take twenty minutes or more. And supposing Miss Lipp came out to the terrace and asked where I was? I gave up, and decided to rely upon dropping the cigarette packet.

The first thing I saw on the terrace was the cardboard box which Harper had brought back with him from Pendik. It was open and discarded on a chair. Harper, Fischer, and Miller were contemplating something laid out across two tables.

It was a block and tackle, but of a kind I had not seen before. The blocks were triple-sheaved and made of some light metal alloy. They were so small that you could hold both of them in one hand. The "rope" was a white cord about a quarter of an inch in diameter and there was a lot of it. On another table there was a thing that looked like a broad belt with hooks at each end, like those you see on dog leashes.

Fischer looked up and stared at me haughtily.

"Miss Lipp told me to come here and have a drink," I said.

Harper waved to a table with bottles and glasses on it. "Help yourself. Then you'd better have a look at this."

I gave myself some *raki* and looked at the cord of the tackle. It was like silk.

"Nylon," Harper said; "breaking strain over a ton. What you have to remember about it is that it's also slightly elastic. There's a lot of give in this tackle. You know how these things work?"

"Yes."

"Show me," said Miller. He picked up the belt and hooked it around one of the terrace pillars. "Show me how you would pull this pillar down."

I hooked one block to the belt, tied the other to the balustrade, and pulled on the tackle.

"Okay," said Harper, "that'll do. Leo, I think you'd better carry the tackle. Arthur's too fat. It'll show on him. He can take the sling and the anchor rope. I don't think Hans should carry anything except his gun and the water flask."

"It is only because my skin is very sensitive that I object," said Miller.

"Well, it won't be for long. As soon as you're inside you can take it off."

Miller sighed irritably but said no more.

"May I know what it is I have to do?" I asked.

"Just pull on this tackle, Arthur. Oh, you mean about taking this gear along? Well, you'll have to carry that sling" —he indicated the belt—"and this extra rope here, wound around that beautiful body of yours under your shirt, so that nobody can see it. It'll be a bit warm for a while, but you'll have plenty of time to cool off. Any other questions?"

I had a dozen and he knew it, but there isn't any sense in asking when you know you're not going to be answered.

"Who is going to carry the bag?" asked Miller.

"You'd better take that, folded in your pocket."

Miss Lipp came out. "Lunch in thirty minutes," she said.

"Lunch!" Miller looked sour.

"You can eat eggs, Leo. You've got to eat something." She took the drink Harper handed her. "Does Arthur know that he's going to have to wait for his dinner tonight?"

"I don't know anything, Miss Lipp," I said calmly; "but I will say this. I was told that I would be given a briefing to-day. So far, all I have been given is a bad attack of nervous indigestion. Whether I eat dinner or not, and, for that matter, whether I eat lunch or not, are matters of complete indifference to me."

She went quite red in the face, and I wondered for a moment if I had said anything offensive; then I realized that the damned woman was trying not to laugh. She looked at Harper.

"Okay," he said. "Come in here." He led the way through a french window into the drawing room. Only Miss Lipp followed with me. I heard Fischer asking Miller to pour him another drink and Miller telling him that he ought to exercise the hand, not pamper it. Then, I no longer listened. Harper had walked to the library table, opened a drawer in it, and pulled out the "map."

"Recognize this place?" he asked.

"Yes."

It was a plan of part of the Seraglio area and of the roads adjacent to the walls. The triangular shape I had noted was formed by the coastline.

"This is what we are going to do," he went on. "When we leave here, we will drive to a garage in Istanbul. Our bags will be in the trunk of the Lincoln. At the garage, Mr. Miller, Mr. Fischer, you, and I will get out of the Lincoln and into a different car, which will be waiting there. I will then drive you to the Seraglio Palace. There, Mr. Miller, Mr. Fischer, and you will get out. The Palace is open to the

public until five. The three of you will buy tickets and enter
in the ordinary way as tourists. You will then cross the Second Courtyard to the Gate of Felicity. When you are sure
that the guides have lost interest in you, you will go through
into the Third Courtyard and turn left. You then have a
short walk—exactly sixty paces—before you come to a big
bronze gate in a courtyard to the left with a small door beside it. Both gate and door are kept locked, but Mr. Miller
will have a key to the door. Beyond the door is a passage
with a stairway leading up to the roof of the White
Eunuchs' apartments"—he pointed to the plan—"here.
Then you lock the door behind you and wait. Clear so far?"

"Quite clear, except about why we're doing all this."

"Oh, I thought you'd have guessed that." He grinned.
"We're just going to have ourselves a piece of the old Sultans' loot. Just a little piece, that's all—about a million dollars' worth."

I looked at Miss Lipp.

"I was being cagey, Arthur," she said. "There is some
obsidian and garnet there, and green tourmaline, too. But a
lot of that stuff's the real thing. There are six pigeon's blood
rubies in that throne room that must be over twenty carets
apiece. Do you know what just one ruby like that is worth,
Arthur? And the emeralds on those Koran caskets! My
God!"

Harper laughed. "All right, honey, I think Arthur has the
picture. Now"—he turned again to the plan—"there are
civilian watchmen on duty, but not very many of them, and
the night shift comes on at eight. You give them an hour
to settle down. At nine you move. You go up the stairs to
the roof and turn left. There are three little domes—cupolas,
they call them—on the roof there, and you walk along to the
right of them. After that the roof is more or less flat until
you get to the gate arch. You go around that over the roof of
the Audience Chamber and on until you see the chimneys

of the kitchens on your right. Then you turn left again, cross the roof of the place where they have the miniatures and tapestries. At the end of it there's a three-foot drop onto the roof of the Treasury Museum. That's where you have to be careful. The Treasury roof is thirty-five feet wide, but it's vaulted. There is a flat area around the cupola though, so you climb down there. All quite safe. The cupola is ten feet in diameter and that'll be your anchor for the tackle. Mr. Miller'll tie the knots for you. When he's got the sling hooked up, he'll sit in it. Then all you have to do is lower him over the side until he's level with a steel shutter eighteen feet below. He'll do the rest."

"Mr. Miller will?"

He looked at me with amusement. "You think he's too old for that sort of thing? Arthur, when Mr. Miller gets busy he makes a fly look like a man in diving boots."

"You said there was a steel shutter?"

"You could open it with a toothpick. The wall's four feet thick and solid stone. I guess it'd stand up to a six-inch shell. But the shutters over the window apertures are just quarter-inch plate with ordinary draw bolts on them. They don't even fit properly. And no alarm system."

"But if this jewelry is so valuable . . ."

"Have you ever looked through one of those window apertures, Arthur? There's a sheer drop of three hundred feet below. It's quite impossible to get up or down there. That's why we're going in from above. The trick is getting out again. What their security setup relies on is the fact that the whole area is walled like a fortress. There are gates, of course, and the gates have troops guarding them at night; but gates can be opened if you know how. That'll all be taken care of. You'll walk out of there just as easily as you walked in." His eyes found mine and held them. "You see, Arthur, we're professionals."

I forced myself to look away. I looked at Miss Lipp; but

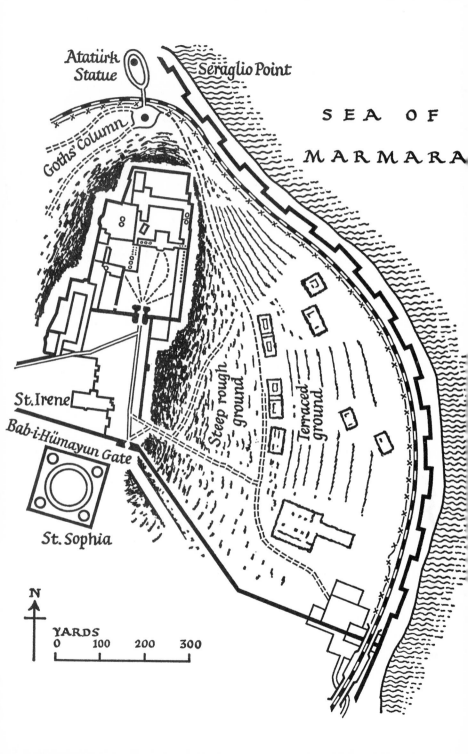

Atatürk
Statue

Seraglio Point

Goths' Column

SEA OF

MARMARA

St. Irene

Bab-i-Hümayun Gate

Steep rough ground

Terraced ground

St. Sophia

N

YARDS
0   100   200   300

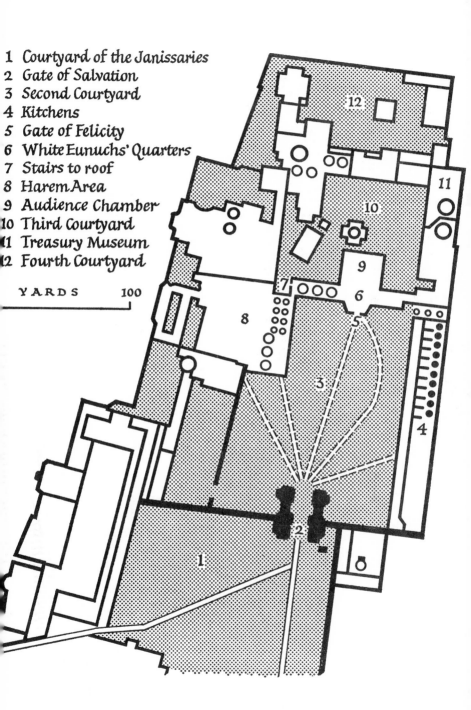

1 Courtyard of the Janissaries
2 Gate of Salvation
3 Second Courtyard
4 Kitchens
5 Gate of Felicity
6 White Eunuchs' Quarters
7 Stairs to roof
8 Harem Area
9 Audience Chamber
10 Third Courtyard
11 Treasury Museum
12 Fourth Courtyard

YARDS   100

her eyes had the same intent look as his. "I'm sorry," I said; "I'm *not* a professional."

"*You* don't have to be," she said.

"I can't do it, Mr. Harper."

"Why not?"

"Because I'd be too afraid."

He smiled. "That's the best thing I've heard you say, Arthur. You had me quite worried for a moment."

"I mean it."

"Sure you do. Who wouldn't be scared? *I'm* scared. In a few hours' time I'll be even more scared. That's good. If you aren't a bit scared you don't stay on your toes."

"I'm not talking about being a bit scared, Mr. Harper. I'm talking about being *too* scared. I'd be no use to you." And I meant it. I was thinking of myself on top of that roof with a three-hundred-foot drop down to the road. I can't stand heights.

There was a silence, and then she laughed. "I don't believe you, Arthur," she said. "You? You with two good arms and hands to hold on with, scared of going where Hans Fischer isn't afraid to go with only *half* a hand? It doesn't make sense."

"I'm sorry," I said again.

There was another silence and then he glanced at her and moved his head slightly. She walked out onto the terrace.

"Let's get a couple of things straight, Arthur," he said. "All I'm asking you to do is take a little ride and then a little walk, and then handle a rope for twenty minutes. You'll be in no danger. Nobody's going to take pot shots at you. And when it's done you get two thousand bucks. Right?"

"Yes, but . . ."

"Let me finish. Now, supposing you chicken out, what do we do?"

"Get someone else, I suppose."

"Yes, but what do we do about *you?*" He paused. "You

see, Arthur, it's not just a question of getting the job done. You know too much now not to be a part of it. If you're going to be on the outside, well, we'll have to protect ourselves another way. You follow me?"

He could see that I did. I had a choice: I could either frighten myself to death on the roof of the Seraglio or take a shorter, quicker route to the police mortuary.

"Now go get yourself another drink and stop worrying," he said; "just think of the two thousand bucks."

I shrugged. "All right. I'm merely telling you how I feel, that's all."

"You'll be okay, Arthur." He led the way back onto the terrace.

It was on the tip of my tongue to ask him how okay Mr. Miller would be if the height got me down and I passed out while I was handling the tackle; but I thought better of it. If he realized that I really wasn't just being timid, that I really couldn't stand heights, he might decide that I was too dangerous a liability in every way. Besides, I was coming to my senses again now. Tufan's "politicals" had turned out to be big-time crooks after all. I had been right all along, and he had been hopelessly wrong; but he was still a powerful ally, and I still had a good chance of being able to stop the whole thing. All I had to do was add just three words—*raiding Seraglio treasury*—to the note in the cigarette packet and drop it for the surveillance people. After that, my worries would be over, and Harper's would begin. I had a pleasing vision of the lot of them, rounded up and in handcuffs, watching Tufan hand me a brand-new British passport.

"What are you grinning at, Arthur?" Harper asked.

I was pouring myself the second drink he had prescribed. "You told me to think of the two thousand dollars, Mr. Harper," I answered. "I was just carrying out orders."

"You're a screwball, Arthur," he said amiably; but I saw a reflective look in his eyes and decided that I had better watch myself. All the same, I couldn't help wondering what he would have said and done if he had been warned, at that moment, that the customs people in Edirne had looked inside the doors of the car, and that every move he had made since had been made with the knowledge and by permission of the security police—if, in other words, he had been told how vulnerable he was. Not that I had the slightest desire to warn him; I hadn't forgotten the caning he had given me in Athens; but if it had been safe to do so, I would have liked to tell him that it was my lousy out-of-date Egyptian passport that had done the job. I would have liked to have seen the bastard's face.

Hamul shuffled out and made signs to Miss Lipp that lunch was served. She glanced at me. "Bring your drink in with you, Arthur."

Presumably I was being promoted to eating with the gentry so that they could keep an eye on me.

Miller was a gloomy feeder, and made the omelet less appetizing than it could have been by talking about infectious diseases all the time. How did they grow virus cultures in laboratories? Why, in eggs, of course! He discussed the possible consequences at length. The others took no notice; evidently they were used to him; but it got me down. I hadn't felt much like eating anyway.

When the fruit came Harper looked across at me. "As soon as the Hamuls have cleared away," he said, "you had better start getting the bags down. They think we're going to Ankara for a couple of days, so it doesn't matter if they see us. The important thing is that we leave ourselves time to clean up the rooms."

"Clean them up?"

"For fingerprints. With any luck we'll never be connected with this place. The rent was paid in advance and the owner couldn't care less if we don't show up again. The

Hamuls will dust off most of it automatically. They're great polishers, I've noticed. But things they could miss, like window handles and closet mirrors, we should take care of ourselves—just in case."

By two o'clock I had all the bags down and asked Harper if I could go to my old room to clean up there. He nodded. "Okay, Arthur, but don't be long. I want you to give Mr. Fischer a hand."

I hurried upstairs. In the bathroom, I completed the cigarette-packet message. Then I went through the motions of "cleaning up"—Tufan already had *my* fingerprints —and returned to Fischer's room.

At a quarter to three Harper drove the car from the garage to the courtyard and I loaded the bags. There wasn't room for all of them in the luggage compartment, so some had to go on the floor by the back seat.

At three, Harper, Miller, and I went up to Miller's room. There, Miller and I took our shirts off and swathed ourselves in the tackle, Harper assisting and rearranging things until he was satisfied that nothing would show. I had the spring hooks of the sling hanging down inside my trouser legs. It was dreadfully uncomfortable. Harper made me walk up and down so that he could see that all was in order.

"You look as if you've wet your pants," he complained. "Can't you walk more naturally?"

"The hooks keep hitting one another."

"Well, wear one higher and one lower."

After further adjustments, he was satisfied and we went downstairs to be inspected by Miss Lipp. She had fault to find with Miller—he had developed the same trouble with the blocks as I had had with the hooks—and while they were putting it right I managed to transfer the cigarette packet from my hip to my shirt pocket, so that it would be easier to get at when the time came.

Fischer was getting edgy now. The bandages prevented his wearing a wrist watch and he kept looking at Miller's. Miller suddenly got irritated.

"You cannot help, so do not get in the way," he snapped.

"It is time we were leaving. After four-thirty, they count the people going in."

"I'll tell you when it's time to leave," Harper said. "If you can't keep still, Hans, go sit in the car."

Fischer sulked, while Miller returned to his bedroom for final adjustments. Harper turned to me.

"You're looking warm, Arthur. Better you don't drive with all that junk under your shirt. You'll only get warmer. Besides, Miss Lipp knows the way. You ride in the back."

"Very well." I had hoped that I might be able to drop the packet while I was making a hand signal; but I knew it was no use arguing with him.

At three-thirty we all went out and got into the car. Miller, of course, was first in the back. Harper motioned me to follow, then Fischer got in after me and Harper shut the door. So I wasn't even next to a window.

Miss Lipp drove with Harper beside her.

From where I was sitting, the driving mirror did not reflect the road behind. After a minute or two, and on the pretext of giving Fischer more room for the arm that was in the sling, I managed to make a half turn and glance through the rear window. The Peugeot was following.

Miss Lipp drove steadily and very carefully, but there wasn't much traffic and we made good time. At ten to four we were past the Dolmabahçe Palace and following the tramlines up towards Taxim Square. I had assumed that the garage Harper had spoken of would be the one near the Spanish Consulate, and within walking distance of the Divan Hotel, which I had heard about from the surveillance man. It looked at that point as if the assumption were correct. Then, quite suddenly, everything seemed to go wrong.

Instead of turning right at Taxim Square, she went straight on across it and down the hill towards Galata. I was so surprised that I nearly lost my head and told her she was going the wrong way. Just in time, I remembered that I wasn't supposed to know the way. But Miller had noticed my involuntary movement.

"What is the matter?"

"That pedestrian back there—I thought he was going to walk straight into us." It is a remark that foreigners driving in Istanbul make every other minute.

He snorted. "They are peasants. They deny the existence of machinery."

At that moment, Miss Lipp turned sharply left and we plunged down a ramp behind a service station.

It wasn't a large place underground. There was garage space for about twenty cars and a greasing bay with an inspection pit. Over the pit stood a Volkswagen Minibus van. In front of it stood a man in overalls with a filthy rag in his hand.

Miss Lipp pulled the Lincoln over to the left and stopped. Harper said: "Here we are! Out!"

Miller and Harper already had their doors open, and Harper opened Fischer's side as well. As I slid out after Miller, I got the cigarette packet from my shirt pocket into the palm of my hand.

Now Harper was climbing up into the driver's seat of the van.

"Move yourselves," he said, and pressed the starter.

The other door of the van was at the side. Miller wrenched it open and got in. As I followed, I pretended to stumble and then dropped the cigarette packet.

I saw it land on the greasy concrete and climbed on in. Then the door swung to behind me and I heard Fischer swear as it caught him on the shoulder. I leaned back to hold it open for him, so I was looking down and saw it happen. As he put out his good hand to grasp the handrail and climb in, his left foot caught the cigarette packet and swept it under the van into the pit. It wasn't intentional. He wasn't even looking down.

Miller shut the door and latched it.

"Hold tight," Harper said, and let in the clutch.

As the van lurched forward, the back of my legs hit the edge of a packing case and I sat down on it. My face was right up against the small window at the back.

We went up to the top of the ramp again, waited a moment or two for a bus to go by, and then made a left turn on down towards the Galata Bridge. Through the window I could see the Peugeot parked opposite the garage.

It was still there when I lost sight of it. It hadn't moved. It was waiting, faithful unto death, for the Lincoln to come out.

Chapter

10

For a minute or two I couldn't believe that it had happened, and kept looking back through the window expecting to see that the Peugeot was following after all. It wasn't. Fischer was swearing and massaging his left shoulder where the door had caught him. Miller was grinning to himself as if at some private joke. As we bounced over the tramlines onto the Galata Bridge, I gave up looking back and stared at the floor. At my feet, amid some wood shavings, there were torn pieces of an Athens newspaper.

Of the six packing cases in the van, three were being used as seats. From the way the other three vibrated and slid about they appeared to be empty. From the way Miller and Fischer were having to hold on to steady themselves on the corners, it looked as if their cases were empty, too. Mine was more steady. It seemed likely that the case that I was sitting on now held the grenades, the pistols, and the ammunition that had come from Athens inside the doors of the car. I wished the whole lot would blow up then and there. It didn't even occur to me, then, to wonder how they were going to be used. I had enough to think of with my own troubles.

As Harper drove past Aya Sophia and headed towards the gate in the old Seraglio wall, he began to talk over his shoulder to us.

"Leo goes first. Hans and Arthur together a hundred yards behind him. Arthur, you pay for Hans so that he doesn't have to fumble for money with those bandages on. Right?"

"Yes."

He drove through into the Courtyard of the Janissaries and pulled up under the trees opposite St. Irene.

"I'm not taking you any nearer to the entrance," he said. "There'll be guides hanging around and we don't want them identifying you with this van. On your way, Leo. See you tonight."

Miller got out and walked towards the Ortakapi Gate. He had about a hundred and fifty yards to go.

When he had covered half the distance, Harper said: "Okay, you two. Get ready. And, Arthur, you watch yourself. Leo and Hans both have guns and they'll use them if you start getting out of line in any way."

"I will think of the two thousand dollars."

"You do that. I'll be right behind you now, just to see that you make it inside."

"We'll make it."

I wanted to appear as co-operative as I could just then, because, although I was sick with panic, I had thought of a way of stopping them that they couldn't blame on me—at least in a dangerous way. I still had my guide's license. Tufan had warned me against attracting attention to myself as a guide in case I was challenged and had to show it. He had said that, because I was a foreigner, that would cause trouble with museum guards. Well, trouble with museum guards was the one kind of trouble I needed at that moment; and the more the better.

Fischer and I began to walk towards the gate. Miller was within a few yards of it, and I saw a guide approach him. Miller walked straight on in without a glance at the man.

"That's the way," Fischer said, and began to walk a little faster.

The hooks began to thump against my legs. "Not so fast," I said; "if these hooks swing too much they'll show."

He slowed down again immediately.

"You needn't worry about the guides," I said. "I've got my license. I'll be your guide."

As we got near the Gate, I began to give him the set speech, all about the weekly executions, the block, the fountain, the Executioner who was also the Chief Gardener.

The guide who had approached Miller was watching us, so I raised my voice slightly to make sure that he heard me and knew what I was up to. What I hoped was that he would follow us and complain about me to the guard at the gate. Instead, he lost interest and turned away.

It was disappointing, but I had another plan worked out by then.

Just inside the gatehouse there is the counter where you pay to go in. When I got to it, I handed the man three separate lira and said: "Two tickets, please." At the same time I showed him my guide's license.

From his point of view I had done three wrong things. I had shown a guide's license, and yet, by asking for two tickets, revealed that I didn't know that guides were admitted free; I had given him three lira, which a real guide would have known was enough to buy six tickets; and I had spoken to him in English.

He was a haggard man with a small black mustache and a disagreeable expression. I waited for trouble. It never came. He did absolutely nothing but glance at the license, push across one ticket, take one of the lira, and give me sixty kurush change. It was maddening. I picked the change up very slowly, hoping he would start to think, but he was gazing into space, bored to death.

"Let's go," Fischer said.

Out of the corner of my eye I could see Harper approaching the gate. There was nothing for it but to go on. Usually there are one or two guides touting for customers inside the Second Courtyard. In fact, it had been there that I had been challenged three years previously. *That* episode had ended up in my being jailed for the night. I could only count on the same thing happening again.

Of course, the same thing did *not* happen again. Because it was the last hour of the museum day, all the courtyard guides were either out with parties of suckers completing tours of the palace or cooling their fat arses in the nearest café.

I did my best. As we walked on along the right side of the Second Courtyard, I gave Fischer the set speech on the Seraglio kitchens—all about the Sung, Yuna, and Ming porcelains—but nobody as much as looked at us. Miller had already reached the Gate of Felicity and was standing there gawking at it like a tourist. When he heard our footsteps behind him, he walked through into the Third Courtyard.

I hesitated. Once we were through the gate, the Audience Chamber and the Library of Ahmed the Third would screen us from the buildings across the courtyard that were open to the public. Unless a guard came out of the manuscript library, and there was no reason why one should, there would be nothing to stop us from getting to the door to which Miller had the key.

"Why are you stopping?" Fischer asked.

"He said that we were to stop here."

"Only if there were guides watching."

There were footsteps on the paving stones behind us. I turned my head. It was Harper.

"Keep going, Arthur," he said; "just keep going." His voice was quite low, but it had an edge to it.

He was only about six paces away now, and I knew suddenly from the look on his face that I dare not let him reach me.

So I went on with Fischer through the Gate of Felicity. I suppose that obedience to Harper had become almost as instinctive with me as breathing.

As he had said, the walk was exactly sixty paces. Nobody stopped us. Nobody noticed us. Miller already had the door open when Fischer and I got there. All I remember about the outside of the door was that it had wood moldings on it arranged in an octagon pattern. Then, with Fischer behind me, I was standing in a narrow stone passage with a vaulted ceiling and Miller was relocking the door.

The passage was about twenty feet long and ended in a blank wall with a coiled fire hose inside a glass-fronted box fastened to it. The spiral stairway to the roof was of iron and had the name of a German company on it. The same company had supplied the fire hose. Miller walked to the bottom of the staircase and looked up at it appreciatively. "A very clever girl," he said.

Fischer shrugged. "For someone who interpreted air photos for the Luftwaffe it was not difficult," he said. "A blind man could have seen this on the enlarged photo she had. It was I who had to find the way to it, and I who had to get a key and make all the other arrangements."

Miller chuckled. "It was she who had the idea, Hans, and Karl who worked out the arrangements. We are only the technicians. They are the artists."

He seemed to be enjoying himself thoroughly, and looked more wolfish than ever. I felt like being sick.

Fischer sat on the stairs. Miller took off his coat and shirt and unwound the tackle from about his skinny waist. There didn't seem any point in being uncomfortable as well as frightened, so I unbuttoned, too, and got rid of the sling and anchor rope. He attached them to the tackle. Then, he took a black velvet bag from his pocket. It was about the size of a man's sock and had a drawstring at the top and a spring clip. He attached the clip to one of the hooks on the sling.

"Now," he said, "we are ready." He looked at his watch. "In an hour or so Giulio and Enrico will be on their way."

"Who are they?" I asked.

"Friends who will bring the boat for us," said Miller.

"A boat? How can a boat reach us?"

"It doesn't," said Fischer. "We reach the boat. You know the yards along the shore by the old city wall, where the boats land the firewood?"

I did. Istanbul is a wood-burning city in winter. The fire-wood yards stretch for nearly a mile along the coast road southeast of Seraglio Point, where the water is deep enough for coasters to come close inshore. But we were two miles from there.

"Do we fly?"

"The Volkswagen will call for us." He grinned at Miller.

"Hadn't you better tell me more than that?"

"That is not our part of the operation," Miller said. "Our part is this. When we leave the Treasury we go quietly back over the kitchens until we come to the wall of the Courtyard of the Janissaries above the place where the cars park during the day. The wall is only twenty feet high and there are trees there to screen us when we lower ourselves to the ground with the tackle. Then . . ."

"Then," Fischer broke in, "we take a little walk to where the Volkswagen will be waiting."

I answered Miller. "Is Mr. Fischer to lower himself to the ground with one hand?"

"He will seat himself in the sling. Only one hand is needed to hold on to the buckles."

"Even in the outer courtyard we are still inside the walls."

"There will be a way through them." He dismissed the subject with an impatient wave of his hand and looked about him for a place to sit down. There was only the iron staircase. He examined the steps of it. "Everything here is very dirty," he complained. "That these people do not all die of disease is incredible. Immunity, perhaps. There was a city here even before Constantine's. Two thousand years or more of plague are in this place—cholera, bubonic, *la vérole*, dysentery."

"Not any more, Leo," said Fischer; "they have even cleaned the drains."

"It is all waiting in the dust," Miller insisted gloomily.

He arranged the nylon rope so as to make a seat on the stairs before he sat down. His exuberance had gone. He had remembered about germs and bacteria.

I sat on the bottom step wishing that I had an irrational anxiety like his to occupy my mind, instead of the real and immediate fears that occupied my lungs, my heart, and my stomach.

At five o'clock, bells were sounded in the courtyards and there were one or two distant shouts. The guards were herding everyone out and closing up for the night.

I started to light a cigarette, but Miller stopped me. "Not until it is dark," he said. "The sun might happen to illuminate the smoke before it dispersed above the roof. It is better also that we talk no more. It will become very quiet outside and we do not know how the acoustics of a place like this may work. No unnecessary risks."

That was what Tufan had said. I wondered what he was

doing. He must, I thought, already know that he had lost everyone and everything, except Miss Lipp and the Lincoln. The Peugeot would have radioed in. The question was whether the surveillance people had remembered the Volkswagen van or not. If they had, there would be a faint possibility of Tufan's being able to trace it using the police; but it seemed very faint. I wondered how many thousand Volkswagen vans there were in the Istanbul area. Of course, if they had happened to notice the registration number—if this, if that. Fischer began to snore and Miller tapped his leg until he stopped.

The patch of sky at the top of the staircase turned red and then gray and then blue-black. I lit a cigarette and saw Miller's teeth gleaming yellowly in the light of the match.

"What about flashlights?" I whispered. "We won't be able to see a thing."

"There will be a third-quarter moon."

At about eight there was a murmur of voices from one or other of the courtyards—in there it was impossible to tell which—and a man laughed. Presumably, the night watchmen were taking over. Then there was silence again. A plane going over became an event, something to think about. Was it preparing to land at Yeşilköy airport or had it just taken off?

Fischer produced a flask of water with a metal cup on the base, and we each had a drink. Another age went by. Then there was the faint sound of a train pulling out of the Sirkeci station and chugging round the sharp curve at Seraglio Point below. Its whistle sounded shrilly, like a French train, and then it began to gather speed. As the sound died away, a light glared, almost blinding me. Miller had a pen light in his hand and was looking at his watch. He sighed contentedly.

"We can go," he whispered.

"The light a moment, Leo," Fischer said.

Miller held the light up for him. With his good hand, Fischer eased a small snub-nosed revolver from his breast pocket, worked the safety catch, and then transferred the thing to a side pocket. He gave me a meaning look as he patted it.

Miller got up, so I stood up, too. He came down the steps with the tackle and looped it around one shoulder like a bandolier. "I will go first," he said; "Arthur will follow me. Then you, Hans. Is there anything else? Ah yes, there is."

He went and relieved himself in the corner by the fire hose. When he had finished Fischer did the same thing.

I was smoking. "Put that out now," Miller said. He looked at Fischer. "Are you ready?"

Fischer nodded; then, an instant before the light went out, I saw him cross himself. That is something I don't understand. I mean, he was asking a blessing, or whatever it is, when he was going to commit a sin.

Miller went up the stairs slowly. At the top he paused, looking all round, getting his bearings. Then he bent his head down to mine.

"Karl said that you may have vertigo," he said softly; "but it is all quite simple. Follow me at three paces. Do not look sideways or back, only ahead. There is one step down from this ironwork. Then there is lead sheet. I will step down, go three paces, and wait a little so that your eyes can adjust themselves."

I had been so long in the darkness that the intermittent glare of the pen light had been almost painful. Outside on the roof, the moonlight seemed to make everything as bright as day; too bright for my liking; I was certain that someone would see us from the ground and start shooting. Fischer must have had the same feeling. I heard him swear under his breath behind me.

Miller's teeth gleamed for an instant; then he started to move forward past the three cupolas over the quarters of the

White Eunuchs. There was a space of about five feet between the cupolas and the edge of the roof. Staying close to the cupolas and looking only ahead as Miller had instructed me, I had no sensation at all of being on a high place. For a while, my only problem was keeping up with him. Harper had compared him to a fly. To me he looked more like an earwig as he slithered round the last of the three cupolas and scuttled on, leaning inward over the slight hump in the center of the roof. He stopped only once. He had crossed the roof of the Audience Chamber, to avoid what looked like three large fanlights over the Gate of Felicity, and was returning to the Eunuchs' roof when another fanlight appeared and the flat surface narrowed suddenly. The way across was only about two feet wide.

I saw the ground below and started to go down on my knees—I might just have been able to crawl across by myself, I suppose—when he reached back, gripped my forearm, and drew me after him. It was done so quickly that I had no time to get sick and lose my balance. His fingers were like steel clamps.

Then, we were level with the kitchens and I could see the conical bases of their ten squat chimneys stretching away to the right. Miller led the way to the left. The flat space here was over thirty feet wide and I had no trouble. There was a four-foot rise then, which brought us over the big room with the exhibition of miniatures and glass in it. Ahead, I could see the whole of one cupola and, beyond it, the top of another smaller one. The smaller one, I knew, was the one on the roof of the Treasury Museum.

Miller began to move more slowly and carefully as he skirted the big cupola. Every now and again he stopped. Then I saw him lower himself over a ledge. When his feet found whatever there was below, only his head and shoulders were showing.

I was following round the big cupola, and had started to

move away from it towards the ledge, when Miller turned and beckoned to me. He had moved a yard or two towards the outer edge of the roof, so I changed direction towards him. That is how it was that when I came to the ledge I saw too much.

There was the vaulted roof of the Treasury, and the cupola with a flat space about four feet wide all around the base of it. That is where Miller was standing. But beyond him there was nothing, just a great black emptiness, and then, horribly far away below, the faint white hairline of a road in the moonlight.

I felt myself starting to lose my balance and fall, so I knelt down quickly and clung to the lead surface of the roof. Then I began retching. I couldn't help it; I've never been able to help it. From what I've heard from people who get seasick, that must be the same sort of feeling; only my feeling about heights is worse.

I had nothing in my stomach to throw up, but that didn't make any difference. My stomach went on trying to throw up.

Fischer began kicking me and hissing at me to be silent. Miller reached up and dragged me by the ankles down over the ledge, then made me sit with my back against the side of the cupola. He shoved my head hard between my knees. I heard a scuffling noise as he helped Fischer down off the ledge, then their whispering.

"Will he be all right?"

"He will have to be."

"The fat fool." Fischer kicked me as I started to retch again.

Miller stopped him. "That will do no good. You will have to help. As long as he gets no nearer the edge it may be possible."

I opened my eyes just enough to see Miller's feet. He was laying out the anchor rope round the cupola and presently he pulled one end of it down between my back and the part I was leaning against. A moment or two later, he crouched down in front of me and began knotting the rope. When that was done, he slipped on the upper block of the lifting tackle. Then he brought his head close to mine.

"Can you hear me, Arthur?"

"Yes."

"If you didn't have to move, you'd feel safe here, wouldn't you?"

"I don't know."

"You *are* safe now, aren't you?"

"Yes."

"Then listen. You can handle the tackle from here. Open your eyes and look up at me."

I managed to do so. He had taken his coat off and looked skinnier than ever. "Hans will be at the edge," he went on, "and with his good hand will hold my coat in place there. In that way the ropes will run smoothly over it and not be cut. You understand?"

"Yes."

"And you will not have to go near the edge—only let out rope and pull in when you are told."

"I don't know. Supposing I let it slip."

"Well, that would be bad, because then you would have only Hans to deal with, and he would certainly make sure that you slipped, too."

The teeth, as he smiled, were like rows of gravestones. Suddenly he picked up a coil of rope from the lead beside him and put it in my hands.

"Get ready to take the strain," he said, "and remember that it stretches. I don't mind how slowly I go down or how quickly I come up. Hans will give you the signals to lower, stop, and raise." He pointed to a ridge in the lead. "Brace your feet against this. So."

The day Mum died, the Imam came and intoned verses

from the Koran. *Now taste the torment of the fire you called a lie.*

Miller slipped the end of the rope around my chest and knotted it firmly. Then he hauled in the slack. "Are you ready, Arthur?"

I nodded.

"Then look at Hans."

I let my eyes go to Fischer's legs and then his body. He was lying on his right side with his shoulder on Miller's coat and his right hand on the tackle ready to guide it. I dared not look any nearer the edge. I knew I would pass out if I did.

I saw Miller put a pair of gloves on, step into the sling, then crouch down and move out of sight.

"Now," Fischer whispered.

The strain didn't come suddenly; the stretch in the nylon had to be taken up first. My hands were slippery with sweat and I had looped the rope round the sleeve of my left arm to give me more purchase. When the full strain came, the loop tightened like a tourniquet. Then the pressure fluctuated and I could feel Miller bouncing in the sling as the tackle settled down.

"Steady." Fischer held his right hand palm downwards over the tackle.

The movement in the block by the anchor rope beside me ceased.

"Lower slowly."

I let the rope slide round my arm and the bouncing began again.

"Keep going, smoothly."

I went on paying out the rope. There was less bouncing now, just an occasional vibration. Miller was using his feet to steady himself against the wall as he descended. I watched the coil of rope beside me growing smaller and had another terror to fight. The end of the rope was tied round my chest. I couldn't untie it now without letting go. If there were not enough rope in the coil to reach the shutter below, Fischer would make me move nearer to the edge.

There was about six feet left to go when he raised his hand. "Stop. Hold still."

I was so relieved that I didn't notice the pain in my arm from the tightened loop; I just closed my eyes and kept my head down.

There were slight movements on the rope, and, after a moment or two, faint clicking sounds as he went to work on the metal shutters. Minutes went by. My left arm began to go numb. Then, there was another sound from below, a sort of hollow tapping. It only lasted a moment, before Fischer hissed at me. I opened my eyes again.

"Lower a little, very slowly."

As I obeyed I felt the tension in the rope suddenly slacken. Miller was inside.

"Rest."

I loosened the rope on my arm and massaged it until the pins and needles began. I didn't try to massage them away. They kept my mind on my arm and away from other things, such as the day the games master had made me dive. When you got into the cadet corps you had to be able to swim, and, once a week, all the boys in each squad who couldn't do so were marched to the Lewisham Public Baths to take lessons. When you had learned to swim you had to dive. I didn't mind the swimming part, but when my head went under water I was always afraid of drowning. For a time I didn't have to, because I kept telling the games master that I had bad ears; but then he said that I would have to get a doctor's certificate. I tried to write one myself, but I didn't know the proper words to use and he caught me out. I expected him to send me with a note to The Bristle, but instead he made me dive. I say "dive." What he did was pick me up by one arm and a leg and throw me in the deep end;

and he kept on doing it. Every time I managed to get out, even while I was still choking up water, he would throw me in again. One of the attendants at the Baths had to stop him in the end. He was married, so I wrote a letter to his wife telling her how he messed about with certain boys in the changing cubicles and pestered them to feel him. I was careless though, because I used the same handwriting as I had used on the certificate, and he knew for certain it was me. He couldn't prove it, of course, because he had torn up the certificate. He took me into a lobby and accused me and called me an "unspeakable little cad"; but that was all he did. He was really shaken. When I realized it, I could have kicked myself. If I had known that he actually had been messing about with boys in the cubicles, I could have put the police onto him. As it was, I had simply warned him to be more careful. He had thin, curly brown hair with an officer's mustache, and walked as if he had springs on the soles of his feet. The term after that he left and went to another school.

Fischer hissed at me and I opened my eyes.

"Take the strain."

I wrapped the rope round my waist this time so that I could use my weight to push away from the edge if necessary.

"Ready?"

I nodded and held on tight. There was a jerk as Miller got his weight into the sling again. Then Fischer nodded.

"Up."

I started to pull. The friction of the rope against the coat on the edge of the roof made it terribly hard. The sweat ran into my eyes. Twice I had to stop and knot the rope round my waist so that I could wipe my hands and ease the cramp in my fingers; but the coil got larger again and then Fischer began to use his good hand on one of the ropes in the tackle.

"Slow . . . slower . . . stop."

Suddenly the tackle ran free and Miller, grinning, was crawling across the roof towards me. He patted my leg.

"*Merci, mon cher collègue,*" he said.

I shut my eyes and nodded. Through the singing in my ears I could hear him reporting to Fischer as he gathered in the tackle.

"All those we counted on and a few more to garnish the dish. I even fastened the shutters again."

I felt him untying the rope from my chest. When I opened my eyes he was clipping the velvet bag to his belt. Fischer was fumbling with the knots in the anchor rope. I crawled over and began to help him. All I wanted was to get away, and I knew that they would have to help me.

Fischer with his injured hand needed help to get back onto the upper roof level. Then, Miller somehow managed to heave me up high enough for me to claw my way over the ledge. I crawled then on my hands and knees to the shelter of the big cupola. By the time Miller reached me, I was able to stand up.

We started back, as we had started out, with Miller in the lead. This time, however, there was no turn to make. We left the White Eunuchs' quarters on our right and went on over the kitchen roofs to the wall by the Gate of Salvation. There was one awkward place—for me, that is—by the old water tower, but I somehow got past it on my hands and knees; then we were on the wall overlooking the Courtyard of the Janissaries.

There was a row of tall plane trees close to the wall, and Miller used an overhanging branch as an anchor for the tackle. He lowered Fischer first, in the sling, and then me; but he wouldn't use the sling himself, because that would have meant leaving the tackle in the tree. It was not the tackle itself he cared about, he said; he didn't want to leave any traces behind of how the job had been done. He got off the wall by looping the anchor rope over the branch and sliding down it. Doubled like that, it wasn't quite long enough to reach the ground, so he dropped the last six feet, pulling one end of the rope with him. He landed as lightly as a cat and began gathering in the rope. After all he had done, he wasn't even out of breath.

Fischer took over the lead now, and headed for the outer wall on a line parallel with the road the tourist cars used during the day. Miller walked behind me. After a minute or two, we could see the lights of the guard room beside the huge Bab-i-Hümayun Gate and Fischer slowed down. We had been walking in the shadow of a row of trees, but now they came to an end. Fifty yards across the road to the right was the bulk of St. Irene; ahead the road forked, the right prong going to the gate, the left prong narrowing and curving inward down the hill towards the sea.

Fischer stopped, staring at the gate.

It was no more than fifty yards away and I could see the sentry. He had his carbine slung over his shoulder and was picking his nose.

Fischer put his mouth to my ear. "What time is it?"

"Five to ten."

"We have time to wait."

"Wait for what?"

"We have to go left down the hill. The guard changes in five minutes. It will be safer then."

"Where are we going to?"

"The railroad—where it bridges the wall."

A section of the railway ran along the shoreline just inside the big wall for about three quarters of a mile; but I knew that there were guard posts at both ends of it. I said so.

He grinned. "Guard posts, yes. But no gates."

Miller hissed a warning.

An oblong of light glowed as the door of the guard

room opened. For an instant two men were outlined in the doorway. Then, as the business of changing sentries began, Fischer touched my arm.

"Now."

He moved forward out of the shadow of the trees and cut across a patch of rough grass to the road. It descended sharply and narrowed to little more than a track. Within thirty seconds the top of the slope hid us from the sentries. Fischer glanced back to see that we were with him, and then walked on at a more leisurely pace.

Ahead was a strip of sea and beyond it the lights of Selimiye and Haydarpaşar on the Asian side. Other lights moved across the water—a ferry and small fishing boats. In the daylight, tourists with movie cameras waste hundreds of feet of film on the view. I suppose it's very beautiful. Personally, I never want to see it again—in any sort of light.

After a couple of minutes' walking we came to another track, which led off to the right towards the outer wall. Fischer crossed it and went straight on down over a stretch of wasteland. There were piles of rubble from archaeological diggings, and part was terraced as if it had at some time been cultivated as a vineyard. At the bottom was the railway embankment.

There was a wooden fence running alongside it, and Miller and I waited while Fischer found the damaged section which he had chosen on an earlier reconnaissance as the best way through. It was about thirty yards to the right. We clambered over some broken boards to the side of the embankment and walked along the drainage ditch. Five minutes later it was possible to see the big wall again. We walked on another hundred feet, and there the embankment ended. If we were to go any farther we had to climb up and walk along the track over the bridge.

Fischer stopped and turned. "What is the time?"

"Ten-fifteen," said Miller. "Where is the guard post exactly?"

"On the other side of the bridge, a hundred meters from here." He turned to me. "Now listen. A train will be coming soon. When it starts to cross the bridge we go to the top of the embankment. As soon as the last wagon has passed us, we start to follow along the tracks at walking speed. When we have gone about twenty meters we will hear a loud explosion ahead. Then we start to run, but not too fast. Have you ever smelled tear gas?"

"Yes."

"You will smell it again, but do not worry. It is our tear gas, not theirs. And there will be smoke, too, also ours. The train will have just gone through. The guard post will not know what is happening. They may think the train has blown up. It does not matter. The tear gas and the smoke will make it hard for them to think, or see. If any of them tries too hard he will get a bullet or a plastic grenade to discourage him. In the confusion we run through. And then, as I told you, the Volkswagen will be waiting for us."

"What about our confusion?" I said. "How do we see where to go with tear gas and smoke?"

Miller nodded. "I asked the same question, my friend. We should have had respirators. But Karl's argument was good. With so much to conceal, how could we carry respirators, too?"

"I made the experiment," Fischer said defensively. "I tried to take a respirator in. They stopped me because of the bulge in my pocket. They thought I was trying to smuggle a camera into the Seraglio. They are strict about that, as you know. It was embarrassing."

"How did you explain it?" Miller asked.

"I said I was a doctor."

"They believed you?"

"If you say you are a doctor, people will believe anything. We need not worry where to go. We simply follow the rail tracks and leave everything to Karl. We have done our work for this evening. Now we only wait for our train."

We waited twenty-five minutes.

It was a mixed train, Fischer said, carrying newspapers, mailbags, local freight, and a few passengers to the small towns between Istanbul and Pehlivanköy. It chuffed towards the bridge as noisily and importantly as the Orient Express. There was a slight offshore breeze blowing. The thick black smoke from the engine rolled along our side of the embankment and engulfed us.

"*Los! Vorwärts!*" Fischer shouted, and, coughing and spluttering, Miller and I scrambled after him up the embankment.

For half a minute we stayed there with the train wheels clacking over a joint in the rails about three feet from our noses. Then, the last axle box went by.

"*Los!*" said Fischer again, and we were stumbling along the side of the tracks between the jutting ends of the ties and the parapet of the bridge.

We must have been about seventy yards from the guard post when the concussion grenade went off, and even at that distance the detonation made my ears sing. In front of me Fischer began to trot. Almost immediately he tripped over something and fell. I heard him gasp with pain as his left arm hit a tie; but he was on his feet and moving again before I got to him.

There was shouting ahead now, and I could hear the plunking, sizzling noise of tear-gas and smoke grenades detonating. The train smoke was still billowing around, but a moment later I got the first whiff of chemical smoke. Three yards more and I saw the white bandage on Fischer's right hand go to his forehead. Then, I was in the tear gas, too, and the first excruciating reaction of the sinuses began to spread into my eyes. I blundered on, choking. As the tears began to blind me, another concussion grenade went off. Then, a shape loomed up out of the smoke and a respirator goggled at me; a hand gripped my arm and steered me to the right. I had a vague, tear-blurred impression of a lighted room and a man in uniform with his hands above his drooping head leaning against a wall. Then, the arm belonging to the hand was supporting me as I stumbled down a long flight of steps.

I was out of the smoke now and I could just see the door of the Volkswagen van. The arm shoved me towards it. I almost fell inside. Fischer was already there, hawking and coughing. More grenades were exploding on the bridge above as Miller scrambled in after me. Then there was a sound of running feet and the men in the respirators piled in. Someone pressed the starter. A moment later the van was on the move. I was crouched on the floor against one of the empty packing cases and somebody was treading on my feet. The stink of tear gas was everywhere. I heard Harper's voice from the front passenger seat.

"Everything okay, Leo?"

Miller was coughing and chuckling at the same time. "The dogs have fed and clothed themselves," he wheezed.

Chapter

II

There were five men besides Harper in the respirators, but my eyes were still so painful that I didn't see any of their faces well enough to be able to identify them. One of them was named Franz and he spoke German as well as Turkish. I know, because I heard him use both languages—the German to Fischer. The other four only spoke Turkish, I think. I can't be certain, because I was only with them a few minutes, and I was coughing most of the time.

The van must have gone about three miles when it slowed down, made a wide U turn, and stopped.

Harper opened the door from the outside.

Miller was nearest the door and he got out first. I followed, with Fischer behind me. The other men just moved enough to make way for us. Then Harper shut the door again and the van was driven off.

"This way," Harper said.

We were opposite one of the big woodyards by an unloading pier and some beached caïques. He led the way along the pier. I was beginning to see well enough again now to recognize Giulio standing up in the *Bulut*'s outboard dinghy. We climbed down into it. I heard Giulio asking who I was and being told that he would find out later. Then the motor started, and we shot away from the pier.

The *Bulut* was anchored a quarter of a mile away, and a man on deck, Enrico presumably, was at the small gangway waiting to help us on board. I followed the others to the saloon.

By the time I reached the bottom of the narrow companionway that led down to it, Harper was already untying the drawstring of Miller's velvet bag, while the others crowded round to look. I saw the glitter of dozens of green and red stones and I heard Giulio draw in his breath. The stones didn't look all that large to me; but, of course, I am no judge of such things.

Harper was grinning his head off. "Nothing but the best, Leo," he said. "You're a great man."

"How much?" said Fischer.

"Better than a million and a half," Harper replied. "Let's be on our way as soon as we can, Giulio."

"*Pronto.*"

Giulio brushed past me and went up the companionway. There were sandwiches and drinks set out at the other end of the table. While they drooled over the stones, I poured myself a large whisky.

Harper looked across at me. "Aren't you interested in the loot, Arthur?"

I had a sudden desire to hit him. I shrugged indifferently. "I'm not interested in counting chickens," I said. "I'll settle for two thousand dollars, cash on the barrel."

They all stared at me in silence for a moment. The deck began to vibrate as the boat's diesels started up.

Harper glanced at Miller. "I take it Arthur behaved himself this evening."

"He was a damned nuisance," Fischer said spitefully.

Harper ignored him. "Well, Leo?"

"He was afraid," Miller answered; "but what he did was enough. Under the circumstances I think he did well."

Harper looked at me again. "Why the cracks, Arthur? What's the problem?"

"How do you imagine you're going to get away with it?"

"Oh, I see." He relaxed again, all smiles. "So our Arthur's worried that the bloodhounds are going to start snapping at his butt, is he? Well, forget it. They won't. All they know so far is that a bunch of armed men in a Volkswagen van roughed up one of their guard posts. So the first thing they'll do is set up blocks on all the roads leading out of the city and look for the van. They'll find it, abandoned, over in Galata. Then they'll start the usual routine—Who's the owner? Where is he? What did he look like?—and get no place. By then, though, they'll have done some thinking, too, and some big brain will be starting to wonder why it had to be that particular post and why nobody got killed —why a lot of things. He may even think of checking out the Treasury Museum and so come up with the right answer. When he does, they'll double up on the road blocks and throw out the dragnet. Only we won't be inside it. We'll be going ashore at a little place sixty miles from here and two hours' easy driving from Edirne and the frontier." He patted my arm. "And where we go ashore, Arthur, Miss Lipp will be waiting to pick us up."

"With the Lincoln?"

"What else? We wouldn't want to walk, would we, or leave without our bags?"

I had to laugh. I couldn't help it. And it didn't matter, because Harper thought that it was the beauty of his plan that I found so amusing, and not the bloody great hole in it. I thought of the customs inspector's face when the Lincoln drove up for clearance—if Tufan allowed it to get that far—and when he saw me again. I laughed so much that Fischer began to laugh, too. It was the best moment I had had in days. I ate some sandwiches and had another drink. There was garlic sausage in the sandwiches, but I didn't even have a twinge of indigestion. I thought my worries were over.

The place we were to go ashore was a port called Serefli, a few miles south of Corlu. Harper said that it would take five hours to get there. I cleaned off the filth I had collected from the Seraglio roof as best I could and went to sleep in the saloon. The others used the cabins. Giulio and Enrico ran the boat between them. I found out later that they had sent the boat's regular crew ashore at Pendik for an evening on the town, and then slipped out of the harbor after dark. The patrol boat that was supposed to be keeping an eye on the *Bulut* missed it completely.

It was getting light when voices in the saloon woke me. Harper and Miller were drinking coffee, and Fischer was trying to make his dirty bandages look more presentable by brushing them. He seemed to be having some sort of discussion with Harper. As it was in German, I couldn't understand. Then Harper looked at me and saw that I was awake.

"Arthur can use a screwdriver," he said, "if you just show him what to do."

"Which door?" Fischer asked.

"Does it matter? How about the right rear?"

"We were talking about a safe place for the loot," Harper said to me. "Inside one of the car doors seems a good place for the customs people to forget about."

"Arthur would not know about such things," Miller said waggishly.

They had a good laugh over that gem of wit, while I tried to look mystified. Luckily, Enrico came in just then and said that we would be entering port in ten minutes.

I had some of the coffee and a stale sandwich. Harper

went up to the wheelhouse. Half an hour later, the sun was up and we were moored alongside a stone jetty.

Fishermen are early risers and the harbor was already busy. Cuttlefish boats were unloading the night's catch at the quayside. Caïques with single-cylinder engines were chugging out to sea. A port official came aboard to collect dues. After a while, Harper came down and said that he was going ashore to make sure that Miss Lipp was there. He left the velvet bag with Fischer.

He returned fifteen minutes later and reported that the Lincoln was parked in a side street beside a café-restaurant on the main square. Miss Lipp was in the restaurant eating breakfast. The side street was a quiet one. Fischer and I could get busy on the door. We would be allowed half an hour to complete the job.

Fischer borrowed a screwdriver from Enrico and we went ashore. Nobody seemed to take any notice of us, probably because we looked so scruffy. I couldn't see the Opel or the Peugeot anywhere about, but that didn't worry me. I knew that one or other of them would be on tap. We found the car without difficulty and I started on the door. It was an ordinary screwdriver I had to work with, but the earlier removals of the panel had eased the screws and I didn't do any more damage to the leather. It took me ten minutes to take the panel off, five seconds for Fischer to wedge the velvet bag in clear of the window mechanism, and fifteen minutes for me to replace the panel. Then Fischer and I got into the back seat. Two minutes later, Miss Lipp came out of the restaurant and got behind the wheel. If she had slept the previous night it could only have been at the inn in Corlu; but she looked as fresh as she always did.

"Good morning, Hans. Good morning, Arthur. The others are just coming across the square now," she said.

They arrived a moment after. Harper got in the front seat

with her. Miller sat on my left. She said "good morning" to
Miller, and drove off the moment she heard the door close.

From Serefli to Corlu, where we would join the main
Istanbul-Edirne road, there are twelve miles of narrow secondary road. The first mile or so is winding, and I waited
until we got to a straighter part before I risked a look back.

The Peugeot was there, and I caught a glimpse of another
car behind it. The Opel was on the job as well.

Harper had started telling Miss Lipp about the night's
work and the size of the haul. Miller was putting in his
word, too. There was a lot of mutual congratulation. It was
like being in the winning team's bus. I wasn't needed in
the conversation, and didn't have to listen to it either. I
could think.

There were several possible explanations for the two cars
being there. Miss Lipp had probably driven straight to
Corlu from the garage, after dropping us the previous afternoon. By the time she had left the Istanbul area, Tufan
must have been told that the men were no longer in the car,
and realized that his only hope of re-establishing contact
lay in keeping track of the Lincoln. The Opel could have
been sent to make sure that there were no further mistakes.
Or it may have been to compensate for lack of radio communication outside the Istanbul area. The two cars could
talk to one another; if an urgent report became necessary,
one car could stop and reach Istanbul by telephone while
the other continued the surveillance. Then a third possibility occurred to me. Tufan must have been told about the
attack on the guard post. As soon as he heard the details—
smoke, tear gas, concussion grenades, six men in respirators
—he would know that the attack and the Lincoln were re-
lated. If he also knew that the *Bulut* had left Pendik and
that the Lincoln had stopped at Corlu, he might have decided that reinforcements were necessary in that area.

The only certainty, I decided sourly, was that Tufan would not be the "big brain" who would think of checking the Treasury Museum. He would still be off on his political wild-goose chase. Well, he would have some surprises coming.

At that moment Miss Lipp said sharply: "Karl!"

Miller had been in the middle of saying something and he broke off abruptly.

"What is it?" Harper said.

"That brown car behind us. It was behind me yesterday when I drove out from Istanbul. I thought then that I'd noticed it before, earlier in the day. In fact, I was so sure that when I stopped at Corlu I waited to get a look at it. When it didn't show up I figured it had turned off somewhere and thought no more about it."

"Don't look around, anyone," Harper said. He swiveled the driving mirror so that he could look behind. After a moment, he said: "Try slowing down."

She did so. I knew what would happen. The Peugeot would keep its distance. After about a minute, Harper twisted the mirror back into position. "Do you think you could lose it?" he said.

"Not on these roads."

"Okay. Just keep going. Doesn't look like a police car. I wonder . . ."

"Franz!" Fischer said suddenly.

"All set for a little hijacking operation, you mean?"

"Why not?"

"He could have done that better last night when he had us in the van," said Miller.

"I'm not so sure," said Harper. "He might have figured that it would be safer to wait until we were all outside the city."

"But Franz didn't know this end of the plan," Miss Lipp objected.

"If he put a tail on you," Fischer said, "he could have guessed."

"Well we'll soon find out," Harper said grimly. "There are only two of them in that car. If it's Franz we're dealing with, that probably means that he's set up an ambush somewhere ahead with his other two mugs. That makes five. We only have three guns, so we'd better take care of this lot first. We'll pick a spot with some trees and then pull off the road. Okay?"

"May I look round at this car?" I asked.

"Why?"

"To see if I recognize it."

I knew that I had to do something. If they started shooting at Turkish security agents, Turkish security agents were going to start shooting back—and they weren't going to stop to ask questions or worry about who got hit.

"Okay," he said; "but make it casual."

I looked back.

"Well?" he asked.

"I don't recognize the brown one," I said; "but there's another one behind it, a gray Opel."

"That's right," Miss Lipp said; "it's been there some time. But so what? The road's too narrow for passing."

"I'm almost sure it was outside that garage yesterday afternoon." I tried to sound like a really worried man. It wasn't very difficult.

"There are many gray Opels," Miller said.

"But not with such a very long radio aerial. That is why I noticed it."

Harper had swiveled the mirror again and was peering into it. "You'd better look, too, Leo," he said grimly. "See the antenna?"

Miller looked and swore. "It could be a coincidence," he said.

"Could be. Do you want to take a chance on it?"

"No," said Fischer.

"I agree," said Miller; "but what do we do about them?"

Harper thought for a moment. Then he asked: "How much farther to Corlu?"

"About three kilometers," Miss Lipp answered.

"Then he must have it set up somewhere between Corlu and Edirne."

"So?"

"So, instead of turning left at Corlu and going to Edirne, we change our plans and turn right."

"But that would take us back to Istanbul," Miller objected.

"Not all the way," Harper said; "only as far as the airport and the first plane out."

"Leaving the car behind?" asked Miss Lipp.

"Don't worry, sweetie. We'll all be able to buy fleets of Lincolns when we cash in this pile of chips."

Suddenly they were all smiles again.

I tried to think. It was barely seven-thirty and the run from Corlu to the Istanbul Airport at Yeşilköy would take little more than an hour. It was Wednesday, which meant that the Treasury Museum would normally stay closed until the following day. Unless the big brain had already started working, or unless Tufan had decided to stop uncovering nonexistent terrorist plots and let the police know what was going on, there was every chance that, within a couple of hours, Harper and the rest would be out of the country. In that case, if anyone were going to stop them it would have to be me. The question was: Did I *want* to stop them? Why didn't I just go along with them and collect my two thousand dollars?

I was still tired and confused or I would have remembered that there could be only one answer to that—my passport was not valid and an airline would not carry me.

But instead of the answer, another stupid question came into my mind; and, stupidly, I asked it.

"Am I included in this?"

Harper turned right round in his seat to face me, and gave me the cold, unpleasant smile I liked least.

"Included, Arthur? Why? Did you have something else in mind—like making a quick deal with Franz, for instance, or even the police?"

"Of course not. I just wanted to be certain."

"Well, that makes five of us who want to be certain. Don't you worry, Arthur. Until we're on that plane with the loot all safe and sound, you're not even going to the can by yourself. That's how much you're included."

Fischer and Miller thought that hilariously amusing. Miss Lipp, I noticed, was keeping her attention divided between the road ahead and the cars behind.

We came to Corlu and turned right onto the main Istanbul road. Harper began to organize the change of plan.

"The first thing is to get the stuff out of the door. Hans, you'd better change places with Arthur. He can get busy now."

"He can't," Fischer said. "There are seven screws on the rear doors. With the door shut he cannot get at them. The door has to be open."

"All the way open?"

"Nearly."

Harper looked at the heavy doors. They were hinged at the rear, and would swing open against the wind. We were doing over sixty. It was obviously out of the question to take the panel off while we were on the move. He nodded. "All right. Here's what we'll do. As soon as we get to the airport, Elizabeth and Leo will take all the passports and get busy buying tickets and filling out passport cards and customs forms for all of us. Right?"

They nodded.

"Then I follow them inside just to check on the flight number and boarding time so that we all know what the score is. As soon as I have that, I return to the car and Arthur drives us to the parking lot. There, we open the door and get the stuff. When it's out, Hans gets porters and we unload the baggage. We leave the car on the park. Any questions?"

"You could unload the baggage first," said Miller; "while the car is in front."

"Maybe. If we have plenty of time. If we don't have too much, I'd sooner make sure of the loot first."

"We must have some baggage for the customs," Miss Lipp put in. "People without baggage get a personal search."

"All right. We'll unload just the stuff from inside the car and leave the rest until later."

There was a murmur of agreement. Miller asked: "If there are two flights available within a short time, which do we take?"

"If one of them flies over a lot of Turkish territory—say, to Aleppo or Beirut—we take the other. Otherwise, we take the first."

They went on discussing which city they would prefer as a destination. I was wondering what would happen if I told them about my passport. From Harper, I decided, there would be only one reaction; if they could not take me with them, yet dared not leave me because I knew too much, I would have to be eliminated from the picture altogether. There would be a corpse on the floor of the car they left behind them. On the other hand, if I waited until the passport was challenged at the airport, there wasn't much they could do. I could yell my head off, demand to see a security official and tell him to contact Tufan. True, the three men had guns; but even if they managed to shoot their way out of the place, I would stand a better chance of coming out of it alive.

"Any more problems?" Harper asked. "No? Okay, then, let's have the passports."

I nearly threw up, but managed to cough instead.

Fischer asked me to get his out of his inside pocket for him. Miller passed his over and Harper flipped through the pages. I gave him Fischer's.

Miss Lipp said: "My bag is on the floor, if you want to put them in it now."

"Okay. Where's yours, Arthur?" *Has any boy not handed in his homework?*

I handed the wretched thing to him and waited.

He lingered over my vital statistics. "Know something, Arthur? I'd have said you were a good three years older. Too much *ouzo* and not enough exercise, that's your trouble." And then, of course, his tone changed. "Wait a minute! This is over two months out of date!"

"Out of date? But it can't be!" *I know I handed in my work with the rest, sir.*

"Look at it!" He leaned over and jammed it under my nose.

"But I had no trouble coming in. You see, there's the visa!"

"What difference does that make, you stupid slob? It's out of date!" He glowered at me and then, unexpectedly, turned to Miss Lipp. "What do you think?"

She kept her eyes on the road as she answered. "When you leave here the immigration people are mostly interested in seeing that the exit cards are properly filled in. He'll get by there. It's the airline-counter check that matters. They are responsible at the port of disembarkation if papers are not in order. We'll have to write in a renewal."

"Without a consular stamp?"

She thought for a moment. "There's a Swiss airmail

stamp in my purse, I think. We could use that. Ten to one they won't look at it closely if there is writing across it. Anyway, I'll keep them talking."

"What about where we land?" asked Miller. "Supposing they catch it there?"

"That's *his* worry," Harper said.

"Not if they send him back here."

"They wouldn't trouble to do that. It's not that serious. The airport police would hold him until the airline could get the Egyptian consul to come out and fix the renewal."

"He has been nothing but a nuisance from the beginning." This was Fischer, of course.

"He was useful enough last night," remarked Miss Lipp. "By the way, that renewal had better be in his handwriting. Would it be in Arabic?"

"French and Arabic, both." Harper stuck the stamp on the renewal space. "Okay, Arthur. Here you are. Write across the center of the stamp. *'Bon jusqu'au,'* let's see— make it April ten of next year. Then do it in Arabic. You can, I suppose?"

I did as I was told—as ever—and handed the passport back to him.

I didn't know *where* I stood now. If the plane went to Athens I might be able to get away with it; I still had my Greek *permis de séjour* to fall back on. But if I went to Vienna, or Frankfurt, or Rome, or (hideous thought) Cairo, then I'd be completely up the creek. I would have to wait until I knew whether they were going to Athens or not, before I decided whether I would go along or try to stay. If I wanted to stay, though, it would be more difficult now. With Harper and Fischer keeping their eyes on me, and no official to single me out because of my invalid passport, yelling for help wouldn't do much good. A quick clip on the jaw from Harper and some fast talking—"So sorry. Our friend tripped and hit his head on a suitcase. He'll be all right in a moment. We'll take care of him"—would be the end of *that*. I would have to rely upon the surveillance cars. The only trouble was that before they regained direct contact with Tufan, we would be at the airport. I would have to give the men in the cars time to draw the right conclusions and issue the necessary orders.

I could only think of one way of causing a delay. When I had finished putting back the door panel, I had slipped the screwdriver into my pocket. There wasn't another one in the car, I knew.

While we were going through Mimarsinan, fifteen minutes or so away from the airport, I managed to ease the screwdriver from my pocket and let it slide back on the seat until I was sitting on it. A minute or two later, I pretended to stretch my legs and stuffed it deep down behind the seat cushion and below the back of the seat. If I wanted to go, I could "find" it; if I wanted to delay, I could look for it in vain on the floor. That way, I thought, I would at least have some sort of control over the situation.

And then Miss Lipp began to worry again about the Peugeot and the Opel.

"They're still tailing us," she said. "I don't get it. Franz must have guessed where we're heading for by now. What does he think he's going to do?"

"Supposing it isn't Franz?" Miller said suddenly.

"If it isn't Franz, who is it?" Fischer demanded irritably. "They can't be police or they would have stopped us. Could it be Giulio?"

"That is an imbecile suggestion," Miller retorted. "Giulio is of our company. You are not. If you were, you would not say such a stupid thing."

I have a unique capacity for self-destruction. I said, helpfully: "Perhaps it is Franz. Perhaps he thinks that we are going back to the villa. If we were, we would still be on this road."

Harper looked back. "When will he know better, Arthur?"

"Not until we turn right for the airport."

"How far is the turn-off?"

"About six miles."

"How far then?"

"A mile and a half."

He looked at Miss Lipp. "Do you think you could lose them so that they wouldn't see us make the turn?"

"I could try."

The Lincoln surged forward. Seconds later I saw the red speedometer needle swing past the ninety mark.

Harper looked back. After a minute, he said: "Leaving them cold."

"We're going too fast for this road" was all she said. It didn't seem to be worrying her unduly, though. She passed two cars and a truck going in the same direction as if they were standing still.

I already knew that I had made a bad mistake, and did my best to retrieve it. "There's a bridge a mile or so ahead," I warned her. "The road narrows. You'll have to slow down for that."

She didn't answer. I was beginning to sweat. If the surveillance cars lost us, that was really the end as far as I was concerned.

She beat a convoy of army trucks to the bridge by fifty yards. On the other side, the road wound a little and she had to slow down to seventy; but when I looked back there wasn't a car in sight. As she braked hard and turned right onto the airport road, Harper chuckled.

"For that extra ounce of get-up-and-go," he announced facetiously, "there is nothing, but *nothing*, like a Lincoln Continental."

There's nothing like feeling a complete bloody half-wit

either. When we drew up outside the airport building, my legs were quivering like Geven's lower lip.

Miller was out of the car and into the building almost before the car had stopped. Miss Lipp and Harper followed while Fischer and I handed the bags inside the car, mine included, to a porter.

I couldn't help looking back along the airport approach road and Fischer noticed. He smiled at my lily-livered anxiety.

"Don't be afraid. They are on their way to Sariyer by now."

"Yes." I knew that at least one of them would be; but I also knew that the men in the cars were not incompetent. When they failed to pick up the Lincoln again, the second car would turn back and try the airport road. How long would it take them to get the idea, though? Five minutes? Ten?

Harper came out of the building and hurried to the car.

"There's an Air France jet to Rome," he said. "Seats available. Boarding in twenty minutes. Let's get moving."

I drove to the car park, a chain-fenced area just off the loop of road in front of the building and beyond the taxi rank. There were only a few cars already there and, on Harper's instructions, I backed into an empty space between two of them.

"Where is the screwdriver?" Fischer asked.

"On the floor." I was still backing the car and could see that he was already searching for it.

"It must have rolled under one of the seats," Harper said impatiently. "Okay, Arthur, that'll do. Let's get the doors open so we can see."

I pulled up, got out, and immediately began trying to peer under the seats. With a Lincoln there is not much to see. The seats are snug against the floor.

"Oh, for God's sake!" Harper said angrily. Suddenly he grabbed at my jacket. "You must have put it in your pocket." He started slapping them to find out.

"I put it on the floor."

"Well, it isn't there now," Fischer said.

Harper glanced at his watch. "It must have been pulled out with the baggage."

"Shall I go back and look?"

"No, get one out of the tool kit."

"There isn't one there," Fischer said. "I noticed that before."

"Okay, see if it's on the ground back there." As Fischer hurried off, Harper looked at the next car to us, a Renault, and tried the front doors. They were locked, of course. Then he tried the front luggage compartment. To my horror, it opened. The next moment he had a tool roll in his hand and was taking a screwdriver from it.

He grinned. "If the owner comes back, we'll buy it off him as a souvenir," he said, and quickly went to work on the door panel of the Lincoln.

I was utterly desperate or I could never have done what I did; but as I stood there gaping at him I became aware of the sound of the engine running. I hadn't finished backing the car into line with the others when he had made me stop. Then I had simply forgotten to switch off.

The door to the driver's seat was open and so were both back doors. He was crouched over the panel of the right-hand one on the opposite side of the car from me.

I glanced at the car-park entrance to make sure that Fischer wasn't coming back; and then I moved. I went to the door by the driver's seat, leaned across it as if I were going to switch off the engine, and looked across the back of the seat.

Harper was bending down to undo one of the screws by the hinge.

I slid into the driver's seat gently so as not to rock the car, and eased the transmission lever from "Park" to "Drive." The car gave a slight jerk. As the same moment I stamped on the accelerator.

I heard a thump as the door sent him flying, then I spun the wheel and was heading for the car-park entrance.

About twenty feet from it, I jammed on the brakes and the two rear doors swung shut with a slam. Through the rear window I could see Harper scrambling to his feet. As I closed the door beside me I accelerated again and went through onto the road. A moment later I was halfway round the loop. Another car ahead slowed me for a moment. In the driving mirror I saw Harper running towards the taxi rank. I leaned on the horn ring and the car in front swerved. Then I was out of the loop and on the approach road.

I had gone about a mile when the Opel passed me going in the opposite direction. I waved frantically, but kept on going. I didn't care whether they thought I'd gone mad or not. All I wanted was to get away from Harper.

I went on driving fast towards Istanbul until I saw in the mirror that the Opel was behind me. Only then did I stop.

It wasn't my fault that they took all that time to catch up with me.

Chapter

12

"The Director is not pleased with you," Tufan informed me.

It was on the tip of my tongue to tell him what the Director could go and do to himself; but I managed to keep my temper. "You got the stuff back," I reminded him sharply; "you have the names and descriptions of the people who took it. You know what was done and how it was done. What more do you want?"

"The woman and the three men," he snapped.

The nerve of it! "It wasn't I who let them get on that plane to Rome," I said.

"It was your stupidity that did. If you hadn't panicked, if you had stopped immediately when you saw the Opel instead of driving off like a madman, they would be in prison now. As it was, they got a close enough look at my men to realize their mistake. We had had no information from you. By the time we were able to re-establish contact with you, naturally they had gone."

"They can be arrested in Rome. You can extradite them."

"Not without a case strong enough to justify extradition proceedings."

"You have it. I've told you what happened."

"And what do you think your evidence would be worth in an Italian court?" he demanded. "You smuggled the explosives in. Who is there to confirm your story of the subsequent robbery? They would have your record from Interpol to discredit you. Is the court to extradite four persons on your unsupported word that you have told the truth? They would laugh at us!"

"What about Giulio and Enrico?"

"Very sensibly, for them, they are saying nothing useful. They chartered a yacht. They decided to go for a night cruise. They were hailed by some men in a caïque who said that their motor had broken down. They took them to Serefli and put them ashore. Is that a crime? Tomorrow the police will have to let them go. There is nothing we can do. Your mistake, Simpson, was in not carrying out orders."

"What orders, for God's sake?"

"The orders I gave you in this very room. You were told to report. You failed to do so. It was unfortunate that the packet you dropped in the garage was overlooked, but you had other opportunities. You could have reported at Serefli. You could have dropped your guide's license at the guard post as you were taken through. There was want of imagination. We have no choice but to abandon the inquiry."

"Including the inquiry about the attack on the guard post?"

He looked like a man who, having just realized that his fly is undone, has decided that he can only ignore the fact. "That," he said loftily, "has already been described officially to the newspapers as an unsuccessful attempt by dissident elements to blow up a train."

There was no polite comment I could make on that one, so I just shrugged and looked over his head at the picture of Abdul Hamid being deposed.

He stood up, as if to end the discussion, and smoothed down the front of his tunic. "Luckily for you," he said, "the Director is not entirely dissatisfied with the affair. The Bureau has recovered the proceeds of a serious robbery which the Criminal Police did not even know about. It shows that *we* are not at the mercy of events, but in charge of them, that we anticipate. You were not entirely useless to us. As a result the Director has authorized the payment to you of a bonus."

"So I should think. How much?"

"Five thousand lira, together with permission to sell them for foreign exchange, dollars or pounds sterling, at the official rate."

For a moment I thought he must have made a mistake.

"Lira, Major? You mean dollars, don't you?"

"I mean Turkish lira," he said stiffly.

"But that's only five hundred dollars—two hundred pounds!"

"Approximately. The fact that your suitcase and other personal belongings were lost has also been taken into consideration. In addition, arrangements are being made to have the various smuggling charges against you withdrawn. A favorable report on you will be made to Interpol. I think you will agree that you have been generously treated."

A kick in the stomach couldn't have been more generous.

I opened my mouth to tell him that I wished now that I had taken my chance in Rome; but then I gave up. These policemen are all piss and wind anyway. Why add to it?

"You were going to say something?" he asked.

"Yes. How do I get out of this country?"

"The Director has persuaded the British Consul-General to issue to you a travel document good for one journey from

here to Athens. I may say that it was not easy. The Consul
agreed in the end only as a personal favor to the Director.
In addition, an air passage has been reserved for you on the
five o'clock Olympic Airways flight to Athens. A representative from the Consulate-General will meet you with the
travel document at the Olympic Airways office by the Hilton Hotel at three-thirty. If you will tell me in what currency you would like the bonus paid, a representative from
the Bureau will also be there to give you the money."

"I'll take it in dollars."

"Very well. That is all, I think. You do not seem as
pleased as you should be."

"What is there to be pleased about?"

He shrugged. "Perhaps you think you would have been
better off in Rome. You wouldn't, you know. If those jewels
had left the country, we would have known enough to get
them back, and you would have been the first to be arrested.
Why not consider yourself lucky?"

"Aren't you forgetting that Harper still has a certain letter of mine?"

"Why should he send it now?"

"To get his own back on me, of course."

He shook his head. "*You* are forgetting. He can never be
sure now how much you found out about them and how
much you told us. Even I cannot be quite sure of that. As
far as he is concerned, the less you see of policemen the
better." He smiled slightly. "You see, you both have an
interest in common."

"Very gratifying."

"You might even consider becoming an honest man."

Work, Simpson, for the night cometh.

I ought to have blown the smug bastard a raspberry; but
I was afraid he might call off the bonus if I did. Even a
crumb is better than no bread. So I just gave him an imitation of Harper's most unpleasant grin, and tried to let him

see how much I despised him. I don't really think I succeeded. He had a hide as thick as an elephant's.

There was a sergeant on duty this time to escort me back to the guard-room gate. He watched me all the time as if he thought I might try to steal one of the pictures. Then, when I got outside there were no taxis. You never can get a taxi from outside the Dolmabahçe Palace. I had to walk a mile before I found one, and that made me angrier still.

The representative from the Bureau looked like a plain-clothes policeman. He watched me carefully as I signed for the money and kept his fingers on the paper all the time in case I snatched it away. There were no flies on *him*. He knew how careful you had to be when dealing with crooks.

The representative from Her Britannic Majesty's Consulate-General in Istanbul was a snotty-nosed clerk who made me sign a paper saying that I understood that the granting of the travel document did not constitute recognition of any claim I had made or might make to United Kingdom citizenship. When I had signed it, I told him what he could do with it.

But on the way back to Athens in the plane, it gave me an idea.

I had been thinking about Nicki and wondering whether I would stop on my way to the flat and buy her a stone-marten stole. She'd been hankering after one for a long while, and I thought that with the American notes I had I might get a good fur really cheap—for thirty or forty dollars perhaps. I would be "papa" for at least a month. That is, if she hadn't moved out while I had been away. I was deciding that I had better make sure of that first when the stewardess stopped by my seat.

"Your nationality, sir?"

"British," I said.

She handed me a passport control card to fill in and moved on to the next seat.

I had said "British" without thinking. Why? Because I consider myself British, because I *am* British.

I took out the travel document and looked at it carefully. It, too, said I was British. And yet they had made me sign a paper which said in effect that I wasn't. Therefore, the travel document could be considered an admission of my claim. The paper was unimportant because I had signed that under duress. You cannot take away a man's nationality by refusing to recognize his right to it. The 1948 Act is quite clear. The only way you can lose British nationality is by renouncing it. I haven't renounced mine at any time. Specifically, I did not renounce it by taking that Egyptian passport. Since the Egyptians say that my Egyptian naturalization is null and void because I made false statements, then it *is* null and void—*all* of it.

The British Government can't have it both ways. Either I am Egyptian or I am British. The Egyptians say I am not Egyptian and never have been. *I* say that I am not Egyptian and never have been. My father was a British officer. I am British.

That is why I have been so completely frank and open. I am not asking to be loved. I am not asking to be liked. I do not mind being loathed, if that will make some pettifogging government official happier. It is a matter of principle. If necessary, I shall take my case to the United Nations. They caned the British after Suez; they can cane them again for me. Sheep I may be; and perhaps certain persons find my breath displeasing; but I am no longer merely indignant. I am angry now.

I give the British Government fair warning. I refuse to go on being an anomaly. Is that quite clear? I *refuse!*

ERIC AMBLER was born in London on June 28, 1909. After his graduation from London University he served a three-year apprenticeship in engineering, followed by short periods as a vaudeville comedian and a songwriter and several years in an advertising agency. His first finished novel was immediately accepted by a London publisher, and his famous four—*Background to Danger* (1937), *Cause for Alarm* (1939), *A Coffin for Dimitrios* (1939), and *Journey into Fear* (1940)—followed in quick succession. He joined the British Army in 1940 as a private, was soon commissioned, and was transferred to an Army film unit in 1942. Ambler finished the war as a lieutenant colonel in charge of the production of all military-training, morale, and education films for the British Army. He then wrote and produced motion pictures for the J. Arthur Rank Organisation in England, and was nominated for an Academy Award for his screenplay of *The Cruel Sea* (1954). Ambler's postwar novels include *Judgment on Deltchev* (1951), *The Schirmer Inheritance* (1953), *State of Siege* (1956), *Passage of Arms* (1960), *A Kind of Anger* (1964), *The Intercom Conspiracy* (1969), *Doctor Frigo* (1974), *The Levanter* (1982), and *The Care of Time* (1981). He also published an autobiography, *Here Lies*, in 1985. Eric Ambler died in London on October 22, 1998.